To my grandson, Liam Ross Anderson, the newest addition to our family, who has filled our hearts with love and our lives with joy. See you soon, little kiwi.

Joseph Simon Paxton, Sr. (1824–1866)
→
Dory Sue Jesperson Keegan (1831–1920)

Ace Keegan
(1855–1932)
married
♥1885♥
→
Caitlin O'Shannessy
(1863–1952)
→
Little Ace Keegan
(1888–1976)

KEEGAN'S LADY, 1996

Joseph Paxton, Jr.
(1858–1953)
married
♥1889♥
→
Rachel Hollister
(1867–1954)

SUMMER BREEZE, January 2006

David Paxton
(1860–1949)
→
Story Yet to Come!!

Esa Paxton
(1867–1933)
→
Story Yet to Come!!

Eden Paxton
(1867–1954)
married
♥1890♥
→
Matthew James Coulter
(1859–1943)
→
Story Yet to Come!!

James Matthew Coulter
(1901–1986)
married
♥1920♥
→
Sarah Beth Johnson
(1902–1989)

Harvey James Coulter
(1942–)
married ♥1967♥
→
Mary Ann McBride
(1946–)

Jake Coulter
(1969–)
married
♥2001♥
→
Molly Sterling
(1972–)
→ ♥
Garrett
Coulter
(2002–)
Cheyenne
Coulter
(2005–)

*SWEET
NOTHINGS*
January 2002

Zeke Coulter
(1970–)
married
♥2003♥
→
Natalie
Patterson
(1973–)
→ ♥
Chad Coulter
(1992–)
Rosie Coulter
(1999–)
(both adopted)

BRIGHT EYES
June 2004

Tucker Coulter
(1970–)
→ ♥
Story Yet to
Come!!

Isaiah Coulter
(1970–)
married
♥2005♥
→
Laura
Townsend
(1973–)

MY SUNSHINE
January 2005

Hank Coulter
(1971–)
married
♥2003♥
→
Carly Adams
(1975–)
→ ♥
Hank
Coulter, Jr.
(2004–)

BLUE SKIES
January 2004

Bethany Coulter
(1974–)
married
♥2000♥
→
Ryan Kendrick
(1970–)
→ ♥
Sylvester
Kendrick
(2001–)
Chastity
Kendrick
(2004–)

*PHANTOM
WALTZ*
July 2001

PROLOGUE

March 15, 2005

Dust billowed up from inside the trunk. Tucker Coulter waved a hand in front of his face and coughed. When the sting cleared from his eyes, he brushed the grit from his dark hair and squinted to see in the dim light of the attic. Either his mother's memory was failing her or he'd opened the wrong camelback trunk. Instead of six baby books, one pink and five blue, he had unearthed what appeared to be a wedding gown gone yellow and fragile with age.

Bewildered, he carefully set the dress aside, hoping that the baby books might be underneath it. No such luck. Instead, he found a thick green tome with gold lettering on the front that read, *My Diary*. His mother's, possibly? Curious, Tucker picked up the book and turned to the first page. In a flowing, feminine cursive someone had written, *My Diary, Thursday, April 27, 1882*. Below was written a name, Rachel Marie Hollister. Tucker had never heard of the woman. Nevertheless, his curiosity was piqued. It wasn't every day that he came across a diary dating back well over a hundred years. Eager to read more, he flipped to the next page. The ink had faded over time, and in the attic twilight, it was difficult for him to make out the words.

> *Today is my fifteenth birthday, and this diary is my present from Ma and Pa. I am going to write in it every single day and keep it in a safe hiding place so Daniel and Tansy will never find it.*

Tucker smiled in spite of himself. He guessed that Daniel and Tansy had been Rachel's brother and sister. Having come from a large family himself, he could sympathize with a young girl's need for privacy. He leafed farther ahead to skim over other entries, impressed by Rachel's perfect spelling and syntax. She spoke of attending school and frequently mentioned her teacher, Mr. Pitt, whom she described as being older than dirt and quick to mete out corporal punishment. It sounded as if Rachel's brother, Daniel, had gotten his knuckles whacked on an almost daily basis.

Tucker found himself smiling again when he came across a passage about Rachel's dog, Denver, who had eaten her new kid boots. Tucker felt as if the years had fallen away and he'd stepped back into another era. It all seemed so real and immediate to him, as if Rachel Hollister had written the words only yesterday.

Impatient to learn more, he skipped ahead again. The next entry chased the smile from his lips. Not only had Rachel's spelling taken a sudden turn for the worse, but the tone of the diary had become gloomy and sad.

> *Monday, December 17, 1888. I am always so lonely at t'is time of year. I cannot 'elp but t'ink of Cristmases past—of t'e wonderful smells of Ma's baking, and Daniel's excitement about going out wit' Pa to find a perfect tree.*

Tucker frowned in bewilderment. The errors in the script weren't so much misspellings as they were deliberate omissions of the letter H, which Rachel had painstakingly replaced with an apostrophe. *Strange.* She'd clearly realized, even as she wrote the words, that she'd left out the letter.

> *I miss t'em so muc'. I yearn to string berries and popped corn for our tree wit' Tansy again, and o', 'ow I wis' I mig't 'ear Pa's voice one more time. I am now twenty-one, soon to be twenty-two. It's been almost five years since t'ey left me and almost as long since I've been able to leave t'e 'ouse. T'ere are days when I'm so lonely I fear I may lose my mind, but I dare not try to leave.*

For the life of him, Tucker couldn't imagine being trapped inside the house for five years. Had Rachel Hollister become agoraphobic? It certainly sounded that way. He read a few more lines, then closed the book and pushed to his feet.

"Mom?" he called as he descended the narrow

drop-down stairway from the attic to the garage. "Hey, Mom?"

Mary Coulter opened the fire door that led into the kitchen. Dressed in gabardine slacks and a cheery pink blouse, partially covered by a white bib apron, she was everyone's picture of a contemporary grandmother, pleasantly plump but still beautiful, her short, curly brown hair only lightly touched with gray. "Did you find your birth certificate?"

Winter doldrums and a bout of depression had convinced Tucker to take a vacation, and he needed the document to get his passport.

"No, I opened the wrong trunk." He held up the book. "Instead of our baby books, I found this diary. Who was Rachel Hollister?"

Mary's blue eyes clouded with bewilderment. "Rachel who?"

"Hollister. This is her diary. The first entry dates clear back to 1882."

Mary pushed the door wide to let Tucker into the house. He went directly to the table and opened the dusty old tome. "Come look at this, Mom. It's fascinating."

"Oh, *my*." Mary's round face creased in a smile. "I had forgotten we even had that. It's Rachel Paxton's diary."

"According to this, her last name was Hollister," Tucker corrected.

Mary wiped her hands clean on her apron as she leaned over the book. "Hollister was her maiden name. She married Joseph Paxton, your great-grandma Eden's brother."

Tucker remembered hearing stories about Eden Coulter. "Dad's grandmother, the one with the fiery red hair and hot temper?"

"That's the one." Mary laughed. "I wish I had known her. If the stories your father tells me are true, she was quite a lady. Sadly, she died in 1954, when your dad was only twelve, and I never got to meet her."

"I never knew my great-grandma Eden's last name was Paxton."

"Eden took the name Coulter when she married your dad's grandfather, Matthew James Coulter." Mary ran her fingertips lightly over the faded handwriting and smiled wistfully. "Goodness. It gives you a strange feeling, doesn't it? To think that this was written so long ago."

Tucker hooked his boot around the leg of a chair to pull it away from the table, motioned for his mother to sit down, and then took a seat beside her. "How on earth did our family end up with Rachel's diary?"

Mary glanced up from the book. "All of her family were slain, and she was the only Hollister left. When she passed away, one of her children sent the diary to Eden as a keepsake because so many of the entries were written by her brother."

"By Joseph? It was Rachel's diary, wasn't it?"

"Yes, but after Joseph and Rachel married, the diary became a joint effort. You know how you kids are always asking your father and me how we met and fell in love?"

Tucker hadn't asked for years because he'd heard all the stories a dozen times. But he nodded anyway.

"Well, Joseph and Rachel told their story in this diary. He recorded his side, and she recorded hers." A distant expression entered Mary's eyes. "I attempted to read it once, but with five kids constantly interrupting me, I finally gave up. It's fascinating reading, as I recall, a he said, she said kind of thing, very sweet and romantic, but very intriguing as well with a murderer still at large."

Tucker wasn't into romance, but he loved a good whodunit. "A murderer?"

"Yes. As I said, Rachel's entire family was killed by a sniper. They were picnicking along a creek, as I recall, and the man came upon them unexpectedly and just opened fire. Horrible." Mary shuddered. "Only Rachel survived."

Tucker leaned closer to read the entries. "Did they ever catch the guy?"

Mary shrugged. "I don't even know if it was a man who committed the slayings, actually. I had three of you boys still in diapers when I tried to read this, and I've forgotten most of it. All I clearly recall is the night Rachel and Joseph met. It stands out in my mind because he broke into her house, and she almost shot him."

"You're kidding." Tucker had been skimming the passages while his mother talked. "This is so incredible. I can't believe it's been in our attic all these years. Won't Bethany love it?" Tucker's only sister Bethany was the genealogy buff in the family. "Once she gets her hands on this, we'll have to fight for a chance to read it."

They both fell quiet. When they reached the bottom

of that page, Tucker turned to the next. Soon they each had an elbow propped on the table, and the kitchen had grown eerily quiet around them, the only sounds that of their breathing and the ticking of the clock.

"Ah, look there," Mary whispered. "Joseph Paxton's first entry. See the difference in the handwriting?"

Tucker nodded. The masculine scrawl definitely wasn't Rachel's. The passage was dated Friday, March 22, 1889, and Tucker was hooked after reading only the first paragraph.

> *I write this after the fact and speak from experience when I say that there isn't any explaining what makes a man fall in love. I liken it to a hornet nailing me between the eyes. I never really thought I'd want to give up my Friday nights in town, playing cards and wetting my whistle with good whiskey. All that poetic stuff about getting lost in a woman's eyes was for my older brother Ace, not for me. I figured I was smarter than that.*

Those sentiments struck a familiar chord with Tucker. All of his brothers were happily married now, but he had no intention of following in their footsteps. Maybe, he thought whimsically, he had inherited his aversion to marriage from Joseph Paxton.

"What relation was Joseph Paxton to me, exactly?" Tucker asked his mother.

Pressing a fingertip to the page to keep her place,

Mary frowned at the distraction. "He was your great-great-uncle."

Joseph went on to write:

All the same, I figured if I ever did fall in love, the lady of my dreams would be someone really special, as pretty as sunrise, sunset, and everything in between, and with a disposition as sweet as fresh-dipped honey. Instead she was totin' a shotgun when first we met, and the little hoyden damned near killed me.

In Tucker's mind, it was no longer the year 2005 but a blustery March day in 1889.

Chapter One

Exhausted from pulling a calf and disheartened because he'd lost the heifer, Joseph Paxton rubbed
the heel of his Justin boot on a clump of grass to rid it
of barnyard muck, then reached into his shirt pocket
for a pack of Crosscuts. Damn, but he was tired. Under
the best of circumstances, hanging and skinning a beef
wasn't his favorite task, but it had been a downright
dismal undertaking today, every flick of the knife
blade reminding him that the Grim Reaper had won
another battle. Over the next week, he would be hard-
pressed to cut up and preserve the meat. There weren't
enough hours in the day as it was.

That was the way of it when a man started his own
cattle operation. Days were long, nights were short,
and come hell, high water, or Election Day, good meat
couldn't be left to spoil. Joseph hoped things would be
easier next spring. This year's heifers would be sea-
soned mothers by then and less likely to have trouble
dropping their calves. He would also have the pro-
ceeds from the fall cattle auction in his bank account,

enabling him to hire more help. As it was he had only two wranglers on the payroll, and both of them had already drawn their week's pay, left for town, and wouldn't be back until Sunday night.

Leaning against a fence post just outside the barn, Joseph struck a Lucifer on the side seam of his Levi's, cupped his hands around the flame to block the wind, and sighed in contentment as he lighted a cigarette. Buddy, his two-year-old sheepdog, brought to Joseph by his mother via stagecoach from San Francisco, flopped down beside him. The breed, which was long-haired, compact, agile, and highly intelligent, had, according to Dory Paxton, first been introduced to California by Basque sheepherders and had quickly become popular as cattle dogs as well.

Mindful of the fact that the animal had put in a hard day, Joseph fished some jerky from his hip pocket. Intelligent amber eyes filled with expectation, Buddy caught the offering in midair, swallowed without chewing, and then pushed to a sitting position to beg for more. Not for the first time, Joseph marveled at how pretty the canine had become, the white markings on his nose, chest, belly, and feet striking a sharp contrast to his thick red-gold fur. Judging by pictures Joseph had seen, the dog most closely resembled an English collie, the exceptions being that his coloring was different, his nose shorter and less pointed, his body a bit smaller. No matter. All Joseph cared about were results, and the dog could flat herd anything, cows mainly but sometimes even chickens.

"That's all I've got on me, you shameless glutton. You'll get nothing more until we call it a day."

Joseph fleetingly wished that he could eat supper in town as he normally did on Friday night, but with calving time fully upon him, he couldn't leave the ranch for fear another heifer might go into labor.

"There'll be no tasty meal for us at Roxie's place tonight, if that's what you're hoping," he informed the dog. "It'll be warmed-up beans and cornbread, and it's lucky we'll be to have that."

At mention of the pretty restaurant owner, Buddy's ears perked up, and Joseph could have sworn the dog grinned.

"You'd best watch your step with that lady," Joseph warned. "All that special grub, and her lightin' up the way she does when we walk in?" He shook his head. "Not many restaurant owners save scraps for a dog and let him eat off a plate in front of the paying customers. Could be she's thinking the way to our hearts is through our stomachs."

Buddy worked his jaws, making a low, growling noise that sounded a lot like talking. So far Joseph hadn't been able to make out any actual words, but he was glad of the dog's responses. Otherwise, he might be accused of talking to himself, and only a crazy man did that.

"Mark my words, that woman has marriage on her mind. Many a confirmed bachelor has met his waterloo over a supper plate." Joseph narrowed an eye at the shepherd. "Chances are she doesn't even like dogs. Females can be treacherous creatures, pretending to be sweet when they're actually not. If she has her way, you could end up sleeping in a drafty doghouse with naught but a bare bone for company."

Buddy whined, dropped to his belly, and crossed his white paws over his eyes. Over the last few months, the dog had become quite a ham, somehow taking his cues from Joseph's tone of voice. His repertoire of acts included sitting up with his front paws held together in prayer, playing dead, rolling over, and lying down with his eyes covered to convey abject misery or dread.

Joseph chuckled and turned to study his newly constructed house, which sat about a hundred yards away. Roxie would undoubtedly insist upon painting the clapboard siding, and she'd want to pretty it up on the inside as well with lacy curtains, braided rugs, knick-knacks, and all manner of other nonsense. *No how, no way.* She was a pretty lady, but Joseph wanted no part of locking down with one woman for the rest of his natural life. Just the thought made the bottoms of his feet itch. He liked things fine the way they were, with only him and Buddy calling the shots.

"Maybe it's just as well that calving season has come on so hard and fast. It'll give Roxie a chance to set her sights on someone else."

Gazing across his ranch, Joseph wondered if he would ever grow accustomed to the fact that it belonged to him. He'd purchased the place only last August. Two full sections of rolling pastureland stretched out on all sides almost as far as he could see, giving him the feeling that he owned the whole world. In truth, the Bar H, better known as the Hollister ranch, lay to the north, and just south of the house was the boundary line of the Circle Star, Patrick O'Shannessy's place. Still, Joseph had plenty of elbow room with the sparsely forested foothills of the Rockies on the western horizon providing limitless open range. A man could saddle up his horse and ride for days without seeing another soul. Joseph had called the ranch Eden after his younger sister, but the name would have been fitting regardless. Finally having his own spread was his definition of paradise.

In the beginning, Joseph hadn't been sure if he could adjust to living alone. He'd spent nearly his whole life surrounded by family, a loving mother, an infuriating and spoiled little sister, and three brothers, one his elder, the other two younger than him by a couple of years. Before settling in here, he'd never come home of an evening to an empty house, let alone passed the night without hearing another human voice.

It had been difficult at first, but with Buddy to keep him company, Joseph had grown used to the solitude after a time. When he hankered for conversation, he could always visit with his hired hands, Bart and Johnny, in the bunkhouse or ride over to his brother Ace's ranch, only a short distance away. Joseph's two younger brothers, David and Esa, still lived there with Ace and his wife, Caitlin, who always seemed pleased to see Joseph when he dropped in for a cup of coffee. Joseph tried to go as often as possible. His nephew, Little Ace, was fourteen months old now and growing like a weed. Since Joseph had no plans to marry and have a family of his own, he wanted to enjoy his brother's children as much as possible.

In his peripheral vision, Joseph caught movement and pushed wind-tossed strands of blond hair from his eyes to get a better look. A horse and rider were slowly approaching. Tossing down the cigarette and grinding it out under the heel of his boot, he pushed away from the fence post and unfastened the holster strap of his Colt .45. Not that he expected trouble. He'd just learned the hard way at a very young age that a smart man always made ready to defend himself when strangers approached.

Sensing Joseph's sudden wariness, Buddy bounded to his feet, sniffed the air, and let loose with a low growl.

"A fine watchdog you are," Joseph scolded.

Concerned at the way the rider slumped forward in the saddle, Joseph struck off to meet the man halfway. When he'd walked about a hundred yards, he recognized him as being Darby McClintoch, the foreman at the Bar H. Joseph had first made the old fellow's acquaintance when they worked together to mend a section of fence that ran between the two properties. Midway through that day, they had shared a patch of shade while they ate lunch. Since then, they'd run into each other only occasionally, a couple of times at the Golden Slipper on a Friday night, other times while out riding fence line or dogging a stray cow.

Joseph had almost reached the oncoming horse when Darby suddenly pitched sideways and fell from the saddle, his right boot hooking dangerously in the stirrup as he hit the dirt. Fearful that the gelding might bolt if startled, Joseph motioned for Buddy to drop and stay. Then he cautiously continued forward, saying, "Whoa, boy, whoa."

The buckskin snorted and tossed his head but didn't sidestep.

"Good boy," Joseph crooned as he covered the last few feet to grab the horse's bridle. "Oh, yeah, you're a steady old gent, aren't you?"

Giving the gelding a soothing pat, Joseph quickly wrapped the reins over the saddle horn with just enough tension to keep the horse from moving. Then he circled around to work Darby's boot loose from the stirrup.

"Darby?" Joseph's first thought was of the old man's heart. Darby was seventy if he was a day. "What's wrong, old friend? You feelin' poorly?" Dumb question. A wrangler by trade, Darby had spent most of his life on the back of a horse. For him to fall from the saddle, something had to be very wrong. "Can you talk to me?"

"Back shot," Darby gasped out as Joseph touched his shoulder. Dust had collected in the countless wrinkles of the old man's face and dulled the nickel-plate shine of his thick silver hair. "Near about—my right kidney."

"Back shot?" The hair at the nape of Joseph's neck tingled. He cast a quick look behind him to scan the horizon. When he was satisfied that no one had followed the old foreman, he rolled Darby partway over to have a look. "Oh, sweet Christ," he whispered when he saw the foreman's blood-soaked shirt. "Who did this to you, partner?"

"Dunno," Darby said weakly. "I was up—at the north end of the Bar H, lookin' for a heifer—that's due to calve." His chest jerked, and a grimace drew the skin over his cheekbones taut. "Thought I heard her—bawlin' up in the rocks. Rode that way—to have a look. Didn't see no tracks. When I turned back toward—the crick—some bastard shot me."

When the older man met Joseph's gaze, his green eyes glittered with pain. He made a loose fist on the front of Joseph's shirt. "You gotta go to the Bar H," he pushed out. "Miss Rachel—she's there all alone."

For the moment, Joseph had far more pressing concerns. Darby had lost a lot of blood. If he didn't get attention straightaway, he'd most likely die.

"First things first," Joseph replied. "You need patching up."

Darby shook his head. "No, you—don't under—stand. I think it was the same fella that murdered—Miss Rachel's folks. Now he's back to—finish the job."

Everyone in the valley had heard stories about the Hollister massacre. It had happened almost five years ago, a few months before Joseph and his brothers had settled in the area. The Hollister family had gone for a picnic one sunny June day at the north end of their property and been slaughtered like toms at a turkey shoot. Only Rachel, the eldest child, had survived.

"Ah, now," Joseph soothed. "You probably just caught a stray bullet, Darby. Someone out hunting, maybe."

"No, you gotta—listen," Darby insisted feebly. "Happened—in damned near the same spot. Too much to be—coincidence. He'll go after Miss—Rachel next."

A chill danced up Joseph's spine. Reason chased it away. The Hollister massacre had taken place way back in '84. So far as Joseph knew, not a lick of trouble had occurred since. It made no sense that a killer would lie low for so long, then suddenly start shooting at people again.

"No need for you to worry about Miss Rachel," Joseph said as he stripped off his shirt. "I'll ride over and make sure she's safe."

Darby shook his grizzled head. "Someone's got to—look after her 'round the clock. She's—in danger. I feel it—in my bones."

Joseph's bones were telling him that Darby's situation was by far the more urgent. "I'll look after her, Darby. No worries."

Darby's face had gone grayish white, and his green eyes had taken on a vacant expression. "Do I got your—word on it?"

"Of course you have my word on it." Joseph folded his shirt, worked it under Darby's back, and then used the sleeves to tie the makeshift bandage around the man's chest. "That's what neighbors are for, to help out in times of trouble."

Darby nodded and closed his eyes, seemingly satisfied with the answer. Taking care to jostle the foreman as little as possible, Joseph helped him back into the saddle. A travois would have provided a smoother ride up to the house, but Joseph didn't have one and couldn't spare the time it would take to make one.

"You steady on?" he asked the older man. "Grab onto the horn if you can."

Darby curled palsied hands over the base of the saddletree. When Joseph was satisfied that the old man could hold his seat, he loosened the reins and led the gelding forward. The house looked to be a mile away, and Darby moaned every time the horse took a step. Finally, the old foreman muttered a curse and lost consciousness, slumping forward with his head lolling against the horse's neck. Joseph made a fist over Darby's belt to keep him from falling and kept walking.

Once at the house, he made fast work of carrying the old man inside. After depositing his burden on the dark leather sofa, he hurried to the linen closet for rags to use as bandages. Until he could fetch the doctor, he needed to get the bleeding stopped, and the only way he knew to do that was to wrap the wound as tightly as possible.

Darby, still gray faced and unconscious, didn't stir as Joseph tended to him. When at last the bleeding had been staunched, Joseph quickly donned a fresh shirt, saddled Obie, his black stallion, and rode, hell-bent for leather, to fetch Doc Halloway.

Twenty minutes later, Joseph brought Obie careening around the last curve of Wolverine Road into No Name's town proper. Main Street, the community's only thoroughfare, swarmed with people. Lying forward along his mount's sweat-flecked neck, Joseph sped past the barber shop, nearly ran over a woman exiting the china shop, and brought Obie to a rearing halt in front of Doc's place. Buddy, who'd run neck to neck with the horse the entire way, barked shrilly and danced circles around Joseph as he alighted.

"Quiet!" Joseph scolded.

Tongue lolling, eyes bright with excitement, Buddy stood up on his hind legs and pawed the air. Brushing past the dog, Joseph looped the reins over the hitching post and cleared the boardwalk in one leap.

"Doc!" The door slapped the interior wall as Joseph spilled into the waiting room. "Doc? You here?"

Joseph had seen the waiting area only once, when Patrick O'Shannessy had been under the physician's care. A hanging shelf to the right held a clutter of thick, dusty medical books. Beneath it, four metal chairs with worn leather seats stood arm to arm along the chipped mopboard. Joseph veered toward the battered oak door that led to the examining rooms.

"Doc!" he yelled, rapping with his fist. "You in there?"

Joseph was about to burst through when the door swung open. Stooped with age, Doc Halloway peered up at Joseph through thick, askew lenses rimmed with gold. The strong smell of disinfectant surrounded him.

"Why in tarnation are you hollering so loud? I'm not deaf, you know."

"Sorry, Doc. I've got an emergency."

"Hmph." Doc pulled a white handkerchief from his pant pocket, gave it a shake, and wiped his mouth. His thinning, grizzled hair was all astir, giving Joseph cause to wonder if he'd caught the doctor napping.

"What kind of emergency?" Doc cast a disapproving look at Buddy, who'd dropped to his haunches at Joseph's heels. "I'm not a veterinarian."

As quickly as possible, Joseph related the details of Darby's injury. "I wrapped the wound as tightly as I could to slow the bleeding, but he's in a bad way."

Doc's kindly blue eyes darkened with concern. "Darby McClintoch, you say?" He shook his head and scratched beside his bulbous nose. "Nice fellow, Darby, minds his own business and as loyal as they come. Who on earth would have reason to shoot him?"

"That's for the marshal to figure out."

"True enough, I guess." Doc jerked up one red suspender strap as he shuffled around a padded examining table. He advanced on a set of drawers along the far wall, which were capped by a crowded countertop that looked remarkably dust free compared to the surfaces in the waiting room. "Did the slug go clear through?"

"No, sir. Went in at an angle on his right flank. I'm hopeful that it missed his kidney and lung."

"Any pink foam on his lips?"

"No, none that I saw."

"Coughing?"

"No, sir. But he was in a lot of pain before he passed out."

"Could be the bullet busted a rib. Damn it." Doc opened a black bag and began collecting items from the shelving over the counter, vials, bandages, and wicked-looking steel instruments. "Means I'll have to dig for the slug. Makes my work a lot easier when the lead goes all the way through." He tugged up the other suspender strap. "Ah, well, I was thinking just this morning that nothing exciting has happened around here for nigh onto a week. Man should be careful what he wishes for. This is the kind of excitement none of us needs."

Impatient to be going, Joseph shifted his weight from one boot to the other. "Is there anything I can do to help you get ready, Doc?"

"You can hook my horse up to the buggy. He's around back."

"It'll be quicker if you ride double with me."

"Never ride astride. Bad case of lumbago."

"But Darby's in a real bad way. Every minute counts."

"If you got the bleeding stopped and the slug hit nothing vital, he'll hang on until we reach him. If not—" Doc sighed and rummaged through another collection of vials until he located one that held something blackish-red. "Well, suffice it to say I'm no miracle worker. Last time I walked on water was when I got drunk in Dodge City and pissed my pants."

Joseph was in no mood for jokes. "I was hoping—" He broke off, not entirely sure now what he'd been hoping. He only knew that arguing about Doc's choice of transportation would waste precious time. "I'll go hook up your buggy and bring it around front, then."

"Fine," Doc muttered as he pawed through his bag. "Just fine. I'll meet you on the boardwalk."

Confident that he could overtake Doc's buggy in no time, Joseph loped up the street to the marshal's office before leaving town. He found his brother, David, kicked back in his chair, his dusty calfskin boots crossed at the ankle and propped on the edge of his desk, his brown Stetson tipped forward over his eyes.

Joseph slammed the door closed with a sharp report that shook the wall. With lazy nonchalance, David nudged up the brim of his hat to pin Joseph with an alert, sky blue gaze.

"What are you doin' here?" he asked. "I thought

you'd given up Friday night gaming until calving seasons ends."

"You see any cards in my hand?" Joseph crossed the bare plank floor. A wanted poster lay faceup on the desk blotter, sporting the sketch of a bearded, craggy-faced stagecoach robber. "I've got a situation out at my place. Darby McClintoch has been shot in the back."

David sighed. "Well, that puts an end to my nap, I reckon."

He flexed his shoulders and rubbed the back of his neck as he dropped his feet to the floor and sat forward on the chair. His starched blue shirt fit snugly over his well-muscled shoulders, crisp creases marking the fold of each sleeve clear to the cuff. The shine of his freshly shaven jaw rivaled that of the badge pinned to his left breast pocket.

"How bad is the old fellow hurt?"

"It's bad," Joseph replied. "Doc's on his way out there now. I thought you might like to be there, just in case Darby comes around again. Maybe he can shed more light on what happened. Might be that he took a stray bullet. Some folks are running low on meat at this time of year, and a few men may be out hunting."

David slipped into his lined sheepskin jacket and then stepped over to lift his Henry from the rifle rack. "Did Darby tell you anything?"

Joseph quickly related what the old foreman had said. "It doesn't seem likely to me that the Hollister killer would wait five years before trying to finish what he started, but Darby seems convinced of it."

A thoughtful frown pleated David's forehead.

"Give me five minutes to saddle my horse. We can ride out there together."

"Make it three minutes," Joseph countered. "I want to beat Doc there. He'll be needing boiled water and an extra pair of hands during surgery."

Joseph just hoped old Darby wasn't dead when they got there.

Chapter Two

Icy gusts of wind buffeted the two-story house. With every creak and groan of the weather-beaten structure, Rachel Hollister's nerves leaped just a little. If she allowed her imagination to get the better of her, it was easy to believe that she'd heard a stealthy footstep or a floorboard giving under someone's weight. To distract herself and hold the collywobbles at bay, she hummed "Oh! Susannah," reminding herself between refrains that no one could enter her living area without first tearing away the barricade over the archway that had once opened into the dining room.

Long, golden hair still slightly damp from her bath and curling in wild abandon around her face, she sat in her mother's reed rocker near the stone fireplace, a wool blanket draped over her shoulders, the toes of her embroidered carpet slippers propped on the edge of the hearth. The hem of her muslin Mother Hubbard nightdress rode high on her shins, allowing the heat of the flames to warm her bare legs.

Hissing softly on a marble-topped table beside her,

an ornate metal parlor lamp with a hand-painted glass dome provided light for her to crochet, one of her favorite pastimes when she didn't have her nose in a book. She was presently working on an Irish lace collar, a delicate creation she planned to give away. Though she could no longer attend Sunday worship services, her elderly ranch foreman, Darby, sometimes did. According to him, Hannibal St. John, the new pastor at No Name's only church, always welcomed donations for the poor. Since Rachel had little else to do, it made her feel useful to address that need in whatever way she could. Keeping her hands busy also saved her sanity.

Over the winter, she had made countless pieces, little pretties to adorn tabletops and garments, along with several pairs of wool stockings for women and children. Indeed, her output had been so considerable that Darby had been teasing her of late about opening a shop and selling her work for a profit.

Rachel frowned slightly, wishing that were possible. She routinely made butter and cheese, which Darby had no trouble selling at Gilpatrick's general store, and the chickens brought in a little egg money as well, but those small infusions of cash weren't nearly enough to offset the lost income of the Bar H. With her father and all the wranglers five years gone, Darby was hard-pressed to handle all the ranch work by himself. Out of necessity, he had cut back the cattle herd to only a few head, and the beef profits had diminished accordingly.

For a time, Rachel had tried to bring in extra money by hiring out as a seamstress, but she'd been in direct competition with Clarissa Denny, who owned the dress shop in town. Later, Rachel had turned to crochet, needlepoint, and embroidery, hoping to sell her creations on consignment at a few of the shops on Main Street, but eventually the items had been sent back to her, via Darby, yellowed and dusty from sitting untouched on a shelf. Nowadays, people who could afford fancywork preferred store-bought items.

Or so Rachel told herself. The only other explanation for her abysmal failure to sell her work—that being reluctance among the townsfolk to purchase things made by a crazy woman—was wholly depressing and better ignored. She couldn't change the attitudes of others, after all, and fretting about it only upset her. As if she *chose* to live this way? As deeply as she yearned to feel sunlight and a soft breeze on her face again, she couldn't breathe and eventually lost consciousness if she went outdoors. Two deadlocks and a thick bar on the front door were all that made her feel safe.

Looking on the bright side, the wolves weren't scratching to get in yet. The ranch made enough to cover expenses and see to her needs, with a little left over for extras. Except for yarn, thread, an occasional bit of fabric, and a weekly dime novel or two, Rachel was careful about her spending. The only other luxuries she allowed herself were scented soap, some extra flour and sugar each month for baked goods and candy, and additional lamp fuel because she detested living like a mole. Light, and lots of it, was her only respite from the darkness, a substitute of sorts for the sunlight she so sorely missed.

With a sigh, she set her crocheting in the basket at her feet and got up to stir the beef stew simmering on the Windsor range. Darby would be along shortly, expecting his supper to be set out for him in the wood safe. She should stoke the cooking fire and get the cornbread in the oven. The old foreman was nothing if not punctual when it came to mealtimes.

Keeping to Darby's schedule was difficult for Rachel sometimes. With her windows boarded over, inside and out, she couldn't tell daylight from darkness, and it was easy for her to lose track of time. Sometimes, if she strained her ears, she could hear the rooster crowing to herald the dawn, and at other times, if she concentrated, she could discern the difference between a morning and afternoon breeze buffeting the house. But overall, she existed in a limbo, the only structure to her days imposed by Darby's growling stomach.

The thought made Rachel smile as she added wood to the firebox and adjusted the stove damper. Her arrangement with Darby was more than fair, preparing his meals her only contribution. In return for tasty cooking and a middling wage, he worked the ranch and saw to her every need. Thanks to him, she never wanted for anything—unless, of course, she counted conversation. Darby turned loose words like a poor man did hard-earned pennies.

Rachel guessed that Darby's quietness resulted from the solitude of his occupation, riding the hills with only cattle for company his whole life long. He occasionally mumbled a short sentence to her through the door or wood safe, but that was the extent of it.

Consequently, her yearning for conversation was only satisfied when she dreamed of her family, her mind recreating life as it had once been, with her parents and siblings talking and laughing over a meal or shouting to each other from different parts of the house.

Her thoughts drifting, Rachel set to work on the cornbread. It always cheered her to bake. She suspected it was partly due to the colorful bags and containers that peppered the counter. A man in a dark suit and top hat, wheeling a barrel, was imprinted on the Gold Medal flour sack. The Royal Baking Powder crock provided a lovely splash of crimson. Her speckled enamel saltshaker added a touch of blue, one of her favorite hues. The cornmeal sack, emblazoned with a cornstalk laden with partially shucked ears of field corn, lent green and yellow to the spectrum, along with GARNER MILLS scrolled across the top in bright red.

But it wasn't only the colors that made her enjoy baking. She loved the delicious smells that filled the room. They reminded her of days gone by when her family had still been alive. Oh, how she missed those times—with her fourteen-year-old brother, Daniel, forever up to mischief, her five-year-old sister, Tansy, running from room to room, and their mother always scolding. Rachel's dog, Denver, had contributed to the confusion as well, his brown eyes alight with affection, his tail wagging. Her pa had complained about the animal being allowed inside the house, but in truth, Henry Hollister had been as guilty of spoiling Denver as everyone else in the family.

As Rachel clipped sugar from the cone into a mixing bowl and crunched it into fine granules, she drew the memories close, a warm cloak around her heart. Life could be tragic. She would be the last to argue the point. But it could also be wonderfully rich. One had to hold tight to the good things and try not to focus on the bad.

When she had whisked the dry ingredients together, she fetched milk and eggs from the icebox, melted some lard, and soon had a batch of bread in the oven. That done, she decided a hot peach cobbler for dessert would be lovely on such a windy March day. Darby had a sweet tooth, and regrettably, so did she, a weakness evidenced by her ever-increasing waistline. Her reflection in the water closet mirror told her that she wasn't actually fat yet, but in another few years she would be. The long walks and horseback rides that had once kept her trim were no longer possible, and the relentless boredom of her existence fueled her appetite. Homemade chocolate drops had recently become her favorite treat.

After collecting the lamp from the table and lifting the bar on the cellar door, Rachel descended the four wooden steps to collect a Mason jar of last year's peaches. Minutes later, she was back upstairs, sipping the extra juice she'd drained off the home-canned fruit while she mixed the cobbler batter. Darby would show up soon. By the time he finished his supper and brought his dishes back from the bunkhouse, the dessert would be cool enough to eat.

The cornbread was done to a turn by the time the cobbler was ready for the oven. While the dessert baked, she sat at the dining table to resume reading

The Adventures of Huckleberry Finn, a fascinating novel that was, in her opinion, every bit as good as *The Adventures of Tom Sawyer*, heretofore her favorite— except, of course, for *Jane Eyre* and *Little Women*.

Dimpling her cheek with a forefinger, Rachel searched for her place on the marked page, and within seconds she was transported to the damp banks of the Mississippi, the blackness of night closing around her with only the light from Jim's lantern to penetrate the darkness.

Some minutes later, the smell of the cobbler jerked Rachel back to the present. "Consternation!"

She leaped up and ran to the stove, praying with every breath that she hadn't burned the dessert. Grabbing a cloth to protect her hand, she hurriedly drew the pan from the oven and sighed with relief when she saw that it hadn't scorched.

"Praise the Lord," she said. "When will I learn not to read while I'm baking?"

After adjusting the stove damper, she dusted her hands. En route back to the table, she glanced at the wall clock. *Five after six.* It wasn't like Darby to be late. She wondered if Poncho, his old buckskin gelding, had gone lame again. Rachel hoped not. Darby fussed over that horse as if it were a child.

Resuming her seat, Rachel found her place in the book, wishing as she started to read that she were actually there on the island with Jim and Huck. The thought no sooner took hold than she scoffed at herself. If she couldn't step out onto her own porch without succumbing to mindless fright, how could she possibly contemplate grand adventures on the fathom-less, churning waters of the Mississippi?

Joseph pulled back on Obie's reins, bringing the stallion to a halt in Rachel Hollister's back dooryard. David drew up beside him, his sorrel snorting and stomping its front hooves. A moment of silence ensued as both men squinted through the deepening shadows of twilight to peruse the large, two-story house. Every window had been boarded up, and not a sliver of light seeped out through the cracks.

"If this don't beat all," Joseph muttered. "I heard she had boards over all the windows, but I had to see it to believe it."

David shivered and turned up the collar of his coat. "You sure we shouldn't go around front? Seems like poor manners to knock at a lady's back door."

"You heard what Darby said. She lives in the kitchen at the back, boarded off from the rest of the house."

"You suppose she'll answer if we knock?"

Joseph swung off his horse and dropped the reins to the ground, confident that Obie would stand fast as he'd been trained to do. "There's only one way to find out."

As Joseph crossed the short expanse of frozen, grass-pocked earth to the wide, covered back porch, which was about two-thirds the width of the house, he marveled at the strangeness of someone who chose to live this way. Since coming to No Name four years ago, he'd heard stories aplenty about Rachel Hollister, all with one common theme: that she had bats in her belfry. But this went beyond crazy. The woman lived in a hidey-hole, cut off from the world.

Studying the modified rear exterior of the house, Joseph heard rather than saw David coming abreast of him. The back door looked to be four inches thick, constructed of oak planks that only a battering ram might penetrate. To the left of the door, next to a boarded-up window, a large iron wood box had been set into the wall. Joseph had a similar setup at his place, a wood safe that could be filled from the outside and opened from inside the kitchen. He guessed that Darby normally kept the box stocked so Miss Hollister never had to venture outdoors for firewood.

Hoping that they might be invited in out of the cold, Joseph stomped his boots clean on the porch as David mounted the steps behind him. When they stood shoulder to shoulder before the door, Joseph glanced at his brother before raising his fist to knock.

When Rachel heard footsteps on the porch, she closed her book, thinking Darby had returned. She almost parted company with her skin when someone started pounding on the door. Not Darby. He only ever rapped on the iron wood safe to let her know he was home.

"Miss Hollister?" a man called out.

Rachel leaped up from the chair and fell back a step. No one ever came to call on her anymore. Her last visitor had been Doc Halloway, and that had been well over four years ago.

"Wh-who is it?" she asked in a voice gone thin with anxiety.

"Joseph Paxton, your neighbor," the deep voice replied. "I own the spread just south of here."

Rachel vaguely recalled Darby's telling her that someone had bought the land due south of her ranch, but the name Paxton didn't ring a bell. She whirled and ran for the gun case that stood between her night table and the armoire. Her hand went straight for the Colt breechloader, a 10-gauge shotgun with shortened barrels that Darby claimed would stop an enraged grizzly dead in its tracks. At close range, all you had to do was point and pull both triggers. Rachel had no desire to shoot anyone, but it only seemed prudent to have the weapon ready, just in case.

Muscles jerking with fear, she spilled a few shells from the ammunition drawer when she jerked it open. *Hurry, hurry.* She broke open the shotgun barrels, shoved a cartridge into each chamber, and snapped the weapon closed again. In the otherwise silent room, the rasp of Damascus steel seemed deafeningly loud.

On wobbly legs, she turned to face the barred door, braced the butt of the shotgun against her hip, and yelled, "State your business!"

She heard boots shuffling on the porch planks. *More than one man?* Her blood ran cold. *Oh, God. Oh, God.* Where was Darby? Had these men harmed him? The old foreman was never this late unless something detained him.

"This isn't the kind of news I want to shout through the door," the man replied. "The marshal is with me, if that eases your mind any."

The marshal? Rachel's heart skipped a beat.

"Can you open up for a minute, ma'am?" another

man asked. "This is David Paxton, the marshal of No Name. I give you my word, we mean you no harm."

Rachel curled her forefinger over the triggers of the shotgun, prepared to start blasting if they tried to come in. "State your business through the door. I can hear you just fine." She swallowed to steady her voice. "My foreman will be along at any moment. If you prefer to speak face-to-face, you can wait a bit and talk to him."

Another silence ensued. Then the first man said, "That's why we're here, Miss Hollister, to bring you news about your foreman. Along about three this afternoon, he rode in to my place, looking for help. He's been hurt."

"Hurt?" Love of Darby had Rachel taking a hesitant step toward the door. Then she caught herself and drew to a stop. She was a woman alone, miles from the nearest neighbor. It would be sheer madness to trust two strangers. "How was he hurt?"

Rachel had grown up on the ranch and knew all the dangers. Darby could have been cut by barbed wire, thrown from his horse onto rocky ground, or kicked by a steer, to list only a few possibilities. Unfortunately, he might also have been bushwhacked by two thieving ne'er-do-wells.

She heard a low rumble of male voices. Then the man who called himself Joseph Paxton finally said, "He was at the north end of your property, tracking a heifer, Miss Hollister. When he left the rocks and headed back toward the creek, someone shot him in the back."

Shot? The word resounded inside Rachel's mind,

and black spots began to dance before her eyes. She knew the place the man described. She saw it in her dreams every night. *Not again, God. Please, not again.* A strange ringing began in her ears, and she could no longer feel her feet. Images of her family flashed before her eyes—of her little sister, Tansy, chasing butterflies—of her father, sitting on the creek bank and playing his fiddle while her mother danced on the grass—and lastly of her brother, Daniel, golden hair gleaming in the sunshine, his grin mischievous as he wrestled with Rachel for the last drumstick in the picnic basket.

She made her way to the table and sank onto a chair. Dimly she heard Joseph Paxton speaking to her, but she couldn't make out the words. It was as if she had water in her ears. *Darby, shot.* She couldn't wrap her mind around it. And to think that it had happened in exactly the same place where her family had been killed. *No, no, no.*

A foggy darkness encroached on her vision. Rachel had experienced it before and knotted her hands into tight fists, determined not to let it happen again. Not *now*, with two strangers on her porch. But the blackness moved inexorably closer, a thick, impenetrable blanket determined to enshroud her.

Chapter Three

"Well, *hell*." Joseph kicked a piece of stove kindling that lay near Rachel Hollister's woodpile. "That got us nowhere fast."

His breath fogging the frigid air, David hunched his shoulders inside his jacket. "It's worrisome, the way she went quiet all of a sudden." He gave Joseph an accusing look. "I knew we shouldn't talk to her through the door. You're supposed to break news like that gently."

"She wouldn't open the door," Joseph reminded him. "And tell me a gentler way to say it. I told her that he was hurt before I told her that he was shot."

"You're too blunt by half, Joseph. She may have a deep affection for that old man. With ladies, especially, you need to sugarcoat things."

"How can you sugarcoat such news?" Joseph demanded. "If you're so damned good with words, why don't you do the talking next time?"

"Thank you, maybe I will."

Joseph kicked at the kindling again. "Like you're

such a charmer? I don't see you with a gal on each arm every Friday night."

"Saloon girls," David countered with a derisive snort. "Like your popularity at the Golden Slipper is a measure of your charm? I haven't seen you with a decent young lady in a good long while."

"The same can be said of you."

Impasse. Neither of them was in the habit of keeping company with respectable young women. Their older half brother, Ace Keegan, the closest thing to a father either of them could clearly remember, had always spoken strongly against it. When a man trifled with a proper young lady, he'd better be prepared to marry her, end of subject. That was the Keegan and Paxton way.

David sighed and toed the kindling back toward Joseph. "I just hope she's all right, is all."

"Anyone who boards herself off from the world like that isn't all right. Alive and halfway rational is the most we can hope for."

"With her family getting killed and all, maybe she's just scared half out of her wits."

Joseph considered that suggestion. "Could be, I reckon." Thinking of what had happened to Darby, he felt a chill inch up his spine. "And maybe with good reason."

Before stopping at the Hollister house to speak to Rachel, Joseph and David had ridden to the north end of the Hollister ranch to have a look around. They'd found the place where Darby had been ambushed, and in their estimation, the shooting couldn't have been an accident. The direction of the hoofprints left by

Darby's horse bore out that Darby had been riding toward the creek when the shot was fired. The prominence of rock behind him would have blocked a stray bullet. Someone had been hiding in those rocks and deliberately taken aim at the old man's back.

"So now what?" David asked.

Joseph knew his brother was referring to the shooting, but he didn't have all of his thoughts about that in order yet. "The lady will need firewood to get her through the night. I'll start with that, I reckon."

As they loaded their arms with split logs, David asked, "Where you planning to spend the night? In the bunkhouse?"

"Too far away," Joseph replied with a grunt. "On the off chance that Darby's right about her being in danger, I need to be close enough to hear if anyone comes around."

Arms filled, Joseph made for the porch, his brother only a step behind him.

"Where will you sleep, then? It's colder than a well digger's ass out here, and there's no windbreak that I can see."

They shoved the wood into the box. On the way back to the pile for kindling, Joseph said, "Darby says Miss Rachel lives in the kitchen, boarded off from the rest of the house. That must mean all the other rooms are unoccupied." He stacked slender pieces of pitch-veined wood on the crook of his arm. "I'll just slip in through a downstairs window and find a spot somewhere inside to shake out my bedroll—preferably as close to the kitchen as I can manage so I can hear if there's any trouble."

As they retraced their steps to the house, a cow lowed plaintively, the sound faint on the evening breeze.

"You think going inside is a good idea?" David asked as they dispensed with their burdens. "The lady's a mite skittish."

Joseph dusted off his hands and straightened his Stetson. "What other choice is there? I'm as happy as a ringtailed possum to play Good Samaritan, David, but I'm not angling to get a bad case of frostbite while I'm at it."

David chafed his arms through the thick sleeves of his coat. "I can't say I blame you. It's not fit out here for man nor beast."

"I'll knock on the door again and explain that Darby sent me over to look after her. If she knows I plan to sleep somewhere in the house, it shouldn't alarm her to hear me coming in." Joseph flashed his brother a sarcastic grin. "You want to write me a speech so I sugarcoat everything enough to suit you?"

"I would if I had paper. You're nothing if not plain-spoken, and that's a fact."

"Yeah, well, flowery speech has never been one of my strong suits." Joseph narrowed an eye at his brother. "Come to think of it, maybe you should be the one to stay. You were born with a lump of sugar in your mouth."

David threw up his hands. "Oh, no, you don't. Darby asked *you* to watch after her, not me, and you're the one who gave him your word."

Joseph had never gone back on his word in his life, and he didn't plan to start now. That didn't mean he couldn't toy with the thought. There were better ways to spend a Friday night than playing nursemaid to a crazy woman.

David collected his gelding and mounted up. Joseph thought about asking him to stop off at Eden and bring him back a jug of whiskey before he headed home, but he already knew what his brother's answer would be. Now that David wore a badge, he was as puritanical as a preacher about the consumption of spirits—and practically anything else that Joseph thought was fun.

"Well," David said in parting. "Good luck. If nothing else, it should be an interesting night."

Sleeping on a cold floor with only hardtack and jerky in his belly wasn't Joseph's idea of interesting, but he couldn't see that he had a choice.

David rubbed his jaw. "I don't have a good feeling about this, big brother."

The comment brought them both full circle to that unsettling moment when they had realized Darby's shooting had been no accident. "Me, either," Joseph confessed. "My theory of a stray bullet was a lot easier to swallow."

"Only it wasn't a stray bullet," David said. "No how, no way could it have been an accident."

The words hung between them in the cold air like ice particles. David stared solemnly at the house. "As much as I hate to think it, she truly may be in danger."

Joseph hated to think it a whole lot worse than his brother did. He was the one who'd promised to protect the woman. "I'm sorry if my frankness put her in a dither," he offered by way of apology. "I know you wanted to ask her some questions."

David turned his gelding to head out, then settled back in the saddle and didn't go anywhere. "Maybe she'll feel more like talking tomorrow."

Joseph doubted it. Insanity didn't normally right itself overnight. "Maybe." Interpreting his brother's reluctance to leave as a sign that he needed to talk, Joseph asked, "In the meantime, what's your gut telling you?"

"That I'm flummoxed. Darby's so drunk on laudanum he can't tell me much of anything, and she refuses to talk. How can I make sense of this mess with nothing to go on?" David rubbed the back of his neck. "What if the shooting today actually is connected to the murders five years ago? We didn't even live in these parts then, and Estyn Beiler, the marshal at the time, never figured out who did it."

"Estyn Beiler was a piss-poor lawman." Just saying the man's name made Joseph's lip curl. "He was so caught up in his own shady dealings that he never did his job. You're dedicated, David, and you're a hell of a lot smarter than he was. I'm confident that you'll get to the bottom of this."

"Without even a suspicion to go on?"

Joseph reached inside his jacket for his pack of Crosscuts. "Ah, now. For the moment, forget the incident five years ago and start with the obvious question. Who might want Darby McClintoch dead?"

"Nobody that I can think of. He comes into town for a couple of drinks every now and again, but he never causes any trouble. He doesn't play cards, which rules out the possibility that he took someone's money and made an enemy. As far as I know, he never goes upstairs with any of the girls, either, eliminating all likelihood of a jealous lover. He's a quiet, inoffensive man, not given to discussing politics or religion, which can cause hard feelings. He just sits at a corner table, enjoys his drinks, and then goes home."

"Okay, then." Joseph offered his brother a smoke. The faint low of a cow reached them again. "Chances are the shooter has nothing personal against Darby."

"Which leads me right back to the incident five years ago and a big, fat nothing in clues." David accepted a cigarette and leaned low over the saddle horn so Joseph could give him a light. As he straightened, he said, "This whole thing is giving me a headache. My thoughts keep circling back on themselves. I have no idea where to start."

Joseph puffed until his Crosscut caught and then waved out the Lucifer. "Start with all the rumors and cast a wide net. A lot of folks hereabouts think that Miss Rachel's great-aunt Amanda Hollister might have killed the family. There was real bad blood between her and her nephew, Rachel's father, Henry. Near as I recall, it had to do with his inheriting the ranch and Amanda getting cut out of the will without a dime."

"That's the story I heard, too," David agreed.

"If Rachel had died with everyone else in her family that day, who stood to gain?" Joseph asked.

David squinted against an updraft of cigarette smoke. "Amanda Hollister. As the only surviving relative, she would have gotten this ranch lock, stock, and barrel and all Henry's money, to boot."

"So there you go, a prime suspect." Joseph spat out a piece of loose tobacco. "She definitely had motive. Maybe she's been keeping her head down the last five years because all the evidence pointed so strongly at her."

David thought about it for a long moment. Then he said, "Too obvious. In the short time I've been marshal, I've learned that the obvious answer is seldom the right one."

"I hear you. The woman would have had to be crazy to think she could get away with it. But maybe craziness runs in the family." Joseph hooked a thumb toward the house. "Folks blame Rachel's strangeness on her getting shot in the head, but maybe she was a little off-plum before it happened."

"Maybe." David exhaled smoke and flicked away ash. "Sort of like red hair running strong in the O'Shannessy family?"

"Yep. Only with the Hollisters, it could be lunacy." Joseph studied the glowing tip of his cigarette. "There again, we could be sniffing up the wrong tree. It's no secret hereabouts that Jebediah Pritchard hated Henry Hollister."

"Jeb's spread is just north of here, isn't it?"

Joseph nodded. "And rumor has it that his tail has been tied in a knot for going on ten years. Something about the flood back in seventy-nine altering the course of Wolverine Creek, leaving him high and dry without running water."

"I remember that, now. The original boundary description between the Bar H and his ranch included the creek and some rock formations. During the flood, the stream moved but the rocks didn't. Jeb wanted Henry Hollister to do a boundary line adjustment to follow the creek, and Henry refused because he would have been forfeiting several acres of prime grazing land."

Joseph pursed his lips. "If I recollect the stories right, Pritchard dynamited the creek a few months later, trying to redirect its course back onto his property. Evidently he didn't know what he was doing and only created a wide spot in the stream."

"Beiler never proved it was Pritchard," David observed.

"Who else had reason to care where that section of the creek flowed? It was Jeb. I'd bet money on it."

Jebediah Pritchard was a mean-natured, hostile man with an irrational streak rivaled only by his cowardice and body stench. His three grown sons, Hayden, Cyrus, and Alan, were apples that hadn't fallen far from the tree. When Joseph encountered a Pritchard in town, he stayed upwind and watched his back.

"I thought Henry Hollister channeled water from the creek into a big pond on Pritchard's property," David said. "That strikes me as being a fair compromise on Henry's part."

"More than fair. But what if Hollister had up and died, and his heir wasn't as generous? Pritchard would have been left with only a well to water his stock and crops. Maybe he decided to get rid of the whole Hollister family with the hope that he could convince Henry's aunt to sell. She'd already purchased a smaller spread on the other side of town, and she was getting up in years. She might have been glad to take the money and have the responsibility of this ranch off her hands."

Warming to the possibilities, David inserted, "Only the bullet glanced off Rachel Hollister's skull, and she didn't die like he'd hoped."

"Exactly. And even worse, she woke from the coma crazier than a loco horse, and never stepped foot outside from then on. Pritchard could never get another shot at her. I've heard tell that he's tried to buy this place several times since the massacre, but Darby's always refused out of hand, knowing Miss Rachel wouldn't agree. That being the case, what's Pritchard to do? He's back to where he started, needing to get shut of Rachel. Only he can't get at her without getting rid of Darby first."

David flashed a grin. "You ever contemplate becoming a lawman? You think like a criminal."

"No, thanks." Joseph chuckled and bent his head to grind out his cigarette under his heel. "I like ranching just fine."

"Any other suspects you can pluck out of your hat?"

Joseph considered the question. "All the neighboring property owners, I reckon. Couldn't hurt to question a few of their hired hands as well. This is prime ranchland. With Darby out of the picture, Miss Rachel would go broke in no time and be forced to sell, leaving someone to pick up this place for a little bit of nothing."

"You've just pointed a finger at yourself, big brother."

Joseph laughed again. "I reckon I did, at that. That's the trouble with casting a wide net. A lot of people fall under suspicion. Take Garrett Buckmaster, for instance. Even though his land is across the road and a little to the north, I believe he's made a couple of offers to buy this place over the last year. He strikes me as being a decent man, but he has no running water at his place, either. Stands to reason you should look at him real close."

David pinched the fire off his cigarette and tucked the butt into his pocket. "I guess I'll be a mite busy tomorrow."

"You mind having some company? I'd like to go along when you question everyone."

"Who'll look after Miss Rachel?"

"You can ask Ace to come over and spell me for a while."

David lifted a shoulder. "I'm not chomping at the bit to face Jeb and his boys alone. They're a shifty lot."

"That settles it, then. I'll ride along with you."

David tugged his hat low over his eyes. With a nudge of his heels, he set his horse to moving. "Tomorrow, then," he called over his shoulder.

Joseph watched his brother ride off. Then, whistling under his breath, he headed for the bunkhouse, where he hoped to find a lantern. He needed to put up his horse for the night and do Darby's chores, the first on the list milking those cows that were bawling so persistently. Making his way through an unfamiliar barn and barnyard would be easier with light to see by.

Joseph had just ripped away the outside boards from what he guessed to be a bedroom window at the front of the Hollister house when he felt something nudge his leg. He glanced down to see his dog standing there.

"What in Sam hill are you doing here? I thought I told you to stay home."

Buddy gave an all-over wag to convey his pleasure at being with his master again. It was difficult for Joseph to scold when he felt equally glad of the company. "All right," he said gruffly. "I'll let it go this time. But after this, when I tell you to stay put, I expect you to stay put."

Buddy worked his jaws and made the growling sound.

"Don't give me any sass," Joseph replied. "Who's the boss of this operation anyhow, you or me?"

Shit. The window was latched closed from the inside. Joseph pushed on the lower sash with all his might, but nothing happened. Resting an arm on the exterior sill, which was rough with peeling paint, he considered his options. To get inside, he would have to break the glass. Given the fact that it was colder than a witch's tit outside, he decided that it would be worth the expense. When Darby was back on his feet, Joseph would replace the pane, no harm done.

Decision made, he drew back his elbow and struck the glass. The thick leather of his jacket sleeve protected him from the shards. A few more elbow jabs finished the job.

"Back," he ordered his dog. When Buddy had retreated to a safe distance, Joseph brushed the fragments from the outside ledge, then swept the ground with the edge of his boot, piling the glass off to one side of the window. "I don't want you getting your paws cut."

The window had been boarded up on the inside as well, Joseph realized as he groped the opening. *Madness.* One layer of wood over the windows wasn't enough to satisfy the woman? Standing at ground level, Joseph couldn't butt the planks with his shoulder to break them loose. Fortunately, he always carried a few tools in his saddlebags.

Within moments, Joseph had set to work with a crowbar to loosen the one-by-fours from the inside casing so he could knock them free. He winced at the racket each time a board fell into the room, but there was no way to do this quietly. He had forewarned Rachel Hollister of his intention to enter her house, so hopefully she wouldn't be too alarmed by the noise.

When the window opening had been divested of barriers, Joseph fetched the lantern, his bedroll, and his saddlebags from where he'd placed them on the ground. After thrusting all his gear through the window, he turned for his dog.

"Come here, you willful mutt. Let's get in out of this dad-blamed wind."

Buddy made the growling sound that Joseph found so endearing. He gathered the silly canine into his arms and gave him a toss through the window. Agile and sure-footed, Buddy was soon bouncing around inside the room, his nails clacking on the floor. Bracing a hand on the sill, Joseph swung up, hooked a knee over the ledge, and eased himself through the opening. A musty, closed-up staleness greeted his nostrils.

After locating his gear, Joseph struck a match and

lighted the lantern. The lamp's golden glow illuminated a bedroom that looked as if its occupants had departed only that morning. A woman's white nightdress had been flung across the foot of the made-up bed, which was covered with a blue chenille spread and ruffled shams that matched the tiny flowers in the wallpaper. The armoire door stood ajar to reveal a man's suit and several white shirts, the remainder of the rod crowded with a woman's garments.

Upon closer inspection, Joseph saw that a thick layer of dust coated everything. He guessed that this must have been Henry and Marie Hollister's bedroom, and he felt like an interloper. A Bible on the night table lay open, a thin red ribbon angled across one page. Recalling the family's tragic end, he could almost picture Mr. and Mrs. Hollister rising to greet the day, never guessing that it would be their last.

"Come on, boy," he said to Buddy. "I'm getting the fidgets."

Joseph's fidgets worsened when he stepped out into a long hallway. A small parlor table, standing against the end wall, sported a vase filled with yellowed, disintegrating flower stalks. Judging by what remained of the leaves and the faded blossom pieces that littered the tatted doily, the flowers had once been irises. It gave him chills to think that Marie Hollister had probably cut the flowers and put them in water right before she died.

Holding the lantern high, Joseph continued along the corridor. He considered calling out to identify himself, just in case all the noise of the breaking glass and falling boards had upset Rachel Hollister. But what more could he possibly say? Before coming inside, he'd rapped on the door three times, once to introduce himself and tell her about Darby's injury, again to inform her that he'd done the chores, filled her wood box, and left two buckets of milk on the porch, and finally to tell her that he was going to enter the house by a front window. Even though she hadn't responded, he'd also explained his reason for being there, namely that Darby had asked him to come over and look after her. If all of that hadn't settled her nerves, nothing would.

He stopped briefly when he came upon what appeared to be a sewing room. The sewing machine was missing, but a half-made dress lay over a table, and an open closet revealed a nude dress form surrounded by lengths of lace and decorative trim looped over wooden pegs.

A little farther up the hall, he found a library. Tall rectangles of lightness in the pine-planked walls told him that several bookcases had been removed. Those that remained were only partially filled with what looked like tomes on animal husbandry and agriculture. Normally Joseph's interest would have been piqued, but tonight he hurried away, still unable to shake the feeling that the essence of the people who had lived here still lingered.

Deep in his heart of hearts, Joseph believed in ghosts. It wasn't something he'd ever talked about with anyone, but the belief was there within him. To his way of thinking, he couldn't very well believe in God and life everlasting without believing in spirits. So far, he'd never come nose to nose with a ghost, thank God, but there had been times in his life, like right now, when the hair on his arms had stood up.

He hurried to the end of the hall, his nerves leaping when Buddy suddenly growled. He tried to remind himself that Buddy *always* growled, but this was different, not a conversational sound but more a snarl of warning. What looked like a large sitting room opened to his right. Swinging the lamp high, he saw that some of the furniture was missing. It looked as if someone had absconded with the sofa, at least one chair, and a couple tables.

As Joseph moved on, his shoulder brushed against the wall, and a picture tipped sideways. The scraping sound startled him, and his skin felt as if it turned inside out. When he reached to straighten the frame, light washed over the photograph. A beautiful young girl stared back at him. Covered from chin to toe in dark muslin, her hair a cloud of light-colored ringlets around her thin shoulders, she looked to be about ten years old. She sat primly on a hassock, her folded hands resting on her lap. She had delicate features and large, expressive eyes, which he guessed to be blue given the lightness of her hair. Rachel Hollister, possibly? The younger daughter had never lived to see her sixth birthday.

Lamp still held high, Joseph stepped through an archway to his left and finally found himself in the dining room, which Darby had told him adjoined the kitchen where Rachel Hollister lived. A large window, which once looked out over the side yard, had been boarded up from the inside, the lace curtains over the planks gone dingy with age. A Louis XV sideboard

graced one wall, the elaborate grape motifs on the
doors reminding Joseph of the furnishings he'd seen as
a boy in San Francisco. Surrounded by ten high-
backed chairs, a long, marble-topped table, dulled by
a layer of grime, sat at the center of the room. The ornate silver candelabra that had served as a centerpiece
was draped with cobwebs, the once white tapers leaning this way and that.

Buddy scampered ahead of Joseph, his paws leaving prints in the film of dust on the fern-patterned burgundy carpet that stretched almost wall to wall.
Clearly, the Hollister family hadn't lived a hand-to-
mouth existence. This peeling, weather-beaten house
had been a pretty grand place.

Joseph lifted the light higher. In the middle of the
north wall was a boarded-over archway. He guessed
that Rachel Hollister's hideaway was on the other side.
After setting the lantern on the table, he tossed his gear
on the floor. No way was he going to sleep in one of
the bedrooms with ghosts as his bed companions.

The thought no sooner moved through Joseph's
mind than the air exploded with sound and flying debris. Buddy yelped in fright. Joseph dived for the floor.
When the dust settled, he was under the table, his Colt
.45 drawn and ready, two overturned chairs providing
him with scant cover.

Holy shit. Disgusted with himself for drawing his
weapon when he knew damned well it was a woman
shooting at him, Joseph slipped the revolver back
into his holster and retrieved his Stetson, which had
been knocked from his head. After putting the hat
back on, he cautiously shifted position to see around

one of the chair seats. Better to make a target of the Stetson than his head, he thought, and then promptly changed his mind when he saw the jagged hole that had appeared dead center in the boarded-up archway. The size of a prize-winning Texas pumpkin, it was well over two feet in diameter, the bottom edge a little over three feet from the ground, telling him that she'd probably fired from the waist instead of her shoulder. Only a shotgun had that kind of blasting power. If aimed anyplace near him, the gun would destroy the table, the overturned chair, his hat, *and* him.

Lamplight poured through the opening, lending additional brightness to the already illuminated dining room. With a shotgun-toting crazy woman on the other side of the wall, Joseph didn't count that as a blessing. Total darkness would have pleased him more.

Judging by the circumference of the hole, he felt fairly sure that Rachel Hollister had emptied both barrels. So far, he hadn't heard the telltale rasp and click of steel to indicate that she'd shoved more cartridges into the chambers. That was encouraging.

Once again, he thought about calling out to identify himself, but then decided it would be futile. If his earlier explanations hadn't satisfied her, telling her his name again wasn't likely to rectify the situation.

This woman wasn't messing around. She meant to kill him.

Chapter Four

Ears still ringing from the blast, Rachel lay on her back, arms and legs sprawled, the weapon lying at an angle across her lower body. Her hip throbbed with pain. For a moment, she couldn't think what had happened. Then her spinning confusion slowly settled into rational thought. She'd been standing in the middle of the room, terrified by the sounds of someone breaking into her house and coming toward the kitchen. Heart pounding, she'd swung the gun toward the boards over the doorway. Then something heavy had struck the wall, she'd jumped in fright, and the next thing she knew, she was staring at the ceiling.

Pushing the weapon off her legs, Rachel struggled to sit up. When she saw the huge hole that the shotgun had blown through her barricade, her heart almost stopped for the second time in as many minutes. *Oh, dear God.* She scrambled to her feet and retrieved the shotgun.

"Who's there?" she called, her voice shaking with

fright. "Get out of my house, or I'll shoot. Don't think I won't!"

No answer. An awful dread squeezed her chest. What if she had killed him? She frantically tried to remember the name of the man who had knocked on her door. *Paxton?* The moment he'd told her about Darby being shot, her head had gone muzzy, and then everything had turned black. Just before that, it seemed to her that the other man had introduced himself as the marshal. *Oh, God. Oh, God.* What if he'd been telling the truth, and she'd just shot a lawman?

Afraid of the sight that might greet her eyes, she inched closer to the opening, the bottom edge of which hit her several inches above the waist, allowing her to look through without ducking. In all her life, she had never harmed anything, not even a spider. To think that she might have killed two men made her stomach roll.

"Mr. Paxton?" She cautiously poked her head through the hole to see into the other room. The silence that bounced back at her was ominous. "A-are you all right?"

Hell, no, I'm not all right, Joseph thought angrily. The woman had almost blown him to Kingdom Come. He wished he could reach the lantern that he'd set on the table so he could lower the wick and extinguish the flame. As it was, the dining room was lighted up like a candle-laden Christmas tree, and all he had to hide behind was a chair seat.

How the hell did he land himself in fixes like this? If she opened fire again, he wouldn't even be able to shoot back. Crazy as a loon or not, she was a female.

No man worth his salt harmed a woman. That wasn't to mention the difficulty he'd have explaining such a thing to a judge. *It was self-defense, Your Honor. When I broke into her house, she started blasting away at me.* Yeah, right. He'd end up swinging from the highest limb of a scrub oak.

At least he hadn't heard her reload the weapon yet. That was a comfort. He inched his head out from behind the chair again.

The sight that greeted his eyes made his breath catch. Then he blinked, thinking maybe his vision was playing tricks on him. Rachel Hollister was beautiful—the kind of beautiful that made men stop dead in their tracks to take a long second look and trip over their own feet.

Never having met a crazy person, Joseph had expected to see a wild-eyed female with matted strings of filthy hair, a skeletal countenance, and soiled clothing. Instead, she looked like an angel. A cloud of golden curls, ignited by the light behind her, framed one of the sweetest, loveliest faces he'd ever clapped eyes on. She had a small, straight nose, delicate cheekbones, a soft, full mouth, a pointy chin, and blue eyes, which, at the moment, were huge with fright.

"I mean you no harm, Miss Hollister. Please don't shoot again."

She jumped as if he'd stuck her with a pin. Then she vanished. Joseph figured she'd gone for more ammunition and muttered a curse under his breath. One second, she was asking if he was all right, and the next she was making ready to kill him again.

Buddy, who had been lying belly-up in front of the

archway, chose that moment to recover from his fright and scramble to his feet. To Joseph's dismay, the dog reared up on his hind legs to hook his front feet over the lower edge of the hole, his snubbed tail wagging in friendly greeting. Rachel Hollister let out a startled squeak.

"Don't hurt him!" Joseph called. "He's harmless, I swear. Still just a pup."

"Go *away*!" she cried. "Get *out*, all of you! I don't want you here."

Joseph had gotten that message, loud and clear. Unfortunately, Buddy hadn't. The dog loved women, fat ones, skinny ones, and all shapes in between. Normally Joseph saw no harm in that. He liked females just fine himself. Only this one was armed, mad as a hatter, and trigger-happy.

The shepherd tensed as if to jump.

"Buddy, *no*!" Joseph cried, but the command came too late. With his usual agility, the sheepdog leaped through the opening. Joseph clenched his teeth and cringed, expecting to hear terrified shrieks, the snap of Damascus steel, and another shotgun blast. Instead, he heard a feminine yelp, followed by, "Go away! No! Bad dog! Get *off*!"

Soon after, a sputtering sound, interspersed by muffled protests, drifted to Joseph from the other room. Bewildered, he inched his head out from behind the chair again. He heard Buddy growling and could only hope Rachel Hollister didn't think the animal was threatening her. Joseph had come to love that silly canine more than was reasonable.

More sputtering. *What the hell?* Muscles tensed to

dive for cover again if necessary, he crawled out from under the table, rose gingerly to his feet, and tiptoed to the hole. Shotgun shells scattered on the floor around her, Rachel Hollister knelt in the middle of the other room, the shotgun lying beside her. Buddy had his front paws planted on her slender shoulders and was licking her face. Rachel kept ducking her head, trying to gather the ammunition, but the dog was quick, agile, and determined to have his way.

Normally the sight might have amused Joseph, but he'd just come close to meeting his Maker.

"Buddy!" he called.

Rachel Hollister jerked and fixed Joseph with a fearful look. The dog wheeled away from her and trotted to the hole. Joseph snapped his fingers, and Buddy obediently leaped back through the opening, coming to land lightly on his feet in the dining room. When Joseph glanced back into the kitchen, Rachel Hollister had retrieved the gun and stood with the brass-plated butt pressed to her shoulder. He wasn't unduly alarmed because he knew she hadn't reloaded the weapon yet.

In Joseph's opinion, she was a mite small to be firing a 10-gauge shotgun, anyway, especially one with shortened barrels. Such a weapon had enough recoil to knock a grown man on his ass. She also seemed to be sorely lacking in weapon know-how. Most people realized that guns worked better with ammunition in them. He guessed maybe she was so scared that she couldn't think straight.

An urge to smile came over him. That gave him pause. Who was crazier, him or her? He decided his urge to smile was partly due to the two-inch ruffles that lined the yoke of her white nightdress and fluffed up over her shoulders like clipped wings, making her resemble a small bird about to take flight. Then again, maybe it was the lamp on the table behind her, which shone through the folds of muslin, clearly outlining her body. He hadn't seen anything so fetching since he'd paid a nickel to watch a peep show in his misspent youth.

She was trembling—an awful shaking that made it difficult for her to hold the gun steady. Remembering the horror in her tone when she'd called out to ask if he was all right, he wondered if she had fired the weapon accidentally. Right before the blast, he'd tossed down his bedroll and saddlebags. Had the thump startled her so badly that her finger jerked?

She didn't have the look of a killer. Joseph firmly believed in the old adage that the eyes were windows to the soul. He saw no meanness in Rachel Hollister's, only terror.

In that moment, his wariness of her abated. Now that he'd had time to assess the situation, he couldn't believe that she'd taken deliberate aim. She was just frightened half out of her wits, reacting without thought to anything that startled her.

Terrorizing females didn't sit well with Joseph. Unfortunately, looking back, he couldn't think what he might have done differently. He'd tapped on her door three different times. Had she registered nothing of what he said?

He held her gaze for an endlessly long moment, waiting for her to look away first. The air between them turned electric, reminding Joseph of the expectant feeling before a storm. When her lashes finally fluttered, he turned aside.

"If you mean to shoot me, Miss Hollister, you'd best reload your gun. Judging by the size of that hole, you already emptied both barrels."

In his peripheral vision, he saw her flick an appalled glance at the weapon. Joseph couldn't help but smile. He went to the table to douse his lantern and then shook out his bedroll, selecting a spot along the wall between the dining room and kitchen so he'd be able to hear any sound coming from the other room. As he arranged his pallet and blankets, a rattling sound told him that Rachel Hollister was trying to retrieve the ammunition that she'd dropped on the floor. A second later, he heard the telltale snap of steel. Oddly, knowing that she'd reloaded the weapon didn't worry him anymore. Unless she accidentally pulled the triggers again, he honestly didn't believe she would shoot him.

He took off his jacket and tossed it at the head of his pallet to use as a pillow. Then he removed his hat and set it on the floor next to his saddlebags. He sensed rather than saw Rachel Hollister return to the opening. He soon felt the burn of her gaze on him. Ignoring her, he sat on the pallet and toed off a boot.

Poking her golden head through the hole to stare at him, she cried, "What are you *doing*?"

"Like I already told you, ma'am, I promised Darby that I'd look after you, and I'm not a man to go back on my word. It's a mite too cold outside for me to sleep on your porch, and the bunkhouse is too far away."

"Well, you most certainly won't sleep *there*."

"I won't?"

"No, you won't!"

Joseph toed off his other boot. Then, after pushing back the wool blankets, he pivoted on his ass and stretched out on his back, the jacket and his crossed arms pillowing his head. Buddy came to lie beside him.

Head angled through the opening, she stared at him with appalled disbelief. He studied her through narrowed eyes. "Do us both a favor, and keep your finger away from those triggers. Think of the mess it'll make if you blow a two-foot hole through me."

What little color remained in her cheeks drained away. "Mess or no"—she hooked a pointy elbow through the hole to better steady the gun—"I'll shoot if you don't get out of my house."

Joseph feigned a huge yawn, wondering as he did if he'd taken total leave of his senses. "You'd best pull the trigger then because I'm not leaving." He tugged the blanket to his chin. "I told old Darby that I'd stay, and that's what I mean to do. If the situation isn't to your liking, take it up with him."

Lowering her head and squinting one eye, she sighted in on him. As if she needed to aim? Joseph watched her with a curious detachment.

"You'd best get your chin away from that gun butt," he warned. "That shotgun will kick back on you like there's no tomorrow and bust your pretty little nose." He waited a beat. "Also—if it's all the same to you, that is—can you pull your aim wide to the left? Maybe then you won't shoot Buddy. His penchant for licking aside, he's a lovable dog, and he's never harmed a living soul. I'd hate to see him get hurt."

"I said you can't sleep there!" she cried.

"Why? You snore or something?"

"No, I don't *snore!*" The shrill pitch of her voice gave measure of her mounting frustration.

"Then I reckon I can sleep here well enough."

Light from the kitchen illuminated the side of her face. Joseph saw her mouth working, but no sound came out. Finally, she gave up on talking and disappeared. Shortly thereafter, he heard a commotion. It sounded to him as if she were tearing something apart.

Angling his upper body to see the doorway, he gazed curiously after her. He wasn't left to wonder what she was doing for long. She soon reappeared at the hole, a half dozen nails clenched between her teeth and a hammer in her hand. He watched as she set to work, nailing the slats of an apple crate over the opening. The sections of wood were barely long enough to span the distance and so flimsy as to provide little protection, but she furiously pounded them into place. Unfortunately, she lacked a sufficient number of slats to completely fill the hole, the result a sloppy crisscross with triangular gaps large enough to accommodate a man's fist. To curtain off her sanctum, she draped two bath towels over the lot, tacking them at top and bottom.

Joseph frowned in the ensuing dimness. A man could crawl through that two-foot hole, but not without making a good deal of noise in the process. With a loaded shotgun handy, she was as safe in there as a babe in its cradle.

Only a dim glow of light penetrated the linen towels. The illumination cast diamond patterns over the room. Settling back on his pallet, Joseph studied the shapes, acutely aware of every sound she made on the other side of the wall. Soft rustles, breathless utterances. "Consternation" seemed to be her favorite byword, "drat" running a close second. She clearly wasn't pleased to have houseguests.

Joseph grabbed his saddlebags, thinking to fetch himself and Buddy some supper. His hand met with emptiness when he reached in the pocket. *Damn.* After a day of wrangling, he always replenished his trail supplies, but somehow or other he'd forgotten to do it last time. Thinking back, he recalled the reason: a heifer in the throes of a breech birth. He'd been out in the field with her until late and had been so exhausted when he reached the house that he'd fallen straight into bed.

Well, hell. Excuses wouldn't fill his stomach. More important, they wouldn't fill Buddy's. Joseph was accustomed to going hungry on occasion, but his dog wasn't. Sighing, he rolled onto his side and rubbed the animal's upturned belly. "Sorry, partner. I'll feed you twice in the morning to make up for it. I know you worked damned hard today. You should have stayed home with Esa. He would have fed you, at least."

Buddy's warm tongue rasped over the whiskers sprouting on Joseph's jaw. *Damn dog.* If there was anything he hated, it was a licker. He pushed at the shepherd's nose. "Stop it," he whispered. "You think I don't know where that tongue of yours has been?"

Buddy whined and nailed Joseph directly on the lips. He almost sputtered as Rachel Hollister had. Instead, he settled for rubbing away the wetness with his shirtsleeve and then changed the position of his upraised arm to guard his face. After a moment, the dog thrust his nose in Joseph's armpit, huffed, and went to sleep.

Joseph's thoughts drifted and circled until his eyelids grew heavy. Buddy snuggled closer, and their combined body heat made the bed cozy warm.

Rachel had turned her mother's rocker to face the archway. She sat poker straight on the chair, the shotgun balanced on her knees. A blanket draped around her shoulders, she stared fixedly at the towels she'd tacked over the crate slats. One question circled endlessly in her mind. *What in heaven's name am I going to do?*

She had no answers. She knew only that her world had been turned upside down. Nothing was as it should be—as she so desperately needed it to be. First and most alarming, her home was no longer safe. The hole in the barricade made her feel horribly vulnerable. When she thought about that man possibly crawling through, her skin shriveled, she broke out in a cold sweat, and she found it difficult to breathe.

He was there, just on the other side of the wall, a threat to her safety—and her sanity. She wanted him gone. Out, out, *out!*

But then what? She had no boards to repair the barricade, and she couldn't go into town to buy more. Darby always went to town and purchased what she needed. Without him, she was helpless, absolutely helpless. What on earth would she do if he died and never came back?

The question was one she couldn't answer, and it also filled her with guilt. What if Joseph Paxton was telling the truth, and Darby had been shot? She loved that old foreman like a father. What kind of person was she to be worrying about boards when he might be dying?

Tears stung her eyes. She began rocking in the chair to maintain her self-control. *Squeak, squeak, squeak.* The whine of the chair came faster and faster until she realized she was pushing with her feet almost frenetically and forced herself to stop. *Darby.* He was much older than she was, and at the back of her mind, she had always known that she would outlive him. She'd just never allowed herself to contemplate the possibility that he might die any time soon. Darby was the closest thing to family that she had left. Oh, how she would miss seeing his craggy face through the peephole that he had installed in her door. And how empty her days would be if he never again tapped on the wood safe for his meals.

The wetness in her eyes spilled over onto her cheeks, creating cold, ticklish trails that made her want to scratch. Only she couldn't pry her hands from the gun. Why hadn't she shot Joseph Paxton when she had the chance? He'd known she couldn't do it, blast him. Even through the shadows, she'd seen the twinkle of amusement in his eyes.

This was all *his* doing. She never would have fired the shotgun if he hadn't made a loud sound and startled her. And just who did he think he was, tearing the boards off one of her windows and breaking the glass? She would never feel safe until the window was repaired and boarded up again.

Anger roiled within her. But before she could get a firm hold on it, worry for Darby assailed her again. If the old man truly was hurt, the least Joseph Paxton could do was apprise her of his condition. Had anyone fetched the doctor? How bad was the wound? And who was caring for the poor old fellow?

Rachel wanted to jerk the towels away from the opening and demand that Joseph Paxton give her answers. But was that even his real name? He'd come here with another man. For all she knew, they could be outlaws. The one she'd seen definitely had the look of a scapegrace. Men who wore sidearms were a dime a dozen in No Name, but there was nothing ordinary about the way he wore his, a pearl-handled Colt .45, strapped low on his thigh. Rachel had read enough novels to know that a gunslinger wore his weapon that way to minimize the distance of reach, thereby maximizing his speed at the draw.

She stared at the towels, which offered her little privacy and even less protection. *Darby.* She had to find out how he fared. Only how? When she contemplated tearing the towels away to confront Joseph Paxton again, she started to shake.

He wasn't really a large man, she assured herself. But he had a large presence, every inch of his lean body roped with muscle, his broad shoulders and well-padded chest tapering to a slim waist and narrow hips. His eyes were particularly arresting, an ordinary blue yet razor sharp, giving the impression that he missed nothing. In the lamplight, they had shimmered like quicksilver.

A frown pleated Rachel's brow as she tried to recall the rest of his face. Exposure to the elements had burnished his skin; she remembered that much. But she couldn't for the life of her envision his features. He'd worn a sand-colored Stetson with a wide brim that dipped down in front. Perhaps that was why. She could remember his hair, which was as blond as her own, only as straight as a bullet on a windless day. Shoulder length, if she recollected right, and tucked behind his ears.

The rapid creak of the rocker told Rachel that she was pushing too fast again. She brought the chair to a stop and then nearly jumped out of her skin at the sound of a low growl. The towels over the hole moved, and the next instant, a liver-colored nose lifted a bottom corner of the linen. *The dog.* She watched the animal's nostrils flare to pick up her scent. Shortly thereafter, another inch of white blaze on the canine's nose became visible.

"No!" Rachel cried softly. "Stop that."

But the reddish-gold dog kept pushing until the bottom of one towel popped free and a slat snapped. His head poked through. Rachel leaped up from the rocker. Leaving the gun on the sofa within easy reach, she advanced on the archway.

"Bad, *bad* dog," she whispered. "I don't want you in here. Away with you. Go on."

Rachel could have sworn that the silly animal grinned. And then he let loose with more growls, working his jaws so the sounds changed pitch, almost as if he were talking. When she reached to push him back, he whined and licked her hands.

Rachel's heart sank. He was such a sweet, friendly fellow, and he truly didn't mean her any harm. He only wanted to say hello. She had always adored dogs. One of the great loves of her life had been Denver, a huge, yellow mongrel with soulful brown eyes. Many had been the time that Rachel wished the killer might have at least spared the dog's life. *Denver, her special friend.* The silly mutt had rarely left her side. In the end, his unfailing loyalty had been the death of him.

The thought always made Rachel sad. Unlike the other members of her family, Denver could have run and saved himself. Instead, he'd stayed to protect her and earned himself a slug between the eyes.

As though her hands had a will of their own, Rachel found herself fondling Buddy's silky ears. Dogs were wonderfully uncomplicated creatures. No subterfuge or pretense. What you saw was what you got. She liked the way his ears stood up, with only the rounded tips flopping forward. He only straightened them when she spoke or made a sound.

He was a handsome fellow, she decided. A snow-white blaze ran the length of his muzzle, and the lighter russet spots above his amber eyes lent his face a pensive look. He was a sheepdog, she concluded, a breed that had proven useful in herding cattle and become popular with the ranchers hereabouts. Rachel had heard it said that most sheepdogs were uncommonly intelligent. Looking into Buddy's alert, questioning eyes, she had little trouble believing it.

"You're a pushy sort, aren't you?" she whispered, wishing that she could let him into the kitchen. As it was, he was about to destroy her makeshift repairs. He shoved with a shoulder and snapped another slat. *"Stop!"* she whispered. "You can't come in. Can't you tell when someone doesn't like you?"

"He's hungry."

Startled by Joseph Paxton's deep voice, Rachel jumped back from the opening.

"Whatever you fixed for supper smells mighty good," he went on. "I thought I had jerky in my saddlebags, but I was mistaken, and he's not used to missing a meal. I've spoiled him, I reckon."

Rachel retreated another step. The dog seemed to interpret that as an invitation. Before she could react, he jumped through the hole, breaking the remaining slats and jerking one towel completely loose. The next instant, she was being accosted by the friendly canine. Fortunately, he was an agile fellow and light on his feet. When he planted his paws on her chest, she barely felt his weight. He growled at her again, a *yaw-yaw-yaw* that sounded absurdly conversational.

It was impossible for Rachel to look into the animal's expressive eyes without wanting to smile.

"So you're hungry, are you? All I have is stew and cornbread, and I don't think that's good for dogs."

Buddy dropped to his belly, put his paws together as if he were praying, and then lifted his head to bark. The message was clear. Stew was very good for dogs, the more the better. Rachel was lost. Maybe it was the prayer position that did her in—or maybe it was the sweet, imploring expression on Buddy's face. She had never been able to turn away a hungry critter. As a girl, she'd loved to feed the wild animals and birds that visited the ranch. One year, her pa had built her half a dozen birdhouses for Christmas so she'd be able to watch the sparrows build their nests and hatch their babies the following spring. Oh, how Rachel missed the birdsong. With her windows boarded up, inside and out, she couldn't hear it anymore.

Just in case Joseph Paxton decided to climb through the hole after his dog, she retrieved the shotgun before advancing on the stove. With the weapon leaning against the wall within close reach, she set to work to feed Buddy. Thoughts of Darby once again assailed her as she filled a serving bowl with stew and added some crumbled cornbread. This was to have been the foreman's supper. Would he ever again tap on the wood safe and enjoy a meal that she had cooked for him?

She cast a considering glance at the damaged barricade as she set the bowl on the floor. Buddy didn't hesitate. With a happy growl, he began gobbling the food as if he hadn't been fed in a week.

Rachel straightened, gathered the blanket closer around her shoulders, took a breath for courage, and said, "I shall strike a bargain with you, Mr. Paxton. In exchange for information about my foreman, I'll feed you supper."

Surprised by the unexpected offer, Joseph sat bolt upright on his pallet. Surely he hadn't heard her right.

"I'm sorry. What did you say?"

"I said that I'm prepared to make a deal with you. Food for information about Darby."

Joseph ran a hand over his midriff. "I'm hungry enough to eat the south end of a northbound jackass, Miss Hollister, but I've already told you everything I can."

"That Darby's been shot, you mean?" Her voice went high-pitched. "Surely you can tell me more than that. Did you fetch Doc Halloway? Was he able to get the slug out? What is the prognosis? Does he think Darby's going to—*die*?"

Joseph had given her all that information earlier. "That's a mighty thick back door you've got. I guess you didn't catch a lot of what I said earlier." Resting his arms over his upraised knees, Joseph once again recounted the events of that afternoon, how Darby had come riding into his place, barely clinging to the saddle, and how Joseph had staunched the bleeding and gone for the doctor. "Doc seems to think he's going to make it. The bullet shattered a couple of ribs, but it missed the lung and kidney."

"What of infection?"

"Doc dressed the wound with honey."

"Honey?" she echoed.

"He swears by it. Says honey fights infection and has healing properties. He slathered all he could over the wound before bandaging Darby up, and he left some for my brother, Esa, to use when he changes the wrappings."

Silence. And then, voice quivering, she asked, "So your brother is looking after Darby?"

"Because I had to come over here, Esa volunteered." Actually, it had been more a case of Joseph's twisting his brother's arm, but he didn't think she needed to know that. Esa had a good heart, and he'd do right by the old man.

"Darby has it in his head that you're in some kind of danger," he expounded. "When he first got to my place, he kept telling me to forget about him and come straight here to make sure you were safe."

Another silence, a long one this time. After a while, Joseph grew concerned. "Miss Hollister? You there?"

He thought he heard her take a taut breath. "Yes. Yes, I'm here, Mr. Paxton." Another silence ensued, and then she added, "That's the first thing you've said all evening that makes me think you may be telling the truth."

That was a step up, Joseph guessed. Only what part of what he'd said had been to her liking? She gave a shrill little sigh that reminded him strongly of his mother. Dory Paxton was a great one for sighing.

"Well, now for your supper," she said. "That was the bargain, after all." He heard the faint clink of china. "I'll hand it through to you. Please stand well back, or I shall have to shoot you. I'm sure you're no fonder of that idea than I am."

Joseph grinned. "Have you shot a number of folks?"

"Not as yet," she informed him. "But don't take that to mean that I will hesitate."

His grin broadened. He was starting to like this lady. She had pluck. He was also starting to wonder if she wasn't crazy like a fox. Someone had shot Darby today, and both Joseph and David agreed that the bullet had been meant to kill. Wasn't it possible that Rachel Hollister had known for years that her life was in danger? Maybe David had hit the nail right on the head, and her hermitlike habits stemmed more from fear than lunacy.

Joseph lighted his lantern and then, honoring her request, stood well back from the hole in the archway to wait for his food. When Rachel appeared at the opening, he noticed that she didn't have to duck her head to look through at him, putting her height at several inches less than his own. He also noticed that she had small, fine-boned hands, her slender fingers gone pink at the tips where they gripped the bowl. Eyeing him warily, she thrust her arms through the opening.

"Here you go."

Not wishing to startle her, Joseph moved slowly forward, taking care to stop when the bowl was within reach. Even then, she was so skittish that she nearly dropped the dish before he could get a good hold on it.

"Thank you."

She retreated several steps, her gaze wide and wary. "You're welcome."

"I know that this is an uncomfortable situation for you," Joseph said as he carried his meal to the table. "You don't know me from Adam. But ask yourself this. Would Darby have sent me here if he didn't trust me?"

Standing some three feet back from the opening, she hugged her waist, the blanket tucked under her arms like the ends of a shawl. "I have no way of knowing if Darby actually sent you."

With a sweep of his hand, Joseph cleaned dust from the far end of the table and sat down facing her. "Why would I lie about it?"

"To gain my trust?"

Joseph fleetingly wished that his brother were present to handle this. A little sugarcoating was definitely in order. "If I meant you harm, Miss Hollister, I already would have done my worst, the devil take your trust." He inclined his head at the barricade. "Do you really believe a few boards would keep me out if I was bent on coming in?"

She stiffened. "You'd run the risk of getting shot."

"Not with an empty gun."

"It isn't empty now."

"But it was, and I knew it. What was stopping me, then, do you think?"

She only stared at him.

"And what stopped me from grabbing your wrist just now when you handed out the food?" He snapped his fingers. "I could have had you then, easy as anything."

She drew the blanket closer. "Are you threatening me, Mr. Paxton?"

"No, I'm making a point. You say you have no way of knowing if Darby actually sent me? I think you do."

"Darby never so much as mentioned your name."

"Yeah, well, Darby's not much of one for small talk. We met at the south end of your ranch when the fence between your place and mine was in sore need of repair. We worked on it together. When it came time to eat, we shared some shade while we had lunch.

Nothing notable happened. Maybe he didn't count it as being important enough to mention."

"You met only the one time?"

"We've run into each other a few times since."

"If he knows you only in passing, why does he trust you?"

Now there was a question Joseph wasn't sure how to answer. "I've got an honest face?"

She didn't smile.

Joseph was starving and wanted to dive into his meal. The stew and cornbread smelled so good that his mouth watered.

"You can learn a lot about a man by mending fence with him," he offered. "If he whines over the bite of barbed wire, you know he lacks grit. If he leans on his shovel a lot, you know he's lazy. If he picks the easier of two jobs more than once, you know he's inclined to be self-serving as well. If he neglects his horse—" Joseph broke off and sighed. "I can't say why Darby trusts me, Miss Hollister. Maybe he liked what he learned about me that day. Or maybe it's because he knows I come from good family. Only he can say."

"Good family? Do your folks live around here?"

"My older brother, Ace Keegan, owns the spread northeast of here."

"The piece of land that Patrick O'Shannessy sold?"

"That's right." Joseph glimpsed a thoughtful look in her eyes. "Ace married Patrick's sister, Caitlin. He also built the railroad spur into Denver."

"Caitlin?"

Joseph nodded. "Know her?"

"She's older than me, but we went to school together for a number of years."

"Did you now?" Joseph picked up a chunk of cornbread and took a bite.

Questions still lurked in her eyes. "How can Ace
Keegan be your brother? You don't have the same last
name."

"We're actually only half brothers. When his pa
died, our ma married my father, Joseph Paxton, senior.
Back in sixty-five, he bought the piece of land that Ace
owns now and moved our family out here from Vir-
ginia to make a fresh start. Unfortunately, things went
sour, my ma took us boys to San Francisco, and none
of us returned to No Name until four and a half years
ago."

Light dawned in her eyes. "Joseph Paxton," she repeated softly. "I remember the name now." A frown
pleated her brow, and her blue eyes sharpened on his
face. "He was hanged."

Joseph winced, thinking that she'd picked a fine
time to put all the pieces together. If she hadn't heard
the entire story, which was a strong possibility, she
might panic for certain. "*Wrongfully* hanged," he
stressed, gesturing with the spoon. "My father was accused of squatting on the land he'd paid good money
for and also of murdering Camlin Beckett, an up-
standing citizen of No Name." Joseph's mouth went as
dry as dirt. To this day, it wasn't easy for him to recall
his father's death, let alone talk about it. "In truth,
Beckett, Conor O'Shannessy, and a handful of others,
including the town marshal, Estyn Beiler, were a

bunch of swindlers, and my father was one of their victims. He just paid far more dearly than the rest."

Her eyes went wide, but she said nothing to indicate what she might be thinking.

"Four and a half years ago," Joseph went on, "all us boys returned to No Name to clear our father's name. But maybe you never heard about that."

She closed her eyes for a moment, and Joseph thought some of the tension eased from her shoulders. "I did hear about it. Darby isn't much for talking, that's true, but he told me about that. It was scandalous what Estyn Beiler and the others did to your father and family."

In Joseph's opinion, scandalous didn't describe it by half, but he was so relieved she'd heard the whole story that he didn't object.

She arched a delicate eyebrow. "Your brother, Ace Keegan—he's a gunslinger of some reputation, isn't he?"

"He gave all that up years ago."

She sent him a dubious look.

"Ace and Caitlin have a son now," he said, hoping to distract her from that train of thought. "Little Ace. He's fourteen months old and cute as a button."

"And you?"

Joseph paused with a spoonful of stew at his lips. "Me, what?"

"You have the look of a gunslinger, too."

"I do?"

"Are you?"

He took the bite of stew. "This is downright delicious, Miss Hollister. Darby's a lucky man if he gets to eat cooking like this every day."

"You didn't answer my question."

He spooned in some more stew, chewed, and swallowed. "What question was that?"

"Are you fast with a gun?"

"Fair to middling. Ace is the one that's fast."

Joseph couldn't see her feet, but he had a notion that she was tapping her toe. "Have you killed anyone, Mr. Paxton?"

Joseph decided then and there that honesty wasn't always the best policy. In self-defense, he had, in fact, taken human life. That wasn't something he wanted to talk about, especially not with a wary woman who might jump to wrong conclusions. "Do I look like a killer?"

"Yes."

Well, hell. He'd finally met someone as plainspoken as he was. Time to turn the tables. "It seems to me it's my turn to ask a few questions."

She looked genuinely surprised. "I am not the interloper in this situation, Mr. Paxton. You've broken into my home, and you refuse to leave. I'll ask the questions until I'm satisfied that you are who you say you are."

"Ah, but I wouldn't be here if Darby hadn't insisted on it." He took another bite of stew and studied her as he chewed. "Even doped up on laudanum, he was so worried about your safety that he was fit to be tied. Can you explain why?"

Her eyes went dark with shadows.

"That strikes me as being a little peculiar," Joseph

pressed on. "Why would Darby instantly conclude that the attack on him today was somehow connected to the attack on you and your family five years ago?"

She closed her eyes and shook her head. "I don't know." Her lashes lifted. "I truly don't know."

Her face had gone as pale as milk, and Joseph didn't miss the fear that had returned to her eyes. "There has to be a reason," he insisted. "He was scared to death for you and absolutely emphatic that your life might be in danger." He studied her closely. "What do you remember about that day?"

"Nothing." She swayed slightly on her feet and splayed a dainty hand over her midriff. "Darby was upset because he was shot near the creek." The pitch of her voice went so low he almost didn't catch her next words. "That's why he made a connection, I'm sure, because that's where it happened before."

Watching her, Joseph tensed on the chair. "Don't faint on me. If you fall, I'm not in there to catch you."

She passed a trembling hand over her eyes. "I'm fine."

Joseph knew better. She looked scared half to death, and his instincts told him that she was holding something back. Yet when he searched her gaze, he saw only frightened confusion.

"You must have some idea who killed your family," he insisted.

The clawing fear in her eyes gave way to anger. "If I did, I would have screamed it to the rooftops years ago, Mr. Paxton."

"I don't buy that. You have a suspicion, at least." Joseph honestly believed that was the only explanation for the way she lived. She was afraid of someone. She had to be. "I don't know why, but you're hiding something."

"I remember nothing. *Nothing,* do you hear? It was my *family* that died!" She made a fist over her heart. "My mother, my father, my brother, and my sister. I *loved* them." Her eyes went bright with tears. "If I had any inkling—even an unfounded *suspicion* of who killed them—do you honestly believe I would keep it to myself?"

Her question struck home for Joseph. He, too, had lost a loved one, and even today it still hurt him to think about that awful night. He'd been—what— eight years old? He couldn't even remember his father clearly. How much more horrible must it be for Rachel Hollister, who'd been sixteen or seventeen at the time? She would have vivid memories of each person's face and of the special moments she'd shared with them, particularly those last, precious moments right before they died. Naturally she would do everything within her power to see their killer brought to justice. He'd been wrong to imply otherwise.

"I don't mean to upset you," he said, his voice husky with regret.

She brushed angrily at her cheeks and whirled from the opening. A moment later, she passed by again, heading for the left rear corner of the room, the shotgun cradled in her arms. Joseph half expected to hear her start sobbing, but instead an awful silence settled over the house.

He finished his meal with one ear cocked, his gaze fixed on the hole. *No sound. No sign of movement.*

When he'd cleaned his bowl, he left the dish on the table and crept over to the barricade.

Prior to this, Joseph had only caught glimpses of her sanctuary. The sight that greeted him was nothing short of amazing. Rachel had transformed the large ranch kitchen into a one-room home, grouping furniture to create different sections. The front of the room still served as a kitchen, the corner to his right had been set up as a parlor, and to his immediate left was her sleeping area, comprised of a double bed, a night table, a chest of drawers, and an armoire. Granted, each area was crowded, but they provided her with all the amenities of a tiny house.

Rachel sat with her back pressed against the headboard of the bed, the shotgun on the mattress beside her. Her eyes were squeezed tightly shut, her fragile jaw set. Joseph took a moment to study her, and what he saw made his heart hurt. No tears, no jerking of her shoulders. Body rigid, she just sat there, hugging her knees as if that were all that held her together. *Memories*. He saw them etched on her face, the grief they brought drawing the skin taut over her cheekbones. He had intentionally forced her to think about that day without considering how painful it might be for her, not just during the conversation, but possibly long after.

Too late, he knew that his brother David was absolutely right. Sometimes the truth went down a little easier if you sprinkled it with sugar. He had no talent for that, never had and never would.

Until now, he'd never thought of it as a serious failing.

Chapter Five

Rachel's eyes burned as if they'd been soaked in lye. She had no idea how long she'd been sitting on the bed, only that she'd been there for hours, listening to the rumble of Joseph Paxton's snores. Her back felt as if the edge of a brutally sharp sword were pressing in just under her shoulder blades. She'd shifted and stretched, but the crick had taken up permanent residence. Quite simply, her body cried out for rest.

Unfortunately, Rachel couldn't bring herself to lie down and try to sleep. Instead, she stared at the hole. It was the proverbial chink in her armor, a weakness in the fortress that had saved her sanity these last five years. Now she felt exposed and vulnerable in a way that made her skin crawl and her nerves leap.

Oddly, the man who slept in the other room was no longer the focus of her terror. His story about Darby rang true, and everything else he'd said rang true as well. He knew things about the old foreman that only a friend might—specifically that Darby wasn't a talker and that he loved Rachel deeply enough to die for her. Rachel was also reassured by the fact that Joseph Paxton had foregone several opportunities to harm her. It was true that he could have grabbed her when she handed out his food. He looked to be a strong man and quick on his feet. There was also no denying that he could easily dispense with the boards over the doorway if he wished. With a couple of waist-high jabs of a boot, he could enlarge the hole, push through, and be on her. In that event, only her willingness to fire the shotgun would save her, and Rachel had a feeling he knew the thought of killing someone gave her the chills.

What had stopped him from entering her quarters? So far as Rachel could see, nothing, which had led her to conclude that he was who he claimed to be and had been sent by Darby, her beloved friend. The old foreman never would have sent a scapegrace to look after her. Rachel knew that beyond a doubt. Darby was nothing if not protective of her. He was also an astute judge of character. In short, Joseph Paxton had come with the very best of recommendations, and she would be foolish to distrust him.

He snorted just then, an abrupt, raucous catch of breath that was so loud Rachel could have sworn it vibrated the walls. It had been so long since she'd heard a man snore that she'd almost forgotten what a comforting sound it was. As a young child awakening from unpleasant dreams, she'd been comforted by the low, rhythmic rumble of her father's snores, which had drifted through the entire house. It was a sound that said, "All is well." And it had always lulled her back to sleep.

Joseph Paxton's snores soothed her, too. Perhaps it was because she sensed that he was an alert, guarded man who slept with one eye open. Or maybe it was simply the sound of the snoring itself, which she'd known since infancy and come to associate with cozy warmth and safety.

His snores made her feel drowsy. Oh, how she wished she could stretch out on her soft bed and close her eyes. But with every creak and groan of the house, her heart shot up into her throat. *Danger.* It lurked beyond her walls, a constant threat.

Joseph Paxton's presence didn't allay her fears. Her father, Henry Hollister, had been a strong protector, every inch of his frame padded with steely muscle from a lifetime of hard work. And yet he had failed to keep his family safe. The danger had come unexpectedly and from out of nowhere, catching him unprepared. No man, no matter how strong and devoted, was impervious to a well-aimed bullet.

Rachel shivered and rubbed her arms. Her skin felt as if it were smeared with drying egg white. *Oh, yes.* The danger was out there. She had no idea where it lurked, only that it might strike again if she let down her guard.

That was the most awful part, the not knowing. It had her jumping at shadows, which went against her nature. Prior to the slayings, she'd been a fearless girl, always off and about, more tomboy than young lady, much to her mother's dismay. One afternoon, a pair of rattlers in the barn had sent all the hired hands scattering, and it was Rachel who'd gone in to remove the snakes. The men had teased her mercilessly about her failure to kill the poor things, but she hadn't let that bother her. It had been her belief then, and still was to this day, that all God's creatures had a purpose and a right to live.

Perhaps that was why the murder of her family and dog still haunted her so—because the senseless violence was so inconceivable to her. Ever since she'd awakened from the coma, her world had been at sixes and sevens, a messy, untidy, chaotic, and askew reality interlaced with an awful unpredictability. And at the root of her confusion there was always a cloying fear—of the sunlight, of a breeze touching her face, even of the air itself—because she knew, deep down, that evil permeated everything beyond the safety of her walls.

Rachel couldn't say how she knew that. The conviction was simply there, hiding behind a black curtain in her mind. She had no clear recollection of the tragic events of that fateful afternoon, only a compilation of facts related to her by Darby, who'd grown concerned when she and her family had failed to return to the house and had finally ridden to their picnic place along the creek to discover the bloodbath, and by Doc Halloway, who'd been summoned to the scene by one of the other ranch hands and had, as a result, treated Rachel's head wound and nursed her back to health over the next few weeks.

Joseph Paxton had accused her of holding something back, of having memories of her family's murder that she'd chosen not to share. In a way, Rachel almost wished that were true. Knowledge would be far better than the blankness that stubbornly shrouded some parts of her mind. Doc Halloway maintained that Rachel must have been the first to be shot that June afternoon. A bullet from out of nowhere, and then only blackness; thus her inability to remember anything about the incident. Rachel had pretended to accept that because it seemed logical. She'd had no better explanation, after all. But deep down, she knew better.

Her nightmares told her that she had seen and felt and heard many things before the blackness had descended. The memories came to her in confusing rushes, blurry images flashing brightly and then going dark, all separate and disconnected but still so horrifying that they brought her bolt upright from sleep with a scream on her lips and rivulets of cold sweat streaming from her body.

Joseph was accustomed to awakening when the first faint light of dawn streaked the sky. But inside the Hollister house, no outside light filtered in. When he first opened his eyes the following morning, he thought for a moment that it was still night. Only the fact that he felt well rested told him otherwise.

He sat up and rubbed the back of his neck, his gaze trained on the barricade. Light still shone through the hole. He sat perfectly still and listened for a moment. He could hear the hum of Rachel's lanterns, but nothing else.

Always eager to greet a new day, Buddy fairly danced with excitement when Joseph's movements awakened him. The shepherd darted in to lick Joseph's face, then pranced to the doorway that led from the dining room into the hall.

Joseph pushed to his feet, hoping the dog would keep quiet for once in his life. But, no, the animal let loose with three earsplitting barks, followed by a series of happy growls.

"Quiet!" Joseph whispered, though he didn't know why he bothered. The dog knew the commands to sit, stay, and drop, but "quiet" wasn't in his vocabulary. Life was an endless celebration, and every incident called for at least one bark or growl to mark the moment.

Joseph escorted the sheepdog to the end of the hall and threw open Henry and Marie Hollister's bedroom door. "Go run off some of that mischief."

Buddy didn't need to be told twice. With three agile leaps, he was across the room and out the window. At a slower pace, Joseph followed, unbuttoning his Levi's as he went. After relieving himself through the opening, he refastened his fly and returned to the dining room. He wasn't surprised to see Rachel standing at the archway.

"I'm sorry if Buddy woke you. He gets a little excited first thing of a morning."

"I wasn't sleeping."

Joseph studied her face, taking in the redness of her eyes and the dark circles beneath them. He wondered if she'd sat up all night. She looked frighteningly fragile—like glass blown so fine that the slightest touch might shatter it.

"Would you like some coffee?" she asked.

Just the thought made his mouth water. "You don't have to bother."

"No bother. I need a cup myself." She turned away from the opening. "If you're hungry, I can make some breakfast, too."

Joseph was pleased to note that she didn't carry the shotgun with her to the range. He leaned a shoulder against the boards to watch while she built a fire in the box and stepped to the sink to rinse out the metal coffeepot.

"Running water?" Joseph had the same luxury at his place, but this house had been built a good many years before the novelty of indoor plumbing, which was still a rarity in these parts. "I'm surprised."

"Darby plumbed it in for me." She gestured at a closed door to his left. "He added on a water closet as well. I have a bathtub, a flushing commode, and a Mosley gas water heater from Montgomery Ward."

Joseph noticed a hand-cylinder laundry machine beside the range, the fill-up hose disconnected from the stove's water reservoir, the drain hose running from the machine to a hole in the wooden floor. That was a step up from his place. He had a fully equipped water closet, but he still did his laundry the old-fashioned way on the back porch. Last autumn, after getting his house finished, he'd thought about ordering a laundry machine, and he still might yet. But it wasn't one of those things that he felt he couldn't live without.

She noticed him staring past her at the door next to the range. It was barred shut with a thick pine plank. "The cellar," she explained. "It used to be Ma's pantry.

Darby ripped up part of the floor, dug it out under-neath, and built steps down into it. I needed a place to cure meat, make pickles and cheese, and store my home-canned goods."

As Joseph took in the details that he'd overlooked last night, he couldn't help but marvel. Darby had added every possible amenity to her confined living area, making sure that she had everything she could need or want. Even more amazing, she'd made it all pretty as could be with colorful rag rugs on the wood floor and curtains over the boarded-up windows, lace panels to the left on the back door, blue gingham to the right over the sink. On the kitchen table there was even a porcelain vase filled with silk and velvet geraniums. He guessed the fake flowers were from Montgomery Ward, too. Caitlin had ordered some a while back to brighten up their house during the winter.

"This is really something," he said.

Turning from the stove, she inspected the room with hollow eyes. "It loses its charm after a while."

She pushed at her hair, which had gone curlier since last night, little golden wisps springing every which way. Joseph wondered if it was as soft as it looked and found himself itching to touch it.

"If you'll excuse me, I need to get dressed," she in-formed him. "Then I'll start breakfast."

Joseph hated to use up her food. He wasn't an in-vited guest, after all. But until Ace showed up to re-lieve him later that day, he was stuck here without any rations of his own. "That'd be nice. I'll be sure to re-place whatever I eat, plus extra to repay you for your trouble."

She gave him a curious look. "You're here at Darby's request to look after me. Providing your meals is the least I can do."

Joseph was pleased that she seemed to have accepted the situation at some point during the night. She wasn't exactly relaxed with him yet, but at least she was no longer jumping out of her skin.

"I'll replace what I eat, all the same," he insisted. " 'Appetite' is my middle name."

Her soft mouth curved up sweetly at the corners. "Well, I'd best get to it, then."

"While you're getting dressed and fixing breakfast, I'll see to the chores. Did you ever empty the wood box and bring in the milk?"

"What milk?"

She truly hadn't registered anything he'd said to her through the door last night, he realized. "I milked both the cows last night and left the buckets just outside the wood box."

"Oh." She pushed at her hair again. "No, I didn't bring it in. I doubt I even can. Unless the buckets are in the safe, they're too heavy for me to lift."

"If you'll take the wood out, I'll put them inside for you."

She shook her head. "Just add the milk to the hog slop for now."

It seemed a terrible waste of good milk. "You sure?"

"I've enough aged cheese and butter to do me for weeks. Until Darby's back to sell the extra to Mr. Gilpatrick at the general store, there's no point in my making more."

Joseph hadn't planned on making frequent trips into town. Now he understood why Darby kept two cows and so many chickens, because the surplus milk and eggs brought in a small income. If Rachel depended on the money to meet her expenses, it might put her in a financial bind if she made nothing during Darby's recuperation.

"I can take your stuff to Gilpatrick's until Darby's back on his feet."

"That's generous of you." A ghost of a smile touched her lovely mouth again. "We'll talk about it. For today, the pigs will enjoy the milk."

An hour later, Rachel was still inside the water closet, unable to open the door to reenter the kitchen. It was madness. She knew that. But the kitchen no longer felt safe, and the water closet did. She wished she'd thought to come in here last night. With the walls all around her, she might have gotten some rest. Tonight, she promised herself, she would gather up her bedding and create a makeshift bed in the bathtub.

First, however, she had to find the courage to open the door and return to the kitchen. Again and again, she grasped the lock to turn it, but each time she lost her courage and dropped her arm. *What if someone's out there?* She knew it was an irrational fear. Joseph Paxton had proven to her satisfaction that he was there to help, not do her harm, and he was probably already back in the dining room standing guard.

Joseph shuffled his deck of cards to play another round of patience, a one-person game that irritated him to no end because he so seldom won. As he dealt the hand, he kept one ear cocked toward the kitchen, wondering what on earth was keeping Rachel. The coffee had been at a full boil when he returned to the house and was still boiling. If the pot didn't go dry, and that was a big if, the stuff was going to be strong enough to peel paint off walls. He'd thought never to meet a woman who stayed in the water closet longer than his younger sister, Eden, but this one took the prize.

Was Rachel ailing? He recalled her pallor and the circles under her eyes. He'd laid both off on exhaustion, but maybe she was sick.

"Mr. Paxton?"

Her voice was so faint that Joseph thought for a moment he had imagined it. Then she called to him again, slightly louder this time. He tossed down the cards and pushed quickly up from the chair. "Yo?"

"Are you back in the dining room?" she asked through the water closet door.

What did she think, that he was answering from outside? "Yes, ma'am, I'm here."

Long silence. Then, "Is there anyone in the kitchen?"

Joseph almost chuckled, but he could tell by her tone that she meant the question seriously. "No, ma'am."

"Would you look, please?"

Joseph poked his head through the hole and dutifully scanned the room. "Uh-oh. I lied. There is someone in your kitchen."

Alarm laced her voice when she replied, "There *is*?"

Joseph eyed his recalcitrant dog, who had taken up squatting rights on Rachel's bed. "Yep," he said. "He's a red-gold scoundrel with a white streak on his nose. At the moment, he's curled up on your sheets, letting fleas hop off, willy-nilly."

The water closet door came ajar, and her pretty face appeared in the opening. She studied the dog. Then she poked her head out to carefully examine the rest of the room.

When she finally emerged from the water closet, Joseph was stunned. Beautiful didn't describe the lady by half. With her golden hair in a swirling coronet atop her head, he could see the fine shape of her skull and the graceful column of her slender neck. Shimmering tendrils had escaped from her hasty coiffure to curl at her nape and above her dainty ears to frame the perfect oval of her face. Despite the ravages of exhaustion, she was absolutely lovely.

Though her outfit was everyday practical, Joseph suddenly felt scruffy. Fingering the stubble on his jaw, he skimmed her figure with purely masculine appreciation. Though he'd glimpsed her delightful curves through the folds of her nightgown last night, there was a lot to be said for a formfitting shirtwaist and a skirt with organ-pipe pleats at the back. The lady was made like an hourglass, with ample breasts and a small waist, enhanced by a wide belt. As she hurried across the room to rescue the coffee, Joseph's eyes shifted with every swing of her hips.

Grabbing a cloth to move the coffeepot away from

the heat, she said, "Consternation! This coffee must be as thick as soup by now." She stepped to the sink for a cup of cold tap water, then returned to pour it inside the pot to settle the grounds. "If it isn't ruined, it'll be a miracle."

To please a woman so lovely, Joseph could have drunk kerosene and sworn he liked it. "I'm not fussy." The moment he spoke, he wanted to kick himself. His voice had gone gravelly with lust. He coughed to clear his throat. "I'm used to coffee made by sleepy cow-pokes over an open fire. It's always boiled to a fare-thee-well."

"Mmm." She filled two mugs. Smiling shyly, she brought one to him. "Nothing smells quite so good as coffee on the crisp morning air."

Joseph remained at the opening, one shoulder resting against the boards. Half expecting her to request that he step back, he was pleasantly surprised when she walked right up to him.

"Here you are."

She smelled of roses, a faint, wonderful scent that drifted enticingly up to him. As he took the cup, his fingertips grazed hers. Joseph had heard of men being poleaxed by the sight of a beautiful woman, but he'd never heard tell of anyone's toes going numb.

His reaction to her troubled him. *Love 'em and leave 'em* had always been his creed. He liked women and particularly enjoyed the generous-natured ones, but that was as far as it ever went, a fleeting, mutual pleasure that began in the wee hours and ended long before the first cock crowed.

"Thank you," he said. "I can't wake up properly without a good cup of coffee."

She wiped her hand on her skirt, whether to remove the taint of his touch or to rub away a bit of moisture from the cup, he didn't know. Joseph wished that he'd thought to bring a clean shirt and razor. Around a pretty lady like her, a man wanted to look his best.

Without thinking, he took a big slug of coffee. *Fire.* The scalding liquid seared the inside of his mouth. He almost choked and spat. Instead, he managed to swallow. Bad mistake. He felt the burn clear to his gonads.

"Are you all right?"

He'd singed all his tongue hairs and blistered the little thingy that dangled at the back of his throat. That wasn't to mention that his stomach was on fire. "I'm fine," he lied. "This is right fine coffee." It was the bitterest coffin varnish that he'd ever tasted in his life.

Bewilderment filled her eyes. Then, as if pushing the questions aside, she hustled back to the stove, the back hem of her skirt trailing gracefully behind her. With well-practiced efficiency, she donned a pretty white apron with a spray of embroidered flowers curving up from the hem to border a large front pocket. Then she vanished into the cellar only to reappear a moment later with a slab of bacon, which she set about slicing.

"Don't cut yourself."

She glanced up. "No worries. In large part, I've spent the last five years perfecting my culinary skills, Mr. Paxton. Aside from needlework and reading, I haven't much else to do, and Darby's a man who enjoys his food."

Weren't most men? Joseph recalled the lecture he'd given his dog yesterday about bachelors who met their waterloo over a supper plate. Somehow, the warning seemed to have lost some of its salt this morning. If it ever happened that he followed in his older brother's footsteps and settled down with one woman for the rest of his days, he hoped she would be as easy on the eyes as Rachel Hollister.

And just what the hell was he *thinking*?

Joseph leaned his head through the hole and gave his dog an accusing glare. *Turncoat.* "Get off that bed, you spoiled mutt." *And don't go making yourself at home.*

This was a temporary situation. The moment that Darby got back on his feet, Joseph would be out of here faster than a cat with its tail on fire. "Come on!" He snapped his fingers. "You're a dirty cur. I'm sure Miss Hollister doesn't want your fleas."

"I haven't noticed him scratching," she observed from her work spot at the table. "And I truly don't mind his being on the bed. My dog, Denver, used to sleep with me all the time."

A woman after his heart. That thought didn't sit well, either. He took a chair at the table to drink his coffee. The purely awful taste made him feel better. A man would have to be out of his mind to tie up with a woman who couldn't make better coffee than this. Coffee was one of the mainstays of Joseph's diet.

Just then he heard Rachel spewing and sputtering. He craned his neck to see her bent over the sink, spitting and scrubbing her mouth with one hand, her other holding a coffee cup out from her body as if it contained poison.

"This is *horrible!*" she cried. She emptied the cup and advanced on the coffeepot. "How can you drink such awful stuff?"

Joseph thought it was a good remedy for what ailed him, namely a purely irrational, inexplicable, imbecilic attraction to a crazy woman.

Rachel was none too pleased when Joseph Paxton informed her that he meant to leave for part of the afternoon. He stood at the opening, ducking his hatless head to see through, his blond hair trailing forward over his sturdy shoulders.

"But one of my windows is wide open!" she reminded him. "And my wall has a huge hole in it! Surely you can't mean to leave me here alone."

"Of course I don't mean to leave you here alone. I told Darby I'd look after you, and I mean to see that you're looked after." He flashed her a cajoling grin. "Have a little faith."

Over the course of the morning, Rachel had catalogued his features, which were chiseled and irregular, his bladelike nose a little too large and sporting a knot along the bridge, his squared jawline accentuated just a bit too strongly by tendon, and his cheekbones just a shade too prominent. Only somehow the overall effect was attractive, especially when he spoke or grinned as he was now. His mouth was full and mobile, a distractingly soft and expressive feature for an otherwise rugged countenance that lent him a boyish appeal. She also liked his blue eyes. When they twinkled with

warmth, she felt as if she'd just swallowed a dozen
live pollywogs.

"While I'm gone, my brother Ace is going to stand
guard," he explained.

His *brother*? Rachel had come to accept Joseph's
presence in the dining room, and she was even starting
to trust him a little. But that was where her high-
mindedness ended. If he had his way, every citizen of
No Name would soon be traipsing through her house.

"*No.*"

"Now, Miss Hollister, Ace is a champion fellow.
You'll like him."

"I don't care how champion he is. I won't have him
inside my house, and that'll be the end of it." She
whirled away from the barricade and advanced on the
sink to finish washing the breakfast dishes. "You tore
the boards from my window, broke out the glass,
frightened me into blowing a hole through my barricade, and now you're *leaving*?"

"I have important business to take care of."

"What important business?"

He took so long to reply that she glanced over her
shoulder. All the laughter had left his eyes, and their
usual sky blue had gone stormy dark. "My brother
David is—"

"How many brothers do you *have*?" she asked, her
tone waspish.

"Three. Ace, David, and Esa. David's the marshal
who was here last night. Today he's going to question
a couple people to see if he can find out who shot
Darby. Since I'm as eager to find out as he is, I'd like
to ride along."

Rachel returned her gaze to the plate in her hands. An iridescent soap bubble slid brightly over the white porcelain surface, caught at the fluted edge, hovered there in trembling splendor for an instant, and then vanished as if it had never been.

She closed her eyes, thinking of her little sister, Tansy, who had glided so brightly through life and then had vanished just as completely as the bubble. No one wanted her killer to be caught more than Rachel did. If there was a connection between the attack on her family and the attack on Darby yesterday, how could she, in good conscience, ask Joseph Paxton not to leave?

Chapter Six

Jebediah Pritchard owned the spread that adjoined the Hollister ranch to the north. The Pritchard home was little more than a one-room shack, its shake roof sagging along the center pitch, the two front windows covered with tattered isinglass, and the porch littered with all manner of objects, most of which needed to be thrown on a garbage heap. A fat brown hen had made her nest in a washtub to the left of the battered front door, inarguable proof that the Pritchards bathed infrequently.

As David and Joseph rode up, Jeb came out onto the dilapidated porch. A short, beefy individual with grizzled brown hair, beady brown eyes, and skin darkened by sun and grime, he stood with his trunklike legs slightly spread, a shotgun cradled in one arm. The creases on his unshaven face were a slightly deeper brown where dirt and body oil had collected. His attire of the day was the same outfit that he'd been wearing for over a year, patched and faded dungarees over white longhandles that had long since gone gray with filth.

Content to let David do the talking since he was the one wearing the badge, Joseph relaxed in the saddle and lighted a cigarette. At least, he pretended to relax. He'd learned early on never to let down his guard around polecats or sidewinders.

"Whatcha want?" Jeb demanded.

Joseph exhaled smoke, thinking that that was a hell of a way to greet one's neighbors. Evidently Joseph and his brother thought alike, for David replied, "That's a downright unfriendly way to say hello, Jeb."

Silver-streaked, stringy brown hair drifting in the crisp afternoon breeze, Jeb leaned slightly forward to spew a stream of brown spittle through a gap in his decayed front teeth. The tobacco juice nearly struck the front hoof of David's gelding. "I'm never friendly to a man wearin' a badge."

"Ah, now."

"Don't you 'ah, now' me. I know why you're here, sniffin' around. It's because Darby McClintoch got hisself shot in the back yesterday. Well, I'll tell you right now, I don't know nothin' about it."

Joseph was pleased when David replied, "That's interesting. If you know nothing, Jeb, how is it you even know Darby was shot?"

"Got it in town from Slim Jim Davidson."

Slim Jim, the bootlack? Joseph dropped his gaze to Jeb's manure-encrusted plow shoes.

David glanced at Jeb's feet, too. "Got your boots shined, did you?"

"Hell, no. What do I look like, a Nancy boy? I seen

Slim Jim when I dropped off my other boots at the cobbler shop."

Jeb's oldest son, Hayden, emerged from the house just then. His weapon of choice was a Smith & Wesson revolver. He wore the gun belt cinched tight at his waist, the holster hanging free. Stocky like his sire, he stood to his father's left, puffed out his chest, spread his feet, and planted his hands on his hips. He wore nothing over his faded red undershirt, the tattered sleeves riding high on his thick, hairy forearms.

The stench coming from the porch grew stronger with Hayden's arrival. Soap and water being cheap, Joseph could only wonder why some folks refused to wash. Though he couldn't imagine it, he guessed there was some truth to the saying that a man stopped smelling himself after three days.

"What's this about the shooting?" Hayden fairly growled the question, displaying the inherent charm that ran so strongly in his family.

David shifted his weight in the saddle. "I just wanted to ask your pa a few questions."

"Why pester Pa?"

That inquiry came from inside the house. Boots thumped loudly to the door, and Cyrus, the next oldest son, came out. The very spit of Hayden and his father, Cyrus positioned himself at Jeb's right side.

"Pa's got no quarrel with Darby McClintoch," Cyrus exclaimed. "Neither does Hayden or me."

"Never said any of you did," David replied. "I'm just sifting through the flour for weevils, so to speak."

"Ain't no weevils around here," Cyrus assured him.

David smiled. "I'm sure not. I just dropped by to

see if you fellows saw or heard anything yesterday. As a crow flies, the scene of the shooting isn't that far from here."

"Happened in the same place where Hollister got his," Jeb interjected. "Leastwise, that's what Slim Jim says."

"Slim Jim seems to know quite a few details," David observed dryly. "That's strange. I've kept a pretty tight lid on things."

Jeb's beady little eyes took on a dangerous glint. "You sayin' I'm lyin'?"

David sat back in the saddle, a clear sign to anyone who knew him well that he wanted fast access to his weapon. The blasting potential of a shotgun still fresh in Joseph's mind, he took his cue from David and tossed down his cigarette.

"I'm just amazed that Slim Jim knows so much about the shooting, like I said," David replied evenly. "Make what you want of it."

"Maybe you oughta talk to Doc," Jeb suggested. The brown hen chose that moment to leave her nest in the washtub. She clucked cheerfully as she hopped off the porch. "Doc was at the Golden Slipper last night, flappin' his lip about Darby to anybody who'd listen."

David's jaw muscle had started to tick. "You never liked Henry Hollister, did you, Jeb?"

"Hated his guts, more like," Jeb shot back. "He was a selfish, connivin' bastard."

"How do you figure that?"

"Just was, that's all, and the devil take his black soul."

"Rumor has it that you had some kind of a boundary dispute with him."

"Dis-pute, hell. It was a flat-out war, and he only won 'cause he hired a highfalutin lawyer outa Denver to twist the facts all around."

"The facts as they actually were?" David asked. "Or the facts as you saw them?"

Pritchard came forward a step, his face flushing red with anger above his scraggly mustache and beard. "Facts is facts, and there's only one way to see 'em. Wolverine Crick marked my south boundary, and that damned flood in seventy-nine moved it. Way I see it, my property line should've moved with it!"

"Not according to the recorded deed that I read last night," David replied. "Your south boundary line description clearly states that the rock formation, once at the center of Wolverine Creek, is the permanent survey monument, with the boundary moving in a straight line, east and west from there, for a certain number of feet in each direction. The stream helped delineate that line, but it didn't legally define it. The rocks did."

"Fancy words! Hollister stole what was rightfully mine!" Pritchard jabbed his chest with a grimy finger. "My land, bought and paid for with my own sweat."

"A lot of folks think it was just the other way around, that it was you who tried to steal from Hollister by insisting that the stream marked your property line, even though it had moved and encompassed several acres of Hollister's prime ranchland."

"Bullshit. It ain't stealin' to demand what's already yourn. I bought a place with runnin' water. Ain't right that the water's gone, leavin' me nothin' but a dry crick bed and thirsty cows. But Henry Hollister refused to set things right."

"He channeled water into a pond on your property."

"Well, whoop-dee-do. Wasn't that just grand of him?"

"Did you kill him?" David fired the question.

"Hell, no, I didn't kill him. But I can't say I'm sorry the bastard's dead. Put that in your pipe and smoke it. I celebrated when I heard what happened. Justice was served, if you ask me."

David's eyes narrowed. "And his wife and kids? You glad they're dead, too, Jeb?"

"The devil take the whole lot of 'em," Jeb volleyed back. "Too bad the oldest girl didn't die with the rest. Maybe then I could've bought that place. As it stands, you couldn't get her off that ranch with a wagonload of dynamite."

"Pa," Cyrus said, his voice cast low. "Watch what you say."

"Watch what I say, be damned. A man can't be thrown in the hoosegow for speakin' his mind."

From the corner of his eye, Joseph saw the youngest son emerge from the barn. Like his older brothers, Alan Pritchard wore a sidearm. There all similarity ended. Pale and flaxen-haired, he was a good fifteen years younger than Hayden or Cyrus, who were pushing forty. He was also the beanpole of the family, so thin that he barely cast a shadow standing sideways.

Gossip had it that Alan took after his mother, who had died giving birth to him. Gossip also had it that shortly before Charlene Pritchard became pregnant with Alan, she had been sneaking off to meet a blond piano player at the Silver Spur, the oldest of No Name's two saloons. Jeb supposedly got wind of her shenanigans, came home reeling drunk, and beat her so severely that she went into early labor and bled to death.

For several reasons, not the least of which was Jeb's charming personality, Joseph believed the gossip. He could well imagine a woman sneaking off from Jebediah Pritchard to be with another man. He could also imagine Jeb using his fists and boots on his pregnant wife. Thirdly, Alan didn't have the look of a Pritchard. Normally, even when a child took mostly after its mother, there were slight resemblances to the father as well. Joseph suspected that Alan had gotten the blond hair and those long, graceful fingers that twitched so eagerly near his gun from his piano-playing papa.

Drawing gently on Obie's reins, Joseph backed the stallion up a few paces to better guard his brother's back. Alan might not be a Pritchard by blood, but he'd been trained up to think like one, and right now he looked to be spoiling for a fight.

"What's the fuss about, Pa?" Alan asked.

"The marshal here thinks I killed Henry Hollister." Jeb jutted his chin to spit again. "Thinks I shot Darby McClintoch, too, I reckon."

Alan's blue eyes glittered. "I'd shoot a man for insultin' me like that. Him wearin' a badge don't make me no nevermind."

"Your father would have to take both of us," Joseph pointed out with a humorless smile, "and he knows that'd be damned near impossible."

"How so?" Posture cocky and challenging, Alan advanced several steps. "There's four of us and only two of you. You may be fast like folks say, Paxton, but nobody's that fast. The odds is in our favor."

Joseph continued to smile. "Draw that gun, son, and you'll find out how fast I am."

"Don't go lettin' your temper get the best of you, Alan," Jeb warned. "He'll clear leather before you even touch your gun."

Alan curled his lip. "He don't look that fast to me."

Joseph sincerely hoped that Jeb got control of this situation. Alan appeared to be somewhere in his early twenties, no longer really a boy, but still too young to die. Joseph had enough regrets to haunt his dreams without adding another to the list.

"Don't be an idiot, little brother," Cyrus interjected. "Everybody in these parts knows his reputation. You got a death wish?"

Joseph remained relaxed in the saddle and kept his gaze fixed on Alan's. The most important part of a gunfight took place during the stare down. A large percentage of the time, the man who blinked first ended up walking away.

Alan blinked.

Holding his hands palm out, he made his way to the porch to stand with his father and brothers. In Joseph's opinion, this party was fast losing its shine. Knowing that his brother would sit tight and watch his back, he turned Obie and trotted the stallion from the littered yard. When safely out of pistol and shotgun range, he wheeled the horse back around, drew his rifle from its boot, and swung down from the saddle.

As David rode from the yard, Joseph kept a close eye on the Pritchards, ready to shoot if he had to but hoping he wouldn't. It was an old stratagem, drilled into both Joseph and David by their older brother, Ace. *Never take your eye off the enemy unless someone you trust is watching your back.*

"That went fair to middling well," Joseph observed a few minutes later as he and David turned their horses onto Wolverine Road toward town.

"I didn't find out much of anything."

Joseph thought about that for a moment. "You found out for sure that Jeb Pritchard hated Henry Hollister's guts," he pointed out, "and that he's glad the man and his family died. Those were pretty strong words, if you ask me. He also said that he wishes Rachel had died with the rest of them."

David shook his head. "Can you believe that? What did she ever do to him?"

"She lived when the others didn't, and her existence is preventing him from buying the Hollister place."

"It's only land. To wish someone dead over it? If I live to be a hundred, I'll never understand how some people's minds work."

"Me, neither," Joseph agreed. "But there you have it, David. There are some folks in this world who have no respect for human life. They can kill and feel no remorse."

David nodded, his expression solemn. "You catch that reference Jeb made to dynamite?"

"Yep. In my opinion, he's definitely the one who dynamited Wolverine Creek."

David removed his hat to wipe his brow. "We can't

prove one damned thing. That's the problem. I can't arrest a man on supposition."

"Nope," Joseph said with a broad grin, "but you can sure as hell make him nervous." He let that hang there for a moment. "Here in a few days, I reckon you ought to go back. Keep him guessing and off balance. If he killed the Hollisters, he's become complacent over the last five years, thinking he got away with it. It must be unsettling to have a marshal in his dooryard again, asking if he did it."

"What good will it do to make him nervous?" David asked.

Joseph touched his heels to Obie's flanks to quicken the pace. "Nervous men make stupid mistakes, especially if they're dumber than dirt to start with."

Rachel had hoped to watch the dogs play through the peephole in her back door, but Ace Keegan sat on the back porch, his broad back and brown Stetson blocking her view of the yard. According to Joseph, Buddy had a brother named Cleveland that belonged to Ace and Caitlin, and the two animals romped nonstop whenever they got together.

Rachel had spent the first thirty minutes after Ace's arrival pacing in circles around the kitchen table, ever conscious of the gaping hole in her barricade. If someone sneaked in through the window that Joseph had broken, Ace Keegan would be none the wiser. Why wasn't he sitting at the side of the house to make sure no one got in?

Pacing, pacing. Rachel couldn't relax enough to sit

down and pass the time reading. She thought about
cooking something special for supper to make the
hours go faster, but that would involve turning her
back on the hole in her barricade. Not a good plan. She
needed to be ready, with her shotgun close at hand,
just in case something happened.

Rachel had paced to the point of exhaustion and
was about to sit in the rocker to watch the barricade
when she heard a strange sound coming from the front
part of the house. A tinkle of laughter? The hair at the
nape of her neck stood on end. Then it came again, a
light, feminine giggle followed by footsteps, not the
imaginary kind that so often set Rachel's heart to
pounding, but real, honest-to-goodness footsteps.

"Raaaa-chel? It's Caitlin!" a feminine voice called
out. "Caitlin O'Shannessy. When Joseph asked Ace to
come over and watch the house, I couldn't resist joining him for a short visit."

Caitlin? Rachel could scarcely believe her ears.

"I won't come any farther, I promise, not unless you
answer and say it's okay. I've got my baby boy with
me."

This was unprecedented. This was *terrifying*. This
was—oh, *God*, it was wonderful, too. *Caitlin.* Rachel
hadn't clapped eyes on her in years and years. Except
for Darby and Joseph Paxton last night, she hadn't
seen anyone.

"Hello?" Caitlin called again. "Can you hear me,
Rachel? I'm just here to visit for a bit. I won't come
into your room or anything. But here's the problem. I
can't come back with my baby until you say it's okay."

Rachel didn't have words. To hear a woman's

voice—to know that a friend from childhood was only a few steps away—was almost overwhelming. Tears sprang to her eyes, so many that she could barely see.

Caitlin. As a girl, the redhead had often sported bruises, which she'd gone to great lengths to hide. Even so, everyone at school had seen the marks at one time or another. When asked about the injuries, Caitlin had always sworn that she'd had an accident, her explanations never ringing true. Her father, Conor O'Shannessy, had been an ill-tempered man with a heavy fist, an unquenchable thirst for whiskey, and little if any regard for his children.

"Hello?" Caitlin called again. "I'm just *dying* to see you, Rachel, and if it was only me—well, I'd be back there, lickety-split. But I have my little boy to think of. Joseph says you have a loaded shotgun. Little Ace, he's such a dear. I can't bring him back there until I know for sure that it's safe. Do you understand?"

Rachel tried once more to speak and simply couldn't. *Caitlin.* A ghost from her past, part of a world to which she no longer belonged but had never stopped missing.

"Okay, fine," Caitlin called. "Visiting is just talking, right? We don't have to see each other to do that. Although I must warn you, Little Ace is active. He's already squirming to get down. If I let him loose and he gets away from me, you won't shoot him, will you?"

Tears streaming, her throat closed off so tightly that she couldn't breathe, Rachel managed one choked word. "No." It came out so faint that she doubted Caitlin even heard.

"Well, then!" Caitlin said cheerfully. "He's down. And, oh, *dear*, he's off and running down the hallway. Don't be startled, please. He just *goes* as fast as his chubby little legs will carry him. He's— Little Ace, come out of there. Is there anything that he can get into in the rooms along the hall?"

The concern in Caitlin's voice had Rachel at the hole in her barricade, trying to remember the contents of the rooms along the corridor. Was there anything that might harm a small child? The *sewing room*. It would be full of dangerous things. Rachel couldn't clearly recall what she had removed from the room or left lying about, but she knew that the child might find something injurious if he were left to explore.

"Go get him, Caitlin!" she cried. "He's either in Pa's library or Ma's sewing room. There are lots of bad things in Ma's sewing room. Scissors, maybe. And needles! I'm sure there are lots of needles."

Footsteps scurried up the hall. Then she heard Caitlin laughing. "You silly boy! What will your pa think if he sees you in that? It's a dress, sweetheart. Dresses are for ladies, not little boys."

Rachel recalled the half-finished dress that her mother had been working on when she died. It had been for Rachel, a graduation dress to mark the end of her school days. More tears sprang to her eyes. *Pain.* Over the last five years, she'd blocked out so many memories, unable to bear thinking of them. Beyond her barricade, the house was filled with them—memories that fairly broke her heart.

Rachel's hands were clenched over the jagged edge of the hole. The shards of splintered wood cut into her fingers and palms. Eyes closed, cheeks wet, she stood rigidly straight, every muscle in her body aching with the strain.

"Pa?"

Her eyes popped open, and there, standing at the other side of her barricade, was a toddler—a pudgy, raven-haired, sloe-eyed little boy with rosy cheeks and absolute innocence shining on his face. He wore a blue shirt without a collar, knickers that drooped almost to his ankles, and a grin to break Rachel's heart.

"Pa, pa, pa, pa, *pa*!" he shouted. And then he grinned, displaying pristinely white bottom teeth, with little ruffles along the edges. "Pa, pa, pa, pa, *pa*!"

"Little Ace, you get *back* here this instant!" Caitlin cried, and then there she was, hovering in the doorway, a mother intent on protecting her baby. Her red hair was done up atop her head, just as Rachel remembered the fashion to be, only now long tendrils dangled before her ears and curls popped out almost everywhere. The latest in vogue? Or was the untidy look a result of motherhood and too few minutes in the day?

"He knows his papa is on your back porch," Caitlin said breathlessly. "If you feel uncomfortable about this, I'll gather him up and go back outside."

The child chose that moment to lift his arms to Rachel, his plump face dimpled in a happy grin. "Pa, pa, pa, *pa*!" he cried.

And somehow Rachel's arms were reaching for him. He was birdsong and sunlight and laughter and all that was lovely—everything she hadn't seen in far too long—a baby, toddling about, with skin so new it glowed. *Oh!* The word echoed and reechoed in her mind, an exclamation of joy she couldn't articulate. That inexpressible joy was amplified a hundred times more when soft, dimpled arms curled trustingly around her neck.

"Pa?"

Rachel could barely see the child for her tears. But she managed to nod and carried him to her back door. In a voice tremulous with emotions she couldn't separate or define just then, she said, "He's out there."

Little Ace was a smart boy. He saw the hole and put his eye to it. Then he promptly started giggling. "Pa, pa, pa, *pa*!"

"Yes," Rachel confirmed, "that's your pa."

The toddler poked his finger into the hole, and then, as if mere pointing wasn't enough, he twisted his wrist to drive his tiny finger deeper into the depression. "Pa!" he said proudly.

And Rachel got lost in his dancing brown eyes. He was so soft and warm and dear, a pint-sized miracle, and she never wanted to let him go.

The peephole quickly became boring. He fastened a bright gaze on Rachel, grinned to display his new front teeth again, and said, "Hi!"

"Hi" was a lovely word, one that she hadn't heard or uttered in far too long. "Hi," she replied softly.

"I am *so* sorry. He can run faster than I can."

Rachel turned from the door. Framed in the hole of her barricade was the face of a longtime friend. "Caitlin," Rachel whispered.

"Yes, it's me. I hope you don't mind the intrusion. When I found out Ace was coming, I begged to come along. Joseph thought you might like the company because you'd mentioned knowing me, but my husband had an absolute *fit*." Her cheeks went high with color, and she flapped her wrist. "The shotgun had him worried. Ace is nothing if not protective, so he left me at home."

"So how—?"

"I hitched up the wagon and came on my own," Caitlin said with an impish grin. "He wasn't happy to see me, but he finally gave in after I promised to be careful." Caitlin rolled her eyes. "As if you'd shoot me. I kept telling him that we've known each other for years and *years*. I've never believed all those silly stories about you being—" Caitlin's blue eyes went wide, and she flapped her wrist again. "Well, you know."

"Crazy?" Rachel supplied.

"Well, there, you know how people talk. I never listened to a word of it. I used to come by once a week and knock on the door." She shrugged. "You never answered, so I'd just leave things on the porch."

Rachel's eyes went teary again. So it was Caitlin who had come calling so often in those early months after the tragedy. "The books," Rachel whispered raggedly. "You brought me *Tom Sawyer*!"

"Did you like it?

Rachel nodded, then laughed when Little Ace touched the wetness on her cheek. "It's one of my favorites. I never knew it was you who brought it. I heard you knocking, but I was afraid to open the door. Finally, the mystery of it bothered me so that I asked Darby to install a peephole, but after that you never came again."

"Oh, lands! I got married." Caitlin rolled her lovely

blue eyes again. "And when I took on a husband, I took on every male in the family. Cooking and laundry and picking up. It took me a full year to train all the bad habits out of them."

Rachel put the squirming toddler down. The child sped off like a pea from a slingshot, heading straight for Rachel's crochet basket.

"Little *Ace!*" Caitlin scolded. "That's a no-no!"

Rachel had no sooner rescued her fancywork than the child turned to the parlor table, his chubby hands reaching for the lamp. If asked, Rachel couldn't have described how she felt in that moment. She only knew that resenting the intrusion wasn't one of her emotions. "Oh, Caitlin, he is *so* precious."

"He's a little pistol, into this and into that, his feet going a mile a minute. He fills up my days, I can tell you that."

He had filled up Rachel's heart, easing the ache in empty places that she hadn't even realized were there. A baby. She'd lived so long within four walls, with only herself for company, that a little boy with dimpled cheeks was the best thing she could have wished to see, even better than sunshine.

Rachel carried the child to the kitchen, opened the cupboard that held her pots and pans, and set Little Ace down in front of it.

"He'll pull everything out," Caitlin warned.

"Exactly," Rachel replied with a laugh, and even that seemed wondrous to her. It felt so fabulous to laugh. She took some large metal spoons from the flatware drawer and showed the child how to pound on the bottom of a pot. Little Ace loved that, and soon the kitchen resounded with noise.

"Oh, *my*. Perhaps I shouldn't have come," Caitlin said. "Your nerves will be completely frazzled." She chafed her arms through the sleeves of her green shirt-waist. "I took off my cloak before Ace boosted me up to climb through the window. Now I wish I hadn't. It's a bit chilly out here."

Rachel had a fire going in the stove and hearth to warm the kitchen, but she guessed only a little of the heat was escaping into the other room. "Would you like to come in?"

Caitlin took visual measure of the hole left in the barricade by the shotgun blast. "Do you suppose I can fit through?"

Rachel was trembling just at the thought. Since the day Darby had finished the modifications to her living quarters, no one besides Rachel had been inside. But this was Caitlin. Even though she was four years Rachel's senior, they'd been educated in the same one-room schoolhouse and had played together in groups during recess.

"If you pull over a chair, it'll be easier to climb through," Rachel suggested. Rushing over to the table, she said, "I'll get a chair for this side and help all I can."

Within seconds, Rachel and Caitlin were giggling like schoolgirls. The hole wasn't quite so large as it had seemed in Rachel's imagination over the last many hours, and it had jagged edges to catch on Caitlin's clothing and hair as she twisted and bent into odd positions, trying to fit through.

"I'm stuck," she pronounced.

Rachel giggled and tugged on Caitlin's elbow, trying to get her loose.

"Is everything all right in there?" a deep, masculine voice called from the back porch.

Rachel nearly parted company with her skin, but Caitlin only laughed. "Yes, darling, everything's fine. Absolutely fine."

Hearing his father's voice, Little Ace scampered toward the door, pounding on a pot with every step.

"What in tarnation is that racket?" Ace Keegan asked.

"Not to worry, sweetheart." Caitlin tugged on strands of her hair that were caught on the wood. "It's only—*ouch*—Little Ace playing with Rachel's pots."

Suddenly—and unexpectedly—Caitlin spilled through the opening and sent Rachel scrambling to catch her. When Caitlin had both feet safely on the kitchen floor, she dissolved into laughter. As her mirth subsided, she said, "I can't believe I just did that." She looked over her shoulder at the hole. "Now the question is, will I be able to get back out?"

That was a worry for later. Rachel stoked the firebox in the range, put on a fresh pot of coffee, and dished up bowls of peach cobbler. Soon she and Caitlin were sitting at the table, and Caitlin was chattering like a magpie, telling Rachel all the news and tidbits of gossip that she'd missed out on over the last five years.

"Remember Beatrice Masterson and Clarissa Denny?" she asked.

"The milliner and dressmaker? Of course I remember them."

"Well," Caitlin said in a low, conspiratorial voice as she spooned up some cobbler, "they're in competition for Doc Halloway's favor."

"Truly?" In Rachel's estimation, both women were too old to be entertaining romantic notions, especially about a stooped, elderly gentleman like Doc.

"You didn't hear it from me, mind you. Normally I try not to carry gossip. It's just that there's so much you don't know about." She tasted the cobbler. "Oh, my, Rachel, this is delicious. May I have the recipe?"

"It's just a bit of this and a dash of that."

Caitlin took another bite. "It's better than mine." She washed the dessert down with a sip of coffee. "Now let me think. What else has happened?" She grinned mischievously and pointed at Rachel with the spoon. "Hannibal St. John, the new preacher."

"What about him?"

"Pauline Perkins carries a torch for him."

"Pauline?" Pauline had been a singularly homely girl, tall, rawboned, and hefty, with frizzy blond hair and as many pimples as freckles. Her father, Zachariah Perkins, published No Name's weekly newspaper, *The Gazette*. "Does the reverend return her fond regard?"

Caitlin let loose with a peal of laughter. *"No,"* she said in a thin, breathless voice. "But Pauline won't leave him be. Last week—I have this on good authority, mind you—she cornered him in the church storage room and kissed him."

"When he didn't want her to?"

"Even worse, her mother, Charlene, caught them in

the act and was absolutely beside herself. She accused Hannibal of compromising her daughter's reputation and demanded that he marry her."

Charlene Rayette Perkins was an older and heavier version of Pauline. Rachel had always been a little afraid of the woman because she wore a perpetual scowl and snapped at people when they spoke to her. "What did Hannibal do?"

"He refused, of course. Would *you* want to get stuck with Pauline?"

Rachel giggled and shook her head. "Lands, no. She used to push me down during recess. I never liked her very much."

"Well, her disposition hasn't gotten any sweeter. Hannibal is a very nice man. Handsome, too—very tall, with golden hair and kindly blue eyes." Caitlin winked. "Not that I'm given to looking, you understand. I have eyes only for Ace."

Rachel couldn't recall ever having seen Caitlin so happy. "Is he good to you, Caitlin?"

A soft, dreamy look filled Caitlin's eyes. "Good to me? He treats me like a queen. I love that man more than life itself, I truly do."

En route to Amanda Hollister's place, Joseph and David chose to bypass town by riding across open country through budding witches'-broom, newly blossoming clover, and more rocks than they could count. Spring was in the air, even though the March temperatures were still chilly enough to make both men shiver when the wind picked up. Joseph thought about tugging his coat free from the straps at the back of his saddle, but each time he started to reach for it, the breeze would slacken.

The sign over Amanda's main gate laid no claims to grandeur, stating only her name, followed by RANCH. As they followed the dirt road toward the house, Joseph took visual measure of the fenced pastures, trying to guess how large a spread it was.

"It doesn't appear that she has much land," he finally commented.

"A quarter section with open range," David replied. "When I went to the courthouse last night, I looked at her deed, too, along with other records of interest. I'm thinking the stories about her quarrel with Henry are true. She can't have been very happy about being left out of her brother's will. Two thousand acres, versus a mere one hundred and sixty? Even with open range for her cattle to graze, it's a big step down for a woman who worked most of her life on a larger spread that she hoped to partly own someday."

"You can bet her father didn't manage to increase his original homestead to encompass that much land without plenty of help from his kids."

"Amanda and her younger brother, Peter James, were his only children. Their mother, Martha, died in twenty-seven, when Amanda was eight and Peter was six. Their father, Luther, never remarried."

"So it was left to only Amanda and Peter to help their pa work the spread."

David nodded. "And according to what Doc told me, Peter inherited his mother's weak constitution, so the giant's share of the work fell to Amanda."

"But the old man left the ranch lock, stock, and barrel to the brother?"

"Yep. Even so, Doc claims that she remained loyal to the family and continued to work like a man, carrying much of the load because Peter was never very robust."

Joseph shook his head. "Peter—he was Henry Hollister's father. Right?"

David nodded. "And he only outlived his and Amanda's father by nineteen years. He was about sixty when he died."

"And he made no provisions for his hardworking sister in his will?"

"Nary a one. He left everything to Henry, consigning Amanda to live on her nephew's charity. She was sixty-two at the time, getting up in years and no longer able to work as she once had. I can't say that I blame her for petitioning Henry to grant her at least a monthly income from the ranch."

"But he refused."

"Flatly." David shrugged. "That was when she moved out and never spoke to him again. Doc says she had a small trust from her grandmother. She used that money to buy this place."

"What goes wrong in some families that they value the boys over the girls?" Joseph couldn't imagine it. "I'd never cut Eden off without a dime."

David grinned. "If there were anything for us to inherit, I wouldn't, either. We're lucky, I reckon. There'll be no haggling in our family when Mom passes on. Everything she has came to her from Ace. It'll rightly go back to him."

Joseph mulled it all over for a moment. "It sounds like Henry Hollister was a selfish man." As Joseph spoke, he remembered the pain he had seen in Rachel's eyes and instinctively knew that Henry had been a kind, just man and a wonderful father. What had gone wrong in the family that a faithful, hard-working female relative had twice been denied her rightful inheritance?

"Maybe so." David pushed up the brim of his hat to meet Joseph's gaze. "Only, no matter what the provocation, what kind of person would kill her own flesh and blood? We've got to remember that it wasn't only Henry who died. His wife and two children went with him, one of them a little girl who wasn't yet six. Read between the lines when we talk with Amanda. Watch for any sign of insanity. Maybe you're right, and it runs in the family."

Even though Joseph had made the same observation last night, he bridled at the suggestion now. Rachel wasn't normal, living as she did. He wouldn't go so far as to say that. But she didn't strike him as being crazy, either. By hiding away, she'd found a way to feel safe, and now she clung to her seclusion like a drowning animal did to a log in a raging stream.

At a very young age, Joseph had learned to be a survivor, and so had everyone else in the family. His father's untimely death had left them without a breadwinner, and the land swindle had rendered them penniless. Supporting the family had fallen to Ace, an eleven-year-old boy, so their circumstances had grown a whole lot worse before they got better. In order to survive, they'd done whatever they had to do, just as Rachel was doing now.

When they reached the end of the road, Joseph saw that Amanda Hollister's house was as neat as a tumbler of straight whiskey. Green shutters bracketed the windows, and a veranda spanned the front of the house. Comfortable-looking wicker chairs flanked a swing, and several flowerpots were strategically placed to get sunlight. Nary a one hosted a plant that had sprouted any blooms yet, but that was Colorado for you. Spring didn't come until almost summertime, and summer died young.

As Joseph and David tethered their horses to the hitching post that ran the length of the front flowerbed, a man came around the corner of the house. He had the look of a ranch hand, his faded Levi's dusty from working with livestock, his gray, collarless shirt stained with sweat. His honey brown hair glistened like bronze in the sunlight, and his fine-featured countenance creased in a warm smile.

"Howdy," he called out. "How can I help you?"

Joseph and David flashed each other a grin. After their reception at the Pritchard place, it was nice to get a friendly greeting.

The man's arresting blue eyes dropped to David's badge, and his eyebrows shot up. "Oh, boy." He thrust out his wrists. "Cuff me and get it over with. I've been found out."

David chuckled, and introductions ensued. The hired hand said he was Amanda Hollister's ranch foreman, Ray Meeks.

"Have we met?" Joseph asked as he shook Meeks' hand.

Ray squinted thoughtfully. "Not that I recall. I'm sure I would remember if we had."

"You look familiar, somehow," Joseph said.

Meeks shrugged and smiled. "We've probably seen each other in town at one time or another. You look sort of familiar to me, too." He hooked a thumb over his shoulder. "Miss Hollister is around back." He motioned for David and Joseph to follow him. "If you want to talk to her, I hope you don't mind a little dust. We're breaking some broncos, and she insists on supervising." Flashing a good-natured grin, he added, "God love her. She needs to leave the horse training to us men, but she won't hear of it."

Joseph had no idea what to expect. Given the fact that Amanda Hollister had motive to have killed Henry and his family—and also to want Rachel dead—he had a picture inside his head of a wicked old crone with calculating eyes and warts on her nose.

Instead, as they walked toward the breaking arena, Joseph saw that she was a much older version of Rachel, a small, fragile woman of about seventy, with delicate features, large, expressive blue eyes, a coronet of white hair that had undoubtedly once been blond, and a bad case of palsy that made her entire body tremble. She sat facing the corral in a wheelchair, head ducked to see through the rails, her divided riding skirt following the unladylike sprawl of her legs. Fists knotted, she pounded on the arms of her chair.

"Stop swinging that lariat at him, you damned fool!

Make him afraid of it and you'll ruin him forever as a
cow pony!"

Joseph seconded that opinion; the man *was* a
damned fool. Chasing the terrified horse around the
corral, the hired hand swung the rope like a whip, hitting the animal on its tender nose and rump. The poor,
confused mustang flinched and darted, trying frantically to escape.

The sight made Joseph furious, and he wanted to
put a boot up the man's ass. Sadly, there were more in-
competent horse trainers than there were good ones,
and it was the horses that paid the price. Too many
greenhorns went into a corral thinking to mimic the
technique of a good trainer, but taming a mustang
wasn't that simple. Horses were large, very powerful
animals and could be dangerous when cornered.
Proper handling demanded a lot of experience, a host
of little tricks, a measure of good sense, and a lot of
compassion.

Amanda Hollister came up out of her wheelchair.
Shaking so badly that it was difficult for her to keep
her feet, she advanced on the rails. "Out of there. If
you strike that animal again, I'll take a whip to you, I
swear." She turned to Ray Meeks, her foreman. "Cut
this imbecile his pay. I never want to see him on this
ranch again."

Ray sent the trainer an apologetic look and motioned for him to exit the corral. Joseph caught the exchange and wondered why Meeks felt bad. When a
man couldn't do the work that he'd been hired to do,
he was damned lucky to get any back pay, and the
apology was his to make.

Still oblivious to the arrival of guests, Amanda Hollister grasped a post to steady herself and took stock of the men who ringed the corral, some sitting on a top rail, others leaning against the fence. In Joseph's opinion, none of them looked highly energetic. At his place, a hired hand was expected to stay busy until daylight waned. It was Saturday, though. Maybe it was the men's day off, and they hadn't chosen to go into town.

"Does anyone here know how to tame a horse, or must I do it myself?" Amanda asked.

None of the men raised a hand. Amanda caught sight of Joseph just then. Without so much as a howdy-do, she said, "You've got the look of a horseman. Do you know anything about taming a mustang?"

Joseph shot David a wondering look, then plucked off his hat to give his head a scratch. "I know a little."

"Don't be modest, young man. How much is a little?"

Joseph almost grinned. Damned if he didn't like the old lady. She had a lot of sass in her frail old bones, and he admired that in anyone. "I've been working with horses most of my life."

"Well, don't stand there with your thumb up your butt. Get to work."

The next thing Joseph knew, he was inside the corral working with the mustang. Though relatively new to cattle ranching, Joseph knew horses and loved the animals as he did little else. As a fatherless boy in San Francisco, he'd hired out as a stable boy at liveries until Ace had mastered the fine art of gambling and started to rake in winnings. After seeing to his family's comfort, Ace had begun spending a portion of his winnings on horses, one of his stepfather's greatest passions. As a result, Joseph had finished out his childhood like a proper young Virginian, working with the animals when he didn't have his nose in a schoolbook.

The first order of business was to get the mustang to stand, and that was tricky business. Never striking the horse, Joseph swung the lariat much as his predecessor had, only with precision, technique, and a purpose in mind, namely to shrink the equine's radius of movement until standing was the only option left to it. An hour of hard work for both him and the animal ensued.

"That's enough for today," he informed Amanda Hollister as he swung a leg over a rail to exit the corral. "He's exhausted."

Back in her chair, Amanda inclined her head at the mustang. "Exhausted, yes, but not terrified. He's beginning to understand what you're asking of him." She turned amazingly clear and beautiful blue eyes on Joseph. "You're very good, young man. What's your price?"

Joseph dusted his Stetson on his pant leg, resettled the hat on his head, and said, "I'm not for hire, ma'am."

"There isn't a man here who holds a candle to you."

Joseph glanced at a nearby holding corral, milling with range-wild mustangs. "Wish I were available. I'd enjoy the challenge. But I have a spread and my own horses to train."

Her eyes sharpened with interest. "Where's your place?"

"Due north of the Circle Star."

"Nice property," she said. "You'll do well there if you put enough sweat into it."

Joseph nodded. She was familiar with the land, certainly. The Hollister place adjoined it to the north. "Sweat's cheap."

Her brilliant gaze came to rest on David's badge. "Marshal," she said by way of greeting as she thrust out a gnarled hand. "Dare I hope that this is a social call?"

David stepped forward to shake her hand. "I'd just like to talk with you for a bit if you can spare me some time."

"Time is a commodity in short supply around here, but I can spare you some." She smiled at Joseph. "One good turn deserves another. Maybe these yahoos learned something. I know the horse did. Please, come to the house. I'll put some coffee on and scrounge up some cookies."

She struggled to move her chair over the uneven ground, her trembling, arthritic hands barely able to grasp the wheels. Joseph grabbed the push handles. With a thrust of a leg, he got the chair out of a rut and soon had his passenger bumping along toward the house. Her voice shook as she talked. He wasn't sure if that was due to the rough ride or the palsy.

"I never got your names," she said. "Forgive my manners. You caught me at a bad moment."

"David Paxton."

She nodded and glanced around at Joseph. "And you, sir?"

"Joseph Paxton. We're brothers."

"I'm assuming that you know my name, or else you wouldn't be here."

"Yes, ma'am," David replied.

"Well, it's pleased I am to make your acquaintance." She settled in the chair. "So, Joseph Paxton, how many acres do you have?"

"Twelve eighty."

"Ah, two full sections. That's a great start. I only have one sixty here, but with the open range, I manage to keep the wolves from my door." She sighed and smiled. "As time wears on, you may be able to pick up more property, Joseph. In this country, you can eke out a living on two sections, but to do really well, you'll need a larger spread." She waved a blue-veined hand. "No worries. For every enterprising man, there's a lazy one, and lazy men can't make it in this country. It's a harsh environment and demands hard work."

Joseph's favorable first impression of this woman hadn't changed. He couldn't help but like her. He found himself wishing that he'd met her under other circumstances, that instead of asking her about the Hollister shootings and the attack on Darby yesterday, he could pick her brain about cattle ranching. He sensed that she had more knowledge in her little finger than he had in his whole body.

By the time she'd served them coffee, the three of them had moved past the awkward stage. Amanda settled back in her chair, gave David a questioning look, and said, "Well, young man, it's time to state your business. What can I help you with?"

David sat forward on the red leather sofa, propped his elbows on his knees, and steepled his fingers. "Have you heard about the shooting yesterday?"

"Shooting?" Amanda glanced at Joseph. "No, I can't say as I have. Did one of my boys cause trouble in town last night?"

"No, ma'am," David replied. "Darby McClintoch was tracking down a stray heifer yesterday afternoon. He was at the north end of the Hollister ranch, between the rock promontory and the creek. Someone up in those rocks shot him in the back."

Amanda's face went ghastly white, and for a moment Joseph feared that the old lady might faint. Instead, she straightened her shoulders, raised her chin, and only closed her eyes briefly. "Darby," she said softly. Her lashes fluttered back up. "He's dead . . . ?"

"No, no, he's not dead," David rushed to clarify. "Not yet, at any rate. Doc patched him up and thinks he stands a fine chance of pulling through."

"Praise the Lord." Amanda passed a trembling hand over her eyes. "Darby and I go a long way back. He came to work for my father down south when I was just a girl. I hope he makes it. The world will be a poorer place without him."

David nodded. "He's a fine man. The problem is, Darby has no idea who shot him."

Amanda's gaze sharpened. "And you think I do."

It wasn't a question, and her eyes suddenly became guarded.

"I'm hoping you can give me some leads," David

clarified. "It happened in almost exactly the same place where Henry and his family were attacked. Darby is convinced the two incidents are somehow connected."

"And since I was the prime suspect five years ago, you're back to pester me with questions again."

David held up his hands. "I'm not here to accuse you of anything, Miss Hollister. Just to see if you can tell me anything. Do you think Darby's right? Could there be a connection? And if so, do you have any idea who hated Henry enough to kill him?"

Amanda leaned forward on her chair to pick up her half-filled coffee cup. Her hands shook so badly that she almost slopped liquid over the brim before she could take a sip. "If I had any idea, do you truly believe I would have kept it to myself these last five years?" Her blue eyes fairly snapped with outrage as she returned the cup to its saucer with a clatter and clack. "I had problems with my nephew. Everyone in this valley knows that. But my problems ended with him. His wife, Marie, was a lovely person, like a daughter to me, and I loved those children like my own, Rachel especially. If I knew who opened fire on them, I'd hunt him down myself."

Joseph searched Amanda Hollister's face for any sign of artifice and found none. She had loved Marie Hollister and the children. There was no doubt in his mind about that.

"I totally agree that it was a heinous crime," David said. "And, please, don't take offense. I'm just trying to do my job. Someone shot Darby in the back. I have to find out who."

"So you start with the person who stood to gain the most by Henry Hollister's death?" Amanda rolled her chair back and wheeled it away from the library table where she'd set out the coffee and cookies. "Good day, gentlemen. You know the way out."

David shot to his feet. "Miss Hollister, please wait!"

"For further insult?" She struggled to turn the chair. "There isn't a piece of land on earth worth spilling blood over, marshal. Now, please, get out. You're no longer welcome under my roof."

Chapter Seven

During the return ride to No Name, Joseph and David went back over their conversation with Amanda Hollister. David was of the opinion that her abrupt departure from the sitting room had been unduly defensive. Joseph's impression had been just the opposite, that Amanda Hollister was a fine woman who had been deeply offended by the implication that she might have killed members of her own family over a piece of land.

"Think about it," Joseph challenged. "She can't take a swallow of coffee without damned near scalding herself. How the hell could she have aimed a rifle at Darby yesterday and hit him in the back?"

"Maybe she hired somebody to do it."

"When it comes to killing, a smart person does it himself," Joseph argued. "Too much risk of being found out, otherwise."

"Maybe she's faking the palsy."

Joseph didn't think so, but he had to concede the point. "Maybe." He thought of Pritchard with his greasy hair and filthy body, a snake if ever he'd met one. "My money's still on Jeb, though."

It was David's turn to make a concession. "He's definitely capable of murder, no question there." He slumped in the saddle with a weary, frustrated sigh. "I guess from here on in, it's a waiting game. We've shaken things up. Now we'll see what falls out."

Joseph drew his watch from his pocket. It was going on four o'clock. "I need to get cooking. Ace has been at Rachel's place for over four hours."

"You heading straight there?"

Joseph clicked his tongue to quicken Obie's pace. "I have some things to take care of in town first, and then I need to swing by home to see how Johnny and Bart have been fairing, running the ranch without me."

"Isn't Esa overseeing things?"

Esa normally worked full-time as a hired hand at Ace's place and knew as much about ranching as Joseph did. "He's getting Bart and Johnny lined out each morning and trying to monitor their work. But taking care of Darby keeps him in the house most of the day. Can't hurt for Bart and Johnny to know that I'm still keeping on top of things. Johnny is on the lazy side. If there's an easy way to do a job, he'll find it. And Bart is too mild-natured to say much if the quality of Johnny's work falls off."

David shook his head. "Used to be that a man took pride in a job well done."

Joseph grinned. "Only when the boss is around. That being the case, I want to drop in on them as often as I can to keep them on their toes. I also need to check on Darby and pick up some stuff."

An hour and a half later, Joseph dismounted in front
of Rachel Hollister's barn and led Obie into his stall.
After rubbing the stallion down, he forked some hay
into the enclosure, filled the trough with fresh water,
and then measured out a portion of grain before turning his attention to the evening chores. He was pleasantly surprised to find that the horses had been brought
in from the paddock and fed, the two cows were already in their stalls and had been milked, the sow was
still standing in the trough, finishing her evening meal,
and someone had recently scattered millet and cracked
corn for the chickens. *Ace.* A fond smile touched
Joseph's lips.

Shakespeare, Ace's black stallion, and two work-
horses from the Paradise had been staked out to graze
near the oak in Rachel's backyard. Joseph was puzzled
by the presence of the two extra equines until he saw
the buckboard parked at one side the house. *Caitlin.*
She very seldom argued with her husband, but she had
this morning, about coming to see Rachel. When
Joseph had left, Ace was laying down the law, forbid-
ding his wife from risking her safety by entering a
house where a crazy woman might open fire on her
with both barrels of a shotgun. Evidently Caitlin had
taken the bit in her teeth, driven over here in the
wagon, and somehow convinced Ace to let her go inside.

The thought made Joseph smile. There wasn't a
man alive who could push Ace Keegan around, but
one small redhead with pleading blue eyes got the better of him every time. Ace seemed content and happy.
That was all that truly mattered, Joseph guessed. He

was glad for his brother and equally pleased for Caitlin. With Conor O'Shannessy as her sire, she'd had a horrible childhood and an even worse girlhood. It was high time she got to have her way the majority of the time and had a man who loved and cherished her as she deserved to be.

As Joseph climbed through the bedroom window, he heard voices coming from the rear of the house. Curious, he made his way up the hallway. As he drew near the dining room, delicious smells made his mouth water. *Fried chicken?* It was one of his favorites.

Ace sat at the dining room table, a plateful of food in front of him. He grinned and saluted Joseph with a half-eaten drumstick. Joseph was about to say hello when a burst of feminine laughter came from the kitchen. Amazed, he went to the barricade, bent his head, and peered inside.

Rachel's tidy world had been turned topsy-turvy. Little Ace was playing with an array of store-bought canned food, Van Camp's pork and beans, Campbell's soup, and some other stuff Joseph couldn't identify, the cans scattered around him helter-skelter. Behind him, an array of pots and pans littered the floor, with Buddy and Cleveland taking a snooze amid the debris. Caitlin and Rachel sat at the table having supper, but it looked as if they were doing more talking and laughing than eating.

"Well, I'll be. Is this an invitation-only party?"

"Joseph!" Rosy cheeked, her red hair attractively mussed, Caitlin sprang up from her chair. "You're late for supper. We didn't expect you to be gone so long."

Rachel came up from her seat more slowly and

blushed when she met Joseph's gaze. "Caitlin came to call," she said, fluttering a hand at the mess around her. "We've had a lovely visit."

"I can see that." And Joseph truly could. Despite the blue shadows of fatigue under Rachel's eyes, she beamed with happiness. It made him feel good to know that he'd played a small part in making that happen by encouraging Caitlin to come calling. "I'm glad you enjoyed yourself."

"How is Darby?" she asked anxiously, her heart shining in her eyes.

Joseph chose not to tell her that the old foreman was running a slight fever. Doc had stopped by to check on his patient, and although he'd been concerned that the fever might worsen, he'd also stressed that it was to be expected. When a bullet invaded the body, it carried with it germs, and a fever indicated that the body was fighting off infection.

"He's doing as well as can be expected," Joseph settled for saying. "Esa made him some beef broth, and he kept that down. Doc stopped by and said the wound looks good. Darby's not quite ready to dance a jig yet, but I think he's on the mend."

Little Ace registered Joseph's voice just then and scrambled to his feet. Chubby legs scissoring, he came running toward the barricade, tripped over a can of pork and beans, and did a face-plant on the floor. Shrieks of distress ensued. Rachel reached the child first, Caitlin not far behind her.

"Oh, no, Ace, he's really hurt!" Caitlin cried. "He's bleeding. I think a tooth went through his lip."

Ace abandoned his meal to bolt toward the hole in

the doorway. Such was Ace's momentum that Joseph feared his brother might plow right through the boards. Fortunately, Ace caught himself short, grasped the jagged edges of wood, and thrust his head through the hole. Peering over his shoulder, Joseph saw Rachel hand the screaming child off to Caitlin and rush to a kitchen drawer. A second later, she plucked out an ice pick and scurried to the icebox.

For the next five minutes, Little Ace was the center of attention while plates of food grew cold. In the end, it was decided that the tooth puncture wasn't all that serious.

When the child's lip had been iced and his mother had doled out enough kisses to soothe a mortal wound, Little Ace suddenly brightened, held out his chubby arms, and hollered, "Seff!"

"Yes, it's your uncle Joseph," Caitlin agreed as she set her son on his feet.

This time, Little Ace ran to the barricade without mishap. Joseph reached through the hole and scooped the child into his arms. "Hey, there, little man. Where did you come by those lungs of yours? My ears are still ringing." Joseph bent his head to nibble under the toddler's chin, which sent Little Ace into fits of giggles. "It looks to me as if you've had way too much fun today without me. Now I'm jealous."

From the stove, Caitlin asked, "Do you want butter or gravy on your potatoes, Joseph?"

"Both." Joseph made a gobbling sound and went after his nephew's belly. The child did an admirable job of fighting his uncle off, all the while lifting his shirt to accommodate the tickling. "Where'd your mama find you, under a cabbage leaf? I was never this ornery."

"The hell you weren't," Ace said from the table.

"I heard that!" Caitlin called. "Unless you want your mouth washed out with soap, Ace Keegan, you'll stop using words like that around your son."

About to take a bite of chicken, Ace said, "All I said was hell. That's not cussing."

"It's not a word that I want our son using," his wife replied. "Imagine how that will go over on his first day at school."

"He won't be in school for another five years," Ace protested.

"Yes, and I shudder to think what his vocabulary will be like by then if you don't get a handle on your language."

Joseph glanced at Ace, awaiting his comeback. Ace just shrugged and resumed eating his meal. Another mark on the chalkboard for Caitlin, Joseph guessed. Personally, he counted hell as being a byword and thought it was a hell of a note that a man couldn't say it when the mood struck.

After Ace and Caitlin left, which was no easy departure given the fact that Caitlin had to crawl back out through the shotgun hole, Rachel set to work tidying her living area. Concerned by the shadows under her eyes, Joseph watched through the opening from his position at the table, wishing he could help her. Mostly it was just busywork, though, putting little things precisely where they belonged, a knickknack here, a rug just there. Before leaving, Caitlin had picked up after her son and helped with the dishes, so the mess was mostly in Rachel's imagination, a result, Joseph felt sure, of her having lived in solitude so long, with little ever happening to disrupt the sameness.

"I want to thank you."

Joseph glanced up from petting Buddy to see her standing at the archway. Her shirtwaist sported spots, either from cooking, eating, or holding Little Ace when his hands were grubby. Even so, she looked beautiful. "Thank me for what?"

Smoothing a hand over the front of her skirt, she smiled and shrugged. "For making today happen. You encouraged Caitlin to come, and I'm ever so glad you did. It was lovely seeing her again."

Joseph could only imagine, and he knew that fell short. She'd been alone inside that kitchen for five long years. The thought boggled his mind. Minute after minute, hour after hour, day after day, with no company and no windows to look outside. If he had been cooped up alone that long, he would have lost his mind.

"I'm glad you enjoyed yourself."

She smiled again and tipped her head as if weighing his words. "Enjoyed? That only skims the surface. I can't tell you how much it meant to me. Little Ace is so darling."

Joseph rocked back in the chair. "You like children, then?"

A thoughtful look entered her eyes. Then she nodded. "Yes, I suppose I must."

It struck Joseph as being a strange answer until he

considered the fact that Rachel had been little more than a girl herself when her family was killed, and she hadn't seen any children since to actually know if she liked them.

"Well, now that Caitlin's come over to see you once, I'm sure she'll be back," he said. "When I take your eggs and cheese into town, I'll be asking Ace to stay with you. Chances are, she'll tag along."

"I hope so." Touching the jagged edges of wood, she added, "I only wish the way in and out were a little less difficult for her."

Ever since asking Caitlin to come visit Rachel that morning, Joseph had been considering that problem and had already taken the initial steps to solve it. Maybe he was wishing on rainbows, but it seemed to him that further modifications needed to be made to Rachel's hidey-hole so she might at least have occasional company. Living as she did was one thing. Even though the measures she had taken seemed extreme, he could understand her need to feel safe. But never to see anyone? There were surely people she trusted, Caitlin being one, who could drop by for coffee sometimes. Just one visitor a week would brighten her life immeasurably. Another thing that troubled Joseph was the constant darkness in which she lived. It was unnatural and couldn't be healthy. Rachel might resent his meddling, but after spending a night and morning in this aboveground tomb, Joseph itched to give her occasional glimpses of sunlight.

"I might could rig up something for you," he offered.

She gave him a curious look. "Like what?"

Still fondling Buddy's ears, he rocked back on the chair. "Has it occurred to you that your barricade didn't hold up very well under that shotgun blast?"

She paled slightly, a telltale sign to Joseph that the barricade's failings had not only occurred to her, but also troubled her deeply.

"I realize now that someone could shoot from the opposite side and do just as much damage, yes."

"Two blasts could make a hole damned near large enough for a man to walk through," Joseph expounded. "If the idea is to keep people out, you need something more than just boards."

"Like what?"

"A solid iron plate bolted to each side of every door, for starters, placed middling high where most people are likely to aim a gun. A shotgun blast can't penetrate iron. On the off chance that someone should try to blast his way in, that would slow him down considerably."

"Yes," she conceded, "I suppose it would."

"And I'm thinking about some iron bars, too, sort of like the cell doors in a jail, something made to fit over the outside of each door as added protection. You got a pad and pencil?"

"Yes." She disappeared for a moment and then returned with the items. Handing them through to him, she pressed close to the hole and watched as he sketched what he had in mind.

He gave her the drawing. "If I could find some long carriage bolts, I could sink them clear through the walls and anchor the barred doors on the inside of the house. In order to remove the exterior bars, a man would need a hacksaw, and it would take forever to cut through even one piece of the iron."

"That would surely increase my security," she agreed.

"And even better, the barred doors could be unlocked. Caitlin may want to come a lot. She enjoys gadding about when she can get away, and she's got only one other good friend, a gal named Bess."

Rachel's eyes brightened. "Bess Halloway, Doc's niece?"

"That's the one, only now her last name's not Halloway."

"Caitlin mentioned today that she'd gotten married."

Joseph nodded. "To Bradley Thompson."

"Do his parents still own the dry goods store?" Rachel asked.

"They do. Brad helps run the place now, and Bess is teaching. With two kids of her own, plus a full-time job, Bess is so busy—even with Brad's mother helping out—that she doesn't have much time for visiting these days. Caitlin could use another friend."

"I'd love it if she chose me," Rachel said with a dreamy smile.

Joseph took the notepad from her hand. "A barred door would simplify her coming and going. Here's what I'm thinking."

Sketching as he talked, Joseph quickly explained how Rachel's damaged archway barricade could be replaced with an extra-thick plank door, similar to the one that opened out onto the back porch. Then barred doors could be installed over both, and the front door of the house as well.

"You could give trusted friends like Caitlin keys to enter the house through the front door," he concluded. "Once Caitlin reaches the dining room, she could knock at the archway door, you could identify her through a peephole, and let her in, locking both the plank and barred door behind her."

"Oh, I never open my doors."

Joseph believed that it was high time she started, if only to allow a good friend like Caitlin to enter. "Ah, but with the added security of a barred door, you could look all around the dining room to be sure it was okay before you unlocked it. Then Caitlin could quickly slip inside, you could lock both doors behind her, and there you'd be, safe as two bugs in a rug."

"I might be able to handle that," she conceded. "It would be fabulous to have a friend come to see me, like a normal person does."

"It'd be safer than the setup you have now," he stressed, "with the added benefit of being able to have a visitor now and again."

She nodded thoughtfully.

"Even better," he went on, "with the bars as an added barrier, you might even feel safe enough to open the back porch door sometimes to enjoy a little morning sunshine."

"And hear the birdsong?" she asked wistfully.

"That, too." The incredulous yearning in her eyes made a tiny place deep inside Joseph's chest throb like a sore tooth. *Birdsong.* He'd not had time to consider all the thousands of things that had been stripped from

Rachel's life—things that he and others took for granted. "Barred doors would be worth a try. Don't you think?"

She sighed and shook her head. "They would be lovely, but I could never afford to have them made."

"It won't cost a thing," Joseph assured her. "Do you remember Bubba White?"

"The blacksmith?"

"One and the same. I stopped by to see him this afternoon. He's got a huge heap of scrap iron left over from when he made rails for the spur Ace built from here to Denver. At present, the iron's rusting and creating an eyesore in front of the shop, and Bubba's wife, Sue Ellen, has been pecking at him to get rid of it. As a result, he's offering the scraps for free to anyone who'll take them off his hands."

"Really?" She frowned thoughtfully. "That would cut the costs, I suppose, but there'd still be Bubba's wages to pay. I don't have much extra money."

Joseph held up a finger to interrupt. "Ah, but you're overlooking one thing. A lot of people in No Name still care about you."

"They do?"

"Of course they do. They've just never known how they might help. Bubba's one of those people. When I told him the barred doors would be for you, he offered to donate his time to make them if I will handle the delivery and installation."

"He did?" She looked amazed. "How kind of him."

"It's not about kindness, Rachel. It's about being a good neighbor. According to Bubba, the attack on your family is the worst thing that's happened in these parts in all the years he's lived here, and he came out from Ohio back in the sixties when Colorado was still just a territory. There have been Cheyenne uprisings and the like, with greater casualties, I suppose, but at least that was during a war. What happened to your family was inexplicable, unprovoked violence that shocked the people in No Name to the core. They're as troubled as you are that the person who did it never was caught."

Dark shadows slipped into her eyes. "I figured everyone would have forgotten about it by now."

"Folks never forget something like that. Bubba is tickled pink to have an opportunity to do something nice for you. 'Some sunlight for Miss Rachel,' he said." Joseph flashed a grin. "In his estimation, it's a worthy cause, and he's more than willing to help me out. I can get everything made for nothing. All I need is a go-ahead from you."

"He actually said that?" Her face fairly glowed. "That it's a worthy cause?"

Joseph searched her eyes and saw the incredulity there. "People haven't stopped caring about you, Rachel."

"I figured they'd all decided I'm crazy."

That, too, but Joseph chose not to go there. "They care about you," he repeated. "Do you remember Sue Ellen, Bubba's wife?"

"Vaguely."

Joseph chuckled. "She's that kind of woman, sort of vague." He held up his hand. "Brown hair, about this tall, a fidgety little lady no wider than a toothpick."

Rachel narrowed her eyes as if to see into the past. "Does she have an eye twitch?"

"That's Sue Ellen. Her and Bubba have to be the most unlikely pair I've ever met, him so big and muscular, and her so itty-bitty. Before I left, she had him and their boy, Eugene, sifting through the scrap iron to find suitable lengths for your doors. I have a feeling she'll ride Bubba's ass until he gets them finished."

Rachel toyed with her collar. An expression of concern suddenly pleated her brow. "What if I can't bring myself to open the back door to let in sunlight? Will it hurt Bubba's feelings, do you think?"

The very fact that she cared about possibly hurting Bubba's feelings told Joseph more about her than she could know. "Nah. He's a tough old fart."

Her cheeks went rosy, and then she laughed. Joseph loved hearing that sound. He had a feeling that levity had been a commodity in short supply for Rachel over the last five years.

"You've a gift with words, Mr. Paxton."

Joseph figured that was her way of telling him he didn't. That was okay. He already knew that talking wasn't his strong suit. "Is that a yes, then?"

She thought about it for a moment and then nodded. "If nothing else, ironwork over my doors will make me feel safer. I'll have to send the Whites some baked goods by way of thanks. A cake and some cookies, maybe."

"There's a plan," Joseph agreed. "But that's for another day. Tonight you need to get some rest."

Moments later, he heard her bustling about. Curious, he returned to the opening and saw her carrying bedding into the water closet. He almost hated to ask. "What are you doing?"

She emerged from the closet. "Making my bed in the bathtub." At his surprised look, she gestured at the barricade. "I couldn't sleep a wink all last night. I don't feel safe with that hole there."

Joseph thought about reminding her of how difficult it had been for Caitlin to crawl through the opening. "I won't sneak in on you or anything."

"It's not you," she assured him. "Well, maybe it is, just a little. I'm not used to having someone here. But mostly it's just the hole." She lifted her hands. "I can't explain except to say that it's part of my sickness. Openness terrifies me. That's why I can't go outside."

"What happens when you try?"

She chafed her arms through the sleeves of her shirtwaist. "My heart pounds, and I can't breathe." She pressed the back of her wrist to her forehead, as if the mere thought made her breathless. "If I don't get back inside straightaway, I pass out."

Joseph couldn't imagine it. "What, exactly, are you afraid of out there, Rachel?"

She fixed him with a wide, bewildered gaze. After a long moment, she whispered, "I don't know."

Why, Joseph wondered, was this card game called patience? Frustration would be a better name. On his third fresh hand, he was already losing again. The cards just wouldn't suit up. Maybe it was his shuffling. Too much, too little. Hell, he didn't know. But he was bored to tears, and that was a fact.

For at least the tenth time in as many minutes, he stretched, rubbed the back of his neck, and thought about hitting the sack. Rachel had retired at least two hours ago. Only he wasn't sleepy. Accustomed to long hours of hard, exhausting work, his body hadn't been taxed enough today. All he'd done was take a ride with David and flap his jaw a little. He needed to do physical work and lots of it in order to sleep well at night.

He had just finished dealing a new row of cards when a bloodcurdling scream rent the air. He shot up from the chair like a jack from its box and reached the barricade in two long strides. There was no sign of any disturbance in the still brightly lighted kitchen.

"Rachel?" he called.

Buddy let loose with a volley of shrill barks and leaped through the hole in the barricade.

"Oh, my *God*!" Joseph heard Rachel cry brokenly. "Oh, my *God*!" And then she screamed again.

Joseph couldn't think how anyone might have gotten inside the water closet. He'd been in the dining room ever since Ace and Caitlin left. But something was horribly wrong.

Reacting instinctively, he backed up and gave the already damaged boards of the barricade several jabs with the heel of his boot. Then he started tearing at the wood with his hands. Within seconds, he was inside the kitchen. Buddy was clawing at the water closet door. Joseph ran over to try the knob. *Damn.* It was locked.

"Rachel?"

Between the dog's frantic barks, Joseph could still hear her sobbing.

"Answer me, honey. Are you all right?"

No response. Trapped in indecision, Joseph stood

there for a moment. But then she whimpered again. He put his shoulder to the door. *Shit.* Tried again.

"Stop it! *Stop* it, *please!*" she cried.

Somebody was in there, Joseph thought. He took a step back and threw himself at the door, putting every ounce of his strength behind his weight.

Chapter Eight

With one more thrust of his shoulder, Joseph heard the door casing split. He threw himself at the panel of wood one more time, and the door burst open.

Swathed in another white gown, her thick night braid falling forward over one breast, Rachel huddled in the bathtub, back to the spigots, her eyes huge as she stared up at him. In so small an enclosure, the single candle, set on a small parlor table in the corner, made the room as bright as day. Joseph scanned the area, saw no one, and relaxed his fists. Buddy leaped into the tub and began sniffing Rachel, as though to check for injuries.

"What?" Joseph asked. "You were screaming. What's wrong?"

Another whimper erupted from her. "N-night— m-mare," she choked out.

All that ruckus over a *dream*? Joseph could scarcely believe his ears. "I thought someone was in here."

She shook her head wildly and pushed the dog's nose away from her face. "Only a n-nightmare."

Joseph turned to assess the damage. He'd flat torn the hell out of the water closet door. The entire casing had come loose, the top rail dangling. He didn't want to think what her barricade must look like. Easing his head out the doorway, he scanned the debris and said, "Well, shit."

"I'm s-sorry. I h-have bad d-dreams."

He raked a hand through his hair. "They must be all-fired awful." He glanced back at her. "What the hell did you dream about?"

She wrapped her arms around Buddy and pressed her face into his fur. "I'm not sure," she confessed raggedly.

If that didn't cap the climax. How could anyone scream that loud when she wasn't even sure what she was screaming about? Joseph felt his temper rising and tried to calm down. She'd scared the bejesus out of him, and after a bad fright, he always got fighting mad for a bit. That didn't give him license to take it out on her.

He left the water closet to assess the damage to her barricade. "Well, that's catawamptiously broken all to pieces."

He heard movement behind him. Then a faint, "Oh, dear *heavens*, what have you *done*?"

The panic in her voice gave Joseph a really bad feeling, and when he turned to her, he forgot all about being pissed off. Her face had lost all color. Her eyes glowed like huge, wet ink splotches on a stark white sheet. Lantern light ignited the recalcitrant curls that had escaped her braid, the golden tendrils creating a nimbus around her head. Buddy paced in nervous circles around her, as if he sensed something was very wrong.

Even as Joseph watched, Rachel's chest started to catch. Her gaze still fixed on the mess he'd made of her barricade, she pressed a hand to the base of her throat.

"With a little bit of fixing, it'll be good as new. I promise."

Her lips were turning blue.

"You're not outside," he cajoled as he moved toward her. Waving a hand, he said, "Rachel? Honey, look at me." But her gaze remained fixed on the scattered boards behind him. "It's still only a hole, just a slightly bigger one than you had a few minutes ago. That's nothing to panic over. I'm here. No one can hurt you."

A horrible rasping whine came up from deep inside her, and her eyes went buggy, like someone choking on a chunk of meat. She extended one slender hand, her fingers curled like claws. Joseph could see that she honestly couldn't breathe. This was bad. This was really, *really* bad. And he had no idea in hell what to do.

For want of anything else, he hollered at the dog to shut up. A lot of good that did. Buddy just barked more insistently, as if imploring Joseph to fix things. Joseph wished he knew how.

When he got within arm's reach of her, Rachel latched on to the front of his shirt, her fingernails scoring his skin through the cloth. Then her knees buckled.

"Christ." It was more a prayer than a curse.

"Sweet Christ," he said for good measure as he barely managed to catch her from falling. Feeling panicked himself, he scooped her up in his arms and hurried into the water closet. "You're safe, Rachel. See? Walls all around."

He sat on the commode seat, putting her back to the doorway so she couldn't see the damaged framework. To his surprise, she hooked both arms around his neck, buried her face against his shoulder, and pressed rigidly against him, still struggling to breathe. Acutely aware of her feminine softness and warmth, Joseph hesitated to slip his arms around her. But then she shivered, and he instinctively embraced her, determined to ignore the reaction of his body and stay focused on her need to be soothed and comforted. Buddy whined and came to rest his chin on her knees.

"No worries," he whispered fiercely. "You've got me, and I'm a whole lot better than a wall. Trust me when I say no one will get through me, not with a shotgun or any other damned thing."

Joseph felt her lungs expand and took heart. He had never been one to blow his own trumpet, but sometimes necessity dictated. She desperately needed to feel safe.

Holding her tightly, he rubbed her back and kept talking. "Remember asking me last night if I'm fast with a gun?" All he got as a response was a labored whistle. "I was afraid to tell you the truth for fear you'd go into hysterics and swoon from sheer fright, but the truth is, I'm very fast." She took another breath. Joseph searched his brain for something more to say. "From the time I was about twelve, Ace insisted that I had to be good with a gun and made me practice every day. Practice makes perfect, as the old saying goes. After nineteen years of practicing, I'm so fast now that you can barely see my hand move when I go for my weapon, and I'm deadly accurate, to boot."

He listened to her breathing and gave himself a mental pat on the back. The whistles were coming less often, and he could feel the rise of her chest occasionally, which told him that her lungs were starting to work properly again.

Warming to his subject, Joseph went on to say, "I can go up against five men who are pretty damned fast and be the only one still standing when the smoke clears."

That was no lie. He had actually done it once. It was one of those memories that still haunted his dreams, a moment in time that he couldn't erase, a regret that he would have to live with for the rest of his life. He closed his eyes and buried his face in her hair. It was every bit as soft as it looked. The scent of roses clouded his senses.

"No one is going to hurt you," he whispered gruffly. "I'll kill any man who tries, Rachel." As Joseph made that promise, he realized he meant it with all his heart. In a very short time, this lady had gotten under his skin. Not a good situation. But that was a worry he would chew on later. "You've got my word on it. If anyone comes into this house, he'll be one sorry son of a bitch."

She made a mewling sound and pressed closer, as if trying to melt into him. "My walls," she said tautly. "I *need* my w-walls, Joseph. I know it's c-crazy, but I c-can't live without th-them."

Though he doubted that he would ever really understand it, Joseph was slowly coming to realize that she truly did need her walls. He guessed some things just had to be accepted whether you understood them or not. There was a sickness inside her head, pure and simple. Not insanity, like he'd thought at first, just a strange, obsessive need to have barricades all around her. He likened it to his obsession about never settling down to sleep along the trail without first checking his bedding for snakes. Even when he'd only just shaken out his blankets, he still had to look. Rationally he knew no snake could possibly be there, but reason held no sway. On some level, Rachel knew that her terror of open spaces was irrational as well, but knowing didn't lessen her fear.

When she was breathing evenly again, Joseph loosened his hold on her, but she clung to him like a baby opossum to its mother. "I thought I might see about fixing your barricade," he whispered. "Where do you keep your hammer and nails?"

"No, *no*. Please don't leave me."

Joseph heard her breath hitch again. He hurried to say, "I won't leave you, honey. A team of wild horses couldn't drag me away. I just need to fix your barricade, is all."

"No boards," she squeaked. "We have no boards."

When a woman couldn't breathe for panic, Joseph could get very creative. He would find something to cover that damned archway even if it meant ripping up floorboards in another room of the house.

Only Rachel wouldn't turn loose of his neck. At the mere thought of his leaving her, she was starting to grab for breath again. In all his days, he'd never seen the like. All of this over a hole in wall? What was it like when she stepped outside? Joseph decided he didn't want to know.

"I won't leave you," he assured her softly. "I'm here, I'm staying. Just calm down, Rachel."

It occurred to Joseph that he might be asking more of her than she could give. Buddy chose that moment to whine and nudge her leg.

"You've got Buddy worried about you," he observed. "He can't figure out what the problem is. Why do you feel afraid when you've got a sterling watchdog like him on duty?"

"Is he a g-good watchdog?" she asked.

Joseph considered the dog's worried face. He guessed Buddy was shaping up to be a fairly good watchdog. He just needed another year of maturity to make him more dependable. As it was, he sometimes grew too interested in food or playing to keep a really sharp eye on his surroundings, and when he fell asleep, he went completely off duty.

"He's the best," Joseph replied.

Hell, if he could brag on himself, he could brag on his dog. In Joseph's opinion, Buddy was the best at just about everything, watching out for danger included. He was just a little young yet. In a few more months, his talents would really start to shine.

"He has hearing like you wouldn't believe." That much was absolutely true. If Joseph touched the cornbread pan to grab a quick snack, the dog came running from any room in the house. "And, boy, howdy, does he raise sand when strangers come around." Sometimes Joseph still had to alert the silly mutt that strangers were approaching, but that was beside the point. "And he's loyal to a fault." Except around golden-haired ladies with big, frightened blue eyes who made stew that smelled too wonderful to resist. Then the dog was a turncoat.

Joseph's spine was starting to ache. He wondered how long she might cling to his neck. Surely not all night. Then again, maybe so. That's what a man got for bragging, he guessed: a woman who counted on him to protect her.

Evidently her muscles were getting cricks in them, too. She squirmed on his lap to get more comfortable. *Uh-oh.* Joseph stared at a curl poking up in front of his nose. Now that she was breathing okay again, a certain part of him, which he'd named Old Glory in puberty, was starting to notice all that warm softness. *This won't do,* Joseph thought. But he couldn't think of a way to rectify the situation. Her butt felt powerful good, and Old Glory had never heeded a single thought in Joseph's head. Nope, Old Glory just did his own thing, and sometimes, like now, that could be pretty damned embarrassing.

He felt Rachel stiffen and knew she felt the hardness. Given the way she'd lived the last five years, Joseph fleetingly hoped that she wouldn't realize the significance. Fat chance. There were some things a female instinctively understood, and a flagstaff poking her in the butt was one of them.

Her head came up, and Joseph found himself being

pinned by an alarmed blue gaze. He couldn't think what to say, but, true to form, he opened his mouth anyway. "Don't let that worry you. Old Glory just stands at attention sometimes." Like *now,* with soft, warm, feminine flesh melting all around him. "In my younger years, I let him influence most of my decisions. Those days are gone forever. I finally figured out that he's got a nose for trouble, and I never pay him any mind."

Her cheeks went bright pink. Joseph was glad to see some color come back to her face, whatever the cause.

"Maybe I should move."

She scrambled off his lap and back into the tub. On the one hand, Joseph was glad to be able to stretch and get the crick out of his spine, but he wasn't pleased to see her gaze shift to the doorway. She locked her arms around her knees, her fingers interlaced and clenched so tightly that her knuckles glowed white. Then she jumped.

"Did you hear that?"

Joseph tipped his head. "Hear what?"

"That."

He listened again and heard only the wind buffeting the house, but the creaks and groans clearly terrified her. "It's just the house settling."

"No, no." Her pupils went large, the blackness almost eclipsing her blue irises. "A footstep," she whispered. "I just heard a footstep."

Buddy whined.

"There, you see?" she said. "He hears it, too."

Buddy was reacting to the fear in her, plain and

simple. Animals could smell it. "It's nothing, honey, just an old house shifting in the wind."

She went quiet, but Joseph could tell that she hadn't relaxed a whit. He found himself wishing he had some of Doc's laudanum. That would relax her. As things stood, it promised to be a mighty long night, and she needed some rest.

A sudden thought occurred to him. "Buddy," he said, "go get my saddlebags."

Fetching the saddlebags was a trick that Buddy had learned out on the trail, a fairly easy one for Joseph to teach him, actually, because the dog knew all their food was in one of the pouches. The shepherd was nothing if not accommodating when it came to getting his treats. He sped off for the dining room.

It took Buddy an uncommonly long while to drag the bags back to the water closet. Joseph figured that the leather probably had gotten hung up in the archway where a few broken boards still protruded.

"Good boy!" Joseph said warmly when the shepherd reappeared, tugging the saddlebags behind him. "First things first." Joseph opened the side pouch, which he had replenished with rations, and pulled out two pieces of jerky. "There you go, partner."

Eyeing Rachel, Joseph opened another bag, found what he sought, and drew it out. Pulling the cork with his teeth, he took a swig, wiped his mouth with his shirtsleeve, and then passed the jug to his charge.

"What's this?" she asked as she grasped the bottle in a shaky hand.

"Ne'er may care," he said with a grin. "A remedy to cure what ails you. Have a snort."

She sniffed the contents and wrinkled her nose. "It smells like whiskey."

"I like 'ne'er may care' better, but whiskey's another name. Bottom's up."

She pushed the jug back at him. Joseph held her gaze and slowly shook his head. "Not an option, darlin'. You're as jumpy as a long-tailed cat in a room full of rockers. The way I see it, we've got two choices. I can go repair that barricade"—he paused and arched an eyebrow at her—"or you can put a brick in your hat and calm down."

She looked back at the jug. "You expect me to become intoxicated?" she asked in a scandalized voice.

"Think of it as getting happy."

"Ladies do not overindulge, Mr. Paxton."

"My name's Joseph, and sure they do when the circumstances call for it. For tonight, think of it as a medicinal remedy. With a few swigs of that under your belt, you won't care if every wall in the place blows down."

"Precisely why I don't choose to obliterate my good sense with drink."

Joseph pushed to his feet. "I reckon I'll see what I can do with that archway, then."

She gave him a glare, put the jug to her lips, and took two dainty swallows. Then she gasped, her eyes went watery, and she started whacking her chest.

"It'll pass," Joseph assured her. "The next swallow will go down like warm honey."

She eyed the jug askance. "I don't care to have any more," she said thinly.

Joseph leaned down to get nose to nose with her.

"You'll drink that whiskey or let me go out there to fix the hole. Your choice. Your eyes look like they've bled onto your cheeks. You have to get some sleep."

She took another gulp of the whiskey. "How much do I have to drink?"

Joseph resumed his perch on the toilet seat. "That'll do for the moment."

She rolled her eyes and made a face. "*Nothing,* not whiskey or anything else, will calm my nerves about that hole."

Joseph had a double eagle in his pocket that said otherwise, but he just shrugged, checked his watch, and winked at her. Holding the neck of the jug clenched in one fist, she remained in a tense huddle, one arm locked around her knees. Every time the house creaked, she wiggled like a Mexican jumping bean.

He liked her nightdress. It was different from the one last night, still a Mother Hubbard but trimmed with lace over the front and at the cuffs. With her knees drawn to her chest, the hem rode high on her shins, revealing shapely calves, trim ankles, and dainty feet, tipped by ten shell pink toes. In all his days, Joseph had never clapped eyes on such tiny toes.

When five minutes had passed, he asked, "How you feelin'?"

She jumped at the mere sound of his voice. "*Nervous.* It won't work, I tell you."

"Try three more swigs."

She lipped the bottle.

"Not sips, sweetheart, *swigs.* By definition, that means big swallows."

He saw her throat working, counted the times her Adam's apple bobbed, and then watched her shudder down the burn. As she settled the jug beside her, Joseph noticed that her fingers limply encircled the neck now. That told him she was starting to relax.

"Now three more," he urged.

She narrowed an eye at him but obediently tipped the jug and took three more gulps. When she came up for air, her cheeks were flagged apple red. She swiped at her mouth with the sleeve of her gown. "Goodness, me."

Joseph grinned. "Feelin' any better yet?"

She fanned her face. "Is it hot in here to you? I'm stifling."

He couldn't very well open a window to let in fresh air. "It'll pass." At least she wasn't listening to the house settle now. "Here in a bit, you'll feel fine as a frog hair."

"Fine as a what?"

"A frog hair. And that's pretty damned fine."

She startled him by pushing suddenly to her feet. Grasping the front of the gown in both hands, she fanned the cloth. "I'm stifling, I say."

When she exited the tub, Joseph gave her a wondering look. "What are you doing?"

She bent over the sink, turned on the tap, and cupped cool water to her cheeks. When she groped for a towel, he tugged one from the rack and handed it to her. "Thank you," she mumbled into the linen. When she lifted her head, she added. "That's better."

"Good." She looked bright eyed and bushy tailed,

which wasn't the effect Joseph had been hoping for. "You ever played poker?" he asked.

"Never."

"You aren't fixing to say that ladies don't play cards, are you? Caitlin does, and she beats Ace's socks off."

"She does?"

Joseph pushed up from the toilet. "Will you be all right while I run get my cards?"

She frowned up at him. "Where are they?"

The very fact that she would consider letting him leave the water closet told Joseph that the whiskey had soothed her nerves some. "On the dining room table."

"Will you hurry back?"

Joseph gave her a mock salute. "Yes, ma'am."

Within seconds he had returned with the cards. Rachel was back in the tub. She wiped her mouth and corked the jug before looking up at him. "It doesn't taste so bad after a while."

Uh-oh. Joseph retrieved the bottle and gave it a shake to check the level. He wanted her relaxed, not pie-eyed. He sat on the commode seat to shuffle on his knee. *Problem.* The rolled edge of the tub wouldn't hold the cards. Joseph eyed the interior.

"Is there room enough in there for you to sit at one end and me at the other if we cross our legs?"

She scooted around with her back to the faucets again. Joseph toed off his boots and crawled in, cards in hand. "I can sit at that end if you like."

"I'm fine."

He handed her the pillow. "Use this to cushion your spine."

He sat cross-legged facing her and settled back. "Okay," he said. "We'll start with five-card draw. It's a pretty simple game." Buddy reared up, hooking his white paws over the edge of the bathtub to eye them. After a moment, he gave a disheartened sigh and curled up on the floor. The dog knew it was time to sleep when he saw his master with playing cards in his hand.

Joseph began explaining the rules. A few sentences in, his student yawned. "You getting sleepy?"

She blinked and sat up straighter. "No, no, I'm fine. With that huge hole in my barricade, I shan't sleep a wink, I assure you."

He dealt the first hand of cards.

She gave him a questioning look. "I pair up the cards, you say?"

Joseph nodded.

"What do you do when you've got three?"

Joseph narrowed an eye at her. "Three what?"

"Three of the same card."

Three of a kind beat his two pairs, hands down. His only hope was to deal himself a third king. That wasn't impossible. He'd seen it happen a number of times. "You keep the three cards and discard the other two," he explained.

"Even if the other two make a pair?"

Joseph gave her another hard look. "You're funning me, right?"

She turned her hand so he could see it. Three aces and two tens. "I'll be a bungtown copper. That's a full house."

She smiled brightly. "Is that good?"

Joseph groaned and bunched that deal. "Beginner's luck," he assured her. "A full house, dealt cold? Never happen again."

Two hands later, Joseph was leaning forward over his crossed ankles, enjoying himself as he hadn't in weeks. "We need something to bet." He studied his cards and bit back a smile. A straight was surely better than anything she had. "It just doesn't feel right without a pot to win."

"I can't afford to gamble with money."

"How about tokens?" Joseph thought for a moment. "You got any hairpins?"

She laid her cards facedown between them and struggled to her feet, treating Joseph to a delightful glimpse of bare thigh when her nightgown rode up. She stepped from the tub to open a cabinet over the sink and returned with a tin of hairpins. Joseph doled out twenty to each of them and schooled her in the fine art of betting. She caught on fast.

"I'll meet your hairpin and raise you"—she pursed her lips as she studied her cards—"two, no, three."

Joseph kept his face expressionless as he eyed his straight. He tossed out three more hairpins. "Call."

With a flick of her wrist, she showed him her hand. Joseph gaped. When he finally found his voice, he said, "A royal flush?"

"Is that good?" she asked innocently.

The question told Joseph he'd been hoodwinked, good and proper. "If you didn't know it was good, why'd you raise me three?"

Her dark lashes swept low, the tips gleaming golden in the candlelight.

"You've played before," he accused.

Her cheek dimpled in an impish grin. "Ma wouldn't let Pa gamble at the saloon, so he taught me how."

"I'll be." He shook his head as he watched her take the ante. "You're having the mother of all lucky streaks."

She giggled, a light tinkling sound that Joseph could have listened to all night. "Luck or know-how. It all depends on if you're winning or losing."

She looked too sweet for words in that lacy Mother Hubbard nightdress with her beautiful hair coming loose from the braid and forming shimmering ringlets around her slender shoulders. Joseph refused to allow his gaze to dip lower, even though he'd done his share of looking earlier. She was all-to-pieces beautiful, make no mistake. And she played poker. He couldn't believe it when she shuffled the cards with a flick of her wrists and started dealing like a pro. He just flat couldn't believe it.

He picked up his cards, arranged his hand, and said, "I'm in for one."

He tossed out a hairpin and discarded. She anteed and stayed, her lips curved in a smug little smile as she dealt him replacements. Joseph perused his hand. He had a full house, kings over deuces. If she had better, he'd gargle salt water while he whistled "Dixie."

He raised the bet by two. She paid to see his hand and raised her delicate brows. "Very nice." Her cheek dimpled again. "But it doesn't beat aces over sevens."

"No way." Joseph stared at the cards she laid down, faceup. "No *way*."

She giggled and collected the ante. "Your deal. Maybe we should change the game."

"Seven-card stud," he suggested.

In truth, Joseph didn't really care if he won. He just enjoyed playing. It was especially pleasurable when his opponent was so lovely to look at. *The perfect woman,* he thought. *Beautiful, a dog lover, a poker player, and a fabulous cook, to boot.* It just didn't get any better than that.

A prickle of alarm worked its way up his spine. He was coming to like this lady a little too much for comfort. In his recollection, he couldn't recall ever having felt this attracted to a female.

She reached over the side of the tub to retrieve the whiskey jug. The cork departed from the neck with a hollow *thunk*. She thrust the bottle at him. "Maybe you need a drink to change your luck."

Joseph guessed he could have one more swig. He didn't want to drink too much for fear that he would sleep too soundly. As unfounded as most of Rachel's fears seemed to be, she hadn't imagined that bullet in Darby's back. He needed to be on guard, just in case the old foreman had it right about her life being in danger.

After taking a swallow of whiskey, he handed back the jug and began the deal. When she saw her first two cards, she burst out laughing and bet three hairpins. All Joseph had so far was a four and a five. Even so, he didn't want to fold. He anteed and dealt her a card faceup.

"An ace?" She grinned and rolled her eyes. "Definitely worth another three tokens."

Joseph's pile of hairpins was dwindling at an alarming rate. She was flat kicking his butt. *His dream woman.* For reasons beyond him, the thought no longer alarmed him. When a man met a woman who appealed to him on so many levels, why run?

A few minutes later, Rachel had most of his hairpins, and her lashes were starting to droop.

"You're exhausted," he said. "We need to quit and get some shut-eye."

"Naturally you'd say that when I'm the biggest toad in the puddle."

Joseph just grinned. "You are, no doubt about it. How about a silly game to cap off the evening? You ever played Injun?"

She nodded. "One card each, on your forehead, face out, without looking?"

Joseph nodded, shuffled the cards, and dealt one to each of them. Without turning hers over to look, she pressed it to her forehead. It took all of Joseph's self-control not to laugh. She had a five. To his surprise, she started giggling so hard when she saw his card that tears came to her eyes. Joseph figured he was holding something pretty pathetic. But what were the odds that it could be worse than a five?

He tossed all his remaining hairpins onto the blanket between them. Still laughing, she met his bet. Then they lowered the cards.

"I don't believe it!" he cried. "No way. You've won every hand so far. I dealt myself a *three*?"

Joseph went to collect his bedding. When he returned to the water closet, his poker opponent's head was lolling. When she heard his footsteps, she jerked erect.

"I think you need to stretch out, darlin'. The biggest toad in this puddle is going under."

"Don't leave me," she murmured as she turned in the tub, punched up the pillow, and drew the blankets over her legs. "If I wake up and you're gone, my heart will stop, I swear."

Joseph shook out his bedroll. "I'll be right here beside you, close enough for you to reach out and touch me. No worries."

She snuggled up to the pillow. "Promise?"

"Absolutely," he assured her. "Buddy and I will be right next to you."

Enough lantern light poured in from the kitchen to dimly illuminate the room. Joseph snuffed out the candle and settled on his pallet, Buddy curled up under the blanket beside him. Within seconds, he heard a faint, feminine snore and smiled to himself. The biggest toad in the puddle was out like a light.

Chapter Nine

When Rachel first opened her eyes the next morning, ice picks stabbed her pupils and it felt as if someone were doing the double shuffle on her skull. Grasping the edge of the tub, she pulled herself up and slumped forward over her knees.

"Oh, *God*."

"Good morning, sunshine."

Joseph's cheerful baritone sent shards of pain lancing through her brain. She held up a hand to silence him. "Whisper. Please. It hurts." Even her own voice hurt. "Oh, God, help me. I'm dying."

"Nah," he assured her in a softer voice. "It's just the Old Orchard, taking its revenge. Drink this. It'll chirk you right up."

Rachel carefully turned her head and squinted one eye at the cup he proffered. "What is it?"

"My remedy. Mostly coffee, with a few other ingredients guaranteed to make you feel better in about a half hour."

With shaky hands, Rachel accepted the cup and

took a gulp of the contents. She sent him a questioning look. "It has whiskey in it."

"That it does. Nothing like some hair of the dog that bit you to set things right."

In thirty minutes, Rachel did feel some better. After leaning the broken water closet door against the shattered frame to afford herself some privacy, she managed to get dressed. Then she moved the broken door to one side to poke her head out the opening to survey the kitchen. To her surprise, the archway doorway was covered with something. The yawning hole that had sent her into a spell last night was gone.

"What is that over the archway?" she asked.

"The dining room table. I stood it on end and walked it over. By way of a barricade, it has its drawbacks, but it'll work for now."

Her skin still crawled as she emerged from the water closet. Joseph motioned for her to sit at the kitchen table and shoved a plate in front of her. She stared dismally at the two pieces of crisp, buttered toast.

"I can't possibly eat."

"You need to. It's part of the cure." He sat down across from her, looking so cheerful that she wanted to shoot him. "Just break off little pieces and wash them down with coffee. You'll feel better with some food in your stomach."

A sound in the other room made her jump. Joseph followed her nervous gaze. "It's nothing. Just the house creaking again. Let me worry about guarding the hole. You eat."

"How do you know eating will make me feel better?"

He winked and grinned. "Experience, darlin'. I've had a few too many tipples in my time."

Rachel broke off a tiny piece of bread and swallowed it with coffee. Her eyebrows shot up. "There's whiskey in this cup, too."

"Like I said, some hair of the dog. It'll help. Trust me."

In that moment, when Rachel looked into his twinkling blue eyes, she realized just how much she *had* come to trust him. If someone had told her two days ago that she'd soon be sitting at the table with a huge hole yawning in her barricade, counting on a stranger to protect her, she would have laughed. Only now it didn't seem ludicrous at all.

When she thought back, she knew she hadn't known Joseph long enough to feel this safe with him, and yet she did. His presence soothed her in some inexplicable way, filling her with a sense of well-being and security that she hadn't felt in a very long while. Even the sound of his voice was a balm to her frazzled nerves.

He gave her damaged barricade a long look, and then he drew out his watch to check the time. "Right about now, your horses are wanting out in the paddock, your cows are bawling to be milked, the hens are demanding breakfast, and that sow is looking in her trough, hoping to see some slop. If Ace comes over today, it'll be later, probably well after noon. I'll have to do the chores myself if they're going to get done."

Just the thought of being left alone made Rachel's heart catch. Evidently he saw the panic in her eyes. "I'm thinking about rigging up a door for your barricade before I leave the house. Would that make you feel any better?"

From the corner of her eye, Rachel could see the archway yawning like a giant mouth waiting to swallow her. The table had been a nice gesture on Joseph's part, but if he had been able to set it there, someone else could just as easily move it. "Yes. Yes, a door would make me feel much better."

"I'm thinking about borrowing an interior door from another room." He let his chair drop forward. "Here's the thing, though. In order to borrow a door and make it work, I'll need the whole unit, doorframe and all. It's liable to do a little damage when I start prying stuff loose."

It had been years since Rachel had ventured into any of the other rooms. A smidgen of damage elsewhere wouldn't matter a whit to her. "That's fine. I don't really care about the rest of the house."

"You sure? Sentimental meaning, and all that. If you ever get well, every nook and cranny will hold memories for you."

Remembering only brought her pain, and Rachel had given up on ever getting well. "I don't think I can handle your going outside unless something is over the hole."

"All right, then." He smiled and shrugged. "I'll need that hammer of yours, all the nails you have on hand, and a screwdriver if you've got one."

Rachel pushed up from the chair. Moments later, she returned to the table with an assortment of tools and a box of nails. Joseph pushed to his feet and went to fetch her shotgun. As he walked back to the table, he motioned to the chair she had vacated.

"I want you to sit right there while I'm gone," he said. "I'll be just up the hall, mind you, but sit right there, all the same."

As she lowered herself onto the chair seat, he handed her the shotgun. "You've got both barrels loaded, right?"

She nodded.

"Well, then. If anyone appears in that archway, point and fire." He leaned down to fix her with a twinkling gaze. "Just don't get spooked and shoot me."

Buddy squeezed through the gap between the lower end of the table and the wall just then. He bounded happily across the kitchen, smelling of fresh air, grass, and oak leaves, scents that Rachel had nearly forgotten. Joseph bent to pat the dog's head.

"Finished with your morning run, fella?" He pointed at the floor. "Sit."

Buddy promptly dropped to his haunches beside Rachel.

"You *stay*," Joseph said firmly. "No deciding different and following me this time, you hear? I want you to stay with Rachel."

Buddy flopped onto his belly, crossed his paws over his eyes, and whined mournfully.

The dog's antics brought a reluctant smile to Rachel's lips. She sent a nervous look at the archway.

"Listen to me." Joseph planted his hands on his knees, once again leaning forward to get nose to nose with her. "I came through your parents' bedroom window when I broke into the house. If I borrow their bedroom door, I'll be working between you and the only window in the house that isn't boarded up. No one will be able to get past me to pester you. I'll be just up the hall, only a few steps away."

A lump of dread filled Rachel's throat. She tried her best to focus on his words and be reasonable. But her fear had nothing to do with reason. She wished she knew how to explain that. Only how could she make sense of feelings that she couldn't understand herself? Her barricade was gone. That was the long and short of it. It was *gone*.

"I'm sorry," she whispered. "I know I'm crazy. You can say it if you want. It won't hurt my feelings or anything."

He took the shotgun and put it on the floor. Then, with a weary sigh, he hunkered down in front of her. Taking her hands in his, he said, "What's crazy and what isn't? What's normal and what isn't? We all have a phobia about something."

"I'm sure you don't."

"Of course I do."

"What is it then?" she challenged.

His full mouth quirked at one corner. "For starters, I'm afraid of ghosts."

Rachel half expected him to suddenly snap his fingers, point at her, and say, "Gotcha." Then she searched his face and realized he was actually serious.

"Ghosts?" she echoed, the revelation so astounding that she forgot about the hole for a moment. *"Ghosts?"*

He nodded. "It's loony, I know. Most folks don't even believe in ghosts." He narrowed an eye at her.

"Tell anyone, and I'll swear you're lying. I've never told anybody, not even my brothers."

A strange ache filled Rachel's chest. "Why are you telling me?"

His lips twitched again. "Now there's a question. Maybe because I know you'll understand and not laugh. And maybe because I think you need to know. You're not the only person on earth with irrational fears, Rachel. If that makes you insane, then all of us are off our rockers."

Tears sprang to her eyes.

"Don't cry. I'm trying to make you feel better, not worse."

Rachel smiled through her tears, for he had made her feel better. Joseph Paxton, afraid of ghosts. Imagine that. "I'm not crying."

He tugged a hand free to thumb moisture from her cheek. "If that's not a tear, what is it?"

"Maybe the roof sprang a leak." She dragged in a shaky breath. "Ghosts? I never would have thought it."

He shrugged. "I believe in God, and I believe in eternal life. How can I believe in those things and rule out the possibility of ghosts? To my way of thinking, I can't. That being the case, if there are good people and bad people in this life, it stands to reason that there must be good spooks and bad spooks in the next life, and it also makes sense that the truly bad spooks may remain true to character, not following any of the rules. So what if they just up and decide not to go to hell? I sure wouldn't if I could weasel out of it."

"So you believe the really bad spooks who are destined for hell sometimes stay here?"

His sun-burnished face flushed to a deep umber. "Yes, and the thought scares the bejesus out of me."

Rachel couldn't feature Joseph as being afraid of anything. "Truly?"

He nodded. "I'm fine with things I can see. I've got my fists and my gun. I'm confident that I can defend myself. But how can you protect yourself from things you can't see or hit or shoot?"

Rachel totally understood that feeling. "I'm afraid of things I can't see, too," she whispered. She glanced past him at the hole and squeezed his fingers with all her strength. "Things I can't even name."

"I know," he said softly.

Her gaze jerked back to his. He was smiling sadly. As she searched his dark face, she realized that he understood her terror in a way that no one else ever had. Darby accepted her strangeness because he loved her, and he'd stood by her through all the bad times for the same reason. But he'd never really understood. More tears sprang to her eyes, the shimmers nearly blinding her.

"I know it's only a hole," she squeezed out. "In the old days, I walked through that archway dozens of times a day. I don't know why it frightens me so to have it uncovered now. It just does."

He brushed the wetness from her cheeks. "That's good enough for me."

It wasn't good enough for Rachel. She wanted to be well again. "When I was a girl, my absolute favorite pastime was to lie under an oak tree on a sunny afternoon and stare at the fluttering leaves until I fell asleep. I watched the clouds drift by, and I fancied sometimes that there were whispers in the wind. And I loved listening to the birds sing. Denver used to lie beside me, with his nose on my shoulder, and snore."

Joseph watched the expressions that drifted across her pretty face, and his heart ached because he could almost feel her yearning. "Denver, your dog?"

She nodded, tears glittering like diamonds on her pale cheeks. "He was my very best friend in the whole world." Her eyes fell closed. "In the end, he died for me." Her voice went thin and taut. "The man was on horseback, and Denver jumped up and sank his teeth into his leg. He wouldn't turn loose, so the man drew his revolver and shot him right between the eyes."

Joseph's insides went suddenly quiet—so quiet that even his heart seemed to stop beating for a second. "You remember that?"

Her lashes lifted. "I've seen it in my nightmares. Not a memory, exactly. Just a picture that moves through my mind and brings me awake, screaming." Her chin quivered. "There are so many horrible pictures, Joseph. But they just flash and then go black."

Joseph squeezed her hands. "You ever get a flash of the bastard's face?"

Her already pale countenance lost all remaining color. "No, I never see that part of him, and the things I do see don't string together." A distant look entered her eyes. "It's like my brain has erased his face."

Joseph wondered if she had known the man. He couldn't imagine anything more horrible than to look into the face of a friend who'd suddenly peeled away his mask to reveal a monster. His stomach turned a slow revolution. If that was the case—if Rachel had known the killer and counted him as a friend or trusted neighbor—was it any wonder that everything once dear and familiar now terrified her?

Holding both her hands in one of his, he pushed forward on his toes, grasped her chin, and trailed his lips lightly over her tear-streaked cheek. He meant to end it there, just a comforting show of affection, but somehow his mouth found hers, and what had begun innocently somehow became a searching kiss. Again that strange quietness filled him, as if everything within his body had gone still in anticipation.

Despite the saltiness of her tears, she had the sweetest mouth he'd ever tasted. It was also the most inexperienced mouth that he'd ever kissed. *Careful, Joseph.* After only a taste, he greedily wanted to plunder every tempting recess. Only the training of a lifetime held him back. This was her first kiss. He knew that, both rationally and instinctively. Yet she surrendered completely, her lips soft, slightly parted, and offering no resistance.

When Joseph drew away, she blinked and swayed on the chair. "Oh, my."

He almost chuckled. Not a wise move. He didn't want her to think he was laughing at her. "I'm sorry. I probably shouldn't have done that."

Her eyes slowly came into focus, the expression in them dreamy and slightly confused. "Why? It was very nice."

Better than nice, Joseph thought, and therein lay the problem. She wasn't a sporting woman at the Golden Slipper who flitted from man to man. She was likely to take a kiss very seriously, possibly even as some kind of commitment from him. He didn't want to give her the wrong impression and end up hurting her. She had experienced enough hurt in her young life.

"Yes, it was nice," he agreed. "Nice enough to get us both into trouble." He leaned in to kiss the end of her nose. "You're a lady from the tips of your toes to the top of your head, Rachel Hollister, and a lady isn't for the likes of me."

She tipped her head to study him questioningly. "Why is that?"

"Because I'm not the marrying kind." Joseph pushed to his feet. "You'll do well to remember that." He walked across the room to the archway. "I take my pleasure where I find it, and then I move on. I don't have it in me to love just one woman. I'm more what you might call a buffet man."

"A what?"

Joseph strained to shift the table. "A buffet man. I like to sample all the dishes and don't have a taste for any particular one." He angled her a warning look. "I love first helpings, but I rarely go back for seconds. I'm the same way with women. You understand what I'm saying?"

"That you're a scoundrel?"

He grinned. "There you go, a scoundrel. When it comes to kissing and that kind of thing, don't trust me any farther than you can throw me. Are we clear?"

"Perfectly clear. What are you doing?"

He managed to scoot the table off to one side so he could squeeze through. "No worries." He returned to collect the tools. "I'll move it back to cover the opening while I'm gone."

* * *

The noise that filtered into the kitchen told Rachel that Joseph was making grand headway on removing the door and casing from her parents' bedroom. She sat on the chair, where he had told her to sit, staring dry eyed at the upturned table, which hadn't budged from the archway. Buddy lay beside her, snoozing. She took comfort from the fact that he seemed to be bored with the whole business.

Finally, she heard footsteps returning to the dining room, interspersed by crashes, bangs, and muffled curses. "Rachel?" he called. "I'm gonna move the table now. Don't get scared and shoot, all right? It's just me."

"Me who?" she couldn't resist asking.

Long silence. "It's me, Joseph." Another silence. "Are you having me on?"

Rachel smiled. "I am, I suppose."

"Will miracles never cease? The woman cracked a joke."

The table grated across the floor, and a moment later Joseph's blond head poked around its edge. He flashed her a grin that made her stomach feel all squiggly. "Howdy. Long time, no see."

"Howdy."

He set to work on installing the doorframe, cussing almost constantly under his breath because the measurements of the archway weren't exactly the same as the doorway in her parents' bedroom.

"Can you make it fit?" she asked.

"Not snug," he confessed. "It's gonna be as loose as a fancy woman's nether regions." He froze and shot her a look over his shoulder. "Pardon me. I forgot for a second who I was talking to."

Rachel went back over what he'd said and couldn't make much sense of it. When he saw her bewildered frown, he chuckled, shook his head, and went back to work, muttering under his breath again.

When the door was finally installed, its swinging edge was an inch shy of touching the jam, and the top rail didn't stretch all the way across. It nevertheless provided a barrier. Joseph had hung it to open into the kitchen. He borrowed the niches and pine plank from the pantry door to bar it shut.

The instant the plank fell into place, Rachel let out a sigh of relief. "Thank you, Joseph."

He came to lay the tools on the table. "Better?" he asked.

"Much better." She felt safer now. "I can't tell you how grateful I am. I know it was a bother."

"Not a problem." He glanced at his watch and then tucked it back in his pocket. "Now here's the question. When I get back from doing the chores, are you going to be able to open up for me?"

Rachel thought about it for a long moment. Normally the very idea of opening a door sent her into a panic, but with Joseph standing on the other side, she thought she might be okay. "I think so."

He flashed her a teasing grin. "It'll be a hell of a note if you can't. I'm leaving Buddy here with you." He bent to scratch behind the dog's ears. "He needs to go out every now and again."

*   *   *

Thanks to Joseph's morning-after remedy, Rachel's headache and nausea were completely gone within the hour. With a door in the archway, she felt relaxed enough while he was off doing chores to follow her usual morning routine, emptying the wood safe, stoking the range fire, and starting breakfast, a working-man's meal of bacon, fried potatoes, biscuits, eggs, and gravy.

A buffet man? Every time Rachel remembered him telling her that, she grinned. He was far too kind a man to possess an inviolate heart. One day soon, when he least expected it, he would meet a lady who would make him forget all that nonsense about second helpings. She'd seen how good he was with Little Ace, a sure sign that he'd make a wonderful father. She also felt confident that he'd be an equally wonderful husband. He just hadn't found the right woman yet.

Rachel refused to let herself wish that she might be that woman. Her situation didn't lend itself well to getting married and raising a family. *Too bad.* She had truly enjoyed that kiss. His fingertips on her chin had made her skin tingle, leading her to wonder how it might feel if he touched her in other places. *Shocking* places. She had no idea where such thoughts had come from, but come they had, and now she couldn't push them from her mind.

Did two people actually *do* stuff like that? A part of Rachel couldn't imagine it, but another part of her thought maybe so. As a girl, she'd sometimes seen her parents caressing each other when they thought she wasn't watching, and though she'd never seen them touch each other in truly intimate places, thinking back on it now, she could remember their coming close. Her father, as she recalled, had been especially fond of touching, running his hands upward from her mother's waist almost to her bosoms and sometimes cupping her posterior in his palms to pull her hips snugly against him. Her ma had always giggled and given him a playful push, as if she hadn't liked it, but it was obvious that she actually had.

Rachel realized that her hands had gone still. She stared stupidly at the dry biscuit ingredients in the bowl, unable to remember what she'd already added and what she hadn't. *Lands.* There was nothing worse than biscuits made bitter with too much baking powder. Dampening a fingertip, she took a taste, trying to determine if the rising agent had already been added. It was hard to tell. To be on the safe side, she measured more in, stirred industriously, and took another taste. No bitterness. That was a good sign. She could only hope she hadn't used twice as much as needed.

Enough woolgathering! She'd end up ruining the entire meal. With determined concentration, she began cutting in the lard, trying her best to think of nothing but the biscuits. Only a picture of Joseph's face crept into her mind again. At some point over the last two days, she'd come to think that he was extraordinarily handsome in a rugged, sun-burnished way. His large, bladelike nose now seemed perfectly right for his face, and she barely noticed the knot along the bridge anymore. She also found his sky blue eyes to be wonderfully expressive and compelling. And his mouth, ah, she loved his mouth. For a man, he had full, beautifully defined lips, and they were fascinatingly mobile, the corners curving up and dimpling one cheek just before he smiled. They were also delightful to watch when he talked, shimmering softly in the light like polished silk.

Rachel realized that her hands had gone still again, and she sighed with frustration. *Enough.* They were just lips, after all. She had work to do after breakfast. If Joseph would take her homemade goods into town to sell them, she needed to make bread, some butter, and a new batch of cheese to start it aging. Otherwise, she'd find herself with nothing in her cellar to replace the blocks of cheddar that were coming ready to be sold now. Her cheddar cheeses were popular items at Gilpatrick's general store, and she needed the money they brought in.

So that was that. No more daydreaming for her this morning.

Cursing to turn the air blue, Joseph kicked an empty oilcan across the barn. What had he been thinking to kiss her like that? Sweet, innocent, decent young ladies were forbidden fruit. He *knew* that. But he'd gone after her anyway, conscienceless bastard that he was. Afterward, she'd looked at him as if he'd just hung the moon. If he didn't watch his step, he'd find himself with a ring through his nose.

Rachel was a sweetheart, and he had to admit, if only to himself, that he liked just about everything about her. Last night, for a fleeting moment, he'd even considered the possibility that she might be *the* woman. That was dangerous thinking, the kind of thinking that could lead him to make a decision he would come to regret.

No way. He liked his life just fine the way it was, and he meant to keep it that way. No fuss and folderol. No female drawers hung to dry over the edge of his bathtub. No grabbing the wrong soap and coming from the water closet smelling like a whore. No woman harping at him like a shrew when he stayed gone all night. Ha. Ace could have it. Joseph enjoyed his freedom.

From now on, that girl was totally off-limits, he lectured himself as he milked the cows. No more looking through her nightgown when she got between him and the light. No more salivating over the taut tips of her breasts when they pushed against her nightdress. No more doing that eye thing, either. He'd always laughed at men who talked about drowning in a woman's eyes. Now here he was, gazing into blue depths himself like some kind of mindless fool.

The lady spelled "trap" in capital letters. Now that he was away from her, he honestly couldn't think what had gotten into him. He felt sorry for her. Maybe that was it. She hadn't asked for the sorrow that life had dished out to her, and she certainly hadn't asked to live as she did. He couldn't be around her without wishing he could make things better for her.

That was it, he assured himself, as he left the barn with a can of chicken feed. He pitied her, and his feelings were all in a tangle. It had been a spell since he'd gone into town on a Friday night. He needed to visit Lucille again. Or was her name Cora? Damned if he could remember. It wasn't about names, after all, or even about being friends. He had needs that couldn't be ignored, and she took care of them, for a price. It was as simple and as awful as that.

Joseph stopped dead in his tracks. *Awful?* And just where had that thought come from? What was awful about two people scratching each other's itch? Nothing that he could see. So why did he suddenly feel guilty?

Shoving his hand into the can, he started throwing feed with such force that the hens squawked and scattered. *Damn it all, anyhow.* She was messing with his mind, making him find fault with himself, with how he lived his life, and with every other damned thing. Like his house, for instance. He'd liked it just fine before he met her. Now he found himself looking at her rugs and doilies and knickknacks, thinking his own place could use a woman's touch.

What was *that* all about?

Chapter Ten

Thirty minutes later when Joseph shoved half of a fluffy, buttered biscuit into his mouth and decided it was equal to none, he knew exactly what his problem was. He'd found the perfect woman.

The realization did not make him happy. He didn't want a woman. Well—he *did* want a woman. What red-blooded man *didn't* want a woman? But he didn't want just *one* woman. He liked variety—plump ones, skinny ones, big-breasted ones and little-breasted ones, tall ones and short ones, bubbly ones and somber ones. *Always* plural.

Only when he looked at Rachel, he didn't think about variety. She was so darned pretty and nice. It almost didn't seem right that she also cooked like a dream, played poker, and loved dogs.

The woman was out to get him.

He chewed and glared at her butt. She was bending over like that on purpose. He knew she was. What woman in her right mind opened an oven door to wash away a few drippings and pushed out her rump like that at a man? Nearly under his nose, give or take a few feet. It was almost an engraved invitation. *Come and get me.* Well, *he* wasn't harkening to the call. Down that path lay marriage, responsibility, and no more Friday nights in town.

He really, *really* needed a night in town. Calving season had kept him at home for going on a month now, and he was as horny as a three-pronged goat. *That* was why her butt looked so good to him, because any woman would tempt him right now.

He pushed another half of a biscuit into his mouth, chomped down, and bit his cheek. Pain radiated. "Damn!"

"Oh, *dear!* What's wrong?" Rachel and her rump raced over to the table. "Did I put in too much baking powder?"

"No, my tooth's just panging." He didn't know where that had come from. But as lies went, it was fair to middling. "The biscuits are fine."

She fixed him with worried blue eyes. He wondered if she practiced in front of a mirror to look that sweet.

"I've got just the thing for that," she said, and raced off to the water closet. "Oil of Cajeput on cotton wool. I keep a few balls from the apothecary on hand. Every now and again, Darby gets a toothache."

Joseph finished his meal in stony silence. When he'd cleared all but two slices of bacon from his plate, he pushed up from the table, tossed the meat to his dog, and advanced on the sink.

"Just never you mind the dishes," she said. "Sit back down so I can doctor that tooth."

If this wasn't a fine predicament, Joseph didn't

know what was. His teeth were fine, but unless he confessed to fibbing, he couldn't very well tell her that. Not knowing what else to do, he sat back down.

She came to hover over him and told him to open his mouth. "Which one is hurting?" she asked.

The scent of roses intoxicated him as she pressed closer and cupped the back of his head with a slender hand. "Naw her," he said. It wasn't easy to talk with his mouth open.

"What?"

One of her breasts was pushing close. He closed his mouth. "I'm not sure."

"Oh, well. That happens sometimes. Open wide, and I'll have a look."

He definitely had an ache now, but it was a long way from his head. Old Glory had gone rock hard and started to throb. He opened his mouth and tipped his head back. She bent to peer in, the pleated front of her shirtwaist grazing his jaw and then the soft, warm weight of her breast coming to rest against his shoulder. God help him, he'd never wanted a woman so badly in his life.

"There it is," she informed him. "Oh, yes, I can see the cavity. You might consider seeing the dentist, Joseph. It needs to be filled, I think."

His eyebrows arched in surprise, but with her fingers in his mouth, he couldn't speak. A nasty smell filled his nostrils, totally obliterating the rose scent. It burned down the back of his throat.

"There you go," she chirped. "Bite down."

He brought his teeth down on the cotton wool, and pain exploded all along his jaw. He came up out of the chair so fast that he almost knocked Rachel over. "Ouch! Oh, *damn*!" He ran a finger into his mouth to scoop out the wool, then ran to the sink and started spitting. "What *is* that shit? *Ouch*. Oh, *damn*!"

"It only hurts for a moment."

Easy for her to say. It wasn't her tooth that was shooting pain clear through her gray matter and out the top of her skull. If he hadn't had a toothache before, he sure as hell did now. "You *knew* it was going to hurt? Why in hell didn't you tell me?" He gingerly prodded the tooth. A cavity? He'd always had perfect teeth. "If that doesn't beat all. I *do* have a cavity back there."

"You really need to keep the wool on it for a few minutes."

Joseph ran some water to rinse his mouth. The pain was finally lessening. "No, thanks. The cure is worse than the toothache."

"It really will help," she insisted.

Free of aches now—in *all* parts of his body— Joseph wiped his mouth on his shirtsleeve and turned to give her a wary look. Old Glory had shriveled up and dived for cover. "It's better already," he assured her.

She beamed a beatific smile. "There, you see? It works for Darby every time."

Accustomed to constant physical activity, Joseph couldn't stand to just sit, so he decided to help Rachel. Over his lifetime, he'd made bread and butter countless times, but he'd never made any kind of cheese.

"This is kind of fun," he said as he minded the large pot of milk heating on the stove while Rachel bustled around him. She had already added a quarter teaspoon of starter to the milk, and here in a bit they would let it ripen while they churned the butter. For now, the milk had to be heated to a certain temperature before she added the rennet to make it curdle. "What'll it taste like when it's done?"

She laughed lightly. "Well, now, it's my hope that it'll taste like cheddar cheese."

He chuckled. "I mean before it ages."

"It's not very good before it ages, just pressed and drained curd that's lightly salted."

Soon Rachel judged the milk to have reached the right temperature, and she added some rennet mixed with a little water. When it was stirred in, they set the pot on the counter by the sink. "It'll have to sit now for about forty-five minutes until the milk breaks clean."

Once again, Joseph found himself with nothing to do but twiddle his thumbs. William Shakespeare had hit the nail on the head, he decided. Dreams were the children of an idle brain. He couldn't keep his eyes off Rachel, and his imagination kept taking him places he didn't want to go. Would she surrender her mouth to him just as completely if he kissed her again? And what would it be like to unfasten that prim little shirtwaist to unveil those soft, full breasts?

In desperation, Joseph reached for the book that lay open on the table. "*The Adventures of Huckleberry Finn*?"

Rachel glanced up from the sink where she was lining a colander with cheesecloth. "Have you read it?"

Since his school days had ended, Joseph seldom

read anything unless it pertained to horses, cows, or raising crops. "No, I can't say that I have."

"How about *The Adventures of Tom Sawyer*?"

"Nope."

She went to one of the bookshelves along the water closet wall and returned a moment later with a leather-bound novel. "You first meet Huckleberry in this story." She sat across from him, turned up the lamp wick, and lovingly opened the book, her graceful fingers caressing the pages as if they were old friends. "Let me just read a bit of it to you."

Joseph was glad of anything that might take his mind off Rachel and her tempting curves. Thirty minutes later, he was lost in the tale, envisioning the small town of St. Petersburg along the shore of the Mississippi River and laughing over Tom Sawyer's shenanigans, which frequently resulted in his receiving a licking from his aunt Polly.

"That darned Sid is a terrible tattletale," he remarked.

Rachel smiled and pushed the book toward him. "It's time for me to drain the curds and churn the butter. Why don't you read aloud to me while I work?"

Joseph took the book and rocked back on the chair while he found their place. Soon he was lost in the story again. As he read, he was dimly aware of Rachel bustling around the kitchen or occasionally coming to sit.

As punishment for skipping school to go swimming, Tom had to whitewash the fence around Aunt Polly's house. Only, being the smooth talker that he was, he convinced some neighbor boys to finish the job for him.

Time flew by on swift wings as the story unfolded. Tom fell wildly in love with a girl named Becky Thatcher, the judge's daughter, and got his heart broken. Then one night, he and Huck sneaked off at midnight to the graveyard to perform a special ritual to cure warts. Convinced that the cemetery was filled with ghosts, the two boys were sore afraid of seeing one.

Joseph chuckled and glanced up at Rachel. "I guess I'm not the only one afraid of spooks."

She grinned. "Keep reading."

Within moments, Joseph's skin had developed goose bumps. Frightened into hiding by approaching voices, the boys accidentally witnessed a trio of grave robbers pilfering a grave. Only soon a fight broke out among the three men, and Tom and Huck witnessed something far worse: a murder. Terrified for their lives, the boys ran. Later they made a pact never to tell anyone of what they'd seen because they were afraid that the murderous Injun Joe might kill them, too.

"This is good," Joseph confessed when he stopped reading to give his voice a rest. "I didn't expect to enjoy it so much."

Rachel worked at the counter, pouring curds into cloth-lined cheese molds. "I absolutely *love* that book, and *The Adventures of Huckleberry Finn* is even better, I think. Truly Twain's masterpiece."

Joseph went back to reading. A while later, Rachel took another turn as the narrator, and before they knew it, it was time for lunch. While helping to make sandwiches, Joseph marveled aloud over the story. "I haven't been back down south since I was knee-high to a tall grasshopper, but that story makes me feel like I'm actually there."

"Reading is one of my favorite pastimes," she confessed, her cheeks going rosy. "Books bring the world into my kitchen. I can feel the sunlight on my skin, feel the summer breeze in my hair, smell the flowers, and hear the birds sing. Without my books, I truly believe I would shrivel up and die."

Joseph was glad that she had had her books to sustain her, but it saddened him deeply that her only glimpses of the world came to her through the written word. He could tell by her tone that she yearned to feel the sun warm her skin again and that she sorely missed dozens of other pleasures that could only be found outdoors. In that moment, he would have given almost anything to make it possible for her to experience those things again. Sadly, he couldn't think how.

Ace showed up shortly after two that afternoon, ready to stand guard duty while Joseph went to town. Rachel's face fell with disappointment when Ace called through the back door that Caitlin hadn't accompanied him this time.

"We had church this morning, and Caitlin had plans for this afternoon," Ace explained. "She said to tell you that she'll try to come next time."

Joseph slipped out through the archway door. When Rachel had barred it behind him, he exited the house via the broken window to go around back to see his brother. Barking joyously, Buddy and Cleveland met in the side yard and tumbled to the ground in a blur of reddish-gold and white fur. When the dogs regained their feet, they raced away, taking turns nipping at each other's heels and knocking each other down. Joseph saw them sail over a pasture fence and then vanish in the tall grass. Knowing full well that they would return when they'd played themselves out, Joseph didn't bother calling them back.

"Howdy," Ace called from where he sat on the steps. "Nice weather we've got today."

Joseph nodded in agreement. "It is a beautiful afternoon. Spring is in the air." He gazed off across the tree-studded pastures that stretched as far as the eye could see, wishing that Rachel could come out to enjoy the sunshine. "It's shirtsleeve warm, and that's a fact. A mighty nice change, if you ask me."

"It being the Sabbath, Caitlin can't do any actual chores, so she's out hoeing her garden rows, getting ready to plant."

Joseph had lived in the same household with his sister-in-law long enough to know that she didn't think of gardening as work. The girl flat loved her plants. Every year at the first of February, she lined every windowsill in the house with her garden starts and could scarcely wait to transplant them.

"I keep telling her it's way too early to put anything out yet," Ace went on, "but she'll have her way about it, I reckon. Then along will come a frost to kill all her sprouts, and I'll have to buy her some chocolate drops to cheer her back up."

Joseph chuckled. "You spoil that girl rotten. No

worries about the seed she'll waste, only about how sad she'll be if a frost kills her plants."

Ace just shrugged. "I can buy her a wagonload of seed and never miss the money. Anything that makes her happy is okay by me."

"She's happy, Ace. The woman thinks the sun rises and sets on your ass."

Ace barked with laughter, throwing back his head so sharply that he lost his hat. His black hair glistened like jet in the bright sunlight. "You do have a way with words, little brother."

"I've been told that a lot lately." Joseph went to sit on the steps to have a smoke before he hooked up the team to Rachel's buckboard and loaded all her commodities. Harrison Gilpatrick always opened the general store after Sunday morning services so churchgoers who came into town only once a week could replenish their supplies. "How's the boy's lip today?"

"Fine, just fine." Ace's eyes softened with warmth. "He's playing in the dirt with his ma and having himself a grand old time."

Joseph could well imagine that. "Little boys do love dirt."

The breeze picked up just then, trailing Joseph's hair across his face in a fan of yellow. He stared through the strands at the swaying branches of the oak tree, which were laden with new buds. Soon spring leaves would unfold and the field grass would darken, painting the ranch in different shades of brilliant green. Rachel would get to see none of it.

"What are you looking so gloomy about?" Ace suddenly asked.

Joseph sighed and shook his head. "Just thinking, is all. It's sad, seeing her live like that." He hooked a thumb over his shoulder at the house. "Day in and day out, never leaving that kitchen. She can't even look out a window to see the sunlight or watch a bird in the tree. I'm already going crazy after being in there with her for only a couple of days. I've been reading a book. Can you believe it?"

Ace drew out his own pack of Crosscuts and lighted one up. "You're growing right fond of her, aren't you?"

"It'd be a mite hard not to," Joseph replied with a sharp edge to his voice. "She's a nice lady."

Ace mulled that over for a moment. "No need to be so prickly."

"I'm not being prickly. Just don't go making something out of it. I'm fond of lots of women. It doesn't mean anything."

"I didn't mean to imply that it did."

Joseph caught him smirking. "What?" he asked, feeling inexplicably angry.

Ace held up his hands. "Nothing. You just seem mighty defensive all of a sudden. That's not like you."

Joseph tossed away his cigarette and jammed his hat more firmly onto his head. "I've got better things to do than listen to this."

Ace gave him a bewildered look. "Damn, Joseph. I haven't said anything."

"You can give a whole dissertation without saying anything. Do you think I can't read between the lines?"

Joseph stomped down the steps, ground out his

smoke, and sent his brother a glare. "You know exactly what you're hinting at."

"No, I don't."

Joseph refused to dignify that with a reply and took off for the barn. He heard his brother following him. "You're supposed to watch the house," he grumped over his shoulder.

"I can see the damned house just fine from here."

Joseph went into the barn. When he emerged a few minutes later leading the two horses, Ace was waiting to help put them in the traces. As they worked in tandem to harness the team, Ace asked, "Are you falling for that girl, Joseph?"

That ripped it. "No, I'm not falling for her!" Joseph realized that he was almost yelling, and that only made him madder. "There you go, making something of it!" He jabbed a finger over the rumps of the geldings at his brother's dark face. "Don't even *think* it. You hear? You're the romantic in this family, not me. I take my pleasure where I find it, and then I move on. That's how it's always been, and that's how it'll always be."

"Boy, howdy, have you ever got a bad case."

Joseph bit down hard on his molars and made his tooth pang again. "I don't, either." He swung into the buckboard, gathered the reins, and kicked the brake release. "I'll see you when I get back. Hopefully you'll be talking better sense by then."

Joseph was almost a mile from the house before he realized that he'd forgotten to load the wagon. "Son of a *bitch*." He drew the team to a stop and just fumed for a moment. *A bad case?* Ace always had known how to put a burr under Joseph's saddle. Well, he who laughed last laughed longest. Joseph Paxton, falling for a woman? Ha. Not in this lifetime.

Simone Gilpatrick was a buxom, sharp-tongued woman with black hair and glittery brown eyes. A lot of folks disliked her for being too bossy and nosy. She also had a reputation for being a gossip. Because Joseph normally shopped at the general store on week-days when Gus, a burly, dark-haired employee, helped Harrison to man the counter, he seldom encountered Simone, and on those rare occasions when he did, he tried to ignore her.

"Good afternoon, Mrs. Gilpatrick," he called as he entered the building.

"The afternoon is waning," Simone retorted from behind the counter. "It being the Sabbath and all, it's lucky you are that we're still open."

Hooking his thumbs over his belt, Joseph skirted the baskets and barrels of grains and foodstuffs that peppered the plank floor, his boot heels scuffing as he walked. "Looks to me like plenty of people are still out and about. I reckon you won't close until the board-walks are clear. You might lose some sales."

She sniffed and puckered her lips as if she smelled something bad. Joseph just grinned. Everyone in town knew Simone was greedy. If not for her kindly, fair-minded husband, Harrison, she would have jacked up all the prices and never felt a moment's remorse as she put the pennies in her till.

She gave him an inquisitive look. "So what can I do for you, Mr. Paxton? If you're here to bend Harrison's ear again about heifers and calving, he's busy cleaning shelves in back."

She wore a pale purple dress of shiny cloth that made her huge bosom look even more gargantuan than usual. Joseph wondered why on earth Harrison allowed her to wear something so unflattering. Then he wondered at himself for wondering. Harrison Gilpatrick was a quiet, peace-loving man who picked his battles and only bucked his wife when he felt he had to.

"I'm not here to visit today," Joseph assured her. "I've got some butter, eggs, and cheese to hawk."

Simone nodded. "I heard you were staying out at the Hollister place with Miss Rachel. Day *and* night, as I understand."

Joseph flicked her a sharp glance. There was an underlying tone in her voice that he didn't quite like.

"There's nothing improper going on. If folks are saying otherwise, they're dead wrong."

She shrugged. "I've no control over what other people say, Mr. Paxton. As for what's going on out at the Hollister place, that's for you to know and the rest of us to only wonder about."

She came out from behind the counter, her manner brisk and businesslike. The shiny dress, when seen from hem to collar, magnified her plumpness until she looked like a garish barn door waddling toward him. "Where are these commodities you'd like to sell?"

Joseph was still stuck on what people were wondering about. "Now look here."

Simone arched an imperious black eyebrow. "Yes, Mr. Paxton?"

"Darby McClintoch, the foreman at the Hollister ranch, is laid up at my place from a bullet wound in the back."

"We heard about that. How is he doing?"

"Doc thinks he'll pull through. That isn't the point." He followed the store proprietress through the maze of baskets and barrels. "Darby believes the attack on him may be connected to the Hollister massacre five years ago, and he's afraid for Miss Rachel's safety. That's why I'm staying at the Hollister place, to protect the lady."

"I see," she said, her tone dubious.

"Miss Rachel lives in a boarded-up kitchen," Joseph protested. "She hasn't opened the door to anyone in years. How can people think anything improper is going on between us?"

Simone swished out the doorway, her broad ass grazing the doorjambs on both sides. "Rachel Hollister is an unmarried young woman, Mr. Paxton, and you are an unmarried man who—if you don't mind my saying so—has something of a reputation for being a womanizer."

A *womanizer*? Joseph was starting to get the mother of all headaches. A womanizer chased anything in a skirt. A womanizer had no scruples. A womanizer would compromise a decent young woman without batting an eye. He had *never* consorted with decent young women.

"That isn't to say that *I* believe anything inappropriate is happening out there." She flashed him a syrupy-sweet smile that fairly dripped venom. "But you may as well know there has been a lot of talk."

And Joseph was willing to bet that her tongue had been wagging the fastest.

"No matter how carefully you slice the pie, Mr. Paxton, some folks are always going to scrutinize the pieces."

Joseph's temples were pounding by the time he joined her at the wagon. The self-righteous, judgmental old bitch. It made him furious to think that anyone in this dusty little town would *dare* to point a finger at Rachel Hollister. She was one of the finest and most proper young women he'd ever met.

"Some people forget the eighth commandment," he told her. "It's a sin to bear false witness against your neighbor."

Simone just lifted her eyebrows again. "Do you want to sell these commodities or not?"

Joseph had been pissed at Ace earlier. Now he wanted to do murder. He couldn't very well strangle the old biddy, so he did the next best thing. He got his revenge by haggling with her over prices.

"Four cents for a dozen eggs? These are from grain-fed chickens, and I know damned well they should go for six cents a dozen. You sell them for nine. I just saw the sign. That's a fair thirty-three percent profit margin for you."

"Go away."

Joseph nodded. "Maybe I'll just do that. I reckon I can stand on the boardwalk, cut your store prices by a penny, and sell out, lickety-split, making not only Miss Rachel's usual profit, but most of yours as well. Care to make a wager?"

Joseph got six cents a dozen for the eggs, eight

cents a pound for Rachel's cheese, which was top price, and six cents a pound for the butter. As he drove the buckboard up Main Street, he grinned like a fool. Who ever said revenge wasn't sweet?

His next stop was at the sawyer's. Ronald Christian was a jet-haired man of medium build with friendly blue eyes. He wore patched but clean overalls, winter and summer, unless he was going to church, where-upon he donned a suit.

As Joseph swung down from the wagon, the little Christian boys came running out to greet him. Richie, a six-year-old, hugged one of Joseph's legs, and Don-nie, a year younger, grabbed the other one. Joseph pat-ted their ebony heads and smiled into their big blue eyes.

"Hello, boys. How are you doing today?"

Ronald emerged from the mill, an open-sided struc-ture, essentially only a roof supported by poles. "Now, Richie, now, Donnie," he scolded. "Let go Mr. Pax-ton's legs. He can't walk with you hanging on him like that."

Joseph ruffled the boys' hair and then focused on their father. "Hi, Ron. I need some planks."

"What kind?"

"I don't much care. I just need them extra thick." He held up his hands to demonstrate. "Miss Rachel Hollister needs a new door."

Ronald nodded. "I heard you were staying out there."

Joseph could only wonder what else Ronald had heard.

"I was real sorry about what happened to Darby. How's he doing?"

"Doc has been dropping by to check on him regularly. So far, so good. He was running a bit of a fever last night. That's a worry. But Doc says it's to be expected."

"Bullet wounds are nasty business," Ronald agreed. "Always liked Darby. I hope he pulls through." He motioned for Joseph to follow him into the mill where he kept his stockpiles. "So what kind of wood are you looking for?"

"I don't rightly care. I just need really thick planks to build a barricade door, something stalwart to fill an archway."

Ronald led Joseph to the far end of the building. His boys swarmed over the stacks of wood like tiny ants, giggling, yelling, and seeming to be everywhere at once.

All of Christian's planed boards were no more than two inches thick. Joseph wanted stuff much stouter than that. He came upon a stack of roughly planed pine that hadn't yet been vertically cut.

"Those are perfect," Joseph said. "Can you plane them more smoothly at that thickness?"

Ronald stroked his jaw. "I can give it a try, but they won't be as smooth as regular planks."

"I can sand them down."

Ronald grinned. "You don't want boards, my man. You want quarter sections of trees."

Joseph nodded good-naturedly. "Can you fix me up with four of them?"

Diana, Ronald's wife, appeared just then. She was a

pretty little woman with brown hair, gentle green eyes, and a slender build. Her gray dress was ready-made from Montgomery Ward and on the cheap side, but she looked Sunday perfect anyhow. She extended a slender hand.

"Mr. Paxton, it is so good to see you. It's not often we get buyers on Sunday."

"I stopped by in the hope that Ron would be out here working."

Diana smiled. "Normally I scold if he works on Sunday, but Garrett Buckmaster is building a new barn, and Ron's got to fill his order no later than Tuesday." Her expression grew solemn. "We were very sorry to hear about Darby, Mr. Paxton. It must be difficult for Miss Rachel. Darby is the closest thing to family that she has left."

Ronald glanced past Diana at his frolicking boys. "Richie, get down off there before you fall and break your neck!"

Diana rushed away to corral her children, leaving Joseph and Ronald to negotiate prices.

On the way out of town, Joseph heard Bubba striking his anvil. It seemed that most all of No Name's business owners worked on Sunday. After turning the team into the yard in front of the shop, Joseph set the brake, swung down from the wagon, and wandered into the building.

"Bubba?"

The huge, muscular blacksmith appeared from around a corner. His grizzled red hair lay wet on his forehead, and his bare, muscular shoulders glistened with sweat. The heat that radiated throughout the building almost took Joseph's breath away.

"Joseph. Hey."

"No rest for the wicked, I see."

Bubba chuckled. "No rest for the blacksmith on Sunday, anyhow. People stop by to place orders before going on to church, and I have my hands full, trying to fill them before they leave town in the afternoon."

Joseph nodded. "I won't keep you, then. I was just wondering if you've started on one of the doors yet, and if you think the idea will work."

"There wasn't much to it," he said, gesturing over his shoulder. "Just straightening and fusing the bars together. They don't look like much. In my opinion, they could use some paint."

"You mean they're done?" Joseph followed the blacksmith into the firing area. The barred doors lay on the ground near the forge. Bubba was right about the call for paint. The rusty iron didn't show well. "These are *great*, Bubba. You must have been up working half the night."

"I did work for a spell after supper." He grinned and winked. "My Sue Ellen is tickled about me getting them done so fast. When she's happy, I'm happy, if you get my meaning."

Joseph chuckled. "Well, you tell Mrs. White that I appreciate her kindheartedness. Rachel will feel much safer with those bars over her doors."

"Me and the wife just hope she can start enjoying a little sunshine." Bubba leaned over to grab a bar in one massive fist. "I'll help you get 'em loaded up."

On the way out to the wagon, Bubba called over his

shoulder, "Now that Sue Ellen knows about Miss Rachel missing the sunshine, she's got a maggot in her brain about building the lady a courtyard."

"A what?"

"A courtyard," Bubba repeated. "A walled-in yard with a barred gate and ceiling. You reckon Miss Rachel would enjoy something like that?"

It was a brilliant idea, in Joseph's estimation. A courtyard. A bubble of excitement lodged at the base of his throat. "I can't rightly say if she would or not, Bubba. She's skittish as all get-out about open places."

"Wouldn't be open, not really. Sue Ellen's talking about tall rock walls, with the ceiling bars set into the mortar and anchored by a final layer of stone. With a heavy iron gate that locks from the inside, it would be an outdoor fortress with walls on all sides."

"I don't know," Joseph said cautiously. "Let me see how she does with the bars over the doors first. No point in our going off half cocked, building something she won't use."

Bubba looked disappointed.

"It's a really grand idea, though," Joseph hurried to add. "Ever since I saw how she lives, I've been racking my brain, trying to think of some way she might enjoy the outdoors. I never would have thought of a courtyard. If Rachel feels safe with the bars and can open the regular door to let in fresh air, there's a good chance that she'll feel safe inside a courtyard, too."

Bubba wiped sweat from his brow. "I'm thinking fifteen feet wide, maybe twenty feet long." He swung a beefy hand toward the pile of rusting metal in the yard. "God knows I've got plenty of scrap iron. Just a little area where Miss Rachel can sit outside for bits of time and maybe even grow a flower garden to attract the butterflies and birds."

Joseph could already picture it. A lovely garden area with a bench and flowers all around, perhaps even a small tree. He wanted to hug Sue Ellen for coming up with the idea. If Rachel could gather the courage, she would be able to sit outside. Sunlight would filter down through the grillwork. She'd be able to feel the summer breeze in her hair. Even better, she'd be able to hear the birdsong again. Joseph knew, deep in his bones, that Rachel would absolutely love that.

"Bubba, your wife is a genius."

The blacksmith's freckles were eclipsed by a blush that suffused his entire face. "Well, now, don't tell her that. She's pesky enough as it is." He rubbed a hand over his sooty leather apron. "Truth to tell, though, I'm convinced it's a pretty good idea myself. This morning, Sue Ellen talked it up at church, and a number of folks have volunteered to bring wagonloads of rock. Everybody seems to have a rock pile from when their land was cleared. All we lack is the mortar, and Jake Lenkins, from out at the quarry, said he'll donate the mixings for that."

Joseph's throat had gone tight. He couldn't push any words out.

"I hope you aren't thinkin' it's none of our beeswax," Bubba said. "I tried to talk Sue Ellen out of it, but once she got the idea in her head, there wasn't any stopping her."

Joseph took off his hat, slapped it against his leg, and then plopped it back on his head. He didn't know if Rachel would ever find the courage to step from her kitchen into a courtyard. But did that really matter? What counted the most to Joseph was that Bubba and his wife had cared enough to come up with the idea. Maybe some people always scrutinized the pieces of pie. But there were others who were just wonderful folks who didn't give a care about gossip and only wanted to make nice things happen for others.

Rachel Hollister had lived in an isolated purgatory for five long years, and now the people of No Name meant to liberate her.

Chapter Eleven

As Joseph left the blacksmith shop and headed for home, his mood had greatly improved. A courtyard for Rachel. He could scarcely believe that Sue Ellen White had already found people who'd volunteered to bring rock. Once it was delivered, all that would remain was for Joseph to start erecting the walls. He felt confident that his brothers would pitch in to help. An almost impossible dream—summer breezes for Rachel—might soon be a reality.

A dozen different plans took shape in Joseph's mind—how to design her flower garden, what plants to order, and the kind of bench to build. And birdhouses, maybe. They'd look cute, hanging from the ironwork over the courtyard, and a few birds might even nest in them. Wouldn't Rachel be delighted if she could watch the eggs hatch and the babies grow?

When Joseph reached his place, he was surprised to see a strange buggy parked in front of his house. Not Doc's, he decided. This one was newer and looked to be something a lady might drive. Joseph parked the buckboard just outside the barn because he wanted to gather some tools before he left for the Bar H. He circled the barn to check in on Johnny and Bart, caught Johnny sitting on his laurels in the shade with his hat pulled over his eyes, and coughed to wake the young man from his nap.

"Mr. Paxton!" the hired hand sputtered as he lurched to his feet.

"Is this what I'm paying you a fair wage to do, Johnny, napping before the day is over?"

"No, sir." Johnny clapped his hat back on his head. "I was just taking a break, is all. I don't know how I managed to drift off like that. Maybe just working too hard."

Joseph doubted that. "Don't let it happen again, or I'll dock your wages," he said sternly. He thumbed his hand toward a heifer out in the field. "You need to be riding the fence lines, looking for cows that are about to calve. Where's Bart?"

"Off doing that, I reckon."

"Well, get out there and help him," Joseph shot back. "I expect a fair amount of work for a fair amount of pay."

The younger man dusted off his pants and went to collect his horse. Joseph gazed after him, glad that he'd stopped by and caught the hired hand lollygagging. It would be a few days before Johnny forgot the reprimand and napped on the job again.

Joseph watched until the hired hand rode from the barnyard. Then he decided to mosey over to the house and find out who'd come calling.

When he entered through the front door, he heard

voices coming along the hallway that led to the back of the house. He'd built three bedrooms, just in case his two younger brothers ever decided to leave Ace's place. Joseph loved David and Esa, he truly did, and he wouldn't mind if they came to live with him, but he'd gotten enough of bunking with them as a boy.

He crossed the sitting room, which was open to the kitchen, and followed the voices to Darby's sickroom, the first door on the right. To his surprise, Amanda Hollister sat on a straight-backed chair beside the bed. With trembling hands, she was sponging Darby's flushed face. From the opposite side of the bed, Esa looked on, his expression concerned.

"How's he doing?" Joseph asked softly.

Amanda glanced up. Joseph was struck once again by her resemblance to Rachel. "Joseph," she said with a smile. "It's good to see you."

Given the fact that they hadn't parted on the best of terms yesterday, Joseph was surprised by the warm greeting. "It's nice to see you, too," he replied and meant it. There was something about this old lady that he instinctively liked. "What brings you over this way?"

Bright spots of color flagged her cheeks. "I'm tempted to say I came only to check on Darby, but the truth is, I also came to apologize. I was unforgivably rude yesterday. I shouldn't have gotten so defensive."

Joseph searched her blue eyes, which were amazingly clear, considering her age. "David and I understood." He glanced at Darby again. The old foreman looked to be asleep. "Is he still feverish?"

"He is, I'm afraid." Amanda dipped the sponge into

a bowl of water on the nightstand. "Burning up, in fact."

"Doc just left a bit ago," Esa said. "He doped him up with laudanum so he can rest. The wound is inflamed and paining him something fierce."

"I hate to hear that." Joseph rested loosely folded arms on the wrought-iron foot of the bed frame. "What's Doc saying?"

"Mostly the same thing, that inflammation and fever are to be expected."

Joseph nodded. "Does he still think Darby's chances are good?"

Esa shrugged. "He didn't say. I take that to mean he's worried. Darby's no spring chicken, and this fever is taking a toll."

Amanda left off bathing the foreman's face. "No spring chicken, you say? Darby McClintoch has more steel in his spine than six younger men." Her eyes fairly snapped when she looked at Esa. "He'll make it through this, mark my words, and he'll go on to work circles around both of you for another twenty years."

Joseph hoped she was right. He wasn't sure how Rachel would handle it if Darby died, and he sure as hell didn't want to be the one to deliver the news to her.

Amanda tossed the sponge back into the bowl and struggled to her feet. She wore a tailored brown jacket and a matching ankle-length riding skirt. She reached out a frail hand to Joseph. "Lend me your arm, young man. I want to take a turn in the yard with you."

Joseph hurried around the end of the bed. Instead of merely lending her an arm, he encircled her back to better support her. She was none too steady on her feet.

After they exited the house, she slowed her pace and then came to a standstill near her buggy. "I barely slept a wink last night for thinking about your visit."

"Don't worry about it. It won't be the last time that David will be invited to leave someone's house, and me along with him. A badge has a way of wearing out a man's welcome in short order."

Amanda shook her head. "I felt bad about asking you to leave, but, in and of itself, that wasn't what kept me awake. Your brother came to me for help, and instead of trying to provide some, I took offense and ordered him out." She gazed for a long moment at the house. "I love him, you know. Darby, I mean."

"So does your great-niece. By all accounts, he's a fine man."

"That's not the way I mean," Amanda corrected. "I mean I *love* him. I have for years."

"Oh."

She smiled tremulously. "I see the questions in your eyes. How and when did we meet, and if I love him, why am I seventy and still not with him?" She drew away to lean against the buggy wheel. Her eyes went shadowy with pain. "Darby went to work for my father back in Kentucky when I was still just a girl. When my father pulled up stakes to come out west, Darby came with us."

"So you've known him almost all your life?"

"Oh, yes. When my father died, Darby stayed on to work for my brother. Over the years, he became like a member of the family, more than just a hired hand."

Joseph nodded to convey his understanding.

She shrugged. "As a girl back in Kentucky, I suppose you might say I was just a mite headstrong."

Joseph could well imagine that. Not many women her age threatened to take a whip to a man for mistreating a horse. "Never met a Kentuckian yet who wasn't just a little headstrong, and we all take the bit in our teeth when we're young, I reckon."

"I was more headstrong than most, and when I was sixteen, I made a terrible mistake." She drew a quivering breath. "A fast-talking, handsome young wrangler came to work on my father's spread, and I fancied myself in love with him. When I got in the family way, the wrangler showed his true colors and lit out for parts unknown. My father was a stern, prideful man. Rather than endure the shame of it, he sent me away to have my child in secrecy. My baby was given up for adoption, and no one at home ever knew about it, not even Darby.

"When I returned home, Darby seemed to sense that I needed a friend. It was a difficult time for me. My father was an unforgiving man. But Darby was always a support to me. He never said much," she added with a smile, "but that's just Darby. With a little maturity under my belt, I began to appreciate the man behind the quietness. He wasn't a slick-talking charmer, to say the least, but he was steady, and he was true, and I came to love him."

"How did your father react to that?" Joseph asked.

"He never knew. He would have objected, I'm sure. Darby's only assets were his horse and saddle, and my father would have wanted me to marry a landowner.

No matter. The relationship was doomed from the start. When Darby eventually asked me to marry him, my answer had to be no."

Joseph frowned. "But why? If you loved him, why didn't you marry him?"

"I said no *because* I loved him," she said softly. Then she waved her hand. "It made sense to me at the time, Joseph. I was ruined—*tarnished* was the word for it back then. I believed with all my heart that Darby deserved better, someone pure and untouched."

"That's plum crazy."

She laughed and wiped her cheeks with palsied hands. "Yes, well, looking back on it, I realize that a woman can bring far more important things to a marriage than her virginity, and I deeply regret that I was such a misguided little fool. But there you have it. I did what I thought was right at the time—a great sacrifice for love. I was all of—what—eighteen? Girls can be very dramatic at that age, and I had no mother to set me straight. If I'd had a mother, maybe I wouldn't have gotten into such a pickle in the first place. But I didn't, and my father hated me for bringing shame upon my family and his good name."

"That seems mighty harsh."

"He *was* a harsh man. My mother's death nearly destroyed him. He was never the same afterward. But that's neither here nor there. When I first came home after my time away, he called me into the barn and gave me an ultimatum. In order to remain in his household, I had to give him my solemn oath that I would never speak of my shame to anyone. As a result, I wasn't free to tell Darby *why* I wouldn't marry him. I

just said no and left him to draw his own conclusions."
Her eyes went sparkly with tears again. "He drew all
the wrong ones, of course, namely that I didn't return
his feelings. It was the end of our friendship, along
with everything else that had grown between us. He
continued to work for my father and later followed us
out here to Colorado, but he always steered clear of
me. It hurt him to be near me, I suppose."

"Why are you telling me this?" Joseph asked.

She looked him dead in the eye. "So you will know,
absolutely and without a doubt, that I didn't shoot
Darby McClintoch. Your brother, David, needs to go
after the real killer, not waste time trying to pin it on
me."

That seemed a reasonable explanation to Joseph.
"You got any idea who might have done it?"

She sighed. "I can think of no one. Darby's as loyal
and true now as he was fifty-two years ago. I honestly
don't believe he's ever had an enemy."

"What about Henry, Rachel's father? Did he have
enemies?"

"He had two that I'm aware of, myself and Jeb
Pritchard."

Joseph admired her honesty. She was under suspicion for shooting Darby, and she knew it, but even so,
she cut herself no slack. "I know why Jeb hated Henry.
But I'm not real clear on why you did."

Amanda smiled. "I didn't *hate* Henry, Joseph. I was
furious with him. There's a big difference."

"Okay, why were you furious with him, then?"

She closed her eyes briefly. "In truth, it wasn't so
much anger at Henry that made me leave the ranch as

it was anger at my father and brother. I worked like a man, back in Kentucky and out here, forever trying to regain my father's high regard. But until the day he died, I remained the *bad seed* in his mind, the one who'd fallen from grace. You can't know what it's like to live with that, day in and day out. Coming in from work at the end of the day and having your father and brother not speak to you over supper. Having your every idea shot down, not because it was flawed, but because it was *yours*. Henry was raised to look down on me. I was the wayward aunt, the one who wasn't quite up to snuff, the one who'd brought shame upon his family."

"So Henry knew about the child?"

"I'm not sure. He never actually said. It was his attitude toward me that rankled and hurt. I thought of his wife as a daughter and loved his babies as if they were mine. But he would never unbend toward me. It had been drilled into him all his life, I guess. I was the outcast. My father died and left me nothing. Then my brother died and left me nothing. I was getting up in years and facing possible poor health." She glanced at her hands. "The shaking had started by then. I asked Henry to grant me a monthly stipend from his inheritance—none of the land or buildings, just a small stipend so I might feel less a beggar when I could no longer work to earn my keep."

"And he refused."

She nodded. "Flatly refused. It wasn't about the money. He was a generous man. But he felt obligated to honor his grandfather and father's wishes. They had cut me off without a cent, and it wasn't up to him to change that."

In that moment, Joseph honestly couldn't blame Amanda for leaving and starting up her own small spread. He would have done the same.

"Henry wasn't a bad man," she went on. "He just clung to the opinions that had been drilled into his head from infancy. He was fair to a fault with everyone else. Jeb Pritchard, for instance. Henry bent over backward for that scapegrace. He just couldn't see his way clear to be equally so to me."

"I'm sorry," Joseph said. In his opinion, everyone was entitled to make one bad mistake. She had been paying for hers all of her life. "It was unfair of your father to hold it against you for so long."

She shrugged and smiled. "When is life ever fair? It was good that it all came to a head after Peter died. I needed to leave the family ranch and put the past behind me. I should have done it years before. I had a very small trust from my grandmother. I put it to work by buying a patch of land. My little spread isn't much, but it brings in enough of an income to sustain me until I die, and it's mine. I bend my head to no one now."

Joseph couldn't imagine her ever bending her head to anyone, but he kept that to himself. "So, in your opinion, Jeb Pritchard was behind the attack on your nephew and his family."

"I can't prove it, but, yes, I've always believed it was Jeb."

Joseph drew out his pack of Crosscuts. When he

tapped one out, Amanda held out her hand. "Don't be selfish. I'll take one, too."

Joseph had never known a woman who smoked.

"Put your eyes back in your head. If a man asked you for a cigarette, would you stare at him like that?"

Joseph tapped her out a Crosscut. After she'd lighted up and exhaled, she said, "I worked shoulder to shoulder with men all my life, sweating with them, getting hurt with them, cursing with them. I guess I'm entitled to have a damned cigarette, if I want."

She was, at that. Joseph chuckled. "You're right. My apologies. I'm just not used to ladies smoking."

"I'm not *just* a lady, Joseph Paxton," she retorted. "I'm one *hell* of a lady, and don't you ever forget it."

"I won't," Joseph assured her. And he sincerely doubted that he ever would. Amanda Hollister was a rare gem. "There's one more thing I'd like to ask you, though. A little off the subject, I suppose, but it troubles me, all the same."

"What's that?"

"Why have you never gone to see your great-niece? You're the only family she has left."

Her eyes darkened with pain again. "I went. Right after she came around from the coma, when she was still at Doc's. I loved that girl like my own. Of course I went."

"What happened?" he asked.

Amanda took a shaky drag from the cigarette. "She took one look at me and started screaming."

*   *   *

When Joseph reached the Hollister place later, the first words from Rachel's mouth were, "How is Darby?"

The anxiety that he saw in her big blue eyes prompted him to lie through his teeth. "He's doing grand. Still weak, of course, but definitely on the mend. He's a tough old fellow."

Rachel beamed a smile, her shoulders slumping with relief. "Oh, I'm so glad. Did you give him my love?"

"I did. Won't be long before he's back over here so you can tell him yourself, though."

The way Joseph saw it, there was no point in worrying Rachel about Darby's condition when there was absolutely nothing she could do for him. The old foreman's chances were still good, after all. If he went into a sudden decline and it appeared that death was imminent, Joseph would have to level with her, but the situation hadn't come to that yet.

She was as pleased as punch when she learned that Joseph had gotten two cents more per dozen for her eggs, three cents more per pound for her cheese, and a penny more per pound for her butter.

"Lands, how did you do it? That woman squeezes a nickel until it squeaks."

Joseph felt a couple of inches taller than he had upon entering the house. "I threatened to set up shop on the boardwalk, undercutting her prices by a penny. She knew damned well that I'd get customers, cutting her out of any profit, so she quickly saw reason."

"Well, then." Rachel wrinkled her nose and looked

at the coins in her hand again. "My *goodness*, such a lot! I can afford to do some shopping."

"Shopping, huh?" Sitting at the table, Joseph dangled a hand to scratch Buddy's head. "And what is it you're dying to buy?"

Joseph expected her list to include feminine items. Caitlin spent hours poring over the Montgomery Ward catalog, dreaming about this and yearning for that. Afterward, Ace sneaked behind her back to order every damned thing she'd wished for.

Rachel surprised Joseph by asking, "How much is Simone asking for flour? Did you happen to notice?"

"Two and a half cents per pound."

"That's highway robbery!" Rachel rolled her eyes. "Whatever is that woman thinking? We're not in a mining town where staples bring premium prices. How about dried peaches?"

Joseph struggled to remember. "Twelve cents a pound, I think."

"Twelve?" She came to sit at the table with a pad and pencil. "Well, that settles that. I can't afford such nonsense. Salt?"

"Last week when I bought some, it was going for three cents a pound."

"You're *serious*? What do the Gilpatricks *do* with all that money?"

"Well, now, I can't say for sure, mind you, but today Simone was wearing a shiny, light purple dress that made her look like a schooner under full sail."

Rachel gave an unladylike snort of laughter and tucked a fingertip under her nose. "Pardon me." Then she snorted again. "A schooner? Oh, my."

"Imagine the cost of all that fabric. It takes more than a swatch to cover hips that broad. She can barely wedge them through a doorway. I thought for a moment she might get stuck. I was looking sharp for some lard so I could grease her up and pop her out."

She snorted again. "Enough!" Then she fell back in her chair, dropped her pencil, and laughed until tears squeezed from her eyes.

"Does she still poke her nose in the air?"

Joseph nodded. "And flares her nostrils. She also puckers her lips all up, like as if someone just stuck dog doo-doo in her mouth."

Rachel burst out laughing again, pressing a slender hand to her midriff and sliding into a slump on the chair. In that moment, Joseph knew beyond a doubt that he'd never clapped eyes on a more beautiful woman in his life.

The realization scared him half to death.

His ma had always told him that the very best things in life happened along when you least expected them. Okay, fine. But what if a fellow wasn't ready? He *liked* Rachel, and there was no question that he felt helplessly attracted to her. But a lasting and enduring affection for someone surely didn't come upon a man this quickly.

"What?" she asked, wiping tears of mirth from her cheeks. "You look so serious suddenly."

Thinking quickly, Joseph replied, "I was just thinking how crazy life can be sometimes." That much was true. "Here you are, pinching all your pennies to spend them at Gilpatrick's so Simone can squander them on dresses that make her look broad as a barn door. There's just no justice."

"I shouldn't have laughed," she said, still struggling to straighten her face. "Someday I'll be old and fat, and I'll look like a schooner under full sail if I wear polished poplin. Especially *lavender*." She shook her head. "A dark color better becomes a hefty person."

"Lavender. Is that what that light purple color is?" Joseph couldn't imagine Rachel ever growing fat, but if she did, he felt confident that she would still be a fine figure of a woman. "You females have a fancy name for everything. What's wrong with light purple?"

"Purple is a deep color. Lavender is much lighter in shade."

In his opinion, purple was purple.

She began making out her shopping a list. "There's no hurry on any of this, mind you. The next time you go into town will be soon enough. I'm just getting low on a number of things." She glanced up. "When I'm finished, I'll draw up a bank draft to cover the cost. Would you mind depositing today's profit in my bank account?"

"Not at all."

She finished her list in short order and pushed it across the table, along with the coins that he'd brought to her. "That should keep me in staples for a spell."

He ran his gaze over the items. Her handwriting was fluid and graceful, as pretty as the lady herself, and she had perfect spelling. His eyes jerked to a stop on one item, "w'eat flour."

"What's this?" he asked.

"Wheat flour."

"You left out the H."

Her face drained of color, and she suddenly pushed up from the table. "I'll fill out that draft before I forget."

She returned to the table, opened a large red ledger, and bent to write. Moments later, when she handed him the draft, she said, "I think that will cover everything. You can redeposit anything left over next week."

She'd written the draft for two dollars, which was plenty enough to cover everything she needed, with some extra. What troubled him was her signature, *Rac'el 'Ollister*. She'd left out both Hs. He angled her a searching look.

"How is your name spelled, Rachel?"

She pushed up from the chair and turned away, presenting him with her back. "My goodness, I didn't realize the time. I need to start supper."

Joseph followed her with a bewildered gaze. The set of her shoulders told him that she was upset about something, but he didn't know what. He went back to studying her list, and there, right at the top, she'd written and underlined *T'ings needed from town*. Again, no H.

Why did she avoid writing that letter? He didn't for a moment believe that she had misspelled her own name or the other words. Her spelling was perfect, otherwise. And she'd also replaced the missing Hs with apostrophes. In each instance, she knew very well that she had made an omission.

For reasons beyond him, she simply hadn't written it in.

Shortly after supper, Joseph heard the faint sound of David's voice drifting to them from the front of the house. Rachel jumped as if she'd been stuck with a pin.

"Did you hear that?"

"I did." Joseph pushed up from the table. "It's my brother David. But where the hell is he?" He stepped close to the archway door. "Ah, he's around the side of the house at the window, I'll bet." He sighed at the interruption to their reading. Tom Sawyer, Joe Harper, and Huck had just developed a distaste for "normal" society and run away to Jackson Island, smack dab in the middle of the Mississippi River. "I'd better go see what he wants."

Joseph went to collect his jacket from where it lay on his pallet in the water closet. When he reentered the kitchen, he gave Rachel a questioning look. "Do you care if I invite him in?"

Rachel jerked her gaze to the door. "In *here*, you mean?"

Joseph didn't know what he'd been thinking. Of course she wouldn't welcome a male guest. It was just—well, she seemed so *normal* here inside the kitchen. It was hard for him to remember that she was terrified of almost everything beyond these walls.

"Never mind." He drew on his coat. "I'll only be a few minutes."

She wrung her hands at her waist. "You can have

him in. He is your brother, after all, and the marshal, to boot. I'm fine with it. He's surely safe."

Safe. Joseph stopped and turned from the archway. He didn't want to push too much at her too quickly. "That's all right. I can have a cigarette while I'm out there."

"No, please. I'll enjoy having him come in for a bit. Just bring him in through the window, if you don't mind. I feel better about lifting the bar on this door because it opens into the rest of the house."

Where there were walls. Here he was, dreaming about building her a courtyard, and just the thought of opening an outside door unnerved her. "Actually, David probably wants to talk about marshaling stuff. You'd find it boring."

"No, really, Joseph. I want you to bring him in. Please."

Joseph could see her pulse pounding at the base of her throat and knew the situation frightened her. But maybe this was something she needed to do.

"Are you sure?"

She nodded. "Yes. Bring him in. I'll put on some coffee."

Joseph grabbed a lantern and slipped out into the dining room. He heard the bar drop behind him. That alone bore testimony to her illness. He'd be right back, but she still needed her barricade secured for the few moments that he would be gone.

David had tethered his horse to a porch post and was smoking a cigarette when Joseph rounded the corner of the house.

"Howdy," he said.

Joseph peered at him through the darkness. "What brings you out so late?"

"It's time for me to visit my suspects again. I was wondering if you might like to ride along with me tomorrow. I'm hoping to visit several of the surrounding ranches to question the owners and their hired hands, plus Pritchard and Amanda Hollister. Ace says that he's wallowed out a spot on the porch step and doesn't mind coming over to sit for a spell."

Joseph chuckled. "If he doesn't mind, I reckon I can be away for a while. I'm willing to let you make a tour of the ranches alone to talk to the landowners and hired hands, but I think it best that you don't go over to Pritchard's place by yourself." He fell into a lengthy recounting of his conversation with Amanda Hollister. "In her opinion, Jeb killed Henry and the others and may have shot Darby."

"You think she's telling the truth?" David asked.

Joseph shivered inside his unbuttoned jacket. "That old woman loves Darby McClintoch. I'd go to the bank on that, and I think she told me true about her falling out with Henry as well."

David chewed on that for a second. "Well, then, I reckon Jeb bears watching. If he shot Darby, he'll come after Miss Rachel sooner or later. It's a good thing you're camping out over here."

"Actually, it's a little better than camping out now. You had supper?"

"Not yet. I keep late hours on Sunday, waiting for all the wranglers to leave town. Caitlin always saves something on the warmer for me."

Joseph clapped his brother on the shoulder. "We

just cleared the table. Rachel boiled up some thick slabs of salt pork, floured them, and fried them to a turn. And there's mashed potatoes, home-canned corn, and apple crisp for dessert, plus fresh coffee."

"You shittin' me?"

Joseph flashed a grin. "I've got it really rough."

"And here I've been feeling sorry for you, having to stay over here with a crazy woman. If she cooks, you can't complain."

Joseph had lost the will to complain about much of anything. "Come on in. It's still a cumbersome entry, through the window like a thief."

Once inside Henry and Marie Hollister's bedroom, David apparently had second thoughts. As Joseph lifted the lantern to light their way back through the house, David said, "This is creepy. It looks like the people just left and will be back at any moment."

"I know. Time has stood still in most parts of this house. But the kitchen at the back is as normal as can be."

"You sure that woman wants me in there?"

That woman? Joseph pictured Rachel's sweet face and knew his brother was in for a big surprise. He led the way up the hall. "If she didn't want you in there, she wouldn't have invited you."

When Joseph tapped on the door, Rachel almost jumped out of her skin. Buddy scampered about and gave a happy bark. It was definitely Joseph, she decided. But even though the dog had identified the person on the other side of the partition, Rachel couldn't go on faith.

"Joseph, is that you?"

"Yes, sweetheart, it's me. Who else would it be?"

Rachel started to lift the bar, but then she froze. His brother, a complete stranger, was with him. She'd felt a lot braver a few minutes ago when she'd insisted on his being invited in. Joseph had been with her then. Everything had come to feel a little less scary with Joseph beside her.

She heard an unfamiliar voice say, "You sure she's okay with this?" And then she heard Joseph reply, "Of course she's okay with it. Would I have asked you in otherwise?"

Rachel lifted the bar, but she couldn't bring herself to actually open the door. She retreated a few steps, hugged her waist, and called, "It's open, Joseph. You can come in."

The door cracked open, and Joseph's blond hair appeared. His blazing blue eyes came next, questioning her before he pushed the portal all the way open. In the next instant, she had a guest walking into her kitchen. He was about Joseph's height, bundled up in a sheepskin jacket with the collar turned up. His Stetson covered him from the crown of his head down to just above his ears. Unlike Joseph, he had closely cropped hair. She couldn't tell the color. But then he nudged up the brim of his hat, and she saw his eyes. *Joseph blue.* And his face was similar, too. Not nearly as handsome as Joseph's, in her opinion, but he had the same high-bridged nose, prominent cheekbones, and strong jaw.

"Howdy," he said and then swept off the Stetson.

Rachel gazed up at him, wondering why on earth she'd felt so afraid. He was cute as a button. His face was still boyishly soft where Joseph's had hardened and become chiseled.

"Hello. You must be David."

David sent Joseph a wondering look. Then he flashed Rachel a broad grin. "Yes, ma'am, that'd be me."

Joseph dropped the bar, clapped his brother on the shoulder, and said, "Take off that jacket. Rachel, I promised him some supper. We have plenty left over, don't we?"

"Of course." She took David's coat. The chill of night clung to it. She ran her hands over the leather. It even smelled of the outdoors. "Please, David, have a seat at the table. The food is still warm, and you're more than welcome."

The two men sat while Rachel bustled around the kitchen, serving David up a plate. Joy surged into her throat, a wonderful warm feeling that soon suffused her entire body. She was serving a guest. And she wasn't having any problem with her breathing at all. He was a stranger, yes, but he wasn't, not really. He was Joseph's brother, Caitlin's brother-in-law. Rachel felt almost as if she knew him.

As David tucked into his meal, Rachel joined them at the table. Joseph had run out of things to talk about and fallen silent. When she sat across from him, he pushed *The Adventures of Tom Sawyer* toward her. "Read to us, darlin'. David's never heard this story, either."

"But we've already read the first part," she protested.

"But now we're at a *good* part," Joseph retorted. "Trust me, he'll like it."

Rachel smoothed the pages and started to read. In the relative silence, she heard David's jaw popping just as Joseph's did when he chewed, and a lovely calm settled over her.

Tom was sneaking off Jackson Island in the dark of night to return home and leave a note for Aunt Polly so she wouldn't think he was dead. Only when Tom entered the house, he heard his aunt and Mrs. Harper making plans for his burial. Tom returned to the island, and he and his friends decided to sneak back into town later so they could attend their own funerals before revealing that they were alive.

Rachel started to turn the page and realized that David had stopped eating. She glanced up, saw that he was staring at her, and asked, "Is the food gone bad?"

David jerked erect and went back to eating. Cheek puffed out with meat, he said, "No, ma'am. The food's delicious. I've just never heard of anybody attending his own funeral."

Rachel smiled and went back to reading. Once back in school, Tom and his friends were the envy of every pupil. But Tom still hadn't won back Becky's heart.

"Who's Becky?" David asked.

Joseph briefly synopsized the story up until that point and then motioned for Rachel to keep reading.

Tom Sawyer caught Becky reading the schoolmaster's book, startled her so badly that she jumped in surprise and accidentally broke the book. Later that day, when the schoolmaster accused Becky of the crime, Tom stepped forward and assumed the blame. As a result, he received the punishment in Becky's stead and finally earned her fond regard.

"What a man won't do for love," David said.

"Quiet," Joseph said. "Let her read."

While David enjoyed Rachel's apple crisp for dessert, Muff Potter's trial began. The entire town had already convicted the innocent man. Tom and Huck were racked with guilt, for they'd seen Injun Joe kill the doctor with their own eyes and knew that Muff was innocent. Their guilt only increased when Muff thanked them for being so kind to him.

David drew out his watch to note the time. "This has been such a nice evening," he said. "But if I don't head on home, I'll be dragging in my tracks come morning. It's after nine o'clock."

Rachel closed the book. In the distant past, she'd once had to worry about time schedules. "It's been lovely having you," she told David. "I hope you'll come again."

David reached out to tap the book. "I'll be back. Just don't read any more without me."

"No way am I holding to that," Joseph protested. "Not unless you come back tomorrow night to hear more. I'm not waiting a week or something."

It was agreed that David would return the following evening for supper, only at an earlier hour so he might eat with Rachel and Joseph. Afterward, it was decided, they would take turns reading the story aloud.

Joseph saw his brother out, taking Buddy along with him for a run before bedtime. Rachel hustled about the kitchen while they were gone, doing up the last-minute dishes and putting the food in the icebox. She was just straightening the table when Joseph tapped on the archway door.

Swallowing down what she knew was irrational

trepidation, she scurried across the room. Leaning close, she called, "Joseph is that you?"

"Nope, it's Injun Joe," he called back.

Buddy answered with a *yaw-yaw-yaw*. She giggled and lifted the bar, allowing Joseph to push into the room, his dog squeezing through ahead of him.

"Well, now," he said, "that was fun. I think David's addicted to *Tom Sawyer*." He turned to secure the door. "Now that you're all buttoned up in here I'll collect my bedroll and sleep in the dining room again tonight."

"But no heat gets in there."

"As long as I've got a windbreak, I can sleep outside in the dead of winter. Buddy and I'll be fine." He cut her a meaningful look. "You and I bunking in the same room isn't appropriate."

That made no sense to Rachel at all. "But, Joseph, who will ever know?"

"I'll know," he replied.

"So sleep in the water closet, then. That's a different room, and it'll be warmer in there."

He cocked an eyebrow at her. "You still feeling nervous?"

For the time being, the barred door over the archway provided a sufficient barrier to make her feel safe. "A little, yes." That wasn't really a lie. She always felt just a little nervous. "I'll feel safer if you're in here with me."

"You sure?"

Rachel had never been more certain of anything in her life.

Chapter Twelve

The following afternoon, David was none too pleased when Joseph confessed that he'd failed to divulge part of the conversation that he'd had with Amanda Hollister the prior day.

"Rachel took one look at her and started screaming?" David wheeled his horse around and gave Joseph an accusing look. "Here I just spent ten minutes bedeviling Jeb Pritchard, and now you tell me?"

"I'm sorry. I didn't think it was important when you and I talked last night."

"Not *important*? You know damned well what this implies, Joseph. Rachel saw something that day, possibly something she doesn't even remember, and it made her terrified of her aunt."

"It's hard for me to believe that," Joseph argued. "I know it's the obvious conclusion, David. But remember what you said? The obvious and easy answer is seldom the right one. There's something about that old lady. I just can't help but like her. And I can't wrap my mind around her being a murderer."

"Well, I can. She wants that ranch."

"For what reason? She's an old, palsied woman. She has no legal heirs. I know a lot of people are sentimental about land that's been in their family for a few generations, but so sentimental that they'd kill for it? I'm sorry. It seemed like a plausible theory in the beginning, but now that I've met Amanda, I just can't believe it of her."

"It's a good thing you aren't a lawman. I never knew you were such a softy."

Joseph gave his brother a narrow-eyed glare. "There's no need to get insulting just because we have a difference of opinion."

David laughed and shook his head. "There's nothing wrong with having a tender heart, Joseph."

"I don't *have* a tender heart. I'm a clear-thinking man who just happens to be a better judge of character than you are."

"Like hell."

Joseph leaned forward over his horse's neck. "Damn it, David, that old lady loves Darby McClintoch. I'd bet my boots on it. I saw her face as she was talking. You can't fake that kind of emotion and regret. She felt it with all her heart. Her palsy aside, how could she have shot the man she loves?"

David held up a hand. "All right, all right. So why'd you tell me about Rachel screaming and get me in a dither, then?"

Joseph swore and pulled out his Crosscuts. "Because there's more."

"More?" David huffed with irritation. "Well, spit it

out, then. I need *all* the facts to solve this case, Joseph, not just the ones you decide to share with me."

"Rachel's a perfect speller," Joseph said. "You heard her reading last night. The girl's got an excellent command of the English language."

"How does that relate to her screaming when she saw Amanda?"

"If you'll shut up and listen, maybe I'll tell you." Joseph swallowed hard because he knew the conclusions that his brother would reach once the words were out. "Rachel can't spell her own name."

David nudged up the brim of his Stetson to pin Joseph with a searching look.

"She leaves out all the Hs. She signed a bank draft and spelled Rachel, R-A-C-E-L. And she left off the H in Hollister as well. Even stranger, she knows she's leaving out the letters. She replaces them with an apostrophe, like we do in a contraction."

"Did you ask her why?"

"She refused to talk about it." Joseph swallowed again. "Why would she revile the letter H?"

"Because her last name starts with it, and Amanda *Hollister* killed her family in cold blood?"

Joseph rubbed his eyes. "I knew you'd think that, because it was my first thought as well. But it feels like I'm missing something. It's there, right in front of me, but I can't put my finger on it."

David sighed. "I'm sorry, Joseph. I know you like that old lady. But I'm going to have to question her again."

"I know it." And Joseph truly did. The evidence

was stacking up against Amanda. David would be a piss-poor marshal if he ignored that.

"If it's all the same to you, I think I'll go alone this time," David said.

"Why? Don't you trust me to keep quiet?"

"It's not that," David replied. "I'm just thinking it'll be easier for you this way. Chances are, it's going to get ugly, and for reasons beyond me, you're fond of the old lady."

After parting company with David, Joseph rode into town to visit the blacksmith shop. He found Bubba hard at work on the ironwork for the ceiling of Rachel's courtyard.

"So you decided to go ahead with the idea, did you?" Joseph said.

Bubba grinned. "Folks will be showing up out there with rock soon, so get yourself in a mind to work."

"I haven't even gotten her barred doors installed yet."

"Well, you'd best get started, son. With my Sue Ellen at the helm, things get done in short order. Spring's coming on. Just look at this pretty weather. She says every day that we delay is one day less that Miss Rachel will get to enjoy the sunshine."

"I really appreciate what all you folks are doing," Joseph said.

Bubba went back to pounding a red-hot bar on the anvil next to the forge. "Not doing it for you. We're doing it for her. And we'll see how grateful you are when you're working from dawn to dark, building those walls."

"I'm hoping to get my brothers to help." A memory flashed in Joseph's mind of the first fireplace that he and his brothers had built out at Ace's place. Along had come a rainstorm, and the whole damned thing had toppled over. Hopefully they'd all learned a few things about working with mortar since then. "Those walls will go up in no time."

"I hope so, or Sue Ellen will be out there building them herself. That's how come she's so skinny, don't you know. The woman's a bundle of nervous energy. Never stands still."

For a time, Joseph and Bubba discussed the particulars of the courtyard design. In snow country, a covered back porch was a must, and Joseph didn't want Rachel's to be removed.

"Why can't we build around the porch?" Bubba asked. "The simplest way would be to encompass the backyard, the courtyard consisting of three stone walls, the house itself providing the fourth, with the porch inside the enclosure. If you build the rock wall shorter than the porch overhang, I can make grid work to stretch from wall to wall until we reach the overhang and support posts. From there, we'll span the distance with individual bars so we can place them around the posts."

"So the rock walls will attach to the house at each corner?"

Bubba nodded. "And the ceiling will come in under the overhang and be flush against the house. When she looks up, there'll be bars spanning from wall to wall, just under the porch roof."

"That'll work," Joseph agreed. And so it was decided.

* * *

Darby was sitting up in bed and sipping a cup of broth when Joseph stopped at Eden thirty minutes later. The old foreman's face crinkled in a weak grin when he saw his visitor.

"Joseph," he said. "Last time I recall seein' you, your face was floatin' around in a laudanum haze."

"Well, now, and howdy. No haze today, I can see. You look as bright eyed as a speckled pup." Joseph swept off his hat and grinned at Esa, who had taken up squatting rights on the chair beside the bed. "Your patient is a far sight better today, little brother. You're shaping up to be a damned fine nurse."

"Not to mention a wrangler," Esa countered. "I delivered two calves this morning, too."

"Any problems with Johnny?" Joseph asked.

"Bart says he's been doing better since you threatened to dock his pay the other day," Esa assured him. "Everything's good on all fronts."

"I wish I had two Barts," Joseph said with a sigh. "Sadly, they don't all have a good work ethic. What else has been happening around here?"

"Doc left about two hours ago." Esa grinned. "He thinks there's a good chance Darby might live. I have ten dollars that says otherwise, and Doc's a betting man, so now he's in town trying to get a pool going. If the majority of folks go with Doc's prognosis, I'll make a killing if Darby goes into a sudden decline."

Joseph chuckled. He was pleased beyond words to see Darby sitting up. "Seems to me like a conflict of interest, Esa. You're caring for the patient."

"Like I'd hedge my bet? I'll take good care of the

old fart." He held out a hand to Joseph. "Who are you betting on, Darby or the Grim Reaper?"

Joseph reached into his pocket and flipped his brother a gold eagle. "My money's on Darby. He's so stubborn, he'll live just to spite you."

Darby shakily set the cup of broth aside. "I've got an eagle. Can I bet on myself?"

"Hell, no," Esa protested. "You'd stay alive just to get a cut."

Darby held his stomach because laughing pained him. "God help me, if I survive, it'll be a miracle. This boy may poison my broth." Then he sobered and looked at Joseph. "How's my little girl doin'?"

"Good," Joseph said. "Except for her stealing my dog, she and I are getting along just fine."

"Your dog?" Darby's eyes filled with bewilderment.

Joseph encapsulated the events that had transpired since Darby's injury. "Buddy has fallen in love, I'm afraid. Miss Rachel's prettier than I am, she's sweeter than I am, and she cooks better than I do. I can't compete with all that."

Darby sighed, let his head fall back against the pillows, and closed his eyes. "Take good care of her for me, Joseph. Whoever shot me will go after her next."

"I haven't left her alone once," Joseph assured him. "When I have to leave, my brother Ace stands guard on the porch."

Esa stood just then and excused himself to go start something for supper. When Joseph had taken his brother's seat, he leaned forward to rest a hand on

Darby's forearm. "Are you too worn out to talk about the shooting, partner?"

Darby's lashes fluttered. "I never saw who done it, if that's what you're wantin' to know. Wish I had. I'd strap on my gun and go after the bastard myself."

Joseph nodded. "David can't prove anything yet, but we've been out to Pritchard's place twice now, mostly just to make the old codger nervous, hoping he'll do something stupid and hang himself." Joseph paused, then reluctantly added, "Amanda Hollister is our other prime suspect."

Darby gave Joseph a sharp look.

"Don't get me wrong," Joseph hastened to add. "I've grown right fond of the lady, and I find it hard to believe she has it in her to kill anyone. It's just that all the evidence seems to be stacking up against her."

"What kind of evidence?"

As briefly as possible, Joseph recounted Rachel's terrified reaction to seeing Amanda shortly after the massacre and how Rachel could no longer bring herself to write the letter H.

"Rachel took to leavin' off the Hs right after her folks was killed," Darby revealed. "It struck me peculiar, but I had so much on my plate back then that her spellin' was the least of my concerns."

Joseph could well imagine.

"It was a hard time after Henry died," Darby went on wearily. "All the hands quit, thinkin' they wouldn't get paid, and left me with all the work. And let me tell you, there was a heap of it. On top of that, I had the girl to think of. She wouldn't come out from behind her bed. Just huddled there in the corner, day and night. I had no choice but to leave off wranglin' and set myself to the task of makin' her feel safe. She grew so thin she looked like a skeleton."

"Hell and damnation," Joseph said softly.

"That don't say it by half. I've never in all my life seen anyone that pale and skinny. She just sat in that corner, starin' out all wild-eyed and afraid. When I tried to leave her to do my work around the place, she'd cry and beg me not to go. It fair broke my heart."

Just thinking about it broke Joseph's heart. "I've seen all your handiwork, Darby. You created a whole world for her in that kitchen. It's nothing short of amazing." A lot of men—hell, most men—would have gone looking for another job where they could have been sure to see payday. "You're a good man, Darby McClintoch."

"Pshaw. She's like family to me. You stand fast with family, son, no matter how lean the times. Her and I got through it."

Joseph sighed. "Back to Rachel screaming at the sight of Amanda and leaving out all her Hs. David and I believe the latter may have something to do with Amanda bearing the Hollister name."

"You don't need to explain your reasonin' to me," Darby said. "If Amanda opened fire on the family and Rachel saw it, everything makes sense, don't it?"

Joseph relaxed back on the chair. "So you think we're on to something?"

"Didn't say that. I just see how you're thinkin' and can understand why."

"But you disagree?"

"Absolutely," Darby answered without hesitation.

"I can tell you right now, son, you and your brother are tryin' to tree the wrong coon."

"Rachel screamed when she saw Amanda, Darby. She must have seen something when her family was killed—something that made her terrified of the woman."

"Maybe so. Rachel loved her aunt Amanda like no tomorrow. There has to be a reason why she screamed. I just know it had nothing to do with Amanda being involved in the killings." A distant look filled Darby's green eyes as he stared at the ceiling. "Only Miss Rachel can give you the answers you're seekin'. All I can tell you is what I know to be fact."

"And that is?"

"Amanda might have been furious enough to shoot Henry, but she loved Marie and never would've harmed a hair on those children's heads. Especially Rachel. She loved that girl like her own. Rachel takes after Amanda, you know."

Joseph had noticed that, yes.

"Before Rachel took to hiding behind her walls, she and Amanda were like two peas in a pod, both of them as pretty as can be and too spunky by half. Rachel drove her mama to distraction. Marie wanted to put the girl in fancy dresses all covered with lace, and Rachel always ruined them first thing, more inclined to be in the barnyard than the parlor. I think Amanda pretended in her mind that Rachel was her own daughter. She lost a child early on, back in Kentucky when she was real young. I don't think she ever quite got over it."

"Who told you about that?" Joseph blurted.

Darby gave him a long, inquisitive study. "I was there, son. Question is, who told you?"

"Amanda."

A slight frown creased Darby's brow. "Did she now? In all these years, I've never known her to speak of it."

"She swore a solemn oath to her father that she wouldn't," Joseph revealed. "He demanded her silence in exchange for allowing her to remain with the family."

Darby's eyes drifted closed. "That heartless old bastard. Is that why she never spoke of it?"

This was a fine kettle of soup, Joseph thought, with more secrets stirred into the mix than he could count. Darby knew about Amanda's child? It boggled Joseph's mind to think that two people who loved each other and should have been together might have been happily married all these years if only they'd been honest with each other.

"I hated that old son of a bitch," Darby said.

Joseph jerked back to the moment. "Who, Luther Hollister?"

"Yes. He didn't deserve Amanda as a daughter. Her little brother, Peter, was a sickly child. She was the only mother he ever knew, nursing him through one sickness after another while she kept the house and worked outdoors with the men every chance she got. Luther never gave her credit for one damned thing. She was such a fine girl. Loyal, clear to the marrow of her bones. But that counted for nothing when she got in trouble. He just washed his hands of her, like as if she was dirt. I honestly believe the only reason he allowed her to come back home was for fear of what folks might say. He didn't care about Amanda, not the way he should have, anyways."

"That's too bad."

Joseph studied the old foreman's weathered face. Darby was a good, honest man and firmly believed in Amanda Hollister's innocence. That probably wouldn't sway David, but it went a long way with Joseph.

"She loves you, you know," Joseph said softly.

Darby's lashes fluttered open. "Who does?"

In for a penny, in for a pound. "Amanda. She never stopped loving you."

"Aw, heck. Go away with you. That's pure non-sense. That girl never loved me. I just thought she did."

Joseph met the old foreman's gaze, saw the glimmer of hope in those green depths, and decided the poor man had been getting the small end of the horn long enough. "She wouldn't marry you all those years ago because she felt unworthy. 'Tarnished,' was the word she used. She believed that you deserved someone pure and untouched, so she refused your proposal. She couldn't tell you why because she'd sworn to her father that she'd never speak of it to anyone. But she never stopped loving you, Darby, not once in all these years."

Darby struggled up on his elbow, clenching his teeth at the pain.

Joseph grabbed the foreman's bare shoulders, which were amazingly well muscled for an old fellow's. "What the hell are you doing?"

"I got some—hash to settle," Darby bit out. "Damned fool girl. I knew—about the baby. What'd she think—that I believed she went off to finishin' school like her daddy said? She didn't come back finished. She came back skinny, with that little belly gone. In addition to bein' stupid, does she reckon I'm blind, to boot?"

Esa heard the commotion and appeared in the doorway. "What's going on?"

"I need my britches and boots," Darby said.

"You can't get up," Esa cried. "Doc said so. Two weeks bed rest, no less."

Darby flung his wiry legs over the edge of the mattress. Hugging his waist with one arm, he sent Esa a fiery look. "I don't care squat what Doc said. Get me my trousers, boy."

"Darby," Joseph tried, "you can't be doing this. You'll start that wound to bleeding again. There'll be time enough later to—"

"Don't talk to me about time. I almost died with that fever. What if it comes back? I have to talk to her *now*. So she'll know I love her back. I can't take that to the grave with me, son. I need her to know my feelin's."

As crazy as it would be for Darby to stand, let alone get dressed and try to ride a horse, Joseph could understand the old man's sense of urgency. That was sobering. A week ago, he would have thought him totally insane. But that was before he met Rachel.

Thinking quickly, he said, "If you're bent on talking to her, Darby, I'll bring her here."

The tension eased from Darby's shoulders. "I'm

bent on it. I love that woman to the marrow of my bones."

"Fine, then. I'll go fetch her. You can't get up. You'll bleed to death before you get there."

Darby lifted his head. "You reckon she'll come?"

"I know it," Joseph assured him.

Darby sank weakly back onto the pillows. "Well, damn it, go get her then. I gotta give her a large piece of my mind."

David's horse was tethered to the hitching post in front of Amanda Hollister's house when Joseph rode in. He swung down from the saddle and looped Obie's reins over the horizontal pole, then ascended the steps two at a time to rap his knuckles on the front door. A few moments later, Amanda answered. She sat off to one side of the doorway in her wheelchair.

"Joseph," she said with a sarcastic edge in her voice. "Have you come to attend the inquisition?"

"No, ma'am." Joseph peered into the room and saw David sitting on the sofa. "I'm sorry to interrupt, little brother, but something important came up. Miss Hollister is urgently needed over at my place."

Amanda's face drained of color. "It's Darby, isn't it?"

"Yes, ma'am, but not in the way you think. The fever broke, and he's on the mend."

She placed a shaking hand over her heart. "Thank God. I thought he'd taken a turn for the worse."

"No, ma'am. But he insists on seeing you, straightaway. If you don't go to him, he'll try to come here. The effort's liable to kill him."

Amanda's eyes filled with tears. "You told him."

It wasn't a question. Joseph nodded and said, "Damn straight I told him. Someone needed to."

"You had no right."

"I know it, and I apologize. But I can't honestly say I'm sorry. He needed to know."

"Is he angry?"

Joseph considered the question. "Well, now, let's just say he'd be whipping wildcats right now if he weren't weak as a kitten."

Amanda rolled her chair back so Joseph could enter. "I trusted you."

"Yes, ma'am, I know you did." Joseph considered trying to explain his reasons for breaking her confidence, but the words just wouldn't come. "But there are some things a man has a right to know, and that's one of them. He knew about the baby all those years ago."

"He what?"

"He knew," Joseph repeated. "He never believed the story your father told about sending you off to finishing school. He knew you'd gone away to have a child in secret long before he asked you to be his wife."

A stricken expression came over Amanda's face. "Why did he never say anything?"

Joseph removed his hat and finger-combed his hair, thinking that she hadn't exactly been the epitome of forthrightness herself. But this wasn't the time for accusations. "I can't speak for Darby. You'll have to ask him why he never said anything. Will you go with me?

If you don't and he tries to come here, it'll be on your head."

Riding alongside the buggy, Joseph escorted Amanda Hollister back to his place and sat in the kitchen while she made her precarious way along the hall to Darby's room. The instant Darby saw her in the doorway, he said, "Come in and shut that door, girl. I don't want everybody and his brother hearin' what I've got to say."

Esa glanced up from pouring Joseph a cup of coffee and whispered, "What's this all about?"

"Love," Joseph said with a broad grin.

"Love?" Esa came to sit at the table across from his brother. "They're old people."

"Just goes to show that love isn't only for us young folks, I reckon."

"He called her 'girl.' How crazy is that?"

Joseph thought about it for a moment. It was true that Amanda Hollister had left girlhood behind her well over a half century ago, but maybe in Darby's eyes she was still as young and beautiful as she'd ever been.

Just then they heard Darby's voice booming through the walls. "I never heard such a bunch of poppycock in all my born days! Unworthy? I oughta tan your fanny for even thinkin' it. You're the finest swatch of calico I ever clapped eyes on, and that's a fact."

"Don't refer to me as a swatch of calico! I don't like it, Darby McClintoch."

"The prettiest thing I ever saw in a skirt, then."

"There's a lot more to me than this skirt."

"Like I don't know it? I loved you with all my heart, and damn it to hell, I still do!"

Amanda's softer voice didn't carry through the walls. All they could hear was a low murmur.

"All these years, I thought you didn't love me back!"

Another murmur.

"And that was the only reason? Damn it, Amanda Grace, what were you thinkin'? You havin' the child never mattered a whit to me. I loved you then, I love you now, and all I can think about is the wasted years."

The front door opened just then and David stepped inside. "You got enough coffee to spare another cup?" he asked.

Esa swung to his feet. "Sure. Come take a load off. The entertainment's above average."

Darby's voice rang out again. "Too *old*? The hell you say. I'm not takin' no for an answer this time. As soon as I get back on my feet, I'm marryin' you, and that's my last word on the subject."

Joseph chuckled. "Church bells are gonna be ringing in No Name."

"We don't have any church bells," Esa pointed out.

"Then we'll all ring cowbells," Joseph retorted. "When two people wait this long to get hitched, they need bells to mark the occasion."

David shoved his hat back to glare at his older brother. "Have you plum lost your mind? The woman may be a cold-blooded killer. If I can prove it, she may hang."

Joseph shook his head. "Are you still stuck on that?

You're never going to prove it. Darby says you're trying to tree the wrong coon, that she couldn't possibly have done it. That's good enough for me."

"So why did Rachel scream when she saw Amanda?"

"I don't know," Joseph replied. "I'd venture a guess that Rachel doesn't even know for sure. But I'm willing to wager every cent I've got that it wasn't because Amanda Hollister committed the murders or was somehow involved."

"You can't be sure," David shot back.

"Yes," Joseph replied. "I'm as sure of it as I've ever been of anything."

Chapter Thirteen

Rachel sat at the table with her chin propped on her fist, staring vacantly at nothing. Joseph had been gone for hours, and she felt lonely. Over the last five years, she'd become accustomed to being alone. But this was different. The silence that had become such a mainstay of her life suddenly seemed almost deafening. She missed the sound of Joseph's voice. She yearned to hear his deep, silky laughter. Even Buddy had deserted her in favor of playing outdoors with his brother.

She had tried to read, but for the first time in her recent memory, her books brought little comfort. Crocheting and needlework held no appeal, either. In a very short time, she'd come to like—no, to *need* the company of others to make her world seem complete.

The realization frightened her. Darby was recovering nicely, and he'd soon come home. When he did, Joseph would leave. There would be no more laughter in her kitchen, no more guests for supper, no more reading aloud long into the evening. She would once

again be alone with the silence. The thought made her
feel almost claustrophobic, which might have been hi-
lariously funny if it hadn't been so sad. A claustrophobic agoraphobic?

Tears filled Rachel's eyes, and the next thing she
knew, she was weeping without really knowing why.
She only knew that she felt desolate and absolutely
forlorn. And trapped. She felt so trapped. Her kitchen,
which had been her safe haven for so long, was now
also her prison. She needed her walls in order to
breathe, but Joseph's intrusion into her life had awakened other needs within her, some of them needs she'd
felt before, others completely new, mysterious, and in-
definable, yet just as compelling.

She loved Darby. She truly did. And she looked forward to hearing his knocks on the wood safe again.
But to go back to living her life around those three
knocks a day? Rachel wasn't sure she could do it
again, not after having Joseph and Buddy there.
They'd made her realize how barren her existence
was, and now she wanted more, so very much more.

Rachel knew it was beyond silly to sit there in her
dim kitchen, weeping over the things that were missing in her life, but that didn't make her want them any
less. Even more horrible was her certain knowledge
that they were all things she could never have or experience. She would grow old without ever knowing
what it was like to be loved by a man. She would never
hold her own baby in her arms. She would never know
the joy of watching her children grow up and become
productive adults. And when she grew old, she would
have no one with whom to share her memories. In

truth, she wouldn't even live a life worth remembering. The days and nights would blend together in a lantern-lighted, silent, empty blur.

And so she wept, her sobs bouncing back at her off the walls that she needed so desperately but had also come to hate.

When she heard Joseph talking to Ace out on the porch some time later, she dried her eyes, patted her cheeks, and leaped up from the chair to tidy her clothing and hair. He would come inside soon, and she didn't want to look a fright. Nor did she want him to know that she'd been crying. He would ask why, and she wasn't at all sure she could explain without bursting into tears again.

Joseph's heart caught when he saw Rachel's face. At a glance, he knew that she'd been crying. Strike that. She'd apparently been sobbing her heart out. Her eyelids were inflamed and puffy. Blotches of red stained her otherwise pale cheeks. Her mouth was swollen.

"Sweetheart, what's wrong?" He stepped into the kitchen, closed the archway door, and dropped the bar into place. "Did something happen?"

"No, no, nothing." She flapped a slender hand and flashed an overly bright smile. "I just spilled the pepper, is all."

"The pepper?"

Joseph stared after her as she scurried away to the kitchen area. Over the years, he'd held his sister Eden in his arms more times than he could count, trying to soothe away her tears, and he instinctively knew that spilled pepper hadn't done that to Rachel's face.

"Lands, yes. I'm allergic. If I get a sniff, I'm sneezing and tearing up for hours."

Joseph didn't buy it. As he moved farther into the kitchen, he remembered Darby's description of Rachel right after the tragic loss of her family—a gaunt, terrified girl, hiding in the corner. Over time, she had put some weight back on and become a beautiful young woman, but in all the ways that counted, she was still hiding. Darby had just given her a much larger area to do it in.

"I have some wonderful news for you."

She turned from the range. "Really? What's that?"

He glanced behind her at the stove. No simmering pot demanded her attention. In fact, judging by the ambient temperature of the room, the fire in the box was dead out. Busywork, he decided, a way to avoid talking about whatever it was that had upset her.

"Darby is looking fit as a fiddle," he said. "Sitting up in bed, laughing, and—you won't believe this one—talking almost nonstop."

She smiled again, this time with a gladness and warmth that made her blotched cheeks glow. "That *is* wonderful news. Did you give him my best?"

"I did. But judging by his progress, I doubt it will be long before you can tell him yourself. Doc wants him to stay in bed for two weeks, but I won't be surprised if Darby is up and about long before that."

"That's my Darby," she said with a wet laugh. And then her eyes filled with sparkling tears.

Joseph moved toward her as if being tugged along

by invisible strings. This wasn't the reaction he had expected. He'd hoped the news would please her. "Honey, what's wrong?"

She cupped a hand over her eyes and shook her head. "Nothing. I'm just being foolish."

In his opinion, anything that had her so upset couldn't be foolish. He grasped her wrist to draw her hand from her face. The pain that he saw in her blue eyes made him feel as if someone were driving a sharp blade straight through his heart. "Can't you tell me? Whatever it is, maybe I can come up with a solution."

"There is no solution." Her mouth quivered and twisted. "I just felt lonely today while you and Buddy were gone. It made me realize that you'll both be leaving soon, and then I'll be lonely all the time."

The blade through Joseph's heart twisted viciously.

"You see? I told you it was foolish. I've been alone for years. It's certainly nothing new. I can't think why I'm suddenly dreading it so."

Joseph had no problem figuring it out. He'd barged into her world and turned it topsy-turvy with a talking dog, dinner guests, a visiting toddler, poker games, and reading out loud. Rachel wasn't a solitary person by nature. Her life choices had been forced upon her by illness. Now that she'd gotten a taste of sociality, of course it was hard for her to contemplate a return to absolute solitude.

He caught her small chin and tipped her face up. "Are you by any chance thinking that once Buddy and I leave, we'll never come back?"

"Why would you want to? If I could leave, I'd never come back."

The fact that she wanted to leave and couldn't made his heart hurt even more for her.

"I'll be back for some of your great cooking, for starters. I also greatly enjoy your company. Do you have any idea how far it is from my house to yours?"

"No," she confessed thinly.

"Hardly more than a hop, skip, and jump. It'll be a lot closer for me to come here to play poker than to go clear to town. And what about Tom and Huck? I'll never find out what happens to those fool boys if I don't come over in the evenings to read."

"The books won't last forever. By the time Darby comes back, we'll probably have finished both of them."

The stories wouldn't last forever; that was true. But Joseph was coming to believe that the feelings he was developing for her might. "There are lots of other books for us to read, Rachel. Until you introduced me to novels, I never realized how entertaining they are. I'm totally hooked now, lady. I can't imagine going back to never reading again."

"Truly?"

In all his life, Joseph had never wanted to kiss a woman so badly, not as a prelude to lovemaking, which was usually his goal, but to chase her tears away and make her smile again.

"Oh, hey, you've made a reader out of me for sure, and David, too, I think. And then there's Caitlin, who'll be coming to visit. Now that she's been here once, she'll be pestering you all the time. Mark my words. Also, don't be surprised if she asks you to watch after Little Ace now and again. She and Ace would like to go places without him sometimes—to have dinner in town or to a hoedown. David, Esa, and I watch him when we can, but we're not always available."

Joseph released her chin and stepped away before he gave in to his urge to kiss her. "Which reminds me. Bubba finished the ironwork to go over all your doors. There's plenty of light left. I should get started installing it."

"Oh, but I was hoping—"

"You were hoping what?" Joseph asked.

"Nothing. I was just hoping we might play cards or something."

"Maybe we can do that this evening. For now, I should work on your doors." He arched an eyebrow at her. "You can't very well have guests coming and going all the time without the proper setup. Now can you?"

Guests coming and going all the time. The words remained with Rachel long after Joseph left the kitchen. She'd been wallowing in dark despair before he returned a while ago, and now, with only a few words from him, she felt buoyant. Visits from Caitlin? Looking after Little Ace? Oh, how she hoped. But what truly lifted her spirits was knowing that Joseph would come to see her often.

In a very short while, she'd become unaccountably fond of him. He was like a ray of sunshine in her dismal little world that chased away all the shadows.

In order to install the ironwork, he had to go in and out a lot. His frequent use of the archway door kept

Rachel running back and forth to lift the bar and drop it again after he left. She'd hoped to make a custard pie for dessert that night, but with so many interruptions, accomplishing that was nearly impossible.

"I'm sorry," he said as she let him into the kitchen again. "I don't mean to be a pest. Working on both sides of the wall like this is a bugger."

He'd chosen to install ironwork over the porch door first, and Rachel knew that he had to climb in and out the window each time he came or went. "You, a pest? I'm the bothersome one. The job would be much simpler if you could just open the porch door and step outside."

He chucked her under the chin as he walked by. "If just opening the door was an option, you wouldn't be needing the bars."

He crouched down next to the exterior door and set to work, drilling through the wall with a handheld auger fitted with a one-inch bit. With each turn of the crank, the muscles across his shoulders and along each side of his spine bunched and flexed under his blue chambray shirt.

As Rachel went back to the table to roll out her piecrust, she found it difficult to keep her eyes off him. Hunkered down as he was, his thighs supported much of his weight, and with each shift of his body, she could see bulges of strength beneath the faded blue denim of his jeans. For such a powerfully built man, he moved with incredible grace, dropping easily into a crouch, leaning sideways with perfect balance, and then pushing effortlessly to his feet.

Watching him brought butterflies fluttering up from

her stomach into her throat. She wanted to place the flat of her hand on his back to feel that wondrous play of tendon and muscle beneath her palm. She also yearned to trace the contours of his arms. Her own body was mostly soft except for where her bones poked out, so everything about his fascinated her. When he wasn't watching, she studied the sturdy thickness of his fingers, the width of his wrists, the distended veins on his sun-browned forearms, the breadth of his shoulders, and the way his torso tapered like a wedge down to his narrow hips.

As Rachel poured the custard into the pie dish, she found herself recalling how lovely it felt when he kissed her, and her cheeks went unaccountably warm. She tried to tell herself it was heat from the oven that had her face burning, but she knew better. It was looking at Joseph that was making her feel warm all over. She also felt deliciously excited, as if something wondrous were about to happen.

"I need to go out and shove the carriage bolts through," he told her as he strode to the archway door. "You want to come drop the bar behind me?"

As Rachel followed him to the archway, even his loose-hipped stride drew her gaze.

"I'll only be gone a minute." He flashed her a grin as he slipped out into the dining room. "When I finish tightening those bolts down on the inside of the wall, I'll get to work on the ironwork over the front door and here. Then you'll be set."

As Rachel dropped the bar, she wished that he would forget the silly ironwork and just kiss her again.

* * *

When Joseph finished installing all the ironwork, he insisted on Rachel's coming to see Bubba's gift to her. When he opened the archway door, she could barely speak. A sturdy crisscross of bars now covered the opening into the dining room.

"Nobody will get past those without a key or hacksaw," he assured her. "Bubba has Pierce Jackson, the local locksmith, make all his locks. They're the same kind they use at the jail."

"Oh, Joseph, it's beautiful."

He chuckled. "I wouldn't go that far. I gave it a scrub and touched it up with some stove black yesterday. It's made of scrap iron, like I said, and the pile has been sitting out in the weather for going on two years. All the bars were rusty."

She reached out a hand to touch the metal. "Thank you so much."

"Don't thank me, darlin'. Bubba did most of the work."

"And I deeply appreciate all his efforts. But it was your idea." She laughed incredulously. "I can't believe I'm standing here, Joseph. I can see into the dining room, and it doesn't frighten me at all."

His voice sounded oddly thick when he replied, "If it helps, that's all the thanks I need."

"Oh, *yes*," Rachel assured him, and she meant it with all her heart. "I feel as if I've been let out of jail." She no sooner spoke than the absurdity of the comment struck her. "Out of jail, but behind bars. How does that make sense?"

"It doesn't have to make sense to anyone but you."

Rachel turned to look at him. In that moment, she

felt certain that she would never forget a single line of his face. "Thank you so much, Joseph. Looking out and not feeling afraid is a fabulous feeling, absolutely *fabulous*."

He handed her two large skeleton keys, pointing out the differences in the notches so she would be able to tell them apart. "This one's for the archway, and this one's for the ironwork over the porch door. I only had one key made for each so you can rest assured that no one else can get in." When she had studied the keys and nodded to let him know she had their shapes memorized, he handed her six more, all of which were exactly alike. "These are for the ironwork over the front door of the house. You can keep one, if you like, and give out the others to special friends like Caitlin. She'll be able to come in without a fuss that way, and once she's inside, with everything locked up behind her, you can let her into the kitchen through the archway."

Rachel tucked the two kitchen keys into her skirt pocket. Then she offered him one of the six front door keys. "You're my most special friend of all, Joseph."

His smile slowly faded, and for a long moment his gaze delved deeply into hers. "Thank you for that. It's a fine compliment."

She pushed the key at him. "Then take it, please."

He reached into his jeans pocket and plucked out a duplicate. "I already confiscated one. Once I board your window back up, I'll be needing a way in." He slipped the key back into his pocket. "I plan to use that front entrance a lot, by the way, even *after* Darby comes home. The next time you start thinking how lonely you'll be when Buddy and I leave, think again. We're gonna pester the daylights out of you, and that's a promise."

"A promise I hope you'll keep."

His eyes went so dark they looked almost indigo. "I never break a promise, darlin'. If I give you my word on something, you can count on it."

Rachel hurried away before he could see the tears in her eyes.

The following day, Joseph got up early, tended to chores while Rachel cooked his breakfast, and directly after he ate went to work on a new, much thicker wooden door for her archway. Using two makeshift sawhorses that he fashioned from boards he'd found in the barn, he set up shop in Rachel's back dooryard, only a few feet from the porch so he could keep a close eye on the house. So far, no attempt had been made on Rachel's life, but it was never far from Joseph's mind that the killer might simply be waiting for an opportune moment. He couldn't afford to forget that and let down his guard.

At around eleven, Joseph heard a creaking sound and glanced up to see the thick back door open a crack. His heart soared, for he knew what it had cost Rachel to lift that bar and disengage the deadlocks. He doubted she'd opened that door in years.

"Joseph?" she called. "Are you there?"

He knew very well that she'd probably just seen him through the peephole, but he answered, all the same. "Right here, darlin'. You've got your bars to protect you. Open on up and enjoy the sunshine. It's a gorgeous morning."

"Oh, no," she said, her voice faint and trailing shakily away. "A crack is fine. I thought maybe we might talk while you work."

Joseph grinned as he grabbed his tape measure. " 'Drink to me only with thine eyes.' "

"You've read Jonson?" she asked incredulously.

Uh-oh. The lady knew her poetry. He used his square to mark his cutting line. "Actually, no. I just memorized certain lines of poetry to woo the ladies. I got them from Ace. He was always the reader in our family. Named his stallion Shakespeare, after a black, leather-bound volume my pa gave him. Damned fool actually *read* it, and I think he memorized half of it. Then he went on to read everything else he could get his hands on, and memorized great lines that he likes to spout all the time to make himself sound learned. I found only a very few to be useful."

"Meaning only a few to impress the ladies? For shame, Joseph Paxton. Poems are ballads for the soul."

"My soul is fine. I know plenty of poems, darlin'."

"Do you now? Recite something then."

" 'Little Bob is a fool, for he don't go to school, and never at work is he seen. And because he don't look inside of a book is the reason he's so very green.' There's some poetry for you."

"That isn't poetry, Joseph. It's a child's rhyme."

"Go ahead. Make light of it. I'll bet you don't know any."

" 'Come here, little kitten,' " she recited back, " 'I

know you love me. I shall put down my sewing, and then we shall see, how smart you will look, when you play and you caper, all over the room, with your round ball of paper.' "

"You like cats?" he asked.

"I love cats, especially kittens. They're so darling when they play."

Joseph filed that information away for later. One of his barnyard cats had recently given birth to a litter of kittens. " 'There was an old woman. And what do you think? She lived upon nothing, but victuals and drink. And though victuals and drink were the whole of her diet, this naughty old woman would never keep quiet.' "

She burst out laughing. "Are you trying to tell me something?"

"Nah. If your new archway door comes out slantindicular because I measure wrong, it makes me no nevermind."

"Perhaps I should be about my business, then." She released a shrill little sigh. "I need to make bread sometime today. We're almost out."

"Don't run off. I won't mess up on my measurements. I was only joshing you."

"But what about the bread?"

"Make a pan of cornbread. That'll do us until tomorrow."

"Are you certain?"

" 'Old mother Ro, she was always so slow that she couldn't even wink in a hurry,' " he said in a singsong voice. " 'But dear little Dick, he is so very quick that he keeps all the folks in a flurry.' "

"I take it back. You do know your verse," she conceded.

Joseph let loose with a gloating chuckle. "Got you whupped, don't I? I know more rhymes than you do."

"You most certainly do *not*."

She launched into several more rhymes from childhood, and then she treated him to some lovely, far more serious poems by famous poets.

"I take it back," he conceded. "I'm flat outclassed. But, hey, book learning isn't the only kind of knowledge that comes in handy. I know a whole passel of things you'll never learn from a book."

"Such as?" she challenged.

"Never squat with your spurs on."

She burst out laughing. Joseph imagined how she might look, throwing her head back and squeezing her eyes closed with mirth. His lips curved in a pleased smile. Damn, but he loved to make the lady laugh.

"What other tidbits of wisdom are floating around in your brain, Joseph Paxton?"

"Some ranchers raise pigs, and some will even admit it. But either way, they're raisin' pigs."

She groaned. "I do not raise pigs. I just have a few kitchen hams and several sides of bacon fattening up in my pigpen. Surely you have something more impressive than that tucked away in your mind."

"Never smack a man when he's chewin' tobacco."

She snorted. "Either that, or be smart enough to duck. What else?"

"Never ask a barber if you need a haircut."

"Hmph. I can tell that you haven't asked that question in a while."

"You making derogatory comments about my hair, woman?"

"No, sir, I like your hair fine. I was just making an observation."

"Never follow good whiskey with water unless you're out of good whiskey," he tried.

"So far, I am not unduly impressed with your store of knowledge."

Joseph thought for a moment. "About the time you get to thinkin' you're a person of some influence, try orderin' someone else's dog around."

"Oh, puh-lease. Surely you've got something better than *that*."

"If you're gonna take the measure of a man, take his full measure," Joseph retorted.

"I'm trying. But so far, I haven't seen a whole lot to measure."

Joseph grinned. He loved that she was plainspoken. When he stuck his foot in his mouth, she'd be likely to understand, at least. "Here's one for you to pay attention to, darlin'. If you're gonna speak your mind, be sure you're ridin' a fast horse."

She giggled again. And so it went. Joseph kept a sharp eye on the door. Over the course of what remained of the morning, the crack widened just a bit.

Miss Rachel was glimpsing a ribbon of sunshine for the first time in five years. Joseph had Bubba White to thank for that. The next time a heifer died at Eden, he'd present the beef to the blacksmith and his family to express his gratitude.

It wasn't often that a forge and anvil could make a miracle happen.

*   *   *

Because he had promised David that he would ride with him over to the Pritchard place that afternoon, Joseph postponed eating lunch until the new archway door was completed. He had just finished sanding the extra-thick planks when Ace showed up to stand guard duty.

"Howdy, big brother!" Joseph called. "You got a strong shoulder I can borrow? I'll need help carrying this thing into the house."

Ace swung down off Shakespeare and sauntered over to peruse the door. "Jumpin' Jehoshaphat. You're never going to fit that thing through the window, Joseph."

"Don't have to. We can take it in through the front door."

Ace rolled up his shirtsleeves. "That's one thick mother. It's a door for a fortress."

"It is, at that." Joseph hooked a thumb at the back door. "Rachel needs barricades, not doors. I figure this will make her feel plenty safe."

"How much protection does she need?"

Not so long ago, Joseph had asked himself the same question. Now he simply accepted and no longer tried to make sense of it.

Once they got the door hefted up onto their shoulders, the two men grunted, huffed, and puffed their way around to the front of the house, whereupon the stout creation had to be lowered to the ground while Joseph used his key to unlock the ironwork that now covered the front entrance.

"I think I've ruptured a gut," Ace said.

Joseph chuckled. "That's a gambler for you. Never turned your hand to hard work."

Ace snorted. "If it weren't for my gambling, you would have starved to death as a young pup."

"That I would have. No aspersions upon your efforts to feed me intended. I was just teasing you."

Once the entrance was opened, they carried the door into the vestibule. Ace kicked the interior door closed behind him, and Joseph called that good enough until they had carried their burden to the dining room. What Rachel didn't know wouldn't hurt her, and he'd be back to lock up soon.

Rachel nearly jumped out of her skin when a deafening crash sounded in the dining room and vibrations rolled through the kitchen floor. She whirled to stare at the archway.

"Rachel?" Joseph called. "Don't shoot us, darlin'. It's just me and Ace with your new barricade. Time to open up. I need to install it."

Rachel had a bad moment. What would she have for a barricade while the installation took place? Nothing, she guessed, and the very thought sent her heart racing. She nevertheless gathered her courage and lifted the bar, opened the interior door, and quickly unlocked the ironwork. Then she scurried away to the water closet.

She'd no sooner moved the broken door to cover the doorway than Joseph said, "Honey, you're perfectly safe. Ace is even faster with a gun than I am. Like we'd let anyone get into the kitchen?"

Rachel inched the door to one side so she could

peer out. The two men were already lifting her new barricade into position, and the sight of it calmed her. It was at least four inches thick, so heavy that both Joseph and Ace strained to maneuver it. "My goodness, Joseph, it's *lovely*."

The comment set Ace to laughing. "Lovely? This door is stout, but that's about all I can say for it."

"What are you saying, that my handiwork is lacking?" Joseph asked.

Soon the men were volleying teasing remarks back and forth, their deep chuckles and laughter filling the kitchen. Their jocularity soothed Rachel's nerves enough that she was able to leave the water closet.

"There she is," Joseph called over his shoulder. "Slipping out to see the finished product. Almost up, darlin'. I just hope you don't bust a gut opening and closing the damned thing. It's heavy, and that's a fact."

Rachel stepped closer to admire her new door. It was three and a half planks wide and every bit as stalwart as the porch door that Darby had fashioned for her years ago. "Oh, Joseph, such a lot of work. You shouldn't have."

"Just took some elbow grease," Joseph assured her, "and I'm used to that. It felt kind of good to break a sweat, actually. I'm used to going from morning 'til night."

While the two finished tightening hinge screws and shaving the door to fit, Rachel fixed lunch. When the door had been installed, she welcomed to her table the third guest in less than a week, and in the doing, she marveled at how Joseph's presence in the house had so greatly changed her life. Only a short time ago, she couldn't have imagined having even one visitor. Now guests in her kitchen were becoming a common occurrence.

"Caitlin's coming later," Ace said around a mouthful of salt pork sandwich. "She couldn't leave until Little Ace woke up from his midmorning nap. She's probably driving over now."

Rachel's heart lifted. "I will be glad to have her."

"She's bringing a bunch of fashion stuff. Recent periodicals with all the latest nonsense in them."

Rachel's heart soared again. She'd had no need to follow fashion, living as she did, and she no longer had any idea what might be in vogue. But a part of her still yearned to look pretty, regardless. Especially now, with Joseph around. She wanted him to— She aborted the notion, horrified at the train of her thoughts. She wanted him to want her.

Joseph caught her eye and gave her a quick wink. "Fabulous lunch, Rachel. You have magic in your fingertips."

Recalling how she felt every time he touched her, she thought it was Joseph who had the magic touch.

"It *is* good," Ace seconded. "Thank you for inviting me to eat."

"Feeding you is the least I can do," Rachel said, collecting her thoughts and forcing them to more practical matters. And as she spoke, she realized that she sincerely meant it. Ace had spent more afternoons at her house recently than he'd spent at his own, and she knew he had a ranch to run. He was also operating minus Esa, one of his full-time hands. "I deeply appreciate all the time you've taken away from your work to be here. Thank you so much."

"Hear that?" Ace gave his brother an arch look. "Some people *appreciate* me and have the good manners to say thank you."

Joseph swallowed and grinned. "What have you done that I should thank you for?"

"I helped carry in the door and install it."

"Oh, that." Joseph shrugged and took another bite of sandwich. "If I were to thank you for every little thing, you might get a big head and start expecting it. That wouldn't do."

Ace turned laughing brown eyes on Rachel. "Do you see what I have to put up with? I think I raised them wrong. Should have kicked their butts more often, I reckon."

Joseph flashed a broad grin and winked at Rachel. "Too late to correct the mistake now, big brother. Nowadays, I kick back."

Ace's expression turned suddenly serious. "You and David going back over to Pritchard's today?"

Joseph sat back on his chair. Not for the first time, Rachel noted how different the two brothers were, one with jet-black hair and brown eyes, the other blond and blue eyed.

"Pritchard's place will be one of our stops," Joseph replied.

Ace wiped his mouth and dropped his napkin on his plate. "You boys be careful. Jeb Pritchard's not just mean; he's crazy, to boot."

Joseph smiled. "We'll be fine, big brother. We were trained up by one of the best."

* * *

"Jesus!"

Joseph dived for cover, praying as he hit the dirt that David had bailed off his horse just as quickly as he had. Jeb Pritchard was shooting at them. Even as the realization registered in Joseph's brain, another bullet plowed into the dirt right in front of his nose. No shotgun today. The son of a bitch had a rifle.

"You okay?" David called from behind a rock.

Joseph kept his head low, using a bush to hide himself. "I'm fine," he yelled back. "But I need more than this for cover." He scrambled sideways to get behind a log. When he felt halfway protected, he drew his Colt, wishing like hell that he had his rifle. No such luck. The weapon was still in the saddle boot, and Obie, being the intelligent animal he was, had galloped away to hide behind some trees. "What's that man's problem?"

Just as Joseph posed the question, Jeb hollered, "You ain't been invited onto my property, you cocky bastards. Until you are, I'll shoot every time I see your faces!"

David sent Joseph a bewildered look. "What's gotten into him? I'm the law, for God's sake. He can't just open fire on the law."

"Looks to me like he's doing just that." Joseph brushed dirt from his eyes. "Means business, too. He's not good enough to place his slug an inch from my nose just to scare hell out of me. I think the ornery old bastard just missed."

David checked his weapon for bullets.

"Why bother?" Joseph called. "He's out of range."

"Damn it," David bit out. "I need my Winchester."

"It's long gone. The horses are off behind the trees."

A bullet hit the rock where David was hiding, the lead making a *ker-chunk* as it sent up a spray of granite. David sank lower to the ground. "Damned horses are smarter than we are."

"I think you're right," Joseph bit out. "Let's pull foot. I don't know about you, but I'm not looking to die today."

"You think we can make it to the trees?"

"If we stay on our bellies and keep our heads down." Crawling away went against Joseph's grain. But, he rationalized, it was better to crawl and live to see another sunrise than take a slug between the eyes. "You ready?"

As Joseph slithered away from the log, Pritchard opened fire again. Geysers of dirt and pine needles shot up all around him. He picked up speed, pushing hard with his feet, grabbing earth with his hands, praying with every inch of ground he covered that his brother hadn't been hit.

When they reached the trees and relative safety, the two men pushed up onto their knees. The instant they came erect, another shot rang out, and David's Stetson went spinning away.

"Holy shit!" they yelled simultaneously and hit the dirt again.

A few seconds later, when they'd crawled beyond the reach of Jeb's bullets, David looked back at his hat. His blue eyes blazed. "That miserable sack of shit came within an inch of blowing my brains out. Now

I'll have to buy a new Stetson. You got any idea how much those things cost?"

It had been a spell since Joseph had purchased a hat. "No, how much?"

"A small fortune, that's what." David brushed dirt and pine needles from his hair. "He'll pay. Now I've got reason to arrest the son of a bitch. He tried to kill a lawman. That's a serious offense!"

Joseph gazed through the trees at Pritchard's shack. "You're gonna need help to take that ornery polecat in."

Silence. Joseph looked back at his brother. David was eyeing him expectantly.

Joseph held up his hands. "Do you think I'm crazy? No way, son. You need a posse."

"And who will I deputize, a bunch of farmers who can't shoot their way out of a flour sack?"

Joseph sighed. "I had plans for later this afternoon."

"Your plans just changed."

Chapter Fourteen

Jeb Pritchard stank up the whole jail and raised so much sand about being locked up that David threatened to shoot him to make him be quiet. Billy Joe Roberts, David's lanky young deputy, was as excited as a kid at Christmas to have an actual criminal in one of the cells.

"You reckon the Pritchard boys will try to break him out?" Billy Joe asked David.

David considered the question. "I hope not. I'd have to lock them up, too. The place already stinks to high heaven." He extended a hand to Joseph. "Thank you, big brother. That went fair to middling well, I think. Not a single shot fired."

Joseph chuckled as he shook David's hand. "I'm glad it went so well. With polecats like them, it could have gotten nasty."

He and David had crept up on the Pritchard place, using bushes as cover until they reached the house. Then they'd each taken up positions outside a door and entered simultaneously on the count of twenty. All four of the Pritchards had been napping, and before they could reach for their weapons, Joseph had had the barrel of his Colt .45 pressed to Jeb's temple.

"I kind of hope the Pritchard boys try something," Billy Joe said. "We could use some excitement around here."

"Not that kind of excitement, Billy Joe." David met Joseph's laughing gaze. "Just in case, though, I should probably stick around here tonight. No reading that book without me, you hear?"

Joseph gave his brother a mock salute as he turned to leave the office. "I'm gone to take a bath. Wrestling with that no-account left me smelling almost as bad as he does."

It took Joseph thirty minutes to reach the Hollister place. When he entered the barn to get Obie settled into a stall for the night, he saw that Ace had already done the evening chores again. Making a mental note to thank him, Joseph headed for the house. When he entered by the front door, the sound of voices and laughter coming from the kitchen area reminded him that Caitlin had come to visit.

"Pugh!" Rachel waved a hand in front of her nose as she let Joseph into the kitchen. "What *is* that smell?"

Joseph plucked at his shirt. "I met up with the south end of a northbound skunk. I'll be taking a bath, if you don't mind."

"Not at all." Rachel flapped her hand again. "Please do. We promise not to peek through the cracks when you lean the door over the hole."

The very fact that she was thinking about peeking

through those cracks heated Joseph's blood. He shot
her a questioning look. She gazed back at him, as innocent as could be. But her cheeks went pink. *Hmm*.
At times when she'd been bathing, he'd been tempted
to peek through those cracks a few times himself. So
he knew how her mind was working. The realization
gave him pause. The attraction he felt for her wasn't as
one-sided as he'd believed.

Caitlin and Ace sat at the table. As Joseph sauntered
over to greet them, he saw that he had interrupted a
poker game. This evening, beans were the token of
choice, the largest pile at the seat Rachel had just vacated.

"Uh-oh. I can see the lady's luck is still holding."

"Luck?" Ace shook his head. "The woman's a card-
sharp."

"I am not," Rachel protested.

Caitlin was frowning over her cards. "I can't *believe* the awful hands I've been getting." She glanced
up and smiled. "Come and join us, Joseph. Maybe
you'll change our luck."

Joseph glanced around for his nephew. The toddler
was fast asleep on the sofa in Rachel's small parlor.
"Looks to me like someone ran low on steam."

"Ace let him play outside with the dogs," Caitlin
explained. "They ran his little legs off."

Forcing himself not to study Rachel's delightful
form and instead look at the cards, Joseph moved
closer. When he saw his brother's hand, he winced and
said, "Ouch."

"Do you mind?" Ace gave him a burning look. "Occasionally I like to bluff."

"You best say your prayers if you're going to bluff with a hand like that."

Ace threw his cards down. "Misdeal!"

"You can't call misdeal just because Joseph gave your hand away," Caitlin cried.

"Sure I can." Ace shot another glare at his brother. "Rachel's right. You stink. What *is* that smell?"

"You are a little odoriferous, Joseph," Caitlin agreed.

"Odor*iferous?* Where on earth did you learn a word like that?" Joseph asked.

"She reads occasionally," Rachel interjected.

Joseph cast her a sharp glance. She flashed a saucy smile and dimpled a cheek. In that moment, he sorely wished the guests weren't present. That bathtub was large enough for two. A vision of Rachel with soap bubbles slipping over her breasts filled his mind. His body snapped taut.

God help me. He marched away, determined to banish all such thoughts from his mind. She was a *lady*. She was *off-limits*. She was marriage bait.

Ace and Caitlin stayed after supper. Playing cards was impossible with two romping dogs and a lively toddler running about the kitchen, so the adults settled for chatting over coffee about nothing in particular.

Watching Rachel interact with Ace and Caitlin did Joseph's heart good, and seeing how gentle she was with Little Ace warmed him through and through. For a young lady who'd spent years in total seclusion, she was taking to company, and to children as well, like a duck to water. Joseph suddenly pictured her holding his child to her soft breast, a golden-haired angel gently stroking the gilded curls of a beautiful baby. And where had that come from? He didn't want a kid. He didn't want a wife.

In short, he didn't want these feelings.

"You ever seen an obedient dime?" Ace suddenly asked.

"Uh-oh," Caitlin said. "Here we go. Prepare yourself, Rachel. Once they get started on this, they just won't quit."

Rachel's eyes fairly danced as she met Ace's gaze. Then she glanced questioningly at Joseph. From his vantage point, it was a guileless look, but the question behind it—"Is this okay?"—only made Old Glory grow harder and throb more painfully. She looked to him for guidance. Knowing that made him ache to hold her in his arms. And how did that make sense? He wasn't in the market for a woman who looked to him for guidance. In short, he wasn't in the market for a wife, and she had "wife" written all over her.

Cheeks still rosy, she finally returned her gaze to Ace. "An obedient dime? No, I can't say I've ever seen one. Mine always jumped right out of my pocket."

Ace rifled through her cupboard for a wide-bottomed glass. Once back at the table, he placed a dime on the tablecloth and flanked it with two half-dollars, leaving about an inch between the coins. Then he perched the glass on the fifty-cent pieces.

"Without ever touching any of those coins," he informed Rachel, "I can make that dime come to my call."

"Ah, go on," Rachel said. "I bet you can't."

She glanced at Joseph again, her big blue eyes shimmering with emotions he didn't want to define. He was having enough trouble dealing with his own feelings, and he didn't need hers to cloud the issue. So why was she flashing those questioning glances his way, making him feel as if she counted on him to make decisions about everything outside her little world?

Because she'd come to trust him, he decided. And the realization brought him no joy. He didn't want her trust. He didn't want that responsibility. She was coming to count on him too much. And he was coming to want her to count on him *way* too much. That didn't fit into his life plan. He wanted to smoke at his table. He wanted to come home at the crack of dawn, drunk as a lord. He wanted to have no obligations to anyone, most especially a trusting woman with big blue eyes that made his heart ache. No matter how pretty she was. No matter how much he wanted her. Nothing about her fit—except the feel of her body against his. And that was Old Glory talking.

Joseph had learned years ago never to listen to Old Glory.

"How many beans is it worth to you to see me do it?" Ace asked.

Everyone burst out laughing. Rachel pursed her lips in thought. "Fifty," she finally wagered.

Ace sat at the table, called, "Come here, dime," and began lightly scratching the tablecloth with one fingernail. The dime walked out from under the glass, just as he had predicted. Rachel slumped in her chair, giggling helplessly as she shoved a mound of beans at him.

Not to be bested, Joseph fetched an egg from the icebox. And why did he care about being bested? As he set up his trick on the table, he scolded himself for being such an idiot, but it didn't stop him from wanting to outshine his older brother in her eyes.

"You got any wine goblets?" he asked Rachel.

"What on earth do you need wine goblets for?"

"To show you an erratic egg."

She wiped tears of mirth from her eyes. "Out in the dining room." She handed Joseph the key to the archway ironwork. "You should find some goblets in Ma's sideboard."

When Joseph returned a moment later, he set the goblets on the table, rims touching, and put the egg in one of them. "Without ever touching that egg, I can make it hop from one glass to another."

"Oh, no, sir!" She flapped her hand at him. "No way." But her eyes told him that she believed he could do anything.

"What are you willing to wager on it?" Joseph asked. And, God forgive him, he wasn't thinking about beans.

She looked at her dwindling pile. "I don't have much left to wager with."

Joseph could think of several other things he'd love to win from her. "I'll take whatever you've got." *Those lovely breasts, for starters.* He wanted to taste her mouth, with no rules of propriety to forestall him. And he wanted to run his hands slowly over her skin, tantalizing her with the dance of his fingertips until she shuddered with pleasure. He wanted to see those blue eyes go foggy and blind with passion.

She nodded in agreement. Joseph bent and blew sharply into the goblet holding the egg, and just as he'd promised, the egg popped out into the other glass. Rachel's eyes went wide with amazement, then she burst out laughing again.

And so went the remainder of the evening. When the Keegan family finally departed, the hour had grown late and Joseph was exhausted. Not because he'd worked hard, but because he'd been wanting the forbidden for hours. *Rachel.* She was so beautiful. His fingers actually ached with his yearning to explore her body. When he glanced at her, his heart knocked.

What in hell was wrong with him? She was just a woman. Until now, any woman would do. Only suddenly he wanted her, and only her, with an intensity that made Old Glory burn. Even worse, she blushed every time he glanced her way, as if she were feeling the same. *No,* Joseph told himself. She was off-limits. It didn't matter if she was attracted to him. Down that path lay obligation—and marriage—and responsibility he didn't want.

Unfortunately, he also instinctively knew that other things also lay in wait if he followed his urges, namely pleasure such as he'd never experienced. He glimpsed the answering desire in her eyes whenever their gazes met and felt the heat between them whenever they moved close. He was drawn to her in a way that defied reason, and that scared the hell out of him. He would have willpower. He would ignore the urges of his body. And most important of all, he would pretend he didn't see that invitation in her eyes.

It was an innocent invitation—the reaction of an untried virgin to biological needs that she didn't understand. It was up to him to be strong and protect her from being compromised.

After locking the ironwork door, Rachel pocketed the key in her skirt and turned a radiant smile on him. Before he could guess what she meant to do, she launched herself at him.

"Oh, Joseph, *thank you*, thank you, thank you, *thank you*. This was the best day, *ever*."

Fiercely hugging his neck, she rained kisses on his face. For an instant, Joseph couldn't think what to do with his hands. Then, as if with a will of their own, they settled at her waist. She felt like heaven against him, all soft, feminine, rose-scented warmth, the fulfillment of an evening-long promise. The yearning for her that he'd been so determinedly holding at bay swamped him like an ocean wave, and he got all the same sensations that he'd experienced as a child playing on the California beach—a feeling of being knocked almost off his feet, then staggering to catch his balance on shifting sand. Oh, *God*, he wanted her.

All his fine principles about never trifling with a lady were forgotten as he settled his mouth over hers. It wasn't a thought or a decision. He just reacted to a need that had been growing within him all evening and had suddenly become bigger than he was. Caught by surprise, she gave a muffled bleep. Then she sighed, relaxed in his arms, and surrendered herself to him.

Joseph was lost. She had the sweetest mouth he'd

ever tasted—her soft lips parting shyly, the tip of her tongue darting away from his for a moment and then hesitantly returning. *Fine silk, drenched in warm honey.* He wanted to taste every delectable inch of her. His pulse slammed in his temples. He ran his hands along her spine, then lowered them to the soft fullness of her hips to pull her hard against him.

At the back of his mind, warning bells went off. He shouldn't be doing this. She wasn't some working girl at the Golden Slipper who'd played the game count-less times and made up the rules as she went along. This was Rachel, sweet, wonderful, innocent Rachel, who'd never even been kissed by anyone but him. But when he tried to make himself pull away, he couldn't. Instead, he deepened the kiss, thrusting deep, tasting and testing the most secret recesses of her mouth. She moaned and stepped up onto his boots to kiss him back with fierce, awkward hunger, taking her cues from him.

She was a quick learner, he thought dizzily, a dear, untried, lovely student who had no idea of the danger into which he was luring her. *Rachel.* She felt perfectly right in his arms, as if she'd been fashioned just for him, and that sense of quiet awareness filled him again, even as he grazed his hands up her sides, feel-ing the soft ladder of her delicate ribs beneath his fin-gertips. *Right for him. All that he'd been searching for.* Dizzily, he assured himself that he'd never hurt her for the world, that this was only a kiss, a harmless kiss. He would stop soon. He would. And that was the last ra-tional thought that went through his head.

And then her breasts were cupped in his hands. Her

breath caught when his thumbs grazed her nipples through her clothing. She moaned and let her head fall back, offering herself to him with childlike trust. The change of position pressed her pelvis forward. He could feel her pliant warmth against his hardness. And the gift was too intoxicating to refuse.

He nipped lightly at her velvety skin, following the graceful column of her neck down to her collar, and then his fingers were at the buttons of her shirtwaist. As the blouse came undone, he trailed kisses in the wake of the parting fabric until he found the taut crest of one breast through the lawn of her simple chemise. She cried out and shuddered with pleasure as he drew on her nipple. Then she made fists in his hair to pull him closer. *Oh, yes.* This was better than anything he could buy. Better than anything he'd ever even dreamed of. *Rachel.* She was the taste that satisfied yearnings he'd never even realized that he had.

"Oh, Joseph!"

He spun in a slow half circle, with her feet riding on his boots. When he lowered her onto the bed and followed her down, he shifted to one side to avoid squashing her. He tugged at the ribbon laces at the front of her chemise to bare her breasts. They were as pale as ivory and as plump as little melons, the tips tinted a deep rose.

When he took one into his mouth, she arched her spine and cried out again. He caught the sensitive tip between his teeth, gave it a gentle roll, and then suckled her again. Her body quivered like a plucked bowstring. Running a hand down the front of her skirt, he made a fist over the cloth, pushed it high, and found the slit in her drawers. His fingertips were instantly drenched with hot, feminine wetness when he parted the soft folds at the apex of her thighs. His mouth found hers again. He kissed her deeply, passionately, as he homed in on the sensitive flange of flesh above her opening. She bucked her hips at the shock of sensation, but he rode her back down with the heel of his hand, lightly flicking and rubbing her, his only thought being to bring her to climax before he sought release for himself.

Ruff-ruff-ruff.

Buddy. The sound of his growling barks barely penetrated Joseph's brain.

But then it came again, a series of deep growls followed by three earsplitting yips. Joseph jerked as if he'd been touched by a red-hot brand. He broke off the kiss and stared stupidly into Rachel's dazed eyes. Felt her heat and wetness under his hand. Saw her bared breasts.

What in the hell was he *doing*?

He sprang to his feet. Bewilderment clouded Rachel's lovely features.

Grinning happily, Buddy scampered back and forth between Joseph and the bed.

Joseph grabbed for breath as if he'd just run a mile. He raked a hand through his hair. "I am *so* sorry, Rachel. I don't know what came over me. I'm so sorry."

She pushed her skirt down and fumbled to close her bodice. Streaks of crimson flagged her cheeks as she sat up. "Please don't," she said softly. "It was as much my doing as yours. I started it, after all."

Joseph couldn't let himself off the hook quite that easily. Granted, she had initiated the embrace, but only with the most innocent of intentions. He was the one who'd taken it to another level. And, God help him, he was shaking with an urgent need to finish what he'd started.

Before he acted on that urge, he had to get away from her. This was *not* happening. He spun away to collect his bedroll and jacket from the water closet. When he emerged, Rachel gave him a bruised, hurt look.

"What are you doing?"

"I'll be sleeping in the dining room from here on out. I don't trust myself to stay in here with you."

She pushed to her feet. "But, Joseph, that's just silly."

Not silly. Had she no idea how devastatingly beautiful she was with her braid coming loose and her mouth swollen from his kisses? He wanted her so bad that he trembled.

"I'll be sleeping in another room, all the same. Do you mind letting me out?"

Joseph rolled his jacket, unrolled his jacket, and punched his jacket. He tried lying on his side. He tried lying on his back. He tried closing his eyes. He tried staring through the darkness at the ceiling. No how, no way could he drift off to sleep. Through the crack under the door, light from the kitchen spilled in a broad swath over the dining room floor to puddle against the wall. He couldn't help thinking that it was almost as golden as Rachel's hair.

What kind of man was he? Wanting her like this was wrong, and yearning to act on it was even worse. What if Buddy hadn't barked? Joseph kept coming back to that, furious with himself because he doubted that he would have come to his senses and stopped. He'd been that far gone.

Young women like Rachel were for marrying. Any man who would take her with no thought of making an honest woman of her wasn't worth the powder it would take to blow him to hell.

Did he want to marry her? Joseph mentally circled the question as if it were a coiled rattlesnake. He cared for her. There was no denying that. He had more feelings for her, in fact, than he'd ever had for any woman outside his family. But did he *love* her? It felt like love. Just a single tear, falling from one of her lovely blue eyes, had him scrambling to set her world to rights, and a single smile from her kissable lips made his heart soar. But couldn't that be only fondness?

And how the hell could he be sure that his feelings for her would last? Maybe he was letting Old Glory do his thinking for him again, and all these confusing emotions would vanish like a puff of smoke the moment he slaked his need for her.

A picture of her face moved through his mind. He didn't want to hurt her. She was too dear. He'd glimpsed pain in her beautiful blue eyes more than once. She'd already suffered enough without his adding to her heartache.

He heard the wood door creak open. The next instant, light poured into the dining room. He shifted his shoulders sideways and tucked in his chin to see

Rachel standing behind the bars over the archway. She'd changed into a nightgown, pale pink and trimmed prettily with lace and ribbons. The lantern light behind her shone through the muslin, outlining every delightful curve of her body.

Joseph fleetingly wondered if one of the temptations that had so tortured Christ during his trial in the desert had been a beautiful woman in a nearly transparent gown.

"Joseph?" she called softly. "Are you still awake?"

He doubted he'd ever sleep again. "Yes, honey, wide awake."

"Can we talk for a bit?"

He almost groaned. "Only if you drape a blanket over your shoulders." *So I can't see your body.* "I don't want you taking a chill."

She spun away and returned a moment later wrapped in a blanket. He could still see the outline of her gorgeous legs, but at least the rest of her was hidden. He recalled the delicate pink of her nipples, and his body hardened.

She sat in the threshold, her back resting against the doorframe, her knees hugged to her chest.

"So what do you want to talk about?" As if he didn't know. Every female he'd ever encountered intimately, in any degree, had wanted to talk about it afterward, especially if the intimate encounter had gone badly. Not that his intimate encounters usually did.

"Anything," she whispered, surprising him yet again. "I can't sleep."

He understood that problem. "Anything, huh?" He

thought of a topic that had recently become dear to his heart. "You ever seen a courtyard?"

"You mean like in rich people's yards? It's a garden of sorts, isn't it?"

"Better than just a garden." Joseph punched at his jacket pillow again and lay on his side so it was easier to see her. "It's a room that's outside. Fancy ladies in big cities can go out in their nightclothes and sit in their courtyards of a morning to enjoy the sunshine and flowers. No one passing by on the street can see them."

She said nothing.

"Just imagine that, a room outside with an ironwork ceiling, made similar to your doors, and tall rock walls all around. You'd be even safer than you are in your kitchen. No shotgun can blow a hole through solid rock, that's for certain."

"Where did you see a courtyard?"

Joseph had seen courtyards in California as a boy. They hadn't been fortresses like he hoped to build for Rachel, but that was beside the point. "A number of people in California have them. They're really some pumpkins."

"Amazing. Too bad I'm not rich."

Joseph grinned. "Just imagine it, an outdoor room as safe as your kitchen where the sunlight comes down through the iron-bar ceiling and the birds and butterflies can come in."

She sighed wistfully. "With flowers all around," she added.

"Absolutely."

She sighed again. "It would be lovely. But there's no point in pining for things I can't have."

"It never hurts to dream a little," Joseph urged. "If *I* had a courtyard, I'd want a birdbath and lots of flowers."

"Roses," she said. "I *love* the smell of roses."

Joseph had recently become fond of their scent, too. Roses went onto his mental shopping list. He had no idea how to get any, but he felt confident that Caitlin did.

"And little stepping-stone walkways," she said dreamily.

Joseph's eyebrows lifted. Stepping-stones? *Whoa, girl. Don't get carried away.*

"And a fountain. If I were rich enough to have a courtyard, I'd want a fountain."

A fountain? That was way beyond anything he could give her. But at least he had her thinking about it and longing for an outdoor garden. "What other flowers do you like?"

"Lilacs," she said straightaway. "And violets. I adore violets. Tulips, too. Do you like tulips?"

Joseph liked all kinds of flowers. "I like tulips fine. What else would you enjoy about a courtyard besides the flowers?"

"The sunlight," she said fervently. "And feeling the wind on my face. Is there anything that smells lovelier than a summer breeze?"

She smelled lovelier than anything he'd ever known, all sweet and clean and dabbed with rose water. He studied her amber-limned features, imagining her sitting on a garden bench with sunlight igniting her golden curls and roses all around her.

"What would you say if I told you that you're about to get a courtyard?"

That brought her gaze to his. "Say what?"

"A bunch of folks hereabouts are going to start bringing wagonloads of rock for your courtyard any day now. The fellow that owns the quarry is donating the mortar mixings. And Bubba White has already started on the ironwork for your roof and gate."

Her eyes widened with incredulity. "You're serious."

"Dead serious. I wish I could take credit for the idea, but it was Sue Ellen White who came up with it. She talked it up at church and got a lot of other folks interested in helping out. 'Sunshine for Miss Rachel' is what they're calling it."

Her eyes went bright with tears. Then she covered her face with her hands.

"Sweetheart, don't cry."

"I can't help it," she said in a muffled voice. "A courtyard? Oh, lands, I can't believe it."

Chapter Fifteen

The first wagonload of rock arrived the following morning, providing Joseph with a perfect excuse to stay outside most of the day, safely away from temptation. Since sexual frustration had his nerves strung tighter than a bowstring, he welcomed the opportunity to do some hard work.

Along about ten, Rachel cracked open the back door, clearly hoping to visit with him, but today he was farther from the porch. "I can't hear you, honey. I'd love to talk, but you'll have to open the door wider."

The door inched open just a little more. "Is that better?"

Joseph could hear her now, but he wasn't about to tell her so. "What was that?"

The crack widened. "Can you hear me now?"

"Come again?"

Finally her face appeared in the opening. "Oh, *Joseph*." She beamed a radiant smile. "I can see *out*!"

"Imagine that." He mixed another batch of mortar

in the wheelbarrow and began adding the second tier of rock to the courtyard wall. "You've got the bars to protect you, honey. Open on up and enjoy the morning."

"I'm good just like this," she insisted.

But soon she was sitting on the floor with the door opened wide enough to accommodate her bent knees.

"I can hear the birds, Joseph. Oh, lands, this is so wonderful!"

"If you'd open the door all the way, you might even see the little buggers."

She didn't find the courage immediately, but within a couple of hours she finally had the door flung wide. The look of utter joy on her face was something Joseph believed he would remember for the rest of his life. She said nothing. Instead, she just sat there, drinking in the sights and sounds for which she'd thirsted for so long.

At last she said, "Oh, Joseph, this is wonderful. Just *listen*."

Joseph paused in his work to cock an ear. At first he heard nothing, but then he realized that wasn't precisely true. He actually heard a multitude of sounds that were so commonplace to him that he mostly ignored them—the buzz of a fly, the raucous call of a jay, the wind whispering through the grass, the creaking of the oak as it shifted in the breeze.

"Pretty incredible, isn't it?" he asked.

"Oh, it's beyond incredible." She flung her arms wide. "The door is open, and I can breathe, Joseph. It's a *miracle*."

Her miracle came to an abrupt end when a new

sound reached them, that of an approaching wagon. Buddy sprang to his feet and started barking. Rachel vanished lickety-split and slammed the door behind her. Squinting against the sunlight, Joseph saw that the driver was Charley Banks, and judging by the drop of the wagon, he had it loaded to capacity with rock. Way off in the distance, Joseph saw another wagon coming in as well.

Rachel's courtyard was about to become a reality.

Over the next two weeks, Joseph's days fell into a repeating pattern. As soon as he'd finished the morning chores and eaten breakfast, he went to work on the courtyard walls, stopping only to eat lunch or when Ace came over to stand guard duty. When the latter occurred, Joseph took care of errands in town, rode the Hollister land to check on Rachel's tiny herd of cattle, and then headed south to monitor his place. Darby was recovering nicely and beginning to grump about staying in bed, which told Joseph that the old foreman would soon be healed enough to come home.

That being the case, it was with a sense of sadness that Joseph saw the courtyard walls grow taller. Before he knew it, the project would be completed, Darby would return, and he would have no reason to stay on with Rachel.

Joseph tried to tell himself that he'd be pleased as punch to have his life back to normal again. Calving season was drawing to an end. He'd be free to go into town on Friday nights to play poker and pursue other pleasures. And, hey, he'd be able to sleep in a regular bed again. But somehow none of those thoughts cheered him. He had a challenging poker opponent in Rachel, and the idea of a two-dollar poke in the upstairs rooms of the Golden Slipper now held little appeal. There was only one woman he wanted. And unless he was prepared to marry her, he couldn't, in good conscience, have her.

One afternoon when Ace came over to lend a hand with the courtyard walls, Joseph blurted out his troubles.

He began with, "How do you know when it's the real thing, Ace?"

Slathering mortar over a section of rock, Ace sent Joseph a sidelong look. "When what's the real thing? If you're talking about gold, you bite it."

Joseph swore under his breath. "You know very well what I'm talking about. Why are you always so dad-blamed difficult?"

Ace chuckled. "The last time I even *hinted* at that, you damned near took my head off. Oh, no, little brother. You want to talk about it, you're going to say the word straight out."

Joseph slapped a rock into place on the wall with such force that the impact jarred his teeth. "What's in a word? It's the feeling that matters."

"Yeah, and if you can't put a name to the feeling, you have a problem."

Joseph added another rock, this time with a little less force. "All *right*, damn it. I think I may be in love with her."

"If you only *think* you're in love with her, you're not. There's no thinking to it when it happens. You can't breathe for wanting her, and the mere thought of losing her ties your guts into knots."

When Joseph thought of leaving Rachel to return home, knotted guts were the least of his troubles. His heart actually hurt. "I reckon I love her, then." He slapped another rock into place. "Only what if I'm wrong? What if my feelings for her fade? I've never had any constancy with women. You know that."

"Before he falls in love, what man does?" Ace wiped a speck of mortar from his lean cheek. "Love brings about changes of heart you can never imagine until they happen to you."

"What kind of changes?"

Ace mused over the question for a moment. "Well, for one thing, if you're really in love, you're ruined for all other females."

Joseph muttered none too happily under his breath again.

"And when you're truly in love, what you once regarded as a huge burden and responsibility, namely a wife and kids, suddenly is a pleasure. You *want* the responsibility, and when that first child comes into the world, instead of thinking of the scary stuff, you're so proud you think you'll bust."

"Little Ace is a fine boy. I don't blame you for being proud."

"I can tell you this. You've never felt love until you hold your own little baby in your arms. If he sneezes, your heart almost stops for fear he's taking sick, and you wake up in the dead of night to poke a finger under his nose just to make sure he's still breathing.

And if by chance he's between breaths and you feel nothing, pure panic seizes you."

"Sounds like a bad case of influenza to me."

Ace grinned. "I reckon that's why we don't *decide* to fall in love. It just happens upon us. Later in the marriage, I reckon there are times when love does become a decision—along about the time your wife gets her monthly curse, and the sweet, angelic little gal you married suddenly snarls at you like a hydrophobic dog. When that happens, you *decide* to love her anyway and don't snarl back."

"When has Caitlin ever snarled at you?"

"Hasn't—yet. But she's been grumpy as all get-out a few times. In short, Joseph, your feelings for a woman do change after a time. It doesn't stay fresh and exciting forever."

"I knew it."

Ace nodded sagely. "One day you wake up, and you realize you know everything there is to know about her. You've heard all her stories. You know what she's going to say before she says it. Your feelings change, plain and simple. The excitement of new love is gone."

"You see?" Joseph slapped another rock into place with such strength that mortar splattered in all directions. "That's exactly my worry, that I'll make a commitment and then wake up one morning with changed feelings."

"It'll happen," Ace said with absolute certainty. "And that's the best part of all, the changes that come with time."

Joseph gave his brother another sharp, questioning look.

"When the excitement fades, the real love takes over," Ace went on. "It's there from the start, I reckon. It's what brings two people together. But in the beginning the real love is overshadowed by all the excitement and newness. When the excitement wears off, you get down to the reality of love, and that's the best part."

"If the excitement goes, how can that be the best part?"

"Don't confuse excitement with passion. Caitlin still excites me that way as no other woman ever has—or ever will. I'm talking about in between those times, when you're troubled and she understands without your ever saying a single word. Or when you sit with her on the porch of an evening to watch the sunset, and you find that just holding her hand and being with her is the best part of your whole day. Love gets comfortable, sort of like your favorite pair of boots."

Joseph braced his hands against the wall and stared down at his Justins. He wouldn't trade them for a dozen new pairs and dreaded when they wore out. "So that's how I'll feel about Rachel in five years—like she's my favorite pair of boots?"

Ace snorted with laughter. "Not exactly, no. But something like that. I've never been good with words, Joseph. You know that. All I'm saying is, the new wears off, and the feelings change. For instance— have you ever seen a really, *really* pregnant woman who walks with her back arched and her feet spread wide to keep her balance, and thought she was the most beautiful female you'd ever seen in your life?"

Joseph shook his head. "No, I can't rightly say I have. Pregnant women mostly just look swollen up and awkward, if you ask me."

"Same here. I'd never seen a pregnant woman I thought was beautiful until Caitlin was big and pregnant with Little Ace. And then, let me tell you, my eyes were opened. In my opinion, she'll never be more beautiful than she was during the last weeks of her pregnancy. I think she's gorgeous now. Don't get me wrong. But she was flat *beautiful* then. Sometimes I'd look at her and get tears in my eyes."

Joseph saw a suspicious gleam of wetness in his brother's eyes even now. Old boots and pregnant women? A part of Joseph just didn't get it, but another part of him—the part in his heart that hurt at the thought of leaving Rachel—sort of understood.

"I don't want to hurt her," he told his brother. "You know what I'm saying? Before I say a word to her, I need to be absolutely sure that my feelings for her are real and lasting."

"You're a good man, Joseph. And knowing you as I do, it's my guess that you wouldn't be wrestling with all these questions if you didn't love the girl. That's part of it, you know, never wanting to cause her pain. When that becomes one of your biggest concerns, you're usually already gone coon."

Later that same afternoon when Joseph was riding in from a tour of Rachel's land, he encountered David on the road that led up to the house.

"Hey, big brother," David called. "What're you doing out here? I thought you had to stay close to Rachel."

"Normally do." Joseph drew Obie into a trot to ride apace with David's gelding. "Ace is spelling me for a bit. I went over to check on things at home. Then I rode the fence line over here and checked on the cattle. Darby runs fewer than twenty head, but they still require a look-see every now and again."

"How's Darby doing?" David asked.

"Chomping at the bit to be out of bed. He's looking real good. What brings you out this way in the middle of the afternoon?"

"The circuit judge came to town. He slapped Jeb Pritchard with a steep fine for shooting at us that afternoon when we rode over to his place, threatened him with a six-month jail sentence if he ever does it again, and turned the old bastard loose."

Joseph wasn't happy to hear that. "Damn it. After all we did to put the son of a bitch behind bars?"

"I hear you," David commiserated, "but once the judge rules on a case, it's out of my hands. I figured you needed to know." He gazed out across the pastureland. "Best be keeping a sharp eye out, just in case. If he's our man, he's fit to be tied right now and spoiling for trouble."

Joseph shook his head. "That's the flaw in circuit judges. They have no idea what's happening locally and make stupid rulings."

"Well, there's one bright note," David replied. "My jail smells a hell of a lot better with that old coot out of there." As they approached the house, David whistled. "You've flat been working, son. Looks to me like you've got that courtyard almost done. Before you know it, Darby will be back to full steam and you'll be free to make tracks."

"In another week, I reckon."

The knowledge that his time with Rachel was running out made Joseph feel as if a steel band were being tightened around his chest.

The last day of the courtyard wall construction, half the town showed up to add the finishing touches. Joseph had told Bubba about Rachel's list of courtyard appointments, and Bubba had passed the information on to Sue Ellen, who evidently had a habit of flapping her jaw almost as hard as she worked. Everybody and his brother seemed to know exactly what Rachel wanted, and they were hell-bent to see that she got most of it.

Bubba brought the ironwork. Sue Ellen came with a second wagon filled with cuttings from her garden. Ron and Diana Christian showed up with a beautiful bench that the sawyer had crafted after hours. In one of his rare moments of defiance against his skinflint wife, Harrison Gilpatrick arrived bearing rosebushes that he had already ordered from Sacramento for the spring planting season. Several ranchers and their wives brought yet more plants that they'd taken from their own yards. Jesse Chandler, the chimney sweep, and his wife, Dorothy, who ran the local candle shop, brought three birdhouses that he had made and she had decorated. Doc Halloway contributed a birdbath that he claimed he never used.

Joseph was overwhelmed by his neighbors' generosity. "Thank you. Thank you so much."

The responses Joseph received all rang with one common note, a generosity of spirit that nearly brought tears to his eyes: "It's nothing." "It's our pleasure." "We just pray she can come out and enjoy the sunlight." He only wished Rachel could find the courage to open her door and personally thank everyone.

But that was wishing for too much. She had already come a long way in a very short time. Having so many people in her dooryard was probably terrifying for her. Fortunately, no one had arrived with any expectations. They'd come to work, and work they did. After the ironwork was laid out over the enclosure, everyone helped lay the final tier of rock to anchor the bars. The bolts to the garden gate were set right into the concrete, making the stout barrier of iron as close to being impenetrable as the rock to which it was attached.

The women worked within the enclosure on the aesthetic aspects of the courtyard. One of them came up with the idea of building small corner shelters atop the wall for nesting robins. Stepping-stones were laid out to wind through the flowers. Bubba's burly son, Eugene, dug a small pond—Sue Ellen's idea, in lieu of a fountain—and Charley Banks lined it with mortar and rock to hold water. Garrett Buckmaster donated some goldfish from his own fishpond. Clarissa Denny, the dressmaker, supplied the fish food, purchased at the general store. Beatrice Masterson, the milliner, brought strips of sod from her own lawn to add small sections of green grass. Shelby Templeton, the cobbler, and his wife, Penny, brought a sapling oak.

When all was done, Joseph teared up, an embarrassing moment for a man who'd always kept his emotions under tight rein. Caitlin hugged his arm and patted his chest. "It is beautiful, isn't it?"

Joseph had such a lump in his throat he could only nod. It was early in the season yet, so only the violets and crocus were in bloom, but the women had managed to make it look like an established garden, equal to anything Joseph had ever seen in San Francisco. It went beyond beautiful. Every inch of that courtyard had been created with loving and caring hands.

Ace saved Joseph the need to speak. "As you all can see, my brother is struck speechless, and well he should be. This is, beyond a doubt, the prettiest little garden I've ever seen. Miss Rachel is going to love it." Ace motioned toward the closed door. "She's got a peephole, you know. I'm sure she's peeking out even as I speak. This is a beautiful gift. There are no words to thank all of you."

The courtyard was so packed with people that Joseph feared the newly transplanted flowers might be trampled. Everyone stepped carefully, though. Sue Ellen White smiled and waved at the door. "Hello, Rachel! Joseph did most of the work, but we hope you enjoy the little things we've added."

Others called out as well, saying they also had contributed very little but hoped she could enjoy the enclosure.

* * *

Rachel collapsed on a chair at the table and sobbed her heart out. All those people! For so many years, she'd felt alienated from everyone in town, convinced that they all thought her insane. To have them band together like this to give her an outdoor garden touched her so deeply that she had no words. She hadn't been forgotten, after all. They simply hadn't known how to help her.

She was still weeping when she heard the wagons begin to pull out. Soon she heard footsteps inside the house. She tried to dry her eyes, but the tears just kept coming.

A knock sounded on the archway door. "Rachel, open up, darlin'."

She didn't want Joseph to see her like this. Oh, *God*. It felt as if her heart was breaking, only for happiness. He knocked again.

"Sweetheart, don't do this to me. I can't get in."

She scrubbed at her cheeks again. "I'm c-coming."

"Why are you crying?" he called. "Have you seen that beautiful courtyard?"

Stifling her sobs, she went to the archway, opened the door, and then struggled to insert the key into the lock with shaking hands. The instant the iron barrier was unlatched, Joseph swept into the room. He took the key from her and locked up after himself. Then he closed and barred the wooden door.

"What is this?" He tucked the key back into her skirt pocket and drew her into his arms. "Don't cry, sweetheart. You should be happy."

It felt so wonderful to be held by him again. Over the last two weeks, he'd scarcely touched her—only an occasional, accidental brush of their fingertips, and he'd absolutely refused to sleep in her water closet anymore.

"Oh, Joseph, it's s-so b-beautiful."

"And that's to cry about?"

He cupped the back of her head in a big, hard hand. Rachel pressed her face into the lee of his shoulder and savored the feeling. She wished the moment might last forever, that he'd never pull away and leave her feeling alone again. He drew her over to the sofa and sat with her still held in his arms.

"Enough, darlin'. I hate it when you cry."

Rachel took a shuddering breath. Then she closed her eyes and sank against him. She loved having his well-muscled body curled partly around her, loved resting her cheek against his heat. She could hear his heartbeat, a strong and sturdy *thump-thump-thump* that was reassuringly rhythmic and even, not thready and erratic like her own.

They sat in silence for a long while, and then he gently set her away from him. "I'm sorry," he said huskily, "but if we stay close much longer, I'll do something we may both regret."

Rachel didn't believe that she would ever regret anything that happened between them. He lived by rules that were important in his world but weren't in hers. She ran a hand over his ribbed chest, pleasuring herself just by touching him. He caught her wrist and shook his head.

"Please don't," he said thickly. "I'm hanging on by a thin thread as it is."

Rachel didn't want him to hang on. "Darby will

come home soon, and you'll leave," she whispered. "Is it so wrong for me to want this time with you, so wrong to want the memories only you can give me?"

His grip on her wrist tightened. "I want to give you more than memories." He took a deep breath, met her gaze with burning intensity, exhaled shakily, and said, "Will you marry me, Rachel?"

The question took her completely by surprise. She tried to free her wrist. "What?"

He kept a firm hold on her. "I spoke plain. Will you marry me?"

She shook her head mutely.

"You talk about me leaving? I don't think I can. I love you, Rachel Hollister. I want you as my wife. I want to give you my babies. I want to grow old with you."

Fresh tears sprang to Rachel's eyes. "Are you mad? I can't marry you, Joseph. What have I to offer you?"

"Everything," he said huskily. "Absolutely everything."

"I can't raise children, living as I do. What would I do, push them out through the wood safe to see them off to school?" She gestured with her free hand to encompass the kitchen. "A family can't live in one room."

"I'll remodel my place and make it one hell of a big room," he said softly. "And I'll build you another courtyard and a vestibule as well, a safe antechamber so you can look out through your bars before you let anyone into the house. The children can come and go through the garden gate."

Rachel shook her head. "No, Joseph. Children need

their own bedrooms. A family can't exist the way I live."

"Sure it can," he insisted. "The water closet is another room. That doesn't bother you. The cellar is another room. That doesn't bother you, either. We could have a regular home, Rachel, you and I together, with bedrooms for our children."

He made it sound so attainable. It was true that the water closet didn't bother her, or the cellar, either.

"I'll make it work," he whispered. "I swear to you, darlin', I can make it work. No hallways to frighten you, just a big room like this with water closets all around, only they'll be bedrooms, with you in the big room, living as you do now, never needing to go outside unless it's to sit in your courtyard or work in your flowerbeds."

The thought of leaving her kitchen and moving to his place terrified Rachel. She shook her head again. "I can't leave here, Joseph. I'm sorry. I want to be with you more than anything. But I just can't leave here."

He sighed and lifted her clenched fist to trail kisses over her knuckles. "All right, then. We'll live here. I can modify this place, adding on water closets as we have babies."

Rachel gaped at him. "But you have your own ranch."

"And the land adjoins yours. Maybe Darby would be willing to live at my place. It's only a house, Rachel. Only a piece of land. I'll sell out if I have to. What I can't do—what I absolutely can't do is go home and be apart from you. I've been wrestling with the problem for two weeks. I just can't do it, darlin'."

Fresh tears welled in Rachel's eyes. "Then don't go. Stay. We don't have to get married for you to stay."

"Oh, yes, we do," he retorted. "I have a set of standards, Rachel Hollister. We'll either do it right, or we won't do it at all."

Rachel wanted so badly to say yes. Oh, how desperately she wanted that. But the whole idea rocked her world. "I can't leave here, Joseph."

"I'm real clear on that, Rachel. I'm not asking you to leave here. I'm just asking you to make what's between us right in the eyes of God."

"But *how*? How would we even get married?"

"I'll bring the preacher here."

"Into my kitchen?"

He smiled. "You've got bars, sweetheart. He can stand in the dining room and say the words. Or we can do it in your courtyard, with him outside the garden gate. He doesn't have to be *in* your kitchen or *in* your courtyard for us to do the deed."

"What if our baby got sick?"

"I'd bring Doc out. You know Doc. Surely you trust him enough to let him inside."

Rachel did trust Doc. She focused on a button of Joseph's shirt. "I don't know. There would be so many problems, Joseph. I've never even considered the possibility of getting married."

He kissed her knuckles again. Then he forced her fingers to unfurl so he could trail the tip of his tongue over her palm. "I want you," he whispered. "I want to hold you in my arms and love on you the whole night long. It's a powerful kind of want, Rachel. So powerful that I'm not sure I'll be able to control it if I'm around you too much."

Jolts of sensation shot up Rachel's arm. With every flick of his tongue, she melted a little more. "Wh-what are you saying?"

"That you have to marry me. Otherwise, I'll have to stay away to keep from taking you." He nibbled at the base of her thumb. "I want to taste you like this all over. I'm dying, I tell you. Put me out of my misery and just say yes."

He tugged her toward him and began nibbling under her ear. Rachel's head went dizzy and her insides turned molten. Her lashes fluttered closed. She remembered how it felt when he'd kissed her breasts—how divine it was when he'd touched her in her most secret place. Her breath began to come in ragged little spurts that didn't quite reach her lungs. She wanted to experience all those feelings again more than she'd ever wanted anything.

"Oh, Joseph," she moaned.

"Say yes," he whispered urgently. "Trust me to make it all work, darlin'. It'll be perfect, I swear. Please, just say yes."

"Yes," she breathed. "Oh, yes, Joseph." She wanted him to open her shirtwaist again, to bare her breasts. "Yes, yes, yes."

He drew her into his arms, enfolding her in a fierce hug that almost crushed her bones. "You're sure?"

"Yes, oh, yes."

"Then I'll make the arrangements." He grasped her firmly by the shoulders and set her away from him. "I want it done as soon as possible. No folderol, no non-sense. We'll keep it simple and just get it done."

Rachel blinked and almost toppled off the sofa cushion. She watched in bewildered confusion as he pushed to his feet and started pacing. "We'll invite Caitlin and Ace, of course, and David, too. I know you've never met my little brother, Esa, but will you mind terribly if he comes?"

What Rachel minded was that he had left her. *Again.* She pushed at her hair, straightened her shirt-waist, and gained her feet. "I thought if I agreed to marry you that we'd—you know. If we're going to get married soon, I thought that we could finish this time."

He settled an implacable gaze on her. "We haven't even started yet. Trust me on that. And we won't, not until I've got a ring on that pretty little finger I was just kissing."

"But what harm is there in—" She broke off. "If we're going to be married, Joseph, why can't we be to-gether that way a tiny bit early?"

"Because that's putting the cart before the horse. When I make love to you, you're going to be my wife, right and proper. I won't have it any other way."

Rachel searched his expression and knew he meant it. "But *why*?"

"Because it's the Paxton way. We're going to do this properly."

She could see that arguing with him would get her nowhere. "How long will doing it properly take?"

The following morning, Joseph opened the back door wide and led Rachel to the ironwork over the opening so she could look out on her courtyard. "It's perfectly safe," he assured her. "Nothing can get in but birds, butterflies, and bugs. Do you feel up to going out there?"

Rachel wasn't sure. "Oh, Joseph, I don't know. I'm fine standing here behind the bars, but—"

"You've got more bars out there, honey." He stepped in close behind her and encircled her waist with his arms. "I'll hold you close. How's that? If you start having a problem breathing, I'll carry you back inside."

Rachel had taken to carrying both keys in her skirt pocket at all times. He loosened one arm from around her and went fishing. When he plucked out the key, she shrank against him and closed her eyes. "Wait!" she cried.

"I'm right here," he assured her. "I won't let any harm come to you, Rachel. I swear it. We'll go out to-gether. I won't turn loose of you unless you want me to."

He reached around her to insert the key into the lock. The mechanism grated loudly as it disengaged. He dropped the key back into her pocket and pushed open the ironwork. Rachel felt like a bit of flotsam being carried forth by a wave. His chest was a wall at her back, his arms like steel bands around her, his legs pushing against hers to make her feet move.

"Joseph?" she said shrilly.

"I'm right here. One little step at a time. You're okay."

They were out on the porch. Panic washed through her in cold waves. She expected her lungs to freeze.

But that didn't happen. He stopped at the steps and just held her close. She felt his heartbeat thrumming against her shoulder, felt his breath sifting through her hair to warm her scalp. She leaned weakly against him and closed her eyes, scarcely able to believe that she was outdoors and not suffocating.

"I love you," he whispered near her ear. "I love you as I never have anyone or anything. Please open your eyes, Rachel. Trust me."

She trusted him as she had never trusted anyone. She lifted her lashes. A little bluebird came down through the ironwork roof just then to light on the back of the bench. Then, with a flutter of his wings, he sailed over to the birdbath. Water flew as he dunked his head and flapped his wings. Rachel watched through a blur of tears.

"Oh, *Joseph.*"

"Pretty wonderful, huh?" Then his body went suddenly tense. "Oh, *shit.*"

"What?" Rachel glanced up and all around, but she saw nothing alarming, only thick rock walls and stout iron bars to keep everything but the smallest of creatures out. "What is it?"

"The fish. When the mortar was set, I was supposed to fill the pond and put them in. I forgot all about them. I hope the little buggers didn't freeze last night."

Rachel's heart caught. "Where are they?"

"In that can by the bench."

"Oh, the poor things." Rachel broke free of his embrace and hurried down the steps. She was halfway across the courtyard before it struck her that she was outside. Oh, God, *outside.* She staggered to a stop, frozen in her tracks. Her heart pounded violently. But nothing else happened. She could still breathe. She just felt a little dizzy and disoriented. "Joseph?"

"You're fine, sweetheart. You've got walls all around you. Look at them. Name me anything that can go through that rock."

The tension eased slowly from Rachel's body. She turned in place, looking all around, and there were walls everywhere. She let her head fall back to put her face up to the sun. The gentle warmth on her skin was beyond wonderful. She held her arms wide and turned again, filling her lungs with fresh, cool morning air. Oh, lands, it smelled so good.

She heard Joseph chuckle. She stopped spinning to face him. A smile curved her lips. She wanted to shout. She felt just that wonderful.

"Have I ever told you that you're the most gorgeous creature I've ever clapped eyes on?" he asked.

Rachel shook her head.

"Well, you are. I think I fell in love with you the first time I ever saw you."

It occurred to Rachel then that she'd never told him that she loved him back. She swallowed to steady her voice. "I love you, too, Joseph. I love you, too."

He said nothing, but that was all right because his eyes told her all she needed to know. "You gonna stand there all day or check on those poor fish?"

"Oh!" The bluebird skittered away as Rachel ran the remaining length of the courtyard. She picked up the can to peer inside. She saw a flash of orange. "They're fine," she cried. "There are three, Joseph. My goodness, they're so tiny."

"They'll grow. They're probably just babies."

"Whatever shall I feed them?"

"Clarissa Denny brought you a tin of food," he assured her. "The first order of business is to fill the pond so they've got a place to swim."

He set himself to the task of hauling water from the kitchen in a milk bucket while Rachel knelt to admire her violets. Joy creased her cheeks as she fingered the delicate purple blossoms. She'd thought never to touch a living flower petal again.

"You okay?"

"I'm fabulous. I've never been better."

After filling the pond, he set the fish loose in the water and scattered granules of food from the tin that he'd fetched from the porch. Rachel sat beside the pond to watch the fish eat. The sunlight played on the water, sparkling like diamonds. It had been so long, so very long, since she'd been outdoors.

The morning breeze drifted in through the garden gate, ruffling her hair. It carried with it scents that she'd almost forgotten—the smell of oak and pine, of grass and manzanita, and fresh air blowing in off the mountains.

"Oh, Joseph."

He sat on the garden bench, one boot propped on his opposite knee, his arms riding the top rail of the backrest. When Rachel glanced up, she knew that she'd never seen any man more handsome. When she said as much, he laughed.

"Yeah, well, you haven't seen many men in a good long while. Could be I'm homely and you just don't know it."

Rachel had more trust in her memory than that. Joseph Paxton was one good-looking fellow. She pushed to her feet and walked slowly toward him. A guarded look entered his eyes.

"Don't even think about it," he said.

Rachel stopped and put her hands on her hips. "How do you know what I'm thinking about?"

He gave her a mischievous wink. "Because I'm thinking about the same thing."

She tapped her toe on the dirt. "Are you now?"

"I am, and thinking about it is all I'm going to do."

Rachel sighed in defeat and went back to admiring her violets.

The wedding took place three days later. Joseph meant for it to be a simple affair, with only the preacher, Darby, and members of his family in attendance, but somehow the word got out that Miss Rachel, presently the most popular lady in town, was getting married, and everybody and his brother came to witness the nuptials. Taking a head count through the garden gate, Joseph saw that everyone who'd worked on the courtyard was there, plus a few extras, and they evidently meant to stay afterward to celebrate, for they'd brought sawhorses and planks to serve as makeshift tables, along with countless dishes of food.

Didn't they understand that Rachel was terrified of strangers? Joseph was afraid that the presence of so many people might force them to have the ceremony inside, and that wouldn't do. He wanted his bride to be standing outdoors in the sunlight when she gave him her hand in marriage. He thought about stepping outside to ask them all to leave but changed his mind when he saw Caitlin's redheaded brother, Patrick O'Shannessy, along with his lovely, newly pregnant wife, Faith, and their daughter, Chastity. Not all were strangers. Some were family who had reason and right to witness this wedding.

As that thought went through Joseph's mind, he saw a woman with a cane standing off by herself under the oak tree. She was dressed all in blue, her day gown mostly covered by a matching double-tiered cape. Atop her head she wore a blue Venice bonnet with a veil covering her face. Through the netting, Joseph had to stare hard to make out her delicate features. He inclined his head to her and smiled. She nodded in return. Amanda Hollister had come to attend her greatniece's wedding.

The knowledge filled Joseph with a sense of rightness that was multiplied a hundredfold when his bride emerged from the kitchen to stand on the porch. She wore a white dress that Caitlin had worked day and night to complete, a delicate, ethereal creation of satin and lace. Sunlight pooled around her like a halo. Joseph took one look at her and knew she was the most beautiful creature on God's green earth. Through the lace veil, she was smiling at him—a radiant, angelic smile made all the more brilliant by the sparkling tears on her cheeks.

A raucous clamor of bells rang out. Joseph was startled by the noise and glanced over his shoulder to find the source. Esa, shaking three cowbells, grinned from ear to ear. "I never thought I'd see this day, my brother Joseph tying the knot. We have to mark the moment."

Joseph winced. He'd been joking about ringing cowbells at Darby's wedding. What was Esa thinking? Only somehow it was the perfect touch, a dash of family craziness tossed in to make the most wonderful day of his life truly memorable. Years from now, when he remembered this moment, he would smile over Esa's idiocy.

Only his brothers weren't done. Oh, no. David unearthed his fiddle from behind the bench, Ace plucked his mouth organ from his shirt pocket, and the three of them filled the air with a blend of sour notes and clanging that sounded a little like the wedding march with church bells ringing in the background—if Joseph used his imagination.

Rachel clung to Darby's arm as he led her down the porch steps. If asked at that moment what her thoughts were, she couldn't have said. She had eyes only for Joseph, who stood waiting for her at the garden gate. In her mind, Bubba's iron bars had come to symbolize freedom and new beginnings, so it seemed fitting that Joseph should be standing in front of those bars. Joseph had made all of this happen for her, after all. Sunlight, fresh air, the scent of new violets, birdsong. He'd filled her life with so many wondrous things, and now he meant to fill it with still more—a future with him, the chance to love and be loved, and possibly to even have babies. Never had she felt so happy.

When the music began, Rachel thought it was so beautiful. *Music.* She'd heard not a single note in over five years. She moved slowly forward, taking her cues from Darby, her oldest and dearest friend, but keeping her gaze fixed on Joseph. He was so handsome. He wore a black, Western-cut suit jacket that showcased his muscular build, a black string tie dividing the starched points of his white shirt collar. Though she'd never seen him in anything but faded denim and chambray, he wore the finery with aplomb.

As Rachel drew closer to him, she glanced at his feet and almost burst out laughing. A woman might take a cowboy out of his jeans, work shirt, and Stetson, but never out of his boots. Though he had polished them up, he wore his Justins, scuff marks, gouges, and all. No spurs, thank goodness. If he accidentally dropped the ring, he might have to squat.

Through the veil, she met his gaze. The burning intensity in his blue eyes made her feel like the most loved woman on earth. Darby put Rachel's hand into Joseph's, then discreetly stepped aside to stand by Caitlin, the matron of honor. As best man, Ace stood at the other side of the gate, opposite his wife. David and Esa also stood nearby, the latter holding Little Ace.

Joseph gave Rachel's hand a gentle squeeze and placed it on the crook of his arm, his fingers resting warmly over hers. Then he turned her so they faced the gate that opened from the courtyard into the surrounding backyard. Rachel leaned closer to him, needing to feel his solid strength as they made ready to say their vows.

Hannibal St. John, No Name's new preacher, stood just outside the courtyard gate, gazing solemnly at them through the bars. He was a tall, fine figure of a man with hair almost as blond as Joseph's. His earnest blue eyes were kind and understanding, which helped soothe Rachel's sudden attack of nerves when she saw all the people gathered in the backyard behind him. *Lands.* Joseph squeezed her hand again, as if he sensed her panic. *I'm here,* that squeeze said. *Don't be afraid. I won't let anyone hurt you.*

Rachel willed the tension away and tried to focus on the preacher.

"Dearly beloved," Hannibal said in a booming voice, "we're gathered together here today . . ."

St. John went on to give a short homily on the sanctity of marriage, but Rachel scarcely registered a word. No matter. She *knew* what marriage was all about. She'd been raised in a loving family by parents who'd taught her with their everyday actions. She also had Joseph to guide her if ever she should falter. *No hallways to frighten you, just a big room like this with water closets all around.* With a husband like that, how could she fail to be a loving, selfless wife?

"Do you, Joseph Simon Paxton, wish to take this woman, Rachel Marie Hollister, to be your lawful wife?"

Joseph squeezed Rachel's hand again and turned to look at her face through the veil. "I do," he said in a loud, certain voice.

Rachel didn't hear the rest of the ceremony. Somehow she managed to repeat her vows on cue, and Joseph got the wedding band on her finger as well.

When Hannibal St. John pronounced them man and wife and then told Joseph that he could kiss his bride, Joseph lifted her veil with shaky hands, drew her into his arms, and kissed her as if tomorrow might never come. Buddy barked, casting his vote of approval. Cleveland echoed the sound. Joseph's brothers hooted, whistled, and cheered. Weeping as if at a funeral, Caitlin rushed over to hug them both.

"Congratulations!" she cried. "Oh, you make such a beautiful couple." Sob, sniff. "Our Joseph, married. I just can't believe it! Your mother will have fits when she learns it happened without her being here."

"I know," Joseph replied, "but I wasn't about to wait for her to travel all the way from San Francisco."

Rachel felt a large pair of hands settle on her shoulders, and the next thing she knew, she was being kissed by her eldest brother-in-law, the fearsome gunslinger Ace Keegan, who, she'd learned, wasn't really fearsome at all. Next, she was passed to David, who teasingly arched her back over his arm and pretended to kiss her deeply.

"Jealous, big brother?" he asked as he allowed Rachel to come upright.

"Hell, no," Joseph retorted.

Esa, who looked more like David than he did Joseph, approached Rachel shyly and thrust out his hand. "Us never meeting before this, I don't reckon it's appropriate for me to kiss the bride today."

Joseph piped in with, "If you're thinking on doing it later, little brother, you'd best think again. I'll let it pass today. Tomorrow I'll rip your ears off."

Everyone laughed. Rachel went up on her tiptoes to kiss Esa's cheek. And then she found herself facing Darby. She loved every wrinkle in his craggy old face. He drew her gently into his arms. Beneath his shirt,

Rachel could feel the bandage around his middle, so she returned his embrace with care.

He turned his nose against her hair, putting his lips just behind her ear. In a choked whisper, he said, "Be happy, little girl. That's only ever been my wish for you, that someday you might be happy."

"Oh, Darby." Rachel put her arms around his neck where she could hug him with no fear of causing him pain. "I love you so. Thank you, thank you, thank you for all that you've done for me. You're my best friend in the whole world, and you always will be."

"Not no more, sweetness. That gent over there who's now your husband will be your best friend from this moment on. He's a good man. You caught yourself a keeper."

Still hugging Darby's neck, Rachel nodded. "I did, didn't I? I can't believe how lucky I am."

"It's high time some luck came your way, darlin'. I only wish your ma and pa could be here today." He drew back to smile down at her. "They would be so proud and happy for you."

"I'm sure they are here, Darby," Rachel replied. Re-calling Joseph's sentiments on such matters, she added, "If we believe in God and a life hereafter, we have to believe that they're here. They'd never miss my wedding."

Darby grinned. "Well, now, I suppose that's right."

Joseph joined them just then. He slipped a posses-sive arm around Rachel's waist. "All my brothers just informed me that they'll be standing in line to kick my ass if I don't treat this lady right," he informed Darby. "Are you gonna threaten me next?"

Darby chuckled. "Nah, I'll leave the ass-kickin' to them. I'm gettin' too old for all that shit."

Joseph smiled and shook the old foreman's hand. "I thank you for giving her away, Darby. You're like a father to her, so that was fitting."

Ace moseyed over to them. He curled a big hand over Darby's shoulder. "Good to see you back on your feet, old friend."

Darby pursed his lips and gave his head a partial shake. "It was touch and go there for a bit. But I'm on the mend now, for sure." He angled a glance at the garden gate, then arched an eyebrow at Rachel. "How do I get out of here, darlin'? There's a lady out there I want to say howdy to."

Joseph knew to which lady the old foreman referred. "I'll let you out through the house. Rachel might have trouble breathing if we open the gate."

Darby nodded. "Nobody knows about that better than me." He bent to kiss Rachel's cheek. "I'll be back shortly, little girl."

Using the key that Rachel had left on the kitchen table, Joseph made fast work of showing Darby out. When he returned to the courtyard, he found his bride, slipped an arm around her waist again, and raised his voice to tell his brothers, "The show's over now, everybody. You can all go home."

Moans and groans followed that announcement. Little Ace grabbed Joseph's pant leg, chortling and grinning as if to say the fun had just begun.

"My sentiments exactly," the child's father called across the garden. "The party's just started. Until we're all good and ready to leave, you can just suffer."

"Oh, boy," Joseph said under his breath to Rachel. "All I want is for everyone to go so we can—"

"Hey, big brother!" David interrupted, jostling Joseph half off his feet with a shoulder jab. "Have a snort." He passed a jug under Joseph's nose. "I want to drink to your happy future."

"No, thanks. I want to keep a clear head," Joseph replied.

"Say what? It's your wedding day." David gave Rachel an imploring look. "Tell him, sis. He's supposed to celebrate."

"You're supposed to celebrate," Rachel informed her groom, pleased as could be that David had just called her sis. "One drink won't hurt."

Joseph sighed and took the jug. After taking a swallow, he passed it back to his brother. "There. I've celebrated."

Only Joseph's brothers hadn't finished with him yet. Ace approached next, insisting that Joseph have a celebratory drink with him. Next came Esa, and then the rotation began all over again. Several snorts later, Joseph had stopped arguing when the jug was passed to him, and Rachel thought he looked a mite too happy. He had doffed his suit jacket, the tie had vanished, and he'd unfastened the white dress shirt to midchest, revealing golden curls and a wealth of bronze skin rippling with muscle that made her want to call the party to a halt herself.

The next thing Rachel knew, a sawhorse table appeared in her courtyard and Caitlin was busy setting out food. Rachel suspected that someone had opened the gate when she wasn't watching, for the sawhorses hadn't been there during the wedding ceremony and none of the dishes belonged to her. She could only assume that they'd been brought by the women from town, who couldn't have passed them in to Caitlin through the bars.

Before Rachel could obsess overlong about someone unlocking her gate, David started playing his fiddle and someone outside joined in with a guitar. Joseph grabbed Rachel around the waist and began swirling her across the garden.

"Joseph, *no*," she cried. "I don't know how."

"Just move with me," he said. "Just let go and move with me."

Rachel looked up at his dark face, then into his sky blue eyes, and she loved him so much that she couldn't possibly refuse. So she let go, just as he'd asked, and danced with him.

Despite the chill in the air after the sun went down, the party went on until long after dark. Lanterns were lighted, both inside the courtyard and out, those outside hung from tree limbs and wagon tailgates to illuminate the area. It had been so long since Rachel had needed a wrap that she couldn't recall where she'd stowed her cape. To keep her warm, Joseph draped a wool blanket around her shoulders.

"I love you," he whispered.

Rachel doubted she would ever tire of hearing him tell her that. "I love you, too."

He leaned down to kiss her, whispering against her lips, "They'll leave soon. I promise."

Rachel couldn't help but laugh. "I don't mind their staying. It's been a lovely party."

"And they're dragging it out just to torture me," he tacked on. "Brothers. You can't live with 'em, and you can't live without 'em."

"I saw that!" David yelled. "No more of that stuff until we leave."

Joseph laughed and straightened away to look at David. "We were just talking."

"Yeah, right."

When Joseph wandered away to speak with someone, Caitlin sidled up to Rachel, cleared her throat nervously, and said, "It suddenly occurred to me that your mother died when you were quite young."

"Yes." Rachel looked up through the bars at the sky, fancying that her parents were up there somewhere, drifting among the stars, looking down. "I had just turned seventeen."

"Oh, *dear*." Caitlin toyed with the buttons of her dress. "Would you mind stepping inside with me for a few minutes? I think we should have a little talk."

Joseph was chatting with Darby when he realized as he scanned the courtyard that his bride had vanished. He excused himself to go in search of her. When he stepped up onto the porch, he saw that the wooden door was closed. When he tried to open it, the thing wouldn't budge.

"Damn." He rapped his knuckles against the oak. "Rachel, you all right in there?"

Her faint reply was, "I'm fine. Caitlin and I are just having a little talk."

"About what?"

"Just things."

Just *things*? Joseph wondered about that.

"What's wrong, little brother?"

Joseph turned a pensive frown on Ace, who stood on the top step behind him. "Rachel and your wife have barricaded themselves off in the kitchen. Rachel says they're having a little talk."

"About what?"

"Rachel said, 'Just *things*,'" Joseph replied.

"Uh-oh." Ace stepped up onto the porch. "Caitlin?" he called through the door. "Can I talk to you for a minute, sweetie?"

"Not right this moment," Caitlin called back. "Rachel and I are having a talk."

"Shit," Ace said.

"What?" Joseph asked.

"They're having a little *talk*," Ace echoed unnecessarily.

"I know that much. What the hell's so important that they've got to hide in the kitchen and talk about it right now?"

Ace sighed and pinched the bridge of his nose. "Wedding night stuff, I'm guessing. And trust me when I say that Caitlin isn't the one to prepare your wife for her first bedding."

Joseph shot a worried look at the door. "She isn't?"

Ace leaned close so their noses were only inches apart. "Do you remember how long it took me to get that girl into bed?"

Joseph remembered Ace being as grumpy as a bear with a sore paw for weeks on end. After Ace got the problem settled, Joseph also remembered having to sit in the barn at crazy times of the day, unable to enter the house because the ropes of Ace's bed were creaking and the headboard was doing a double shuffle against the wall.

"I remember it being a tough time, but it all came right between you in the end."

"It came right between Caitlin and me, Joseph, but her first experience was a nightmare. She was *raped*, remember? Trust me when I say she isn't the person to tell Rachel what her first time is going to be like."

Joseph saw his point. He hooked a thumb at the door. "Well, get her out of there, then. Rachel's fine as things stand. *Eager*, in fact. I don't need Caitlin filling her head with horror stories."

"She won't. Caitlin has a kind heart. She's just liable to paint a pretty grim picture of how bad the virgin pain is."

Joseph pounded on the door again. To his brother, he said, "God damn it, Ace. She's your wife. Get her away from mine before she causes all kinds of grief."

"How?"

"How what?" Joseph asked, impatience lending an edge to his question.

"How do you expect me to get her out of there?" Ace expounded.

"Tell her to come out. Just put your foot down for once. You wear the pants in the family."

Ace arched his eyebrows. "That isn't how it works. It's true that I wear the pants, but Caitlin wears the drawers. If I want in to them, I don't strut around like I'm the boss, issuing orders to her."

"Make an exception this one time. It's my wedding night."

Ace pounded on the door again. "Caitlin, sweetheart, Little Ace is crying and I can't make him stop."

Joseph rolled his eyes. "That is *so* weak. I can't believe it. My big, tough brother can't assert himself with a woman half his size."

They heard the bar lift. Ace smiled. "Worked, didn't it?"

The door opened and Caitlin appeared. When she saw her son happily romping with Buddy and Cleveland in the courtyard, she sent her husband a questioning look. "I thought you said he was crying."

"He suddenly stopped." Ace shrugged. "You know how little boys are, crying one minute, happy as bugs the next."

Rachel exited onto the porch after her sister-in-law. Joseph half expected her to give him an accusing glare, but instead she only smiled secretively and stepped close to hug his arm.

Joseph patted her hand. He felt the curve of her hip pressing against his and the soft warmth of her breast against his arm. The delicate scent of roses curled around him like tendrils of silk. God, how he wanted her. The need was so intense he ached.

He wished the public celebration would end soon so the private one could start.

Chapter Sixteen

W hen all their guests had left, Rachel and Joseph adjourned to the kitchen, leaving Buddy outside in the courtyard. Rachel was a whole lot more nervous than she had expected to be. Caitlin, whose husband was wealthy, had given her a gorgeous gossamer negligee to wear tonight, one she'd ordered for herself but hadn't yet worn. It fell in voluminous folds to tease a man's eye.

Joseph strode slowly toward her. "What did Caitlin talk to you about?"

Rachel released a shaky breath. "About how wonderful tonight will be."

He gave her a dubious look. "And nothing else?"

Rachel shrugged. "She warned me that it may hurt dreadfully for a moment."

His eyes darkened with concern. "Are you worried about it?"

Rachel considered the question. "Not unduly. Caitlin assured me that after the first bit of pain, it's like dying and going to heaven if you're with the right man." She reached up to press her fingertips to his jaw. "You are definitely the right man, Joseph. I love you so much it pains me."

He dipped his head to kiss her palm. "And I love you so much that if this hurts you, it's going to half kill me."

"I know." And Rachel truly did. Joseph was nothing if not caring about her feelings. Indeed, she felt that he understood her better than anyone ever had. "And I can't imagine that it will be that bad. If it were, no one would ever go back for seconds."

A twinkle slipped into his eyes. "Do I hear an echo?"

Rachel recalled his warning to her after they'd shared their first kiss, that he wasn't the marrying kind, preferring instead to flit from woman to woman. She giggled. "Ah, yes, the buffet man. Sadly for you, you're now tied down to one lady."

"And happy to be tied down. I never thought it'd happen, but now that it has, I'm looking forward to seconds"—he nibbled at the inside of her wrist—"and thirds"—he trailed kisses along the cuff of her sleeve—"and fourths, and fifths. I'll never tire of you."

All the folds of gossamer weren't concealing, after all. Horrified, Rachel couldn't lift her chin and stop gaping at herself. The gown was as transparent as glass. She could see her bosoms, her belly button, her nether regions, and even the freckle on her knee. What on *earth* had Caitlin been thinking? Rachel couldn't leave the water closet wearing this.

"Is everything all right in there?"

Rachel almost jumped out of her skin. The door still wasn't fixed, and propping it up over the opening left cracks, which she'd taken to covering with linen towels. It sounded as if Joseph was standing right outside.

"Caitlin bought me a special negligee for tonight," she confessed, "and I thought it was lovely until I put it on."

"What's wrong with it?"

"It's just—" Rachel couldn't think how to describe it. "It *isn't*."

"It isn't what?"

"It just *isn't*. Imagine if I stood naked behind glass, and there you have it."

"Hmm."

"I can't wear this, Joseph. It'd be *too* embarrassing."

"Then don't."

"I didn't bring another gown in with me."

She heard his boots thumping. Then came the scrape of a drawer opening. A moment later, he pushed a white Mother Hubbard through to her. Rachel hugged it gratefully to her breasts. "Thank you."

"You're welcome, darlin'. And no matter about the nightgown. I don't care what you wear."

Rachel sighed dreamily. To please him, perhaps she could wear the negligee, after all.

Joseph had resumed his seat at the table and, as was his habit, had rocked back on the chair to straighten his legs and cross his ankles. He had just finished stretching and folded his arms behind his head to flex and roll his shoulders when Rachel finally emerged from the water closet.

She wore nothing but a see-through shimmer of soft stuff that made her completely nude body look as if kissed with morning dew. His startled gaze dropped to her beautiful, rose-tipped breasts and then trailed in stunned amazement to the dark gold thatch of curls at the apex of her shapely thighs. His breath whooshed from his chest like air from a bellows, his entire body snapped taut, and somehow the teetering chair got away from him.

Just like that, over he went, hitting the floor so hard that it rattled his brains.

"Joseph?"

A vision of gossamer scurried across the room to stand over him.

"Oh, lands, are you all right?"

Joseph gaped at the pretty little breasts dangling and bouncing above his nose as she leaned over to look down at him.

"Sweet Christ," he said stupidly.

Hands aflutter, she knelt beside him. "Did you hit your head? Are you injured?"

Joseph couldn't rightly say if he was injured. He only knew one part of him was in fine working order. He rolled toward her to get free of the chair, hooked an arm around her neck to pull her to the floor, and straddled her hips as he came to his knees. "My God, you're beautiful. You are so damned beautiful."

Her cheeks went pink as he slid his gaze over her breasts. "This isn't fair. You're fully clothed. I want to see you, too."

That was a request Joseph could deliver on. Buttons went flying as he jerked off his shirt, the tiny mother-of-pearl disks going *tick-tick-tick* as they struck the floor. He tossed aside the shirt and braced his arms to lean over her. His whole body jerked when she trailed her slender fingers over his chest.

"Oh, Joseph, you're pretty, too."

Pretty wasn't a word he would have chosen to describe himself, but coming from her, it would do.

With the first kiss, Rachel forgot all about feeling shy. *Silken caresses of lips and tongues.* Being in Joseph's arms eclipsed all her worries, allowing her to focus only on the sensations that his mouth, hands, and hard body evoked within her. He was lantern light and shadows, his sculpted torso gleaming in the amber illumination like burnished oak.

At some point, he swept her up into his arms and carried her to the bed, where he proceeded to make love to her just as he did all else: straightforwardly, thoroughly, and masterfully. She wasn't sure when he peeled her negligee away, only that he replaced the tease of netting with his hands and mouth, touching and kissing her in places she'd never dreamed he might, until her body quivered with delight and throbbed with need.

When he trailed his lips down her torso and settled his hot mouth over her secret place, she was too far over the edge to feel embarrassed, and soon his clever ministrations obliterated every rational thought in her mind. With every sweep of his tongue, her body jerked and quivered, a hot, electrical, urgent ache building within her until she arched upward, frantically seeking release.

With a fierce growl, he gave her what she sought with harder, quickening flicks of his tongue until the throbbing ache inside her shattered like thin glass, shooting shards of sheer ecstasy all over her body.

"Joseph?" Disoriented and suddenly uncertain, Rachel reached for him as he drew away to kick off his boots and remove his trousers. "Don't go."

"Not on your life, darlin'." He returned to her then, kneeling between her parted thighs. When their gazes met, she saw his concern for her beneath the glaze of passion in his eyes. "You're as ready as I can get you, sweetheart. If this hurts too much, just tell me, and I swear I'll stop."

Rachel wasn't worried. No matter how much it might hurt this first time, she wanted it over with so he would never have that worried look in his eyes again.

"Just do it," she whispered.

He slowly nudged himself into her, and Rachel did indeed feel pain. She clenched her teeth and clutched at his muscular shoulders, braced for the invasion. Only it didn't come.

"I'm hurting you," he whispered raggedly. He started to withdraw. "I can't do this."

Rachel locked her bent legs around him and bucked forward with her hips to finish it herself. Pain exploded through her. It hurt so much that it fairly took her breath.

"Oh, *shit*." Joseph gathered her into his arms. His body was shaking, shaking horribly. "Oh, sweetheart. Why did you do that?"

She'd done it because he couldn't. Tears stung Rachel's eyes. He would have stopped rather than cause her pain. That told her how very much he loved her, as words never could. And the pain was receding now, becoming more a dull ache than an actual hurting.

"It's better now, Joseph." She trailed kisses along his jaw. "Make love to me. Make me feel as if I've died and gone to heaven."

He pushed up on his arms and moved tentatively within her. "How's that?"

Rachel's breath caught at the sensations that darted through her. "Good, very good."

He thrust with more force, magnifying the delight. "Oh, *yes,* Joseph, *yes!*"

Joseph had never felt so drained in his life. His bride was an insatiable bed partner. Not that he was complaining. Holding her close, he lay on his side, facing the kitchen. Her soft, naked bottom was nestled against Old Glory, who'd given up the ghost and didn't stir even when she wiggled. Joseph tried to remember how many times they'd made love over the course of the night. One time blended together with another, creating a glorious blur in his mind. He could only say with certainty that he'd loved her well and thoroughly.

The kitchen looked as if a storm had come along and rained clothing. He smiled and buried his face in Rachel's curls. Oh, how he loved her. Never in all his life had he imagined himself capable of loving anyone this much. She was so wonderful—and so brave—

and so openly honest about her feelings. *I want to see you, too.* How many virgin brides faced their first bedding with such enthusiasm? *Oh, Joseph, you're pretty, too.* Was it any wonder he loved the girl?

Exhaustion settled over Joseph like a black blanket. He gave himself up to it, moving from consciousness into sweet, rose-scented dreams.

When Joseph awakened some time later, Rachel had left the bed. As he sat up, he realized that the day had long since dawned, the porch door was flung wide, and the ironwork was hanging open. He slipped from bed, drew on his trousers, and padded barefoot to the doorway. The sight that greeted his sleepy gaze— Rachel, strolling barefoot about the garden, wearing nothing but the gossamer gown—nearly took his breath away.

Weeks ago, he had tried to picture how she might look in her courtyard, but his imagination had failed him on two counts. The garden was far prettier than he had envisioned, and the woman in it was even more beautiful. Her hair fell in a glorious cloud of golden curls to her narrow waist. Her body could have been sculpted in ivory.

Mesmerized by her, Joseph moved out onto the porch. She gave a tinkling laugh when she saw him. "Come look, Joseph. We have a rosebud."

The only rosebuds he was interested in were at the tips of her breasts, but he obediently followed the path of stepping-stones until he reached her side. After giving the rosebush due attention, he caught his wife around the waist and kissed her. She melted against him in eager surrender, then stiffened slightly and glanced uneasily around the courtyard.

"I'm not sure this is the place for this. I feel self-conscious."

Joseph nibbled the silken slope of her neck. "No need for that. Except for Buddy, it's completely private here." He skimmed his hands up her sides to cup her breasts and then lifted them to his searching lips. "Ah, Rachel, you're so beautiful."

She moaned and arched her spine. "Joseph?"

"It's all right. Trust me," he whispered.

She moaned again, and by the sound, he knew that he had won. He proceeded to make love to her in the sunlight on a patch of new grass—and then on the porch—and then on the kitchen table.

A man needed breakfast, after all.

Darby remained at Eden for a week after the wedding to give the newlyweds privacy, and Joseph made the most of each day. Because he couldn't take Rachel anywhere for their honeymoon, their activities were limited. They talked, they ate, they completed the few chores that they absolutely had to, and then they spent the rest of the time doing what they enjoyed most, making love.

Rachel continued to surprise Joseph with her unabashed enjoyment of physical intimacy. Most ladies in his acquaintance adhered to strict rules of social conduct that he suspected followed them to the bedroom. Such was not the case with Rachel. Joseph didn't know if it was because she'd been sequestered for so long, or if she simply possessed a free spirit. He only knew she never said no to anything.

One evening, upon request, she happily cooked his supper while wearing nothing but her apron. That ended with the meat scorching. Not that either of them cared about eating when the meal was finished. Another evening, they bet articles of the clothing they were wearing while playing poker. When Rachel lost her drawers to Joseph, he threw in his hand.

In all Joseph's life, he couldn't recall a time when he'd laughed so much. If ever he'd had doubts about getting married, they vanished during that week. Rachel was his companion, his wife, his lover, and his confidante. He loved to hear her giggle. He loved listening to the inflections of her voice when she read to him. He loved watching the myriad expressions that entered and left her beautiful blue eyes while they conversed about any subject. In short, he just loved the girl. She was everything he could have wanted in a woman, and she made him feel complete, as if he'd found the other half of himself. Even better, he knew that Rachel felt the same way. They were meant for each other, plain and simple.

Darby's appearance at the garden gate on Monday morning, a week and one day after their wedding, marked the end of Rachel and Joseph's honeymoon, but Joseph didn't expect it to end their happiness. While Rachel stayed in the kitchen behind her bars, Joseph let the old foreman into the courtyard, patted him on the shoulder, and invited him to join them for breakfast.

"That'd be good," Darby said as they followed the

stepping-stones to the porch. "I have some news to share."

"What kind of news?" Rachel beamed a smile through the ironwork as she inserted a key into the lock. Pushing the bars wide, she beckoned Darby inside. "Something wonderful, I hope."

Darby swept off his hat and nodded. "I think so. I ain't so sure how you're gonna feel about it."

Rachel's smile faltered. She wore a pink shirtwaist tucked into a gray skirt with organ-pipe pleats at the back. Joseph suspected what Darby was about to say, and a premonition of doom came over him like a gray cloud.

"You're leaving," Rachel said softly. It wasn't really a question. The sadness in her eyes bespoke certainty. "Oh, Darby, not because I'm married, surely. You'll always be welcome here."

Darby slapped his hat against his leg. "I know that, honey. This isn't about me feelin' unwelcome. It's about me havin' a life of my own. You've got a husband to love you and look after you now. I'm not needed here like I used to be. I'm finally free to do other things and go where the wind takes me."

Rachel nodded. And then she smiled just a little too brightly. "Of *course*." She clamped a hand over the swirl of braid atop her head. "Oh, of *course*, Darby. How selfish of me. I never thought. I just never thought. Have you found another job, then?"

Joseph wanted to gather Rachel up into his arms and shield her from what Darby was about to tell her, but the rational side of him realized that he couldn't protect her from everything.

"Not another job, exactly, although it will mean me workin' somewhere else." Darby's larynx bobbed. "There's a lady I've loved for a good many years, and I've asked her to be my wife. I know it's a little late in life for me to be tyin' the knot, but I'm gonna get hitched anyhow."

Rachel's mouth formed an O of surprise. Then all the clouds of regret vanished from her eyes. She clapped her slender hands, laughed with absolute gladness, and threw her arms around Darby's neck.

"Married? Oh, Darby, that's so lovely. And it's never too late! I'm so happy for you, so very happy! Joseph, did you hear? Darby's in love."

"I heard," Joseph replied solemnly. He thrust out a hand to the foreman. "Congratulations, Darby. I'm happy as I can be for you. I truly am."

Rachel loosened her arms from around Darby's neck and fairly danced in front of him. "Who is she? Tell me all about her. Is she pretty? Is she good enough for you? When did you meet her?"

Darby moistened his lips. Then he shot a look at Joseph. "I met her years ago, honey, long before you were ever born. As for whether she's pretty or not, I think she's beautiful, and that's all that counts."

Rachel's smile faded again. "You don't act very happy about it, Darby."

He sighed and smoothed a gnarled hand over his hair. "That's because I'm afraid the news is gonna hurt you, and you gotta know I'd never hurt you for anything."

"That's just silly. I'm delighted for you. Why would the news hurt me?"

"Because the woman I plan to marry is your aunt Amanda."

All the color drained from Rachel's face.

"I'm sorry, honey. I know you've got hard feelings toward her. I'm not sure why, but there it is. You've got a right to your feelings, just like I've got a right to mine."

Rachel swayed on her feet. Joseph stepped in close to grasp her arm.

"Amanda," she whispered. "You're going to marry Amanda Hollister?"

"I've waited well over half my life to be with her," Darby replied. "I'm an old man, and time's runnin' out. Forgive me, little girl. I know you're gonna hate me for it."

Rachel squeezed her eyes closed. "Never that, Darby. Never that."

"For the last five years, I've made all my choices for you," the foreman went on. "I don't regret a single minute, mind you. Please don't be thinkin' that. But now that you have Joseph, I can make some choices for myself. I hope you can find it in your heart to understand."

Rachel wrapped her trembling hands around Joseph's arm as if she needed his strength to support her weight. "I do understand, Darby. You've given five years of your life to me. I shan't begrudge you a chance at happiness, no matter who it's with."

Darby's green eyes filled. He nodded and looked out through the ironwork at the garden. "I'll be stayin' on here for about a week, if that's okay. If you'd rather

I didn't, I can sleep in Amanda's barn until our nuptials."

Rachel's nails dug into Joseph's arm. "This is your home, Darby McClintoch. You can remain here however long you wish."

Darby left without joining them for breakfast. The tension in the air was so thick it could have been eaten with a spoon. Rachel sank down on a chair at the table, braced her arms, and covered her face with her hands. Joseph sat across from her.

"I'm sorry, sweetheart." It was all he could think to say.

She didn't look up. "I want him to be happy," she said in a strained voice. "I truly do, Joseph. Only why must it be with *her*?"

Joseph chose his words carefully. "Can you tell me why you hate her so?"

She shook her head.

"There has to be a reason, darlin'." Joseph sincerely believed that. Rachel had such a loving and caring heart. He couldn't envision her hating anyone without good cause. "There just has to be."

"My dreams," she whispered raggedly. "It's something in my dreams. She was behind it. I know it. I just don't know for sure *how* I know it."

"Can you tell me about your dreams? Maybe if we talk about them, maybe if you can describe to me what you see in them, we can come up with some answers."

Long silence. Then, "*Blood*. I see *blood*. Everywhere, Joseph, everywhere. On the grass. On Denver's yellow fur." Her shoulders jerked. "Tansy's pink dress, drenched in blood. And Ma. Oh, *God*. Oh, *God*. No face. Pa's p-playing his fiddle, and she's d-dancing over the grass, laughing and smiling at him. But then she has no face."

Joseph's stomach rolled. "You mentioned once that you see Denver leaping up to bite the man's leg, and that the man pulls his revolver and shoots him between the eyes. What else do you see, sweetheart? Picture his boot. Picture his leg. Is there anything special about the gun—or possibly the saddle? If you see his leg, if you see his hand holding the gun, you must see other things."

No answer. Joseph studied her bent head for a long moment. Then he sighed. "If it's this painful for you, honey, just let it go."

Still no reply. A cold, itchy sensation inched up Joseph's spine. "Rachel?"

She didn't move. Concerned, Joseph reached across the table and drew her hands from her face. Her lashes fluttered open, but even though she appeared to be looking at him, she didn't seem to see him.

"Rachel?" he whispered.

Nothing. He looked deeply into her eyes, searching for any sign that she heard him. It was as if everything within her had been snuffed out.

"Oh, Jesus."

Joseph carried his wife to the sofa and sat with her cradled in his arms. Morning came and went, and still Rachel didn't move or speak. She just lay there against him, limp, eyes open but unseeing, not hearing when he spoke to her. As the hours dragged by, Joseph began to fear that she might never return to herself.

His fault. He'd pushed her into thinking of that day. He'd forced her to describe what she saw in her dreams. Her mother, without a face. He closed his eyes, so sorry for pressuring her that he ached.

It was nearly three o'clock in the afternoon when Rachel finally stirred. Pushing against his chest, she sat straight, stretched as if she'd just awakened from a long nap, and beamed a smile at him.

"My goodness. How long have I been asleep?"

Joseph glanced at the clock. "For a bit." Over nine hours, to be exact.

"Lands, just look at the time. I should have made bread today." She swung off his lap. "It's far too late for that now, Joseph. Will cornbread do for supper?"

Joseph's body was cramped from sitting still for so long. He worked his arms to get the achy cricks out, his gaze fixed on his wife. She didn't seem to recall their discussion, leading him to wonder if she even recollected Darby's news. If so, she gave no sign of it. Humming the wedding march, she tied on her apron and hurried about the kitchen.

"I am *so* hungry. I'd swear I had no lunch."

Or breakfast, either. A cold, crawling fear moved through Joseph. Rachel was not only hiding behind walls, but also behind memory loss. He'd never known anyone who could simply erase unpleasant memories from her mind, but that seemed to be what she was doing.

He wanted to confront her, to ask what she recalled of the morning. But fear held his tongue. What if he upset her and she went away from him again? Even worse, what if she stayed away next time? Joseph had heard of people going into trances. Sometimes they never came right again. He loved Rachel too much to take that chance.

And so he pretended with her that the events of the morning had never happened.

That evening when Joseph left the house to do chores, he went looking for Darby and found the old fellow resting in the bunkhouse.

"I still tire easy," Darby explained as he swung his legs off the bed and finger-combed his hair. "Do a little bit, then I gotta sleep."

"You lost a lot of blood, and you're still not completely healed yet." Joseph made a mental note not to allow Darby to overdo it during the week he planned to remain there. "Something happened up at the house this morning, partner. You and I need to talk."

Darby gave him a questioning look. Joseph briefly explained about his conversation with Rachel and how she'd blinked out on him when his questions upset her. "I don't think she remembers any of it," Joseph said in conclusion. "Not our talk—or your news about marrying Amanda."

"I'll be." Darby shook his head. "That's beyond strange."

It was the strangest thing Joseph had ever witnessed, and it made him scared to death of losing his wife. "I'm thinking it might be best if you don't make any further mention of your marriage."

Darby sighed and pushed to his feet. "I can't for the

life of me understand what's going on in that girl's head. Amanda still loves her with all her heart. She came to your wedding, hiding behind a veil."

"I know. I saw her there, Darby."

"It's so sad. She'd give anything to hug that girl and cuddle her up. How did Rachel get it into her head that Amanda was behind the killings?"

Joseph had no idea, and he was coming to accept that he never might. He also realized that his first loyalty had to be with his wife. "I know that it'll pain Amanda that I've asked this, but when next you see her, please tell her that I don't want her coming around here again, veil or no. If Rachel were to recognize her—well, I just don't know how she might react. That trance she was in today scared the bejesus out of me. I never want it to happen again."

The following morning when Joseph went out to milk the cows and feed the stock, he found Darby in the barn, saddling up his gelding, Poncho.

"Where are you off to so early?" Joseph asked.

"Thought I'd ride fence line," the old foreman replied. "Maybe count cows if I don't tucker out before I get around to it."

Joseph hadn't been out to check on the cattle since his marriage. The livestock grazed for feed and had water aplenty, so during his honeymoon he'd let them fare for themselves. "How about trading jobs with me? That's a lot of fence line to ride."

"It is, at that, but I'm no invalid, son."

"I never meant to imply that," Joseph replied. "But those cows are my worry now. If you'll stick close to the house to keep an eye on Rachel, I'll be happy to get out for a while, truth to tell."

"All right, then."

Darby started to loosen the saddle cinch. Joseph brushed the old man's hands aside and handed him the milk bucket.

"I can lift my own saddle," Darby protested.

"Never thought for a minute that you couldn't." Joseph quickly swept the saddle from Poncho's back and settled it over a stall rail. "The cows are bawling to be milked. I'll take care of your horse and saddle my own."

Muttering about bossy young pups, Darby sauntered away to do the milking.

After finishing the chores and eating a breakfast that Joseph handed out through the garden gate, Darby took up squatting rights under the oak tree, his rifle resting across his outstretched legs, which were comfortably crossed at the ankle. As Joseph left to ride fence line, the old foreman yelled, "No need to worry while you're gone. I won't get caught with my back turned twice."

Joseph nodded. He had every confidence that Darby would keep a sharp eye out for trouble. He rode close to say, "Been a week since I counted the stock. I'll be taking my dog along to help sniff them out."

Darby lifted his hat in farewell. "Have a good ride."

It was a beautiful April morning, and Joseph had every intention of enjoying it. He was never happier than when he was in the saddle, especially when the mount beneath him was Obie. The stallion, sired by

Ace's black, Shakespeare, had his daddy's fine conformation and even gait. Joseph had never owned a horse who gave him a smoother ride, and Obie was steady and trustworthy, to boot, never spooking, always responsive, and as sure-footed as any animal Joseph had ever seen.

During the ride around the perimeters of the property, Buddy did what he did best: running with his nose to the ground to sniff out cattle. Into copses, over rocks, into gullies, the dog maintained an easy lope, never seeming to tire of the hunt. By noon, when Joseph took a break for lunch, the shepherd had routed out ten of Rachel's eighteen head.

"Good boy." Joseph made over the dog for a few seconds. "It's been a spell since we worked. But you haven't lost your knack for it."

Buddy happily growled in reply.

The dog kept a sharp eye out for treats as Joseph lifted the flap of his saddlebag. "Yes, Rachel sent you lunch. Same as she sent for me. Spoiling you, isn't she?" Joseph sat in the shade of a tree to eat. After laying out Buddy's food on the grass, he tucked hungrily into his own, appreciating every bite. "Damn, but that girl has the magic touch. No bread for sandwiches, so instead we get biscuits. But mine's still good enough that I could go for seconds."

Joseph unfolded another cloth and gave a satisfied sigh when he saw turnovers, fried golden and still slightly warm from the skillet. He sank his teeth into the gooey peach center and closed his eyes in pure pleasure.

Buddy barked and pranced with his front feet, his lolling tongue dripping drool as he eyed the dessert.

"This is people food," Joseph protested. "Besides, she only sent two."

The dog pranced again and licked his chops. *Ruff!*

Joseph groaned and handed over the second turnover. "All I know is, you'd better work for it this afternoon. We've got a lot more fence to ride and eight more cows to find."

Joseph reached the creek around two in the afternoon. He'd ridden through there several times since Darby had been shot, but never without an eerie sensation crawling up his spine. Jeb Pritchard's place wasn't far away as a crow flew—or as a horse walked, for that matter—and Joseph couldn't turn his back to the mountain of rocks without half expecting to take a slug in the back.

Today was no exception, which was why, when Buddy suddenly started to bark, Joseph leaped from his horse and hit the dirt with his weapon drawn. Joseph squinted to see into the deep shadows cast by the projections of stone that reached toward the sky like gigantic arrowheads.

"Buddy!" he yelled.

But the red-gold dog was already gone up the steep hill. Joseph could hear him up in the rocks barking excitedly. Then came a shrill yelp and silence. Joseph was on his feet and running before common sense could make him think better of it.

"You rotten old son of a bitch!" he yelled as he charged for the rocks. "If you hurt that dog, I'll tear you apart with my bare hands." Joseph took cover behind a boulder. "Buddy?" he called.

He heard nothing but the wind. His heart squeezed with fear for his dog. He wanted to race up there with no thought for his own safety, but with the ebb of that first rush of rage, he knew how stupid it would be. So he went slowly, darting from one rock to another, trying to shield himself as he ascended the hill.

After Darby's shooting, he and David had scoured this area and found the place where they believed the sniper had hidden to take aim. It was an opening of about forty feet across, encircled by boulders, which offered a broad view of the flat and creek below. When Joseph reached it, he searched the ground for any sign of disturbance to indicate that a man had recently been hiding there, but he saw nothing, not even a turned blade of grass.

Believing that they'd found what they sought, Joseph and David hadn't climbed any higher that other afternoon, so Joseph was surprised as he pressed upward to find that the mountain wasn't all rock as it appeared to be from below. There were grassy openings aplenty between the clusters of stone.

Joseph was about halfway to the top when he heard the thundering tattoo of a horse's hooves. At the sound, he almost ran back down the hill to jump on Obie and give chase. But Buddy was above him somewhere, and Joseph strongly suspected that the shepherd might be badly hurt. He had to find his dog. He could track the horse later.

Joseph found Buddy lying before what looked like the opening of a cave. As Joseph approached, he had eyes only for his dog, searching for blood, dreading what he might find. To his relief, Joseph saw that the shepherd was still breathing. He holstered his gun, dropped to his knees, and gently ran his hands over red-gold fur to check for wounds. No blood that he could see.

Bewildered, Joseph made a second pass over the dog's body, this time parting the animal's coat, thinking that perhaps a puncture wound might not bleed heavily enough at first to soak through the thick fur. *Nothing.* Turning his attention to Buddy's head, Joseph soon found what he was seeking: a small gash along the dog's temple.

"Bastard," Joseph muttered. "I don't know what he hit you with, partner, but he flat snuffed your wick."

Buddy whimpered and shuddered. Joseph's temper soared. The dog didn't have a mean bone. How could anyone do this?

And why?

When Buddy's eyes came open and Joseph felt confident the dog was going to be all right, he turned a more observant eye to his surroundings. Not just a cave, after all. A long wooden box lay nearby, and it was still wet. A portable mining sluice?

Buddy pushed up on his haunches. Joseph ran his hands over the animal's fur. "Sorry about that, my friend. I didn't know anyone was up here. Next time I call you back, maybe you'll think smart and do as I tell you, huh?" Joseph carefully scratched behind the dog's ears, avoiding the small gash. "You did good, though. Damned good. It looks to me like you've sniffed out more than cows today."

Joseph pushed to his feet and approached the mouth of the cave. He couldn't see very far inside, but what he did see confirmed his suspicions. Tracks and an ore cart. This was a mine—a gold mine, if Joseph guessed right. Only whoever had been doing the digging had taken great pains to keep his activities hidden. At day's end, Joseph suspected even the portable sluice would vanish inside the cave. To the eye of a casual passerby—if anyone ever happened to have reason to come up here, which was doubtful—they would see only an opening in the rock.

Joseph stepped deeper into the cave. After his eyes adjusted to the dimness, he saw a lantern, a miner's light, and all manner of other paraphernalia lying about. Joseph grabbed the miner's light, struck a match to illuminate it, and tossed away his Stetson to don the headgear.

"Just what do we have here?" he mused aloud. His voice bounced back at him, echoing and reechoing. That told him that the cave ran deep. "Well, well, well. Suddenly it all makes sense."

Joseph's excitement grew apace with his footsteps. *Gold.* Who would have thought it? But it wasn't beyond the realm of possibility. No Name itself was a mining town that had gone bust so quickly that the folks who'd swarmed there hoping to get rich left for better digs before giving the community a name. But then there was Black Jack, Colorado, where fortunes had been made in the foothills of the Rockies, a fellow named Luke Taggart topping them all. Joseph had heard stories that the man had more gold in just one bank than Midas could ever conceive of.

But that was the stuff dreams were made of. Years ago, folks around No Name had settled down to a more grueling reality, scratching out a living on the land, very few of them doing well. Ace's railroad spur had changed that immensely, making it easier and far more profitable for cattle ranchers to get their stock to auction in bustling Denver. Even so, the mind-set of folks had remained the same. To put bacon on one's plate, nobody looked at the dirt hoping to find gold. They prayed to see sprouts of grass hay or alfalfa if they had water, and wheat or oats if they didn't.

The light that blazed from Joseph's headlamp played over the rock walls of the tunnel. He could see where someone had chipped at the rock until it played out, and then had moved deeper. Occasionally he saw traces of gold, but nothing to shout about. Then he rounded a corner and saw where someone had blasted with dynamite. Now he was in business. Tresses had been built to support the tunnel, and as he moved deeper into the bowels of the mine, the air became ever colder and thinner.

Someone had been chipping away at this rock for a spell, Joseph decided. One man, possibly two, all under cover of secrecy. His boots slid on the obliterated pieces of stone, left behind by a weary digger who had exhaustively removed possibly tons of rock to some other location to hide the goings-on here. *Years,* Joseph concluded. Small extractions of gold, over time, had occurred here. In a regular mine, countless men swung picks to break out the ore, and dynamite was used whenever they needed to go deeper, ever in search of the mother lode. But this person or persons hadn't been able to search for the precious metal aggressively for fear of discovery. A little here, a little there, day in and day out, week after week, and year after year.

Joseph rounded a corner in the tunnel. "Sweet Christ."

The miner's light played over a wall of solid rock that was ribboned with gold, some of the veins thicker than Joseph's wrist. The sight fairly boggled his mind. He couldn't recall how much an ounce of pure ore was selling for right then. *A lot.* Enough that a greedy man or men might kill to keep a rich vein like this a secret.

The thought made Joseph sick. *No face.* Five years ago, a family had come here to picnic along a creek on their own land. Father, mother, sisters, and brother, they'd had no inkling that they were so close to a deadly fortune. Had Denver, Rachel's beloved dog, run up here, much as Buddy had, with her little sister, Tansy, at his heels? Neither child nor dog would have understood the significance of this find if they had come upon it.

But greedy men often had no sense. With a fortune hanging in the balance, what might they do to protect their treasure from discovery? Even though Tansy probably hadn't realized the significance, she would have seen enough to go back down to the creek where her family was picnicking and mention what she had seen to her father.

So they had slaughtered the Hollisters. All of them except Rachel, who, by some miracle, had lived. Joseph believed in God with all his heart, and in that moment of revelation he also believed with utter conviction that God had put the projectile of that one bullet slightly off, possibly by sheer divine will, so that it glanced off her skull. God, in all His wisdom, knew, even then, that Rachel Hollister would be the salvation of Joseph Paxton, a young man who didn't want a wife, wasn't looking for a wife, and believed he didn't need a wife. Only he had, and somehow God had saved her—out of all the members of her family, he'd somehow saved Rachel, for Joseph.

Tears burned in his eyes. Tears of absolute, mindless rage. *No face.* His sweet Rachel had seen her mother's face blown away while she danced over the grass on a sunny afternoon. *Holy Mother of God.* Marie Hollister, who'd read her Bible the night before she died and marked her place with a ribbon so she could live her life according to Scripture, observing every code of decency, had died a violent, senseless death right before her daughter's eyes. And for what? For gold. So a selfish bastard could line his filthy pockets.

Joseph leaned against the cold rock. He'd never clapped eyes on any of Rachel's family, but he'd seen that vacant look in her eyes and held her in his arms while she was overcome by the horror of their deaths. *Jeb Pritchard.* That stinking, immoral, hell-bent *bastard.* He'd killed his own wife. Why hesitate to spill more blood? Now Joseph knew how the fools could afford to buy whiskey and nap in drunken stupors on a spring afternoon. They'd done their labor, and it didn't involve cows. Their whiskey money was a crow's flight away, deep in the bowels of a cave.

Joseph didn't need to see any more. He exited the dig, gathered his injured dog in his arms, and hurried down the hill. The circuit judge could hang up his hat. Jeb Pritchard was going to pay for what he'd done.

Chapter Seventeen

Darby was still lounging under the oak tree when Joseph returned to the Bar H. Joseph drew up near the tree to dismount and set his dog down. Buddy wasn't his usual energetic self. He just sort of stood there, looking around.

"What's the matter with him?" Darby asked.

"He got beaned a good one."

"Beaned?"

Joseph quickly gave Darby a recounting of the afternoon.

"I'll be damned. Gold, you say?" Darby shook his head. "I knew there was a cave up on that hill, but I paid it no nevermind. Nosin' around in places like that's a good way to get snake bit or come nose to nose with a badger."

Joseph normally avoided caves himself for the same reasons. "Somebody went nosing around in there. Some time ago, if I'm any judge. Mining on the sly, you can't move a lot of rock at once, and a considerable amount of digging has taken place up there."

"And you reckon it was Pritchard?"

"Who else? Jeb's been in a snit about that creek since way back in seventy-nine. He had reason to be down there, walking the property, trying to figure out how to alter the course of the stream back onto his land. At one point or another, he came across that cave, realized there was gold in there for the taking, and started helping himself. Chances are his boys have been aiding him in the endeavor."

Darby narrowed his eyes. "And on the day of the killings, the Hollister family chose a picnic spot just a little too close to his treasure."

"And one of the children wandered up into the rocks," Joseph added. "My guess is that it was Tansy, the five-year-old. Pritchard knew the game would be up if the little girl realized the significance of what she'd seen and blabbed to her daddy."

Darby shook his head again. "So, to make sure that didn't happen, Pritchard opened fire on the whole family." His eyes glittered with anger as he met Joseph's gaze. "Hangin's too good for the bastard."

"I totally agree," Joseph replied. "But we've got to abide by the law, all the same. Otherwise, we're no better than they are."

"So what's your plan?"

"I need to ride into town and talk with my brother. He's wearing the badge. He needs to make the decisions about how to best handle it, I reckon."

Darby drew his watch from his pocket. "How late you think you'll be?"

"I should be back in a couple of hours. My guess is David won't want to make a move tonight. Not enough daylight left to get organized and ride out there before dark. We're going to need manpower this time around, if for no other reason than to help search the property. If Pritchard's been filching gold from Bar H over the last several years, there'll be evidence of it somewhere on his place."

Darby closed his watch. "I promised Amanda I'd come see her tonight. If I run a little late, she'll be sure to understand."

Joseph caught hold of Obie's reins and prepared to remount. "I appreciate you looking after my wife for me, Darby. If she should ask where I went, it might be best if you tell her I had business in town."

"No details." Darby nodded. "I gotcha. As for thankin' me, son, there's no need. I love Rachel, too. Watchin' after her ain't a chore."

David rocked back on his office chair to prop his boots on the edge of his desk. Frowning pensively, he said, "So you were right all along. It was Pritchard."

"It sure looks that way to me." Joseph paced back and forth in front of the window. "I can't think of anyone else who might have had reason to be in that area and come upon that cave. Can you?"

David sighed. "It's not beyond the realm of possibility that Amanda Hollister knows about it. She worked on the Bar H for years."

"Are you back on that again?"

David held up his hands. "Not really, no. I'm inclined to think you're right about it being Pritchard. I'm just trying to look at it from all angles."

"If we find nothing at Pritchard's place to implicate him, we can consider other angles then."

"Jeb isn't gonna sit on his porch having a smoke while we search his place," David pointed out. "He'll raise holy hell and possibly start shooting at us again."

"I've considered that," Joseph said. "We're going to need reinforcements. A small army, if you can round one up."

"Most men hereabouts are willing to stand in as deputies when I need them. I'll send Billy Joe out to ride from house to house while I go knocking on doors here in town. What time in the morning do you want to join up with us?"

When Joseph got back to the Hollister place, Darby pushed to his feet and walked out to meet him.

"David's rounding up a posse," Joseph said. "I'll meet up with them on Wolverine Road at ten tomorrow morning. We'll descend on the Pritchard place en masse. If Jeb sees a huge group of riders, maybe it'll discourage him from getting trigger-happy."

"I hope so." Darby hooked a thumb toward the house. "Don't go makin' a widow of that girl, son. You'll flat mess up my plans."

Joseph chuckled. "I have a few plans of my own that I don't want messed up, so I'll do my best to stay safe."

Darby's green eyes twinkled. "I just want to enjoy my last years with someone special. If you're home to stay, I think I'll go callin' on her for a bit." The old foreman returned to the tree to collect his rifle and a handful of wildflowers. "Just a little nonsense I picked while you was off gallivantin'."

Joseph grinned. "A little nonsense, huh? Looks to me like you're thinking sharp. Most ladies love flowers."

Darby nodded. Then he squinted up at Joseph. "How long's it been since you gave some to Rachel?"

"I gave her a whole courtyard full of flowers."

"That don't count. You gotta pick 'em, son. Makes a gal melt every time."

An hour later, when Joseph finished the evening chores, he walked a wide circle around the house to collect any wildflowers that Darby had missed before he went indoors to greet his wife.

The following morning shortly after Joseph left to run some unspecified errands, Rachel went out in the courtyard to tend her garden. Each little task brought her joy: watering the roses and counting the tiny buds, carefully plucking weeds from around her violets, admiring the cheerful and showy blooms of the crocus, and feeding her three fish, which she could have sworn had already grown a bit. Though the air was crisp, requiring her to drape a blanket over her shoulders, she smelled spring on the breeze, and, oh, how wonderful that was.

"My roses have six buds, Darby. *Six.*"

The old foreman, who stood guard outside the gate, came to peer through the iron bars. "Well, now, ain't that somethin'?"

"It *is*, it surely is." Rachel beamed a smile at him. "And just look how my violets are flourishing!"

"Pretty as can be," he agreed. "And just lookee at that. You got a barn swallow checking out that birdhouse yonder. Could be she'll make a nest inside."

Rachel watched the small bird hop in and out of the hole. "Oh, wouldn't that be grand?" She held her arms wide and twirled in a circle. "He's given me heaven right here on earth, Darby. You just can't know how much I love that man."

"I think I've got an inklin'. And I'm happy for you, honey. So very happy."

Rachel tugged the blanket back around her shoulders. Sobering, she asked, "How are you feeling? I'm so selfish, only thinking about me. Is your wound healing fine?"

"I'm feelin' stronger every day. And you're entitled to be just a little selfish for a spell, darlin'. That's how it's supposed to be right after gettin' married, more so for you than for most."

They chatted a while longer before Rachel went inside to check on her rising loaves of bread. She'd just returned to the garden to laze on her bench in the sunshine for a bit when she heard a horse fast approaching. Buddy started to bark rather furiously, which she decided was just as it should be. Someone was coming, and it was the dog's job to raise an alarm. Rachel wondered who might be calling. Someone from town, possibly, bringing something more for her courtyard? Harrison Gilpatrick was supposed to bring her some tulip bulbs, and Garrett Buckmaster had promised her some pond lilies. She was greatly looking forward to receiving both.

A little over a week ago, Rachel might have rushed

into the house to bar her door and hide at the sound of an approaching horse. But she'd come to feel quite safe inside her courtyard. As Joseph was fond of reminding her, the walls out here were made of stone and almost a foot thick. No one could get in. Only she and Joseph had a key to the gate. If anything alarming happened outside the courtyard, she'd have enough advanced warning to escape into the house.

Rachel no sooner thought that than she heard Buddy snarl. It was so unlike the dog to be unfriendly. She turned on the bench to stare at the gate. The dog let loose with another snarl, prompting Darby to say, "Silly fool pup. You need to learn the difference between friends and foes. Mind your manners." Then, "Buddy! Get back here!" Darby whistled. Then he cursed. "Joseph will have my head, you dad-blamed mutt. You're supposed to stay here today!"

Rachel pushed slowly to her feet. She felt frightened suddenly without knowing why. No, that wasn't precisely true. *Buddy.* He was a friendly fellow, always ready for a pat on the head from friend or stranger. It wasn't in his nature to snarl at anyone—or to ignore Darby's calls.

She heard the horse slowing to a trot out front.

"Howdy, Ray," Darby said. "What brings you out this way so bright and early?"

"It's the boss, Darby. She's gravely ill. Came on her real sudden like. I sent one of the men for Doc Halloway, but she's asking for you."

Rachel shot up from the bench. *That voice.* Her heart was pounding hard, and an awful coldness trickled over her skin like ice water. *That voice.* Black spots danced before her eyes. *Oh, my God.* It was the voice in her nightmares. Her breath suddenly hitching, she stumbled backward toward the house. *Him*—it's *him.* She fell on the steps. Scrambled back to her feet. The world swirled upside down and then came right again. Oxygen, she needed oxygen. She hugged a porch post to hold herself erect, fighting frantically for breath. Staggered away, trying to reach the doorway. Fell into the house, her legs so watery that they would no longer support her weight. *Him, him, him.*

Sprawled on her belly, she grabbed the ironwork to swing it closed. Dragged herself to her knees and tried desperately to fit the key into the lock, only in her panic she couldn't hit the hole. Her numb fingers lost their grip on the metal bow, and the key fell to the floor. With a sob, she twisted sharply at the waist to seize hold of the thick wooden door, shifting out of the way to pull it closed. The portal slammed shut with a loud thunk. Pulling herself to her feet, she engaged the deadlocks. Then, with violently trembling hands, she dropped the bar into place.

Him. If she lived for another hundred years, she would never forget that voice. Panic swamped her. She staggered to a corner, dropped to her rump, and pressed her back to the walls. *Him.* He'd come to kill her. She knew it. *Oh, God.* She needed Joseph. *Joseph.* Thinking of him calmed her somewhat. She was safe inside her kitchen, just like always. She had the shotgun to defend herself. She wasn't sitting unsuspecting on the grass along the creek this time. Oh, no. This time, she could fight back.

The thought sent her crawling across the floor to the

gun rack. She struggled to her feet, still dizzy from lack of breath. Shells, she needed shells. She pulled so hard on the ammunition drawer that it came clear off the runners and crashed to the floor. She grabbed handfuls of ammunition and shoved it into her skirt pockets. Then she wrested the gun from its niche. With violently trembling hands, she managed to break open the barrels, load both, and snap them back into place.

On weak legs, she made her way to the wood safe, flung open the door, and dropped to her knees to peer out. *Joseph.* She had a wonderful life to look forward to now—a husband who loved her, the possibility of children and happiness and laughter. She wasn't about to die and miss out on all that. Oh, no. She would be ready. He wouldn't have such easy pickings this time.

She tried to listen, but her breathing was so ragged that it was hard to hear anything. She gulped and tried to hold her breath. Was that a horse trotting off? She gulped again and closed her eyes on a silent prayer. Then she peered out the wood safe again.

"Darby?" she called softly. "You there?"

No answer. Had he left? *No, no, no.*

"Darby," she called just a little louder.

What if *he* was out there? The thought had her slamming the door of the wood safe closed. As the latch dropped, she pressed her back to the wall. *Okay.* She was fine. Darby wasn't answering, but she was safe. Her familiar kitchen was just like always, everything locked and barred closed. No one could get in. She was just fine. Let him try to come in one of the doors. Let him just *try*.

Time passed. Rachel's heartbeat slowed. Her

breathing became regular again. More important, she was able to think more rationally. *Ray.* Darby had called the man Ray. She would tell Joseph when he got home. Joseph would go after him. Ray would be removed from the face of the earth. That was a good way to think of it. *Removed.* She'd never have to worry again. Joseph would go after him, and from now on she'd be safe because she finally knew his name.

A gray fog clouded her vision. Rachel blinked, tried to focus. *No,* she told herself. No more running away in her mind. She had to hold on to his name. *Ray.* And he worked for Amanda Hollister.

The gray fog grew thicker. Rachel blinked, passed a hand over her eyes. *No.* After the grayness came blackness. She knew that all too well. It had come over her the first night when Joseph had knocked on her door to tell her Darby had been shot. She had to be strong this time. She had to keep her head. Her life might depend on it, and she needed to live so she could have Joseph's babies. She had to live because he had given her so much to live for. She couldn't let herself succumb to the blackness when that awful man might be out there.

Ray. She knew his voice, and now she knew his name. A terrible pain lanced through her head. She rested the shotgun across the bend of her lap and drew up her knees to rest her throbbing brow on them. Images pelted her. Horrible images. *No face.* Her ma, falling—falling—falling. Her head bouncing on the grass when she landed on her back. *No face. Blood— everywhere blood.* Visions of crimson-soaked pink flashed through Rachel's mind. *Tansy's pretty little dress.* And then red on yellow. *Denver, her loyal dog, lying limp on the ground.* And Daniel. A picture blinked. *Daniel, with a chicken drumstick still caught between his teeth and a reddish-black hole suddenly appearing between his blank blue eyes.*

The blackness tried to move over her, but Rachel kept fighting against it. *Ray.* She would forget his name if she gave in to the blackness. She'd wake up and she wouldn't remember anything. She couldn't allow that to happen, not this time. Oh, how it *hurt.* Remembering *hurt* so much, and it was horrible beyond comprehension. But she had to do it. For Tansy. For her ma. For Daniel. And for her pa, who'd used the only weapon he had, his beloved fiddle, to try to protect them. He'd sprung up from the grass and charged the shooter, shattering the string instrument on the man's shoulder.

Rachel raised her head, staring blankly at nothing, her mind replaying events that she had blacked out for years. She and Daniel had been arguing over the last piece of chicken in the basket, and Daniel, being stronger than she, had wrestled the drumstick from her hand. Grinning impishly, he'd sunk his teeth into the meat. *Kaboom.*

Rachel shuddered and closed her eyes. *Oh, God.* Daniel's head. Blood, all over the blanket, even before he fell. Blood, splattered all over her. Rachel remembered staring stupidly at the blood, not understanding where it had come from, and then seeing Daniel fall as if a gigantic force had struck him. She had scrambled to her knees, screaming, "Daniel? Daniel!"

Rachel's stomach convulsed, and she gagged,

bringing up only gall to wet her skirt. *Daniel.* The blackness edged close again. She shoved it away. Joseph's voice whispered in her mind. *You mentioned once that you see Denver leaping up to bite the man's leg, and that the man pulls his revolver and shoots him between the eyes. What else do you see, sweetheart? Picture his boot. Picture his leg. Is there anything special about the gun—or possibly the saddle? If you see his leg, if you see his hand holding the gun, you must see other things.*

Rachel gagged again, bringing up more than bile this time. But she scarcely noticed because she was seeing Denver, her wonderful, loyal Denver, throwing himself at the man's leg, seeing the man reach for his gun, seeing him point the barrel at her dog's head. *Push past it. Don't think of poor Denver. See the man's leg, his boot, the saddle.* And there it was, the horror that had skirted at the edges of the blackness for so long, a brand on the rump of the sorrel horse, an H within a circle.

Rachel started to shake so violently that she could barely hug her legs. Her family's brand, only altered. The Bar H ranch had always used an H underscored by a bar to brand their animals. When Amanda had left the family fold, she had altered that brand, keeping the H but encompassing it with a circle. It had been different enough from the original Hollister brand to be legally recorded, enabling her to use the first letter of her surname to mark her horses and livestock, just as she always had. *The Circle H.* And Rachel had seen it on the rump of the killer's horse. For all these years, she'd blacked it out, but it was there in her mind now, like a photograph hanging on the wall. He'd been riding a Circle H horse.

As a very small child, Rachel had adored her aunt Amanda. No one had understood her so well. Mannie, Rachel had called her, still so young that she couldn't say Amanda. In her mind's eye, she could see herself racing toward her aunt, much as Little Ace ran toward Joseph now, her arms spread wide, her heart swelling with love. She had wanted nothing more than to feel Mannie's arms around her.

Rachel had loved her mother. No doubt about that. But she had adored Amanda, who'd never scolded when she got her dress dirty and who'd always seemed to take pleasure in her mischievousness as Rachel's mother never could.

A sob jerked through Rachel's body. *Mannie*. Long after Amanda had left the Bar H, Rachel had frequently gone to see her. Her aunt had always been ready to drop everything and spend time with her. Once, she might show her the new foals. Another time, she might take Rachel into the house for milk and cookies. When Rachel had had problems, she'd always been able to count on Mannie for solutions. Mannie, her best friend.

Rachel's mother, Marie, had always understood. Looking back on it now, Rachel wished she could give her ma just one more hug for being such a wonderful mother. They'd been so different, Rachel and her mother, Marie always fussing about every little thing, Rachel ever ready to traipse through the pigpen with no thought for being a lady. Whenever Rachel had had a problem that her mother couldn't solve, Marie had sent Rachel to town on silly errands—to buy special ribbon for a dress, or to pick up a book that Marie was yearning to read, or to purchase some peppermint to satisfy a sudden craving. And while in town, Rachel could slip over to visit Mannie, her father none the wiser.

Love. It was strange how it went every which way and doubled back on itself. Rachel had loved her ma very much, but it had been only Mannie who could chase away her tears and make her laugh. There was no explaining it. Her ma had just shrugged, saying that Rachel and Amanda were kindred spirits, one the very spit of the other. Sometimes it made Rachel feel guilty, for on some level she'd always known that no one loved her as much as her ma did.

When Rachel had first started growing breasts, she was so upset that her mother sent her off to stay all night with Katy, a childhood friend. Only Rachel didn't go to Katy's, and her mother had known she wouldn't. It had all been a plot to fool Rachel's pa, so he'd never guess that his daughter was off with Mannie, getting her head filled with all manner of nonsense. Rachel and Mannie had talked grown-up, female talk about the unwelcome growths that were appearing on Rachel's chest, and by morning Rachel had been able to look at herself in the mirror and shrug. *Teats.* Cows had them. Mares had them. And Rachel was growing some, too. It was necessary because, someday, she'd have babies, and she'd need teats to feed them. Until then, they were just *there,* and she had to put up with them.

Rachel's ma had somehow understood that nobody

could communicate with Rachel better than Mannie.
And so it went until that fateful day along the creek
when nearly everyone Rachel loved had died.

Remembering, Rachel clenched her teeth against
the pain. Losing all of them would have been unbearable no matter *what*. But to grab her brother and then
look up to see a CIRCLE H on his killer's horse? Rachel
had *known* that brand. Every time she visited Mannie,
she would see it—on the cows, on the horses, and
even on Mannie's saddles. It was so familiar, a variation of the brand that had been in her family for generations, a trademark that signified *Hollister*.

For years, Rachel had been unable to write the letter H. Now she knew why, and a murderous rage
roiled through her. *Mannie*. It had been the worst kind
of betrayal. Her aunt hadn't been there that day to fire
the rifle. But she had hired it done.

That was what Rachel had been running from for
the last five years. *Mannie,* her beloved aunt, had paid
someone to slaughter all of Rachel's family—and
even Rachel herself. It was too horrible to accept.

She raised her head, feeling weak and shaky, but
also stronger. Mannie had betrayed her, but Joseph
never would. She couldn't huddle forever in a corner,
afraid because one wicked woman had broken her
heart and destroyed her ability to trust.

An odd smell reached Rachel's nostrils. She
blinked and focused, staring for a moment at a table
leg. What *was* that smell? She sniffed. Then she set
the shotgun aside and pushed to her feet. The smell
was really strong, and it grew stronger as she circled
the kitchen and came to the water closet, which Darby

had added on to the house after her parents' death. *Kerosene?* Rachel stepped fully into the enclosure. Kerosene, definitely kerosene. She knew the scent so well. For five years, all she'd had for light were kerosene lanterns and an occasional candle.

She heard a faint whoosh. Spun in a full circle. What was that? She stepped back out into the kitchen. *Whoosh, whoosh, WHOOSH.* She spun again, her eyes bulging from their sockets, her ears straining to hear. *Kerosene, igniting.* She'd heard the sound a thousand times if she'd heard it once. After touching a match to a kerosene-soaked wick, a whoosh always followed. Only now it wasn't a wick that had been lighted.

Rachel moved to the center of the kitchen, knowing even before she saw smoke squeezing up through the floorboards that someone had set fire to the house. A crackling sound surrounded her. *Oh, dear God.* He didn't plan to force his way into her sanctum. He meant to incinerate it. With her *inside.*

Chapter Eighteen

"If this doesn't beat all," David said. "They're gone?"

Joseph scanned the area, taking in the Pritchard shack and the outbuildings. Not a sign of any human movement. Pigs rutted in the hog pen. A chicken high-stepped across the yard. A cow bawled in the barn. But he saw no sign of the Pritchards anywhere.

"Sure looks like they're gone to me." Joseph swung down off his horse. "That'll make our job easier. Let's get it done before they come back."

David dismounted. Turning to the group of men behind them, he began giving orders, sending one bunch of deputized volunteers to the barn, another to search the rest of the outbuildings, and still another to walk the property.

"We're looking for mining equipment," he barked. "Or anything else connected with mining, possibly even gold. There has to be evidence here somewhere." To the men who were about to walk the grounds, he added, "Be watchful for recently turned earth where something might be buried." To the men about to search the barn, he yelled, "Look in the stalls, under the tack room floors, up in the hayloft. Leave nothing unturned."

When the search parties had been dispatched, Joseph and David descended on the house. As Joseph stepped onto the porch, a loose board rocked under his boot. He jerked the plank free to look under it. *Nothing.* But they'd only just started. They would find the evidence they needed to see justice done. Every last one of the Pritchards might soon be swinging at the end of a rope.

Tansy. As he entered the Pritchard shack, he kept remembering Rachel's face as she had described the child's blood-soaked dress. And her mother, with no face. Rage roiled within him. How could these filthy excuses for human beings have done such things? It went beyond evil. To sight in on a little girl and pull the trigger? Joseph shuddered as he upended beds, opened cupboards, rifled through drawers. *Bastards.* He wanted to find enough evidence to see them hang. Nothing less.

David stepped on a loose floorboard and dropped to his knees to rip at the planks like a madman. As Joseph went to help him, his nostrils were filled with the stench of the men who frequented the house.

They ripped up half the floor. David had just jumped down to search beneath the remaining planks when a shout sounded from outside. It was Charley Banks. "We found it! Gold! A bunch of gold!"

David and Joseph raced outside. Charley stood outside the barn doors, holding up two partially filled burlap bags. Joseph could see by the strain on the man's face that the sacks weighed a great deal. He and his brother ran across the pocked yard.

"Are you sure it's gold?" David demanded.

Charley dropped the bags at his feet and reached into his shirt pocket to extract a chunk of yellow. "It's gold, all right." He turned the piece of ore in the sunlight. "Christ almighty, that must be a thick vein."

Joseph had seen the vein, and Charley was right; it ran deep into the rock. The tension eased from his body. The Pritchards were finished. Justice would be done. The blood on a little girl's pink dress would be avenged. And perhaps, somewhere along the way, Rachel would finally find peace, knowing that her family's killers had been punished.

David opened both bags, stared at the contents, and cursed vilely. Turning to Joseph, he said, "You had it right all along, Joseph. Those filthy bastards slaughtered the Hollisters."

Following that pronouncement, Joseph heard a shout. He turned to see Jeb Pritchard and his boys riding in on sweaty horses. Jeb swung down from the saddle before his sons even got their horses reined to a stop.

"So it was *you*!" he cried. "You cut our fence wire and chased our cattle off our land!" He turned a fiery gaze toward his house, saw the dismantled porch, and shook his fist. "What in God's name have you done? You come in here and tear apart our home? What's the matter with you?" He sent Joseph an accusing glare. "Enough of this *bullshit*. I ain't done nothin' wrong. My boys ain't, either. You've bedeviled me for *weeks*. I'm

thinking you learned nothin' from what happened to
your pa. Hanged, he was! And for somethin' he didn't
do! Now you're hell-bent to do the same to me and
mine!"

For just an instant, Joseph wondered if he'd been
wrong. He disliked Jeb Pritchard. The man was so
filthy that Joseph could have scraped the crud from his
skin with the dull edge of a knife blade. But did Jeb's
failure to bathe regularly make him evil?

Then Joseph's gaze shifted to the burlap bags at
Charley's feet. Hard evidence didn't lie. Pritchard had
been caught red-handed. Bags of gold, hidden in his
barn. That hen nesting in his bathtub hadn't laid two
bags of golden eggs.

"Hands behind your back," David ordered. "And
I'm warning you, Pritchard, if you give me a moment's grief, I'll shoot you and dance on your grave."

Men surrounded Jeb's sons. Alan started to reach
for his gun.

"I wouldn't if I were you," Joseph warned him.

Charley Banks jerked the thin younger man off his
horse and none too gently pulled his arms behind his
back while Garrett Buckmaster tied his wrists.

"You'll regret this!" Jeb cried. "And, by God, you'll
fix all that you tore up. You got no right to come onto
my land and destroy what's mine."

"We found the gold in your barn, Jeb," David said
coldly.

"What gold?"

"*That* gold." David pointed to the bags. "And I'll
venture a guess that we haven't found the half of it."

"You're crazy. Gold in my barn? You think I'd wear

shoes with holey soles if I had gold stashed away? And where would I get it? Huh? Ain't like it grows on trees."

"I found the mine," Joseph inserted. "You didn't kill my dog, by the way, and it's lucky for you."

Just as Joseph spoke, he heard a distant barking and turned to see a red-gold ball of fur streaking through the trees. Buddy, in a flat-out run, barking every inch of the way. As the dog skidded to a stop, Joseph cried, "When are you gonna learn that stay means *stay*?"

Buddy lunged at Joseph's boots, snapping and snarling. Then the dog whirled, ran off a ways, and stopped to look back.

"What's gotten into you?" Joseph asked.

The shepherd dashed back, circling Joseph, nipping at his calves, and barking wildly. Buckmaster laughed. "Damn, Joseph. Dog needs lessons on the difference betwixt people and cows. He's trying to herd you."

When Buddy ran off again, Joseph gazed thoughtfully after him. "He got knocked into a cocked hat yesterday. Maybe his brains are still rattled." Only even as Joseph spoke, he looked into his dog's intelligent amber eyes and doubted his own words. "What's wrong, boy?"

The shepherd wheeled in a circle, then darted back toward the trees—and home. Joseph knew it was crazy, but his gut told him that the dog was trying to tell him something. "I gotta go," he told David.

"What?" David cried incredulously. "We aren't finished here yet."

Joseph was already racing for his horse. "Something's wrong at home. I gotta go!"

Joseph swung up into the saddle, turned Obie, and urged him forward into a run. Buddy barked and took off through the trees, his white paws moving so fast his legs were a blur. Feeling just a little foolish, Joseph leaned low over Obie's neck, guiding the stallion to follow the dog.

When they reached the fence line that divided the Bar H from Pritchard's land, Buddy sailed over the four strands of barbed wire as if they weren't there. Joseph nudged Obie with his heels. The stallion's powerful muscles bunched to leap, and over the wire they went.

As they neared the creek, Joseph saw the smoke— a huge mushroom of roiling grayish black reaching ever higher into the blue sky. *Oh, Jesus.* He became one with his horse, bent legs supporting his weight, torso parallel to Obie's back, his cheek riding the animal's sweaty neck. *Rachel.*

Joseph's heart almost stopped beating when he saw the house. The place was a blazing inferno, flames leaping far higher than the oak tree. He was out of the saddle and running before Obie skidded to a complete stop. He saw Ray Meeks, Amanda Hollister's foreman, racing back from the spring, water sloshing from the bucket he carried.

"Help me!" Ray yelled. "You gotta help me!"

But Joseph knew it was already too late. The entire house was afire, the heat rolling from it so intense that it seared his face. *Rachel.* He dropped to his knees and screamed, "No! No, God, *no-oo-o!*"

And then he heard wild barking. Buddy was at the courtyard gate, frantically trying to dig under it.

Joseph staggered to his feet. Since his marriage to Rachel, he'd had duplicate keys made for the kitchen doorways and courtyard gate so he could let himself in and out. Digging in his pocket as he ran, he pulled out the three skeleton keys. Which one went to the gate? He was so terrified that he couldn't remember their shapes.

He reached the ironwork, shoved in one of the keys, and sobbed with relief when the lock turned. The metal was so hot that it blistered his hands as he jerked it open. "Rachel? Rachel!"

He ran into the courtyard, looking everywhere for her. The plants were already scorched. A birdhouse hanging from an iron bar burst into flame and exploded like an Independence Day firework. Joseph threw up an arm to protect his face, knowing that Rachel couldn't have survived this, not even if she'd come out into the courtyard. He moved toward what had once been the porch, yelling her name, wanting to throw himself into the flames and die with her. But something inside the burning house exploded just then. The force of it knocked him clear off his feet and backward.

He lay sprawled on the ground for a moment, dazed and disoriented. Then he rolled onto his knees. As he came erect, he saw Buddy in a corner of the enclosure digging at the dirt. Joseph scrambled over on his knees. Not dirt. A pile of wet blankets. Joseph prodded the hot wool, felt firm softness underneath. *Rachel.*

He grabbed her up in his arms, blankets and all, lunged to his feet, and ran from the courtyard with his shoulders hunched around his burden. When he reached the old oak, he dropped back to his knees, pulled away the blankets, and saw her pale, soot-streaked face.

"Rachel?" He grabbed her up into his arms again. "Don't be dead. You can't be dead. Rachel!"

Her body jerked. Then she coughed. Joseph made a fist in her wet hair and cried like a baby. "Oh, sweetheart. I'll never leave you again. I swear to God, I'll never leave you again."

"Joseph," she croaked. "Tried—to—kill me. Wet the bl-blankets in the p-pond." She coughed again. "Saved myself."

Then she looked past his shoulder and he felt her whole body tense. Joseph knew it had just dawned on her that she was out in the open. He quickly drew the blanket back over her face. "You're all right, honey. You're all right. I'll get you somewhere safe. I'll get you somewhere safe."

She turned her face against his shirt, her hands knotted on his arms. Joseph was about to reassure her again when Buddy let loose with a low, vicious snarl. Joseph darted a surprised glance at his dog. The shepherd's hackles were up. Turning, Joseph saw that Ray Meeks was staggering toward them. The closer the man came, the more viciously Buddy growled.

Such behavior was completely unlike Buddy. Joseph felt his wife trembling against him. Was she terrified by the openness, as he'd first thought, or by the man? He spoke softly to his dog and told him to sit. Buddy obeyed and stopped snarling, but Joseph could tell the animal was ready to attack if Meeks made a wrong move.

"Ah, Jesus, Joseph, I'm so sorry." Tears trailed down the man's cheeks, leaving pale tracks. "I am *so* sorry. Amanda took gravely ill. I promised Darby that I'd look after Rachel while he went to be with her. And I *tried,* I swear to you. I only went as far as the barn to unsaddle my horse and give it some water, and I never took my eyes off the house the entire time."

Wariness tightened every muscle in Joseph's body.

"I don't know how they sneaked in on me like that. The first I knew they were here was when I saw them riding away, and then flames started shooting up from the house. I tried my damnedest to put the fire out, but they'd doused the whole place with kerosene." Ray held out his hands, which looked to be charred. "I tried, partner. I put everything I had into saving her. I'm so sorry."

Meeks had missed his calling as an actor. If Joseph's wife and dog hadn't been telling him different, he would have believed the man was sincere.

"Who rode away?" Joseph asked, stalling for time. He had never in his life been afraid to draw down on another man, but he held Rachel in his arms. He was fast enough to take Meeks out. He had every confidence in that. But he couldn't slap leather with Rachel in the line of fire. "Who set fire to the place?"

Ray passed a sleeve over his tear-filled eyes. "I can't be positive. They were some distance off and riding fast. But it looked like Jeb Pritchard and his boys."

Meeks glanced at the sodden lump of wool in Joseph's arms. "I'd give my right arm to undo this. I'm so sorry about your wife. I should never have gone to the barn."

Joseph prayed that Rachel wouldn't move. Meeks had tried to kill her and clearly believed that he'd been successful in the attempt. Joseph bent his head. He needed to put distance between himself and Rachel before Meeks realized she wasn't dead and went for his gun. Only what if Rachel cried out when Joseph tried to move away from her?

Before Joseph could think what to do, he heard the sound of approaching horses. Meeks turned to squint into the distance. When he recognized the riders, his blackened face went pale.

Amanda Hollister and Darby McClintoch rode in. Despite her palsy, Amanda swung out of the saddle with the skill and grace born of a lifetime on horseback. She quickly jerked her rifle from its boot, turned aching blue eyes on Ray, and said, "I dumped the tea in a potted plant."

Ray licked his lips, gave a shaky laugh. "Pardon me?"

"What was in it?" Amanda's whole body was shaking. "Arsenic? You were so worried about making sure I drank it that I grew suspicious. Then I noticed an odd taste. While you had your back turned, I dumped it out. You thought I'd swallowed it all when you left to come here for Darby. You figured I'd be dead by the time he reached my place, that I'd never be able to say I hadn't sent for him."

Joseph looked back and forth from Ray to Amanda, not understanding any of the exchange. *Poisoned tea?*

"You killed my nephew." Amanda raised the rifle to her shoulder. "You murdered his wife and Daniel and little Tansy. Shot them down in cold blood. I never wanted to believe it was you. The very thought broke my heart. God forgive me, it was so much easier to lay the blame on Jeb. So I turned a blind eye and told myself that my son, my long-lost child, couldn't have done such a heinous thing."

"Put that gun down, Ma." Meeks laughed again. "You aren't going to shoot me."

It hit Joseph then, like a fist to his jaw. Ray's eyes. The first time Joseph met the man, he'd experienced an odd sense of familiarity and asked Ray if they'd met before. Now Joseph knew what it was about Ray that had struck a chord in his memory. *His eyes.* He had Rachel's arresting blue eyes and her fine features as well.

"Now you've killed my Rachel," Amanda went on, her voice beginning to shake as badly as her body was. "I loved that girl like my own. How could you do this?"

Ray held his hands out to his sides and retreated another pace. "You're talking crazy. Arsenic in your tea? You're my mother. I love you. Why would I do such a thing?"

"That's a good question." Amanda curled her finger over the trigger. "Stand fast, Raymond. If you take another step, I'll drop you in your tracks."

"This is insane!" Ray cried.

"Is it? I noticed that someone had been in my desk last week. Then I discovered that my will was missing. I thought I might have misplaced it. But then it reappeared in the drawer, right where I always kept it. Even then, I didn't want to believe what my common sense was telling me. What a sentimental old fool I was, hoping against hope that my boy was everything he pretended to be. But the truth was, you took the will to get legal counsel to see where you would stand if I married Darby. I'm sure you learned that everything I own will become his, leaving you with nothing."

Amanda shook her head sadly. "You wanted it all. Didn't you, Ray? A little gold here and there wasn't enough to satisfy your greed. Getting my little spread after I died wasn't grand enough for you, either. You wanted the gold, you wanted this ranch, you wanted *everything*. And time was suddenly running out. I was days away from marrying Darby. You had to stop that from happening, and you had to kill Rachel, as well, to take possession of this ranch. Joseph had found the mine. You knew you'd be able to do no more digging without running the risk of getting caught."

"You gave me up!" Ray yelled. Swinging an arm to encompass the ranch, he cried. "It should've been mine. I had as much right to it as Henry, maybe more! You worked harder to make a go of this place than his father ever did. But what did I get? A tiny little spread where I'd have to scratch out a living for the rest of my life. Oh, yes, and the gold! Some compensation that was, none of it really mine to take, and me taking a huge chance every time I came over here to chip rock."

Ray moved back another step. "You talk about your family. What about *me*? Then, to add insult to injury, you decide to get married when you're seventy years old with one foot already in the grave. I've worked that meager, parched piece of land for almost eight years, waiting for you to die so it'd be mine, and you were going to take even that from me."

"What happened in the past is over. I eventually found you, didn't I? And I didn't willingly give you up. My father forced me to do it."

"A lot of comfort that is to me. I got cheated out of everything, even the Hollister name!"

"It's no excuse, Raymond. You've wrongfully taken human life. You have to pay for that."

"Hang, you mean?" Ray shook his head. "No way. For once in your life, be a decent mother and just let me go."

"I can't do that," Amanda said sadly.

Ray went for his gun.

"Don't, Raymond!" Amanda cried. "Please, for the love of God, don't."

Joseph rolled sideways to cover Rachel with his body, but before he could draw his weapon, Amanda Hollister fired her rifle. Ray's blue eyes filled with incredulity. He dropped his chin to stare stupidly at the blood blossoming over the front of his gray shirt. The revolver fell from his hand.

"You shot me," he whispered.

And then he dropped facedown on the dirt, shuddered, and died.

The rifle slipped from Amanda's trembling grasp. On unsteady legs, she made her way to her son, dropped to her knees, wrapped her arms around his limp body, and started to sob.

"God forgive me. My baby boy. God forgive me. God forgive me."

Darby knelt beside her. As he laid a hand on her

heaving back, he sent Joseph a tortured look. There were no words. Amanda Hollister had just killed her own son. Joseph sorely wished that it hadn't been necessary. But sadly it was. Ray had gone for his gun. He wouldn't have hesitated to shoot. Amanda had done what she had to do to keep her son from hurting any more innocent people.

Nevertheless, the memory of this day would haunt her for the rest of her life.

Chapter Nineteen

Rachel came slowly awake. Nearby she heard the crackling of a fire, which terrified her for a moment, but then she felt Joseph's big, hard hand curled warmly around hers and she knew that she was absolutely safe. She slowly lifted her lashes. His darkly burnished face hovered above hers, his beautiful blue eyes cloudy with tenderness.

"There she is, finally coming around," he said softly. "I thought you were gonna sleep until sometime next week. I tried to tell Doc not to dose you with that much laudanum, but he wouldn't listen."

Rachel only dimly recalled Doc's being there. She glanced uneasily around. She lay on a dark leather sofa in a strange room. A fire crackled cheerfully in the hearth of a large river-rock fireplace. "Where am I?"

"My place. Don't panic. Every window in this section of the house is boarded over, inside and out. Esa and David's handiwork. And Ace blocked off the hallway just beyond the water closet. It's not quite as good as your kitchen, but almost. We brought in a bed be-

fore he blocked the hall. We have the place trimmed
down to one room, more or less." He smiled and lifted
her hand to trail silky lips lightly over her knuckles.
"When I built this house, I think I was building it for
you and just didn't know it. I made the kitchen and sitting room all one area."

Rachel turned onto her side to better see his face.
Moving made her hands hurt. When she glanced down
at her knuckles, Joseph said, "You kept them out from
under the wet blankets to hold them close around you.
The heat from the fire was pretty intense and blistered
the backs of your fingers."

Rachel sank back against the pillows. It all came
back to her then—the fire, throwing blankets into the
fishpond and draping them around herself to stay safe
from the flames, smoke, and heat. "Oh, Joseph." She
gave him a questioning look. "Ray's dead, isn't he?"

He nodded, his expression going solemn. "Amanda
shot him."

Rachel squeezed her eyes closed. "Poor Mannie."

"Who?"

"Mannie. It's what I've always called Aunt
Amanda. Ray was her son?"

Joseph kissed her knuckles again. "It's a long
story," he said.

"Tell me," she whispered, and so he began. Much
later, when he finally stopped talking, Rachel said, "So
that's why my pa always said Mannie had brought
shame upon the family name. Because she had a child
out of wedlock."

Joseph nodded. "I guess she never stopped pining
for the baby boy she gave away. When she had the

falling out with your father and left the ranch, she hired a detective to try to find her son."

Rachel sighed. "I remember when Ray came to work for Mannie. She was always patting his arm and smoothing his hair. I wasn't that old back then, about fourteen, I think, but I thought it was odd. I decided that she probably just liked him a lot."

"A whole lot. He was her son, and she loved him."

"But she never told anyone?"

Joseph ran a hand through his hair. The strands fell back to his shoulders, glistening like threads of spun gold. "Darby rode over a bit ago. He has the whole story now, straight from Amanda, and he wanted me to hear it first so I might explain it all to you."

Rachel searched his gaze. "Is it bad?"

"Let's just say your aunt Amanda isn't entirely innocent in all of this. But let me start from the first. All right?"

Rachel nodded.

"Years ago, when Amanda was still a fairly young woman, she had a secret place on the Bar H where she often went to be alone. Your great-grandfather Luther Hollister and your grandpa Peter didn't treat her very well. They never quite forgave her for getting pregnant. When their coldness toward her got to be too much, she'd go to her secret place, a cave that she'd found up in the rocks near the creek. One afternoon, she took a lantern with her to see how deep the cave went, and she discovered that there was gold in the rock.

"To spite her father, who'd already informed her that he had cut her out of his will and meant to leave her nothing, she kept the gold a secret, never telling anyone. It was her one little bit of revenge. In her defense, I have to also add that Amanda never thought there was a lot of gold. She had no way of knowing how deep into the rock the vein went, and generally speaking, this area hasn't proved out to be rich, No Name being a perfect example. Keeping the discovery to herself was more an act of defiance, her only way of striking back at two men who had made her life a misery. She'd not only been forced to give up her baby, but she'd lost the only man she ever truly loved."

"Darby."

Joseph reached to smooth Rachel's hair. She so loved the feel of his touch that she turned her cheek into the palm of his hand.

"Yes, Darby. There's been a lot of sadness in her life. Finally locating Ray was one of the few things that ever went right for her, or so she thought. He had been adopted by a Kentucky farmer and his wife, mainly so he could help with the work around their place. Ray had a terrible childhood, according to the story he told Amanda, getting whipped for the least infraction, sometimes not getting fed as additional punishment." Joseph sighed and shrugged. "Who knows the real story? Maybe he was horribly abused, maybe he wasn't. He could have made it all up to make Amanda feel even more guilty for giving him up as a baby."

"So he could control her," Rachel whispered.

Joseph nodded. "We'll never know. But Amanda did feel terrible for him. She had so little to offer him, really, a small spread that made barely enough to keep the wolves from her door. He was her son, a Hollister by birth, and, in her mind, deserved so much more. She saw no point in legally claiming him as her child. She had no other children to contest her will. At that time, your father had the family ranch and was doing well. She knew he wouldn't care who got her meager little patch of land. Claiming Ray as her child would have caused a scandal that might have reflected on her loved ones." He smiled and trailed a fingertip over Rachel's mouth. "Namely you. She saw no point in causing a bunch of gossip that might hurt you. So she just made Ray Meeks her sole beneficiary so he would get what little she had when she died."

"Which wasn't much," Rachel observed.

"No, not much. So to make up for it, Amanda told Ray about the cave on her family's land. If he was careful, he could sneak in and chip out some gold now and again. Small compensation, in her mind. She had no way of knowing that Ray would discover a veritable fortune inside that cave, enough gold that he would kill to protect the secret."

Joseph stared at the fire thoughtfully. "The day your family was killed, I believe one of you children went up into the rocks and came upon the cave."

Memories flashed through Rachel's mind in a dizzying rush. "Tansy," she whispered raggedly. "I remember that now. She went traipsing off right before lunch, and Ma sent me and Daniel to find her. She was already coming back down the hill when we came upon her. I remember her saying that she'd found a dark, scary place, and had seen a spook looking out at her. She was fanciful and often told whoppers. Daniel and I pretended to be interested, but we didn't take her seriously." An awful pain moved through Rachel's chest. "We went back down to the creek and had lunch. Daniel and I were still eating when the first shot rang out."

"It stands to reason that Tansy's spook was Raymond Meeks," Joseph said thickly. "Tansy had seen the cave and possibly his mining paraphernalia. He knew she would probably tell. He couldn't take that chance, so he rode down the hill and opened fire on all of you, his hope being that Estyn Beiler, the marshal back then, would think it to be a random act, some drunked-up plug-ugly who happened onto your land and decided to do a little target practice."

Rachel felt sick, physically sick.

"Only that wasn't how it went. Instead, Amanda Hollister was the prime suspect. If all of you had died, she was next in line to inherit everything. She was the only person who really stood to gain by your deaths— or so everyone believed. You can bet Ray Meeks sweated bullets, terrified that Beiler would start digging and discover that another person stood to gain as well, namely Ray because he was the sole beneficiary of Amanda Hollister's will."

Rachel cupped a hand over her eyes.

"You okay?" Joseph asked softly. "We can let this go, honey. I know it has to be difficult for you to hear."

Rachel lowered her hand. "No, no. I need to know, Joseph. Then I just want to put it behind me if I can."

He sighed and resumed talking. "Ray left you for dead that afternoon, not realizing that the bullet glanced off your skull. He was probably in a hell of a snit when he heard you survived. It wasn't as if he could finish the job, not without raising suspicion again. You went into seclusion, making it almost impossible for him to try to kill you and make it look like an accident. One good thing came of it for Ray, though. With your father dead, all the hired hands quit, and only Darby was left to work your ranch. By exercising a little caution, Ray was able to go to and from the mine with scarcely any risk of being seen. That's a big spread, and Darby couldn't be everywhere at once."

"So he contented himself with that and worked the mine for all these years."

"Precisely. It wasn't an ideal situation. He had to do all the picking and digging and hauling on the sly. But judging by what I've seen, it was very profitable. Maybe he hoped to eventually play the mine out, pull up stakes, and live like a king somewhere else. I only know that he left you and Darby alone for a good long while."

"Until Darby rode up into the rocks, searching for a stray."

"Ray apparently believed that Darby had seen the mine. A fortune was at stake. So Ray shot him in the back. When Darby came riding into my place, my first thought was that he'd taken a stray bullet. But Darby insisted it was too much to be a coincidence and believed he'd been shot by the same person who murdered your family."

"And you came to my house to look after me." Rachel smiled sadly. "Something lovely to make up for all the bad, that. I met you."

He lifted her hand to nibble at the base of her thumb. "Yeah, and just for the record, Mrs. Paxton, I'm as thankful for that turn of events as you are. But I want to finish this." He smiled and winked at her. "Contrary to what Ray evidently thought, Darby hadn't seen the mine. And the new marshal, David, was as baffled as Estyn Beiler had been five years ago, with no real clues to solve either shooting incident. It's highly unlikely that Ray would have done anything else to arouse suspicion if Buddy hadn't seen or heard him up in the rocks yesterday, raised sand to alert me, and then taken off up there.

"I'll never know how that dog knew that Ray Meeks was a polecat, but somehow he did. He wasn't barking a friendly hello, like he normally does. Buddy knew the man was dangerous. When I called him back, he didn't listen. He just charged on up the hill, and Ray hit him in the head with something to shut him up. When I went looking for my dog, I found the damned mine."

"And the secret was out."

"Essentially, and Ray stood to lose a veritable fortune in gold. Even worse, everything else was going to hell in a handbasket as well. His mother had suddenly up and decided to get married. He realized that Darby, as her husband, would have legal right to her property and could probably contest her will, cutting Ray out cold. They were planning to marry in less than a week. He panicked and hatched a plan to kill his mother and you both. He hoped to make Amanda's death look natural—she is old, after all, and Doc might have thought her heart just stopped. And your death could appear to be the murder it actually was, with all the evidence carefully laid by Ray to implicate the Pritchards.

"It was a pretty clever plan, actually. He apparently eavesdropped on Darby's conversation with Amanda last night and knew of my and David's decision to round up a posse to search Jeb's property at ten this morning. Sometime last night, Ray sneaked into Jeb's barn to plant a couple bags of gold. Then bright and early this morning, he cut Jeb's fence wire, herded the Pritchard cows off the property, and then went by Jeb's place to tell him that his cattle were running all over hell's creation. When we got to Jeb's, no one was there. Then Buddy came racing in, acting deranged and trying to make me follow him." Joseph's eyes went bright with wetness. "I'm so glad now that I had the good sense to pay attention to that dad-blamed dog. He knew you were in danger."

Rachel shivered, remembering. "Right after Ray showed up, Buddy started snarling. When Darby scolded him, he ran off and wouldn't come back. I didn't know he was going to find you, but I'm ever so glad he did. If you hadn't come—"

Joseph laid a finger over her lips. "Don't say it, Rachel. It's a miracle you survived. Right after I entered the courtyard, a birdhouse exploded from sheer heat. I've never seen anything like it."

"Buddy saved my life by going for you, Joseph. I can't leave that unsaid. He knew Ray meant to harm me. Somehow he *knew*."

"Maybe dogs can smell evil in a person just like they smell fear. When I reached your place and got you out of the courtyard, I would have believed Ray's story in a heartbeat if it hadn't been for Buddy snarling at him. If not for that, everything Ray told me would have played into what I already believed, that the Pritchards were behind everything. I knew Jeb and his boys had been gone from their place when we got over there. Then Ray said he'd seen them riding away from your house right before it went up in flames. It all fit, and I would have believed him, I think." He sighed. "I feel bad about that now. Jeb's dirty and unlikable. I almost made a terrible mistake, something I never would have forgiven myself for, all because I don't like the man."

Rachel glanced around. "Where is Buddy, by the way? I owe him a big thank-you hug."

"I figured he deserved a treat and let him go home with Ace tonight so he can play with Cleveland until he drops."

Rachel laughed softly. "Good. He does deserve a reward. When he comes home, you need to kill a steer so I can feed him steak until it comes out his ears."

"What about me? Don't I get a reward?"

Rachel pushed up on an elbow to hook an arm around his neck. "Oh, yes, but I've something better in mind for you."

Rachel smoothed his hair, kissed him just below his ear. "It's over, Joseph. It's finally, truly over. From this moment forward, I don't want to think about Ray Meeks ever again. I want to concentrate on our life together and on making you happy."

"I can go for that," he said with a growl. "You sure you're feeling up to it? You had a pretty horrible experience today."

A nightmarish experience, and Rachel wanted to put it completely, forever behind her. "I feel fine, thank you. I just need you to help me think about something else."

Within seconds, he went from serious to passionate, tearing at her clothing, laving her body with kisses. Rachel forgot about the fire—forgot about Ray Meeks—forgot about Mannie.

She was alive, and that had to be celebrated.

Later when they lay satiated in each other's arms with only a film of sweat separating their naked bodies, Joseph whispered, "Shit."

"What?"

"I just ripped your shirtwaist, getting it off you."

Rachel tasted his ear, wanting him again. "It's okay. I didn't like that shirtwaist very well, anyway."

He nibbled just below her jaw. "It was your *only* shirtwaist. Every other stitch of clothing you owned went up in flames."

Rachel realized he was right and burst out laughing. "Oh, dear. I guess I'll have to run around the house stark naked."

"Hmm. Now there's a thought. Stupid me. I was thinking more along the lines of going shopping to get you new clothes."

She nipped the underside of his chin. "Shame on you."

He grinned and kissed her. Against her lips, he whispered, "No worries. I'll get you one of my shirts to use as a nightgown for tonight, and tomorrow I'll go shopping." He trailed his mouth toward her breasts. Then he went still and let loose with another curse.

Rachel grinned and ran her hands into his hair, trying to direct him to where she desperately wanted to have his mouth. "What now?"

His wonderful hands cupped her breasts. "Ace boarded off the hallway. I forgot to get any of my clothes out of the bedroom."

Rachel started to giggle. She was still laughing when Joseph thrust himself deeply into her. Suddenly all thought of laughter abandoned her. *Heaven on earth.* Caitlin had told her exactly right.

Some time later, Rachel stood before the fire, her only covering a blanket from off the sofa. A loud crash of breaking glass came from the back of the house. She smiled and turned to warm her backside. *Joseph, breaking through a window again.* Except for it being in his house instead of hers, it seemed they'd come full circle, with one small difference.

This time, she wouldn't shoot at him when he reached the kitchen. The man had his fine points and was definitely a keeper.

Chapter Twenty

Three months later

Rachel sat in her new courtyard on a bench fashioned for her by No Name's only sawyer, Ron Christian. It was a gorgeous July afternoon, and she had nothing better to do than enjoy the sunlight that poured down through the iron bars to warm her skin and make her roses and violets bloom.

Heaven. Jesse Chandler, the chimney sweep, had built her another trio of birdhouses, and his wife, Dorothy, a gentle, soft-spoken blonde who made gorgeous candles, had decorated each of them. Harrison Gilpatrick had defied his wife yet again to bring her several more rosebushes, and the first spring buds had now matured into gorgeous full blooms. The patches of lawn were a brilliant summer green. Her new school of goldfish loved their new pond. Everything in Rachel's world was absolutely right. Joseph had seen to that.

Just as he'd promised, he'd created a safe world for her at his ranch. She had everything she could possibly need at her fingertips within her living area: a

water closet, a brand-new washing machine, re-
tractable clotheslines to dry the laundry, and designated areas for comfortable living—a kitchen, a
dining room, a bedroom, and a parlor—the only remarkable difference being that now her area was larger
because, without knowing it, Joseph had built his
house just for her, combining his kitchen, dining area,
and sitting room into one large open section. In the
days since her near brush with death, he had added on
a vestibule, just as he'd promised, and Bubba White
had fashioned more ironwork for the doors, ceiling,
and gate, making her feel absolutely safe.

Everyone had worked so hard to create this world
for her, and Rachel loved it. She truly did. The courtyard was even larger than the first one. Joseph had
slaved from dawn to dark building the walls, taking
them out much farther from the house this time so she
wouldn't perish in the event of another fire. The
thought brought tears to her eyes. So much love, and
so much *work*. When she thought of all the hours of
labor that had been invested, she didn't know how to
tell Joseph that she no longer needed any walls.

Directly after Ray Meeks' death, Rachel had needed
the barricades, just like always. Boards over the windows. A shotgun within easy reach. No doors that
opened onto the outdoors. Only somehow, over the
weeks that followed the fire, something within her had
inexplicably healed, and she awoke one morning wanting the boards off the windows so she could see out.
And once outside in her courtyard, where before she
had always felt so miraculously free, she suddenly felt

imprisoned, all that was within her yearning to see the world beyond the walls.

She didn't know what to do. Joseph had spent a small fortune adding on to the front of his house to build her a vestibule. And he'd neglected his ranch to build these fabulous, impenetrable walls of rock for her. How could she tell him that she no longer needed or even wanted them?

She heard a conveyance pull up out front. No urge came over her to run into the house to hide. The demon that had haunted her dreams for so very long no longer existed. Maybe it was Doc, coming to check on her again. Or maybe it was someone from town, bearing yet another sweet gift to make her little world more beautiful.

Only she wanted the real world now. She wanted to go walking through the fields with her wonderful husband. She wanted to go horseback riding and lie on her back in a shady place, watching the clouds drift by and listening to the birds.

Rachel had prayed for so long to get well. For *years*. And she had despaired, convinced she never would. But that was before Joseph. Before Buddy. Before Joseph's wonderful family. Maybe she would pretend to be sick a while longer. She'd lived in a dark cave for so long. She could surely do it for a few more months. Then everyone who had worked so hard on this beautiful courtyard might not feel quite so deflated when she informed them that she no longer needed it.

"Rachel?"

That voice. It was one that Rachel had adored all

her life. She sat frozen on the bench for a moment. Then she twisted to look over her shoulder. There, gazing at her through the bars, was Aunt Amanda.

"I'll go if you want," she said shakily. "I'll understand if you hate me. I truly will. But I had to at least try to see you one more time."

Tears filled Rachel's eyes, nearly blinding her. "Mannie."

"Yes, it's me. I'm a little worse for wear, I'm afraid." She curled a shaky hand around a bar. "I won't stay but for a minute, sweet girl. Only for a minute. I just want to say that I'm so very sorry. I loved him, you know. My Raymond." Amanda grabbed for breath and shakily exhaled. "Sometimes when we love a child so very, very much, we're blinded to his faults. I won't lie to you. Deep down, I think I always knew. But I couldn't *believe*. Does that make any sense?"

Rachel tried to nod, but the muscles in her neck seemed to have turned to stone.

"As a mother," Amanda continued, "I couldn't believe it of him. So I found others to blame, and I pretended he was all that I wanted and needed him to be, the wonderful son that I had lost and found again."

Rachel pushed slowly to her feet. Her throat had closed off, and she couldn't speak.

"I just need you to know that I never stopped loving you. *Never.* I was an old fool, and you and your family paid the price for it. I can never undo that. I will never forgive myself for the pain I've caused you. I just hope that someday, when you hold your own little boy in your arms, you'll come to some sort of understanding and finally be able to forgive me. There's no

then? Darby can work the ranch as long as he feels up to it, but you and Joseph will actually own it and manage it. And the gold will be divided equally between you and me. Darby and I will build a grand little house over there and live out our last years like a king and queen, working only when and if we please. What we don't manage to spend before we die will go to your children, although I have to warn you that I've always had a hankering to see far-away places. Maybe we'll spend it all traveling."

Rachel hoped so. No one deserved to see far-away places more than her aunt Amanda. "It's a deal," she replied.

And they shook on it.

As they moved on to talk about other things, Rachel felt like a child again, confessing her troubles to always understanding Mannie.

When Rachel had told her the entire story about no longer needing any walls, Amanda threw back her head and chortled with laughter. Flicking Rachel an apologetic glance, she wiped tears of mirth from under her eyes and said, "What a pickle."

"I already know it's a pickle. Joseph will want to strangle me when he finds out."

Amanda laughed some more.

"It's not funny, Mannie. I'm well, and I can't tell anyone. Joseph has been so wonderful. You just can't know. He's created a safe world for me here, doing everything within his power to make me happy. How can I tell him it was all for nothing?" The back of Rachel's throat burned. "I always thought I'd be so happy if I got well. Now I just feel awful and wish I were sick again."

Amanda shook her head. "Sick again? Rachel Marie, bite your tongue. Where is the man?"

Rachel jumped up from the bench. "Why? You aren't going to tell him?"

Amanda laughed. "No, but you are. Right now, this instant. Where is he?"

"Out in the fields. I think he's plowing."

"Well, then. Plowing means he hasn't turned dirt everywhere yet, and you can still find some grass. Run out there and make best use of it."

"The best use of grass?" Rachel asked, completely baffled.

"Yes, the grass. Where's your head at, young lady? By the time you finish with him, he won't care about the damned courtyard. He'll only be delighted that you're well. How can you think otherwise?" She glanced around the courtyard. "You got a lovely garden out of it. Be thankful for that and count your blessings."

"But what of all the people from town?"

Amanda rolled her blue eyes. "They wanted to give you sunshine. Do you think caring hearts like that will nitpick? They are going to be happy as can be that you're well."

Rachel cast a dubious look at the gate. "Oh, Mannie, I've never been so scared in my life."

"Pshaw." She flicked her fingertips at the gate. "Off with you. Are you the daughter of my heart or not? Sometimes you have to dig deep for courage, girl. Start digging."

Rachel ran over to hug her aunt. "Oh, Mannie, I have missed you so."

Amanda gathered her close for a long, tight embrace. Then she pushed Rachel away. "Go on. Give the man something to smile about. You can tell me about it later."

Rachel let herself out the gate. *Deep breath.* And, oh, that felt so wonderful. She was *free*. After five long years in prison, she was absolutely free. Way off in the distance, she saw Joseph shuffling along behind the mules, his strong shoulders braced to control the plow as it dug deep into new earth.

"Joseph!" she called.

He didn't look up.

"Joseph?" she called again.

Her voice must have carried to him on the summer breeze, for he drew the team to a halt and looked up. Rachel ran faster, her arms held wide. She saw him pull the gear off over his head and start toward her, haltingly at first, as if he couldn't quite believe his eyes, and then surging into a flat-out run, as if every second that passed might be their last.

They collided in the pasture between the house and the field. Rachel locked her arms around his strong neck. "I'm well, Joseph. I'm well! I didn't know how to tell you."

She babbled on about the courtyard and the vestibule and all the boarded-up windows and how terrible she felt for not needing them anymore. And then Joseph locked an arm around her waist, dropping to his knees and taking her down with him.

"You're well? You're well and you couldn't tell

me? Sweet Christ, woman. Like I care about that damned courtyard?" He caught her face between his hands. Dirty hands, ingrained with the soil that provided their livelihood. "Being out here doesn't bother you? You can breathe?"

Rachel took a deep breath, just to show him. "I'm so sorry, Joseph. I didn't realize. Not until the courtyard was almost finished. And then I felt so *awful*. All that work for nothing. I didn't know how to tell you, and I just—"

His hungry mouth cut off the rest of the sentence. The next thing Rachel knew, she was on her back in pink clover, with the most wonderful, handsome, sexy man on earth braced on his arms above her.

"I love you," he whispered raggedly as he trailed kisses down her throat. "It's a miracle, Rachel. A miracle. We won't have to shove our kids out the wood safe to send them to school."

Rachel snorted with laughter. And then as his hot mouth found one of her breasts, she forgot what she was laughing about. *Joseph.* She loved him as she'd never loved anyone. As he shoved up her skirts and thrust himself deeply into her, Rachel drank in the blue sky above them, reveling in the wondrous feeling of a summer breeze flowing gently over her bare skin.

Joseph's gift to her.

When their passion was spent and he collapsed beside her, Rachel whispered, "It's a good thing the grass is tall. I'll bet anything that Mannie stayed to watch."

"What?"

Rachel giggled and then told him about her aunt's

visit. "She still hadn't left when I ran out here to tell you."

Joseph jerked his pants up. "You mean I was flashing my bare ass at your aunt?"

"Oh, I doubt that. I think the grass is tall enough to have covered you."

"You *think*. You don't know for sure. You just *think*? I've a good mind to turn you over my knee and paddle your bare butt."

"Hmm. That sounds fun."

He grabbed her and wrestled her across his lap. Rachel shrieked and burst out laughing when he threw up her skirts and playfully pinched her bottom instead.

Laughter. Wrestling with her husband in the grass, with clover forming a pink blanket all around them. If she lived to be a hundred, she doubted that life would ever get better.

Everything, absolutely everything, was perfect just as it was.

EPILOGUE

Tucker stared long and hard at the last page of Rachel Hollister's diary, feeling oddly empty inside, as if the last few pages of her memoirs had been dribbles of water, spilling from inside of him, leaving nothing. Such an incredible story, with such happiness at the end, the kind of happiness he had never experienced and wasn't sure he ever would.

He turned to look at his mom. On this, the fifth afternoon of their diary reading, she was smiling dreamily, staring at the curtains over her kitchen bay window, as if remembering something.

"What are you thinking?" he asked.

Mary Coulter shrugged and grinned. "About your dad. About the first time I ever saw him. About our courtship." She sighed. "What a glorious thing true love is. It only gets better with time. Comfortable, like Ace tried to explain to Joseph, and ever so precious after all the excitement wears off. I nag at your father to change his shirt, and I chew him out whenever he messes up, never sparing any words. But I love him more now than I ever dreamed possible when we were young and just starting out."

She patted Rachel's diary. "It's so good to read something like that. They lived and loved so long ago, but even then they found a happy ending. Isn't that wonderful?"

"How can you know that?" Tucker asked. "Maybe Joseph woke up one morning and his feelings had changed. Maybe the excitement all wore off." It had happened to Tucker more times than he wanted to count—a sizzle, thinking he'd found the woman of his dreams, and then the inevitable fizzle. "They got married so *fast*. What was it—a month after they met, maybe? They barely knew each other."

His mother looked at him as if he were an alien and rapped him sharply on the forehead with her knuckles. "They were together almost constantly for all that time. Trust me, they knew all the things they needed to know about each other, and the love they felt was real."

Tucker shook his head. "Ten years later, I'll bet Joseph Paxton was sweating behind a plow, wishing he'd never bitten off all that responsibility. A wife and kids and bills to pay. The romance doesn't last. If you buy into that, you're in for a big fall."

Mary smiled. "I knew you'd say that." She turned on her kitchen chair and plucked something off the counter behind them. "Read that, you doubting Thomas. It's Joseph's last letter to Rachel, shortly before he died."

"What?" Tucker was so into the story by now that he reverently took the yellowed paper from his mother's hand. Unlike the paper in the diary, these sheets looked familiar, lined in blue and from a tablet, much like the sheets of paper he'd used to do his lessons in grade school.

His mother's eyes shone. "He was ninety-four when he wrote that letter. It's dated 1952. Your grandma Eden received it from one of Joseph and Rachel's children, and she saved it in the family Bible. I've never read it without crying. It's so beautiful."

My darling Rachel: the letter read in spidery, faded ink, clearly written by an old, palsied man. *I fear that I may leave you soon.*

"He died a year later," Mary whispered reverently. "He knew his time with her was almost over, and he wanted her to know all the things in his heart. Isn't that beautiful? She passed on about a year after he did, but she had this to sustain her."

As Tucker read on, his throat got tight, and he wasn't the sentimental sort.

> *You have given me so much. When I first met you, I thought I was opening up the world for you, but I was so wrong. You were the one who opened up all of my windows so I could see the beauty beyond the glass. Holding Little Joe in my arms, watching him grow into a man. Then Paul, Peter, Mary, Sarah, and John. When did we start giving them biblical names? We never reached our goal of replicating the twelve apostles, my darling, but each one is so very special.*
>
> *I am afraid now as the end draws near, not of dying, but of growing so weak that I'll have to*

leave you. I feel the time coming close. But even though I will leave you in the flesh, I will never leave you in spirit. I'll be a ghost to haunt you, my sweet Rachel. I will be the scent of roses in the summer breeze. I will be your comfort in the shadows. I'll be the creak you hear when the house settles at night. I am going to stay with you as long as you remain here, a good ghost who can't bring himself to depart for heaven until you can go with me. I have unfinished business here, the other half of my heart. Heaven won't be heaven if you aren't there with me. I guess I'll be one of those disobedient spooks I once told you about, refusing to follow all the rules, only I won't be an evil one. Just the spirit of a man who isn't complete without his Rachel beside him.

Fortunately, I won't have to be a spook for long. You'll join me on the other side soon, and then we'll go to heaven together. I swore once that I would never leave you again. I meant it. I will never, ever leave you, my darling. You can go to the bank on that. And I know that God will allow me to keep that promise. I will be the wind in your hair. I will be the bark of Buddy's great-grandson many times removed. I'll be the softness of a rosebud against your sweet cheek. I'll be the warmth of the blankets around you at night.

When I'm gone and you cry for me, dry your tears and feel my presence. I'll be right there beside you, unable to touch you as I did in this life, but there all the same.

I love you, sweet Rachel. I always will. My body may die, but that which is between us never will.

Your loving husband, into eternity,
Joseph

The signature blurred in Tucker's vision, for he feared that he would never write such words to a woman. Maybe true love—the genuine article—had died out in modern times. Or maybe he was just unlucky. He'd never found anyone who meant a fraction as much to him as Rachel had meant to Joseph.

"Isn't that incredible?" Mary whispered.

It was, indeed, incredible. Tucker saw the proof, right there in his hand, that true love could actually happen. At least it had way back in the 1800s. Maybe women had changed, becoming more selfish and self-serving. Or maybe men had changed, becoming more focused on physical pleasure than meaningful relationships. He didn't know. He only knew that nothing so precious and lasting had ever come his way.

"When I was younger, I used to hope that your father might one day write a letter like that to me," his mother whispered.

Tucker turned to study Mary's sweet face. Her eyes were closed, and her smile glowed with happiness.

"But now that I'm older, with so many years behind us," she added, "I no longer need him to write the words. He loves me just that much, and I love him just as deeply. We'll go on, and one day we'll be at the last of our lives, as Joseph was when he wrote this letter to

Rachel, but even though our bodies are dying, what we feel for each other never will."

Tucker had a lump in his throat. And a yearning. He'd seen his sister and brothers find such happiness in their marriages. They'd found the magic. What was wrong with him that he hadn't found it, too? Soon he'd turn thirty-fire. His good years were almost gone. God, he'd be forty before he knew it.

What did he have? Only one half of a veterinary practice. Rather than talk about that with his mother, he asked, "Do you think they're still there in Colorado, living near No Name?"

"Rachel and Joseph?"

"No, their descendants. Paxtons and Keegans. They must still be there."

Mary thought about it for a moment and then nodded. "It's a branch of our family that we've never kept in contact with, but they surely must be. People like us, who have bits and pieces of the past hidden away in their attics."

Tucker had a sudden yearning to go there—to No Name, Colorado.

Maybe there he would find the magic that eluded him in Oregon.

The Cup
and the Crown

❦ 1 ❧

King Alaric the Younger

THE GREAT HALL WAS MUCH as she remembered it: the tapestries, the massive iron candle stands, the enormous fireplace, the great gilt screen behind the dais. But the rushes were gone from the floor now, in keeping with the latest fashion. And there were sentries posted at the entrance to the royal chambers. They followed her with their eyes as she paced in restless circles, waiting. What was taking Alaric so long?

There had never been guards in the old days, when Godfrey the Lame was king. Molly knew this for a fact. She'd once pressed her ear to that very door and listened to young Prince Alaric quarreling with his

mother, unobserved by anyone but Tobias, who'd come to mend the fire. He'd been scandalized that a scullery maid should presume to eavesdrop on a queen.

Molly smiled, remembering how intensely she'd despised them both. "Mind who you look at, wench," Prince Alaric had said to her as he stormed out of his mother's room. And "You aren't fit to be here," Tobias had added later. What *she'd* said didn't bear repeating—but then she'd only been seven at the time, and inclined to say whatever popped into her head, however outrageous it might be.

Come to think of it, that last part hadn't changed so very much.

She circled past the dais and was musing on the screen when the door flew open and a large, imposing man came out, thunder on his face, his boots striking the flagstones with the force of his anger. As he passed, he shot Molly a look of pure revulsion. Then he turned away, as from something loathsome, and continued with long strides down the length of that cavernous room, the stink of his fury trailing behind. She watched him, appalled, till he was long out of sight. Only when she heard her name did she look back at the door and see Alaric standing there.

He didn't greet her with a smile or apologize for making her wait. Indeed, he scarcely looked at her at all.

"Come," he said. "We'll walk in the garden. I need a change of air."

⁂

He took her arm and held it close to his side. Whether he did this out of affection or was merely stiff with rage, Molly couldn't tell. Either way, she liked it. She cast a quick glance up at his pale, narrow face, his sun-bright curls and gray eyes, and judged him as handsome as ever—despite the scowl and the crease between his brows. She sighed to herself in quiet satisfaction and leaned her head against his shoulder, just a touch.

It was high summer, and the flower beds were bright with lilacs, roses, and lilies. Ancient trees arched over their heads, offering welcome shade as they followed their winding course, fine gravel crunching beneath their feet.

Molly had never been there before, though she'd lived half her life at Dethemere Castle. Common servants had no business in the king's garden, unless it was to plant, and prune, and tend that private little patch of paradise. Her place had been in the kitchen, scrubbing pots and polishing silver.

All that had changed this past half year. And nothing about her transformation from scullion to lady had struck her quite so forcibly as this: that she walked the

paths of the royal garden on the arm of the king of Westria—just the two of them, alone.

Never mind that he was in a mood.

"So, how do you like your new estate?" He said this distractedly, his mind on something else.

"It's very beautiful, my lord."

"I should certainly hope so. It was to have been my sister's dower house. You're happy there?"

"Not especially, my lord."

He stopped and looked down at her, *really* looked for the first time that morning.

"'*Not especially*, my lord'?"

"It's too grand for me, Alaric. I don't belong. And those highborn servants, brought in to attend a princess, being asked to serve the likes of me . . ."

"You're a lady now, by royal decree."

"Yes. And you could royally decree that henceforth eels shall fly and magpies shall swim in the sea. But even *you* have not the power to make it so. My ladies of the chamber certainly know what I am. They correct my manners at table and express amazement that I can't do embroidery, or play the lute, or dance, or read romances. And there's nothing for me to do all day but meet with my steward and my chamberlain to talk about things I don't understand, and choose which gown to wear, and sit staring into the fire or out

the window while my ladies drive me mad with their never-ending chatter."

"Merciful heavens! You're *bored* as well?"

"Unbearably."

She could feel the tension in his body. He held her arm in a viselike grip.

"Any minute now you're going to say that you're awfully sorry, you know you've been shockingly rude, but it's all because you were ill raised."

"I suppose that would be—"

"Well, *a plague* on your upbringing! I'm sick of hearing about it. I can see you now in your dotage." He took the high, nasal voice of an old crone, hunching his back for added effect. "Oh, I'm *so* sorry I insulted you, my lord, but when I was a small child—*fifty years* ago—I was not taught how to behave."

She took a deep breath. "Your Majesty," she said, "I truly *am* sorry that I seem so ungrateful when you have been so generous and kind. But I spoke the truth: I don't have the makings of a lady. You'd have done better to set me up as a shopkeeper—"

"If you say another word, I shall bite off your head."

How was it, she wondered as they continued to walk in stormy silence, that she'd been so careful of what she said to the cook when she'd worked in the palace kitchens and cowered under the haughty gazes

of her ladies of the chamber—yet with the *king of Westria,* well, she'd say just *any* old thing!

"I'll find you some better attendants," he muttered, "and see that they treat you with respect."

When she didn't respond, he added, "You may speak now."

"Thank you, my lord, but you can leave them as they are. In the end I found it rather amusing to torture them."

"*Torture* them? Good God!"

"Not with thumbscrews, never fear. I just developed a sudden fondness for exercise—taking long walks to the village or the next town over, in foul weather whenever possible. And as I cannot go out alone, it being unfitting for a lady—"

"—they have to accompany you."

"Yes. Such a lot of mud this year."

She'd finally made him laugh. And it felt for a brief spell like the old times, before he'd become king and the burden of great responsibility had been laid on his young shoulders, along with his royal robes.

"Alaric," she said softly. "Tell me why I'm here." She already knew, of course. She'd known for weeks, long before the royal messenger had arrived at Barcliffe Manor, calling her back to court. She knew because she'd seen it in a vision.

The first time it had happened, she'd taken it for a dream. But it had been too clear, too perfect; and when she'd sat up in bed, it had stayed with her, not fading away like smoke into air as dreams always do. It had returned the following night, and every night thereafter, always exactly the same: a handsome boy of eighteen or twenty, dressed in fine clothes, holding a beautiful goblet. And though she'd never seen the cup before, she knew exactly what it was—and what it meant for her, and for the king.

As for the boy, he was a mystery.

"I want you to go to Austlind," Alaric said, "to find one of your grandfather's Loving Cups."

"I thought that must be it," she said. "You were so keen to have one last winter—then not another word. I kept expecting . . . but I suppose you've had a lot on your mind these past months."

"Learning to be a king, you mean? And taking control of my country, and choosing my counselors, and fending off officious busybodies who say I'm too young to rule and I must have a regent do it for me?"

"Yes. And I suppose that terrible man who came out of your chambers just now is one of the busy-bodies?"

"Lord Mayhew? Oh, yes. You know what he calls

me behind my back? King Alaric the Younger. Isn't that charming?"

"You should chop off his head."

"Oh, please, Molly, be serious. I'm sending him with you to Austlind, by the way, to see to your safety on the road. That's why he was so angry. He feels the mission is beneath him."

"Then why send him? If he mocks you in secret, surely he cannot be trusted."

"I trust him to keep you safe. As for the rest, I just told him you're going to Austlind to find a certain silver cup, which I want to send as a gift to the king of Cortova. Anything regarding the princess or the special properties of the cup—please keep that to yourself."

They'd reached an opening in the boxwood hedge that led to the heart of the garden. Here was a pond with a stone fish rising out of the center, standing upright on its tail, water spouting from its mouth.

They sat on a long stone bench in the shade of a chestnut tree. The king released her arm.

"Now, in addition to Lord Mayhew, I'm sending my valet. His name is Stephen, he's fluent in the language of Austlind, and he has my complete trust. You may speak freely with him in all things. But do it in private."

She nodded.

"You'll need a chaperone, of course. Winifred will do, if you wish."

"Yes. And I want Tobias, too."

He scowled. "Whatever for?"

"Have you some personal objection to Tobias?"

His hands flew up, impatient. "Fine," he said. "By all means, bring Tobias."

She waited a spell for his ruffled feathers to settle before making them rise again.

"Alaric?" she began carefully. "May I ask you a question?"

"I suppose that depends on what it is."

"I know you feel you must marry soon and get yourself an heir, as there is no one left in your family to inherit. What I don't understand is why you must resort to enchantment in order to get yourself a bride. I would think there'd be princesses waiting in line—"

He gripped his head with both hands as if fearing it might come off. "By all the saints in heaven, Molly— is there nothing you will not ask? God's blood, but your impertinence takes my breath away!"

She flushed. "I see I overstepped." And then, because she couldn't help it, "I thought I was your friend."

"Don't," he said, getting up from the bench and going to stand by the pond. He stayed there, not

speaking, for an age and more. Then he came back and sat down beside her again.

"It will not be an easy match to make," he said. "When Princess Elizabetta was betrothed to my brother Edmund and came to Dethemere Castle in advance of the marriage, she was in the great hall that night, at my brother's side—"

"I know all that, Alaric. For heaven's sake, I was there."

"Then you will understand that after witnessing the slaughter of my family, including my poor brother whom she was meant to marry—and at such close hand that she was spattered with his very blood—the princess will not look warmly on a match with another king of Westria."

"I agree. It's hopeless. So why not just choose someone else?"

"Because it must be her."

"Oh, come now! She stole your heart in a single day? I know she's beautiful; I saw her myself. But you can't have exchanged a dozen words with the lady. How do you know she's not a shrew, or stupid, or wicked?"

"Neither my heart nor her beauty has anything to do with it, Molly. The kingdom of Cortova controls the Southern Sea. I can't afford to have them turn away from us and make an alliance elsewhere. And

there's been talk of a match with Prince Rupert, my cousin Reynard's eldest son."

"That little runt? He can't be more than thirteen!"

"He's fourteen, just two years younger than I; and where royal marriages are concerned, age doesn't matter. If Rupert is matched with Elizabetta, it'll be a disaster for us. Austlind is already allied to Erbano through Reynard's marriage to Beatrice. If they combine with Cortova too, they'll be so powerful, I fear we could not stand against them.

"So I must have an alliance with Cortova. To achieve that, I must wed the princess. And to wed the princess I must, as you so graciously put it, resort to enchantment. Is that clear?"

"As a mountain stream, my lord."

"Good. Now, you'll be going to a crafts town called Faers-Wigan, where your grandfather worked his trade. If one of his cups is still to be had, you should find it there. But I'm a little concerned—"

"—that I won't be able to tell a true cup from a false one?"

He nodded. "There are a lot of dishonest traders who'll be eager to make a sale, and they'll claim—"

"I know. But they won't fool me. I've been seeing the cup in my dreams this past month and more. I could describe it to you down to the finest detail."

The king brightened upon hearing this. He trusted her magical gift, innocent of the dreadful price she'd paid for the knowledge it brought her. He didn't know—because she'd never told him—how profoundly she dreaded those visions, which came to her unbidden, forcing her to look on unspeakable things. And he certainly couldn't imagine that brash, bold, tough little Molly was haunted by the murder of her grandfather, which she'd witnessed in one of those visions, and the terrible fate of her gentle mother, locked up as a madwoman in a small, dim, noisome room till she was released by death—all because they shared the same magical gift that Molly now carried.

She gazed thoughtfully at the play of water in the pond, thinking not about the cup but the boy who held it: that face, with its straight nose and fine chin, those clear gray eyes, that dark, curly hair—it was like looking into a mirror. He was *herself*, had she been older and a boy.

It had to mean something—that uncanny resemblance, the nightly insistence of the vision. Wouldn't it be wonderful if, just this once, it portended something good?

Best not to count on it, though.

❦ 2 ❧

A Lonely Road

THE WEATHER WAS PERFECT for a journey: the cloudless sky a brilliant blue, the warm air sweet with the smell of clover, the road shaded by ancient plane trees, which rustled in the breeze. And overhead, a pair of ravens danced together—swooping in tandem, dipping and rising, floating on currents of air. It was as if they were joined by invisible strings.

"Look at that!" Molly said, craning her neck to watch. "See how they stay together so perfectly."

"They're courting," Stephen said. "Ravens pair for life, you know."

"Oh, I wish I could do that, just once!"

"Go a-courting?" asked Winifred with a wicked smile.

"*No*, you goose! Fly! I want to rise up into the clouds and float on the air."

"Wouldn't we all?" Stephen said.

They continued in silence, watching in fascination, listening to the birdsong in the meadows and trees and the soft plodding of the horses—all but Tobias, who stared down the road deep in thought.

When he and Molly had first met, he'd been the kitchen's donkey boy, an unkempt, scruffy, troubled child of nine who'd just lost his family to the plague. She'd been the lowest of the scullions, an unkempt, scruffy, impetuous, mannerless child of seven who'd lost her mother to madness and her father to drink and disinterest. She'd told Tobias to wipe his nose and shut his mouth so people wouldn't take him for a half-wit; he'd said she didn't deserve to work at Dethemere Castle and probably wouldn't last there a week.

They'd been inseparable ever since.

When, exactly, things had started to change, Tobias couldn't quite remember. It came to him at odd moments, this sense that she was something more than a friend. There were times when he was gripped with a terrible foreboding that he might lose her some-day, as he'd lost his family; and he knew he could not

survive it. From this he understood that she'd become essential to his life.

There was a word for that, but he'd never spoken it. He was afraid to, and rightly so. That wasn't how they related to each other. The most affectionate thing she'd ever said was "Don't you die on me, Tobias! I couldn't bear it."

He'd wondered many a time whether she felt the same things he did but kept it close to her chest as was her nature. She hadn't grown up with affection. It must seem strange to her. But was the thought of courting really such an outrage that she'd call Winifred a goose for even suggesting it?

"And what are *you* so glum about, prune-face?" Molly said. "On this beautiful day, when ravens are courting and we're off on an adventure?"

"Nothing at all," he said.

Just then a breeze kicked up and caught the brim of Molly's hat—a disreputable-looking thing she'd bought from one of the gardeners—and sent it flying. Tobias, ever quick, caught it in midair and returned it to Molly with a bow from the waist. She smiled at him like an angel, then crammed it gracelessly back on her head.

And suddenly his dejection vanished. *Of course* she loved him, in her own strange way, and that was more

than enough. Indeed, he wondered, in a surge of emotion, if one day, looking back on his life as an old man, he'd choose this moment to have been the happiest of all, the time when he felt the most hopeful and at peace with the world.

⁓ ❦ ⁓

As the days passed, the landscape began to change. The air grew cooler and pines began to replace the plane trees, the chestnuts, and the oaks. In the distance were great, rugged mountains, half shrouded in mist. And then, shortly before sunrise on their sixth day, they crossed the border into Austlind.

Only then did Mayhew announce the change of plans.

They would not be taking the common route that skirted the mountains, winding through the southern foothills before turning north again. Instead, they'd cut directly across the range through a narrow mountain pass. The road was rarely used, being steep and in poor repair; but if they rode hard before the climbing began, they might reach Faers-Wigan by nightfall.

This was contrary to Alaric's explicit instructions. And considering all the precautions they'd taken against being robbed—dressing as common folk, hiding the king's gold in many secret compartments—it

seemed odd to choose the very sort of lonely road where thieves were most likely to be lurking. But no one dared argue with Mayhew, not even Molly.

The short route it would be, then.

Around midmorning they left the broad highway, crossed the river, and continued north and east on a narrow horse path. Trees, tall grass, and scrub grew thickly on both sides, encroaching on the roadway. Here and there potholes, fit to break a horse's leg, were hidden by the undergrowth. Mayhew reined in his horse and they proceeded at a walk.

Above them a raven circled, riding the warm updraft of air. "He's following us," Tobias said.

"*Leading* us, more like," said Winifred. "He flies straight along the path till he gets too far ahead, then he circles back over us, like now."

Stephen laughed. "The countryside is full of ravens, and they all look exactly the same."

"No," Molly said. "Winifred's right. I've been watching him too, and it's the same bird, no question."

Stephen shrugged. "Whatever you say."

"Our raven guide," Molly muttered to herself, pleased with the image.

Before long the path began to rise. In places it was too narrow even for two to ride abreast, so they formed a single file and continued at a walk so as not

to overtax the horses on the steep incline.

Mayhew looked back to see how it had fallen out. Molly was close behind him, followed by Tobias, then Winifred, with Stephen taking the rear. He would rather have had Tobias in back—for though the boy had no apparent skill with a sword, he was tall, strong, and probably quick, while Stephen was none of those things. But it would take time to stop and rearrange the order, so he let it go.

That was a mistake. And he compounded it by failing to notice how much stronger his mount was than the others. It might not look like a warhorse, but that's what it was. And so, as the way twisted and turned through the steep and rocky terrain, the space between them grew, particularly a gap between Tobias and Winifred, who'd stopped to pull out her cloak.

⚞ ⚟

The thief had been hiding in the wilderness since escaping from prison, living off the land and waiting for someone to pass on that godforsaken road. Now the moment had arrived, bringing with it the chance to get both money and a horse. He might lose his life in the attempt, but that would be better than dying of starvation in the woods.

The girl would be easy. The only problem was the man behind her. He was armed, though the sword was

probably just for show. There was a softness about him that was telling; he wouldn't put up much of a fight.

The man in the lead, though, he was a knight for sure. The thief would have to work fast before he could ride back to the rescue. But it was doable: he'd just have to take the little fellow by surprise, knock him off his horse, grab his purse, then leap into the saddle and ride like the devil. By the time the girl had finished screaming and the knight had made his way back—working his way around the girl and the boy in the middle—the thief would have disappeared.

He knew the woods now, and the hiding places.

Winifred was just fastening her cloak—Stephen watching uneasily, aware of the growing space between her and Tobias—when the raven came swooping down and gave a loud, anxious cry. It was a warning, Stephen was sure of it; but when he looked around, he saw nothing.

That was because the thief had come in from behind and was hiding under the horse's rump. Now, still crouching down, he reached up and grabbed the hem of Stephen's cloak. Yanking hard, he pulled him out of the saddle. But Stephen's left foot caught in the stirrup, and the terrified horse danced away to the right, trying to free itself of this unnatural burden. Winifred screamed.

The thief decided to leave the man dangling where

he was and take the girl's horse instead. But she proved more quick-witted than expected. She gave her mount a vicious kick and darted out of his reach, crying "Help, help!" and nearly colliding with the tall boy who'd already turned back.

There was still a chance to get what he wanted if he acted fast. He easily cut the purse from his victim's belt; now all he had to do was get the boot out of the stirrup. But it wouldn't come; the weight of the man's inert body was holding it in place. The thief had just decided to cut his losses and run—at least he had the purse, and with all the trees and underbrush, they couldn't follow him on horseback—when the tall boy came thundering in and leaped out of the saddle, dagger at the ready.

It wasn't even a contest. By the time Mayhew arrived and made a more practiced leap from his mount, Tobias had the man pinned to the ground, the knife at his throat.

"Move," Mayhew said, pulling Tobias roughly away by the collar and dispatching the thief with a single slash of his sword. Then, once he'd satisfied himself that Stephen was all right, he grabbed hold of the dead man's feet and started dragging the body away.

"What are you doing?" Tobias asked.

"What does it look like?"

As there was no obvious response to that question, Tobias didn't give one; but it was plain that Mayhew wasn't simply clearing the road. He was hauling the corpse into the forest.

"But we can't just leave him there," Molly said when Mayhew returned alone. "Shouldn't we give the hue and cry?"

He stared at her, incredulous.

"That's the law," Tobias said.

"All right. And who, pray tell, will hear our hue and cry? That blasted raven there? Perhaps we should turn back and ride to the nearest town—we might get there by nightfall—and see if they want to send a coroner up here to determine the cause of death, then carry the body back down the mountain so they can dump it into a pauper's grave."

"I see your point," Molly said.

❦ 3 ❧

Faers-Wigan

THE GOLDSMITHS' GUILD had the largest and grandest trade hall in Faers-Wigan. It looked more like a palace than a business establishment, with floors of marble, walls hung with tapestries, and torch stands plated with gold. The building served as a gathering place for the members of the guild—goldsmiths and silversmiths alike—and held offices for its many officials.

The guildhall also had a library where the archives were kept, an airy, pleasant room with bookshelves running along the walls. In the center was a large oak table, at the far end of which sat the guild's librarian, whose name was Joseph.

Light streamed in through tall windows onto the dome of his balding head. He was old and pale, as though the sun had bleached him out, and what little hair he had was fine and fair. But his eyes were bright, and so were his wits. Not only could he find the information they were seeking, he could do it in their own language.

He went to a shelf, quickly found the correct volume, and brought it back to the table. Then he started turning pages, leaning forward now and again to squint at an entry, shaking his head and turning to the next one. At last he seemed to have found something, but he didn't say a word; he just opened a little box and took out a thin stick of yellow wood. This he carefully laid between the pages to act as a bookmark, then continued with his search.

Molly sat quietly, watching him and waiting. After a while she noticed that Stephen was looking down at the table, or gazing idly around the room—not staring unendingly at Joseph as she was doing. *Of course,* she thought; he was being polite. No one likes to be stared at. So she looked down at her hands, noticed a smudge, and was just wetting her fingers in her mouth to wipe the smudge away when she heard a gravelly snort. She turned to see Winifred, her head lolling forward, her mouth agape, and her eyes closed. Oh, they were such a hopeless pair of bumpkins! She nudged her friend

with an elbow, then discreetly wiped her fingers on her skirt.

Joseph still studied the book in silence, flipping pages, stopping, reading, moving on. Now and then a look of triumph would cross his face and he'd tuck in a strip of wood to mark a page. At last it seemed he was done. He turned back to the beginning, folded his hands on the tabletop, and spoke.

"The first mention of your grandfather, William Harrows, is in May of 1358," he said. "It's in regard to a contract of employment in the workshop of Artur Volkmann. At the same time William was entered into our rolls as a journeyman silversmith, though there's no record of his apprenticeship and no mention of who his master might have been. We must therefore assume that he came here from somewhere else. Harrows is probably a place-name, his town of origin."

"Oh," Molly said, disappointed. "I'd hoped to find some relatives here."

"That's very unlikely," he said, tapping a bony finger thoughtfully on a corner of the book. "Wherever he came from, William should have had a document of release showing that he'd completed his term of service. But the records just say that he'd proved his competence to Master Volkmann's satisfaction. Quite frankly, I find that suspicious."

Molly's hackles went up. "What do you mean, 'suspicious'?"

"It suggests that your grandfather may have broken his contract and run away. In a case like that, who can tell what other crimes he might also have committed— thievery, for example, or worse—that forced him to leave his master, and indeed his native country? Of course, it's also possible that he was set loose by some tragedy or other: plague, or fire, or accident. "

He stared into the distance for a moment, eyes half closed, quite unaware that Molly was red-faced and scowling.

"There's something else that strikes me as odd," he said, lifting his brows in emphasis. "William Harrows was only seventeen at the time. His apprenticeship would have taken seven years. He would have to have started at ten, which is . . . unusual."

"Perhaps the rules were different in his home country," Stephen suggested.

"Perhaps." Joseph turned to the next marked section. "This should please you, my lady," he said. "Remarkable—truly remarkable! At the age of twenty-two your grandfather submitted a masterpiece to the guild. That was very bold of him, being so young and new to the town. He cannot have imagined he'd be accepted. But he applied all the same. The work is

described as"—he leaned forward and read, following the text with his finger—"'a silver-gilt cup with a lid decorated with pearls set in filigree and embellished with transparent enamels of astonishing quality.' Master Volkmann testified under oath that the work was wholly William's own and he had not assisted him in any way.

"The piece must have been extraordinary for it to have been accepted," he went on. "The old men on the committee would have been hard set against it: *'This will set a dangerous precedent! He must wait his turn!'* And yet it *was* accepted, and William Harrows became the youngest master in the history of our guild."

"Oh!" Molly said. "That does please me, very much."

"I thought it would. Now, right below that is a second entry. Artur Volkmann and William Harrows entered into a partnership that same day—which is, again, highly unusual. Buying half a share of a large, established business would be beyond the means of a young man on a journeyman's salary."

"Are you suggesting—?"

"It's just curious, that's all—or at least it was till I read the next entry. On August 12, 1366, William married his new partner's daughter, Martha."

"That means Artur Volkmann was—"

"Your great-grandfather. Yes." He turned to the next page.

"This one is dated February 3, 1368: 'Master Artur Volkmann departed this life at the age of fifty-three. He was accompanied to the churchyard by his family and the members of the guild, etcetera, etcetera. . . . His last will and testament was established by probate, etcetera, etcetera . . . the beneficiary being his partner, William Harrows.'" He looked up at Molly. "That made him a very wealthy man. Quite a feat for a boy who arrived here . . . well . . ."

Molly heaved a loud sigh of disgust. Joseph didn't seem to notice.

"'On December tenth of that same year, a daughter was born to William Harrows, master goldsmith, and his wife, Martha.' No name is given."

"It was Greta," Molly said.

He nodded and turned to the final entry but paused for a moment before reading it. "'November 23, 1369, Master William Harrows was found dead in his workshop. In the absence of any family, the funeral was arranged by the guild.'"

He folded his hands on the table again. "That's everything in the records. But it was common knowledge at the time that William was murdered."

"I know."

"Indeed?" He looked at her pointedly. "Well, since the wife and child were nowhere to be found, it was assumed that they had been taken, and most likely killed, by whoever had done the murder. Yet now here you are, saying you are William's granddaughter. So I gather that the child at least—"

"Greta."

"You claim that she survived."

"Yes, I *do* claim it, for it is true. My grandmother fled to Westria with the baby and settled there."

"Ah. I suppose you've come for the inheritance, then."

"No!" she said, rising to her feet. "I have *not* come for his money. I came to learn my grandfather's history."

"All the same," Joseph said, rising as well out of politeness, "I should tell you that William's fortune was seized by the crown, there being no surviving heirs. So if you change your mind and decide to pursue it, you'll have to prove that you are indeed William's grandchild. And even then—"

"I will *not* pursue it."

"As you wish. Is there anything else you need?"

"No," said Molly.

"Yes," said Stephen at exactly the same time. "The address of William's shop."

❦ 4 ❧

The Workshop of William Harrows

THEY LEFT THE GUILDHALL and headed for the commercial district, Stephen leading the way. He took Molly's arm and leaned over to speak softly into her ear. "The man didn't mean to offend you," he said.

"Really? He all but said my grandfather slit his master's throat, then robbed him and ran away."

"Excuse me, my lady, but you exaggerate."

"I didn't like him."

"Well, he was useful, was he not?"

"I suppose."

They turned down Silk Row and continued at an unhurried pace, admiring the goods on display: furs,

lace, velvets, brocades, cloth-of-gold, and silken veils as fine as spiderwebs. Apprentices waiting outside shop doors perked up as they approached. "Something for the ladies?" they'd ask. "Won't you come in and have a look?"

But Stephen would just nod and smile. "Not today, thank you," he'd say.

At last they came to Goldsmith's Lane, where he paused, looking thoughtfully up and down the street, wondering from which end the blocks were numbered.

"I think they start from the center of town," Mayhew said.

"Yes. You're right. In that case we should turn to the left."

Winifred stopped to stare at a window display of brooches, belt fittings, signets, and sword hilts, all made from silver or gold, engraved or worked with fine enamels, inlaid with ivory, or set with precious jewels. "Oh!" she moaned. "Will you look at that?"

Instantly the apprentices were upon them.

"Just looking," Stephen said, gently taking Winifred's arm and urging her forward. "It's best to keep moving," he whispered.

They continued in the same leisurely manner, trying not to stare, until Stephen stopped before a particularly handsome doorway framed by a stone arch,

its double doors open wide. Above the entrance was a painted wooden sign. The image was simple: the silhouette of a goblet rendered in silver on a field of blue. Molly recognized the shape at once. It was the Loving Cup, exactly as she'd seen in her dreams.

And perched on the post that held the sign was her raven.

"This is the place," she said.

⁂

The sound of hammering filled the workshop—*tink, tink, tink*—as busy hands worked to form the shape of bowls or cups against the curved necks of little anvils. One man was pressing designs into a silver tray, carefully placing his punch, then striking it smartly with a hammer: *thunk!* Over by the forge, a journeyman and an apprentice did double-duty with the bellows.

Molly closed her eyes and tried to recall her grandfather's workshop as she'd seen it in her visions. There'd been shelves to display his fine silver pieces against the right-hand wall, and the central worktable had been smaller. But the forge was in the same place, and she remembered the graceful arched window that filled the end wall of the long, narrow room. Yes, she was sure. This had once been the workshop of William Harrows, the place where Molly had watched him die.

"My lady?" Stephen said, gently touching her arm. "Will you please step this way?"

He guided her back toward the front of the room where a stocky man waited, looking very grand in saffron-colored silk. Pinned to his wine-red velvet cap was a handsome brooch: four pearls set in a diamond shape with a single ruby drop hanging from its lowest point.

"Lady Marguerite," Stephen said in his best courtly manner, "may I present Master Frears, the owner of this shop."

The man bowed and his ruby danced.

"Master Frears purchased this shop from another goldsmith, who had bought it years before from the crown. But he's certainly heard of William Harrows, who is something of a legend in Goldsmith's Lane, and assures me that this used to be his workshop."

"Did you ask about the Loving Cups?" she said in Westrian.

"Not yet. I'll do it now."

While Stephen asked the question in flaw-less Austlinder, Molly scanned the countertops and shelves. There were any number of goblets on display, but all of them were in the new style, slender and tall. So unless Master Frears had some old pieces locked away somewhere . . .

Suddenly she realized how unlikely that was. The workshop and all of its contents had been seized by the crown. Besides the building, that would have included the tools and furnishings; William's stock of silver and gold, jewels, ivory, pearls, coral, and onyx; and any finished pieces that had not been sold. It would have been the same with the family's home. The king's men would have come and carried everything away, from Greta's cradle and Martha's gowns to the pots and andirons in the kitchen. If there'd been a Loving Cup in either place, King Reynard had it now.

Disheartened, she turned back to Master Frears just as Stephen was rounding off his question. She saw the goldsmith cast a quick glance around the room, trying to decide which of several goblets he could pass off as a Loving Cup.

Was it even worth the effort of going through the motions, looking at what he had to offer, shaking her head, watching as he grew ever more desperate and offered her still more expensive cups her grandfather hadn't made? Yet they'd come so far to find the cup. And what if Master Frears should suddenly remember: "Oh, you must mean *that* old thing—excuse me, I meant that *classically beautiful* piece up there on the top shelf hidden behind the silver-gilt bowl?"

It wasn't likely, but it *might* happen.

She was staring at the floor, trying to decide what to do, when she had the distinct impression that she was being watched.

I see you! said a voice in her head.

Molly looked up and saw a stooped old man sitting in a corner at the back of the shop. He was polishing a small bowl with a white cloth and gazing fixedly in her direction. She tugged gently at Stephen's sleeve to get his attention. "There are no Loving Cups in this shop," she whispered, "but keep him busy, will you? There's something I need to find out."

Stephen nodded and returned to the goldsmith while Molly wandered away.

The old man's face didn't change as she came closer. He just continued to stare straight ahead. And then she understood. He hadn't been looking at her at all—the man was stone-blind.

Yet he spoke to her again in that strange way. His lips weren't moving and she wasn't hearing a voice, yet she knew exactly what he was saying.

You're one of them, ain't you?

She squatted down so they were face to face. "What did you mean, 'You're *one of them*'? One of who?"

He rocked back and forth on his stool.

One of them magical folk from Harrowsgode.

"No. I've never heard of Harrowsgode. But my grandfather was called William Harrows, and he wasn't born here; he came from somewhere else. Is that the place, then? Harrowsgode?"

Aye. He was magical, too. He's dead now.

She caught her breath, trying to stay calm. "Did you know him—William Harrows?"

I was his shop boy, till he were murdered. I saw him lyin' right there. He pointed to a spot by the forge. *Right there he was. Strangled.*

Molly shivered, picturing this man, just a young boy then, coming in to sweep up the shop and finding his master's body. No, she suddenly realized—more likely he was there all along. He watched the murder through a keyhole. Then when it was safe, he came creeping out and rifled through her grandfather's pockets, looking for coins. Or slipped the rings off his fingers.

He didn't need it anymore.

She started. "What? What didn't he need?"

The old man wouldn't say.

"I won't tell anyone," Molly promised.

You'll take it.

"No, I won't!"

But he seemed unconvinced, his face suddenly that of a sullen child.

"Why would I want it?" she said. "I'm magical, remember? I can make anything, any old time: money, rings. . . ."

The old man shook his head, a knowing expression on his face. Then with fumbling fingers he reached into the leather bag he wore strapped to his belt. Finding what he was searching for, he grinned, displaying three brown teeth, one of them broken.

"You're wasting my time, you know. Either show it to me or don't. It's of no concern to me."

He pulled his hand out of the bag, but he still kept his fingers curled around whatever it was he held. Then slowly he loosened his grip. Molly leaned in and stared.

At first she took it for a giant opal and was calculating what it must be worth—a stone like that could be the centerpiece of a great king's crown. She could see right into its heart, as you can see the pebbles on the bottom of a clear, deep spring. Only this wasn't the pale transparency of water; it was alive with color— deep blues and brilliant greens, with tiny flashes of red. And it didn't just capture the light as even the finest jewels do—this stone had its *own light*. It glowed like a candle.

The old man closed his fingers around it again. Molly thought hard.

"Did William make that?"

Aye. He were magical, like I said.

"What's it for? What does it do?"

William talked to it. Muttering all the time, he was. Having conversations.

"He had conversations with a stone?"

No. He squinted, trying to remember. *More like talking to people who was far away. Old friends, it sounded like.*

"And they answered back? Could you hear them?"

No, but he could.

"That's very magical indeed."

Yeh. I just thought it was pretty.

"It is. It's beautiful."

But now . . . His face brightened. He took his balled fist, still clutching the opal, and pressed it to his lips and then to his eyes. *I can see you and speak to you.*

"Yes."

Ain't never happened afore. That's how come I know you be one of 'em.

"This place," she said. "Harrowsgode. Do you know where it is?"

Up north.

"Where, up north?"

By the sea.

"Due north? How far?"

He seemed distracted now, troubled. *I shouldn't of took it. I shouldn't of.* He rocked slowly back and forth, humming a tuneless melody, not looking at her anymore.

Finally Molly left him and returned to the front of the shop, where Master Frears was making a drawing for Stephen on fine vellum. The picture showed a lidded cup with rubies around the base. He'd gone to the trouble of painting the stones in red, which is how she knew what they were. It was a handsome piece, and the drawing was fine. But it wasn't a Loving Cup.

Stephen gave her a questioning glance.

"We're leaving," she said. "Say something polite."

"That's it, then? Back to Westria?"

"On the contrary. We're going to Harrowsgode, where my grandfather was born. *That's* where we'll find a real Loving Cup."

"Ah," said Stephen. "And where exactly is that?"

"North."

And when Stephen raised his eyebrows, hoping for more, "By the sea," she added.

❦ 5 ❦

North, by the Sea

THE LANDLORD AT THE INN had never heard of Harrowsgode. He hadn't thought there were any cities in the northlands at all. The region was said to be barren and wild, with just the occasional village, maybe a few sheep and goats on the hillsides. They *might* come across an inn or tavern along the way, but probably not. He advised them to take along plenty of provisions.

The north of Austlind proved to be everything the landlord had described, and more. Before the first day's ride was ended, the terrain had grown desolate and rocky, with nothing but the occasional decrepit cottage and a rutted path for a road. And with so little

grass for sheep and goats to graze upon, the hillsides were bare.

Lord Mayhew rode ahead of them, keeping a sizable distance between himself and the others. If he could so much as hear the sound of their voices, he'd give his horse a nudge with his spurs. He'd been cold and aloof from the start. But since Faers-Wigan, he'd progressed from aloof to sullen, brooding, and hostile.

It was Molly's proposal—that they should head off into the wastelands of the north, with no real directions, in search of a city that might not exist, to buy a fancy cup for the king—that had done it. He'd refused to go, firmly and absolutely, till Molly finally called his bluff.

"All right," she'd said with a shrug, "then we'll just have to go on our own. But good luck explaining to the king why you came back to Westria without us, the people he'd sent you to protect."

It had been heavy-handed, Molly knew; no doubt she'd made an enemy for life. But she didn't really see that she'd had a choice. Alaric wanted an alliance with Cortova, and to get it he needed the cup. It would have been so much easier if Mayhew had known the importance of their mission. But he didn't. Mayhew couldn't be trusted.

She asked Stephen about it later, and he'd agreed she'd done the right thing. "Though for a while there I

was afraid he'd break with us entirely, go home, and do God knows what—start an insurrection or something. He felt so strongly about it; and he's accustomed to giving orders, not taking them."

"Especially from a trumped-up—"

"From anyone, Molly. Even the king. But Mayhew, for his many faults, is a man of honor. He's a knight, and a great one, trained since childhood to give everything he has to the task he's been assigned. Usually that means risking great bodily harm, but in this case it was harder: he had to lay down his pride and go against his firm convictions. Few men of his stature would have done it, but Mayhew did. I'm still thinking about that, but it gives me hope.

"But you've stirred him up. You know how it is when our horses cross a stream: they kick up mud and silt from the bottom, and the water turns cloudy? Then after a while it settles, and the water is clear again? That's how it is with Mayhew. Let's leave him alone for a while and let the anger subside."

"I'll do my best not to annoy him in any way."

"I think that would be very wise."

On their fifth day of wandering in the wilderness, they left the barren plain and started to climb. The air grew crisp and clear again, the dull brown landscape giving

way to green. And straight ahead of them loomed a seemingly endless range of mountains.

For the first time Molly began to wonder if she'd imagined all that business about the blind man, and the magical stone, and the city to the north, by the sea. If so, then she had failed Alaric utterly and absolutely, while making Mayhew even more resentful than before and embarrassing herself past bearing.

Then, late in the day, they came quite unexpectedly upon a tidy village. It even had an inn of sorts—small, but remarkably clean. After nights of sleeping on the ground wrapped in their cloaks for warmth and using their saddlebags for pillows, they would sleep indoors on real beds.

The landlord sent a lad up to their rooms with towels and bowls of steaming water so they could wash before coming down to dinner. And as summer nights were cool in the highlands, he'd built a roaring fire in the hall and brought a pitcher of warm, spiced ale to their table. They began to hope that the food might even be good.

"One travels," Stephen said, "and one comes to expect certain things. Occasionally one is surprised."

"Yes," agreed Mayhew with something approaching a smile, "it's a pleasant change. Did you ask the landlord about Harrowsgode?"

"I did. It's in a valley on the other side of those mountains."

"He's heard of it, then? Good. How do we get there? I've been staring at that blasted range for days, and for the life of me I can't see a pass or a road of any kind."

"The landlord couldn't tell me. Apparently no one ever goes there."

"And why is that?" There was an edge to his voice that said he was sure he wasn't going to like the answer.

"Because . . ." Stephen paused and sighed, his face wiped clean of expression. "It is an evil place, and all who enter the valley are turned to stone."

Silence followed, each of them trying to digest this curious morsel of information.

"How does he know that," asked the logical Tobias, "if he's never been there?"

"It's common knowledge, part of the local folklore for hundreds of years. There are actual stone people, right there at the entrance to the valley, for anyone to see."

"Oh, pish," said Winifred.

"I'm just telling you what the fellow said."

"And this *entrance* to the valley, the way *in*—that isn't part of the folklore?"

"Unfortunately not. But it stands to reason that if

the people here know about the city and fear it as they do, then someone from this village must have gone there once, however many years ago, and come back with fanciful tales. It has to be close. And I doubt he climbed over the mountains. There must be a way in."

"Well if there is, it's bloody impossible to see. And unless there's a road leading to it—which there won't be, since no one ever goes there—we'll be traveling blind."

Tobias cleared his throat and said, "Um."

"Um, what?" said Mayhew.

"The raven. I think he knows. I think he's been leading us there this whole time."

Nobody moved then; nobody spoke. All eyes turned toward Mayhew, waiting for him to object—strongly and with curses. But he just stared into the fire, nodding slightly.

"Yes," he finally said, laughing darkly. "We *do* still have that bloody raven."

❧ ❦

As they feared, no road led north from the village, not even the trace of an overgrown path. They had nothing to guide them now but the large black bird that continued to fly toward the mountains, never very far ahead. Then, after hours of riding in anxious silence,

The harvest had just begun. Teams of workers were out in the fields swinging their sickles rhythmically, spreading the new-cut wheat, speckled with the last of the wildflowers, out on the stubble to dry in the sun. They stopped their work to stare as the strangers rode by.

The streets of the little town were neatly cobbled, with no horse flop on the road, no filth in the gutters, no animals running wild. And the shops were uncommonly plentiful for a village of that size. They passed a cobbler, a tanner, a weaver, a tailor, two bakers, a cooper, an ironmonger, and a butcher—and that was just the high street. What else there might be on the side lanes could only be imagined.

There weren't many shoppers on the street—most were probably busy with the harvest—but those who were, together with the merchants, also stopped to stare.

"Stephen," Molly whispered, "I think they're afraid of us."

"It's possible. I doubt they see strangers very often."

"We should smile so as not to look threatening."

"Molly, my dear, I don't believe you could look threatening if you tried."

Tobias laughed at that, rather louder than was absolutely necessary. Molly made a face at him.

They continued through the village and out again, where the street opened into a broad avenue leading to the moat that gave added protection to the city—at which point the road ended. The drawbridge was up.

"That's bloody inconvenient," Mayhew grumbled. "Do you suppose it's been raised on our account?"

"Maybe they keep it up all the time," Stephen said. "No one ever comes here, remember?"

"All right, let's turn back. We'll have to ask one of the villagers how to get inside the city—though who's likely to tell us, I can't imagine. They gape at us like we're carrying the plague."

"I saw a wineshop back there," Winifred said. "Near the square, on a lane to the right. The sign over the door showed a bunch of grapes, and there was a trestle table out in the yard under a big old tree."

"Good. A wineshop is perfect. Stephen, you and Winifred go down there and order yourselves some dinner. Ask the appropriate questions. You know Austlinder."

"All right," Stephen said. "But I think I should take off my sword. Nobody wears them here."

"I noticed that, too. But in case they're not as peaceful as they seem, I'll keep watch from the other end of the street. If you get your hackles up, give me a sign."

Stephen unbuckled his scabbard and handed it to Mayhew. Then he offered Winifred his arm and they sauntered back up the high street like an old married couple out for a Sunday stroll. Mayhew left Molly and Tobias to mind the horses while he skirted the edge of the town in search of a watching spot.

They found a small copse of trees and tied up the horses. Tobias tossed his wineskin to Molly, unfastened the bag of provisions, and took out some bread and cheese. Side by side, they sat in the shade, eating their rustic dinner.

Kerrokk!

"Oh!" Molly cried, scrambling to her feet and searching among the leafy branches. "Where are you hiding, raven dear?"

Kerrokk!

"Ah, there you are!"

Having shown himself, the bird now took flight, rising high into the air, making a wide circle over a cluster of animal pens, then landing on a distant fence post. From there he called to them, his grating voice loud and insistent.

They didn't hesitate. Grabbing Molly's hand, Tobias led her down the path that followed the fence line, turning left the first chance he got, then right again. The raven was on the far side of the enclosure,

where a large black bull stood with his back to them, his head low and at an angle. With the tip of one horn he was prodding something that lay on the ground.

It was a man, they realized, and he was almost certainly dead.

Tobias dropped Molly's hand and ran. It wasn't till he'd turned the second corner that he got a proper look at the body: crumpled and stained with blood, the bull standing over it, nudging, nudging with the vicious point of his horn.

Tobias picked up a large rock and threw it at the bull, but he missed. It'd been too heavy, and his hand was trembling. Molly handed him a smaller one, and this time his aim was true. The beast stepped back, fixing them with a venomous stare. When the next rock hit the mark again, the bull turned and slowly walked away.

"Warn me if he's coming back," Tobias said, climbing over the fence and squatting beside the figure: a young man, maybe seventeen or eighteen, his fine saffron doublet ripped and soaked with gore. Tobias touched a cheek and found it cold. Then he licked the palm of his hand and held it over the boy's mouth and nose. Like putting a finger to the wind, he would feel the slightest movement of air. There wasn't any.

"He's dead."

"I know, Tobias. I can see that from here."

"Should I move him, so the bull won't—?"

"No," Molly said. "We must raise the hue and cry. And the coroner needs to see him as he lies so it'll be plain to everyone what happened. But first, get out of that blasted pen. I'll get some more rocks. We can keep the bull away till help arrives."

They hallooed till their throats were sore, and before long a man arrived. He stayed just long enough to size up the situation, and gape at the strangers, before running back to summon the coroner and the four nearest neighbors as required by law.

The neighbors, all women, were the first to come; they were followed by a man whose carroty hair sprung out from his head on all sides like a rusty dandelion puff. Unlike the women, who were more interested in Molly and Tobias than in the poor dead boy, the man was visibly distressed. He had to lean on a fence post to keep from collapsing.

"The boy's father," Tobias whispered.

"No," Molly said. "The owner of the bull."

"Why do you say that?"

"The boy is rich, for one thing—look at his clothes—whereas that man is a peasant. And they don't resemble each other at all."

Tobias looked at the weeping man, with his

peculiar hair and weak chin, then down at the handsome youth. "You're right," he said quietly. "The boy looks nothing at all like that man. . . ."

His thought sounded unfinished, so she asked, "What, Tobias?"

"He looks exactly like you."

More people came. Ropes were brought and the bull was restrained at the far end of the paddock. Finally the coroner arrived (he was also the village butcher, by the looks of his apron), and the crowd gave way to let him pass. He climbed over the fence, as Tobias had done, and came to the same conclusion.

"He's one of theirs," the butcher said. "It's not our business. I'll go to the tower and have them sound the alarm. Meanwhile, someone call up to the ramparts and tell them what's happened. Say they need to send out their coroner."

"Let's go," Tobias said. "This is none of our business, either."

But apparently it was, because the crowd was quite insistent that they stay right where they were.

"Are we under arrest?" Molly whispered.

"No. I think they need us to testify at the trial."

"Why should there be a trial? It was an accident."

"I don't know. Maybe the owner of the bull is being held responsible."

"But it wasn't his fault."

Tobias shrugged. "We'll find out, I guess."

"I wonder where . . ."

Molly turned to one of the women then and asked in fractured Austlinder, "Where we is for this thing we go?"

"The trial?"

"Yes."

"Harrowsgode," she said, pointing.

Molly smiled.

7

The Trial

THE ENTRY GATE OF Harrowsgode didn't open onto the street, as it would in any other city. Instead, they came first to a small atrium, where they waited while the gate was locked, the portcullis lowered, and the drawbridge raised. Then they waited some more. Though there was another door in the little room, the guard made no move to open it.

"They're summoning the court and a jury," said Stephen, who'd been permitted to accompany Molly and Tobias and act as their translator. "They assure us it won't take long."

"Good," Molly said. "It's bloody close in here."

The villagers stood clustered together, as far from the strangers as the limited space would allow; they talked in low voices and stared at Molly.

"Why do they keep looking at me like that?" she whispered to Stephen. "What are they saying?"

"They think you must be one of the Harrowsgode folk. They say you look just like them, and your skin glows the same as theirs does."

"Oh, horse flop!"

"You asked me what they were saying. You do resemble them, though."

"I suppose," she said. "But I don't glow. Not in the least."

Tobias studied her, head at an angle as if trying to judge whether she glowed or not. Molly flicked his arm and gave him a look.

"Stephen," he asked, "did anyone mention who exactly is being tried?"

"You really don't know?"

"Would I have asked if I did?"

"It's the *bull*, Tobias."

"No!"

"Yes. I've seen a pig hanged for wandering into a cottage, upsetting a cradle, and devouring an infant."

"Lord, Stephen, that's horrible!"

"Which part?"

"All of it. As for hanging a pig—it's absurd. It was just a beast doing what beasts do. Surely it's the parents who ought to be punished for letting the pig run free and leaving the infant alone with the door open."

"The law is not always wise, Tobias, and the bull is indeed being tried for murder."

"Will they hang it?" Molly wondered. "I can't imagine."

"Ha! What a scaffold *that* would be. No, they'll probably slit its throat, then destroy the meat so none may partake of its evil flesh."

"Gaw!"

"I thought you'd be amazed."

The room had grown uncomfortably warm, and the smell of so many sweating bodies was strong. Molly leaned against Tobias—the top of her head just reaching his collarbone—and groaned. "How much longer can this possibly take? It's hard to breathe in here."

"You've been in worse places," he said, and she agreed.

Finally they heard a key turning in the lock; and the door swung open to reveal not the city but a great, cavernous hall, with floors and walls of stone and a high ceiling supported by massive wooden beams. At one end was a dais covered with a velvet cloth. And built into the two side walls were long benches with wooden back rests six feet high and decoratively carved

at the top. They were led to the nearest bench and told to sit down.

The court was already assembled. The judge sat on a raised chair at the center of the dais dressed in a scarlet gown, like a bishop on his throne. To his left and right were the barristers, dressed in similar robes. There was also a scribe and, on the far edge of the dais, an official holding a staff. On the bench directly across from them sat the jury.

It was the first time Molly had seen so many Harrowsgode folk gathered together—and indeed they *did* all look remarkably alike. Despite differences in age, dress, and social standing, they might have been one great family—the wealthy uncle, his up-and-coming nephews, and the poor relations—all of the same seed, however differently they'd grown. And it wasn't just the dark curls and the pale gray eyes. There *was* something about them that was bright and fresh: the clear skin with its perfect sheen picking up the light from the windows overhead and the torches along the walls.

Molly studied her own familiar hands, turning them palms up, then palms down. They didn't seem exceptional in any way. Tobias, who sat beside her, noticed. He reached over and took one of those ordinary hands and kept it in his. She found this a comfort.

Stephen, on her other side, leaned over and

whispered in her ear. "They don't intend to let us into the city at all. When the trial is over, they'll take us out again."

"How do you know that?"

"One of the neighbors told me. Harrowsgode is a closed city. Not even their villagers may enter, which explains this room, I suppose. This is where they bring their crops, and get paid, and so on."

"That's a problem, then."

"Maybe not. If they regard you as one of their own, they might make an exception. They've all noticed the resemblance. So when the time comes, you need to step forward quickly and try to get someone's attention, tell him your grandfather was born here, that you've come back searching for relatives—that sort of thing."

"But who?"

"I don't know yet. Let's see what happens during the trial."

There came a great thumping noise; the official with the staff was pounding the floor of the dais, calling the people to attention.

"The court is now is session," he cried. "May justice be done!"

"Know ye," said the judge, "that we are gathered here to rule on the death of our brother, Kort Gunnarson. Master Coroner, please give your report."

The coroner stood, made a respectful bow, then described the scene of the crime: the position of the body, the nature of the wounds, and the presence of blood on the bull's horns. He was questioned briefly by the two barristers, then the coroner bowed a second time and resumed his seat.

"Witnesses next," whispered Stephen.

"Tobias, Lord Worthington of Westria," called the judge. "Please stand and give your testimony."

Tobias squeezed Molly's hand, then released it and got to his feet. "I not speak you language well. Friend Stephen with me help," he said.

"That will be allowed," said the judge. "Master Einar, you may begin the prosecution."

"Lord Worthington," Master Einar said, "you arrived here this morning from outside the valley?"

"That's correct," Tobias said.

"And you happened to come upon the body of the deceased?"

"Yes. We were some distance away, so we went to investigate."

"And what did you find?"

"A young man lying near the fence covered in

blood. A bull was probing the body with his horn. We drove the beast away with stones. Then I went inside the enclosure and determined that the boy was dead."

"Did you see anyone else nearby? A man with a weapon, perhaps? Someone running off into the wheat fields in a suspicious manner?"

"No."

"Just the bull."

"Yes."

"What did you do then?"

"We gave the hue and cry. Someone came, then he notified the four neighbors and the owner of the bull. The village coroner too."

"Did you notice, by chance, if there was any blood on the bull's horns?"

"I heard the coroner say there was. I didn't see it myself."

"Have you anything further to add?"

"No."

"Remain standing please, Lord Worthington," said the judge. "Master Pieter will speak for the defense."

Master Einar took his seat and Master Pieter now stepped forward.

"Lord Worthington," he said, "when you and Lady Marguerite first noticed the body, was it inside the bull's enclosure or out?"

"Inside."

"When you drove the animal off and climbed in to check on the boy, did you move the body at all?"

"No. Since he was already dead and there was nothing to be done for him, we felt it was best to leave the scene as it was—for the coroner, you understand."

"Yes. You did the proper thing. That's all I have for now."

Master Pieter returned to his seat, and Tobias sat down. Now it was Molly's turn.

"Lady Marguerite," Master Einar said, "you were with Lord Worthington during the entire time in question?"

"Yes, I was."

"And did you see anything that hasn't already been mentioned?"

"Not really."

"No one running away from the scene? You didn't stumble upon a dropped weapon?"

She shook her head.

"Just the bull standing over the victim, jabbing the body with his horn."

"Yes."

"Thank you."

That was it? As Einar sat down and Pieter took his place, Molly started to panic. As the second witness,

with nothing new to add, she was clearly being dispensed with quickly. And this would be her last chance to mention her grandfather. She'd just have to keep her wits about her and work the information in somehow, no matter how silly and irrelevant it seemed.

"Please tell me, Lady Marguerite," Master Pieter began, "how it is you came to our valley. Were you lost?"

Molly blinked. He had given her the perfect opening!

"No, Master Pieter, we were not lost. We were searching for Harrowsgode most particularly."

"And why is that?"

"My grandfather, a silversmith of great renown, was said to have come from this city." Stephen struggled with a grin as he translated this for the court. It really had been too easy. "He went by the name of William Harrows and lived his latter days in the town of Faers-Wigan, but I believe he—and I—have family here. I came with my companions to seek them out."

There—it was done! Her foot was firmly wedged in the door.

"I rather suspected as much, my lady," Master Pieter said. "You greatly resemble us Harrowsgode folk."

"Please stick to the defense, Master Pieter," said the judge.

"Of course. My apologies for straying off the topic. Now, Lady Marguerite, your friend Lord Worthington said you drove the bull away with stones. Can you tell me why you did that?"

"So Tobias could get into the enclosure to look after the boy, to see if he still lived."

"And you couldn't do that while the bull was near?"

"Of course not. It wouldn't be safe."

"But it was safe where you were, outside the enclosure?"

"Yes."

He nodded thoughtfully as if this were a tricky puzzle. "Normally, if you saw a bull inside a pen surrounded by a strong fence, would you be alarmed?"

"I don't understand your question."

"Well, suppose you saw a bull walking down the street or in the fishmonger's shop—would you be alarmed then?"

"Anyone would."

"Because?"

"It would be dangerous." Where was he going with this? Everything he said was so obvious it didn't bear mentioning at all.

"Is the bull not also dangerous within his enclosure?"

"Yes, but there's a stout fence to keep him in,

whereas on the street or in a shop there's nothing to restrain him from doing harm."

"Very good. Now tell me—you seem a clever young lady—do you think a bull has the right to exist? Keeping in mind that he is a dangerous beast."

"I should hope so—else we'd have no cows or calves." There was a titter of laughter from the jury.

"Master Pieter?" said the judge, a warning note in his voice.

"Please have patience a little longer, my lord; I am about to make my point."

"Make it soon. We haven't got all day."

"Thank you, my lord, I shall. So would it be fair to say, Lady Marguerite, that the bull should be allowed to dwell alongside his masters—we of the human race—so long as he is confined and can do us no harm?"

"Yes. Though in this particular case—"

"I was just getting to that. I believe we all agree that the bull, to exist at all, must have some place of his own in which to live; that place is within his enclosure. The humans who control him, and use him for their purposes, live everywhere else. Correct?"

Molly nodded, entranced.

"So the young man, by climbing into his pen, was *trespassing*, was he not?"

Ah. She saw where he was going now. "It was

certainly a foolish thing to do."

"No one questions that it was foolish. But had he the *right*?"

Molly shrugged.

"A king may not cross the threshold of the humblest man's cottage unless he is bid to enter. Is it not so with our bull, who has no choice but to stay where he is put and no choice in his warlike nature, which was endowed by his creator? Can we truly call it murder when the bull was defending his home?"

"I . . . suppose . . ."

"That was a rhetorical question, lady," said the judge. "You are not expected to answer."

After that it went quickly, a mere formality. The neighbors had nothing of interest to say. The owner begged for the life of his bull, as it was a valuable animal and the loss would tax his household greatly. The prosecutor and the defense each came forward and summed up the case. Then the jury rose and the official with the staff led them across the hall to a room where they could discuss the case in private and come to their decision.

"I think," whispered Stephen, "Master Pieter is our man."

"I think so, too," Molly said. "Wasn't it amazing how he led me directly to the very thing I'd wanted to

say? I was afraid I would never get the chance."

"He did it on purpose. Whether out of curiosity or for some other reason, I cannot guess. But for sure you may safely approach him. I would not be surprised if he came to you himself."

"Nor would I. Listen, Stephen, I think he might be more open if I speak to him alone."

"Can you manage the language?"

"I understand a lot of what I hear now so long as the words aren't too fancy. Speaking is harder, of course—"

"It always is."

"But I think I can make myself clear. You and Tobias stay nearby, but not too close. I'll nod to you if I need help."

"All right. Have you thought of what you will say to him?"

"Stephen, I've thought of nothing else since we came into this place."

The decision must have been an easy one; minutes later the door opened and the jury filed back out.

"Who is your spokesman?" asked the judge.

"I am, Your Honor," said a heavyset man.

"Then give us your verdict, please."

"Your Honor, we find the beast innocent of murderous intent."

"So be it. We thank you for your service."

The official struck the dais three times with his staff, then suddenly everyone was in motion. The jury rose to their feet, the judge and barristers stepped down, and the official headed over to the witness bench to lead the villagers out. But Master Pieter didn't follow the others to the far side of the room, where they stood in a knot by the great double doors that almost certainly led into the city. Instead, he remained in the middle of the room, apparently waiting for her.

"Now!" said Stephen. "Go!"

Molly grabbed her saddle pack and hurried over to the barrister.

"Master Pieter," she said. "I talk you, please?"

"Of course. I would be delighted." He said this in flawless Westrian.

"You speak my language?"

"Oh, yes. There are many in Harrowsgode who do. We are a scholarly people."

"Good," Molly said. "For I am *not* scholarly in the least, and I've been making rather a muddle of speaking Austlinder."

"Lady," he said, brushing this aside, "I want you to know that you are welcome here. Harrowsgode is, in

the truest sense, your home. And there is much I am eager to tell you—about your family, and about our people. If you'll just wait here with me until the others have gone, I'll take you into the city."

"But what about my friends?"

"I'm sorry. They are not permitted."

"Why? They traveled all this way with me so I could find my grandfather's people; now we're here and you say they can't go inside?"

"Harrowsgode isn't an open city. Only our people may enter. You are one of us; they are not."

"They won't do you any harm."

"It's interesting that you say that since you came accompanied by a knight, and all your men were armed."

"That had nothing at all to do with you," she said, wondering how he knew so much. "Lord Mayhew— the knight—just came along to protect us on the road. I don't care if he stays behind now that we're here. But I do need Winifred for propriety; she's my lady companion. And Stephen is my translator. And Tobias—"

"We will find you a lady companion, one of your own kind. And as you will have noticed, I speak your language. You won't need a translator here."

She felt a rush of panic; her face went damp with sweat. She looked into Pieter's gray eyes, her

desperation unmasked, and said in a voice that was deep and urgent: "Then I must have Tobias."

"But, lady—"

"Please believe me: I want to go with you into the city, but *I will not go without him.*"

"Why—are you betrothed?"

Her breath caught. She paused. She heard herself say yes.

"You are very young. Was this arranged by your father?"

She paused again.

"Yes," she said. "Yes, it was."

Oh, how she choked on that dreadful lie—as if her father gave a goose's fart about whom she married, or if she even married at all! Why, she hadn't so much as laid eyes on the man since she was seven, when he'd decided it was time she earned her own bread and dragged her off to Dethemere Castle to work as a scullery maid.

"You are aware, my lady, that no maid can be compelled to marry against her will—not by her father, or anyone else. That is the law."

"I have no desire to break my bond. Tobias is my dearest friend—and besides, we are sworn to each other."

"Already sworn? Truly?"

The villagers had left the room by then. Now the official came back for the foreigners—Stephen, Tobias, and Molly—who seemed to be lingering.

"Not the tall one," Pieter said to the official. "Lord Worthington and the lady will remain here. But you may take the other one out." The official raised his eyebrows in surprise. But as no explanation was forthcoming, he did as he was told.

"Lord Worthington," Pieter called, waving Tobias over. "Will you come and join us, please."

Tobias had been staring dumbfounded as Stephen was ushered out of the room. Now he came forward, looking to Molly for assurance that everything was all right. She responded with something between a twitch and a wink.

"My lord," Pieter said, "you know that Lady Marguerite is descended from the folk of this city. She testified to that effect not an hour ago."

He nodded.

"And so, being one of us, she is granted free entrance here."

Tobias had always been good at silence. He proved this once again. He waited for the rest of it as unmoving as a mountain, looking down at the little barrister with solemn eyes.

"You, of course, would not normally be permitted beyond this room. We're a closed city. Our gates

stay shut, our drawbridge raised, unless business is to be done with our villagers. Even then they may only come so far as this chamber and never through those doors."

Tobias still waited. He scarcely seemed to breathe. "However . . ."

Heaven help me, Molly thought, *here it comes!*

"The lady has expressed the strongest unwillingness to go unless you, her betrothed"—Tobias blanched—"should be allowed to come with her. And as we will never turn away one of our people who has returned to us, we will make an exception and allow it."

"Master Pieter," Tobias said, his face now transformed by a foolish grin, "as *her betrothed*, I am most happy, most grateful, truly honored to be admitted into the city where my future wife's family—"

"Tobias?"

"Yes, my dearest?"

"You have said enough, I think."

The outer gates were shut and bolted. The grinding of chains said the portcullis was down and the drawbridge was being raised. Molly glanced over at the crowd by the door that led into Harrowsgode: the judge, the prosecutor, the official, the scribe, and the jury. All were watching them with unvarnished curiosity.

"Excuse me," Pieter said. "I must go and explain.

Please don't worry. It'll be all right."

"Control yourself," Molly hissed when Pieter had gone.

"It's very hard to do, sweetheart. Under the circumstances."

She covered her mouth to hide a grin. "Well, you must try. This is important."

"I know, my darling."

"If you darling-dearest me one more time, I'll tell him the truth, and he'll send you packing."

"No you won't. But all the same, I promise to behave. I was just overcome by a wave of giddiness. I'm completely recovered now. Rather bored by it, actually."

"Good. We're sworn, just so you know. My father made the arrangements."

"Your father? *Really?*"

"Tobias!"

"He's coming back now, Molly. You'd best control yourself."

The official produced a ring of keys and unlocked the door. The jury filed out, followed by the prosecutor and the scribe. Only the judge remained—standing in the open doorway, backlit by the warm light of a late summer afternoon—glaring at them. The man with the keys waited.

Something wasn't right. Molly wondered if the barrister actually had the authority to let them in. Certainly the judge disapproved. But Pieter was standing his ground. Finally the judge shook his head, slowly and solemnly as if in warning, then turned on his heel and left.

Pieter watched him go. At last, his face flushed and his voice dark with feeling, he turned to them and spoke. "He's old-fashioned in his views. I respect him, but in this case he is wrong. We can never, ever turn away one of our own—and a child of the Magnus line!" His voice broke and he cleared his throat. "He will be gone now. No need to fear any unpleasantness. Will you follow me?"

Just as they were about to step over the threshold, Pieter paused. "My lady," he said solemnly, "welcome home."

❦ 8 ❧

The Tale of King Magnus

PIETER'S OFFICE WAS a pleasant chamber with a wide bank of leadlight windows looking out onto the great courtyard of the university. Everything about the room was tidy and bright, the personal space of a thoughtful man who was not lavish but who loved pretty things.

He introduced them to his mother, who sat by the window with her needlework. She was small and elegant like her son, her dark hair streaked with silver. "Mother will serve as your lady companion for now," he said to Molly. "Later we will make other arrangements. It's not our custom here, but I wouldn't want you to feel uncomfortable."

Molly wished like the devil that she'd never brought the whole thing up. It had just been an excuse to bring Winifred.

Pieter led them over to a pair of handsome chairs facing a large wooden desk. "Please," he said. "Make yourselves comfortable." Then he went around the desk and sat across from them.

"If you will excuse me for just a moment, I must make some arrangements. I promise it won't take long. Then we will talk."

He took several sheets of vellum out of a drawer and laid them on the desk. Then he unstopped his inkwell, dipped the point of his pen into it, and began to write, taking great pains with his swirls and loops. When he was finished, he blotted the ink, turned the paper over, and addressed it on the top edge. But he didn't fold and seal it as was done in other places. He just rolled it up and tied it with a ribbon.

Now he took up his pen again and started on a second letter. When he was done with that one, he wrote a third. At last he flashed a smile at them that said *Almost done!* and rang a little brass bell that sat on his desk. An assistant popped out of an adjoining room, and Pieter handed him the letters.

"Deliver the one to the Council first, then the one to the Magnussons. After that you can go to

Neargate. It's a lot of ground to cover, so you may take the spinner."

The boy's face brightened.

"And, Robbin, if you damage it, I'll take it out of your hide. You understand?"

"Yes, Master," the boy said. "I'll bring it back as good as new." He hurried out, shutting the door behind him with exaggerated care.

"There," Pieter said. "Everything is now in motion. Like the heavens," he added with a chuckle. "Now draw your chairs closer, if you will. While we wait, I have something to show you."

He brought out a much larger roll of vellum and spread it out on the table. As it wanted to curl back up again, he set little velvet bags filled with sand on each of the corners to hold it down.

They leaned forward to look at the scroll. It was covered with curvy letters, some in writing so small you couldn't possibly read it even if you knew how. There were lines connecting one word to the next and little pictures rendered in color. Everything was embellished with gleaming gold paint.

"That's beautiful," Tobias said. "I never saw anything like it."

"Well," said Pieter, "thank you for saying so. It's my own little project, not anything to compare with the

great Map of the People that is kept in Harrowsgode Hall. But it will suffice for our purposes."

"*You* made that?" Molly asked, astonished.

"Well, yes, I did. I rather fancied myself an artist in my youth, but there's little call for such skills in my profession. So I entertain myself with a brush and pen—in my spare time, you understand. Now let me tell you about it; I brought it out for a reason.

"Here at the top you see three thrones, and upon them sit three kings. This one, whose throne is raised above the others, let us call him the Great King for the sake of simplicity. He was the father of the two below. We shall come to them in a moment.

"Now the Great King was strong in war, very powerful and clever with weapons. When he was still a young man, the crown hardly warm from the touch of his brow, he gathered an army and sailed across the waters to conquer our people. That was long ago, hundreds and hundreds of years."

Molly loved a story. She leaned in, her elbows resting on Pieter's desk, for a closer look at the three small images of kings on their thrones: one above, two below; two fair, one dark.

"Now the Great King married a lady of his own race, and she bore him a son, Harald—also several daughters, but they were of no account, for women

could not rule. This is Harald: the fair one who sits below his father on your left.

"Now in time the queen died, as queens do, giving birth to yet another daughter; and the Great King married again. Only this time he chose a lady from the conquered race, one of our own. Here is *their* son, on the right, with the dark hair. He was called Magnus.

"Now the Great King loved his second wife, and the son she bore him, more than he loved the first. And when his life's thread had worn thin and was near to breaking, he made his desires known regarding the succession; to the astonishment of all, he chose Magnus as his heir instead of the firstborn son.

"Well, you can imagine what happened after that. It was war all over the kingdom, with Harald, who claimed to be the rightful heir (and surely you can see his point), driving Magnus off the throne, after which the once-conquered people rose up in revolt. Many died in those terrible times.

"And it was all utterly pointless, for Magnus was a mystic and a scholar, not a warrior or a man of the world; he had no desire to rule a country or lead an army. Yet all over the kingdom his people were dying in his name, dying to defend his right to an unwanted throne. So he formally renounced the crown and acknowledged his brother as king.

"But it was already too late. The pot was boiling; everyone was angry—conquered and conquerors alike. *Our* people were convinced that their king had been forced to abdicate. *Their* people were sure the crown had been stolen from the rightful heir.

"Finally Magnus made a proposal. There was a large island belonging to the kingdom called Budenholme, just off the coast. As the soil was poor and rocky, it was mostly uninhabited. Magnus said it was all the land that he would claim. He would go and live there, never to return, but any of his people who wished to follow him must be permitted to do so. He would become the ruler of his own tiny kingdom.

"Harald agreed to this, and provided Magnus with ships to carry everything he and his followers would need to start their new life on the island. Then he left them in peace to live as they wished, just as he had promised.

"But there were others, wild raiders with fast ships who swore allegiance to no king. They noticed that the once-barren island was now sprouting cottages and wheat fields; the hillsides were covered with herds of grazing sheep. And so they came sweeping in time after time, stealing sheep, pigs, grain, and now and then a comely maiden. It was so easy—why, the innocents who lived there didn't even have an army! They

had no weapons at all!"

"Horrible!" Molly said.

"Yes, it was. So clearly they would have to find another home, someplace safe, quiet, and remote. But where?

"Magnus needed to consider the matter, and to do this he needed to be alone. So he climbed to the top of the highest hill and built himself a crude little shelter, just enough to keep off the sun and the rain. And there he stayed—we don't know how long—living on nothing but the bread and water that were set outside his door every morning. And during that time King Magnus had a vision."

Molly gasped.

"He saw a lush valley fed by rivers and guarded by mountains on all four sides, the coastal range dropping precipitously down to the sea. He saw a few peasants living there, growing crops, cut off from the rest of the world since the time before time. He saw dense, honey-colored stone ready to be quarried for building. And he saw his men at the top of soaring cliffs with a system of winches and ropes, hauling their things up from the ships below, animals and bedsteads alike. And best of all, he saw the way in to that sweet, protected spot: a narrow canyon near impossible to find if you didn't know the way, cutting right through the

southern mountains.

"When he came back down the hill—ragged and dirty, no doubt, and with a scraggly beard—he told his people to pack up their belongings and get the ships ready to sail. That is how they came to settle in this place and build this beautiful city. It was a labor of many generations, but these walls and these mountains have kept us safe ever since." Pieter took a deep breath, his face glowing with pride.

"That's amazing," Molly said. "What a wonderful story."

"Indeed. And as you shall see, we have created a paradise here, untouched and untroubled by the world."

Molly stared thoughtfully at the great sheet of vellum.

"But what about all the rest of the scroll—that part, and that? All those little pictures and lines?"

"It's a map of our people, showing the leaders of the seven clans, from the time of Magnus to the present generation."

"What does that mean—clans?"

"They grew out of family groups long ago. There would have been a patriarch named Gunnar, for example, who was a great hunter, so his descendants became the Gunnarclan, who now serve as the archers

on our ramparts. We don't allow weapons here, as you know, but we have made that one exception. As we are not a warlike people and have no army, we need at least *some* protection. Just in case."

"No army?" said Tobias, astonished.

"We have mountains instead." Pieter smiled. "So, that's the Gunnarclan. In the same way, long ago, there was a man named Stig, who was a sailor. His descendants are the Stiggesclan, from which our Voyagers are chosen. They don't sail in ships, not anymore; but they are the only ones who are permitted to leave our valley and go out into the world—secretly, you understand—to learn of new things and bring back wisdom to our people."

"And you?"

"I'm of the Visenclan. We are scholars, mostly. This is my family line, here."

"But what about the one in the middle? It has more names than the others. And so many lines lead to it, and there's so much gold paint."

Pieter smiled. "That is *your* clan, lady—the descendants of King Magnus."

"Gaw!" cried Tobias, forgetting himself entirely. "You're a royal princess, Molly!"

"Is it true?" she asked.

"In a way. Not exactly. The king's line is here." He

showed them where the Magnus clan had split several times, some lines dying out, a few running side by side all the way to the bottom. "See the little gold crown I have painted here? That's our king, Koenraad; and below him you see his son, Prince Fredrik. You are part of this other line, here. But it's true you are of royal lineage—noble, I believe you'd call it in your country."

Molly was struck speechless. Royal blood—who would have thought it?

Pieter now opened a drawer and took out a strange object. It was like half of a ball made out of glass. He positioned it carefully at the end of her branch of the Magnus line, peering down and adjusting it slightly. "There!" he said. "Don't touch it, lady. Just—it's better if you stand and look straight down. Now tell me, what do you see?"

"Oh, you have made the words larger."

"Not me, the magnifying glass."

"Is it magic?"

"No. It's science, the science of optics. But what I wished you to notice is the word that's being magnified."

"Oh. I don't know how to read."

"That's all right. I'll help you. Now imagine two valleys, side by side." He drew the shape with a finger

in the air. "That is the letter *W.*"

"But I know that one already!" she cried. "I also know the letter *M.*"

"Well, how clever of you!"

She flushed then, hearing her own words and hearing his reply. No doubt he'd meant to be kind, but to say to a man who could read *anything*, a man who knew *all* the letters and could write them down as well—to say *I know* M *and* W as though that were some great accomplishment . . .

"I had a necklace," she explained. "The king of Westria has it now. My grandfather made it as a love-gift for my grandmother, so he worked both of their initials into the design: *M* for *Martha* and *W* for *William.* That's the only reason I know. Otherwise, I'm as ignorant as a toad."

"No you're not. You just haven't had an education. But you're as sharp and clever as any young lady of my acquaintance. Now look again—don't move it; I have it perfectly placed—and tell me what you see."

"The letter *W.*"

"Exactly. And combined with the others that follow, it spells out the name William."

"Like my grandfather?"

"That *is* your grandfather, lady."

"Oh." And then, after studying it a while, "But

there's nothing under it, no little lines running down . . ."

"Not yet," Pieter said, turning the scroll around so the top part, with the three kings, was on their side of the table now and the word that said *William* was in front of him. From out of his pocket he pulled a new device—two metallic rings, each holding a circle of glass just as strips of lead hold the panes of a window. The rings of metal and glass were connected by a squiggly bit of wire in the middle.

"Eyeglasses," Pieter said, slipping the squiggly bit onto his nose. "They magnify as the glass dome does, so I can see to work small." Then he sharpened his pen with a knife, wiped it clean with a cloth, and dipped it into the ink.

"You must tell me the names. William begat—?"

"What is 'begat'?"

"William's issue. His children."

"Oh. There was just my mother."

"And her name?"

"Greta."

He nodded and carefully began to write the name on the scroll. When he was done, he drew a remarkably straight line running down from it and looked up again at Molly.

"How would you like to be listed, lady?" His eyes,

as seen through the circles of glass, were distorted.

"You look like a demon in those eyeglasses."

"I assure you I am nothing of the kind. Now how shall I list you? As Marguerite? Or your full title? It'll be tight, but I think I can manage."

Molly pinched her lips and thought. "Not the title, no." She chewed on a fingernail, thinking some more. "Just Molly," she decided. "That's who I really am."

"All right." She watched, scarcely breathing, as he slowly, carefully, made the tiny strokes on the paper that spelled out her name, and enrolled her for all time as one of the people of Harrowsgode.

"Oh, Master Pieter—is that really my name? Tobias, you must come and see!"

"It's wonderful," he said, leaning over to look. "Exactly the way a princess's name ought to be written."

"I'm not a princess," she said, though her face fairly glowed with pleasure.

Just then the assistant returned, closing the door very gently again—no doubt he'd been scolded for slamming it—and handed Pieter a single scroll.

"Only one reply?" he asked. Then, checking to see who'd sent it, "Nothing from the Council?"

"No, Master. They were very busy. They just took the letter and sent me on my way."

"I understand." He opened the scroll and scanned

it quickly, nodding with satisfaction. "What about Richard Strange?" he asked. "Did you not go to Neargate?"

"I did. He's agreed to host the gentleman."

"All right, then," Pieter said to Molly and Tobias. "It grows late, and all is now arranged. Shall we away?"

"Where?"

"To your lodgings. We have no inns in Harrowsgode, as we have no travelers; but you'll be quite comfortable, I promise. Marguerite—excuse me, Molly—you'll be the guest of a near relative, Claus Magnusson, a professor at the university. His father was William's brother, so that would make him a cousin of sorts. The family knows Westrian, so language won't be a problem."

"What about me?" Tobias asked.

"You'll be staying with a gentleman named Richard Strange. He was born in Westria, so he knows the language. I'm sure you'll suit each other splendidly. Now, come. Get your things. Robbin, you take Lord Worthington over to Neargate. I'll see to the lady. Do you want my mother to accompany us?"

"No," Molly said. "It's just a stuffy old custom."

"As you like, my dear. Shall we go?"

And then they were out the door and through the gates of the university, where they parted—she to go

one way and he another. It had all happened too fast.

"But how will I see Tobias?" she asked. "We didn't make any plans. I don't even know where he's staying."

"Don't worry. Dr. Magnusson will arrange it. No problem at all."

❧ 9 ❧

The Great Seer

KING KOENRAAD WAS VERY OLD. He was nearly blind, profoundly deaf, and too frail to walk without assistance. He'd completely forgotten his once-beloved queen, dead now these many years; and he didn't recognize Prince Fredrik, the son she'd borne him. Every night he'd ask his gentlemen of the chamber where his mother was and why she hadn't come to kiss him before he went to sleep. He mostly stayed in bed, except on good days, when he'd have himself carried to a large leather chair in which he'd sit by the fire, a woolen blanket draped across his lap, summer and winter.

This was a tragedy for Harrowsgode. For though

Prince Fredrik was everything you'd want in a king—sensible, judicious, and wise—he was not permitted to step into the breach and rule in his father's place. The law quite clearly stated that a king's position was absolute so long as he drew breath. That left the Privy Council in charge, since their official duty was to assist and advise the king.

The Council, all Magi, held their meetings in the Celestium, an airy chamber in the central tower of Harrowsgode Hall. There, all matters concerning the city were thoughtfully discussed, sometimes for hours, until consensus was reached and a decision made.

If the Celestium was the city's reasoning mind, the buzzing hive of government offices below on the second floor was unquestionably its beating heart, for here those decisions were put into action.

The heart and mind were linked in the person of Soren Visenson, the chief counselor of Harrowsgode, whose title was Great Seer. Every morning he went downstairs to meet with his principal ministers to hear their reports and pass along the will of the Council.

On this particular day he'd stayed later than usual due to a meeting with the designers and engineers of a new citywide hot-water system soon to be up and running. They were just finishing their discussion when the Minister of Security came rushing in without even

bothering to knock. He was flushed and breathing hard.

"Your Excellency," he said, "please excuse the interruption, but I just received word that strangers have been seen entering the valley. There are five of them: three men and two women. The men are all carrying swords."

A chill fell over the room—for though their city walls were strong and high, their moat deep and wide, and their ramparts always manned with well-trained archers, they'd never wanted, and had never had, an army. They'd counted on magic and mountains to protect them. And now, for the first time in the hundreds of years since they'd settled in the valley, magic and mountains apparently had failed them.

"It could mean nothing, my lord. There aren't enough of them to do us any harm; and they came quite openly, bringing women. That's not what you'd expect from a raiding party."

"You said they were armed."

"Yes, but I'm told that foreigners always carry swords for protection when they travel. Most likely they're commonplace travelers who happened to lose their way."

Soren shook his head. "Impossible. No one finds this place by accident. We need to question them

closely and find out how they came here, and why. But disarm them first—and take care how you do it. If you frighten them they'll fight back, and someone might be harmed."

The minister nodded. "I understand. I'll take my strongest men; we'll go in the guise of a welcoming party and explain that we don't allow weapons here. I doubt they'll resist. They have a similar custom in Austlind, I believe—something about a visitor offering his sword to his host to show that he comes in peace."

"Good. Then once they're disarmed, arrest them. I presume there is someplace in the village where criminals can be confined."

"I suppose; I'll ask. But I'll need a warrant to do it."

"I'll write one out now—for their arrest and for their execution. I'm sorry, but it can't be helped. If they leave this valley they'll carry tales, and others are sure to follow. But question them thoroughly first—one at a time would be best, I think—then come and report to me. I'll be here all day."

"Your Excellency," the minister said with obvious discomfort, "such actions require the approval of the Council. And for execution, it has to be unanimous."

"We don't have time for that. I'll explain to the Council later. For now my signature will be sufficient."

"But, Your Excellency, I really can't—"

The Great Seer shot him a look of cold rage. "Then I'll have to find someone who can."

The minister flushed with anger and embarrassment. "I'm sorry, Your Excellency. I only meant—"

Just then they heard the pealing of the bell in the village tower.

"We know, we know," Soren muttered to himself. "Now go and round up your men—unless, of course, you'd rather resign, in which case please do me the favor of sending in your deputy."

"No need of that, my lord."

"I'm glad to hear it. Now go. By the time you're ready, I'll have the warrant."

As the Minister of Security turned to leave, a messenger arrived. He, too, stepped through the open doorway without asking permission to enter. Protocol had fallen by the wayside that day.

"Your Eminence . . . Lord Minister," he said, giving each of them a hasty bow. "The villagers have called up to the ramparts to say that there's been a death. One of our own."

"Not again!" The Great Seer leaned back and gazed at the ceiling, fighting for his composure. "Drowned?"

"No, sire. He survived the plunge, but then he took a shortcut through an enclosure, and a bull was in it. The animal killed the boy, or so it appears."

Soren turned to his minister, who'd been edging toward the door. "How could your men have missed him?" he roared. "Up there on the wall in plain sight, climbing over—"

"Perhaps he did it in the dark of night."

"And no one heard the splash?"

"I . . . it does seem rather unlikely, Your Eminence. Maybe the sound of the wind—"

"Oh, the devil take you, Lord Minister! This was a needless tragedy, and a precious life was lost—all because of your incompetence."

The minister shut his eyes. He'd moved beyond fear and resentment now to complete and hopeless submission. Had the Great Seer asked him to pitch himself out of the window, he would have done it right away.

"I am deeply ashamed," he said.

The Great Seer studied his minister in silence, considering whether the man was too dispirited to perform his duties properly in this moment of great emergency, and if so, whether the deputy was up to the task. He quickly came to the conclusion that a broken horse was a useful and obedient horse, and decided in favor of mercy.

"All right," he said. "We'll discuss it later. For now, you and your men can go out with the coroner. The

strangers won't suspect you. It'll give you an advantage."

"Your Eminence," said the messenger. "Lord Minister. Please excuse me, but there's something else. It appears that one of the principal witnesses in the case . . ."

⚜

And so the day went, from one appalling development to the next, until crisis was capped by disaster in the form of two letters, one arriving hard on the heels of the other.

The first, hastily written, came from the judge who'd presided over the trial. He wished to inform the Council that Pieter, the barrister for the defense, had taken it upon himself to invite two foreigners into the city, an outrageous breach of Harrowsgode law and custom.

Then they heard the same news a second time, in more measured tones, from the barrister himself.

Pieter explained that the girl in question wasn't really a foreigner but a lost descendant of the Magnus clan. She was, in fact, the granddaughter of William Magnusson, who'd so famously hidden his prodigious gifts in the guise of a simpleton and then when his little charade was up, escaped through the river channel.

The Great Seer nodded as he read this. Pieter had done the right thing—though he shouldn't have made the decision on his own. The girl could have waited in the anteroom till the Council had been consulted.

Then he came to the second paragraph and despair washed over him. He dropped the letter on the table and cradled his head in his hands. Was incompetence spreading through Harrowsgode like the very plague? What in the name of Magnus had the barrister been thinking—letting a foreign lord into the city? It was absolute madness!

He looked up. The room was filled with officials, among them the Deputy Minister of Security, who was standing in while his superior was away in the village.

"I want the barrister Pieter arrested," the Great Seer said, unable to keep the fury out of his voice.

"I'll see to it, Your Excellency, as soon as—"

"Yes, I know. The bloody papers."

"And the foreign gentleman?"

"He's included in the warrant I issued earlier. But don't arrest him yet. We might need to trot him out to reassure the lady till we've brought her safely into the fold. I should have that taken care of by tomorrow."

"And after that?"

"We won't need him anymore."

❧ 10 ❧

The Ratcatcher

THE RATCATCHER OF HARROWSGODE, Richard
Strange by name, sat in solitary splendor eating his
dinner. He enjoyed the small luxuries his salary made
possible; and though he regrettably had no lady-wife
or friends to join him at table, he dined on quail
stuffed with almonds and dates, a selection of fine
aged cheeses, rare fruits, white bread, and some pretty
little butter cakes he hadn't been able to resist. He ate
them off a silver plate and drank his wine from a crystal goblet etched with a floral design and rimmed with
gold (a recent purchase, one of a pair).

He'd lingered rather longer than usual over his

meal, it being a warm and lazy afternoon. Now he got up, fetched a silver tray, and carefully set his platter, goblet, knife, and fork upon it, ready to carry them out to the kitchen where—since he was his own servant as well as lord of the manor—he would wash them all himself and put them away.

He was perfectly aware of how comical it was: a ratcatcher putting on airs. He'd discussed it many times with Charley, his ancient and beloved rat terrier. They'd agreed that the incongruity added a layer of delight to the situation.

He'd just set the tray on the kitchen worktable when Charley announced with a frenzied bark that someone was coming up the path. A messenger no doubt, carrying news of suspicious droppings found behind the flour sacks in a bakeshop storeroom. Or perhaps it was merely a rustling in the eaves, a darting rat-shape spied in the shadows at night. Whatever it was, it would mean a trip across town to meet with the client and size up the situation.

But he opened the door to an unfamiliar face, a lad dressed in some kind of livery; the scroll he carried was prettily tied with a rose-colored ribbon. And, Richard noted with widening eyes, there was a shiny new spinner leaning against the tree out front. Not your commonplace summons, then.

"Richard Strange?" said the boy.

"That's me," Richard said, taking the scroll and stepping back into his house.

"Favor of a reply is requested, Master says."

"And who might your master be?"

"Pieter, the barrister."

"All right. I'll give you my answer as soon as I've read it. You can wait in the garden."

"Might I go to the pen there and have a look at your dogs?"

"If you want. But don't go trying to pet 'em lest they think you're a rat and bite your hand off."

The boy stared back in horror.

"That was a joke," Richard said, and shut the door.

He untied the ribbon, spread the scroll out on his table, and studied it with squinty eyes. He was literate, but only just, having left school at the age of nine; and this florid script was nothing at all like his schoolmaster's neat, simple hand. Richard had an eye for beautiful things, but those blasted loops and swirls made it hard to make out the meaning—which was, after all, the point of writing things down: so someone else could read them.

Skipping over the salutation, Richard attacked the words one at a time, moving down through a string of niceties till he reached the heart of the message.

"Oh, crikes!" he muttered, then. "Oh, no! They can't do this to me. They can't!"

He got up, made a circuit of the room, then sat down again, slapping his thigh for emphasis, and returned to the offending words. But they still said the same thing they had before: that Richard was requested—politely instructed was more the tone of it—to play host to some bloody arrogant Westrian lord who had just arrived in the city and who, like lords the world over, would find fault, demand when he should rightly ask, sneer at Richard's hospitality, then forget to say thanks when he left.

By the saints! And here Richard thought he was finished with lords for life!

What in blazes was a nobleman from Westria doing in Harrowsgode anyway? Some mystery lay hidden there, no doubt about it, made all the more mysterious by the barrister having chosen to lodge him with the ratcatcher. It wasn't fitting, not fitting at all, and Lord Worthington was sure to be offended. Was that the point? Had they *meant* to insult him?

At least the man would be unarmed—that was something—as weapons were forbidden in Harrowsgode. A great lord in a mad rage could be a very dangerous animal, inclined to swinging swords about and never mind who got in the way. Richard had

hard experience with lords and their moods, and made a mental note to hide the dinner knives.

Well, there was no help for it. He got up from the table and opened the door again. The lad was still on the doorstep, having apparently changed his mind about looking at the dogs.

"Tell your master," Richard said, "that I will offer up my bed to the gentleman. The lord won't be well pleased at being housed with the ratcatcher—but then I suppose your master knows that already."

The boy gaped. "Am I to tell him *that?*"

"No," Richard said. "Just say I'm willing."

He watched as the boy mounted his spinner, pressed down on one of the pedals to start it in motion, then moved slowly forward—wobbling a bit at first, then gaining speed and balance as he continued up the street. How he managed to stay upright on that fantastical contraption was utterly past imagining, but it was a joy to watch him do it.

Richard went back inside and stood in his hall, admiring once again its sturdy construction, its fine proportions, the attention that had been given to small details: the carving on the corbels, the handsome floor, each stone neatly fitted to its neighbor. They did things very well in Harrowsgode, even in the Neargate District. Even for a ratcatcher.

Then he saw it all through Lord Worthington's eyes—the house was small, there were no tapestries, his table would seat only eight—and his pleasure was utterly spoiled.

Muttering curses to himself, Richard went into his sleeping chamber and began to empty the wardrobe of cloaks, boots, doublets, and long woolen gowns, carrying them to the storeroom by the armful. Next he fetched a basket from the kitchen and filled it with the contents of his chest: gloves and hose, linen shirts, a velvet cap, and those satin slippers he'd never had occasion to wear.

Now he stripped the linen from the bed and put on fresh, fluffing the pillows, arranging the coverlet just so, straightening the bed-curtains. Would a small vase holding a rose be too much? Yes, he decided. It would smack of subservience, of eagerness to please, and he was done with that.

He *would* give the floor a quick sweep, though, for pride's sake.

As he worked with the broom, Richard thought back on the two noblemen he'd known best in his life. Both had borne the title of Lord Carnovan of Bergestadt, father and son, one after the other.

Richard had been born on the Bergestadt estate, where his pa served in the lord's kennels, looking after

the hunting hounds. As soon as Richard had been old enough, he'd gone to work there as a page, bedding down with the dogs at night, filling their water bowls, changing the straw, and taking them out when they needed to do their business.

Lord Carnovan the father was a big, coarse, impatient, red-faced, shouting sort of man, an accomplished and passionate hunter. He wasted no affection on his lady or his son; he lavished it all on his purebred horses and his splendid hunting dogs.

Most days he'd come striding into the stable yard preceded by his booming voice: "Oh, the devil take you, what's-your-name-Matthew; I don't want the *mastiff*! The lyam-hound, you fool! I want the *lymer*!"

Richard had thought him an ogre back then and trembled at the sound of his arrival. But later, after the old man pitched off his courser one day while vaulting over a hedge, and struck his head on a boulder, and was killed, he'd gained a whole new perspective on the matter. Lord Carnovan the father had been what a lord should be: confident, capable, and strong. He had, in a manner of speaking, earned the right to be rude and demanding.

But Lord Carnovan the son was something altogether different. He had not his father's wit, nor his father's skill, nor his father's competence—just his

father's title, and the lands and fortune that came with it. Little Lord Peacock was his whispered name. Puffed up with pride and drunk with power, he'd brandished his new estate like a toddling child who'd gotten hold of a sword.

"I am master now," he'd announced that first day, "and it's of no consequence to me how things were done in my father's time. You will do as I say or you shall be sacked. Am I clear?"

He carried a whip; he liked to use it, too.

Richard heaved a sigh and put the broom away. The bedroom was presentable enough, considering the short notice he'd been given. Now he went into the kitchen and set about arranging a light meal on the silver tray—fruit, cheeses, and sliced cold meat—thinking how glad he was he'd bought himself a *pair* of cups in case he actually had a visitor someday. That was one small humiliation averted, at least.

Suddenly his heart filled with rage—that this, of all things, should be forced upon him now when he was so happily settled, that ugly business all behind him. He was so overcome with horrible memories that he dropped onto the kitchen stool, breathing hard.

The Peacock had been uncommonly proud of the fine dogs and horses he'd inherited—though he'd had no hand in breeding, buying, or training

them. They were like the heavy gold chain that hung around his neck and the ruby he wore on his thumb—possessions, things that cost a lot of money. He didn't love them.

Within the kennels, where Richard and his pa worked, the dog most valued by the Peacock was the beautiful greyhound Aurora, and Aurora was expecting puppies. When the time came near for her to drop her litter, she was moved into a private room with a fireplace, away from the other dogs, where she could be cared for tenderly night and day until the birth was accomplished and the pups were well out of danger.

Richard's pa had been given the evening shift. Though he wasn't the senior man, he had a natural way with dogs and was well schooled in veterinary physic. Since Richard was coming up in the dog trade, too—he'd been given charge of the ratters and showed great promise—he'd been allowed to stay with his father and learn what he could.

"It'll be tonight," Pa had said to Richard, "or tomorrow morning at the latest. She's turned away from her food all day—and see how moody she is?"

"If I fall asleep, will you wake me?"

"I will, Son. I promise."

"I wouldn't want to miss it."

Everything was ready. There was a large nest for

Aurora filled with fresh straw, a bowl of water nearby. There was a roll of silk thread and a clean, sharp knife—the one to tie off the cord and the other to cut it should Aurora fail to do it with her teeth. Water and linen cloths were ready to wipe the puppies clean, and a brass bell as big as your hand to ring for help should anything go wrong.

Richard was young, and he'd worked all day; it'd been hard to stay awake. So he hadn't heard Aurora's panting, nor her little whimpers. He hadn't seen his father rise up from his chair to go to her. But he *had* heard, through the mist of a dream, a strange, guttural sound, followed by a crash and a moan.

He'd woken then to see his father lying, as still as death, sprawled across the greyhound, crushing her with his body.

Richard hadn't had the breath to scream. He'd just leaped off the bench and run to his pa, pulling him off the stricken greyhound with all the strength he had—though his father was a heavy man and Richard was still small. He'd laid him out on the floor and knelt over him. Pa's face had been red, and his mouth slack—but he breathed; he was still alive. Richard had found the bell then and rung it hard, setting up such a clamor that it should have woken the dead. But it hadn't woken his pa, nor the greyhound, either.

First a groom had come running, then another, and finally the marshal of the stables himself. By the time he got there, two puppies had been saved, cut from Aurora's belly. She'd felt no pain; nor would she ever feel anything again.

Only then had anyone attended to Richard's pa.

"Apoplexy," the marshal had pronounced. "I doubt he'll walk or speak again, if indeed he lives at all." He'd laid a hand on Richard's shoulder. "We'll call a physician, lad; but I wouldn't store up too much hope."

It was nearly morning by then, and someone had decided that they must inform the Peacock. Richard had been kneeling over his father, stroking his hand and whispering encouragement, when the lord had come storming in. He'd seen the dog, her belly sliced open and the three dead puppies. Then he'd turned to the prostrate man lying in the straw by the birthing box.

The circumstances were explained: a horrible tragedy, an accident, unanticipated, and most certainly unintended. Richard remembered looking up at the Peacock, watching the emotions play across his face and realizing with horror that the man was stoking the fire of his rage. Once he had it blazing hot, the Peacock had started swinging his whip at the comatose man—who had loved that dog with a tenderness her

owner could never feel, who would not have harmed Aurora or her puppies for the world. It was as though the lord had been taken with a fit, so out of control had he been that morning, striking the unconscious man over and over.

Richard had screamed for him to stop, even tried to grab his arm, at which point the lord had struck him across the face and kicked him to the ground.

They'd buried Richard's pa that afternoon. That evening Richard had packed up his few belongings and such money as his father had saved. Then when all was quiet, he'd slipped into the kennels and stolen his two favorite ratters, a breeding pair.

He'd traveled east all through that night, the ratters trotting happily behind him. Three days later they'd crossed the border into Austlind. There he'd made a life for himself going from town to town, ratting for room and board. Eventually he'd settled in a midsize town where he was so well regarded that folks from miles around would call him to rid their barns of vermin. He'd even been able to buy himself a little house with a yard for his dogs to run in.

It was there that the Voyager from Harrowsgode had found him and made him that offer—with the astonishing salary, and a house besides—that Richard had accepted. He'd become his own man at last, never

again to cower before a master.

And now here he was, all those years later, giving house-room to another Peacock, giving up his bed to the man, bringing him food on his precious silver tray—all of which the lord would sneer at because it wasn't good enough. Why, *why* had he not just refused? They could have found someplace else for the man to stay. Lots of people spoke Westrian. The city was chock-full of scholars.

Charley set to barking again and dashed to the door. Richard hauled himself up from the stool, the arrangement still unfinished on the tray, and went reluctantly to open it.

Had the messenger brought him a dancing bear, Richard couldn't have been more surprised. Why, this fellow was just a *lad*, probably not eighteen. And though he was fair of face and manly made, he looked for all the world like the gardener's boy, come hat in hand to ask was there anything more that needed doing just now?

As Lord Worthington came through the doorway, Richard saw him turn to the messenger who'd guided him there and give him a friendly nod. Not a bow, most certainly not a bow, but an acknowledgment that the boy had walked across town on his account and thanks for doing it.

That was one mistake too many. The shy smile had been one thing—unlikely, to be sure, though perhaps he didn't yet realize what a lowly sort of fellow Richard was. But to give the messenger a second thought, let alone a nod and a smile—*that* had been bloody careless.

Why, you precious fool, Richard thought as he shut the door behind Tobias, *you're no more a lord than my Charley is!*

❦ 11 ❧

Tobias

THE MAN WAS APTLY NAMED: Richard Strange. He bowed and scraped as though the king himself had come to stay. "Here is your bedchamber, milord." "Here is a small tray of humble food, milord." Yet he said it all with an edge of—what? Irony? *Malice?*

Probably both, Tobias decided.

It was galling to accept food that was so grudgingly offered. But Master Pieter, for all his attention to ancient history, and maps, and magnifying domes, had neglected to offer them any dinner, and Tobias was famished. So he did eat, though he tried not to seem overeager about it.

The little dog kept sniffing at his boots—he probably caught the scent of horses—and he reached down quite naturally and scratched him behind the ears.

"Come away, Charley," Richard said, scooping up the dog and holding him in his lap. "You mustn't bother the great gentleman."

It was all Tobias could do not to scream—or stalk out of the house, slamming the door behind him. But instead he drew a deep breath and continued to eat while his host watched—as though Tobias were some kind of loathsome but fascinating creature: a large, hairy spider or a slimy water-leech bloated with blood.

Finally Richard leaned forward and posed a question.

"If it wouldn't be too probing to ask, *your lordship*—where lies your estate? I know sommat of Westria, as I was born there."

"It's in the south, on the River Seren. Where in Westria were you born?"

"At Bergestadt, in the north. So your estate, my lord—is it a *large* place? Do a bit of hunting down there?"

"No, not large," Tobias said. "And I've done a little hunting. Not much."

"I see. Lots of dogs in your kennel? I have a particular interest in dogs, as you can imagine."

Tobias set his slice of cheese back on the tray and studied Richard openly. "A small kennel," he said, "on my small estate."

"You could build it up, my lord, buy yourself some purebred stock, get yourself a first-rate huntsman. Money is of no importance, I'm sure, to a great nobleman like you."

Tobias closed his eyes in despair. It was as though the man suspected him of lying and was trying to catch him out. And though he wasn't especially proud by nature, he hated being mocked. So he carefully moved aside the tray and folded his arms on the table.

"You can stop calling me 'my lord,'" he said.

"Ha!" Richard cried, exultant. "I *knew* you weren't a lord the minute I saw you!"

"Then you were mistaken, for I am a lord. And I really do have a rather nice, rather small estate on the bank of the Seren River. But I wasn't born a gentleman, as you rightly suspected. I was given my lands and title by royal decree for doing the king a favor."

"What sort of favor?"

"Saving his life. Before that, I worked in the stable yard."

Richard was grinning now. Not the gardener's boy, but close enough. "So what shall I call you if not 'my lord'?"

"My name is Tobias."

"Well then, Tobias, I've been appallingly rude, and I beg your forgiveness. It had nothing at all to do with you, just a misunderstanding—and an old ghost that haunts my soul sometimes and makes me foolish. Can we start over again? All forgiven, all forgotten?"

"Of course we can."

Tobias looked away, thinking, then turned back to his host again, resolved to speak plainly. "Richard, I'm afraid I may need your help."

"I think you very well might. But I won't know for sure till you tell me your situation—how you came to Harrowsgode and why they let you into the city."

Tobias ran his fingers through his hair, grabbing a clump and giving it a tug. He'd done this since childhood whenever he was nervous or afraid—as he was now. "We were sent to Austlind by the king of Westria to buy a special cup made years ago by my lady's grandfather, William."

"What lady?"

"Her name is Molly, and she likewise served the king and was raised to great estate. She was a scullion before, if you wish to know."

"It doesn't matter in the least," Richard said, solemn now. "So it was just the two of you on this journey?"

"No. We had a knight to protect us as well as a translator, and Molly's lady companion. They're still in the village."

"All right. Go on."

"We went to Faers-Wigan first; that's a crafts town where the grandfather lived in his later years. But when William died, his family having fled to Westria, the entire estate reverted to the crown. There was nothing left for us to find."

"But?"

"William wasn't a native of Faers-Wigan; he was already full-grown when he arrived. Molly learned that he'd come from the far north—"

"—a place called Harrowsgode."

"Yes."

"But how did you manage to find it? Did someone give you directions?"

Tobias gave a little snort. "North. By the sea."

"And yet you found your way across a pathless plain and discovered that clever little cleft in the mountain?"

Tobias picked up a strawberry and nibbled at it thoughtfully. "A raven led us," he said.

"You're joking."

"No."

"And then they invited you into the city, though

it's closed to foreigners. This is all quite fantastical, Tobias."

"All the same, it's true. Molly's one of them, remember. Descended from the Magnus clan by way of her grandfather. They seemed right eager to have her."

"That much I understand. But what about you?"

"Well, Molly and I are . . . um . . . betrothed." He still couldn't say that without blushing. "She refused to come without me."

"And where is she now?"

"Staying with a distant relative, Claus Magnusson. But I don't know where he lives, nor how to contact her; and I'm beginning to be afraid. . . ."

Richard nodded as if in agreement. "Is that all?"

"Yes."

"Well, there's a lot I need to tell you. But bear with me a moment. It grows dark, and my eyes aren't what they used to be."

He set Charley down on the floor and went to the sideboard for a small silver pitcher. He carried it over to one of the peculiar candlesticks that sat on the table. Tobias had noticed them earlier and wondered what they were—for at the top of each one, where candles should have been, was a shallow silver cup; and resting in each cup was a stone. You'd think they were

something precious, being displayed like that, yet they looked like common river stones.

Tobias watched as Richard poured a thin stream of clear liquid into each of the cups. In the time it took to draw a breath and let it out again, the stones began to glow, filling the room with a soft, greenish light.

"Coldfire," Richard explained. "Don't know how it works exactly, but it's a great improvement on candles. Safer, you know, less chance of setting yourself and your house on fire."

"I'm amazed."

"They're very advanced, these Harrowsgode folk." He put the pitcher back on the sideboard and returned to his seat. "That's better," he said. "I can see you now."

He sat for a moment, gathering his thoughts.

"I'm afraid that what I'm going to say will be rather hard to hear. And there's a lot to tell."

Tobias nodded, dread creeping over him.

"You'll have noticed how the Harrowsgode folk keep to themselves. But they set a great store on wisdom, and they want the best of everything. So they send a few of their people—they call 'em Voyagers—out into the world to learn about new things and bring back all manner of treasures. They're big on books and maps, but it could be anything, really: seeds for new plants, precious stones, musical instruments,

paintings, scientific devices. Ideas, too: ways of doing things that are different from their own."

He paused, rolled his neck, and shook out his shoulders. "I *am* getting to the point."

Tobias waited.

"Sometimes they bring back people, foreigners like me. They want us for our particular skills: the knowledge of how to make fine, hand-knotted carpets, or fluency in a language that the Harrowsgode folk don't know. In my case they wanted my ratting dogs and my knowledge of how to use them.

"There are about thirty of us here. They give us nice houses to live in and pay us handsomely—more money than we need, really, in case you were wondering about my silver tray, and the cups, and whatnot. But we all live here in the Neargate District, and we don't have the freedom of the city. I'm the sole exception since I can't do my work unless I go wherever the rats are."

Richard sat up straighter now and looked Tobias hard in the eye.

"So that's the bargain. In return for wealth and comfort, we commit to spending our lives here, passing on our skills so the Harrowsgode folk will have them when we're gone."

"Are you saying—?"

"Foreigners never leave Harrowsgode. I shall die here, Tobias, and so shall you."

"But why?"

"Because people talk. And if word ever got out about this hidden city with its great, rich silver mine, and its abundant harvests, and its hoard of priceless treasures—all unprotected, you see, for they have no army—well, you can imagine what would happen. And so they rely on secrecy, as they have for hundreds of years."

"But—"

"I'm not finished, Tobias. There's more. You saw how glad they were to have your lady here, especially as she's one of the Magnus clan. Why, that's like—"

"—royalty?"

"That's it. She's very special. So naturally they'll want her to marry one of her own, someone carefully chosen. Not an outsider, Tobias."

He waited.

"That makes you something of a problem, don't you see? What to do with the foreign gentleman the lady has sworn herself to? They'll go about it as they do everything here—with tact and discretion. They'll keep you apart, bring her into their charmed circle, and try to win her over. Then when the moment seems right—"

"I understand, Richard. You don't need to say any more."

"As for the other three—the rest of your party . . ."

"What about them?"

"They'll be the first to go."

Tobias buried his face in his hands and let despair wash over him. For one brief moment he lost hold of the fierce determination that had sustained him all his life—helping him bear the death of his baby brother, then his parents, and finally sweet little Mary; keeping his wits sharp in the midst of a royal slaughter so he could get the prince to safety; and giving him the strength and endurance to battle an army of demons and go on fighting long past the point of exhaustion. Now he just felt hopeless. . . .

"Mind you," Richard said, "I won't say there isn't a way out of this predicament."

Tobias looked up, all attention.

"It's just that at the moment I don't exactly know what it is."

❧ 12 ❧

A Family Dinner

MOLLY STOOD IN THE CENTER of the large, handsome room she'd been given at the Magnussons' house. With bare toes she probed the softness of a downy silk carpet while Ulla, her lady's maid, unlaced the sides of her gown. When it was loose, the girl offered Molly a hand as she stepped out from the circle of russet-colored wool that had dropped to the floor. Ulla folded it carefully over a bench as though it were something fine, then went to work on the buttons that ran down the bodice of her kirtle.

Molly blushed to think of Ulla trying to make her garments presentable again: brushing them, airing

them, mending them, scrubbing out the stains. She might be a servant, but it was highly doubtful that she'd ever handled anything so shabby in her life. The clothes had been humble to begin with—they'd dressed as common travelers so as not to attract the attention of thieves—and Molly had been wearing them for many, many days. And for all but one of the past five nights, she'd slept in them out on the ground.

Maybe she should tell the girl to burn the blasted things. She had plenty of money to buy new clothes for the trip back to Westria.

The buttons undone, Ulla helped Molly off with her kirtle and then her shift. As it passed over her head, Molly caught the stench of her own unwashed body. Finally the maid untied the laces of her under-drawers—and there Molly stood: on a silk rug, in an elegant room, completely naked.

She would never get used to it, standing there like a wooden saint while a servant took her clothes off and then put new ones on. She'd much rather have done it for herself, but that wasn't how ladies behaved. So she stayed where she was, arms held away from her scrawny frame, while everything happened again in reverse: on with the fresh underdrawers; then the hose, held in place with garters tied right below the knee; now the clean shift that went on over her head;

then another helping hand as she stepped into her finer kirtle and all the buttons were fastened up the front; and over that her good gown—the one she'd brought to wear in Faers-Wigan, since only people of quality shopped there—which was fastened with a wide belt, buckled in the back. Finally, Ulla knelt at Molly's feet and helped her on with her little satin slippers.

"I've brought you some ribbons for your hair, lady, if you'd like to wear them. They're the same blue as your gown. Would that please you?"

"Very much," Molly said, thinking back to the afternoon of Princess Elinor's wedding.

It seemed ages ago, though it had only been a matter of months. Winifred had done up Molly's hair for the occasion, weaving the ribbons Tobias had given her through the braids as she went. When she had finished, Winifred stepped back to admire the results and declared that Molly was a perfect beauty—and why had Winifred never noticed that before?

People say things like that all the time, just to be kind, without really meaning it. But no one had *ever* said such a thing to Molly before that day. It had made her heart sing with pleasure.

Then, just a few hours after, King Edmund had been slain, along with his mother and the poor princess bride. Molly shivered, remembering the rest:

Tobias carrying the wounded and unconscious prince down the stairs into the storeroom, where a boat was tied at the water gate—and, oh, the blood, and the sheer terror of it, and the fear that Alaric would die . . .

"Lady?"

"I'm all right," she said, and shivered again.

⚜

As Molly descended the stairs to the great hall, she was surprised to hear loud voices and boisterous laughter. She'd met Claus and Margit Magnusson earlier in the day; and though they'd greeted her warmly, they'd struck her as the quiet sort, stiff and formal. Apparently she'd misjudged them.

She stopped just outside the door, listening. They were speaking in Austlinder, but she understood most of it.

"Now, Papa," a girl was saying, "you are *absolutely forbidden* to be pompous tonight. We cannot have you boring our guest."

"I am never boring or pompous. I merely offer such insights as I've gained through a lifetime of study, and—"

"See! Exactly!"

"That's enough, Laila." Molly recognized Margit's voice.

"She has a point, Mother," came the voice of a young man. "The lady should be allowed to find wisdom for herself—not have it dumped into her lap like spilled soup."

"Spilled soup! Oh, Lorens, how apt! May I use that in a poem?"

A titter from a younger child.

They sounded like the kind of family Molly had wished for as a child: lively, affectionate, and happy. Then it came to her with a sudden thrill that they really *were* her family. Distant, yes, but the fruit of the same tree.

She peered around the doorway and saw them gathered around the fireplace. Master Claus stood, one hand resting on the shoulder of his younger daughter. The little girl's face, as round and shining as the moon, was framed by a mane of fluffy curls. Margit sat near the fire, busy with some needlework. And behind Margit, leaning on the back of her chair, was a beautiful girl of eighteen or so, with a straight back and large, prominent eyes. She looked as though she was just about to tell a funny story or play some wicked prank. Molly liked her instantly.

A little apart from the rest stood a lad of perhaps twenty-five. He was dressed in a silk robe of deep midnight blue, embroidered all over with silver thread in a

pattern of bursting stars. The silver badge on his velvet cap was shaped like a crescent moon.

Rich, beautiful, elegant, and happy—*her* family! Molly took a deep breath and stepped into the room.

"Ah, here she is!" cried Claus in a booming voice. "Welcome, welcome!"

It was only then, as they turned to greet her, that Molly noticed another boy, much the same age as the beauty. He'd been standing in the shadow of his star-clad brother. Even now she couldn't see his face very well.

"Children," Claus said, switching to Westrian for Molly's sake, "may I present your cousin, Lady Marguerite of Barcliffe Manor, the granddaughter of my late uncle, William Magnusson. Come, my dear, we'll take our seats at table"—Claus indicated a chair between the fluffy angel and the younger boy—"and then I'll introduce my little brood."

"Your *brood*!" cried the angel, pretending to be offended. "Are we *poultry* now, Father?"

"You are indeed," Claus said. "But you'll have to wait your turn, my little chick. Oldest first, remember? Marguerite, this magnificent creature to my right is Lorens Magnusson. We called him home especially to meet you; and it's quite a treat for us as well, for we don't get to see him very often anymore. He lives

at Harrowsgode Hall and is studying to be a Magus Mästare."

"Papa is very proud," said the beauty.

"As he has every right to be," Claus returned. "And this impertinent young lady is our daughter Laila. She is at the university studying natural philosophy, and she talks of nothing but *chem*icals and *cor*puscles and *car*bonates—" He leaned hard on those explosive *c*'s for comic effect. "And she says *I* am dull!" He said all this with the greatest affection and pride; the beauty took it with a smile.

"Now on your right is Laila's twin, Jakob. And on your left—"

"Father," said the boy, "aren't you going to list *my* accomplishments?"

He had turned to address his father; all Molly could see was his hair, his ear, and the curve of his cheekbone and chin.

"I *am* the family disappointment, after all. Surely that counts for something."

"Oh, spare us, Jakob, please," Claus said.

"But it's true. Every family must have one. Don't you agree, Marguerite?"

He turned as he said this, and Molly stifled a gasp—for it was the boy in her dream! And from the way he locked eyes with her, it was clear that he had

recognized her, too.

"Are you all right, my dear?" asked Margit.

"No," Molly said. "I mean yes. Yes."

A hand reached in and set a bowl of soup before her. Molly looked down, then up at Jakob again.

"I'm not at the university with my sister," he went on mechanically. "I failed my exams, you see—quite spectacularly, in fact. So I'm apprenticed to a silversmith. A tradesman in *this* family—only think of it! Papa is so disappointed."

"That's enough," Claus said. "You're making our guest uncomfortable. And do stop staring at her, will you? She'll want to turn around and go straight back to Westria this very night."

The boy sniffed as if that was somehow darkly amusing.

"Jakob!" Margit snapped. "I'm sorry, Marguerite. He's not himself tonight."

"You forgot about me," said the little sprite. "You left me out entirely."

"I was trying to get to you, child, but your brother was insistent upon—"

"Father," said the beauty, "let's move on."

"Indeed. This lovely creature to your left is Sanna, our youngest. She is a first-year scholar."

Sanna knew how to sparkle, and she did so now.

She turned to Molly, eyes wide, and asked with wonder in her voice, "Are you *really* from Westria?"

Molly said she was.

"Ohhhh—what's it like?"

"Well, we don't have as many mountains as you have here. Actually, now that I think of it, there aren't any mountains at all. Just some very big hills."

"What else? Is it very large?"

"About the same size as Austlind."

"And does it have a king?"

"Most certainly."

"Is he old?"

"Not at all! He's younger than Jakob and Laila. His name is Alaric, and he's very, *very* handsome."

"Oh!" Sanna clapped her hands, wild with excitement. "Ours is old. Have you seen him in person, then—the king of Westria?"

"Why, yes, Sanna; I've seen him many times. In fact, I shall tell you something that will amaze you; just the other day we were walking together in his private garden—"

"Alone?"

"Well, there were guards outside, but yes, we were alone. And he took my arm, just like this, and he held me close . . ."

Sanna flopped back in her chair in exaggerated

amazement, rolling her eyes up into her head, her mouth open wide. Then Molly realized that the others had stopped drinking their soup; spoons in hand, they were staring at her—what? Dumbfounded? *Scandalized?*

"In a brotherly sort of way," she added. "Nothing improper. We're just very good friends."

"I have no doubt of it," Margit said, and changed the subject.

As dish after dish came out of the kitchen and then was carried empty away, the conversation rolled cheerfully on, Jakob's outburst and Molly's indiscretion long forgotten. Soon the family drifted back to their accustomed subjects: the university, philosophy, and corpuscles. Even Sanna, who had little to offer on such subjects, made an effort to join in.

Only Jakob and Molly held back. They sat, eating in silence, pretending interest in the discussion. Finally, at a particularly noisy moment when Laila was making everyone laugh, Jakob leaned in and whispered in Molly's ear.

"In the garden," he said. "By the bench, after dinner."

❦ 13 ❧

Jakob

WHAT A FOOL HE'D MADE of himself at dinner. He hadn't pulled a stunt like that in years. True, it had hurt to be discounted so transparently, especially in front of his cousin; but he ought to be used to it by now.

Jakob understood his father very well, better than most sons did. He knew Claus to be a proud man: proud of his clan, his position in society, and the accomplishments of his children. But Jakob also knew that beneath that pride lay a deep well of disappointment—that he, Claus Magnusson, had been granted no gift at all. He was nothing more than a university

professor, and not even a great one at that.

There was the root of the family tragedy: Because, of the four children, Jakob should have been the one to fulfill his father's hopes. Instead, he'd been difficult; he'd denied his prodigious gift, pretending to be a slow-wit and setting himself on a path that led to service in a trade. He'd taken the very thing that Claus valued and wanted most in the world—and thrown it away. Of course the man was angry. But if Claus had tried to understand his son, as the son understood the father, he might have found it in his heart to forgive, and gained a measure of peace for himself into the bargain.

Jakob heard the sound of footsteps on gravel and saw a figure moving slowly down the path, feeling her way in the darkness.

He crossed his arms protectively over his chest. He was trembling a little, wondering whether his cousin would be a kindred soul—and certainly Jakob needed one—or a threat to his very life and happiness. Well, he'd know soon enough.

She was waving at him now, with big, wide sweeps of her arm as though hailing a ship at sea. She seemed so young and childish—and that was odd, considering who and what she was. But then she'd been raised common, according to Claus, and had been given no

education. That might account for it.

"Jakob?" A loud whisper.

"Over here."

Now she was standing in front of him—such a little thing, all skin and bones and enormous eyes, like some wild creature. Not timid, though. Not timid at all.

"Well, cousin," Jakob said. "Here we are. We don't have a lot of time."

"Then we'd best get right on with it, hadn't we? You've seen me before. In there, just now, you recognized me."

"We recognized each other, Marguerite. It went both ways."

"Yes. I've been seeing you in my dreams this last month and more."

"They were visions, I think."

"All right, visions. You were always dressed in a fawn-colored doublet, embroidered with soft green vines. And the sleeves were some sort of stiff brocade, burgundy and gold, puffy at the shoulder and narrow at the wrist. Do you have a doublet like that?"

"I do—exactly like that."

"Ah." She drew in a deep breath and let it out. "And you were holding a silver goblet up against your chest, like so." She raised her hands to show him, fingers

enclosing empty air. "The base is very fancy—some parts gilded, with enamels framed in filigree. But the cup itself is plain."

"I've seen the same goblet," he said, "except it was *you* who held it."

He could hear her slippers shuffling the gravel as she thought about this.

"Listen, Jakob," she said after a while, "I must tell you something. I was sent to Austlind by the king of Westria to find a special cup, of a kind my grandfather used to make. We went to Faers-Wigan, a crafts town to the south, because that's where he lived and practiced his trade. But while we were there I found out that he hadn't been born in Faers-Wigan; he'd come there from someplace else. Yet right from the start, before Alaric even called me back to court, before I'd even *heard* of Harrowsgode, I was dreaming of you. Don't you see? I was *meant* to come here."

"I think you're right."

"And there's something else. The cup we both saw—"

"—is a Loving Cup. And that's what your king is after."

"Yes. It all fits together. I saw you holding the cup because you were meant to make it. And you saw me in your visions—"

"—because I'm supposed to make it for you."

"Oh, Jakob, I'm so glad I found you! There are only two people in the world I completely trust—my friend Tobias and Alaric, the king of Westria. But even they can't understand what it's like to be the way we are. Talking to you feels so natural. It's almost like talking to myself."

And there it was, the answer to his question: a kindred soul.

They were quiet then for a while, aware that something important had just happened, and feeling a little bashful at the intimacy of it.

"Jakob," Molly said at last, breaking the silence. "I want to ask you something. I don't mean to pry, but . . ."

"Go ahead."

"Why are you a silversmith? No, wait—let me ask this in a different way. Why are you *also* a silversmith, like my grandfather was, when both of you might have been—well, what Lorens is, only greater? Where I come from, having visions and knowing the future are seen as marks of the devil. Here it's a sign of greatness. So, why?"

Jakob turned away and studied the rosebushes, trying to decide what to say. That had been the most personal and painful question anyone could have

asked. Did he really trust her that much?

"Let's sit down," he finally said, having made up his mind. "It's not going to be a short answer." He took his time, ordering his thoughts, deciding what to tell now and what he could put off till later. Then he took the plunge:

"When I was very small, I was playing with Laila, here in the garden. I had a toy horse, with a real horse-hair mane and tail, and big, button eyes. It was my very favorite thing. So naturally Laila, being devilish, took it away from me and ran away—waving it in the air, you know, just to torment me. I ran after her, growing angrier by the minute, until I was positively beside myself with rage and frustration. She was a fast little thing, but I finally caught up with her and grabbed her by the arm . . . and I remember feeling this strange sensation: the heat of my fury just *pouring* out of me, through my hand, and into her body till she screamed and fell to the ground. And she lay there, not breathing, her skin very white. I thought she must be dead—and that I had killed her.

"I couldn't think what to do—I was very young and stupid—so instead of calling for help I just knelt down and touched her cheek, stroked it gently. I was sobbing the whole time because I loved her—I still love her—like nobody else on earth. Then suddenly

she gasped and opened her eyes."

"Oh!" Molly said.

"She didn't remember any of it, didn't understand what had happened. She thought she'd just fallen down. And I was glad, because I was sure she'd hate me if she knew. I've told her since, some of it; but back then I had to carry it alone, and the pain of it nearly destroyed me. I took to hiding in dark places and wouldn't let anyone near. I'd go out into the garden sometimes and touch things—caterpillars, beetles—to see if they would die, but they never did.

"Then I started having these visions of another little boy. I saw him playing with a kitten once. He'd ask it questions, and it would answer. Another time I saw him telling his mother that the dustman wouldn't be coming that day because he'd died in the night. And she scolded him, saying he mustn't make up dreadful stories like that. But later it turned out to be true. And once I saw him make the fire burn brighter, just with the wave of his hand.

"I realized then that we were alike, this boy and me. We both had these inexplicable powers. I found it comforting, as you can imagine."

"Yes, I can. I've felt like a freak since I was seven years old. I would have been glad back then to know there were others like me."

"The boy was with me all the time, but he was always a few steps ahead. He became my guide, my model. When he turned himself into a thick-wit at school—took to asking foolish questions and giving the wrong answers—I did the same. I failed my exams, just as he did. And I followed him into the same trade."

"It was my grandfather, wasn't it?"

"Yes. But William was different from me in one important respect: his gift was not merely great—it was extraordinary, such as only comes along once in a hundred years. So if *I* could kill my sister with an angry touch, then bring her back to life with my grief—for William it must have felt like holding lightning in his hands. It frightened him terribly. That's why he kept it hidden. He knew that if he ever learned to *harness* those powers, they might consume him and drive him to do despicable things."

"Oh, Jakob!"

"What?"

"Did you see—in your visions—the whole of his life?"

"No. I saw him dive into the river—over in Neargate, where the canals come together and flow under the walls—and swim underwater for what seemed like hours, through endless darkness; then there was just a hint of light, and he rose up and out of

the water and took this deep, gasping breath, floating in the still waters of the moat. And he was wild with joy, thinking, *I'm free! I'm free!* And that was the end of it. After that vision I never saw him again."

"Oh." He could hear the sadness in that single word.

"Tell me."

"I think he was right to be afraid. He never meant to do harm—indeed, he did a lot of good. He made Loving Cups that caused people to love each other. But in doing that he revealed himself and his powers to the world. Someone forced him to use them in a horrible way—they threatened to kill his family if he didn't. So he made a beautiful silver bowl as a baby gift for a prince and filled it with a hundred curses."

Jakob shook his head, refusing to believe it.

"But the prince didn't die as he was supposed to. William was too smart for that. The curses he made were innocent things, like scraped knees and cold porridge. And he put a guardian spirit in the bowl to make sure everything went as planned—a little man, allover silver, and very kind. He was like a little"—she pressed her thumb and forefinger together as if holding a pinch of salt—"a little fragment of my grandfather, all his wisdom and sweetness, dressed up in a silver suit." She smiled, remembering. "My grandfather always

tempered the metal with his own blood to make the enchantment work. That made us blood relatives, the Guardian said. So he asked me to call him Uncle."

"You met him—inside the bowl? I don't understand."

"It's a long story. Things didn't go as planned, and he called me for help. When it was over and all the curses were destroyed, his spirit was released. His body melted back into the bowl. Now his spirit is"—she waved a hand at the sky—"*out there* somewhere. I miss him, Jakob. I miss him very much."

The bright tip of a full moon was rising over the eastern mountains. Jakob watched it emerge and grow until it hurt his eyes. He knew she hadn't finished the story. She'd come close, then changed the subject. But he had to know.

"Molly," he said. "What happened when the curses failed?"

She took a deep breath and let it out, then sat in silence for a while. "William was murdered," she said.

He covered his face with his hands and felt tears stinging his eyes. "That breaks my heart," he said. "I always imagined he lived a long and happy life, that he found a girl he fancied, and married her, and spent his days making beautiful things out of silver and gold. . . ."

"He did all that."

"But not for long."

"Long enough. He found kind friends and was a great success at his work—he was the youngest master silversmith in the history of the city's guild. He had a wife and a child he loved. And he died saving their lives."

"I'm glad. It's strange—I never met him, just saw him in my visions, but I loved him very much. He was like my closest friend."

"I understand," she said.

"Marguerite—"

"Molly, please. Marguerite is for strangers."

"All right, Molly. It's my turn to tell you something hard."

"I thought you just did."

"This is different. And I've been putting it off, because . . ." He plucked a leaf from a lilac bush and rolled it in his fingers. He couldn't bring himself to look her in the face. "You came here in search of a Loving Cup, and I'll gladly make you one. But you can't give it to the king of Westria, because you'll never see him again. Like death, this is the undiscovered country from which no traveler returns. I'm sorry, but that's the truth."

"No!" she said.

"Listen to me: I told you I saw you holding the cup, but I didn't say what you were wearing. Molly, you were dressed in the robes of a Magus Mästare, and my visions never lie. That's your future, and the reason you were called here. You possess the Gift of King Magnus, as your grandfather did; and you will spend your life in Harrowsgode Hall, growing your powers and learning—"

She was shaking her head. "That's not true! I just see things sometimes, same as you."

"No. You're altogether different from me. I can sense your power just sitting here beside you. It pours off you like heat from a bonfire. Even my parents know you have the Gift, and they have no powers of perception at all."

"But how could they possibly—even if it were true?"

"Tell me, when you came to our house, how did they welcome you?"

"Like this," she said, holding out her hands. "I thought it was a Harrowsgode greeting."

"Well, it's not. No one touches hands here without consent. For most people it means nothing; but for those with the Gift, it's like water running downstream—their spirit flows out of them, revealing their secrets. To take their hands without permission is like

going through their underclothes or reading their private letters. We only touch those we love and trust.

"It's disgusting what my parents did. They were testing you because they sensed you had some of William's fire, and they wanted to be sure. They didn't think you'd know the difference."

"Your mother trembled when she took my hands."

"I'll bet she did. I'm glad. I hope it gives her nightmares."

"Jakob! Marguerite!" They'd finally been missed.

"In a minute, Father!"

"Quick, Jakob—what about Tobias? Will they keep him from leaving, too?"

"Tobias? The friend you mentioned before?"

"Yes. He came with me on the journey."

"And they *let him into Harrowsgode*?" He was astonished.

"I lied and said we were betrothed. I refused to come without him."

"Oh, Molly!" He shook his head. "No, they will *not* let him leave."

That was the least of it, Jakob suspected, but he wouldn't say any more. He'd heaped enough grief on her already, and there was nothing she could do to help her friend.

"Come *inside*!" Claus called again.

"We have to go, Molly. We'll talk again tomorrow."

"All right. But promise you'll make me the cup, and as quickly as you can. I'll figure out the rest. Will you do that for me, please?"

"Of course I will. But it won't change a thing."

"They can't force me to stay here. I won't let them."

"Oh, little cousin, you have *no idea* who you're dealing with."

"Really, Jakob?" She raised her chin with such childish defiance, it almost made him laugh. "Well, neither do *they*!"

❦ 14 ❦

Watching

HE ARRIVED AT the house before dawn. Lights were already glowing in some of the windows—servants, most likely, making preparations for the day ahead. At sunup the porter came out to sweep the steps, and not long after that a servant left, a basket on her arm. When she returned, the basket was so full she needed both hands to carry it. After that nothing much happened for a while.

Then Claus Magnusson came out with his two daughters. The younger one gripped her father's hand, skipping and bouncing along as they made their way down the street. The older one walked gracefully

beside them, her shoulders back, her head held high, and her eyes wide with interest. She reminded him of Molly—they had the same boldness, the same strong spirit. But while the Magnusson girl was confident and serene, Molly was fierce and full of fire.

Well, they'd led very different lives.

He continued to wait.

Mornings came slowly to Harrowsgode, the mountains and tall buildings casting long, cool shadows till the sun was well up in the sky. But by midday the cobbles would be shimmering with heat, and warm currents of air would begin to rise, the ones that lifted his wings and allowed him to soar so effortlessly through the sky.

But not quite yet. The River District was deep in shadow still.

At last something unexpected: a man was approaching the house. He had gray hair and wore academic robes. The raven felt sure that he'd come to visit Molly. A tutor perhaps?

He'd been avoiding the windowsills, which were narrow for a bird of his size, but he needed to hear what the man said. Clapping the air with his great black wings, he rose and circled once, marking a spot on a sill to the right of the entry door, calculating the angle and speed of his descent, then sliding in with

a little sideways hop so that he stood pressed close against the window glass. It wasn't comfortable, but he was steady.

The man looked up for a moment, startled by the sound of wings; then he looked down again as the door opened.

"Dr. Larsson to see the lady Marguerite," he said.

The porter bowed and ushered the man in.

❧ 15 ❧

A Little Outing

THE TUTOR, GEROLD LARSSON, was older than she'd expected, and more distinguished in appearance. He looked as if he ought to be teaching at the university, not giving private lessons to someone like Molly.

"Dr. Magnusson tells me that you were never taught your letters," he said. "Can this possibly be true?"

"Yes," she said as if it were a matter of pride. "I was taught nothing at all."

"Then we shall have some catching up to do." He said this with relish, as if helping ignorant girls catch up was the thing he liked most in the world.

"I'd rather you taught me Austlinder. I have great need of speaking and no need whatsoever for reading and writing."

"I think you'll find, once we get started, that knowing how to read and write is surprisingly useful. But we will do both, never fear."

There was a thump and rustling at the window just then, and both of them turned to see a raven clinging precariously to the narrow ledge.

"Shoo!" Dr. Larsson shouted, clapping his hands.

With a flutter of wings, the bird disappeared from sight.

"Why did you *do* that?"

He seemed surprised that she should ask. "Birds are filthy creatures," he said as if stating the obvious. "They leave their droppings on the window ledges and down the sides of the house."

She went over to the window and looked down into the garden, searching for any sign of the raven. At last she heard a froglike *croooawk*—and there he was, half hidden in a lilac bush.

"I like ravens," she said without turning around. "And they're not filthy."

"I'm sorry, Marguerite. I didn't mean to offend."

"They're beautiful birds."

"I suppose they are."

"Stephen says they're very intelligent."

"Yes, I've heard that too."

"They court by dancing side by side with their sweethearts in the air. And they mate for life."

"Well, once you've learned to read, you can study books on natural philosophy and learn all there is to know about ravens."

She finally turned away from the window and found him waiting with a gentle smile.

"Excuse me, my dear, but I'd be very grateful if you'd take a seat. Courtesy requires that I remain standing as long as a lady does, and I have very troublesome knees."

"Oh," she said, "I didn't know."

She walked around the little desk and plopped herself down behind it, then waited while Dr. Larsson lowered himself cautiously into a chair. He massaged his knees for a minute, then looked up at Molly and thanked her.

"Now, I believe there's no better place to start than at the beginning—with the letters of the alphabet. I've asked for our meal to be brought in on a tray at twelve-bells. After that we might move on to a bit of language study, using the skills—"

Only now did Molly understand that he planned to stay all day. And no doubt he'd be back again

tomorrow and the day after that, leaving her no time to find Tobias and work out a plan or to roam about Harrowsgode searching for a way to escape.

"Master Tutor," she said, interrupting his flow of words, "I really don't think I could learn anything at all today. I've been traveling for a long time and didn't sleep well last night. I'm bone-tired, and my wits are like curdled cream. Maybe you could come back later—next week, perhaps."

"I quite understand. But let me make an alternative proposal. Suppose we put off your studies for today and go on a little outing instead? There are many things in Harrowsgode that will amaze you, but there's one particular sight that stands above the rest and is positively not to be missed: the Great Hall of Treasures. It's not far from here, and we needn't stay long—though once you get there and see it, you may want to."

"What is it—the Great Hall of Treasures?"

"Exactly what the name implies: a beautiful building with priceless treasures on display. Anyone in Harrowsgode may go there. You don't even have to pay."

"What sort of treasures?"

"Every kind you can possibly imagine—and countless more you cannot. In my opinion, the library is the greatest treasure of all, but that will not interest you

just yet. We'll peek in so you can say you've seen it, then move on to the treasures.

"The library is in the center of the building and is very large. The treasure-house wraps around it on all four sides. There are rooms dedicated to paintings from all over the world, and one room filled with marble sculptures. There are works in silver and gold, artifacts from ancient times, new inventions, musical instruments, native costumes from distant lands, tapestries, and curiosities from every age and corner of the world. I promise you will be astonished."

"I've never seen anything like that."

"Nor has anyone else who hasn't been to Harrowsgode. What do you say? Would you like to go?"

As she stood gazing up at the building, Molly realized that she'd seen it before. It was when they'd just come out of the narrow canyon and were standing on the rim, looking down at Harrowsgode. It was the city's most distinctive feature, so grand and imposing she'd thought at first it must be a cathedral, though it didn't really look like one. Enormous at the base, it rose story by story, each level smaller than the one below: a sort of giant's staircase capped by five domed towers.

Leading to the entrance was a broad staircase, which they now began to climb.

Dr. Larsson asked if she'd lend him her arm, as she was young and strong and he was old, with troublesome knees. He held it firmly, just as Alaric had, but the experience was altogether different. This was not the intimate thrill of touching the king of Westria; she felt a tingling in her arm rather like the sensation of clasping hands with Claus and Margit, only very much stronger. She didn't think he'd done it on purpose, as her relatives had—but surely he must feel it. And if what Jakob had told her was true, he must even now be reading the secrets of her heart. Molly turned to look at him, but the only expression she saw on his face was the occasional wince at the pain from climbing the stairs.

"Going down is even worse," he said as if reading her mind. "They really should build a ramp, maybe with some sort of pulley system to haul pathetic old fellows like me up and down the stairway." He gave her a wan smile. "I think I'll write a note to the Council suggesting it."

At last they reached the landing and Dr. Larsson released her arm. They waited a moment while he caught his breath, then he gave her a quick little nod.

"Shall we go in?" he said.

Large buildings, in her experience, were usually dark. But the entrance to the Great Hall of Treasures was astonishingly bright. And looking up, she saw why. The stout walls that held up the enormous structure were straight ahead of her. The entry hall, and the corridors that extended beyond it on either side, wrapping all around the building, were simply an elaborate porch. Since nothing rested on top of it, the ceiling could safely hold countless skylights, as well as a string of small, angled windows placed where the wall met the ceiling on the outer side. She'd never seen anything like it. And all that glass—it must have cost an absolute fortune!

Dr. Larsson had gone to speak with one of the officials, who wrote something on a small slip of paper and handed it to him. Now he returned. "A pass for the library," he explained. "We'll just take a *very* quick look, I promise. But you cannot come here and miss the finest thing in all of Harrowsgode, perhaps even the world—the wisdom of every land, and every age, gathered in a single place." He said this with such high emotion that Molly almost laughed.

"Just wait," he said. "You'll see."

The library door was as stout as a castle gate and made of dark, gleaming wood, reinforced by masses of astonishing ironwork: cunningly wrought vines

curling into spirals, sprouting leaves and delicate whorls touched up here and there with spots of gold.

A guard kept watch beside it. And even though he'd seen his fellow official write out their pass, he made Dr. Larsson show it anyway.

"There was a library like this in ancient times," he said as the guard was pulling out his keys to unlock the door. "Nearly two thousand years ago. It had the finest collection of manuscripts in the world. The greatest minds of the age flocked there to give lectures, and read, and discuss what they had learned. It is said that carved upon the walls was an inscription: 'This is the place that cures the soul.'"

The guard had the door open now and was waiting for them to walk through. Once they were inside, he shut and locked the door behind them. Molly was just wondering why they were so protective of a room full of books when anyone might walk in and look at the treasures—but then she looked around and understood.

The place was immense, supported by thousands of stone pillars, each as broad and high as the oldest tree that ever grew. Running along both sides of these rows of columns, as far as the eye could see, were bookshelves, so tall that ladders had been provided for reaching the upper shelves.

This was no dreary tomb of dusty books. It was alive, like a hive of bees, humming with the soft voices and quiet footsteps of scholars. They sat at tables, books laid out before them, talking with one another. They wandered through the stacks and climbed the ladders.

Against her will, Molly felt the tremendous power of the place: all the knowledge of the world collected in that very room, and all those scholars scurrying about, drinking the knowledge in as bees suck nectar.

The place that cures the soul.

"I want to show you something of special interest," Dr. Larsson said, guiding her past more shelves holding an inconceivable number of books until they finally reached the heart of the library. Here was a great stone box, a room within the room, its marble-clad walls rising to the ceiling on all four sides. High above the level of their heads the box had barred, unglazed windows, probably to let in light and air.

"This is the sanctum sanctorum," he said, showing his slip of paper to the guard at the door, who was not so fastidious as the first one had been. He merely glanced at the pass before fishing out his key. Once he'd unlocked the door, though, he followed them inside and was joined a moment later by a second guard.

"What do you keep in here?" she asked. "The crown jewels?"

"Oh, dear, no. Those are on display in the Hall of Treasures. The documents in *here*"—he indicated the rows of locked cabinets—"are of *much* higher value. They're truly priceless, irreplaceable, the rarest of the rare." Then, to the first guard, "The Pinakes of Callimachus, please."

The man unlocked one of the cabinets—there were no open shelves here—and took out a scroll. He handed it to Dr. Larsson, who carried it to a small, round table where light-stones were already glowing. He unfurled it for Molly to see.

"This is a copy. The original is also here in this room, but we never handle it. Old papyrus scrolls are extremely delicate."

Molly nodded.

"Remember the famous library I was just telling you about? Well, this is a list of all the books it contained. If you were an ancient scholar and you wanted to read a certain work by a particular author, you could look it up on the list to see where it was kept. It's an extraordinary document, the very first of its kind."

"What happened to it?" Molly asked, staring down at the tiny writing, the unfamiliar letters. "The library, I mean. Is it still there?"

Dr. Larsson straightened, allowing the scroll to wind itself up again, and said with a strange, fierce dignity, "There was a war. It burned. Everything was destroyed."

"Oh," she said. "That's very sad."

"'Sad' is too small a word to describe such a terrible loss."

"But why didn't this burn up?" She pointed to the scroll on the table.

"The Pinakes was in constant use. There were many copies, widely distributed. A few of them survived."

He returned the scroll to the cabinet, then nodded to the guard, who nodded back. She thought they were about to leave. But the guard, having finished locking the cabinet, now crossed the little room and opened yet another door. She hadn't noticed it till now since it was small and matched the cabinets around it. A quick glance told her that the space in which they stood wasn't square. On the other side of that wall there must be yet *another* room, holding the rarest treasures of them all. She looked up at her tutor, brows raised in question.

"You shall see," he said, ushering her through the door.

It opened—how unexpected!—onto a spiral staircase.

She heard the turn of a lock and looked behind her. Both guards had entered and were standing with their backs to the door.

"You will forgive me one day," Dr. Larsson said. "I'm sorry. But we can no more afford to lose you than we could these precious scrolls."

"I don't understand." She looked up the stairway lit from above by a warm golden light. "What *is* this place?"

"Why, didn't you know? It's Harrowsgode Hall."

❧ 16 ❧

A Plan

RICHARD LEANED HIS RAT-STAFF against the wall and took off his official cloak. "Bad news, I'm afraid," he said. "The barrister's been arrested."

Tobias groaned. "It's because of me, isn't it? Because he let me into the city."

"Master Pieter made his own decision. It wasn't your idea. And before you fall all over yourself with remorse, consider the spot he's put you in. He'll spend a couple of months in prison till the Council gets over its annoyance, but they won't spill a drop of his precious blood. He's one of their own, and from the highest class. You, on the other hand . . ."

"I know, Richard. You've made that point already, and there's nothing wrong with my memory."

"Then you understand that we can't just have you sitting here waiting for the Watch to pick you up. We need a plan, and we need it bloody quick."

"I was already thinking along those lines while you were away."

"Oh? And did you come up with anything?"

"Not exactly. But let me ask you this—as a foreigner living in Neargate, are you permitted to send personal letters to people in the town? By messenger, I mean."

"Yes. Messengers come and go from here all the time. It's how my clients contact me and how I set up meetings."

"Could you send one to the home of Claus Magnusson, even though we don't know his address?"

"The messenger would know where to take it. But can your lady read?"

"No, but she could get someone to read it to her, someone she trusts."

"Well, I don't much like it; I'll be honest with you, Tobias. There are lots of things that could go wrong. But let's just say for the sake of argument that we did compose such a letter. What would be the gist of it?"

"That she's in danger. That she won't be allowed to

leave. That she should forget about the cup and escape if she can. That Master Pieter has been arrested. I'm not sure I should tell her the other bit . . ."

"About the Council probably wanting you dead?"

"It would only upset her."

"It might, yes."

"Then I'd set up a meeting somewhere dark and quiet, and hide there till she comes. Molly's clever. She'll manage to get out of the house. Then we can work out a plan together."

Richard grinned. "It's a beginning. And as it happens, I know a score of dark and quiet places."

Tobias gave him a questioning look.

"That's where the rats live."

❧ 17 ❧

An Amazing Stroke
of Luck

It was perfect flying weather.

He floated effortlessly in the sky, held aloft by a cushion of warm air rising from the cobbles and slate on the streets and rooftops below. He had no need to beat his wings—just a delicate movement of the feathers now and then, that's all that was required, and slight adjustments to the angle of his widespread tail.

He hadn't chosen this body any more than a human child decides whether it will be born in a cottage or a castle. He might have stayed as he was—a disembodied spirit—after the spell was broken and his obligations were fulfilled. But he'd formed deep

attachments during that time, and even a spirit hungers for love. So he'd willed himself another life, and his wish had been granted.

He'd laughed—well, actually he'd gone *kraaaaa*—when he saw what he'd become. How darkly amusing! Weren't ravens said to be the ghosts of murdered people or the souls of the damned?

It had taken some getting used to. His raven-body craved the most disgusting things: dead mice, maggots, beetles. But his vision was sharp and his hearing keen; and best of all, he could fly. He could go wherever he wanted, the world spread out below him—what a blessing after the life of seclusion he'd endured for so many years!

Now he'd even chosen a mate. They'd been courting since the spring, flying together, dancing through the air, dipping and rising in perfect unison. When he returned—*if* he returned—they'd find their own little spot of land. He'd defend it, and together they'd raise their young, feeding them and keeping them safe till they were fledged and ready to go out on their own.

But that would have to wait until this final task was done. For now he was just one of the countless birds that circled Harrowsgode Hall. Rooks in particular congregated there, but so did jackdaws, ravens, and crows.

He'd been watching the entrance for a long time—since Molly had first gone in—and she still had not come out. This troubled him, because the man—the one who'd driven him off the ledge and had later escorted Molly to Harrowsgode Hall—had left within an hour of their arrival. Why would he do that? What did it mean? The raven was sure he hadn't missed her.

He continued his vigil till the building was shut for the night and the people who worked there had gone home for their dinners. Disheartened, he left Harrowsgode Hall and flew back to the Magnussons' house.

At least he knew where her bedroom was. He'd found it that morning. After the tutor had so rudely shooed him away, he'd circled the house a few more times. In one of the rooms, where a servant was making the bed, he'd spotted something familiar: Molly's comical straw hat perched on top of the wardrobe.

He returned there now and was preparing himself for a tricky landing when he saw that the window was open. He perched on the sill and looked inside.

The room was dark; the maid hadn't attended to the light-stone yet, which was surprising in a household like that. You'd expect the staff to be highly trained and quick to . . . *what was that?*

He stuck out his head and blinked. Over in the

shadows, blending in with the carpet and difficult to see—if you weren't a sharp-eyed raven—was a bit of dark blue ribbon. He stared at it for a moment, tilting his head thoughtfully. Then he had a brilliant idea.

He could see Tobias inside the house. He was seated across a table from an older man with a large nose, presumably the ratcatcher. Their heads were together, studying something. The raven tapped on the window glass.

Tobias looked up, squinted, then looked down again.

The raven signaled a second time: *tap-tap-tap-tap-tap-tap*.

The little dog that rested at their feet jumped up and started barking. The ratcatcher turned in alarm.

"It's just a raven," Tobias said, going over to have a look.

"Then leave it be," the host said. "Stop it, Charley! Come here!"

But Tobias ignored him. He leaned down and stared through the window.

"Richard, hold the dog. I'm going outside."

The raven flew down from the windowsill and waited. Tobias came out, and for a moment he just

stood there staring. Then the raven hopped forward, dropped the ribbon, and hopped back.

Tobias picked it up.

"This is Molly's," he said as if speaking to himself. Then he stared at the raven some more.

Oh, come on, Tobias. You can figure it out! He nodded and made another little hop. *Please, don't be such a dullard!*

"You brought this to me on purpose."

The raven dipped his head.

"Talking to birds now, are we?" It was the rat-catcher, standing behind Tobias. Inside, behind the closed door, the dog still barked.

"As you see, Richard."

"Should I be concerned—for your sanity, I mean?"

"Not at all." He held up the ribbon; Richard took it.

"Crikes!" he said. "Is this the magical raven that led you here?"

"I'm rather sure it is. Now will you please—?"

"Sorry." Richard stepped back, but he didn't go inside. "I'll let you finish your conversation."

Tobias ignored the remark. "Did Molly send this to me?" he asked.

The raven thought quickly. The answer was *Not really.* But he dipped his head anyway to get things started.

"Do you know who I am?"

Dip.

"Am I Matthew?"

Nothing.

"Am I Stephen?"

Nothing.

"Am I Tobias?"

Dip, dip, hop.

"Crikes!" whispered Richard.

"And do you know where Molly is staying?"

Dip.

Tobias turned to Richard, then back to the raven. "If I asked you to take her a message, could you do it?"

Dip, dip.

"Will you wait till we're ready?"

Dip.

Tobias stood and turned to Richard. "What do you think?"

"I think it's an amazing stroke of luck, and we should go finish that letter right now."

❦ 18 ❦

Dusk at the Magnussons' House

ONCE AGAIN THE RAVEN stood on the window ledge, peering into Molly's chamber. Tied carefully around one of his legs was a slender strip of paper—the message from Tobias. He'd come to deliver it, but the room was still dark and empty. She must be at dinner, then. He'd just have to wait.

After a while the door opened and the servant came in, carrying a small silver pitcher. She went to the light-stone on the bedside table and poured a slow stream of coldfire over it; the room was now filled with a strange, greenish light.

The maid went over to the wardrobe and took out

Molly's blue gown. She laid it on the bed and began to fold it with care. Then she picked up the traveling bag, opened it wide, and packed the gown away. In the same methodical manner she folded and packed the kirtle, shift, underlinen, garters, and stockings. Finally, she went back for the satin slippers and tucked them in at the sides.

For a moment the girl stopped and leaned against the wardrobe, her hand over her mouth. The raven saw that her cheeks were wet with tears. But she didn't rest there long; she sucked in a deep breath and went back to her work, gathering Molly's few personal items from the nightstand—her comb, some hairpins, the small leather box that held her earrings—and setting them on top of the other things in the bag. At last she closed and fastened it, reached up for the straw hat, and set everything down outside the door.

Was Molly going somewhere?

Now the girl was folding back the coverlet, exactly in half, smoothing out any wrinkles. She folded it in half again, and again, till it formed a neat strip at the foot of the bed. Then she removed the linens from the bed and set them outside the door on the floor beside Molly's bag.

The raven felt the feathers rise all over his body. How had he been so slow to understand? The maid

was closing up the room! Something had happened to Molly.

The girl noticed him then. She wiped her eyes and went over to open the window.

"Be that a message for my lady?" she asked, pointing to the strip of paper he carried.

The raven nodded his head.

"I'm sorry. She's not here. Nor will she be returning."

The raven cocked his head, and she seemed to understand.

"She's gone to Harrowsgode Hall, that's what Master said. I don't know where exactly, and it's a great, large place. But I think you can find her; she'll have a window, wherever she be." The girl smiled then. "I'm glad she has a little friend. She touched my heart when she were here, even such a very short time."

And then, softly, "I'm sorry, but I have to close the window now."

Downstairs, the family was at dinner. Claus and Margit had been doing their best to warm the chill in the air, but they had not been successful. Laila was solemn and glum, speaking only when addressed and in as few words as she could manage without being rude. Even the subject of corpuscles couldn't draw her

out. Jakob wouldn't speak at all. And little Sanna, no longer sparkling, had turned as fierce and tenacious as a bulldog.

"But *why*?" she kept wailing, refusing to be hushed or even to lower her voice. The servants had long since been told to leave the room.

"Because she must learn," Claus said. He was repeating himself, but then Sanna kept repeating herself too. "She's not had your advantages. She's almost grown, yet she cannot so much as read or write. And she's one of *us*, Sanna, with a special gift!"

"But why couldn't she stay here and go to school?"

"She's too old. Would *you* like to go to school with crawling infants?"

"She could have a tutor."

"And so she will. She'll have the very best tutors to be had, at Harrowsgode Hall."

"Will she see Laurens there?"

"I would imagine. Of course. They'll both be Magi."

"Will she come back and visit?"

"Yes, darling."

Laila snorted.

"Stop that," Claus said. "It's disgusting."

"*You're* disgusting!" Jakob muttered under his breath.

But he hadn't said it softly enough. His father heard, and he looked as though he'd just been slapped. Claus jumped to his feet, red-faced and trembling, not caring that he'd overturned his chair. Eyes fierce with anger, he lunged toward Jakob, his hand raised to strike.

"Papa!" Laila screamed. "Don't!"

Claus froze, and Laila hurried around the table, laying her hands protectively on her twin brother's shoulders.

"Come with me, Jakob," she said, glaring defiance at her father. "You, too, Sanna. We'll go to the kitchen and get some honey cakes like we used to do—remember? Then we'll eat them in the garden and watch the stars come out."

✤ 19 ✤

In the Tower

MOLLY HAD LED A hardscrabble life and was familiar with raw emotions: rage, despair, misery, terror, pain. But she'd never felt them all in the course of a single afternoon. Well, maybe that one time.

Now she lay on her little bed, too spent to move, or weep, or think. She'd passed beyond hopeless; indeed, if the floor were to open up beneath her, sending her plunging to a certain death, she'd welcome it.

All she could manage now was to breathe.

Apparently they'd thought it would be easy. They'd explain the situation in a reasonable manner, and she'd see the wisdom of their words. Then everything would be fine.

They certainly hadn't expected her to fight.

They'd overcome her eventually (though not before she'd broken the guard's nose and given that arrogant, egotistical, haughty, conceited, patronizing fellow with the beard a good, solid, satisfying kick in the groin). And it'd been worth it too, though afterward they'd tied her to a chair. Twice she'd vomited, and servants had to be called in to clean her up and dress her in fresh clothes. Yet in all that time not one of them had raised a voice—well, no, that wasn't true; the guard and the man with the beard had screamed. But the other three, they'd just talked, and talked, and talked. Sometimes she had screamed just to drown them out. But they had just gone on being logical, explaining, pretending to be kind.

Even now those calm, reasonable voices echoed in her head: Molly had been granted a prodigious gift that, like the very sun that sustains life on earth, was bountiful, and beautiful, and good, a blessing to her people—and a great deal else, all much along the same lines. She would get over her "reluctance" soon, very soon, and discover a happiness and sense of purpose she could never have imagined before.

In time they'd broken her, like a wild creature whose spirit must be tamed so it can spend its life working in the service of a master—except that she was too weary and heartsick just then to serve anyone

or do anything except lie there in her little round room on the very top floor of a tower and gaze up at the ceiling.

She heard a tapping and ignored it. If they wanted to come into her room and talk at her some more, they'd bloody well have to open the bloody door themselves, because she was bloody well locked in. And even if she hadn't been, she bloody well wasn't going to move a muscle to help them.

The tapping came again. It wasn't really a knock, she decided, more of a *toc-toc-toc*, like a tree branch rattling against a window. And it wasn't coming from the stairway door but from the other side of the room.

There still remained in her crushed spirit the tiniest spark of curiosity. She made the enormous effort of opening her eyes.

The sound came for the third time: *toc-toc-toc*. Now she made a greater effort still; she turned her head to look at the open window. It was round, like the room, and was covered by an ornamental iron grille—to keep bats and birds from flying in, according to the man who'd escorted her up the stairs to her little prison.

Molly squinted. Something was out there: a dark shape against the failing light. Now it was moving; it made that sound again: *toc-toc-toc-toc*.

A thrill rushed through her then, carrying with it

a burst of energy. She knew what it was: the hollow knocking that ravens made deep in their throats. She pushed herself into a sitting position, then dropped her feet to the floor. The thrill came again, with such a rush this time that she almost couldn't catch her breath.

Oh, please don't leave! her mind was screaming. *Please, stay where you are!*

Now she stood at the open window, and the raven—her raven—slipped his head through a hole in the grillwork. She reached out and stroked it gently.

"Have you come to teach me to fly?" she crooned. "For I would gladly fly from this tower if I could."

The raven gazed at her for a moment, blinked, then pulled his head back out. Then, grabbing hold of the grille with his beak, he lifted one leg, closing his talons into a bird-fist, and threaded it awkwardly through one of the open spaces.

Molly stared dumbly for a moment before noticing the strip of paper that was wrapped around the bird's leg, fastened with a bit of thread. "Oh," she said, scanning the room for a tool, any tool, that might help her break the thread. "Don't move." She'd spotted a comb, the one they'd given her along with the new clothes. Quickly she fetched it and slipped one of its teeth under the thread, tugged until it snapped, then

removed the little scroll—at which point the raven pulled his leg back out, let go of the grille with his beak, and disappeared. Outside she heard the flutter of wings, and soon he was back on the sill, rearranging himself.

Molly looked at the paper with dismay. It was just a sea of meaningless letters. "Someone sent this to me?" She asked it rhetorically. She didn't expect the raven to answer. And yet he did—he nodded as any person might: yes.

"Was it Master Pieter?" she tried. The bird turned his head away. She took that for a no.

"Jakob, then? Claus?"

No and no.

"The girls—Laila or Sanna? Ulla, then?"

But the raven continued to stare away into the growing darkness, and she began to wonder if she'd imagined that nod or taken it to mean more than it did. Birds nodded their heads all the time—bobble, bobble, bobble. And though her grandfather conversed with animals, she never had.

The raven rattled the bars with his beak as though urging her to keep on trying. So she asked about Stephen and Mayhew. When he still looked away, she threw up her hands.

"That's it, raven dear. I can't think of anyone else.

Winifred can't write, and neither can Tobias."

Now he was all motion, bobbing his head, tapping the bars, and bobbing his head again.

"Tobias?"

An unmistakable yes.

"Someone wrote it for him, then. Somebody he trusts. And . . . he thinks, he hopes, I also have such a person, like Ulla or Jakob, who will read it to me—which means he doesn't know what happened. He thinks I'm still at the Magnussons'—"

The raven croaked, looked down at the message and up at her again.

"What?"

He danced on the window ledge; she could feel his agitation. But what was he trying to tell her? How she *wished* she could understand!

It came to her suddenly that if she had such a bloody wonderful gift that the Magi had seized and detained her, then perhaps she could use it to save herself.

"Give me a minute," she said, stepping back from the window and shutting her eyes. Then she let herself go, slipping into the unknown depths of her own spirit.

It was like being in a windowless room; and though there was no light, she could sense movement around

her. She waited for them to come, whatever they might be. She could feel them all around her, pulsing with energy, like bubbles rising in boiling water. Somehow she knew they were part of her, her own latent powers—waiting for her to reach out and claim them.

Come, she whispered, terrified. *Help me.* The throbbing increased, like a pounding heartbeat. *Come,* she kept saying, *come. I'm ready.*

From far away she could hear the raven's froglike croak—but it was soft, soft, hardly above a whisper. *You must learn to read and develop your powers. And you need to do it quickly.*

"I will," she said as though in a trance. "But please, don't leave me."

I didn't want to leave you before, but I didn't have the power to stay. Now I'm back, and this time I can fly. I will go anywhere you want me to.

She continued to stand there, eyes squeezed shut, clinging to the last wisps of her heightened powers as they threatened to fade away.

Is it possible that you don't recognize me in my beautiful new feathers?

She looked around in the darkness now, beyond the pulsing shapes, where something glowed faintly in the distance. It was the thing she wanted—the understanding, the answer to the riddle. She moved toward

it with painful lethargy, as in a dream. And when her way was inexplicably blocked, she reached out, her hands spread wide . . . and then the dam broke; a flood of clarity washed over her. She felt it enter her body like a cleansing breath. It seemed to lift her off her feet, and she was restored, as if waking from a much-needed sleep.

She opened her eyes and looked at the raven again. He cocked his head to the side. And she did—she *did* recognize him, then!

"Oh," she said, tears stinging her eyes.

Say my name.

"Uncle."

Say it again.

"Uncle! Oh, Uncle!"

Yes.

"We'll fight side by side, the way we did before."

I'll do everything in my power. I can carry messages and gather information.

"And comfort me so I won't feel alone."

Yes. But, Molly—you have to do the rest.

She reached through the grille and stroked his wing feathers, thinking. What could she send to Tobias that would tell him where she was?

You can do it. You're the clever one.

"I'm trying." It didn't have to be wonderful, just

something he would recognize.

And finally it came to her.

"Uncle," she said, "you must be patient. This will take a little time."

I am always patient.

"So you are."

She went to her desk, a beautiful piece of carpentry, dark wood inlaid with light, rounded in the back to fit against the wall of the room, curving in front as if to embrace her. On the desktop sat a penholder with several quills, sharpened and ready for use. There was a crystal bottle filled with ink, several sheets of paper, a blotter, and a neat stack of books. This was to be her place of study, then. They'd provided her with everything she'd need.

She tore a thin strip off one of the sheets of paper, small enough to fit around Uncle's leg. Then she opened the bottle of ink and chose a pen. She'd seen people writing before and knew there were tricks to avoiding splatters and inkblots. So she followed their example, not dipping the pen into the bottle too deep and tapping it gently against the rim to release any surplus of ink. Finally, poised to write for the very first time, she looked up at the raven.

How I missed you, Molly!

"Don't distract me, Uncle dear," she said with a

grin, then leaned over and, with fierce concentration, began to draw a circle on one end of the strip. It was not as round as she would have liked, but Tobias would understand. Then inside the circle, side by side, she wrote the only letters she knew: *M* and *W.* It was a crude picture of her necklace. He couldn't possibly mistake who it had come from; it was practically like signing her name.

Now, on the other end of the narrow strip, she drew a little picture: a sort of box, and on top of it another, smaller box, then a third that was smaller still. And on top of all that—she was running out of room—she drew towers. They looked more like beehives, and she only had room for three, but she thought he'd understand. Finally, at the top of one of the towers, she drew a line pointing to a round window.

She was rather enjoying this. In a stab of inspiration, she added a bird, not a very good one, flying through the air. And she was done. Her message said, *This is from Molly, I am in a tower at Harrowsgode Hall, and the raven will help us.* What more, really, was there to say?

When she was done, Uncle repeated his contortions—balancing on one foot, holding on with his beak, slipping claw and leg though the grille. Molly grabbed her linen coif from the floor where she'd flung it when

they'd locked her in and tore off one of the ribbons that hung down on either side. Then she delicately wound the paper around the raven's leg and secured it firmly with the ribbon.

"You'll come back?" she said, missing him already.

Your tower shall be my roosting place. You have only to call.

And then he pushed off from the sill, wings spread wide. *Whosh, whosh, whosh* came the sound of his flight—silken, like the rustle of a lady's gown. Out over the city the raven flew, touched by the light of the rising moon, until he was lost in the darkness.

❧ 20 ❧

The Ratcatcher's
Apprentice

"**TOBIAS,**" **RICHARD SAID,** "I don't mean to alarm you any more than you are already, but this is really not a good development."

"Not *good*? She's confined in a tower at Harrowsgode Hall, and you're telling me that's *not good*?"

"For you, lad," Richard said. "I meant for you. I never thought they'd move so quickly. The business with the barrister was troubling, a sign of things to come. But *this*, well, it's an altogether different matter. And though naturally you're brooding about it and feeling hopeless—"

"I'm *not* brooding, Richard," Tobias mumbled into

his hands. "I'm thinking."

"Well, that's good. Glad to hear it. Now if you'll just pick up your head and give me a moment of your attention, I believe you'll find what I have to say worth hearing."

Tobias did, admitting to himself that he *had* been brooding, just a little.

"Now that they've got your lady where they want her, you're of no use to them anymore so we need to move fast, before the Watch shows up and—"

"Richard! You've made that point endlessly. I've fully grasped it. Move on."

"All right, then. Can you swim?"

"Not really. I've bathed in a river. I know that if you beat your hands against the water, it helps you stay afloat."

"Good enough. Now, the walls are high, but the moat is deep and will protect you somewhat from your fall. It's not a sure thing, but people have gone over before and survived. The problem will be the guards. They're always up on the ramparts, day and night, and—"

"Are you suggesting that I leave the city?"

"I'm suggesting that you save your own life."

"I won't do it."

"Why not? Do you really think you can rescue

Molly from a tower at Harrowsgode Hall?"

"No. I think that if I leave her behind and save myself, then my life will not have been worth saving."

"Even if you can't possibly help her?"

"Even then."

"The saints protect us from heroes," Richard muttered. "All right, I'd expected nothing less from you, so it happens that I've thought of something else."

"Good. Tell me."

"I've got a job tonight—a silk merchant over in the Western District has rats in his warehouse. I've been out there these last few days getting things set up. Now I'm ready to start with the trapping. For that I always bring my apprentice along, to help carry the gear, and set the traps, and so on. Tonight that will be you. I've never worked for this client before, so he won't know the difference. Nor will my apprentice, because he only ever learns that I have a job when I summon him to come."

"But what's the point?"

"To get you to a safe hiding place. I've already told the merchant he's to leave the storeroom alone, to not so much as set a foot inside it until I'm finished. I always insist on that; if I don't, they're sure to make a mess of my preparations.

"Now, get off that bench and come with me. We

need to turn you into a credible apprentice, and I think we'd best begin with your hair. It's altogether the wrong color for a Harrowsgode lad. But some ashes and a little goose grease ought to do the trick. And don't look at me like that! This is no time to be vain about your beautiful hair—"

"I'm not!"

"—because you're likely to look a good deal worse before this business is over. Now, I'll lend you my old cloak, and you'll be carrying the traps, and the bag of meal, and the lanterns, and so on. You'll look the part—but curse you for being so tall, Tobias; it's really most inconvenient! When I'm conversing with my client, you'll have to sit on a wall and hunch over. Or better still, hide in the shadows."

"And keep my mouth shut."

"That too. Now, I should catch a good number of rats tonight, which'll keep the merchant content. I'll explain that he has to be patient till I've gotten 'em all, and that will take some time. You'll be safe in the storeroom for a week or more, with me coming and going day and night. I'll bring you food and water, and empty your chamber pot, and bring such news as comes my way. After that we'll just hope I get a new job, and a new hiding place."

Tobias sighed.

"It won't be pleasant, lad, I understand. But unless you have a better idea, it seems you have only two choices: go over the wall or hide in the dark."

"I'm useless either way."

"You'll be even more useless without your head."

"So you keep mentioning. What about you? What'll you say when the Watch comes asking for me?"

"I'll tell 'em lies. I'll say you left on account of great lords not much liking being lodged with ratcatchers. They'll know I'm spinning 'em a story, and they'll try to scare me with threats. But rest assured, they won't do me any harm. They need me to kill their rats—which they believe carry the plague, so it's important to them—and my apprentice isn't near ready to take over. I'll be all right."

"Is that true, Richard, or are you spinning me a story, too?"

"Yes, it is."

"Then slather me with grease and ashes and let's be on our way."

❧ 21 ❧

In the Dark

TOBIAS KNEW AS MUCH about ratcatching as he knew about the art of war—that is to say, absolutely nothing. But it seemed to him, as he surveyed the field of combat in the silk merchant's warehouse and Richard described his tactics in rather painstaking detail, that the two were very much the same—except that this battlefield was small, and dark, and filled with empty crates.

The floor of the storeroom was flagstone, so Richard hadn't been able to dig down to bury his traps. But he'd encountered this problem many times, and like any good commanding officer he had

an alternate strategy at hand.

He'd positioned the empty crates to form two walls, one on either side of the rathole, so the creatures would be forced to run between them, along a path of Richard's choosing. Then he'd hauled in dirt and built a ramp that rose to the height of the traps. These he'd buried, one every couple of feet, covering them first with half an inch of dirt, then a pile of sawdust mixed with meal. Over this he'd sprinkled a few drops of aniseed oil to whet their little rodent appetites. Then he'd waited, letting them feed for a few nights, putting out fresh bait every morning, till they'd grown bold and trusting.

Now hostilities had been officially declared; combat was about to begin. Quietly, the lantern shielded so as not to alarm the rats, Richard started near the rathole and worked his way back: setting each trap, arranging fresh piles of meal upon them, then moving on to the next one.

Tobias had been disappointed that Charley couldn't come. But Richard had said no. Charley was old and had suffered a rat-bite two years before. It had gone bad, as rat-bites so often did, and Richard had all but given him up for dead. But he'd survived, brave Charley, and had earned his retirement as a house pet, eating scraps from his master's table.

"You don't want to get bitten by a rat, Tobias," Richard added unnecessarily.

So they'd left Charley at home and brought Constance instead. She was the smallest of the dogs, young and eager to perform the task that she'd been bred and trained to do. Now they waited in the dim light, perched on a crate at the far end of the room, Constance in her master's arms, quivering with excitement.

"Richard," Tobias whispered, "what happens when you leave?"

"You'll go to sleep. Then, come morning, you'll wake and use the chamber pot, then open the little iron box of food we brought and break your fast—"

"You know what I mean."

"Actually, I don't. Waiting is waiting, lad. You pass the time and manage not to get arrested. What else is there?"

"Doing something. Coming up with a plan. Getting Molly out of the tower."

"Perhaps the solitude and the darkness will help you think of something. I find ideas often come to me quite unexpectedly in the night, when I'm restless and can't sleep."

"I hope so. Waiting goes against my nature."

"A man of action, are we?"

"You may laugh, but—"

"Shhhh. Listen."

There was a scrabbling sound, then a nibbling, then a soft metallic *twang* followed by a thump and a snap: the first casualty of war.

Now more rats came, one or two at a time, some skirting the edges of collapsed piles where a fellow rat had just disappeared, continuing down the run to the next pile, or the next, until they stepped on a metal plate and were swallowed by a trap. Tobias found it all mildly disturbing.

Rats, as Richard had pointed out more than once, are intelligent creatures; and after a while they became more guarded. They refused to go near the meal anymore. It was time to wrap things up.

Richard had hung a board, hinged to the wall, directly over the entrance to the rathole. It was held in the raised position by a hook, to which a long string was attached. Now he gave it a tug, yanking out the hook and causing the door to drop. With the rathole blocked, and with no avenue of escape, the creatures began to scatter—out the far end of the run, up the sides of the crates, anywhere their little rat-brains told them might be safe.

Now came the mopping-up operation, Constance's moment of glory. And if the trapping had been

disturbing, this was truly disgusting.

When it was over, Richard unshielded the lantern and went about gathering the little corpses and tossing them into a sack. That done, he went from trap to trap, pulling out the live ones and putting them into a cage. In all there were thirty-seven rats.

"An excellent haul for one night," he said. "It should more than satisfy my client. I'll come back in the morning and set it all up again. But for now we both need to get some sleep."

"What'll you do with the rats?"

"Kill 'em, bury 'em. Folks here aren't like the Austlinders, who were always wanting the live ones so they could try their dogs against 'em in the rat-pits. Sometimes I keep a few for training my young ratters—"

Suddenly he stopped speaking. He stood, a cage of cowering rats in one hand, a sack of dead ones in the others, and stared at his boots, mouth open. Tobias followed his gaze but saw nothing unusual. Then Richard set down his burdens, sat on the nearest crate, and smiled.

"Y'see?" he said. "What'd I say just a minute ago about ideas popping into your head? They're like dry tinder; they just need a spark to set them alight. So when you asked, 'What'll you do with the rats?'—why it was just such a spark, don't you know."

"Does that mean you have an idea?"

"Yes, lad, it does. I have a great mountain of an idea."

"Do you plan to tell me what it is?"

"Hold still. Let me enjoy myself."

"It's *that* good?"

"No, it's better."

"Richard!"

"All right, now listen to this. Some years ago I was called to a house in the oldest part of Harrowsgode. The city walls have been extended many times over the years to make room as the city grew. But this, as I said, was the original part. The buildings are old and in poor repair—small doors and windows, you know, in the old style. Now this particular house was a good deal larger and handsomer than the rest. The man who lived there claimed it had once been part of the palace of old King Magnus—which was just a lot of puffery, of course.

"At any rate, the owner called me in about the rats, and I looked around the property, getting the lay of the land. The creatures had set up house all over the place: the kitchen, the storeroom, you name it; but they seemed to be coming and going from a single location, a little shed out back. I cleared away all the tools and whatnot and found a heap of rubbish, so I

cleared that away, too—at which point I found their hole. They'd burrowed through the dirt, which is uncommon for rats, so I figured there must be a pipe or a drain down there, or an old sewer line, sommat like that. Naturally, I got to work with a shovel—"

"And what did you find?"

"A tunnel. Well built, too, or it had been once upon a time. It was crumbling in places, and full of mud and rubbish such as rats carry in—and the rats themselves, of course, swarms of 'em."

"What did you do?"

"I walled the whole thing off nice and tight. If they died down there, so be it. The stink wouldn't travel, not through all that dirt and stone."

"And now you're thinking that tunnel might lead under the wall. That it was built in the old days as a means of escape in the event of an attack or a siege."

"Clever lad!"

"Richard, how did my question about your caged rats and what you intended to do with them make you think of that house and that tunnel?"

"Well, you know how a person's mind jumps from one thing to t'other? When you asked that, it reminded me of this ratcatcher I'd heard of once who'd keep such rats as weren't wanted for the pits and hold on to 'em. Then whenever work was slow and he was running

short on cash, he'd sneak over to a bakery, say, or an inn, and let the whole lot of 'em out. He'd be guaranteed another job, see? But he got caught at it, and serves him right. Gave all of us a bad name."

"And?"

"Then I thought it might be well to hold on to these once I've shown 'em to the silk merchant. They could be useful in gaining entrance to some place we might need to go, like the Magnussons' house, for example—though there's no point now since your sweetheart isn't there anymore. But it did start me wondering if there were any *other* places that it might be advantageous to get into. And that ancient palace—which now that I think on it may really *have* been part of the palace—just popped right into my head."

"Amazing."

"Isn't it? So, as soon as the client has counted and admired my rats, I think I'll just run on over there and give 'em their freedom."

"And the owner will call you, and we'll open up the tunnel—"

"Yes, Tobias, that's the plan. Ain't it ingenious? As soon as I get the job, I'll move you over there by night, and you can be useful to your heart's content, clearing out rubbish, and reinforcing walls, and seeing how far the thing goes."

"That's marvelous, Richard. I shall do it gladly."

"But?"

"Molly's still in the tower. Have you forgotten?"

"No, I have not. But you're safe, and we may have found a way out of the city. Is that not enough for one night? Can't you take your miracles one at a time?"

"Richard, I shall try."

❦ 22 ❧

The New Magus Mästare

THEY SENT LORENS to fetch Molly in the morning, apparently hoping she'd be more compliant with him than she'd been with the others. He seemed relieved to find her already dressed and seated at her desk, copying words out of a book.

"Lorens!" she said. "Where are your beautiful stars?"

"They only come out at night, cousin. This is my day robe, and here's one for you." Hers was made of fine wool, in a deep garnet color, not blue like his. "Let me help you put it on. Your robe of occasion should be ready by this evening. It had to be altered. They didn't

have any that were quite so small."

"Will it have silver stars like yours?"

"No, better—you get golden sunbursts." Then, after a pause, "Are you . . . recovered, Marguerite?"

She barked out a bitter laugh.

"I'm sorry," he said. "I wasn't told till this morning that you were here—or, well, the circumstances under which . . ."

"Never mind. I'm here now. Just tell me what happens next. I'm ready to work as they want me to—though first I'd like something to eat."

"As it happens, I've come to bring you down to the hall to eat with the others if you're willing. If not—"

"I just *said* I was willing, Lorens—to learn *and* to eat. Can't you see I'm ready?"

"I can indeed, cousin. After you?"

~❧ ❦~

The great hall was dark and gloomy, with a low arched ceiling, small windows, and a glowing brazier in the center. The walls were adorned with frescoes darkened by age and smoke, cracked and peeling in places, hard to see in the dim light.

The hall was furnished with four long tables, two on either side of the brazier, at which the Magi now sat, dressed identically in plain robes of garnet-colored wool. It felt more like a monk's refectory than a

nobleman's dining hall—except for the fact that there were women among them.

Molly searched their faces, looking for any that might be familiar from the day before. She spotted only one, the tall man with the irritatingly pleasant voice who'd kept begging her to be calm.

"The room looks ancient," Lorens whispered, "but it's not. It's an exact replica of King Magnus's hall, copied many times over the years, always the same."

"But there's no dais. The king didn't sit at a high table?"

"No. He always dined with his Council of Magi— just as you will, cousin. See the handsome white-haired gentleman at the far end of the table there? That's Soren Visenson, the Great Seer. And notice the empty place on the bench? They've put you right beside him. It's quite an honor."

"Where will you sit?"

"Downstairs, with the other Magi Postuläre. I'm still in training to be a Magus Mästare—sort of like an apprentice. That's why I wear blue and silver while you wear garnet and gold."

She stopped and looked up at him, pointedly touching her robe. "Then why . . . ?"

"You get to wear garnet because you're already a Magus Mästare."

"But how can that be? I just got here yesterday—

kicking and screaming, I might add. And I'm an igno-rant bumpkin, whereas you can read and write, and went to the university—"

"Lower your voice," he whispered. "You were made a Mästare because you have something they value far more than education: the Gift of King Magnus."

"But—"

"Shhhh. Here we are. This is where we part ways."

Molly remained where Lorens left her, watching him walk away, feeling abandoned and utterly over-whelmed. Only when the door had closed and he was gone did she turn around, slide onto the bench, and look up.

She'd expected grim, disapproving faces, at the very least curious stares. But instead she was greeted with smiles and words of welcome. The Great Seer, who said she must call him Soren, not Lord Seer, smiled even more broadly than the others. He introduced her in turn to each of the members of the Council, some of whose names she remembered. Then he made a graceful gesture with his hand, directing her attention to the platters of food, and urged her to take whatever she wanted.

"We follow the custom of King Magnus here," he said. "We help ourselves. Magnus felt that servants at table were a distraction from thoughtful conversation. So, please, go ahead. You must be hungry."

Molly gazed at the feast set out before her—sliced oranges, strawberries bathed in cream, fragrant loaves of white bread fresh from the oven, tubs of butter, three different cheeses, and slices of cold roast pork— and didn't know where to begin. As the bread was closest to hand, she took two large slices and smeared them thickly with butter. Then she spooned an ample portion of berries onto her plate, where cream and crimson juices oozed onto her buttered bread.

"You really must try the oranges," Soren said. "I believe they're uncommon in your country."

"I had them once, at a royal banquet. They came all the way from Cortova."

"Yes, orange trees are tender plants, native to the south, where winters are mild. But we grow them here in great glass houses; they get plenty of sunshine, you see, yet they stay warm in the winter." He reached for the platter of oranges, to pass it. "We have lemon trees too," he added.

Just then his eyes flicked away for a second, and a flash of annoyance crossed his face. Molly followed his glance, curious to know what incoming cloud could have brought such a sudden change in the weather. As soon as she saw that it was Sigrid, she understood.

Sigrid had been the only one of the councilors who hadn't greeted Molly warmly. She'd simply nodded; and there had been such a lack of expression on her

great, pale slab of a face, it had put Molly in mind of something dead and frozen, drowned perhaps. Only Sigrid's eyes had been alive; and they'd burned with such a fierce, knowing intelligence that Molly had quickly turned away, half fearing the woman might steal her soul.

But it was something else, something quite unexpected, that had drawn Soren's attention and rattled his composure. Sigrid was smiling. And not the sort of smile one friend gives to another, or even the false kind you put on out of politeness. This was the smile of a poisoner watching her victim take his first bite.

Soren met her gaze and held it as long as he could. Then, with a shudder, he turned back to Molly. But he was trembling now, and it seemed that he might drop the platter of orange slices, so she reached out to take it from him. As she did, their fingers touched, and a jolt ran through her as from an unexpected blow. She struggled to catch her breath, but already the vision was rising before her: the Great Seer, sitting behind a gleaming desk in a beautiful room with tapestries on the walls.

There was no doubt it was Soren—he had the same handsome, angular face, the same aristocratic nose, the same close-cropped silver hair—but in her vision he wasn't smiling and he didn't look pleasant. He was talking to his ministers, and he was angry.

Molly seemed to be floating above the scene, watching everything that happened and hearing every word that was spoken in that room. When the vision finally faded away, she felt fried in the middle, as though she'd been struck by lightning. For a moment she just sat there, blinking stupidly, wondering why there was a broken platter lying on the table with half-moon slices of orange scattered around it, and why everyone was staring at her. Maybe she *had* been struck by lightning.

Then her mind cleared. Sucking in a ragged breath, she swung around to face the Great Seer. "You—" she howled. "You arrested my friends. You signed their death warrant!"

A ripple of silence moved across the room. Soren's face went ashen.

"You even locked up poor Master Pieter, who was so kind to me. And then, just now, you dared to *smile at me?*"

The Great Seer rose, trembling with rage, and looked down at her with the same cold fury she'd seen in her vision.

"Be careful what you say and who you say it to," he said. Then as he turned to leave the room, "I really would be a lot more careful."

⚡ 23 ⚡

The Gift of King Magnus

AND THEN EVERYONE around her was gone, scattered like sheep in a thunderstorm. Soren had stormed off in one direction, the rest of the Council in another, deep in whispered conversation. Molly remained, alone on the bench, sick with fear and embarrassment.

Then, from behind her, "Lady?"

His voice was soft, hard to hear over the scraping of benches and the scuffling of feet as the other Magi rose and left the hall. He'd had to say it twice: "Lady?"

Molly turned and saw a small, plain man with a kind face. "Excuse me," he said. "My name is Mikel. I've been asked to serve as your teacher."

She was still too dazed to speak.

"Come," he said gently. "They've given us a room downstairs to work in. We'll discuss it there, in private."

"You heard, then—what happened?"

"Yes."

Well, of course, everyone had. Her voice was loud at the best of times, and she'd been shouting.

"Please, lady? They need to clear the tables now."

The room was bright and spacious, equipped with a large desk, two chairs, and shelves filled with scrolls and books. Across from the entrance was another door, which led to a balcony with a view of the northernmost mountains and beyond them, the sea. Mikel opened it, letting in the cool morning air. Then he urged her to sit at the desk and—just as Master Pieter had done two days before—took his place across from her.

"I understand you had a vision," he said.

She nodded.

"Our visions are deeply personal, the gifts of our spirits and meant for us alone. So when you and I are working together, I shall *never* ask what you've seen or experienced. But in this case, as you've already shared it and as it clearly troubled you, I wonder if you'd like to discuss it."

She nodded again.

"Sometimes, especially with those who are young and inexperienced, visions can be unreliable. You might see the thing you fear the most, or something you deeply long for. I don't mean to discount what you saw, but I have to tell you, it's contrary to everything I know about Soren and the people of Harrowsgode."

"What do you mean?"

"Our people abhor bloodshed. We have no murders here, nor any other violent crime. We don't execute people. As for Soren, though I don't know him well, he's been our Great Seer for many years; and he's always held the good of Harrowsgode very close to his heart."

"That may be, and I hope you're right. But, Mikel, I've been having visions since my seventh year. That first time, I was chasing a playmate in a game. I touched him on the shoulder, and suddenly I saw him dead of the plague. Everybody laughed when I screamed and ran away. But the next day it happened exactly as I'd seen it. The neighbors started talking, saying I was a witch, so Father sent me away.

"Then I had a vision of my mother's death, and after that they started coming thick and fast, one after the other. I saw my grandfather murdered. I saw evil people plotting against the royal family. I saw the

horrible death of a king. And I saw my cousin Jakob, who lives here in Harrowsgode, before I even knew that I *had* a cousin or that this city existed.

"Mikel—I have never had a vision that didn't turn out to be true. So I can't just dismiss it. I *really believe* that Soren is planning to execute my friends . . . and I don't know what to do!"

She was blinking back tears now.

"I understand," he said. "Let me see what I can find out. The Council is meeting this morning; and while their deliberations are secret, their final decisions are not. They're our elected representatives, after all. We have the right to know what's being done in our name."

"How soon will you know?"

"Not till this evening, I would guess. They have a lot to discuss; they'll probably be at it most of the day. But even if you're right and your vision *was* true, warrants issued without consent of the Council are invalid. Your friends should be safe, for the moment at least."

Molly took a deep breath and let it out. "Good," she said.

"So perhaps while we're waiting for more information, we could pass the time with a few lessons?" It was a dark little joke, and it actually made her laugh.

"Why is everyone so dead set on giving me *lessons*? I've gotten along quite well without them all these years."

"You have a great gift, lady, and it would be a crime to let it lie fallow."

"What—you mean that bloody Gift of King Magnus everyone's always talking about?"

"Yes, the very same."

"I don't even know what it is."

"Would you like me to *tell* you?" Something about the slow, calm way he said this, and the little twitchy half smile at the corners of his lips, made Molly laugh again.

"Yes," she said. "I would."

"Good. To begin, then, all Harrowsgode folk have a touch of the Gift, to a greater or lesser extent. But some, like you, have visions; they can see the future and look into the past. Such people are chosen to be Magi Mästare."

"So *you* have the Gift of Magnus, too? And all those people in the hall?"

"Wait. I'm not finished. Even among the Mästare there are differences. Most are like me: useful and talented, but nothing more. Then there are great ones; they are very powerful and are often elected to the Council. And finally there are the rare few with

truly prodigious gifts. Magnus was the first. He saw this valley in a vision, you know, and led his people to it, though he'd never been here before. And when he was old and near death, he rose up from his bed and summoned his powers one last time. He split open the side of the mountain with the force of his mind and caused the very stone within to be changed to silver. It's been a blessing to us ever since, the source of our great wealth.

"Of course that was a special case since it was done by the king himself. But the Magi have done amazing things too. We have harnessed nature so that the rains come only when we want them to, watering our fields in spring and summer, though never so often as to rob the growing crops of sunshine. We never have floods, or droughts, or hailstorms. You will have noticed, I'm sure, how green the fields are. It's done by magic."

"What else?"

"We've kept our city safe from invasion for hundreds of years."

"The stone figures?"

"Yes. That's just a few examples. There are many others."

"Did *you* do any of those things?"

He smiled. "No. Those feats were all done long ago by great sorcerers of the past. We still make use of their

enchantments—Master Soren continues directing the rainclouds, for example; but he's just using the same old spells. We're no longer capable of anything that ambitious, and with each generation we grow weaker. No one knows exactly why."

He drummed his fingers on the desk.

"But every now and then someone comes along, quite unexpectedly, who is blessed with the powers of the ancients. *That's* what we call the Gift of King Magnus. Your grandfather had it; and when we lost him, it was a terrible blow. Who could tell how many years would pass before we saw his like again?"

"And you think *I* . . . ?"

"Yes. Claus Magnusson has assured the Council that it was so, and Dr. Larsson confirmed it."

"By grabbing my hands? And taking my arm?"

Mikel sighed. "I'm sorry. That was unspeakable. But they felt it was so important, they had to be sure. We've been waiting a very long time for someone like you—since William left us, never to be seen again. But he carried with him the seed of his greatness, and it's found fertile ground in you, lady: the Gift of King Magnus."

"Well, I'm sorry to disappoint you. I possess no powers at all."

"Surely—"

"*They* possess *me*, Mikel. I can't summon them. I can't make them go away. And I certainly can't make stone turn to silver or summon the rain."

"That's because you're a beginner," he said. "It's the same for everyone. But if you're willing to do the work—and I shall help you—your powers will grow, and you'll learn how to bend them to your will. Right now they're carrying you, like a runaway horse or a ship blown off course in a gale. But soon you'll grab the reins, take the helm—then you will truly possess your great and powerful gift. Don't you see?"

She thought back to the previous night, how she'd forced herself to probe the hidden depths of her spirit—not waiting to receive but reaching out her greedy hands to grasp the thing she wanted. She'd called up the shadow of the bold, relentless, swaggering, ignorant, savage little beast she'd once been, back in the days when she'd roamed the streets, slinging insults at her playmates, wrestling in the mud with the boys, laughing when she got the best of them, picking herself up when they got the best of her, always ready for another go: tough, hard, brash, resilient, joyful little Molly—her own true self.

She *had* grabbed the reins then, taken the helm of just the smallest fragment of that which pulsed within her, yet to be tamed.

"Yes," she said. "I do see."

"Good. Then here is what I propose: we will work in the mornings on reading and writing. In the afternoons we'll do the spirit work: learning to develop your natural gifts. What do you say? Will you give it a try?"

"On one condition."

"And what is that?"

"Please stop calling me 'lady.' I'm Molly to my friends."

❦ 24 ❧

The Tale of the Prince of Chin

"**JUST AS A MASON BUILDS** a wall," Mikel said, "by piling up stone upon stone, so we make words by putting one letter after the other. But while the mason needs hundreds and hundreds of stones to build the simplest wall, we only need twenty-six letters to write any word in our language."

"I already know how to write most of them," she said. "I copied them out of books up in my room. But I don't know their names—except *W* for *William* and *M* for *Martha*."

"*M* is also for *Molly*, you know. Look."

Molly, he wrote. "That's you."

She stared at the word, enchanted.

"Now you write it—you'll want to do it several times, till you have it down by heart."

Molly, she wrote. *Molly Molly Molly Molly*

How often had she said, with defiant pride in her own ignorance, "I can't even write my own name!"? What a load of horse flop! Why be proud of that?

Suddenly she understood fully, and for the first time, the power of the written word. It could bridge the gap that separated her from her friends outside the tower. Once she'd learned how to read and write, she could say anything she liked to anyone she wanted, even though they'd locked her up and the others were far away. And they in turn could tell her things: whether they were safe or not, what plans they might be hatching, or simply that they missed her. As long as she had a window—and a raven to carry her letters— Molly would be able to speak to the world.

She threw herself into her lessons with a passion that astonished her teacher; and by midday, when a servant arrived bringing their meals on a tray, she'd mastered all the letters, and the sounds they commonly made, and had moved on to writing easy words.

After they'd finished their bread and mutton stew and the trays had been cleared away, Mikel sketched out his plans for the afternoon. "You've crammed a lot

of new things into your head this morning; now you should give them a chance to settle in. Practice a bit in the evening if you like, and we'll start again tomorrow. But there is such a thing as overdoing."

"I'm not tired. I could work all day."

"I have no doubt of that. But if you'll indulge me, I'd like to show you a few things. I believe they'll help you see your task from a broader perspective. Our work this morning was like kneeling down and gazing at a single blade of grass. Now let's stand up and take a look at the whole meadow." When she seemed reluctant, he added, "It's interesting, I promise."

Mikel went to the bookshelf and came back with a scroll. He stood by her chair and unrolled it in front of her—just as Gerold Larsson had shown her the Pinakes of Callimachus before luring her through that little door into the prison of Harrowsgode Hall.

"This is a replica of a manuscript that is more than a thousand years old. It was written by a Gracian scholar in an alphabet that's different from ours. The title of the book is *Geometry*—that's a branch of mathematics—and here is how the word looks in ancient Gracian."

He took her pen and carefully wrote:

Γεωμετρία

Molly stared at it, tilting her head this way and

that. Most of the letters looked strange, but not all of them did. "I see a *t*, and a *p*, and an *i*."

"Yes, very good. Our alphabets are related—distant relatives, you might say."

He put the Gracian scroll away and came back with a different one.

"Now, this comes from the ancient kingdom of Chin," he said. "And I'm sure you can see that it's entirely different—not only from the alphabet you learned this morning, but also from the Gracian writing I just showed you. That's because the Chin don't use an alphabet at all. They write with pictures, a special character for each word. You read it from top to bottom and from right to left, see?"

"A picture for every single word—how could anyone learn them all?"

"Well, it *is* difficult, but not as hard as you'd think. I hesitate to go into it too deeply for fear I'll give you false information. You might want to discuss it with Sigrid; she's an expert on the Chin."

Molly shuddered at the thought. "I'd rather not."

"Well, all right. Let's pretend there's a certain character that means 'building.' If you start with that character and add, say, two strokes on top, it becomes 'palace.' If you leave off the strokes but put a dot in the middle, it means 'cottage.' And so on, for all the

different kinds of buildings. Do you see?"

She nodded.

"Now, this book is a history—that means it's a collection of stories about things that really happened. And the title is written—"

"What kind of stories?"

"Mostly about kings and wars, I believe—though I've never actually read the book, not even in translation. Sigrid has, of course, and she's told me a few."

"Do you remember any of them?"

"Yes. There's one about a prince . . ."

She folded her hands and looked up at him expectantly.

"Oh, all right," he said, smiling. "Though I'm no great storyteller, I warn you.

"There was once a prince of Chin who went to war. He was captured in battle and taken prisoner by his enemies." Mikel stopped suddenly, his face flushed with embarrassment. He'd only just realized how inappropriate the story was, considering the parallels to Molly's situation. "Oh!" he said, "I'm sorry."

"Well, I'm not," she said, "but I *will* be if you don't finish. I'll pout and be difficult for the rest of the afternoon."

He managed a wan smile. "Are you sure? I would never want to cause you any more distress than—"

"Just tell the story."

He closed his eyes, sucked in a lung full of air, and launched back into the shockingly inappropriate tale of the prince of Chin.

"The prince was confined in a high place, the Tower of the Golden Phoenix"—another deep breath, followed by a wince—"with no possible means of escape. But he came up with a clever plan. He attached himself to a kite, leaped from the tower, and soared away through the air as birds do, out over the city walls and into the countryside, where he landed safely."

"Now, see—that was a wonderful story! What's a kite?"

"An invention of the Chin people made of sticks and paper, and tethered by a string. You throw it up in the air, and the wind catches it and carries it into the heavens. We have one downstairs, in the Great Hall of Treasures."

"I never got to see the treasures. I was supposed to, but Dr. Larsson brought me here instead."

There seemed no end to Mikel's discomfiture.

"I'm truly sorry," he said. And then, after an apparent struggle, "There are many among us who feel quite ashamed of . . . the way you were treated. It did not become us. Believe me, that's not who we are."

She almost asked if, that being the case, she was

actually free to go; but she already knew the answer, and it wasn't Mikel's fault.

"I'm glad to know that" was all she said. "So what happened next? Is that the end of the story? Or did the prince return to his father, the king, and go on to rule the land of Chin and have more adventures?"

"No."

"Why not?"

"He was captured again and put to death."

"Oh."

"Such a story to tell a young girl!" Mikel muttered, shaking his head in dismay. "I beg you to forget it if you can."

"I will," she said. "It's forgotten already."

It wasn't, of course—not in the least. The tale of the prince and his marvelous escape had lodged itself firmly in her mind. And while she appeared to be listening as Mikel continued with his lesson, she was actually thinking about the kite. If she was going to build one—as she now intended to do—and risk her life on having built it correctly, then she needed to know what they looked like and learn what made them fly. And to do that she'd have to go downstairs to the Hall of Treasures.

"Mikel?" she said, apparently interrupting him in midsentence, or so she judged by his startled

expression. "Could I ask you a question?"

"Of course."

"The Hall of Treasures . . ."

"Yes?"

"As I said before, I never got to see it. I was supposed to; that's what I was told. But then I was whisked away instead. So naturally I was very disappointed—"

"Molly?"

"What?"

"Would you like to see the treasures?"

"Yes, I would."

"Then I will see that you do, this very night. And unlike Dr. Larsson, *I* shall keep my promise."

❦ 25 ❧

An Incident in the Celestium

THE FIVE TOWERS OF Harrowsgode Hall varied in style from the rest of the building. They were more ornate and were covered with fanciful carvings; they rose, level by level, in a series of concentric rings, each smaller than the one below, forming a smoothly tapered dome that came to a point at the top.

There was a tower at each of the four corners of the building with a fifth, much broader and taller than the others, in the middle. And near the top of this central tower was a large, handsome room: the Celestium.

On this particular morning, every rook, jackdaw, raven, and crow in Harrowsgode seemed to have

gathered there, all of them perched on the very same ring. So it was with some difficulty that Uncle managed to find a place to land, starting a wing-flapping scuffle with a pair of rooks. But they quickly settled down; none of them wanted to miss the show.

The windows of the Celestium were tall and wide, separated by slender columns of stone. The effect was that of a space entirely walled with glass. In the center of this round room was a round table at which thirteen Magi now sat, dressed in their ceremonial caps and robes, the gold embroidery sparkling in the sunlight. They were deep in heated conversation.

"And when exactly had you planned to tell us, Soren?" asked a red-faced Magus. Both his question and his anger were directed at a man with silver hair and the face of an aristocrat.

"As soon as I was able," the man said. He seemed surprisingly calm, considering the fact that everyone in the room was looking daggers at him. "It was a crisis situation. I had serious matters to deal with, and new information was coming in by the minute. There wasn't time to convene the Council, let alone hold a meeting."

"Then you should have called us into your office, or at the very least told us what was happening."

"If I had, Oskar, we'd still be down there talking in

circles, and nothing would have gotten done."

"Well, that would have been a blessing," said another Magus, leaning in closer, jutting out her chin. "Because what you did was illegal. You had no authority to issue those warrants—not on your own, not without approval by the Council."

There was a hum of agreement from others in the room.

"I'm afraid you're mistaken. As Great Seer, I have the authority—indeed the responsibility—to act on my own in times of peril—"

"Peril?" Oskar laughed. "From five people—two of them women—who came here to shop for a cup? Is *that* the terrible menace that caused you to throw all law and custom aside and sign, without consulting us, warrants for *execution*? Unbelievable!" He slapped a meaty hand on the table for emphasis, causing several of the Magi to jump.

"It was not a decision lightly made," the Great Seer said, "but I assure you it was the right one. If those foreigners are permitted to leave, they'll carry tales; and sooner or later we'll be invaded. So put these two on the balance scale, members of the Council: the lives of four strangers—foreigners who intruded where they did not belong—against the loss of our city and our whole way of life. Which tips the heaviest?"

"First of all, Soren," said a plain, big-boned woman, "they aren't 'foreigners'—they're people. And the very foundation of our 'way of life'—which you're so eager to protect—is that we never shed human blood. Twice King Magnus walked away from a kingdom he might have ruled—first from his ancestral homeland and then from Budenholme—because he would not fight and kill in order to keep them. What you did yesterday wasn't just some minor breach of protocol. It was a betrayal of everything we are."

The Great Seer leaned back in his chair and cocked his head as though the acrobats had just come in and he expected to be delighted.

"So. We should just let them go back to Westria, is that it? Though maybe before they leave we ought to ask them to swear an oath—you know, promising never to reveal our location, or our wealth, or the curious fact that we don't have an army, that sort of thing. Well, here's a bit of hard truth, Sigrid: people lie. People break their oaths. And I'm not willing to risk everything we've built, and the lives of all our citizens, on the very slim chance that these particular strangers happen to be paragons of virtue."

Sigrid didn't flinch. "I'm well aware of the frailties of human nature. And no, that is not what I propose. I think we should find another, better way, as we have

for hundreds of years."

"And what would that be?"

"Enchantment."

They were both standing now, staring at each other as though they were the only two people in the room.

"Got something up your sleeve, Sigrid? Some old charm, long forgotten, just turned up in a dusty corner of the library the other day?"

"I do, Soren—have *something up my sleeve*. I'm glad it amuses you."

"And what sort of charm would this be?"

"Forgetfulness. I've been studying it for over a year, mostly in texts of the Chin. My purpose was to ease the pain of dark remembrance. But with some slight adjustments—"

"Ah. Not quite ready yet."

"I need a little more time, yes—to be sure that it will work."

"What a pity, Sigrid. We don't *have* time."

"Yes, we do. The three in the village will wait for the others, at least for a while."

"And what if they don't? What if they decide that it's been too long, that they ought to go for help— while you're still down in the library tinkering with your little charm?"

She didn't reply, and no one spoke. For a long time

they just stood there, motionless, their eyes locked in a silent exchange of intense and mutual loathing. Then Soren squinted as an animal does—lip raised, canines revealed—just before lunging at your throat.

"I challenge you," Sigrid said.

Soren laughed, and the tension broke. "But that's absurd! No one's done that for a hundred years. Maybe two."

"All the same, it's spelled out quite clearly in the Edicts of the Magi, composed by King Magnus himself."

"You *have* been a busy girl."

"Do you accept?"

"Sigrid, those birds out there are more qualified to be Great Seer than you are. Why, you haven't been on the Council more than six or seven years."

"And you've been on it far too long. You're required to accept my challenge, you know, or refuse and step down. That's in the Edicts, too."

"When this is over," he said, "I shall have you removed from the Council."

"I'm afraid you can't do that. If I defeat you, I become Great Seer; if I fail, we remain as we are. Do you accept my challenge, or will you step down? I'm asking now for the third time. You must say yes or no."

There followed a long pause. The birds outside

leaned in expectantly.

"This is such a waste of precious time."

"Nevertheless."

"All right. I accept your challenge."

"Here it comes," said one of the rooks.

"Are they going to fight? With swords?"

"I don't think so. Wait and see."

The other Magi rose from the table and went to stand against the stairway door. Soren and Sigrid stayed as they were, facing each other across the table.

Slowly the rumbling began, growing deeper and louder till it was painful to hear: an ominous sound, like an avalanche, an earthquake, or the end of the world. Now the room began to fill with mist, and the light streaming in through the windows turned it to golden fire. It grew brighter and brighter, almost blinding to look at—and then it began to pulse.

Uncle drew himself into his feathers as he did in stormy weather, shutting his eyes tight. But this storm penetrated every pore of his being till he feared for his very life. He would have flown away, but he doubted he had the strength. So he remained there, trembling, until suddenly there came a great, loud *whoosh*, as when a great, old tree goes down in a tempest. And then—utter silence.

He blinked. Inside the room, Soren stood as

before, though he trembled; and his handsome face was drained of all of its color. Sigrid had dropped to the floor, where she crouched, arms protectively over her head. And for the longest time no one moved. Finally two of the Magi came forward and helped Sigrid rise.

"Does the Council agree that all was done in accordance with ancient law and that I remain Great Seer?"

Solemnly, the Magi nodded assent.

"Sigrid, this has to be unanimous—or would you like to do that again?"

"I admit defeat," she said. "Your powers are greater than mine."

"So they are."

"But I am still a member of the Council," she said. Her voice was so weak the birds could hardly catch the words. "So I hereby propose that the warrants illegally issued yesterday be declared null and void, that the barrister be released, and that the prisoners in the village stand under no threat of execution. They should be closely watched but given their freedom. I believe, in this case, unanimity is not required."

"I so move," said Oskar.

"All in favor—"

❦ 26 ❧

Hard Things

THE GREAT HALL OF MAGNUS was transformed by night. The green glow of light-stones—in silver stands on every table and along the back wall in little niches—pierced the darkness like a hundred brilliant stars. Heavy damask linen was draped over the tables, and the Magi were dressed in their robes of occasion: garnet silk embroidered with gold. Above the hum of quiet voices, Molly heard the plaintive sound of a lute.

It was early yet. They all stood around talking in little groups, waiting for the others to arrive. Molly went straight to find Mikel.

"It's been arranged," he said. "We'll go down right after dinner."

"Good," she said. "Thanks."

"There won't be time to see everything, but I've drawn up a list of the finest pieces in the collection. And I've asked a few Magi—experts on those particular items—to come with us and say a few words. It should be very nice."

"Have you heard anything about the Council meeting?"

"Yes." He lowered his voice now, so she had to lean in to hear. "You have nothing to worry about. There will be no executions, and Pieter is a free man."

"But what does that mean? That my vision was wrong, and Soren—"

"Shhh."

She dropped to a whisper. "—and Soren never signed those warrants? Or was everything I saw really true, but he later changed his mind?"

"I don't know. It was worded exactly as I told you: there will be no executions, and the barrister is free."

"What about my friends in the village? And what about Tobias? Are *they* free?"

"Who is Tobias?"

"My friend, part of our group. He came into the city with me. Soren said, in my vision, that Tobias was to be watched until I was brought 'safely into the fold,' then treated like the others."

Mikel gave a little shudder of disgust. "Well, there won't be any executions; that much is clear."

Out of the corner of her eye she saw Soren enter the room. He moved with swanlike grace, his head held high, his face radiant.

"Mikel, can't I eat at your table?"

"No," he said. "You'll just make things worse."

"I'll go upstairs then, pretend I'm sick."

"Molly, look at me! This morning you publicly charged that man with grievous crimes. The *Great Seer*, in front of all the Council! Now, until you know for certain that he did any of those things, you'd best keep your tongue and be gracious. He'll do the same, I imagine. Soren's not a man to hold childish grudges."

"I can't."

"Yes, you can. There are times in life when we have to do hard things. This is one of them. So be pleasant—and if you can't manage that, keep quiet." Mikel leaned in so close now, she could feel his breath on her cheek. "You *don't* want Soren for an enemy. Do you understand?"

⋞ ⋟

Molly slipped into her place at the end of the bench, keeping her eyes down, feeling the heat in her cheeks.

"Well, look at you!" Molly recognized the youthful

voice of Liv, the Magi with the large, handsome eyes. "Your first night to wear the robe of a Magus Mästare! It suits you perfectly, like you were born to wear it. But then I guess you were."

"Congratulations," said the man with the heavy eyebrows whose name she couldn't remember. "The first time is always a great occasion. You should be very proud."

Molly nodded, not yet able to speak.

"I understand you worked with Master Mikel today." Molly felt a jolt go through her. It was Soren's voice. "Were you pleased?"

"I liked him very much," she said, meeting Soren's eyes, surprised to find no anger there.

"We thought it would be a good fit."

"He's very patient and kind."

"So he is. Did you make progress?"

Waiters were bringing in the food now, reaching in to set platters on the table, pouring the wine.

"I did." Then, with a sheepish smile, "I can write my name now. I couldn't before."

She wondered if they would laugh at her or cast little glances of amusement at one another, but they didn't. They seemed genuinely pleased, even Soren.

"Two milestones in a single day," he said. "You've become a Magus and a writer both."

Platters were passed, conversation flowed, and Molly thought with amazement how masterfully it had all been done. No going straight at it with blunt words, her accustomed way. No awkward silence or piercing stares. Just courtesy, warmth, and reassurance, then, "Won't you pass the carrots?"

Was it real, she wondered—or just manners?

❦ 27 ❧

The Hall of Treasures

THEY PROCEEDED DOWN the long, silent corridor like priests in procession. Molly was in the middle—Magi ahead of her, Magi behind—like an effigy of the Virgin being carried through the streets on Lady Day. Each of them held a light-stone in a small silver cup, casting eerie shadows against the floors and walls.

They went first to the gallery of pictures and stopped before a scroll, perhaps ten feet long, which was laid out on a table. It had already been prepared for viewing, a string of light-stones glowing behind it in wrought-iron stands.

The scroll was one single, continuous drawing

of a river and the road that ran beside it. There were many small figures traveling from one village to the next with their oxcarts and horses, their children and dogs. Boats floated on the water; fishermen stood on the shore. And in the trees perched tiny birds.

The Magi stepped back to give Molly space to admire the scroll—all except Sigrid, who came forward to address the group.

"This scroll comes to us from the land of Chin," she began. "It was painted with colored inks on silk—"

Molly leaned down, her nose nearly touching the paper, and studied the pictures, a tapestry of scenes from the everyday life of those long-ago people. There was a man whipping a boy, a woman shopping at an outdoor market, an overturned cart, a young couple kissing, an old man peeing into the river.

"—in the court style, which is marked by a meticulous technique and is noticeably less spontaneous than—"

Molly suddenly wondered whether she was supposed to be looking at the scroll or paying attention to the lecture. Her first instinct, to look at the pictures, had probably been wrong since she was habitually rude. So she stood back up, clasped her hands in front of her, and pretended to be interested as Sigrid continued to speak, woodenly, using lots of big words.

"Please observe the difference between this scroll and the picture that hangs above it."

There followed a weighty pause till Molly noticed that everyone was looking at her. Had that been a question? Was she supposed to say something? Should she be *looking* at the painting that hung above the scroll?

Probably yes to all.

"Um," she said, giving it a quick glance. "The one up there looks more, um, real."

"Yes. That's exactly what the artist was striving to achieve, in accordance with what his culture considered to be the highest purpose of art: to capture reality in the form of ideal beauty.

"But the people of Chin have an altogether different tradition, a concept of art that is based on spontaneous lines, drawn with a brush. They learn it from childhood, since they write their characters, not with a pen as we do, but with brush and ink. They regard beautiful writing to be high art in itself—"

Then it slammed into Molly like a punch in the gut: Sigrid wasn't there to talk about the *kite*! She'd been invited to do what she was doing now: give a boring lecture about a stupid scroll!

Molly hadn't *asked* to see the kite, not specifically. She'd already shown too much interest in the prince of Chin and his escape from the tower. She didn't want

to raise any suspicions that she was planning to follow his example. She'd just assumed that since Sigrid was on the list, the kite would be, too.

"—so that every stroke is clearly seen, nothing is hidden, and the artist is revealed. They would never pile one brushstroke on top of another till they all blended together, as this painter has done. It's not in keeping with their sense of beauty."

Molly had stopped listening; she just gazed at the floor, desperate for the lecture to be over. She didn't care about the bloody Chin and their bloody brushes. All she'd ever wanted was—

It was quiet again. She looked up and saw that Sigrid was waiting, with that same flat expression, for Molly to answer—what? Another question?

"That's very interesting," she said, at a total loss.

God's bones, what a tragic waste of the Gift! The girl has the brains of a goat.

Molly gasped, and, without intending to, covered her mouth with her hand. In the brief moment that followed—while she was wondering if anyone had noticed, and hoping they hadn't—she saw that Sigrid's half-closed eyes, which made her look so condescending, had widened, and her mouth was open.

Sigrid knew about "the bloody Chin and their bloody brushes," just as Molly knew that Sigrid

thought she had "the brains of a goat."

They were reading each other's thoughts!

"Yes," Sigrid said. "That is extremely interesting." And Molly knew she wasn't referring to the Chin and their sense of beauty.

They were connected somehow, Molly and this dreadful woman—not as friends or kindred spirits, but as the owl and the field mouse are. So what did the mouse do when the owl's great shadow passed across the moonlit meadow? It darted into its hole, that's what.

Where was hers?

The group was moving now, on to the next item on the tour, oblivious of the remarkable exchange that had just taken place.

They stopped before a stone carving of a foreign god. He had the plump cheeks of a baby and too many arms, which made him look like a fat, jolly spider. It was Oskar's turn to stand up front and explain things, none of which Molly heard. She was still puzzling over Sigrid, whose mind had gone silent. Did she have a mousehole too? Seeing the danger that Molly posed to her, had she hidden somewhere safe?

Well, if she could do that, so could Molly—as soon as she figured out how.

The carving was followed by a handsome apparatus

made of gleaming brass that had something to do with ships at sea—but Molly still wasn't paying attention. She was deep inside her mind, hauling imaginary blocks of ice, piling one atop the other. Even if her wall was a failure and offered no protection, her thoughts (*Lift, stack; lift, stack; lift, stack*) would be as interesting as watching mold grow on cheese.

She kept it up for the rest of the tour, learning nothing whatsoever about the tapestry, the saltcellar, or the thumb harp shaped like a tortoise. Only when it was over and they were turning to go back did Molly realize that in building her imaginary wall of ice she'd forgotten about the kite.

"Wait!" Sigrid said. Everyone turned to stare. "I believe we've left something out. Mikel, weren't you telling young Marguerite about kites this afternoon?"

"I . . . yes."

"Well, apparently you piqued her curiosity. She mentioned it to me earlier—that she couldn't so much as imagine a kite and would very much like to see one. Isn't that so, my dear?"

Speechless, Molly nodded.

"It's just around the corner. What do you say? I'd hate for her to miss it."

This was so unlike the Sigrid they thought they knew, she of the closed expression and the acid

tongue, that for a moment everyone was stupefied. But they quickly recovered themselves and agreed that certainly they could go see the kite.

Sigrid charged ahead and the others followed till they finally came to the famous kite from the land of Chin. As it had not been prepared for viewing, they set their small light-stones around it.

Molly didn't move. She just stared in disbelief. Why, it was just a toy, hardly bigger than a serving platter! True, it was shaped like a butterfly, and prettily painted; but beyond that it was nothing but sticks and paper. What a crushing disappointment!

"But—" She gasped. "That little thing couldn't carry a cat, much less a man!"

"It wasn't designed to carry a cat. Or a man."

Mikel cleared his throat. "I told her a story this afternoon, the one about the prince of Chin. . . ."

Sigrid nodded. "I know the one. An unusual choice, I'd think, under the circumstances."

"Yes," Mikel said. "A very poor choice indeed. But after I told her the story she asked me what a kite was, and I mentioned that we had one in our collection. She assumed it was the same one from the story."

"I can see how that would have happened," Sigrid said. "Well, Marguerite, that kite would have been much larger, with a sturdier frame, and made of

stronger material. Silk, I'm guessing—something else that came to us from the land of Chin.

"Now notice that the kite has a tail. And while it's certainly charming, with all the little bows, it's not there for decoration. Its weight keeps the kite upright and balanced as it flies. Notice also that a string is attached, here at the front; that's how the flier controls the kite. By keeping the string taut, the flat surface is held against the wind, which then carries the kite up into the sky."

"Did the prince of Chin have a flier?"

"I expect his kite was of a different sort, more of a glider. You've watched birds soar?"

"Yes."

"Well, it would have been something like that."

"Ah," said Molly.

"That's it, then. Thank you all for indulging us."

They returned the way they had come. Light-stones in hand, they climbed the winding stairs, one at a time, back to the private quarters of the Magi.

You know, there's a science to building kites.

Sigrid was out of her mousehole again. Molly went on alert.

Why don't you try building some and see if they will fly?

Up, up, up they went, silent but for the tread of feet on stone. And Sigrid in her head.

There are books in the library on the principles of flight.

Molly turned and looked into that cold, expressionless face, now drained of the false cheer of only a moment before.

Yes, Molly said, without words. *I would like that very much.*

Sigrid just blinked.

❦ 28 ❧

A Visit from the Watch

RICHARD HAD BEEN OUT very late the night before, so he was hard asleep when the pounding started. He woke, confused. It was daylight, but a glance at the shadows outside told him it was early yet—too soon for the gentleman in the Old District to have noticed the rats, written out a summons, and had it delivered across the city to Neargate.

The pounding came again.

"Be right there!" he called, hurriedly pulling on his braies for decency. There was no time to dress; he'd have to go in his shirt. *Crikes!* Did they mean to break down his door?

He ran quick fingers through his hair, slapped himself on the side of the head to wake things up a little, then went to open the door. There stood a burly man dressed in the blue and gold livery of an officer of the Watch. His balled fist was raised, ready to pound again; and behind him stood two more officers.

"Good morning, gentlemen," Richard said, pointedly scratching a rib. "Rather early for a visit."

"We've come for the foreign gentleman." Before Richard could reply, they entered his house, stepping right around him. "Where is he?"

"Well, I don't know," Richard said, shutting the door and tugging at his shirt, which was embarrassingly short. "Lord Worthington took rather high offense at being lodged with the ratcatcher. So he cursed me to hell, then turned on his heels and went away. He hasn't been back since, and I can't say I'm sorry to see the last of him. Hope he went over the wall and drowned himself in the moat."

The watchmen exchanged suspicious looks. They didn't believe a word.

"Search the house," the chief officer said to one of his men. "You look around outside," he said to the other.

"What's the fellow done, officer? He's a lord, you know, not a petty thief."

"I know exactly what he is."

"A foreigner?"

"Right."

Richard stopped talking then and started thinking. Once you've committed to a lie, then you'd better arrange the furniture around it, so to speak. He did so now, because there were one or two questions he hoped he wouldn't be asked; but if they were, well, it would be better if he didn't have to come up with the answers on the fly. That's how mistakes were made.

"Mind if I finish getting dressed?" he asked. "I was still abed when—"

"Stay where you are. I have some questions to ask."

"Have a seat, then?"

"No."

The Harrowsgode Watch could be a stern lot, but never as hard as this. Tobias must be serious business, then.

"You were nosing around the university the other day, asking about the barrister."

"I'm allowed the freedom of the city so I can work at my trade. I have an official badge given me by the Council, attesting to my right—"

"Then you went over to the River District and were seen watching—"

Ah, one of the questions he'd been dreading, and

the furniture not yet in place.

"—a particular house belonging to—"

"Claus Magnusson, yes." Richard pressed his lips together and waited for the rest.

"And as it happens, a lady who was staying there is betrothed to this same Lord Worthington. All kind of suspicious, don't you think?"

"I do. Absolutely."

"Perhaps you'd like to offer an explanation?"

"Look, officer, I was instructed, very official-like, to give house-room to this Westrian gentleman. I got this letter—all loops and swirls and hard to read, not like the usual summonses I get, and delivered by a lad in livery riding a shiny new spinner. He was sent by a master barrister, name of Pieter. Well, I'm not used to none of that, see. And in the letter—besides the part where the barrister informed me I was to make the gentleman comfortable—he happened to mention that Lord Worthington was betrothed to the lady you just spoke of and said where she was staying."

Oh, please, please, don't ask to see that letter!

The watchman watched, frowning.

"So I was worried, as you can imagine—having lost the fellow on the very first day, and within an hour of his arrival—that I might be held accountable for it. It wasn't my fault. I was courteous as could be. And I didn't look like this, neither, when he came. I was

dressed all properlike, not half naked, as I am now—"

"I don't want the story of your life, ratcatcher; just make your point."

"So I went there to find him." *Short enough?*

"Why?"

"To ask him to come back so I wouldn't be blamed on account of his leaving."

The watchman who'd been sent to search the house came back into the hall and shook his head. The chief officer nodded and returned his attention to Richard.

"We came here last night. Nobody was home. Where were you?"

"Catching rats. It's what I do, and night is when I do it."

"Where?"

Richard told him.

"Will this silk merchant vouch for you?"

"He will, and gladly, too. I caught thirty-seven rats for him."

"Where are they now?"

"The rats?"

"Yes."

"Buried in the rat-pit out back. I'll dig 'em up if you'd like to see."

"Did you go alone?"

Oh, crikes! Here was the other one! How he wished

he'd started with a better story! All the furniture in the world wouldn't make this one look good. But you can't put the milk back into the cow; he'd have to do his best with what he had.

"I brought my apprentice, as I always do. I'm required to have an apprentice by Harrowsgode law, so he can learn the trade and carry on—"

"What's his name and where does he live?"

Richard gave him the name and address, desperately hoping they wouldn't bother to contact the boy. Chances of that were good, especially after his client had sworn that Richard had been in his storeroom the night before, exactly as he'd claimed, catching thirty-seven rats.

The third man came in from the yard now; he hadn't found anything, either.

"All right," said the inquisitor, disgusted with Richard and bored with the whole business. "If you want to know, I think your story smells. I'd watch your back, ratcatcher, if I were you."

When the men had gone, Richard went into the pantry and sliced himself a large hunk of bread. He ate it quickly, leaning over the wash-sink. Then he got properly dressed and left the house.

❦ 29 ❧

Spirit Work

MIKEL WAS WAITING in the study-room, an open letter in his hand. He looked up when Molly came in, his expression grave.

"What?" she said.

"I have a message here. It seems you're to be moved from your quarters in the tower to a larger room downstairs—as you've apparently decided to take up kite building and will want to do some of the work in your chamber at night. Do you . . . is there something . . . can you explain this to me at all?"

"It's true. I do want to build a kite and see if it will fly."

"Instead of learning to read?"

"Can't I do both?"

"There are only so many hours in a day, and you're already so far behind—almost grown and just starting to learn your letters. To waste your precious time on children's games—"

"Who was the message from?"

"Sigrid."

"That's what I thought. It was her idea, you know."

"*Sigrid's* idea."

"Yes."

"Really?"

"Yes."

"Well." He looked away and sighed at the walls. "Who am I to question . . . ?"

"I only need a little help—just see if you can find some books about kites and the principles of flight, then read out the important parts. I'll do the rest on my own, in the evenings. In my new, large room. Then everything will be as before."

He nodded, tapping his knee with the letter—*slap, slap, slap*. He probed his teeth with his tongue and looked thoughtfully out the window.

"What? There's something else."

Mikel sighed. "The Great Seer has offered to begin your spirit work. He's too busy to take it on as a regular

thing, but he wanted to get you started."

"When did this happen?"

"This morning. You've certainly captured every-one's attention."

"Mikel—"

"I know. And my answer is the same as it was last night. And there's something more, if you'll hear it."

She had the feeling she was going to hear it whether she liked it or not.

"Molly, you tend to say exactly what you think and show the world everything you feel. I'm sure you're just being honest and straightforward, and that's an admirable thing; but there's tremendous power in keeping your thoughts and emotions to yourself. Let others spill their secrets, then use what they reveal to your advantage. Think of it as buckling on your armor."

Molly was appalled. "I should be like that with *everybody*? I might as well be dead!"

"No, not with everybody. Just be careful whom you trust."

"I trust you."

"You do me honor, then. And, if you've been paying close attention—something else you need to learn—I have given you my trust as well."

"What about Soren. Should I trust him?"

He was quiet for a very long time.

"If you have to ask . . ."

❧ ☙

Soren arrived a little after noon. There was a brisk, bustling air about him, as if he'd just come upstairs after a busy morning, which in truth he probably had. He smiled at Molly, not too broadly, friendly but not fawning. She decided that smile had been carefully chosen. Inwardly, she began strapping on her armor.

"Thank you, Mikel," Soren said with a curt little nod and a slightly altered smile—as between colleagues, though slightly dismissive. Mikel took the hint and left the room.

"Well, Marguerite, I'm quite looking forward to this. I hope you are, too."

"Yes," she said.

"So many new beginnings in such a short time."

She nodded, carefully arranging her expression.

"You are—as I'm sure you know—a very gifted young lady, with enormous potential. But a gift only grows into greatness through hard work." He raised his eyebrows as if to ask *Do you understand?*

"I'm willing to work. You won't find me wanting."

"That's what I hoped to hear. Now, let's suppose that I spoke to you in a whisper—*like this*. Let's also

suppose that you were bustling about, gathering your papers together, sliding books across the desk, scooting in your chair—that sort of thing. Would you be able to hear me?"

"Probably not."

"Well, it's the same with the voice of your inner spirit. You must learn to listen for its faintest whispers—for unless you hear it calling, you can't draw it out and help it to grow. Do you see?"

"Yes."

"We're going to start with an exercise in stillness and concentration. I want you to close your eyes and let your muscles relax: your shoulders, arms, hands, neck, jaw, tongue, fingers, and toes. Imagine you're melting into the carpet."

He waited as she concentrated on one part of her body after another, bidding each to release and go limp. When Soren judged that she was fully relaxed, he began to speak in a soft, mellow voice.

"Now stay as you are, calm and peaceful; but I want you to move your consciousness away from your body. Empty your mind completely so it becomes like a great, cavernous space with a wide, welcoming door. Then you must have patience. Wait for whatever comes. And when it does, give it your full attention and hold on as long as you can. *Begin.*"

Molly was floating in a warm sea, deep below the surface. Everything around her was still. Soft light penetrated her world from above, but there was no sound except for her own steady breathing: in, out; in, out.

She drifted like this for a long time, as though in a dreamless sleep. Then gradually she sensed a change. She still floated, but now she felt the touch of fresh, cool air; and when she opened her eyes, everything was white.

She was in a cloud. It had dark places and bright places, soft edges and great patches of nothingness. And then it was gone. She squinted against the sudden light.

Her arms were outstretched, but they didn't feel like arms exactly. They were more . . . complicated. She turned her head and saw that they had become wings—glossy and black. They trembled with a subtle vibration, reacting to little movements in the air.

She angled her body and banked to the right—knowing how to do this without being taught— swooping down, circling the towers of Harrowsgode Hall, then rising again. She was conscious of every feather-twitch, each small adjustment she made in the set of her tail. It all came as naturally as breathing.

She looked down on the city spread out below her and the patchwork of fields in the valley. It would be so easy to fly there, to land amid the barley stubble. But why not go higher, farther, out over the very mountains themselves to the villages of Austlind and beyond, to Alaric in his garden back in Westria? How amazed he would be when she flew in!

But her wings weren't responding anymore; she couldn't move her primary feathers. They'd become nothing but outstretched arms again, she realized; and her hands were gripping something. Her chest and hips were cradled by strong bands. And above her, holding her aloft, was a great canopy of silk—the color of garnet, embroidered all over with sunbursts in thread-of-gold. New wings of her own design, the wings of a Magus Mästare. But they weren't as clever as her bird-wings had been. All they could do was soar, floating gently down, always down. . . .

Molly opened her eyes. A stack of books lay on the desk, and beside it a basket of materials for building a kite. Someone must have come into the room, probably knocking first, and put those things down on the table. Then whoever it was had gone out again and shut the door. Yet she'd heard none of it.

"How do you feel?" Soren asked.

"Fresh as springtime." She looked out the window and was startled. "It's almost dark!"

"Yes. You held on for a very long time."

"It didn't seem long."

"It never does."

She nodded. She'd spent a whole day flying.

"So, tell me," he said, leaning forward on the desk, wearing a friendly smile, "what did you see?"

Molly felt the hair rise up on her arms. Then, quick as lightning, the armor was back on again.

"I was in a barn," she said, "very big and very dark. And there were all these cows. . . ."

❧ 30 ❧

The Silversmith's Shop

RICHARD STOOD AT the entrance to a silversmith's shop, his hat in his hand. He'd been directed to go there by Molly, who'd sent another message by her raven.

He'd never been to this particular workshop before. He'd bought his own little treasures—the tray, the cups—in the Neargate District, where they didn't stare at foreigners or ignore them altogether as they did in the city establishments. So this visit made Richard uncomfortable. He'd had to nerve himself just to walk through the doorway.

"You the ratcatcher?" asked a very young apprentice,

noting Richard's cape and badge.

"Yes, I am."

"Well, you've got the wrong place, then. Nobody called you here."

"I'm not on official business," Richard said, feeling once again a boy of eight years, a lowly servant expected to bow and doff his cap to his betters.

"Then why have you come?"

"To spend my gold, lad—which I earned by honest labor in the service of Harrowsgode. I believe it's as good as any other man's."

The boy was taken aback by Richard's boldness. "Shall I call the master?" he asked.

"No. We won't bother him. I just want a few brief words with one of your fellows, Jakob Magnusson."

"Oh," said the boy. "He's over there."

"Jakob," Richard said, pulling up a stool and settling himself on it, "I have come at the request of a lady whose name I shall not mention." He kept his voice very low so only Jakob could hear. "She is related to you—a cousin, I believe."

"That lady is in no position to request anything, or send anyone anywhere."

"So one would naturally assume. All the same, she has found a way to get messages out of . . . the place where she is."

"Yet I still don't believe you."

"And why not?"

"Because she's just as incapable of writing a letter as she is of sending one."

"Well, see, that's changed. They've got teachers up there at . . . the place where she is, and she's rather a quick study. Now why don't we just move on to the point, which is this: the lady wishes me to ask you about a certain cup. How soon will it be ready?"

Jakob put his hand over his mouth, a small gesture of astonishment, then disguised it by rubbing his jaw. Richard had his attention now.

"I worked on it for a while after she left—or to be more precise, after my father arranged for her to be taken. After that there seemed no point. So I stopped." He gave a little snort and shook his head. "She wanted it for the king of Westria, you know."

"I was aware of that, actually."

"Well, the king won't be getting his cup, alas. My cousin isn't going anywhere."

Richard allowed a smile to creep onto his lips. He leaned forward and lowered his voice even further. "I wouldn't be so sure of that."

"What do you mean?"

"Exactly what you think."

"There's a plan?"

"Two."

Jakob started. "Two plans?"

"Think about it."

He did. It took a minute.

"One to get her out of . . . her current location, and one to get . . . away?"

Richard smiled and gave the slightest nod.

"Can you tell me what they are exactly?"

"No."

"Is time important?"

"You mean the cup? The answer is yes. The sooner, the better."

Jakob sighed, more in resolve than despair. "I still have the gilding to do on the base, and the last of the trim. Then there's all the enamel work—very precious business; it can't be rushed."

"How long?"

"A week, maybe more. I'll have to come in early and stay late. It's my own personal project and must be done on my own time." He smiled now. "Tell her I'll try to finish it in a week, and it will be *everything* she expects. Make sure you tell her that part."

"I will, and she'll be right glad to hear it. Now, there's one other thing. The lady has no access to her money at present—"

"I know," he said bitterly. "It's in her bag, with her

things, in my house."

"Yes, well, the point is that she has asked me to pay you myself, and she'll reimburse me later. I've brought—"

"Don't!" he snapped. "I owe her—*my whole family* owes her—far more than the price of a chalice, considering how she was betrayed. It disgusts me to live there. It'll be a pleasure to come to the workshop early and stay late."

"All right, then. I'll be back in a week to pick up the cup. In the meantime, if you should happen to be accosted by a raven—"

"Excuse me?"

"A raven, with a slip of paper wrapped around its leg—?"

"Of course!" he said, rather too loud. Then he dropped back to a whisper. "I understand now, about the messages. Very clever."

"She is, apparently—clever. Tobias keeps mentioning it."

"I'll be especially friendly to ravens from this moment on, though how this particular bird will know who I am and where I am to be found—"

"I'm sure it already does. This particular raven is also quite clever. If I didn't know better, I'd say it was a human living under an enchantment. Most certainly it

serves the lady with impressive devotion. Now, I'd better go. You can frown when I leave, as though I forced my conversation upon you." Richard made to rise.

"Wait."

He sat down again.

"One last question. This plan . . ."

"Yes."

"Is it . . . limited? To the number of persons who can . . . you understand me?"

"I do. And no. It is not like . . . a boat, say, where there are only so many seats." He knew what Jakob was asking, but he'd let the boy do it himself.

"In that case, would you ask the lady if I might go with her?"

"I will, and I'm sure she'll say yes." Then, after weighing it in his mind for a moment, he added, "I'll be going, too."

❦ 31 ❧

The Tunnel

CONSTANCE ALWAYS SEEMED to know when morning had arrived, though the shed in which they slept was as dark as a cave, having no windows whatsoever. Perhaps she possessed some secret dog-knowledge to which he was not privy. Or maybe she just had better ears and could hear the cocks crowing in the village. However it was, Tobias could depend on her to wake him early by walking across his chest and nuzzling his cheek with her warm, wet nose.

He gave the dog a friendly squeeze and a scratch behind the ears, then sat up and felt in the darkness for the lantern and flint.

Richard was very particular when it came to his equipment, and he insisted that light-stones, while an admirable invention, weren't nearly bright enough for ratting at night. Nor could you adjust the degree of their light by turning a flame up or down as you could with a lantern. So he'd petitioned the Council for a special dispensation to continue using oil lamps, and his request had been granted.

When the room was lit, Tobias opened the rat-proof iron box and took out some bread and cheese. Richard always brought him the best his neighborhood cookshop had to offer: juicy meat pies, ripe cheeses, fresh fruit, plump sausages, and bread that was whiter than white—all a complete waste of money. It might have been cakes made of sawdust for all Tobias cared. Food was just fuel for his body, giving him strength for the labor ahead.

Having fed himself and the dog, Tobias dressed, rolled up his pallet, and stashed it in the corner along with the rat-proof box. Then he slipped on Richard's heavy leather gloves and went to work removing the boards that covered the entrance to the tunnel. Constance stood, her senses primed, her muscles quivering with desire. As soon as the first board was off, she shot through the opening like an arrow, scrabbling down the stairs and into the long, dark, wonderful hole where the rats lived.

When he had the entrance completely uncovered for the day, Tobias followed with the lantern, hunching over since the ceiling was low. His back ached constantly from working in that unnatural position. But Tobias didn't care about that, either. He just thought about the work.

When he and Richard had first started clearing the entrance, they'd noted with growing excitement that the walls and ceiling were sturdily constructed of stone blocks, most of them still intact. But breaking up the hard-packed dirt and rubble that filled the tunnel, then carrying it all out bag after bag, was slow, tedious work. And Tobias did most of it alone, since Richard had his two ratting jobs to attend to, plus disposing of the bags of rubble and running back and forth across town to get food and other supplies. If the tunnel was like this all the way through, the job could take a year or more—and even Richard couldn't explain *that* to the owner of the house.

Then one evening when Tobias was in the tunnel, working late, swinging his pick for the thousandth time that day, he felt the barrier give way. After that, he went at the little hole like one possessed until the opening was wide enough to reach his lantern through. Only then did he know for sure that they wouldn't have to dig the whole way out. As far as he could see by the lantern's light, the passageway was clear, if you didn't

count the mess carried in by countless generations of rats, and their desiccated corpses, and the droppings they'd left behind.

"From now on," Richard had said when he'd arrived later that night, "we go at it quick and dirty. No need to clear out the muck. I seriously doubt your lady cares what she walks through so long as she comes out beyond the walls at the other end. We can finish the last bit tonight, you and me together—just enough to get through, that's all we really need. Then we go to work like demons on the far end."

Left hanging in the air, unspoken, had been the Great Uncertainty: what they would find on the other side. Tobias had tried not to think about it as he slammed his pick into the slowly receding back wall day after day. Yet think about it he had, asking himself how *he* would have gone about hiding the egress from a tunnel. He'd have rolled in enormous boulders to cover the fill, that's what; and the thought of that was horribly depressing: to work so hard and get so far only to run into solid rock.

Well, he told himself, they'd cross that bridge when they came to it. For now his mission was simple and clear: to break down the wall at the end of the tunnel, shovel the dirt and rocks into canvas bags, and haul them up to the storeroom for Richard to dispose of later. Then, after stretching out his back for just a

moment, he'd go back in and do it all over again.

Constance helped break the tedium, trotting along beside him with her boundless energy, always on the lookout for anything ratlike, eager to show Tobias how beautifully she did the disgusting thing she'd been bred to do. (In addition to the bags of rubble upstairs, there was also a smaller one filled with the lifeless bodies of her vanquished prey.)

The "rat-muck" Richard had mentioned so lightly was more plentiful and revolting than Tobias could have imagined. The tunnel stank of it; so did Constance and Tobias. For all his care—leaving his boots and tools inside the tunnel at night, boarding it up, washing himself and the dog as well as he could with what water he had—the smell of rat urine was in his nostrils day and night.

And then there was that other thing, which was worse.

Richard had told him that the Harrowsgode folk thought plague was carried by vermin. Since then, the very sight, sound, and stink of rats became forever linked in his mind with a single terrible image: his parents laid out on their marriage bed, the baby placed between them, their spirits gone, their bodies ruined—and his little sister, Mary, not yet showing any symptoms, looking up at him and asking why Mama wouldn't get up and make her porridge.

But none of that erased the fact that unless they finished clearing the tunnel, they would never get out. Tobias would die, probably soon, and Molly would be a captive all her life. So he offered up his suffering as a sacrifice, knowing it to be superstitious nonsense, knowing that all the rat-stink in the world couldn't buy Molly's freedom. But it helped to play tricks with his mind, so he chose to think that way.

Around midday Richard arrived, more than usually jolly. He'd brought some pork pies for Tobias and a pig's knuckle for Constance.

"Sit down and have a rest," Richard said. "And have yourself something to eat. You'll be no use to anyone whatsoever if you pitch over dead from overwork. And you'll be in the way, too. We'll have to climb over your body on our way out."

Tobias laughed, feeling the tension drain out of him. He sat and ate as he'd been instructed—though not before washing his hands—and was quite miraculously restored.

Richard went on smiling. He plainly had something to tell and was waiting for Tobias to ask.

"All right," Tobias said, "what is it?"

"This!" He produced a strip of paper with an enormous grin.

"From Molly?" He took it from Richard's hand and saw that it was covered with words, not pretty written,

but bold as brass—Molly through and through. He looked up at Richard pleadingly. *Don't tease me, not now! Just tell me what it says.*

This only served to encourage him.

"Now, you've told me rather a lot about that girl of yours, Tobias; and I confess I've doubted whether she could be as amazing as she's been presented: battling demons, rescuing princes—"

"Richard, for heaven's sake!"

"She's beautiful, of course, and clever, clever, clever—"

"I could strangle you with one hand, you know, while eating this pie with the other; and I'm quite inclined to do it, too, if—"

"Patience, lad. Who would bring you food if you strangled me?"

"No need. I'd slice you up and eat you raw."

"That's the spirit! I'll tell you—though, mind, this is something that deserves to be told right—"

"And you're the very man to do it."

"I am indeed. So here it is: your beloved has sent me to a silversmith's shop to see about a cup, which I have done. It will be ready within the week."

"That's why you're grinning?"

"No. I told you it must be enjoyed slowly, like a fine dinner."

Tobias glared at him in silence.

"What else? Let me see. She is gratified to know that you are safe and that we have found an escape route. I was so exceedingly careful in my choice of words, in case the message was intercepted, that I rather feared I might have been too subtle altogether. But she made my meaning out perfectly and was nearly as cagy in her reply, so that I had to read it over a time or two before I got it entirely straight in my mind."

Tobias folded his hands as if in prayer, the very model of quiet patience.

"Oh, dear, I shan't do it justice, but I really can't bear to drag it out."

Tobias raised his eyebrows, just a little.

"Prepare yourself, man, to be knocked over with amazement. Are you ready? You are? Good. Well *your lady*—who I have vastly underestimated, I confess it now, without reservation—is at this very moment . . ."

Tobias unlaced his fingers from their prayerful pose and reached out a hand as though to grasp something—a ball, say, or Richard's throat.

". . . is building herself some wings."

Tobias froze, stupefied. "Wings?"

"Yes, Tobias. Wings. *Your* lady is going to *fly* out of bloody Harrowsgode Hall. Now, what do you think of that?"

❦ 32 ❧

Wings

HER NEW ROOM WAS twice the size of her chamber in the tower. And while the windows there had been small and covered by a grille, here she had a large double casement. When both of the panes were opened, it provided a fine, wide sill—a perfect place to perch while arranging one's flying apparatus before flinging oneself off the building.

It was also a more comfortable spot for Uncle to land; he'd managed with difficulty before.

All she'd lacked was privacy, and that would be essential once she started constructing her Magus wings. To that end, she'd had a few words with the

chambermaid, begging the girl to stay out of her room and never mind the mess. Because otherwise the maid was sure to tread on one of the kites, or be tripped up by a bit of string, or knock over a pot of glue. The girl had not minded in the least—that much less for her to do.

Now Molly sat on the floor with her pile of willow wands. Winifred had gathered them at her request; and Uncle had carried them by night, one at a time, to her new room at Harrowsgode Hall. Then he'd gone back to Winifred for one last package containing a penknife, a needle, and six spools of thread.

The choice of willow had been brilliant; it was supple, light, and strong. But tying the individual branches together to form a perfect curve, making sure that at each connection point the thread was wound tightly many times, then finished with a stout knot—that wasn't so easy. And her life would depend on having done it right.

She laid out the first willow branch on the floor, admiring its graceful curve. Then she nested a second one against the first and slid it down about a handsbreadth so that its thin end extended beyond that of the first. Now she bound them together at four points. In this way, with each addition, the structure would grow in length and sturdiness.

She worked in a dream state, with utter concentration, effortlessly harnessing something within her that guided her busy hands, correcting the shape of the curve as needed, alerting her if the thread was too loose at any of the connection points. When it was, she'd unwind it and start again.

Time was suspended. The slender moon, a bright shallow cup, hung motionless outside her window as she worked.

When the two wings were completed, their supporting struts attached and the trailing edges perfectly formed, they proved to be equal in length, exact mirror images of each other, each with a delicate curve from side to side and front to back, as when you cup your hands to splash water on your face.

Now she started on the central structure that would join the wings and support the harness.

Still the moon remained a fixed point in the sky. Still Molly worked under the guidance of her inner spirit. The world around her was hushed.

She'd reserved the thickest branches for this final step. Simple though it was—a box shape, longer than it was wide, reinforced by crosspieces and the overlapping origin of the wings—it had to be strong.

Her hands knew exactly what to do.

When at last it was finished, lacking only its silken

skin, she lifted it and felt its weight. It was heavier than she'd expected, but still she believed. From working with her kites she knew the astonishing power of wind against a broad surface. It would hold her weight and that of the wings, and carry them over the city walls to freedom.

As soon as the cup was ready, as soon as the tunnel was finished—then she would cut apart her beautiful Magus gown and attach the silk to the frame with careful stitches, using the scraps to form a harness—one loop to support her chest, one to support her hips, and a small handle on either side to grip with each of her hands.

Now she had only to wait, and sleep.

Outside, the little sliver of moon began to move in the sky again.

⅙ 33 ⅋

Rats

AS BEFORE, TOBIAS was alone in the tunnel when his pick bit through the fill.

He'd found the first stair earlier that morning and known that he was close. Perhaps by dusk, when Richard arrived, he'd have broken through altogether. Excited, he'd redoubled his efforts, clearing step after step.

But it was trickier digging up than it had been digging down. There was always the danger that a large chunk would break away from the wall and bury him in a heap of rubble. So the nearer he came to the top, the more careful and analytical did his process

become—working in from the side, for example, instead of starting in the middle.

It was going well. He allowed himself to hope. Any minute now his pick might cut right through that wall like a knife through butter; light would come streaming in from the outside world, bringing with it the sweet smell of sun-warmed grass.

But instead his pick met stone, and the unexpected impact sent him tumbling down the stairs. He lay there for a moment, catching his breath. Then he got to his feet again and held the lantern up to the wall. There wasn't much to see. Stone, yes, undoubtedly—in one particular place. But that wasn't the whole story, not yet.

And the more he thought about it, the more hopeful he became. They couldn't possibly have moved a single boulder large enough to cover the entrance. It must be a pile of rocks, then, in varying sizes. There might be gaps between those rocks. Some of them might be small enough to move. To find out, he'd simply have to keep knocking rubble away till the true state of affairs was revealed.

He continued chipping away with the pick, exposing more and more rock. He worked all the way to the ceiling and found that the rock extended beyond the opening. He would have to work laterally, then. But

nothing he found brought him joy. So far it was all the same: one single, enormous stone pressed against the opening.

Constance had been busy at the other end of the tunnel, doing what she did best. Now she came to join Tobias, bringing her usual offering.

"What a bloodthirsty, precious little monster you are," he said, using the point of his pick to fling the rat corpse off the stairs. Then he went back to clearing the stone, the endless, enormous, giant, hopeless—

Constance was at it again, this time over on the corner, right at the top of the stairs. She made a fierce little growl and began scratching frantically at the dirt with her forepaws. Well, Tobias thought, at least that was one section he wouldn't have to clear.

She barked twice, then returned to her digging: *scritch-scritch-scritch-scritch-scritch*—very fast.

Tobias stopped and stared.

Scritch-scritch-scritch-scritch-scritch! Bark-bark-bark!

"Constance!" he said, but she ignored him. Rats always came first. So he went and squatted beside her, loose bits of dirt flying out as she dug, covering his boots. Finally she reached the nest-hole and a rat darted out. Constance caught it on the run; and there followed the familiar screech, the creature's death throes, and then it was over. She dropped it, limp, on

the flagstone. Another gift.

But this time the gift had been one of hope. Because a rat couldn't dig through stone any more than Tobias could. "My turn," he said, nudging the little terrier away with his foot so he could see what lay beyond the nest.

❦ 34 ❧

Messages

DEAR M.—

The vessel you ordered is finished, and the person who made it wishes to join us. Is this all right with you?

R.

Dear R—

Yes. Take him with you, and I will meet you at our destanashun. tamarro I think after noon mabe mid day.

M.

Dear Win—

I am redy. You need to by 2 more horses with sadels and have plenty of ~~proviz~~ food. Do this rite now. I will come tamarro after the mid day meal. Look up at the sky.

M

Dear M.—

Your gentleman friend wishes you to know that he is rather the worse for goose-grease, ashes, and rat-muck. He hopes you will not mind. He also says that if you die on him, he will never forgive you.

I cannot wait to meet you.

R.

Dear M.,

Everything will be ready. Be careful.

Yours,

Lord M.

❦ 35 ❧

Escape

MOLLY STOOD AT THE window watching the clouds. Uncle had said she must wait for the puffy kind, the ones that looked like mountains with flat bases, darker at the bottom. They were a sign that warm air was rising, and that meant perfect flying weather.

But she wasn't worried. She'd been watching for mountain-clouds every afternoon since Uncle had first mentioned them, and never had they failed to form. She recalled that it was Soren who managed the weather, and that made her laugh. If he only knew that he was making it easier for her to escape! Thunderclouds right now would be very inconvenient.

She'd been holed up in her chamber, the door locked, since dinner the previous night, at which she'd complained, in a loud voice, of a headache and a roiling gut. She'd spent the rest of the night taking her Magus gown apart and attaching it to the framework of the wings. It had been tedious work, stitch after painstaking stitch; but when she'd finished, Uncle had said it was perfect. She'd collapsed onto her bed, still in her clothes, and slept till midmorning.

Mikel, bless him, had knocked politely and asked if she was all right. But he'd woken her, and she'd been a bit snappish. *No*, she didn't want to eat. *No*, she wasn't up to studying today. *Please go away!*

She felt bad about that now. He'd been so kind to her. He'd taught her how to write her name and how to buckle on her armor. And now, if all went well, she'd never see him again. But she had the feeling he'd know that she was grateful even though she'd never said it.

The clouds were just about perfect now, the warm air ready to support her. She was ready, too. She'd plaited her hair and pinned it up so it wouldn't blow in her face. And she'd turned the skirt of her day gown into makeshift pantaloons by stitching it up the middle between her legs, fastening the hem tightly around the ankles and across the middle. It looked ridiculous, but at least her skirt wouldn't catch the

wind and slow her down.

Now there was nothing left to do but lean on the windowsill, look at the clouds, and wait for Uncle. And that was hard. Molly was restless, and she couldn't stop thinking about all the things that might go wrong. It was a long list, and she had a gruesome imagination when it came to picturing disasters. What she really needed was to get this over with *now*, get up on that bloody ledge and bloody well jump off into—

There he was! Finally!

He landed gracefully on the sill beside her.

"Where in blazes have you been?" she scolded. "I've about lost my mind with waiting."

I was having a word with some rooks and jackdaws.

That left her more or less speechless. Saying good-bye to his little friends? Getting some tips on wind direction? "Well, I've been ready this last hour or more. Shall we go?"

Yes. But before you put the wings on, let's review this one more time: your window faces north, but you want to go south. So first—"

"I know, Uncle: fly straight toward the mountains till I've caught the wind and feel I'm in control, then bank to the left, not dropping any more than I have to, and head straight south and over the walls—"

And the landing?

"It'll be hard, and I might tumble. I need to find a bare field, then drop down, arching my back at the last minute so the wings will tilt and slow my progress—then run."

Good. I believe you are ready.

It was harder than she'd expected. The wings were wider than the window opening, so she had to stand at an angle—one wing inside, one out. Just climbing onto the sill had been tricky since she'd needed to keep a grip on the handles so the contraption wouldn't slide down. Then once she'd made it up there, she had no way to steady herself; and the wind started tugging at the outside wing, throwing her off balance. She'd looked down, always a mistake, and was suddenly jolted by a moment of terror such as she had never known before—which, considering the life she'd led, was saying something.

"Uncle, am I going to die?"

No, Molly dear. You're going to fly. Just follow me.

He pushed off the sill and rose with beats of his powerful raven wings, then flew straight north. Now it was her turn. Molly took a deep breath, bent her knees, and sprang into empty air.

But it wasn't working, she realized with a stab of terror. She was falling, falling, falling—until suddenly

there was a lurch and a loud *whomp* as the wind caught her silken wings, and fear gave way to elation. She was flying—the wind rushing at her face and lifting her up, the sun shining through the crimson silk like a blessing. *Oh, my stars,* she thought, *this is wonderful!* Up ahead, Uncle banked to the left and Molly followed, doing it neatly, staying high. She was in control. Like that ancient prince of Chin, she had harnessed the wind to do her bidding.

Below she saw rooftops, streets, people—and not too far ahead the city walls, and beyond them the fertile valley, greener than green. She began searching for a landing spot. Two or three stubble fields side by side would be ideal, in case she couldn't stop herself fast enough and had to keep on going. And it should be away from the village; she definitely didn't want to go crashing into somebody's chicken coop.

Suddenly Uncle gave a distress call—*Kraaaaaaw! Watch out!*—but Molly couldn't see any sign of danger. "What?" she shouted, her words almost swallowed by the wind.

Below, on the ramparts!

She saw the archers then, staring up at her, their bows drawn; and the first arrow had already been loosed. It missed, but the second one pierced her right wing, very near her elbow. And then, as if someone

had written it there, three amazing words came into her mind: *Archers, stand down!*

To Molly's astonishment they *did* stand down, lowering their bows as one. But at the same moment she heard the sickening rip of fabric as the pressure of the wind tugged against the arrow hole, tearing the silk from the front edge to the back. She began to tilt, her balance lost as the right wing spilled air through the gap. She knew what happened to kites when they lost control: they went spiraling down with alarming speed till they crashed against something hard and broke into pieces. Now that was happening to her.

Except it wasn't. Something was holding her aloft, guiding her straight toward the valley. Above she could hear a fierce beating of wings—*whomp, whomp, whomp, whomp, whomp*! She looked up and saw bird-shadows against the garnet silk; and through the tear in the fabric she could see the movement of wings. Uncle's rooks and jackdaws, it had to be!

As she continued over the city walls, she saw the archers up close; they still gazed at her, but their threatening manner was gone. They simply gaped with amazement at the flying girl in Magus wings being carried by a flock of large black birds. Not something you saw every day, even in Harrowsgode.

Down they glided, quickly but gracefully, Uncle

still in the lead. He had chosen a landing spot and was guiding her there. Molly watched, her gut in a knot, as the ground rose up to meet her. *Arch your back,* she remembered, *then run as fast as you can.* But when? Now?

Never mind—they were doing it for her. The wings jerked back, rather suddenly, so that she was upright now, her legs circling in the air until the moment they touched the ground.

A stubble field is nothing like a smooth, flat meadow. It's all lumps and dips, and is full of hard, dry stalks. Molly staggered as she ran, twisting an ankle, the rough stubble catching at her pantaloons. She was going to fall—there was no help for it—and the whole apparatus would land on top of her, pressing her down into the dirt and the sharp things sticking out of it. But no, the birds still held her wings aloft, steadying her until she finally came to a stop, let go of the handles, and slipped out of the harness. They were like an army of very small servants helping a gentleman off with his cloak.

When she was free of her wings, they let the contraption fall and rose in unison. She looked up at them, raising her arms in gratitude. "Thank you, oh, thank you!" she called to the rooks and the jackdaws as they flew back toward the city, filling the air with

their raucous cries. Then she trudged across the field in the direction of the village, Uncle still showing her the way.

Villagers had gathered outside their cottages to watch. They clapped and waved as she passed by. She felt for just a moment like a queen in procession—a very ragged queen with wild hair, dressed in pantaloons—so that she couldn't resist a few head nods, acknowledging their acclaim. When she saw Stephen running up the road to meet her, she laughed out loud.

"Stephen!" she shouted. "Did you see? I flew through the air!"

"Yes!" he said, breathless, taking her arm and urging her to pick up speed, hurrying her back toward the town. "It was astonishing—we really must hurry, my dear—and when the archers . . . oh, and the birds! Well now, *that* was something!"

"Are the horses ready?" She was gasping now, too.

"They have been since this morning."

"And everybody got out?"

"Yes."

"And Jakob has the cup?"

"Yes."

"Tobias? Is he all right?"

"Can you run, lady? We don't know what they're likely to do next now that they've seen you escape."

The others were already mounted, hidden behind a large barn at the very edge of town—Winifred, Mayhew, Jakob, and another man who had to be the wonderful Richard. Hanging on each side of his saddle was a wicker basket, each holding a little dog with pointed ears. Three riderless horses stood ready and waiting. That would be hers, Stephen's, and—

"Where's Tobias?"

"He stayed behind," the man who must be Richard said, "so he'd be there to help you if you didn't make it over the walls."

"And you let him do that?"

"I had no choice. He's bigger than I am, and very stubborn. But he'll be on his way now, I'm sure."

"Then we'll wait."

"No," Mayhew said. "We won't. We need to get up that blasted narrow trail and into the safety of the canyon before darkness sets in—or they'll lower their blasted drawbridge and send an army in our wake. Don't worry about Tobias. He knows the way."

"That makes perfect sense," Molly said. "Absolutely. You go ahead. I'll wait for Tobias."

"Oh, for heaven's sake, you're impossible!"

"Go!"

"I will not!"

"Suit yourself then. I'm not leaving without him."

Finally Mayhew took a deep breath, snorted, and directed his troops. "Stephen, you get the others up to safety. We'll follow as soon as we can."

Stephen nodded, and without a word he turned his horse into the road. The others stared at Molly, unsure what to do, until Mayhew roared at them to go and do it bloody quick.

"You take care, Molls!" Winifred said as they rode away.

"Don't I always?" she replied.

❦ 36 ❧

Skulking

TOBIAS HAD CALCULATED the probable trajectory of Molly's flight from the tower. From that he'd determined the most likely landing spot, in the event she couldn't make it over the walls. With this in mind, he'd chosen a good spot to hide: a cluttered yard behind a bakeshop in the southern part of the city. It had the advantage of being close to an alley, so he could run out quickly when the moment came. It also offered a good view of the towers of Harrowsgode Hall.

There he now waited, skulking in a dark corner, a cap pulled low over his head. He'd traveled there by night and had been waiting all morning, though

she'd said she wouldn't leave till midafternoon. Several times people had come out of the bakeshop to use the privy, and Tobias would always duck behind a ruined butter churn. It was small and he was large, so half of him was still in plain sight, but so far no one had noticed him.

The shadows grew shorter, gradually moving from west to east, marking the passage of time; and still Tobias stayed at his post, gazing upward, going over and over in his mind the many problems that might occur. As each of them occurred to him, he searched for some way to help. But in this he was unsuccessful. If she'd been prevented from leaving, for example, or if she dropped like a stone to her death—well, there was really nothing anyone could do.

And then, finally, there she was, soaring out into the open from the back of Harrowsgode Hall with the savage grace of a hawk on the hunt, her wine-red wings, lit from behind, glowing like the sunset. Tobias reached the alley, then, sprinting out onto the road, followed her with his eyes. How splendid she was, so unbelievably brave!

But what was that—an arrow? Surely it was—yes! And there went another one, with a truer aim this time, barely missing Molly and tearing a wing. He started to run now, with such dangerous speed that people

leaped out of his way as they would from a runaway horse. His heart almost burst with the effort. Then it registered on his consciousness that the archers had lowered their bows. But it was already too late; a wing was torn. . . .

What happened after that had been so miraculous that he and everyone else in Harrowsgode could do nothing but gaze in wonder at the flying girl with the wounded wing being held aloft by a flock of ink-black birds, floating over the great walls of Harrowsgode and out into the countryside!

Tobias turned and dashed back toward the tunnel. But he didn't get far before an officer of the Watch shouted and stepped in his way. Deftly, Tobias danced to the side and kept on going. Soon others joined the chase. He could hear their shouts and the sound of hurried footsteps. They didn't know what he had done that deserved pursuit, only that he was a foreigner, out where he didn't belong, and his behavior seemed suspicious.

Tobias ran with the endurance of youth, taking great strides with his long legs, drawing steadily ahead of the crowd. He was heading straight for the windowless shed where he and Constance had spent so many nights. He reached it, slammed the door behind him, and since it couldn't be locked from the inside,

dragged a couple of rubble sacks over to block it.

But he doubted that would keep them out for long. There seemed to be a lot of them, and if they worked together they could easily push his makeshift barricade aside. Then they'd see the tunnel entrance straight ahead of them, and the chase would simply continue—down the tunnel, out the narrow opening, and into the village, complicating everyone's escape.

He found the lantern where he'd left it, just by the door, and lit it with the flint. Then he set it on the floor in the middle of the room, swinging down the metal shields on three of the sides so it would only shine straight ahead and not on the back wall where the tunnel entrance was. When his pursuers entered, they'd be blinded by the jarring blast of light out of a sea of darkness.

But that would only slow them down, he realized, and he needed to stop them altogether. He could hear their shouts in the distance. He probably had a minute, maybe a little more, before they'd have the door opened. He hauled another bag of rubble to his barricade. It might help a little. And as he was doing it, inspiration struck. He knew exactly what to do.

He grabbed another sack from the far corner and scattered its contents in a broad semicircle around the glowing lamp. He paused for the briefest moment to

admire his ghoulish tableau: a sea of dead rats rather past the time when they ought to have been buried in the rat-pit—some of them bloated, all of them stinking, the whole lot of them brilliantly lit.

Thanking Constance one more time, Tobias fled, hands outstretched in the darkness, running—running through rat-muck, running toward the faint light that beckoned at the end of the tunnel.

❦ 37 ❧

The Canyon

MOLLY SAT SPRAWLED in the dirt, graceless as a guttersnipe—picking, picking, picking at the stitches that held her skirt together. If she was to sit in a saddle, they must come out. If she ruined her gown, so be it.

She was glad Mayhew was looking elsewhere—first at the castle gate to see if the drawbridge had been lowered, then to the western corner of the city walls around which he hoped to see Tobias coming, preferably very soon. Back and forth he went, from one side of the barn to the other, peering around the corner, saying nothing.

Rip, rip, rip, tear—Molly would break the thread,

then take hold of a free end and pull again, the fabric of her gown pleating itself until it would go no farther, at which point she'd break the thread and start again.

She heard a hiss from Mayhew. "I see him!"

"Tobias?"

"Yes."

He unhitched his horse and the other one for Tobias. Seconds later he was away, leading the riderless mount by the reins.

Molly gave her skirt one last heartless rip, then climbed onto her little mare and trotted after him, searching the landscape for any sign of Tobias. But she saw nothing. Mayhew must have the eyes of a hawk. And then she caught the movement, a head and shoulders plowing through a sea of barley. She set heels to her mare and caught up with Lord Mayhew as Tobias emerged into the lane. He stood there for a moment, gasping for breath.

"Merciful heavens, Tobias!" said Mayhew. "What have you been doing in there? You'll frighten the horses with your stink."

His hair—no other word would do—was disgusting: greasy, grimy, and matted. His clothes were soiled with sweat and filth, his face and hands covered with mud. And even from a distance they could smell the rat-muck.

"I've been digging a tunnel," Tobias said, looking not at Mayhew but at Molly, who was trying very hard not to laugh. Then, with all the dignity he could muster, he took the reins and mounted his horse.

⚼ ⚼

As they climbed the steep trail, Mayhew kept looking back at the drawbridge, and was astonished every time to see it still closed. Tobias was searching the west side of the city walls for any sign that his pursuers had made it past the rats to the tunnel, and noted with satisfaction that they had not.

But Molly just looked down at the beautiful valley below, and at Harrowsgode, the city of her people. As eager as she'd been to leave, being there had changed her; and now she felt a strange tug of sadness. She thought of all the people who'd been kind to her— Mikel, Pieter, Ulla, Laila, Sanna, Lorens—and knew she'd never see them again, would never know the end to their stories. Had William felt the same, she wondered, as he climbed this very trail on his way to a new life?

She saw her abandoned Magus wings, still lying in the stubble field like the carcass of a giant, dead insect. She hoped that someone would go out there and haul them in, use the beautiful embroidered silk

for the bodice of a gown. That would be nice.

The sun had already dropped behind the western mountains, but it seemed rather darker than it ought to be. The coming of night, like the coming of morning, was gradual in the valley. Long after the sun set the sky would still be bright, slowly fading into twilight, then finally into the almost-dark of northern summer.

"I don't much like the look of that," Tobias said.

Looking up, Molly saw that the perfect mountain-clouds of less than an hour before had now turned heavy, lowering, and black. You never saw thunder-clouds in Harrowsgode, not at this time of year. So why now?

Her breath caught as she suddenly understood. She squinted at the distant towers of Harrowsgode Hall. She could almost *feel* Soren up there, watching their ascent, waiting for the perfect moment. Of course. He'd never had any intention of letting them leave. But how was she going to explain this to Mayhew?

The trail made another of its many zigzag turns. The enormous stone figures loomed straight ahead and they heard the first rumbling of thunder.

When they finally left the narrow trail for the wide, flat ledge above, Mayhew looked angrily around. "Fie on Stephen!" he said. "I told him to wait!"

"No," Molly corrected, "you said to take everyone up to safety. He probably wanted to get them through the canyon while there was still light."

"All right," he said, grumbling. "Let's go."

"No, wait. There's something I have to tell you first."

"Molly, it grows dark, and it's threatening rain."

"Yes. But this is important. And you're going to have to trust me though you won't—"

"Skip the preamble," he said. "Make it fast."

"I'll do my best. There's a man up there in one of those towers. He's a very powerful Magus, the Great Seer. He uses ancient magic to control the clouds." Mayhew stared at her, incredulous, just as she'd expected. Another growl came from the darkening skies. "Think—why didn't they send anyone after us? Because this is so much easier. All he has to do is wait till we're in the canyon, then send in a thunderstorm."

Mayhew was still staring, but he seemed to half believe her. At least he was turning it over in his mind. "Well, magical or not," he said, "I think we should stay here on the ledge until this storm has passed. We'll get wet, but we won't be drowned in the canyon."

"I don't know," Tobias said. "We're awfully exposed."

"What do you mean?"

"Lightning. Molly—can the Great Seer control that, too?"

Before she could answer, a thunderbolt struck, barely missing Tobias and throwing the horses into a panic.

"Let's go!" Mayhew shouted, and dashed into the canyon.

They rode as fast as they could, but the floor was covered with small, smooth stones that slid beneath the horses' hooves, causing them to scramble and slide.

"Can you swim?" Mayhew shouted back to Molly. "No."

"Well, your horse can, if the rush of water doesn't overwhelm her. Stay on her back as long as you can. If you're washed away, then kick your legs and flap your arms. That'll keep your head above water."

"All right."

"Pass it on to Tobias."

She did.

Now it began to rain softly, the high walls of the canyon protecting them from all but a few errant drops. But they knew this was only the beginning. Soon it would start to pour, and the water would stream down the mountain slopes and into their narrow cleft in the rock—water with nowhere to go but out the two

narrow passages, one on either end. It would rise with alarming speed, the space being so narrow, covering first the horses' hooves, then their knees, and then their chests. This would be no dip in a still-water pond on a warm summer afternoon; it would become a raging torrent, surging along the downward slope, carrying them with it to their deaths.

They urged their horses on as the rain picked up, little runnels already streaming down the sides of the canyon.

"Molly!" Tobias called. She turned to see him holding up his wineskin. Then he pulled out the cork and emptied it, and showed it to her again.

"*What?*"

He held up his hand: *Wait.* Now he blew air into it, his cheeks puffing out with the effort; the leather sack grew round as he filled it with his breath. Then, holding his thumb over the opening to keep it from deflating again, he quickly slid the stopper in and pressed it down hard.

"It'll float," he called. "Do the same with yours. Keep the strap around your wrist."

Molly nodded and felt for her own wineskin, but it was hard to concentrate now. The rain was coming down the cliff walls with tremendous force, beating on their heads, their backs, the tops of their knees;

running into their eyes and making it hard to see. She finally found the wineskin and did as Tobias had showed her. But half of the air escaped before she got in the stopper, so she had to do it a second time. Even then it wasn't as plump as Tobias's was, but she stoppered it successfully and felt its roundness. Better than nothing.

The horses pressed stoically on, heads down, heaving with the strain. Then a surge of water caught them from behind, lifting horses and riders alike, driving them forward, knocking them against the narrow walls as they went. Molly lost her wineskin and watched as it floated away. Her mare was paddling frantically, trying to stay afloat; but only her head remained above the flood. Molly could feel the force of the water tugging at her skirts.

"Stop it," she screamed into the darkness, "you putrid, stinking sack of maggots!" Water streamed onto her upturned face and into her mouth, making her gag. "You weeping sore, you pestilent toad. Do you *hear me*, Soren? You're nothing but an arrogant, stone-hearted, prideful old—"

Another surge came, and now she was out of the saddle, hanging on with only one hand. This part of the canyon was especially narrow; she was afraid of being crushed between her horse and the wall. And

her gown, heavy with water, was dragging her down. She reached behind with her free hand and tugged at the sodden lacings, but they wouldn't budge. Then she was slammed against the wall again. *God's breath!* She would probably be crushed before she had a chance to drown!

If you are the great Magus I think you are, then you can find your powers even now.

She hadn't heard this exactly—the words had just come into her mind fully formed.

Such as *Archers, stand down!*

And *The girl has the brains of a goat.*

She gasped, trying to make sense of it while searching with her fingers for something, anything she could get a grip on.

But Molly dear, you will at least have to try!

"Well, yes, you *do* have a point there!" she muttered, finding a second handhold at last, a strap that had once held a basket of provisions. Then she drove everything else from her mind—the raging storm; the sound of Tobias screaming behind her; the heaving gasps of her poor, wild-eyed, overburdened mount; the absolute hopelessness of their situation—and dived deep into herself, deeper than she'd ever gone before.

She didn't feel the next great surge of water as it rushed over her head, slamming her against the wall;

she didn't see Tobias springing from his horse, beating the wild water with powerful arms, making his way toward her with desperate determination; she didn't feel his strong grip as he hauled her up onto the saddle, where she lay draped over it like a felled deer being carried home from the hunt. She was unaware of everything but the dark place inside her spirit and the thing that she had to do.

She pictured the looming clouds, heavy and black, emptying themselves of moisture in great, steaming, drowning gushes of water. Then she reversed it, and the clouds became a giant dishcloth, soaking up a spill from a giant kitchen table. She focused her mind on the rain as it began to rise in vast, beautiful, silver sheets, stroking them softly as it passed. She clung fiercely to her vision, eyes shut tight, teeth clenched, till the great black cloud had sucked up every drop that had fallen, then slowly faded and began to dissipate like morning fog.

Then all was silent. The sky was clear, ablaze with stars—and moving across that dazzling light show she saw the dark form of a solitary raven.

Well! That . . . was very . . . impressive!

⁅ 38 ⁆

Sigrid

SIGRID?

Of course.

You made the archers stand down.

Yes. But I take no credit for the birds.

You let me escape. You helped me escape. Why?

Because you wanted to. No one should be a prisoner, least of all you.

Soren tried to kill me!

I know. Because you destroyed all his plans and broke his heart. He thought he could mold you in his own image and use your powers against the forces of change. How ironic that you should be the one to bring him down.

But I didn't hurt him, not at all!

On the contrary, my dear; you destroyed him. Because you defeated him by feat of combat, he has lost his position as Great Seer. And because he used his sacred powers with the intention of taking lives, he will be banished from the Magi altogether.

I did all that?

All that and more; I think you may have saved Harrows-gode.

We've hidden behind our walls too long, living like misers, taking from the world and giving nothing back. It has weakened us, and what once made us great is dying. It's time we went out and engaged the world. It's time we opened our gates to let our restless spirits fly. Soren alone stood against it. Now everything is possible.

You aren't at all what you seem.

Neither are you, my dear.

I'm going to miss you, Sigrid; I never would have thought it.

Miss me—we've only just begun!

I don't understand.

Come now, Molly—do you really have the brains of a goat?

At the moment, yes. I probably do.

Through feat of combat you have taken Soren's place.

I'm on the Council?

You're the Great Seer of Harrowsgode.

Sigrid, no!

It's already done, my dear.

But why? Why would I want to rule a city that kept me a prisoner?

Because it's your ancestral home. Because there is so much here that is good, and we need your guidance. Because you were chosen to do it.

Well, I can't. I don't know how, and I won't even be there. I'm going back to Westria.

Your deputy can handle most of the work—meeting with the ministers, passing on the will of the Council, seeing to the general business of the city.

You?

Goodness, no. That wouldn't be appropriate at all. What I propose is that you choose a chief minister, someone who is not on the Council, nor even a Magus.

And you have someone in mind?

Yes. Prince Fredrik. By Harrowsgode law he is not permitted to rule while his father still lives; and since he's not a Magus he can't serve as Great Seer. But as your deputy, he can guide the city as he was born to do. It's quite legal, and it's what we should have done years ago—but Soren wouldn't allow it.

And don't worry. I'll guide you and teach you as best I can. I'll be by your side, watching you grow into your

marvelous Gift. In return, wherever you might be, you will lead us out into the world.

But I think you've done quite enough for one day, and your young man seems to need some reassurance. I'll just slip back into my mousehole now.

Molly opened her eyes. Tobias was holding her close in his arms. It was hard to see his face in the darkness; but she could feel his grief. She could hear his sobbing breaths.

"Tobias, you're crushing me!" she said, her voice scarcely more than a whisper.

"Oh," he said. "Oh, Molly. I thought you were dead!" He touched her cheek and sobbed some more. "You didn't answer when I called."

"I was . . . busy, but I'm all right now. Just very tired."

"Look!" He gestured with his hand to indicate the dry stones beneath them, the bright, starry sky above. "That was you, wasn't it?"

"Don't tell anyone. You have to promise."

"All right."

She coughed and stirred, tried to get up, and found she didn't have the strength.

"Tobias, you're going to have to help me into the saddle. I don't think I can do it myself, and I want to get out of this bloody canyon."

He gathered her up as tenderly as a father carries a sleeping child, then gently set her down beside the mare. When she was steady, he laced his hands and leaned down. She set her boot into them, and he helped her rise till she could swing her leg over the saddle. He guided her feet into the stirrups and collected the reins, placing them in her hands. Then wordlessly he turned and walked back to his mount, knowing in his heart that she had passed out of his universe that night. She was beyond him now, and all the devotion in the world could never bring her back.

⚄ 39 ⚄

Incantations

SIGRID CAME AGAIN IN THE NIGHT.

If anyone had been watching, they'd have heard Molly talking softly in her sleep, would have noticed the restless movements of head and hands, the play of expressions across her face. But nobody was. They were all asleep.

She woke now and sat up, pulling her blanket around her shoulders and hugging her knees. For a long time she stayed like that, staring into the dying coals, trying to work out her story. When she was ready, she went quietly over to the clearing where they'd built their fire and ran her fingers through the dirt, searching for two smooth stones of equal size,

smaller than a walnut but not as round.

Sigrid had been most specific, and Molly had feared she wouldn't be able to find them. Smooth stones were found in low places, where water ran. But they had camped on high ground. Yet there they were, side by side, half buried in the hard-packed earth at the very edge of the fire ring as though Sigrid had put them there.

She wiped them clean on her skirt. Then she held them as instructed—one in each hand, palms up—and began the Incantation of the Stones.

The words felt foreign on her tongue, and she didn't understand them. She'd merely learned them by rote, repeating after Sigrid many times. But when the stones grew warm and began to give off light, she knew she'd done it right.

She took a deep breath, shaking off her nervousness. This was a good beginning.

Now she went over to Tobias. Constance, who lay curled in the crook of his arm, woke and looked up; but he slept on, mouth slightly open, breathing heavily. The torrent in the canyon had washed him clean. His hair was tangled, but golden again.

With her right hand she carefully set the first stone on his forehead. With her left she laid the second on his chest, for remembrance and forgetting were matters of heart as well as mind. You cannot change the

one without the other.

They glowed softly in the darkness.

Now she set a thumb on each stone and began the Incantation of Forgetfulness. It was longer than the first, and some of the words had to be spoken with an uplift of the voice while others slid down, then up again. She focused all her attention on doing it perfectly. Then she lifted her thumbs, lowered them again, and repeated the incantation a second time.

Tobias's heart and mind were open now.

"You will forget everything about Harrowsgode," she whispered, "even its name. You will forget that I flew from a tower and what happened in the canyon tonight."

Twice more she repeated the Incantation of Forgetfulness, and it was complete. She'd erased a part of his life, robbed him of memories. It was a heavy thing to do, and it frightened her. But she trusted Sigrid, and Sigrid had said it must be done.

Now came the final charm, the Incantation of Remembering.

Molly sang the magical words softly, in a pure, sweet voice. When she came to *aii-kah,* she remembered to press down on the stones, as one does when planting a seed. When she came to the word *chi-ahn-o,* she raised them to the skies, as if calling forth the sun and the rain.

Now she filled the empty spaces in his heart and mind with a new reality, a new memory. Tobias would go through his life believing it had really happened—and she could never tell him otherwise.

She'd never lied to Tobias before. She didn't like to do it now. But she did.

"We left Faers-Wigan and went to the town where my grandfather was born. It's to the north and east of Austlind, and it's called Einarstadt. We met my cousin Jakob there, and he agreed to make us a cup. But it took him several weeks, so we had to wait. Einarstadt didn't have an inn—it'd burned down the year before—so we lodged with the villagers. I stayed with my cousin. You stayed with Richard Strange. We all became very fond of one another, and they decided to come back with us to Westria. Now we're on our way home.

"That's what you will remember."

She gazed down at Tobias, deep in unguarded sleep, the little dog cradled in the crook of his arm and a small stone glowing on his forehead. He seemed at peace now, and she was glad, for those long days he'd spent in that tomb of a tunnel, alone but for Constance and the rats, digging his way out, fearing for Molly's safety, knowing he was powerless to help her, had damaged him somehow.

Now those memories were gone, and with them the pain. They were erased forever from his heart and

mind. For good measure, just in case, she gave him one final gift.

"You were helpful to everyone, especially to Molly. You said funny things and made her laugh. And the whole time—every single minute, waking or sleeping—you were happy."

There. It was done.

As she sang the Song of Remembrance again, closing the loop and completing the enchantment, her voice broke; and she felt a wave of unaccountable grief pass over her. She didn't understand it, but it had something to do with the sweetness of his sleeping face and the surety that nothing would ever be the same again.

She removed the stones from his forehead and his chest. And then, impulsively, she leaned down and kissed his stubbly cheek. He sighed in his sleep and smiled.

⁂

As the night drew on, Molly worked the same magic on Winifred, Stephen, and Richard, adjusting the story slightly for each one as needed.

Mayhew she'd left for last. And as with Tobias, she gave him an extra gift: a vivid memory of a day he'd gone out riding in the countryside. He'd been restless hanging around Einarstadt while Jakob made the cup, so he'd

gone down to the river and rested there for a while.

Alaric had come into his mind then, and it had struck Mayhew suddenly, with the force of a blow, how very wrong he'd been about him. Yes, he was young and inexperienced in war, but he had a subtle mind and enormous courage. Mayhew might have acted as a father to the boy, supporting and encouraging him, helping him to grow into a great king. Instead, he'd schemed against him, mocking him behind his back and stirring up discontent among the nobles.

Oh, the tragedy of lost opportunity! He would confess it all to the king as soon as he returned to Dethemere. If it cost him his life, so be it.

Just then a fish had leaped out of the water, glittering silver in the afternoon sun—and Lord Mayhew had known, without the whisper of a doubt, that it had been a sign. Alaric would forgive him. They'd make a new beginning.

Molly smiled as she gave him this memory. It would do a powerful lot of good. It hadn't been part of the plan, and Sigrid might disapprove, but she didn't think so.

Now she sang the Song of Remembrance one final time. When she'd finished, Mayhew's enchantment complete, she left him and knelt in the grass, one stone in each hand, palms toward the sky. As she said the Incantation of the Stones in reverse, they grew dull

and cold, their magic gone. She put them back where she'd found them and went to sit beside her cousin.

"Jakob," she whispered into his ear. "Jakob!"

"What's the matter?" he said, startled.

"Shhh. Don't wake the others. I have something to tell you."

He rubbed his face, then sat up and crossed his legs.

"The secret of Harrowsgode is safe now," she said. "I laid an enchantment on each of them, removing all memory of their time in the city. They think we've been in a place called Einarstadt, in the northeast corner of the kingdom. Try to remember the name. That's where we met you and Richard."

"They taught you that at Harrowsgode Hall—how to do spells and charms?"

"No. I learned it from Sigrid tonight."

"Sigrid Morgansson? Of the Council?"

"Yes."

"Is she hiding behind a bush somewhere?" He smiled as he asked it.

"No. She's here. And here." She touched her head and her heart, knowing that he would understand. "She guides me now."

"You are a true Magus Mästare, then, whether

you're in Harrowsgode or not."

"I'm more than that, as you shall hear. But listen, Jakob. Wouldn't you like to see Laila again? See Sanna all grown up? Lorens, too—maybe in garnet robes next time? You might even find it in your heart to forgive your parents. I have."

"Don't, Molly! Do you think it was easy for me to walk away from them like that, knowing I could never return?"

"But you can—that's what I'm trying to tell you. Something happened tonight that changes everything. Jakob, remember in the garden when you said Harrowsgode folk only clasped hands with those they love and trust?"

He nodded.

"You said it was because Harrowsgode folk reveal ourselves when we touch; and for those with the Gift it comes pouring out of us like —"

"—water running downhill."

"—laying all our secrets bare. Well, tonight I'm like that water, so full of things to tell you that it wells up in me fit to bursting and must come rushing out. I ask you to clasp hands with me tonight, as cousins, with love and trust. And I will show you everything."

Then she reached out her hands, and Jakob took them.

⚡ 40 ⚡

The Cup

THEY'D ARRIVED AT THE INN late that afternoon.
Dinner was over now, the landlord had cleared away
the dishes, and the others had gone upstairs to bed.
Only the cousins had remained behind.

Jakob held a plain wooden box. It had been beside
him on the bench all during dinner. Now he handed it
nervously to Molly, wishing there'd been time to commission a proper presentation case—something made
of ebony, say, carved with initials or a coat of arms.

She looked up at him and smiled.

"Go ahead," he said. "Open it."

She took off the lid, handed it to Jakob, then lifted

out the package that lay nestled inside.

He'd wrapped it in layer after layer of silk, each of a different color, so that first there was emerald green, then scarlet, then saffron, then robin's-egg blue. Molly admired each one—so lovely—but really, he needn't have gone to all that trouble!

The final layer of silk—cloud white—dropped into her lap, and at last she held it in her hands: the Loving Cup. And it was a marvel.

The base, bold and masculine, was gilded and embellished with translucent enamels, pictures of delicate flowers and mythical beasts, framed in silver filigree. But the bowl of the cup was disarmingly simple, made of beaten silver. So perfect was its shape and size, so glorious its luster, that the base with all its knobs, and cartouches, and ornate decorations seemed to be reaching up in praise of the vessel itself, which was too perfect to require any ornament at all.

Molly said not a word, just laid the cup in her lap and gazed thoughtfully at the fire. Jakob felt the waves of disappointment rolling off of her.

"It's not right, is it? There's something wrong."

Still she was silent.

"I tempered the metal with my blood, just as William did."

"It's beautiful, Jakob," she finally said. "A masterpiece. A fitting gift for the greatest princess in the world."

"But . . ."

"That's all it is. A sip from this cup will not join two people together for life."

"Are you sure?"

She nodded. "Jakob—is this the cup you saw in your vision?"

"Yes. To the last detail."

"The inside of the bowl was silver, not gold?"

"Absolutely. That isn't what you saw?"

"No. In my vision, it was gilded. It glowed like the very sun."

"I don't understand that."

"Nor do I, but it has to mean something. You were supposed to make this cup, just as you saw it. And I was meant to give Alaric . . . a different cup. . . ."

"No," he said, "the same cup. It just—"

"—isn't finished!"

"Yes. I was meant to do what only a silversmith can. And I did. I made the cup that was shown to me in my vision. But *you* saw the cup in its final form. Molly, we were meant to finish it together."

"But how?"

"You'll see," he said.

⟨ 41 ⟩

Blood and Fire

THEY SAT SIDE BY SIDE at a long worktable, each
wearing a leather apron. They were in a famous goldsmith's workshop that had served the royal house of
Westria for many generations. But on this particular
day the shop was quiet, the apprentices and journey-
men off for the day and the doors shut to customers.
Molly and Jakob were alone there except for the master goldsmith, who sat politely at the far end of the
table and never left off watching them. They'd paid
him handsomely for the use of his shop; but he didn't
know them, and he had a fortune in jewels and precious metals to protect.

"In this bowl," Jakob was explaining to Molly, "we have powdered gold. And in this one we have mercury."

"It looks like liquid silver."

"Yes. It's called 'quicksilver' for that very reason. Now in a moment I'll heat them both in the furnace. The gold will melt into a liquid, and the mercury will become thinner and more watery. Then I'll mix them together—six parts of mercury to one part of gold."

"What am I supposed to do? We were meant to do this together."

"And so we will," he said, pulling his knife from its scabbard and setting it down before her. "We'll start right now, in fact—because there's a third ingredient that's not in the usual formula."

She cocked her head.

"Blood, Molly—remember? And apparently it has to be yours. That's why you saw gold inside the cup when I saw silver. The enchantment comes with the gilding."

She nodded, then studied her hand, back and front. At last she took up the dagger and made a neat slice, not too deep, right over a web of tiny veins near the spot where her thumb met the wrist. Holding her hand over the bowl, she watched the scarlet drops fall onto powdered gold. When she judged it was enough,

she looked up at Jakob, who was ready with a strip of gauze to bind her wound.

"Excuse me," said the goldsmith, rising to his feet. "Why did you do that?"

"Ah," said Jakob. "We temper the metal with blood. An old trick from Austlind."

"Wouldn't chicken blood do just as well?"

"No doubt. I didn't think you'd have any on hand."

"But the lady—"

"The lady is fine," Molly said.

He sat down again.

Jakob set the two bowls into the forge with tongs, then pumped air onto the coals with a bellows. When enough time had passed, he removed them again and set them on the table. Then he poured the molten gold into the bowl of mercury, raising up a cloud of smoke.

"Now stir it with this," he said, handing her an iron rod. "Faster. Mix it really well."

While she stirred, Jakob opened the box that held the cup. He made rather a ceremony of removing the silk wrappings, for the entertainment of the goldsmith, who was leaning forward now, curious.

"Where did you get that, young man?" he asked.

"I made it," Jakob said, smiling at the man's astonishment. "Now, I'll need some aqua fortis, if you please, to prepare the cup for the gold. And a strip of chamois too."

When the inside of the cup was ready, cleaned of oils and dirt, the surface bitten by the acid in the aqua fortis so the gilding would stick, Jakob squeezed the mercury out through the chamois, leaving mostly gold behind. It was thicker now, the consistency of butter, and yellower than before; but it didn't really look like gold.

"Don't worry," he told Molly. "There's still a lot of mercury in with the gold. We'll burn it off in a minute. But for now we have a nice soft paste you can easily paint onto the cup."

"Me?"

"Yes. I'll show you."

Molly worked with careful, patient strokes, smoothing out ridges, filling in any spots she'd missed. But it wasn't perfect, and it didn't look gold.

"Well done," Jakob said, making a few minor touch-ups.

Once again the goldsmith interrupted. "Excuse me, young man, but I'm a bit concerned about your enamels. Might I suggest—?"

"It's all right. I have a solution. See what you think."

"What's the matter with your enamels?" Molly asked.

"We have to heat the cup to drive off the mercury. It'll turn to smoke and fly off into the air, leaving just the gold behind. Normally we'd put the cup right into

the furnace, but we can't do that because I've already done the enamels; and since they're made of glass, they'll melt. But we can work around it. It'll take a lot longer, and we'll sweat like a pair of lost souls in hell; but it's more poetic, I think. You shall hold the fire, and I shall hold the cup."

Jakob took a clean linen cloth and folded it, as though to make a bandage or a blindfold, and tied it around Molly's mouth and nose to protect her from the fumes. Then he made a mask for himself. Finally he wrapped the base of the cup in many layers of wet rags to keep it cool and to protect the enamels.

"All right, cousin," he said, "I want you to take those tongs and find yourself a nice, hot coal. Good. Now hold it inside the cup, but try not to touch the surface of the gold. It's not easy, I know. I'll take a turn when you get tired."

It *wasn't* easy, and it took hours. Their arms ached, the fumes stung their eyes, and the heat was almost unbearable. At one point the goldsmith offered to help, but Molly sent him away. And slowly, coal by coal, the mercury was driven off into the air, leaving gleaming gold behind.

"What do you think?" Jakob said as he wiped the cup clean. "How does it look?"

"It glows like the sun."

"Pick it up."

"I don't need to. I already know the answer."

"Pick it up anyway. I want to do this properly."

"All right." She stood and held the cup exactly as she'd seen him holding it in her visions, at about chest height, like an offering. "This chalice," she said softly so only he could hear, "is not merely a beautiful work by a great artist; it is a true Loving Cup. It has the power to bind two souls together for life, to bless their children and their children's children down through the generations. Thank you, Jakob."

While Molly was wrapping the cup in its silken swaddling clothes, the goldsmith came over to Jakob. "Are you a licensed journeyman, lad? I believe you must be, though you look quite young."

"I've served out my apprenticeship, but I left Austlind before I was able to prove my competence."

"Would you like to work for me? I'll see you through the approval process with the guild. It should be easy. You have only to show them that cup, and they'll grant you journeyman status right away."

"The cup is not available," Molly said. "It's a gift for the king."

"For the king! Well, I imagine he'll be very glad to own such a beautiful piece."

"He will," she said. "I'm sure of it."

"Then you'll just have to make something new. I'll pay you full journeyman's wages, right from the beginning, even before you receive your papers. Watching you just now, I was most impressed."

"He isn't interested," Molly said, setting the lid on the box.

"I don't mean to offend, lady, but shouldn't the young gentleman speak for himself?"

"I suppose. But I rather think he'll be setting up his own shop. He'll be coming into a lot of money soon. The king is famous for his gratitude."

"A partnership, perhaps. We might consider—"

"Thank you, Master Goldsmith, for your generous offer. And thank you, Cousin, as well. But I'd rather wait a while before deciding what to do. I just might be going home."

⟨ 42 ⟩

Once Again in the Garden

THE GARDEN WAS FADING now. The roses and the lilies were over, and some of the beds were bare, the withered plants cut back to the ground. But the trees were bursting into autumn color. Red and yellow leaves covered the ground. As they walked the paths arm in arm again, Molly could feel the change. The world was shifting toward winter.

Nothing in nature ever stayed the same. Not even Alaric. Not even Molly.

"Stephen says you returned three days ago," said the king. "I'm sorry I wasn't here. I was up north hunting, if you can believe it, entertaining a pompous duke

and a brace of arrogant lords."

"Did you kill anything?"

"I did, much to the astonishment of my guests, who think me a pup and a weakling—though one could hardly grow up at King Reynard's court, as I did, without learning how to use a bow."

"It was a success, then?"

"No one pulled a dagger on me."

"Is it really that bad?"

"No. I exaggerate. A little."

He ran his fingers through his hair, thinking.

"Molly, I had a private interview with Lord Mayhew this morning. At his request."

"I see."

"Yes, I imagine you do—better than I, most likely. I should have been more forthright with you, about why I chose him to guide you into Austlind."

"That's all right. I figured it out."

"You did?"

"It wasn't that hard. How did the interview go?"

"I won't reveal everything he said, though I doubt any of it would surprise you. He confessed things to me that he needn't have, practically laid his head out on the chopping block and invited me to have the thing off. Pride, I suppose. He's a man of honor, determined to take his licks when he feels they're deserved."

"And?"

"I forgave him, and he was grateful. He knelt, and kissed my hand, and swore his undying fealty. I rather think you had something to do with all that."

"In a roundabout sort of way."

"Then, once again I am in your debt. I don't know how I would have managed if he'd gone on working against me like that, stirring up ill feeling. I might have had an insurrection on my hands—on top of my cousin Reynard nipping at my heels. Now I have a very useful ally where I once had an enemy. All thanks to you, Molly. I sometimes wonder if there's anything you cannot do."

"A bargain, Your Highness?"

"A bargain?"

"I'll stop blaming my upbringing, such as it was, for my every rude remark if you'll stop saying that I can work miracles."

"But I truly believe you can."

"And I truly believe that I was ill raised."

"A bargain, then." Alaric smiled as he said this, but the smile slipped quickly away.

He'd grown solemn since becoming king, but he was more solemn now than before. The weight of responsibility, which had come to him so tragically and while he was yet so young, was with him every

hour of the day. It had snuffed out the bright joy that once had been a part of his nature. For never was there a more ardent king, determined to rule with wisdom and courage, no matter what it cost him. He looked older now, and exhausted.

"Stephen's not really your valet, is he?" she said.

He stopped on the pathway, threw back his head, and laughed. "No, Molly, he is not. When my parents sent me to Austlind as a boy, they sent Stephen, too—as my 'minder,' to make sure I didn't disgrace myself at Reynard's court. In time he became more like a father. Now he is my close adviser and trusted friend. Acting as my valet gives him good cover. People discount him and speak freely when he's around—just a servant, you know. It's very convenient."

"I can see that. I like him very much."

"I thought you would. So—that box you're carrying. I assume it holds the cup?"

"Yes. Why don't we go over to that bench by the pond. It'll be easier for you to open it if you're sitting down."

"All right. But tell me, is it the real thing? Made by your grandfather?"

"Yes and no. It's the real thing, but my cousin Jakob made it. And don't look so disappointed. It was made especially for you."

They turned a corner and walked through the boxwood arch. Straight ahead was the pond, the stone fish still standing on its tail, still spouting water. They sat on the bench, and Molly handed Alaric the box.

"Jakob wishes me to tell you that he's sorry the case is so plain. There wasn't time to order a proper one."

"It doesn't matter. I'll have a cabinetmaker build me a presentation case, with the arms of Cortova on it and Elizabetta's initials."

He took off the lid and started unwrapping the layers of silk.

"It's very powerful, Alaric. The bond it forms can never be broken."

He looked up at her. "What are you saying?"

"Just use it carefully, that's all. Use it wisely."

"That has always been my intention."

"Good. Because once the princess sets her lips to the cup, there's no turning back."

"I will take that under advisement."

The last layer of silk came off, and now the cup was revealed. He held it up to the sunlight, turning it in his hands. "Your cousin made this?"

"Yes. And he refused any payment. I believe a handsome reward might be appropriate."

"Without question. This is astonishing work. I am overcome."

"And while you're at it—being generous, I mean—you might do something for Richard."

"The ratcatcher who followed you home? Why?"

"Because you're in my debt, and that's how I wish to be paid."

"Are you *serious*?"

"Yes."

"All right, then. What does the fellow want?"

"Nothing at all. This is entirely my idea, and he doesn't know I'm asking. Alaric, Richard is an amazing man, very generous and kind. A good storyteller, too. He entertained us wonderfully on the road during our return. But he told me one story in private that wasn't comical at all—quite sad, in fact—about his childhood. And, well, it set me to thinking."

"What?"

"I believe Richard would find it . . . very amusing, and deeply satisfying, if you were to make him a lord."

The king laughed at that quite merrily. "Sir Richard, Lord Rattington?"

"Perhaps something a little more conventional would be better. Alaric, I *did* think twice before asking this of you. I know you're in a delicate position just now, and you took a risk when you raised Tobias and

me to high estate. But perhaps you could do it quietly, not call undue attention to it. And you needn't give him lands or a house. He'll be staying on with Tobias at his estate."

"All right, then. Consider it done."

She grinned. "You will make a good man very happy."

"Then I'm glad it's in my power to do so. Now listen, Molly. I'd like you to remain at court this time and not go back to Barcliffe Manor. I trust you will not mind."

"Not in the least."

"The others may go home, of course—Winifred and Tobias. And I have *nothing* against the boy, Molly. I just don't need him."

"I understand you, Alaric."

He studied her for a moment, his head cocked at an angle. "What have they done with Molly, and who is this person they've put in her place?"

She laughed.

"Truly. You've grown up in—what has it been? Five, six weeks?"

"Horse flop! I'm just not my usual annoying self today. And I brought you the thing you wanted."

"Oh, Molly—*please* don't play a part with me."

"I'm sorry. I did it out of habit. It's . . . my armor."

He was looking at her now straight on, with something on his face she'd never seen before. It was the most intimate moment they'd ever shared. Molly felt as if she'd taken in a deep breath and couldn't let it out.

"Something happened to you in Austlind," he said.

She didn't speak. Still he held her eyes.

"And it's changed you. It lifts you up, even as it weighs you down. And you can't tell me what it is."

Oh, help me, Sigrid! Molly thought.

"It has set you on a path for life and laid a great burden on your shoulders. It was thrust upon you unexpectedly, but you accepted it all the same."

Sigrid? Is it permitted?

"It came at a heavy price. And now it's breaking your heart."

Do you trust him to keep our secret?

Oh, yes! With all my heart!

Then what are you waiting for, child?

❧ 43 ❧

Ravens

HE'D ALREADY SAID his good-byes, but he had to see Molly one last time. So he circled Dethemere for several hours till he saw them in the garden. They were sitting together on the bench beside the pond. Neither of them looked up.

So he rose into the sky and banked toward the east. He knew where to find her, and it wasn't far. She'd promised she would wait.

Soon they would soar through the skies together again side by side, dancing in the air, dropping and rising, one form mirroring the other. They would lock their talons and fly in loops, like a pair of acrobats. It

would be wonderful.

Then they'd find a home and build a nest. She would be his, and he would be hers, for as long as they lived. A bond that could never be broken.

And at last he would be complete.

CONTENTS

This book is dedicated to Peter,
who is always there to listen
and who says wonderful things, like,
What if you had a ratcatcher?

Library of Congress Cataloging-in-Publication Data is available.
ISBN 978-0-06-196321-6 (trade bdg.)

Typography by Adam B. Bohannon
12 13 14 15 16   LP/RRDH   10 9 8 7 6 5 4 3 2 1
❖
First Edition

The
Cup and the Crown

Diane Stanley

HARPER

An Imprint of HarperCollinsPublishers

DYLAN THOMAS. Before his tragic death at 39, Dylan Thomas was already recognized as the greatest lyric poet of the younger generation. Wide appreciation of his fiction and other prose writings has been largely posthumous.

Born in 1914 in the Welsh seaport of Swansea, he was early steeped in Welsh lore and poetry, and in the Bible, all of which left their mark on his rich, startling imagery and driving rhythms. As a boy, he said he "was small, thin, indecisively active, quick to get dirty, curly." His formal education ended with the Swansea Grammar school; and thereafter he was at various times a newspaper reporter, a "hack writer," an odd-job man, a documentary film scriptwriter.

The rich resonance of his "Welsh-singing" voice led to Dylan Thomas reading other poets' work as well as his own over the B.B.C. Third Programme. It also brought him to the United States, in 1950, '52 and '53, where he gave readings of his own and other poetry in as many as 40 university towns, and made three magnificent long playing records published by Caedmon. "I don't believe in New York," he said, "but I love Third Avenue."

Since Dylan Thomas's death in 1953 his reputation and popularity have steadily increased. His poetry is studied in hundreds of American colleges, and his prose books such as *Adventures in the Skin Trade, Portrait of the Artist as a Young Dog, Quite Early One Morning* and *A Child's Christmas in Wales* are paperback bestsellers. Many books have been written about his life and work, while a play about him, in which Alec Guinness portrayed Dylan, was a Broadway hit. New Directions has also published an anthology of the poetry of other poets which Thomas recited at his famous readings entitled *Dylan Thomas's Choice.*

UNDER MILK WOOD

ALSO BY DYLAN THOMAS

Collected Poems
Adventures in the Skin Trade
The Doctor and the Devils
The Notebooks
Portrait of the Artist as a Young Dog
Quite Early One Morning
Selected Letters
Letters to Vernon Watkins
A Child's Christmas in Wales,
illustrated by Fritz Eichenberg
A Child's Christmas in Wales,
illustrated by Ellen Raskin

———•—•———

Dylan Thomas's Choice

Dylan Thomas

UNDER MILK WOOD

A PLAY FOR VOICES

A *New Directions* PAPERBOOK

THIRTEENTH PRINTING

Contents

PREFACE

On the ninth of November, 1953, a few days after his thirty-ninth birthday, Dylan Thomas died in New York. At the time of his death a new poem was still unfinished, and the collaboration with Stravinsky, planned for the end of the year, had not even begun. The survival of *Under Milk Wood* is a remarkable piece of good fortune, for it was not completed until Thomas came within a month of his death, though he had worked intermittently on the play for nearly ten years. There was no time for any final revision of the text by the poet himself, but we are justified in regarding what he has left as a complete work.

The publication of Thomas's *Collected Poems* in 1953 marked the end of one period of his literary development; after this, according to his own words, he intended to turn from the strictly personal kind of poetry to a more public form of expression, and to large-scale dramatic works, in particular, where there would be scope for all his versatility, for his gifts of humour and characterisation as well as his genius for poetry. It is fortunate that at least one of these projected works has been preserved for us.

Under Milk Wood, a Play for Voices grew by a slow and natural process, and the story of that growth, known only to a few friends of the poet, is most interesting. Thomas liked small towns by the sea best, and small Welsh towns by the sea best of all. Before the war, he lived for many years in Laugharne, and during the war, for a time in New Quay; there is no doubt that he absorbed the spirit of these places and, through imagination and insight, the spirit of all other places like them. When, more than ten years ago, a short talk was commissioned by the B.B.C., the description of a small Welsh seaside town was a natural choice of subject. *Quite Early One Morning*, short as it is, and written so many years ago, is closely related to *Under Milk Wood*. There is the same sequence of time, though limited to the morning hours and in winter, not spring; we hear the dreams of the sleeping town and see the sleepers getting up and going about their business. Captain Tiny Evans and the Reverend Thomas Evans are pygmies beside the blind seacaptain and the reverend bard of Llareggub, but Miss Hughes "The Cosy" recalls Myfanwy Price, Manchester House stands ready for Mog Edwards, and the husbands of Mrs. Ogmore-Pritchard are already at their tasks: "Dust the china, feed the canary, sweep the drawing-room floor; and before you let the sun in, mind he wipes his shoes."

The success of this broadcast talk suggested to Thomas a more extended work against the same kind of background. At first he was unable to decide upon the form of the work, and there was much discussion with friends about a stage play, a comedy in verse, and a radio play with a blind man as narrator and central character. The blind man, a natural bridge between eye and ear for the radio listener, survives in

Under Milk Wood, with the difference that Captain Cat is made to share his central position with two anonymous narrators. But the simple time sequence of *Quite Early One Morning,* which resembles the pattern of *Under Milk Wood* so closely, at first appeared inadequate; some kind of plot seemed to be necessary. Thomas thought he had found the theme he wanted in the contrast between Llareggub and the surrounding world, the conflict between the eccentrics, strong in their individuality and freedom, and the sane ones who sacrifice everything to some notion of conformity. The whole population of Llareggub cannot very well be accommodated inside the walls of a lunatic asylum; so the sane world decrees that the town itself shall be declared an "insane area," with all traffic and goods diverted from it. Captain Cat, spokesman of the indignant citizens, insists that the sanity of Llareggub should be put on trial in the townhall with every legal formality; he will be Counsel for the Defense and the citizens themselves will be witnesses. The trial takes place, but it comes to a surprising end. The final speech for the Prosecution consists of a full and minute description of the ideally sane town; as soon as they hear this, the people of Llareggub withdraw their defense and beg to be cordoned off from the sane world as soon as possible.

Once more settled in his house overlooking Laugharne Estuary, Thomas began working according to the plan of "The Town Was Mad," as he called it, and brought the action up to the delivery of letters by Willy Nilly, the postman; but by that time he had changed his mind, and there was no letter for Captain

Cat about the sanity or the insanity of the town. When this first part of *Under Milk Wood*, with the provisional title *Llareggub, a Piece for Radio Perhaps*, appeared for the first time in *Botteghe Oscure,* * Thomas had returned to the plan of *Quite Early One Morning;* his intention was to limit the picture to the town itself, with hardly a suggestion of a world beyond the town, and to extend the time sequence to form a complete cycle.

Before Thomas's third visit to the United States in 1953, the title *Under Milk Wood, a Play for Voices* was decided upon, the first part, *Llareggub,* was revised, and the work had been extended to the end of Polly Garter's Song, where it first appears. In this form, the play was read at the Kaufmann Auditorium of the Young Men's Hebrew Association on the fifteenth and the twenty-ninth of May; the poet himself read the parts of the First Voice and the Reverend Eli Jenkins.

As soon as Thomas returned to Britain, the B.B.C. urged him to complete the work without further delay, and, by omitting some projected ballads and unfinished material for the closing section, he was able to supply a finished version at the end of October. The first broadcast of the whole work, produced by Douglas Cleverdon with a distinguished all-Welsh cast, was given on January 25, 1954, with a repetition two days later.

In case *Under Milk Wood* falls into the hands of a Welsh philologist, it must be made clear that the

*Quaderno IX, edited by Marguerite Caetani (Rome, 1952).

language used is Anglo-Welsh. Dylan Thomas spoke no Welsh, and the reader must imitate his inconsistency if he wishes to hear the words as they were pronounced by the poet himself. Notes on pronunciation will be found at the end of the text.

Daniel Jones
January, 1954

A trial performance of *Under Milk Wood* was given on May 14, 1953, under the auspices of the Poetry Center of the Young Men's and Young Women's Hebrew Association, New York City. Dylan Thomas directed the production and read the parts of the First Voice, Second Drowned, Fifth Drowned, and the Reverend Eli Jenkins. The other parts were played by Dion Allen, Allen F. Collins, Roy Poole, Sada Thompson, and Nancy Wickwire.

CAST OF CHARACTERS

First Voice
Second Voice
Captain Cat
First Drowned
Second Drowned
Rosie Probert
Third Drowned
Fourth Drowned
Fifth Drowned
Mr Mog Edwards
Miss Myfanwy Price
Jack Black
Waldo's Mother
Little Boy Waldo
Waldo's Wife

Mr Waldo
First Neighbour
Second Neighbour
Third Neighbour
Fourth Neighbour
Matti's Mother
First Woman
Second Woman
Third Woman
Fourth Woman
Fifth Woman
Preacher
Mrs Ogmore-Pritchard
Mr Ogmore
Mr Pritchard

Gossamer Beynon	Lord Cut-Glass
Organ Morgan	Voice of a Guide-Book
Utah Watkins	Mrs Beynon
Mrs Utah Watkins	Mrs Pugh
Ocky Milkman	Mrs Dai Bread One
A Voice	Mrs Dai Bread Two
Mrs Willy Nilly	Willy Nilly
Lily Smalls	Mrs Cherry Owen
Mae Rose Cottage	Cherry Owen
Butcher Beynon	Sinbad Sailors
Reverend Eli Jenkins	Old Man
Mr Pugh	Evans the Death
Mrs Organ Morgan	Fisherman
Mary Ann Sailors	Child's Voice
Dai Bread	Bessie Bighead
Polly Garter	A Drinker
Nogood Boyo	

UNDER MILK WOOD

UNDER MILK WOOD

[*Silence*]

FIRST VOICE (*Very softly*)

To begin at the beginning:

It is Spring, moonless night in the small town, starless and bible-black, the cobblestreets silent and the hunched, courters'-and-rabbits' wood limping invisible down to the sloeblack, slow, black, crowblack, fishingboat-bobbing sea. The houses are blind as moles (though moles see fine to-night in the snouting, velvet dingles) or blind as Captain Cat there in the muffled middle by the pump and the town clock, the shops in mourning, the Welfare Hall in widows' weeds. And all the people of the lulled and dumbfound town are sleeping now.

Hush, the babies are sleeping, the farmers, the fishers, the tradesmen and pensioners, cobbler, schoolteacher, postman and publican, the undertaker and the fancy woman, drunkard, dressmaker, preacher, policeman, the webfoot cocklewomen and the tidy wives. Young girls lie bedded soft or glide in their dreams, with rings and trousseaux, bridesmaided by glowworms down the aisles of the organplaying wood. The boys are dreaming wicked or of the bucking

1

ranches of the night and the jollyrodgered sea. And the anthracite statues of the horses sleep in the fields, and the cows in the byres, and the dogs in the wet-nosed yards; and the cats nap in the slant corners or lope sly, streaking and needling, on the one cloud of the roofs.

You can hear the dew falling, and the hushed town breathing.

Only *your* eyes are unclosed to see the black and folded town fast, and slow, asleep.

And you alone can hear the invisible starfall, the darkest-before-dawn minutely dewgrazed stir of the black, dab-filled sea where the *Arethusa*, the *Curlew* and the *Skylark*, *Zanzibar*, *Rhiannon*, the *Rover*, the *Cormorant*, and the *Star of Wales* tilt and ride.

Listen. It is night moving in the streets, the processional salt slow musical wind in Coronation Street and Cockle Row, it is the grass growing on Llareggub Hill, dewfall, starfall, the sleep of birds in Milk Wood.

Listen. It is night in the chill, squat chapel, hymning in bonnet and brooch and bombazine black, butterfly choker and bootlace bow, coughing like nanny-goats, sucking mintoes, fortywinking hallelujah; night in the four-ale, quiet as a domino; in Ocky Milkman's lofts like a mouse with gloves; in Dai Bread's bakery flying like black flour. It is to-night in Donkey Street, trotting silent, with seaweed on its hooves, along the cockled cobbles, past curtained fernpot, text and trinket, harmonium, holy dresser, watercolours done by hand, china dog and rosy tin teacaddy. It is night neddying among the snuggeries of babies.

Look. It is night, dumbly, royally winding through

2

the Coronation cherry trees; going through the grave-yard of Bethesda with winds gloved and folded, and dew doffed; tumbling by the Sailors Arms.

Time passes. Listen. Time passes.

Come closer now.

Only you can hear the houses sleeping in the streets in the slow deep salt and silent black, bandaged night. Only you can see, in the blinded bedrooms, the combs and petticoats over the chairs, the jugs and basins, the glasses of teeth, Thou Shalt Not on the wall, and the yellowing dickybird-watching pictures of the dead. Only you can hear and see, behind the eyes of the sleepers, the movements and countries and mazes and colours and dismays and rainbows and tunes and wishes and flight and fall and despairs and big seas of their dreams.

From where you are, you can hear their dreams.

Captain Cat, the retired blind seacaptain, asleep in his bunk in the seashelled, ship-in-bottled, shipshape best cabin of Schooner House dreams of

SECOND VOICE

never such seas as any that swamped the decks of his S.S. *Kidwelly* bellying over the bedclothes and jellyfish-slippery sucking him down salt deep into the Davy dark where the fish come biting out and nibble him down to his wishbone, and the long drowned nuzzle up to him.

FIRST DROWNED

Remember me, Captain?

3

You're Dancing Williams!

FIRST DROWNED
I lost my step in Nantucket.

SECOND DROWNED
Do you see me, Captain? the white bone talking?
I'm Tom-Fred the donkeyman ... we shared the same
girl once ... her name was Mrs Probert ...

WOMAN'S VOICE
Rosie Probert, thirty three Duck Lane. Come on
up, boys, I'm dead.

THIRD DROWNED
Hold me, Captain, I'm Jonah Jarvis, come to a
bad end, very enjoyable.

FOURTH DROWNED
Alfred Pomeroy Jones, sealawyer, born in Mum-
bles, sung like a linnet, crowned you with a flagon,
tattooed with mermaids, thirst like a dredger, died of
blisters.

FIRST DROWNED
This skull at your earhole is

FIFTH DROWNED
Curly Bevan. Tell my auntie it was me that
pawned the ormolu clock.

CAPTAIN CAT
Aye, aye, Curly.

SECOND DROWNED
Tell my missus no I never

THIRD DROWNED
I never done what she said I never

FOURTH DROWNED
Yes, they did.

FIFTH DROWNED
And who brings coconuts and shawls and parrots
to *my* Gwen now?

FIRST DROWNED
How's it above?

SECOND DROWNED
Is there rum and lavabread?

THIRD DROWNED
Bosoms and robins?

FOURTH DROWNED
Concertinas?

FIFTH DROWNED
Ebenezer's bell?

FIRST DROWNED
Fighting and onions?

SECOND DROWNED

And sparrows and daisies?

THIRD DROWNED

Tiddlers in a jamjar?

FOURTH DROWNED

Buttermilk and whippets?

FIFTH DROWNED

Rock-a-bye baby?

FIRST DROWNED

Washing on the line?

SECOND DROWNED

And old girls in the snug?

THIRD DROWNED

How's the tenors in Dowlais?

FOURTH DROWNED

Who milks the cows in Maesgwyn?

FIFTH DROWNED

When she smiles, is there dimples?

FIRST DROWNED

What's the smell of parsley?

CAPTAIN CAT

Oh, my dead dears!

From where you are, you can hear in Cockle Row in the spring, moonless night, Miss Price, dressmaker and sweetshop-keeper, dream of

her lover, tall as the town clock tower, Samson-syrup-gold-maned, whacking thighed and piping hot, thunderbolt-bass'd and barnacle-breasted, flailing up the cockles with his eyes like blowlamps and scooping low over her lonely loving hotwaterbottled body.

MR EDWARDS
Myfanwy Price!

MISS PRICE
Mr Mog Edwards!

MR EDWARDS
I am a draper mad with love. I love you more than all the flannelette and calico, candlewick, dimity, crash and merino, tussore, cretonne, crépon, muslin, poplin, ticking and twill in the whole Cloth Hall of the world. I have come to take you away to my Emporium on the hill, where the change hums on wires. Throw away your little bedsocks and your Welsh wool knitted jacket, I will warm the sheets like an electric toaster, I will lie by your side like the Sunday roast.

MISS PRICE
I will knit you a wallet of forget-me-not blue, for the money to be comfy. I will warm your heart by the

7

fire so that you can slip it in under your vest when
the shop is closed.

MR EDWARDS

Myfanwy, Myfanwy, before the mice gnaw at
your bottom drawer will you say

MISS PRICE

Yes, Mog, yes, Mog, yes, yes, yes.

MR EDWARDS

And all the bells of the tills of the town shall ring
for our wedding.

[*Noise of money-tills and chapel bells*

FIRST VOICE

Come now, drift up the dark, come up the drifting
sea-dark street now in the dark night seesawing like
the sea, to the bible-black airless attic over Jack Black
the cobbler's shop where alone and savagely Jack
Black sleeps in a nightshirt tied to his ankles with
elastic and dreams of

SECOND VOICE

chasing the naughty couples down the grassgreen
gooseberried double bed of the wood, flogging the
tosspots in the spit-and-sawdust, driving out the bare
bold girls from the sixpenny hops of his nightmares.

JACK BLACK (*Loudly*)
Ach y fi!
Ach y fi!

Evans the Death, the undertaker,

laughs high and aloud in his sleep and curls up his toes as he sees, upon waking fifty years ago, snow lie deep on the goosefield behind the sleeping house; and he runs out into the field where his mother is making welshcakes in the snow, and steals a fistful of snow-flakes and currants and climbs back to bed to eat them cold and sweet under the warm, white clothes while his mother dances in the snow kitchen crying out for her lost currants.

And in the little pink-eyed cottage next to the undertaker's, lie, alone, the seventeen snoring gentle stone of Mister Waldo, rabbitcatcher, barber, herbalist, catdoctor, quack, his fat pink hands, palms up, over the edge of the patchwork quilt, his black boots neat and tidy in the washing-basin, his bowler on a nail above the bed, a milk stout and a slice of cold bread pudding under the pillow; and, dripping in the dark, he dreams of

This little piggy went to market
This little piggy stayed at home
This little piggy had roast beef
This little piggy had none
And this little piggy went

9

LITTLE BOY
wee wee wee wee wee

MOTHER
all the way home to

WIFE (*Screaming*)
Waldo! Wal-do!

MR WALDO
Yes, Blodwen love?

WIFE
Oh, what'll the neighbours say, what'll the neighbours . . .

FIRST NEIGHBOUR
Poor Mrs Waldo

SECOND NEIGHBOUR
What she puts up with

FIRST NEIGHBOUR
Never should of married

SECOND NEIGHBOUR
If she didn't had to

FIRST NEIGHBOUR
Same as her mother

SECOND NEIGHBOUR
There's a husband for you

FIRST NEIGHBOUR

Bad as his father

SECOND NEIGHBOUR

And you know where he ended

FIRST NEIGHBOUR

Up in the asylum

SECOND NEIGHBOUR

Crying for his ma

FIRST NEIGHBOUR

Every Saturday

SECOND NEIGHBOUR

He hasn't got a leg

FIRST NEIGHBOUR

And carrying on

SECOND NEIGHBOUR

With that Mrs Beattie Morris

FIRST NEIGHBOUR

Up in the quarry

SECOND NEIGHBOUR

And seen her baby

FIRST NEIGHBOUR

It's got his nose

SECOND NEIGHBOUR
Oh, it makes my heart bleed

FIRST NEIGHBOUR
What he'll do for drink

SECOND NEIGHBOUR
He sold the pianola

FIRST NEIGHBOUR
And her sewing machine

SECOND NEIGHBOUR
Falling in the gutter

FIRST NEIGHBOUR
Talking to the lamp-post

SECOND NEIGHBOUR
Using language

FIRST NEIGHBOUR
Singing in the w.

SECOND NEIGHBOUR
Poor Mrs Waldo

WIFE (*Tearfully*)
... Oh, Waldo, Waldo!

MR WALDO
Hush, love, hush. I'm *widower* Waldo now.

MOTHER (*Screaming*)
Waldo, Wal-do!

LITTLE BOY
Yes, our mum?

MOTHER
Oh, what'll the neighbours say, what'll the neighbours . . .

THIRD NEIGHBOUR
Black as a chimbley

FOURTH NEIGHBOUR
Ringing doorbells

THIRD NEIGHBOUR
Breaking windows

FOURTH NEIGHBOUR
Making mudpies

THIRD NEIGHBOUR
Stealing currants

FOURTH NEIGHBOUR
Chalking words

THIRD NEIGHBOUR
Saw him in the bushes

FOURTH NEIGHBOUR
Playing mwchins

13

THIRD NEIGHBOUR
Send him to bed without any supper

FOURTH NEIGHBOUR
Give him sennapods and lock him in the dark

THIRD NEIGHBOUR
Off to the reformatory

FOURTH NEIGHBOUR
Off to the reformatory

TOGETHER
Learn him with a slipper on his b.t.m.

ANOTHER MOTHER (*Screaming*)
Waldo, Wal-do! What you doing with our Matti?

LITTLE BOY
Give us a kiss, Matti Richards.

LITTLE GIRL
Give us a penny then.

MR WALDO
I only got a halfpenny.

FIRST WOMAN
Lips is a penny.

PREACHER
Will you take this woman Matti Richards

SECOND WOMAN

Dulcie Prothero

THIRD WOMAN

Effie Bevan

FOURTH WOMAN

Lil the Gluepot

FIFTH WOMAN

Mrs Flusher

WIFE

Blodwen Bowen

PREACHER

To be your awful wedded wife

LITTLE BOY (*Screaming*)

No, no, no!

FIRST VOICE

Now, in her iceberg-white, holily laundered crinoline nightgown, under virtuous polar sheets, in her spruced and scoured dust-defying bedroom in trig and trim Bay View, a house for paying guests at the top of the town, Mrs Ogmore-Pritchard, widow, twice, of Mr Ogmore, linoleum, retired, and Mr Pritchard, failed bookmaker, who maddened by besoming, swabbing and scrubbing, the voice of the vacuum-cleaner and the fume of polish, ironically swallowed disinfectant, fidgets in her rinsed sleep, wakes in a dream, and nudges in the ribs dead Mr Ogmore, dead Mr Pritchard, ghostly on either side.

MRS OGMORE-PRITCHARD

Mr Ogmore!
Mr Pritchard!
It is time to inhale your balsam.

MR OGMORE

Oh, Mrs Ogmore!

MR PRITCHARD

Oh, Mrs Pritchard!

MRS PRITCHARD

Soon it will be time to get up.
Tell me your tasks, in order.

MR OGMORE

I must put my pyjamas in the drawer marked pyjamas.

MR PRITCHARD

I must take my cold bath which is good for me.

MR OGMORE

I must wear my flannel band to ward off sciatica.

MR PRITCHARD

I must dress behind the curtain and put on my apron.

MR OGMORE
I must blow my nose.

MRS OGMORE-PRITCHARD
In the garden, if you please.

MR OGMORE
In a piece of tissue-paper which I afterwards burn.

MR PRITCHARD
I must take my salts which are nature's friend.

MR OGMORE
I must boil the drinking water because of germs.

MR PRITCHARD
I must take my herb tea which is free from tannin.

MR OGMORE
And have a charcoal biscuit which is good for me.

MR PRITCHARD
I may smoke one pipe of asthma mixture.

MRS OGMORE-PRITCHARD
In the woodshed, if you please.

MR PRITCHARD
And dust the parlour and spray the canary.

MR OGMORE
I must put on rubber gloves and search the peke for fleas.

MR PRITCHARD

I must dust the blinds and then I must raise them.

MRS OGMORE-PRITCHARD

And before you let the sun in, mind it wipes its shoes.

FIRST VOICE

In Butcher Beynon's, Gossamer Beynon, daughter, schoolteacher, dreaming deep, daintily ferrets under a fluttering hummock of chicken's feathers in a slaughterhouse that has chintz curtains and a three-pieced suite, and finds, with no surprise, a small rough ready man with a bushy tail winking in a paper carrier.

GOSSAMER BEYNON

At last, my love,

FIRST VOICE

sighs Gossamer Beynon. And the bushy tail wags rude and ginger.

ORGAN MORGAN

Help,

SECOND VOICE

cries Organ Morgan, the organist, in his dream,

ORGAN MORGAN

there is perturbation and music in Coronation Street! All the spouses are honking like geese and the babies singing opera. P.C. Attila Rees has got his truncheon out and is playing cadenzas by the pump, the cows from Sunday Meadow ring like reindeer, and on the roof of Handel Villa see the Women's Welfare hoofing, bloomered, in the moon.

FIRST VOICE

At the sea-end of town, Mr and Mrs Floyd, the cocklers, are sleeping as quiet as death, side by wrinkled side, toothless, salt and brown, like two old kippers in a box.

And high above, in Salt Lake Farm, Mr Utah Watkins counts, all night, the wife-faced sheep as they leap the fences on the hill, smiling and knitting and bleating just like Mrs Utah Watkins.

UTAH WATKINS (*Yawning*)

Thirty-four, thirty-five, thirty-six, forty-eight, eighty-nine . . .

MRS UTAH WATKINS (*Bleating*)

Knit one slip one
Knit two together
Pass the slipstitch over . . .

FIRST VOICE

Ocky Milkman, drowned asleep in Cockle Street, is emptying his churns into the Dewi River,

OCKY MILKMAN (*Whispering*)

regardless of expense,

FIRST VOICE

and weeping like a funeral.

Cherry Owen, next door, lifts a tankard to his lips but nothing flows out of it. He shakes the tankard. It turns into a fish. He drinks the fish.

FIRST VOICE

P.C. Attila Rees lumps out of bed, dead to the dark and still foghorning, and drags out his helmet from under the bed; but deep in the backyard lock-up of his sleep a mean voice murmurs

A VOICE (*Murmuring*)

You'll be sorry for this in the morning,

FIRST VOICE

and he heave-ho's back to bed. His helmet swashes in the dark.

SECOND VOICE

Willy Nilly, postman, asleep up street, walks fourteen miles to deliver the post as he does every day of the night, and rat-a-tats hard and sharp on Mrs Willy Nilly.

MRS WILLY NILLY

Don't spank me, please, teacher,

SECOND VOICE

whimpers his wife at his side, but every night of her married life she has been late for school.

Sinbad Sailors, over the taproom of the Sailors Arms, hugs his damp pillow whose secret name is Gossamer Beynon.

A mogul catches Lily Smalls in the wash-house.

LILY SMALLS
Ooh, you old mogul!

SECOND VOICE
Mrs Rose Cottage's eldest, Mae, peals off her pink-and-white skin in a furnace in a tower in a cave in a waterfall in a wood and waits there raw as an onion for Mister Right to leap up the burning tall hollow splashes of leaves like a brilliantined trout.

MAE ROSE COTTAGE (*Very close and softly, drawing out the words*)
Call me Dolores
Like they do in the stories.

FIRST VOICE
Alone until she dies, Bessie Bighead, hired help, born in the workhouse, smelling of the cowshed, snores bass and gruff on a couch of straw in a loft in Salt Lake Farm and picks a posy of daisies in Sunday Meadow to put on the grave of Gomer Owen who kissed her once by the pig-sty when she wasn't looking and never kissed her again although she was looking all the time.

And the Inspectors of Cruelty fly down into Mrs

21

Butcher Beynon's dream to persecute Mr Beynon for selling

BUTCHER BEYNON

owl meat, dogs' eyes, manchop.

SECOND VOICE

Mr Beynon, in butcher's bloodied apron, spring-heels down Coronation Street, a finger, not his own, in his mouth. Straightfaced in his cunning sleep he pulls the legs of his dreams and

BUTCHER BEYNON

hunting on pigback shoots down the wild giblets.

ORGAN MORGAN (*High and softly*)

Help!

GOSSAMER BEYNON (*Softly*)

My foxy darling.

FIRST VOICE

Now behind the eyes and secrets of the dreamers in the streets rocked to sleep by the sea, see the

SECOND VOICE

titbits and topsyturvies, bobs and buttontops, bags and bones, ash and rind and dandruff and nailparings, saliva and snowflakes and moulted feathers of dreams, the wrecks and sprats and shells and fishbones, whale-juice and moonshine and small salt fry dished up by the hidden sea.

The owls are hunting. Look, over Bethesda grave-stones one hoots and swoops and catches a mouse by Hannah Rees, Beloved Wife. And in Coronation Street, which you alone can see it is so dark under the chapel in the skies, the Reverend Eli Jenkins, poet, preacher, turns in his deep towards-dawn sleep and dreams of

REVEREND ELI JENKINS

Eisteddfodau.

SECOND VOICE

He intricately rhymes, to the music of crwth and pibgorn, all night long in his druid's seedy nightie in a beer-tent black with parchs.

FIRST VOICE

Mr Pugh, schoolmaster, fathoms asleep, pretends to be sleeping, spies foxy round the droop of his night-cap and pssst! whistles up

MR PUGH

Murder.

FIRST VOICE

Mrs Organ Morgan, groceress, coiled grey like a dormouse, her paws to her ears, conjures

MRS ORGAN MORGAN

Silence.

She sleeps very dulcet in a cove of wool, and trumpeting Organ Morgan at her side snores no louder than a spider.

FIRST VOICE

Mary Ann Sailors dreams of

MARY ANN SAILORS

the Garden of Eden.

FIRST VOICE

She comes in her smock-frock and clogs

MARY ANN SAILORS

away from the cool scrubbed cobbled kitchen with the Sunday-school pictures on the whitewashed wall and the farmers' almanac hung above the settle and the sides of bacon on the ceiling hooks, and goes down the cockleshelled paths of that applepie kitchen garden, ducking under the gippo's clothespegs, catching her apron on the blackcurrant bushes, past bean-rows and onion-bed and tomatoes ripening on the wall towards the old man playing the harmonium in the orchard, and sits down on the grass at his side and shells the green peas that grow up through the lap of her frock that brushes the dew.

FIRST VOICE

In Donkey Street, so furred with sleep, Dai Bread, Polly Garter, Nogood Boyo, and Lord Cut-Glass sigh before the dawn that is about to be and dream of

DAI BREAD
Harems.

POLLY GARTER
Babies.

NOGOOD BOYO
Nothing.

LORD CUT-GLASS
Tick tock tick tock tick tock tick tock.

FIRST VOICE
Time passes. Listen. Time passes. An owl flies home past Bethesda, to a chapel in an oak. And the dawn inches up.
[*One distant bell-note, faintly reverberating*

FIRST VOICE
Stand on this hill. This is Llareggub Hill, old as the hills, high, cool, and green, and from this small circle of stones, made not by druids but by Mrs Beynon's Billy, you can see all the town below you sleeping in the first of the dawn.

You can hear the love-sick woodpigeons mooning in bed. A dog barks in his sleep, farmyards away. The town ripples like a lake in the waking haze.

VOICE OF A GUIDE-BOOK
Less than five hundred souls inhabit the three quaint streets and the few narrow by-lanes and scattered farmsteads that constitute this small, decaying watering-place which may, indeed, be called a 'back-

water of life' without disrespect to its natives who possess, to this day, a salty individuality of their own. The main street, Coronation Street, consists, for the most part, of humble, two-storied houses many of which attempt to achieve some measure of gaiety by prinking themselves out in crude colours and by the liberal use of pinkwash, though there are remaining a few eighteenth-century houses of more pretension, if, on the whole, in a sad state of disrepair. Though there is little to attract the hillclimber, the healthseeker, the sportsman, or the weekending motorist, the contemplative may, if sufficiently attracted to spare it some leisurely hours, find, in its cobbled streets and its little fishing harbour, in its several curious customs, and in the conversation of its local 'characters,' some of that picturesque sense of the past so frequently lacking in towns and villages which have kept more abreast of the times. The River Dewi is said to abound in trout, but is much poached. The one place of worship, with its neglected graveyard, is of no architectural interest.

[*A cock crows*

FIRST VOICE

The principality of the sky lightens now, over our green hill, into spring morning larked and crowed and belling.

[*Slow bell notes*

FIRST VOICE

Who pulls the townhall bellrope but blind Captain Cat? One by one, the sleepers are rung out of sleep this one morning as every morning. And soon you

26

shall see the chimneys' slow upflying snow as Captain Cat, in sailor's cap and seaboots, announces to-day with his loud get-out-of-bed bell.

SECOND VOICE
The Reverend Eli Jenkins, in Bethesda House, gropes out of bed into his preacher's black, combs back his bard's white hair, forgets to wash, pads barefoot downstairs, opens the front door, stands in the doorway and, looking out at the day and up at the eternal hill, and hearing the sea break and the gab of birds, remembers his own verses and tells them softly to empty Coronation Street that is rising and raising its blinds.

REVEREND ELI JENKINS
Dear Gwalia! I know there are
Towns lovelier than ours,
And fairer hills and loftier far,
And groves more full of flowers,

And boskier woods more blithe with spring
And bright with birds' adorning,
And sweeter bards than I to sing
Their praise this beauteous morning.

By Cader Idris, tempest-torn,
Or Moel yr Wyddfa's glory,
Carnedd Llewelyn beauty born,
Plinlimmon old in story,

By mountains where King Arthur dreams,
By Penmaenmawr defiant,

27

Llareggub Hill a molehill seems,
A pygmy to a giant.

By Sawddwy, Senny, Dovey, Dee,
Edw, Eden, Aled, all,
Taff and Towy broad and free,
Llyfnant with its waterfall,

Claerwen, Cleddau, Dulais, Daw,
Ely, Gwili, Ogwr, Nedd,
Small is our River Dewi, Lord,
A baby on a rushy bed.

By Carreg Cennen, King of time,
Our Heron Head is only
A bit of stone with seaweed spread
Where gulls come to be lonely.

A tiny dingle is Milk Wood
By Golden Grove 'neath Grongar,
But let me choose and oh! I should
Love all my life and longer

To stroll among our trees and stray
In Goosegog Lane, on Donkey Down,
And hear the Dewi sing all day,
And never, never leave the town.

SECOND VOICE

The Reverend Jenkins closes the front door. His
morning service is over.

[*Slow bell notes*

28

Now, woken at last by the out-of-bed-sleepy-head-Polly-put-the-kettle-on townhall bell, Lily Smalls, Mrs Beynon's treasure, comes downstairs from a dream of royalty who all night long went larking with her full of sauce in the Milk Wood dark, and puts the kettle on the primus ring in Mrs Beynon's kitchen, and looks at herself in Mr Beynon's shaving-glass over the sink, and sees:

LILY SMALLS

Oh there's a face!
Where you get that hair from?
Got it from a old tom cat.
Give it back then, love.
Oh, there's a perm!

Where you get that nose from, Lily?
Got it from my father, silly.
You've got it on upside down!
Oh, there's a conk!

Look at your complexion!
Oh, no, *you* look.
Needs a bit of make-up.
Needs a veil.
Oh, there's glamour!

Where you get that smile, Lil?
Never you mind, girl.
Nobody loves you.
That's what *you* think.

Who is it loves you?
Shan't tell.
Come on, Lily.
Cross your heart, then?
Cross my heart.

FIRST VOICE

FIRST VOICE

And very softly, her lips almost touching her reflection, she breathes the name and clouds the shaving-
glass.

MRS BEYNON (*Loudly, from above*)
Lily!

LILY SMALLS (*Loudly*)
Yes, mum.

MRS BEYNON
Where's my tea, girl?

LILY SMALLS
(*Softly*)   Where d'you think? In the cat-box?
(*Loudly*) Coming up, mum.

FIRST VOICE
Mr Pugh, in the School House opposite, takes up
the morning tea to Mrs Pugh, and whispers on the
stairs

MR PUGH
Here's your arsenic, dear.
And your weedkiller biscuit.

30

I've throttled your parakeet.
I've spat in the vases.
I've put cheese in the mouseholes.
Here's your ...   [*Door creaks open*
          ... nice tea, dear.

MRS PUGH

Too much sugar.

MR PUGH

You haven't tasted it yet, dear.

MRS PUGH

Too much milk, then. Has Mr Jenkins said his
poetry?

MR PUGH

Yes, dear.

MRS PUGH

Then it's time to get up. Give me my glasses.
No, not my *reading* glasses, I want to look *out*.
I want to see

SECOND VOICE

Lily Smalls the treasure down on her red knees
washing the front step.

MRS PUGH

She's tucked her dress in her bloomers—oh, the
baggage!

31

P.C. Attila Rees, ox-broad, barge-booted, stamping out of Handcuff House in a heavy beef-red huff, black-browed under his damp helmet . . .

MRS PUGH

He's going to arrest Polly Garter, mark my words.

MR PUGH

What for, dear?

MRS PUGH

For having babies.

SECOND VOICE

. . . and lumbering down towards the strand to see that the sea is still there.

FIRST VOICE

Mary Ann Sailors, opening her bedroom window above the taproom and calling out to the heavens

MARY ANN SAILORS

I'm eighty-five years three months and a day!

MRS PUGH

I will say this for her, she never makes a mistake.

FIRST VOICE

Organ Morgan at his bedroom window playing chords on the sill to the morning fishwife gulls who, heckling over Donkey Street, observe

DAI BREAD

Me, Dai Bread, hurrying to the bakery, pushing in my shirt-tails, buttoning my waistcoat, ping goes a button, why can't they sew them, no time for breakfast, nothing for breakfast, there's wives for you.

MRS DAI BREAD ONE

Me, Mrs Dai Bread One, capped and shawled and no old corset, nice to be comfy, nice to be nice, clogging on the cobbles to stir up a neighbour. Oh, Mrs Sarah, can you spare a loaf, love? Dai Bread forgot the bread. There's a lovely morning! How's your boils this morning? Isn't that good news now, it's a change to sit down. Ta, Mrs Sarah.

MRS DAI BREAD TWO

Me, Mrs Dai Bread Two, gypsied to kill in a silky scarlet petticoat above my knees, dirty pretty knees, see my body through my petticoat brown as a berry, high-heel shoes with one heel missing, tortoiseshell comb in my bright black slinky hair, nothing else at all but a dab of scent, lolling gaudy at the doorway, tell your fortune in the tea-leaves, scowling at the sunshine, lighting up my pipe.

LORD CUT-GLASS

Me, Lord Cut-Glass, in an old frock-coat belonged to Eli Jenkins and a pair of postman's trousers from Bethesda Jumble, running out of doors to empty slops—mind there, Rover!—and then running in again, tick tock.

Me, Nogood Boyo, up to no good in the wash-house.

MISS PRICE

Me, Miss Price, in my pretty print housecoat, deft at the clothesline, natty as a jenny-wren, then pit-pat back to my egg in its cosy, my crisp toast-fingers, my home-made plum and butterpat.

POLLY GARTER

Me, Polly Garter, under the washing line, giving the breast in the garden to my bonny new baby. Nothing grows in our garden, only washing. And babies. And where's their fathers live, my love? Over the hills and far away. You're looking up at me now. I know what you're thinking, you poor little milky creature. You're thinking, you're no better than you should be, Polly, and that's good enough for me. Oh, isn't life a terrible thing, thank God?

[*Single long high chord on strings*

FIRST VOICE

Now frying-pans spit, kettles and cats purr in the kitchen. The town smells of seaweed and breakfast all the way down from Bay View, where Mrs Ogmore-Pritchard, in smock and turban, big-besomed to engage the dust, picks at her starchless bread and sips lemon-rind tea, to Bottom Cottage, where Mr Waldo, in bowler and bib, gobbles his bubble-and-squeak and kippers and swigs from the saucebottle. Mary Ann Sailors

34

praises the Lord who made porridge.

Mr Pugh

remembers ground glass as he juggles his omelet.

Mrs Pugh

nags the salt-cellar.

Willy Nilly postman

downs his last bucket of black brackish tea and rumbles out bandy to the clucking back where the hens twitch and grieve for their tea-soaked sops.

Mrs Willy Nilly

full of tea to her double-chinned brim broods and bubbles over her coven of kettles on the hissing hot range always ready to steam open the mail.

The Reverend Eli Jenkins

REVEREND ELI JENKINS
finds a rhyme and dips his pen in his cocoa.

FIRST VOICE
Lord Cut-Glass in his ticking kitchen

LORD CUT-GLASS
scampers from clock to clock, a bunch of clock-keys in one hand, a fish-head in the other.

FIRST VOICE
Captain Cat in his galley.

CAPTAIN CAT
blind and fine-fingered savours his sea-fry.

FIRST VOICE
Mr and Mrs Cherry Owen, in their Donkey Street room that is bedroom, parlour, kitchen, and scullery, sit down to last night's supper of onions boiled in their overcoats and broth of spuds and baconrind and leeks and bones.

MRS CHERRY OWEN
See that smudge on the wall by the picture of Auntie Blossom? That's where you threw the sago.
                    [*Cherry Owen laughs with delight*

MRS CHERRY OWEN
You only missed me by a inch.

CHERRY OWEN
I always miss Auntie Blossom too.

Remember last night? In you reeled, my boy, as drunk as a deacon with a big wet bucket and a fish-frail full of stout and you looked at me and you said, 'God has come home!' you said, and then over the bucket you went, sprawling and bawling, and the floor was all flagons and eels.

CHERRY OWEN

Was I wounded?

MRS CHERRY OWEN

And then you took off your trousers and you said, 'Does anybody want a fight!' Oh, you old baboon.

CHERRY OWEN

Give me a kiss.

MRS CHERRY OWEN

And then you sang 'Bread of Heaven,' tenor and bass.

CHERRY OWEN

I *always* sing 'Bread of Heaven.'

MRS CHERRY OWEN

And then you did a little dance on the table.

CHERRY OWEN

I did?

MRS CHERRY OWEN
Drop dead!

CHERRY OWEN
And then what did I do?

MRS CHERRY OWEN
Then you cried like a baby and said you were a poor drunk orphan with nowhere to go but the grave.

CHERRY OWEN
And what did I do next, my dear?

MRS CHERRY OWEN
Then you danced on the table all over again and said you were King Solomon Owen and I was your Mrs Sheba.

CHERRY OWEN (*Softly*)
And then?

MRS CHERRY OWEN
And then I got you into bed and you snored all night like a brewery.
[*Mr and Mrs Cherry Owen laugh delightedly together*

FIRST VOICE
From Beynon Butchers in Coronation Street, the smell of fried liver sidles out with onions on its breath. And listen! In the dark breakfast-room behind the shop, Mr and Mrs Beynon, waited upon by their treasure, enjoy, between bites, their everymorning

hullabaloo, and Mrs Beynon slips the gristly bits under the tasselled tablecloth to her fat cat.

[*Cat purrs*

MRS BEYNON
She likes the liver, Ben.

MR BEYNON
She ought to do, Bess. It's her brother's.

MRS BEYNON (*Screaming*)
Oh, d'you hear that, Lily?

LILY SMALLS
Yes, mum.

MRS BEYNON
We're eating pusscat.

LILY SMALLS
Yes, mum.

MRS BEYNON
Oh, you cat-butcher!

MR BEYNON
It was doctored, mind.

MRS BEYNON (*Hysterical*)
What's that got to do with it?

MR BEYNON
Yesterday we had mole.

39

Oh, Lily, Lily!

MR BEYNON
Monday, otter. Tuesday, shrews.
[*Mrs Beynon screams*

LILY SMALLS
Go on, Mrs Beynon. He's the biggest liar in town.

MRS BEYNON
Don't you dare say that about Mr Beynon.

LILY SMALLS
Everybody knows it, mum.

MRS BEYNON
Mr Beynon never tells a lie. Do you, Ben?

MR BEYNON
No, Bess. And now I am going out after the corgies, with my little cleaver.

MRS BEYNON
Oh, Lily, Lily!

FIRST VOICE
Up the street, in the Sailors Arms, Sinbad Sailors, grandson of Mary Ann Sailors, draws a pint in the sunlit bar. The ship's clock in the bar says half past eleven. Half past eleven is opening time. The hands

of the clock have stayed still at half past eleven for
fifty years. It is always opening time in the Sailors
Arms.

SINBAD
Here's to me, Sinbad.

FIRST VOICE
All over the town, babies and old men are cleaned
and put into their broken prams and wheeled on to
the sunlit cockled cobbles or out into the backyards
under the dancing underclothes, and left. A baby
cries.

OLD MAN
I want my pipe and he wants his bottle.
[*School bell rings*

FIRST VOICE
Noses are wiped, heads picked, hair combed, paws
scrubbed, ears boxed, and the children shrilled off to
school.

SECOND VOICE
Fishermen grumble to their nets. Nogood Boyo
goes out in the dinghy *Zanzibar*, ships the oars, drifts
slowly in the dab-filled bay, and, lying on his back
in the unbaled water, among crabs' legs and tangled
lines, looks up at the spring sky.

NOGOOD BOYO (*Softly, lazily*)
I don't know who's up there and I don't care.

41

He turns his head and looks up at Llareggub Hill, and sees, among green lathered trees, the white houses of the strewn away farms, where farmboys whistle, dogs shout, cows low, but all too far away for him, or you, to hear. And in the town, the shops squeak open. Mr Edwards, in butterfly-collar and straw-hat at the doorway of Manchester House, measures with his eye the dawdlers-by for striped flannel shirts and shrouds and flowery blouses, and bellows to himself in the darkness behind his eye.

MR EDWARDS (*Whispers*)
I love Miss Price.

FIRST VOICE
Syrup is sold in the post-office. A car drives to market, full of fowls and a farmer. Milk-churns stand at Coronation Corner like short silver police-men. And, sitting at the open window of Schooner House, blind Captain Cat hears all the morning of the town.
[*School bell in background. Children's voices.
The noise of children's feet on the cobbles*

CAPTAIN CAT (*Softly, to himself*)
Maggie Richards, Ricky Rhys, Tommy Powell, our Sal, little Gerwain, Billy Swansea with the dog's voice, one of Mr Waldo's, nasty Humphrey, Jackie with the sniff . . . Where's Dicky's Albie? and the boys from Ty-pant? Perhaps they got the rash again.
[*A sudden cry among the children's voices*

42

CAPTAIN CAT
Somebody's hit Maggie Richards. Two to one it's Billy Swansea. Never trust a boy who barks.

> [*A burst of yelping crying*

Right again! It's Billy.

FIRST VOICE
And the children's voices cry away.

> [*Postman's rat-a-tat on door, distant*

CAPTAIN CAT (*Softly, to himself*)
That's Willy Nilly knocking at Bay View. Rat-a-tat, very soft. The knocker's got a kid glove on. Who's sent a letter to Mrs Ogmore-Pritchard?

> [*Rat-a-tat, distant again*

CAPTAIN CAT
Careful now, she swabs the front glassy. Every step's like a bar of soap. Mind your size twelveses. That old Bessie would beeswax the lawn to make the birds slip.

WILLY NILLY
Morning, Mrs Ogmore-Pritchard.

MRS OGMORE-PRITCHARD
Good morning, postman.

WILLY NILLY
Here's a letter for you with stamped and addressed envelope enclosed, all the way from Builth Wells. A gentleman wants to study birds and can he

have accommodation for two weeks and a bath vegetarian.

MRS OGMORE-PRITCHARD
No.

WILLY NILLY (*Persuasively*)
You wouldn't know he was in the house, Mrs Ogmore-Pritchard. He'd be out in the mornings at the bang of dawn with his bag of breadcrumbs and his little telescope . . .

MRS OGMORE-PRITCHARD
And come home at all hours covered with feathers. I don't want persons in my *nice clean* rooms breathing all over the chairs . . .

WILLY NILLY
Cross my heart, he won't breathe.

MRS OGMORE-PRITCHARD
. . . and putting their feet on my carpets and sneezing on my china and sleeping in my sheets . . .

WILLY NILLY
He only wants a *single* bed, Mrs Ogmore-Pritchard.

[*Door slams*

CAPTAIN CAT (*Softly*)
And back she goes to the kitchen to polish the potatoes.

Captain Cat hears Willy Nilly's feet heavy on the distant cobbles.

CAPTAIN CAT

One, two, three, four, five . . . That's Mrs Rose Cottage. What's to-day? To-day she gets the letter from her sister in Gorslas. How's the twins' teeth? He's stopping at School House.

WILLY NILLY

Morning, Mrs Pugh. Mrs Ogmore-Pritchard won't have a gentleman in from Builth Wells because he'll sleep in her sheets, Mrs Rose Cottage's sister in Gorslas's twins have got to have them out . . .

MRS PUGH

Give me the parcel.

WILLY NILLY

It's for *Mr* Pugh, Mrs Pugh.

MRS PUGH

Never you mind. What's inside it?

WILLY NILLY

A book called *Lives of the Great Poisoners.*

CAPTAIN CAT

That's Manchester House.

WILLY NILLY

Morning, Mr Edwards. Very small news. Mrs Ogmore-Pritchard won't have birds in the house, and

45

Mr Pugh's bought a book now on how to do in Mrs Pugh.

MR EDWARDS
Have you got a letter from *her?*

WILLY NILLY
Miss Price loves you with all her heart. Smelling of lavender to-day. She's down to the last of the elderflower wine but the quince jam's bearing up and she's knitting roses on the doilies. Last week she sold three jars of boiled sweets, pound of humbugs, half a box of jellybabies and six coloured photos of Llareggub. Yours for ever. Then twenty-one X's.

MR EDWARDS
Oh, Willy Nilly, she's a ruby! Here's my letter. Put it into her hands now.
[*Slow feet on cobbles, quicker feet approaching*

CAPTAIN CAT
Mr Waldo hurrying to the Sailors Arms. Pint of stout with a egg in it.
[*Footsteps stop*
(*Softly*) There's a letter for him.

WILLY NILLY
It's another paternity summons, Mr Waldo.

FIRST VOICE
The quick footsteps hurry on along the cobbles and up three steps to the Sailors Arms.

MR WALDO (*Calling out*)
Quick, Sinbad. Pint of stout. And no egg in.

FIRST VOICE
People are moving now up and down the cobbled street.

CAPTAIN CAT
All the women are out this morning, in the sun. You can tell it's Spring. There goes Mrs Cherry, you can tell her by her trotters, off she trots new as a daisy. Who's that talking by the pump? Mrs Floyd and Boyo, talking flatfish. What can you talk about flatfish? That's Mrs Dai Bread One, waltzing up the street like a jelly, every time she shakes it's slap slap slap. Who's that? Mrs Butcher Beynon with her pet black cat, it follows her everywhere, miaow and all. There goes Mrs Twenty-Three, important, the sun gets up and goes down in her dewlap, when she shuts her eyes, it's night. High heels now, in the morning too, Mrs Rose Cottage's eldest Mae, seventeen and never been kissed ho ho, going young and milking under my window to the field with the nannygoats, she reminds me all the way. Can't hear what the women are gabbing round the pump. Same as ever. Who's having a baby, who blacked whose eye, seen Polly Garter giving her belly an airing, there should be a law, seen Mrs Beynon's new mauve jumper, it's her old grey jumper dyed, who's dead, who's dying, there's a lovely day, oh the cost of soapflakes!

[*Organ music, distant*

47

Organ Morgan's at it early. You can *tell* it's Spring.

FIRST VOICE

And he hears the noise of milk-cans.

CAPTAIN CAT

Ocky Milkman on his round. I will say this, his milk's as fresh as the dew. Half dew it is. Snuffle on, Ocky, watering the town . . . Somebody's coming. Now the voices round the pump can see somebody coming. Hush, there's a hush! You can tell by the noise of the hush, it's Polly Garter. (*Louder*) Hullo, Polly, who's there?

POLLY GARTER (*Off*)

Me, love.

CAPTAIN CAT

That's Polly Garter. (*Softly*) Hullo, Polly, my love, can you hear the dumb goose-hiss of the wives as they huddle and peck or flounce at a waddle away? Who cuddled you when? Which of their gandering hubbies moaned in Milk Wood for your naughty mothering arms and body like a wardrobe, love? Scrub the floors of the Welfare Hall for the Mothers' Union Social Dance, you're one mother won't wriggle her roly poly bum or pat her fat little buttery feet in that wedding-ringed holy to-night through the waltz-ing breadwinners snatched from the cosy smoke of the Sailors Arms will grizzle and mope.

[*A cock crows*

Too late, cock, too late

for the town's half over with its morning. The morning's busy as bees.

[*Organ music fades into silence*

There's the clip clop of horses on the sunhoneyed cobbles of the humming streets, hammering of horse-shoes, gobble quack and cackle, tomtit twitter from the bird-ounced boughs, braying on Donkey Down. Bread is baking, pigs are grunting, chop goes the butcher, milk-churns bell, tills ring, sheep cough, dogs shout, saws sing. Oh, the Spring whinny and morning moo from the clog-dancing farms, the gulls' gab and rabble on the boat-bobbing river and sea and the cockles bubbling in the sand, scamper of sander-lings, curlew cry, crow caw, pigeon coo, clock strike, bull bellow, and the ragged gabble of the beargarden school as the women scratch and babble in Mrs Organ Morgan's general shop where everything is sold: custard, buckets, henna, rat-traps, shrimp-nets, sugar, stamps, confetti, paraffin, hatchets, whistles.

Mrs Ogmore-Pritchard

la di da

FIRST WOMAN

got a man in Builth Wells

THIRD WOMAN

and he got a little telescope to look at birds

SECOND WOMAN

Willy Nilly said

THIRD WOMAN

Remember her first husband? He didn't need a
telescope

FIRST WOMAN

he looked at them undressing through the keyhole

THIRD WOMAN

and he used to shout Tallyho

SECOND WOMAN

but Mr Ogmore was a proper gentleman

FIRST WOMAN

even though he hanged his collie.

THIRD WOMAN

Seen Mrs Butcher Beynon?

SECOND WOMAN

she said Butcher Beynon put dogs in the mincer

FIRST WOMAN

go on, he's pulling her leg

THIRD WOMAN
now don't you dare tell her that, there's a dear

SECOND WOMAN
or she'll think he's trying to pull it off and eat it.

FOURTH WOMAN
There's a nasty lot live here when you come to think.

FIRST WOMAN
Look at that Nogood Boyo now

SECOND WOMAN
too lazy to wipe his snout

THIRD WOMAN
and going out fishing every day and all he ever brought back was a Mrs Samuels

FIRST WOMAN
been in the water a week.

SECOND WOMAN
And look at Ocky Milkman's wife that nobody's ever seen

FIRST WOMAN
he keeps her in the cupboard with the empties

THIRD WOMAN
and think of Dai Bread with two wives

one for the daytime one for the night.

Men are brutes on the quiet.

And how's Organ Morgan, Mrs Morgan?

you look dead beat

it's organ organ all the time with him

up every night until midnight playing the organ

Oh, I'm a martyr to music.

FIRST VOICE

Outside, the sun springs down on the rough and tumbling town. It runs through the hedges of Goose-gog Lane, cuffing the birds to sing. Spring whips green down Cockle Row, and the shells ring out. Llareggub this snip of a morning is wildfruit and warm, the streets, fields, sands and waters springing in the young sun.

SECOND VOICE

Evans the Death presses hard with black gloves on the coffin of his breast in case his heart jumps out.

52

EVANS THE DEATH (*Harshly*)
Where's your dignity. Lie down.

SECOND VOICE
Spring stirs Gossamer Beynon schoolmistress like a spoon.

GOSSAMER BEYNON (*Tearfully*)
Oh, what can I do? I'll *never* be refined if I twitch.

SECOND VOICE
Spring this strong morning foams in a flame in Jack Black as he cobbles a high-heeled shoe for Mrs Dai Bread Two the gypsy, but he hammers it sternly out.

JACK BLACK (*To a hammer rhythm*)
There is *no leg* belonging to the foot that belongs to this shoe.

SECOND VOICE
The sun and the green breeze ship Captain Cat sea-memory again.

CAPTAIN CAT
No, *I'll* take the mulatto, by God, who's captain here? Parlez-vous jig jig, Madam?

SECOND VOICE
Mary Ann Sailors says very softly to herself as she looks out at Llareggub Hill from the bedroom where she was born

53

MARY ANN SAILORS (*Loudly*)

It is Spring in Llareggub in the sun in my old age, and this is the Chosen Land.

[*A choir of children's voices suddenly cries out on one, high, glad, long, sighing note*

FIRST VOICE

And in Willy Nilly the Postman's dark and sizzling damp tea-coated misty pygmy kitchen where the spittingcat kettles throb and hop on the range, Mrs Willy Nilly steams open Mr Mog Edwards' letter to Miss Myfanwy Price and reads it aloud to Willy Nilly by the squint of the Spring sun through the one sealed window running with tears, while the drugged, bedraggled hens at the back door whimper and snivel for the lickerish bog-black tea.

MRS WILLY NILLY

From Manchester House, Llareggub. Sole Prop: Mr Mog Edwards (late of Twll), Linendraper, Haberdasher, Master Tailor, Costumier. For West End Negligee, Lingerie, Teagowns, Evening Dress, Trousseaux, Layettes. Also Ready to Wear for All Occasions. Economical Outfitting for Agricultural Employment Our Speciality, Wardrobes Bought. Among Our Satisfied Customers Ministers of Religion and J.P.'s. Fittings by Appointment. Advertising Weekly in the *Twll Bugle*. Beloved Myfanwy Price my Bride in Heaven,

MOG EDWARDS

I love you until Death do us part and then we shall be together for ever and ever. A new parcel of

54

ribbons has come from Carmarthen to-day, all the colours in the rainbow. I wish I could tie a ribbon in your hair a white one but it cannot be. I dreamed last night you were all dripping wet and you sat on my lap as the Reverend Jenkins went down the street. I see you got a mermaid in your lap he said and he lifted his hat. He is a proper Christian. Not like Cherry Owen who said you should have thrown her back he said. Business is very poorly. Polly Garter bought two garters with roses but she never got stockings so what is the use I say. Mr Waldo tried to sell me a woman's nightie outsize he said he found it and we know where. I sold a packet of pins to Tom the Sailors to pick his teeth. If this goes on I shall be in the poorhouse. My heart is in your bosom and yours is in mine. God be with you always Myfanwy Price and keep you lovely for me in His Heavenly Mansion. I must stop now and remain, Your Eternal, Mog Edwards.

MRS WILLY NILLY

And then a little message with a rubber stamp. Shop at Mog's!!!

FIRST VOICE

And Willy Nilly, rumbling, jockeys out again to the three-seated shack called the House of Commons in the back where the hens weep, and sees, in sudden Springshine,

SECOND VOICE

herring gulls heckling down to the harbour where the fishermen spit and prop the morning up and eye the fishy sea smooth to the sea's end as it lulls in blue. Green and gold money, tobacco, tinned salmon, hats with feathers, pots of fish-paste, warmth for the winter-to-be, weave and leap in it rich and slippery in the flash and shapes of fishes through the cold sea-streets. But with blue lazy eyes the fishermen gaze at that milkmaid whispering water with no ruck or ripple as though it blew great guns and serpents and typhooned the town.

FISHERMAN

Too rough for fishing to-day.

SECOND VOICE

And they thank God, and gob at a gull for luck, and moss-slow and silent make their way uphill, from the still still sea, towards the Sailors Arms as the children

[School bell

FIRST VOICE

spank and scamper rough and singing out of school into the draggletail yard. And Captain Cat at his window says soft to himself the words of their song.

CAPTAIN CAT (*To the beat of the singing*)
Johnnie Crack and Flossie Snail
Kept their baby in a milking pail
Flossie Snail and Johnnie Crack
One would pull it out and one would put it back

O it's my turn now said Flossie Snail
To take the baby from the milking pail

And it's my turn now said Johnnie Crack
To smack it on the head and put it back

Johnnie Crack and Flossie Snail
Kept their baby in a milking pail
One would put it back and one would pull it out
And all it had to drink was ale and stout
For Johnnie Crack and Flossie Snail
Always used to say that stout and ale
Was *good* for a baby in a milking pail.

[*Long pause*

FIRST VOICE

The music of the spheres is heard distinctly over
Milk Wood. It is 'The Rustle of Spring.'

SECOND VOICE

A glee-party sings in Bethesda Graveyard, gay
but muffled.

FIRST VOICE

Vegetables make love above the tenors

SECOND VOICE

and dogs bark blue in the face.

FIRST VOICE

Mrs Ogmore-Pritchard belches in a teeny hanky
and chases the sunlight with a flywhisk, but even she
cannot drive out the Spring: from one of the finger-
bowls, a primrose grows.

Mrs Dai Bread One and Mrs Dai Bread Two are sitting outside their house in Donkey Lane, one darkly one plumply blooming in the quick, dewy sun. Mrs Dai Bread Two is looking into a crystal ball which she holds in the lap of her dirty yellow petticoat, hard against her hard dark thighs.

MRS DAI BREAD TWO

Cross my palm with silver. Out of our housekeeping money. Aah!

MRS DAI BREAD ONE

What d'you see, lovie?

MRS DAI BREAD TWO

I see a featherbed. With three pillows on it. And a text above the bed. I can't read what it says, there's great clouds blowing. Now they have blown away. God is Love, the text says.

MRS DAI BREAD ONE (*Delighted*)

That's *our* bed.

MRS DAI BREAD TWO

And now it's vanished. The sun's spinning like a top. Who's this coming out of the sun? It's a hairy little man with big pink lips. He got a wall eye.

MRS DAI BREAD ONE

It's Dai, it's Dai Bread!

Ssh! The featherbed's floating back. The little man's taking his boots off. He's pulling his shirt over his head. He's beating his chest with his fists. He's climbing into bed.

MRS DAI BREAD ONE

Go on, go on.

MRS DAI BREAD TWO

There's *two* women in bed. He looks at them both, with his head cocked on one side. He's whistling through his teeth. Now he grips his little arms round one of the women.

MRS DAI BREAD ONE

Which one, which one?

MRS DAI BREAD TWO

I can't see any more. There's great clouds blowing again.

MRS DAI BREAD ONE

Ach, the mean old clouds!
[*Pause. The children's singing fades*

FIRST VOICE

The morning is all singing. The Reverend Eli Jenkins, busy on his morning calls, stops outside the Welfare Hall to hear Polly Garter as she scrubs the floors for the Mothers' Union Dance to-night.

59

I loved a man whose name was Tom
He was strong as a bear and two yards long
I loved a man whose name was Dick
He was big as a barrel and three feet thick
And I loved a man whose name was Harry
Six feet tall and sweet as a cherry
But the one I loved best awake or asleep
Was little Willy Wee and he's six feet deep.

O Tom Dick and Harry were three fine men
And I'll never have such loving again
But little Willy Wee who took me on his knee
Little Willy Wee was the man for me.

Now men from every parish round
Run after me and roll me on the ground
But whenever I love another man back
Johnnie from the Hill or Sailing Jack
I always think as they do what they please
Of Tom Dick and Harry who were tall as trees
And most I think when I'm by their side
Of little Willy Wee who downed and died.

O Tom Dick and Harry were three fine men
And I'll never have such loving again
But little Willy Wee who took me on his knee
Little Willy Weazel is the man for me.

REVEREND ELI JENKINS
Praise the Lord! We are a musical nation.

And the Reverend Jenkins hurries on through the town to visit the sick with jelly and poems.

FIRST VOICE

The town's as full as a lovebird's egg.

MR WALDO

There goes the Reverend,

FIRST VOICE

says Mr Waldo at the smoked herring brown window of the unwashed Sailors Arms,

MR WALDO

with his brolly and his odes. Fill 'em up, Sinbad, I'm on the treacle to-day.

SECOND VOICE

The silent fishermen flush down their pints.

SINBAD

Oh, Mr Waldo,

FIRST VOICE

sighs Sinbad Sailors,

SINBAD

I dote on that Gossamer Beynon. She's a lady all over.

And Mr Waldo, who is thinking of a woman soft as Eve and sharp as sciatica to share his bread-pudding bed, answers

MR WALDO

No lady that I know is.

SINBAD

And if only grandma'd die, cross my heart I'd go down on my knees Mr Waldo and I'd say Miss Gossamer I'd say

CHILDREN'S VOICES

When birds do sing hey ding a ding a ding
Sweet lovers love the Spring . . .

SECOND VOICE

Polly Garter sings, still on her knees,

POLLY GARTER

Tom Dick and Harry were three fine men
And I'll never have such

CHILDREN

Ding a ding

POLLY GARTER

again.

FIRST VOICE

And the morning school is over, and Captain Cat at his curtained schooner's.porthole open to the Spring

sun tides hears the naughty forfeiting children tumble
and rhyme on the cobbles.

GIRLS' VOICES

Gwennie call the boys
They make such a noise.

GIRL

Boys boys boys
Come along to me.

GIRLS' VOICES

Boys boys boys
Kiss Gwennie where she says
Or give her a penny.
Go on, Gwennie.

GIRL

Kiss me in Goosegog Lane
Or give me a penny.
What's your name?

FIRST BOY

Billy.

GIRL

Kiss me in Goosegog Lane Billy
Or give me a penny silly.

FIRST BOY

Gwennie Gwennie
I kiss you in Goosegog Lane.
Now I haven't got to give you a penny.

Boys boys boys
Kiss Gwennie where she says
Or give her a penny.
Go on, Gwennie.

GIRL
Kiss me on Llareggub Hill
Or give me a penny.
What's your name?

SECOND BOY
Johnnie Cristo.

GIRL
Kiss me on Llareggub Hill Johnnie Cristo
Or give me a penny mister.

SECOND BOY
Gwennie Gwennie
I kiss you on Llareggub Hill.
Now I haven't got to give you a penny.

GIRLS' VOICES
Boys boys boys
Kiss Gwennie where she says
Or give her a penny.
Go on, Gwennie.

GIRL
Kiss me in Milk Wood
Or give me a penny.
What's your name?

THIRD BOY

Dicky.

GIRL

Kiss me in Milk Wood Dicky
Or give me a penny quickly.

THIRD BOY

Gwennie Gwennie
I can't kiss you in Milk Wood.

GIRLS' VOICES

Gwennie ask him why.

GIRL

Why?

THIRD BOY

Because my mother says I mustn't.

GIRLS' VOICES

Cowardy cowardy custard
Give Gwennie a penny.

GIRL

Give me a penny.

THIRD BOY

I haven't got any.

GIRLS' VOICES

Put him in the river
Up to his liver

Quick quick Dirty Dick
Beat him on the bum
With a rhubarb stick.
Aiee!
Hush!

And the shrill girls giggle and master around him
and squeal as they clutch and thrash, and he blubbers
away downhill with his patched pants falling, and his
tear-splashed blush burns all the way as the triumphant
bird-like sisters scream with buttons in their claws
and the bully brothers hoot after him his little nickname and his mother's shame and his father's wicked-
ness with the loose wild barefoot women of the hovels
of the hills. It all means nothing at all, and, howling
for his milky mum, for her cawl and buttermilk and
cowbreath and welshcakes and the fat birth-smelling
bed and moonlit kitchen of her arms, he'll never
forget as he paddles blind home through the weeping
end of the world. Then his tormentors tussle and run
to the Cockle Street sweet-shop, their pennies sticky
as honey, to buy from Miss Myfanwy Price, who is
cocky and neat as a puff-bosomed robin and her small
round buttocks tight as ticks, gobstoppers big as wens
that rainbow as you suck, brandyballs, winegums,
hundreds and thousands, liquorice sweet as sick,
nougat to tug and ribbon out like another red rubbery
tongue, gum to glue in girls' curls, crimson cough-
drops to spit blood, ice-cream cornets, dandelion-and-
burdock, raspberry and cherryade, pop goes the
weasel and the wind.

Gossamer Beynon high-heels out of school. The sun hums down through the cotton flowers of her dress into the bell of her heart and buzzes in the honey there and couches and kisses, lazy-loving and boozed, in her red-berried breast. Eyes run from the trees and windows of the street, steaming 'Gossamer,' and strip her to the nipples and the bees. She blazes naked past the Sailors Arms, the only woman on the Dai-Adamed earth. Sinbad Sailors places on her thighs still dewdamp from the first mangrowing cock-crow garden his reverent goat-bearded hands.

GOSSAMER BEYNON

I don't care if he *is* common,

SECOND VOICE

she whispers to her salad-day deep self,

GOSSAMER BEYNON

I want to gobble him up. I don't care if he *does* drop his aitches,

SECOND VOICE

she tells the stripped and mother-of-the-world big-beamed and Eve-hipped spring of her self.

GOSSAMER BEYNON

so long as he's all cucumber and hooves.

SECOND VOICE

Sinbad Sailors watches her go by, demure and proud and schoolmarm in her crisp flower dress and

67

sun-defying hat, with never a look or lilt or wriggle, the butcher's unmelting icemaiden daughter veiled forever from the hungry hug of his eyes.

Oh, Gossamer Beynon, why are you so proud?

he grieves to his Guinness,

Oh, beautiful beautiful Gossamer B, I wish I wish that you were for me. I wish you were not so educated.

She feels his goatbeard tickle her in the middle of the world like a tuft of wiry fire, and she turns in a terror of delight away from his whips and whiskery conflagration, and sits down in the kitchen to a plate heaped high with chips and the kidneys of lambs.

In the blind-drawn dark dining-room of School House, dusty and echoing as a dining-room in a vault, Mr and Mrs Pugh are silent over cold grey cottage pie. Mr Pugh reads, as he forks the shroud meat in, from *Lives of the Great Poisoners*. He has bound a plain brown-paper cover round the book. Slyly, between slow mouthfuls, he sidespies up at Mrs Pugh, poisons her with his eye, then goes on reading. He underlines certain passages and smiles in secret.

MRS PUGH

Persons with manners do not read at table,

FIRST VOICE

says Mrs Pugh. She swallows a digestive tablet as big as a horse-pill, washing it down with clouded peasoup water.

[*Pause*

MRS PUGH

Some persons were brought up in pigsties.

MR PUGH

Pigs don't read at table, dear.

FIRST VOICE

Bitterly she flicks dust from the broken cruet. It settles on the pie in a thin gnat-rain.

MR PUGH

Pigs can't read, my dear.

MRS PUGH

I know one who can.

FIRST VOICE

Alone in the hissing laboratory of his wishes, Mr Pugh minces among bad vats and jeroboams, tiptoes through spinneys of murdering herbs, agony dancing in his crucibles, and mixes especially for Mrs Pugh a venomous porridge unknown to toxicologists which will scald and viper through her until her ears fall off like figs, her toes grow big and black as balloons, and steam comes screaming out of her navel.

MR PUGH

You know best, dear,

FIRST VOICE

says Mr Pugh, and quick as a flash he ducks her in rat soup.

MRS PUGH

What's that book by your trough, Mr Pugh?

MR PUGH

It's a theological work, my dear. *Lives of the Great Saints.*

FIRST VOICE

Mrs Pugh smiles. An icicle forms in the cold air of the dining vault.

MRS PUGH

I saw you talking to a saint this morning. Saint Polly Garter. She was martyred again last night. Mrs Organ Morgan saw her with Mr Waldo.

MRS ORGAN MORGAN

And when they saw me they pretended they were looking for nests,

SECOND VOICE

said Mrs Organ Morgan to her husband, with her mouth full of fish as a pelican's.

70

MRS ORGAN MORGAN

But you don't go nesting in long combinations, I
said to myself, like Mr Waldo was wearing, and your
dress nearly over your head like Polly Garter's. Oh,
they didn't fool me.

SECOND VOICE

One big bird gulp, and the flounder's gone. She
licks her lips and goes stabbing again.

MRS ORGAN MORGAN

And when you think of all those babies she's got,
then all I can say is she'd better give up bird nesting
that's all I can say, it isn't the right kind of hobby at
all for a woman that can't say No even to midgets.
Remember Bob Spit? He wasn't any bigger than a
baby and he gave her two. But they're two nice boys,
I will say that, Fred Spit and Arthur. Sometimes I
like Fred best and sometimes I like Arthur. Who do
you like best, Organ?

ORGAN MORGAN

Oh, Bach without any doubt. Bach every time
for me.

MRS ORGAN MORGAN

Organ Morgan, you haven't been listening to a
word I said. It's organ organ all the time with you...

FIRST VOICE

And she bursts into tears, and, in the middle of
her salty howling, nimbly spears a small flatfish and
pelicans it whole.

And then Palestrina,

says Organ Morgan.

Lord Cut-Glass, in his kitchen full of time, squats down alone to a dogdish, marked Fido, of peppery fish-scraps and listens to the voices of his sixty-six clocks—(one for each year of his loony age)—and watches, with love, their black-and-white moony loudlipped faces tocking the earth away: slow clocks, quick clocks, pendulumed heart-knocks, china, alarm, grandfather, cuckoo; clocks shaped like Noah's whirring Ark, clocks that bicker in marble ships, clocks in the wombs of glass women, hourglass chimers, tu-wit-tu-woo clocks, clocks that pluck tunes, Vesuvius clocks all black bells and lava, Niagara clocks that cataract their ticks, old time-weeping clocks with ebony beards, clocks with no hands for ever drumming out time without ever knowing what time it is. His sixty-six singers are all set at different hours. Lord Cut-Glass lives in a house and a life at siege. Any minute or dark day now, the unknown enemy will loot and savage downhill, but they will not catch him napping. Sixty-six different times in his fish-slimy kitchen ping, strike, tick, chime, and tock.

The lust and lilt and lather and emerald breeze and crackle of the bird-praise and body of Spring with its breasts full of rivering May-milk, means, to that lordly fish-head nibbler, nothing but another nearness to the tribes and navies of the Last Black Day who'll sear and pillage down Armageddon Hill to his double-locked rusty-shuttered tick-tock dust-scrabbled shack at the bottom of the town that has fallen head over bells in love.

POLLY GARTER

And I'll never have such loving again,

SECOND VOICE

pretty Polly hums and longs.

POLLY GARTER (*Sings*)

Now when farmers' boys on the first fair day
Come down from the hills to drink and be gay,
Before the sun sinks I'll lie there in their arms
For they're *good* bad boys from the lonely farms,

But I always think as we tumble into bed
Of little Willy Wee who is dead, dead, dead . . .

[*A silence*

FIRST VOICE

The sunny slow lulling afternoon yawns and moons through the dozy town. The sea lolls, laps and idles in, with fishes sleeping in its lap. The meadows still as Sunday, the shut-eye tasselled bulls, the goat-and-daisy dingles, nap happy and lazy. The dumb duck-ponds snooze. Clouds sag and pillow on Llareggub Hill. Pigs grunt in a wet wallow-bath, and smile

73

as they snort and dream. They dream of the acorned swill of the world, the rooting for pig-fruit, the bagpipe dugs of the mother sow, the squeal and snuffle of yesses of the women pigs in rut. They mud-bask and snout in the pig-loving sun; their tails curl; they rollick and slobber and snore to deep, smug, afterswill sleep. Donkeys angelically drowse on Donkey Down.

MRS PUGH

Persons with manners,

SECOND VOICE

snaps Mrs cold Pugh

MRS PUGH

do not nod at table.

FIRST VOICE

Mr Pugh cringes awake. He puts on a soft-soaping smile: it is sad and grey under his nicotine-eggyellow weeping walrus Victorian moustache worn thick and long in memory of Doctor Crippen.

MRS PUGH

You should wait until you retire to your sty,

SECOND VOICE

says Mrs Pugh, sweet as a razor. His fawning measly quarter-smile freezes. Sly and silent, he foxes into his chemist's den and there, in a hiss and prussic circle of cauldrons and phials brimful with pox and

74

the Black Death, cooks up a fricassee of deadly night-shade, nicotine, hot frog, cyanide and bat-spit for his needling stalactite hag and bednag of a pokerbacked nutcracker wife.

MR PUGH

I beg your pardon, my dear,

SECOND VOICE

he murmurs with a wheedle.

FIRST VOICE

Captain Cat, at his window thrown wide to the sun and the clippered seas he sailed long ago when his eyes were blue and bright, slumbers and voyages; ear-ringed and rolling, I Love You Rosie Probert tattooed on his belly, he brawls with broken bottles in the fug and babel of the dark dock bars, roves with a herd of short and good time cows in every naughty port and twines and souses with the drowned and blowzy-breasted dead. He weeps as he sleeps and sails.

SECOND VOICE

One voice of all he remembers most dearly as his dream buckets down. Lazy early Rosie with the flaxen thatch, whom he shared with Tom-Fred the donkey-man and many another seaman, clearly and near to him speaks from the bedroom of her dust. In that gulf and haven, fleets by the dozen have anchored for the little heaven of the night; but she speaks to Captain napping Cat alone. Mrs Probert . . .

from Duck Lane, Jack. Quack twice and ask for
Rosie.

SECOND VOICE

. . . is the one love of his sea-life that was sardined
with women.

ROSIE PROBERT (*Softly*)
What seas did you see,
Tom Cat, Tom Cat,
In your sailoring days
Long long ago?
What sea beasts were
In the wavery green
When you were my master?

CAPTAIN CAT
I'll tell you the truth.
Seas barking like seals,
Blue seas and green,
Seas covered with eels
And mermen and whales.

ROSIE PROBERT
What seas did you sail
Old whaler when
On the blubbery waves
Between Frisco and Wales
You were my bosun?

CAPTAIN CAT
As true as I'm here

Dear you Tom Cat's tart
You landlubber Rosie
You cosy love
My easy as easy
My true sweetheart,
Seas green as a bean
Seas gliding with swans
In the seal-barking moon.

ROSIE PROBERT
What seas were rocking
My little deck hand
My favourite husband
In your seaboots and hunger
My duck my whaler
My honey my daddy
My pretty sugar sailor
With my name on your belly
When you were a boy
Long long ago?

CAPTAIN CAT
I'll tell you no lies.
The only sea I saw
Was the seesaw sea
With you riding on it.
Lie down, lie easy.
Let me shipwreck in your thighs.

ROSIE PROBERT
Knock twice, Jack,

At the door of my grave
And ask for Rosie.

CAPTAIN CAT
Rosie Probert.

ROSIE PROBERT
Remember her.
She is forgetting.
The earth which filled her mouth
Is vanishing from her.
Remember me.
I have forgotten you.
I am going into the darkness of the
    darkness for ever.
I have forgotten that I was ever born.

CHILD
Look,

FIRST VOICE
says a child to her mother as they pass by the
window of Schooner House,

CHILD
Captain Cat is crying.

FIRST VOICE
Captain Cat is crying

CAPTAIN CAT
Come back, come back,

up the silences and echoes of the passages of the eternal night.

CHILD

He's crying all over his nose,

FIRST VOICE

says the child. Mother and child move on down the street.

CHILD

He's got a nose like strawberries,

FIRST VOICE

the child says; and then she forgets him too. She sees in the still middle of the bluebagged bay Nogood Boyo fishing from the *Zanzibar*.

CHILD

Nogood Boyo gave me three pennies yesterday but I wouldn't,

FIRST VOICE

the child tells her mother.

SECOND VOICE

Boyo catches a whalebone corset. It is all he has caught all day.

NOGOOD BOYO

Bloody funny fish!

79

Mrs Dai Bread Two gypsies up his mind's slow eye, dressed only in a bangle.

NOGOOD BOYO

She's wearing her nightgown. (*Pleadingly*) Would you like this nice wet corset, Mrs Dai Bread Two?

MRS DAI BREAD TWO

No, I *won't*!

NOGOOD BOYO

And a bite of my little apple?

SECOND VOICE

he offers with no hope.

FIRST VOICE

She shakes her brass nightgown, and he chases her out of his mind; and when he comes gusting back, there in the bloodshot centre of his eye a geisha girl grins and bows in a kimono of ricepaper.

NOGOOD BOYO

I want to be *good* Boyo, but nobody'll let me,

FIRST VOICE

he sighs as she writhes politely. The land fades, the sea flocks silently away; and through the warm white cloud where he lies, silky, tingling, uneasy Eastern music undoes him in a Japanese minute.

The afternoon buzzes like lazy bees round the flowers round Mae Rose Cottage. Nearly asleep in the field of nannygoats who hum and gently butt the sun, she blows love on a puffball.

MAE ROSE COTTAGE (*Lazily*)
He loves me
He loves me not
He loves me
He loves me not
He *loves* me!—the dirty old fool.

SECOND VOICE
Lazy she lies alone in clover and sweet-grass, seventeen and never been sweet in the grass ho ho.

FIRST VOICE
The Reverend Eli Jenkins inky in his cool front parlour or poem-room tells only the truth in his Lifework—the Population, Main Industry, Shipping, History, Topography, Flora and Fauna of the town he worships in—the White Book of Llareggub. Portraits of famous bards and preachers, all fur and wool from the squint to the kneecaps, hang over him heavy as sheep, next to faint lady watercolours of pale green Milk Wood like a lettuce salad dying. His mother, propped against a pot in a palm, with her wedding-ring waist and bust like a black-clothed dining-table, suffers in her stays.

REVEREND ELI JENKINS

Oh, angels be careful there with your knives and forks,

FIRST VOICE

he prays. There is no known likeness of his father Esau, who, undogcollared because of his little weakness, was scythed to the bone one harvest by mistake when sleeping with his weakness in the corn. He lost all ambition and died, with one leg.

REVEREND ELI JENKINS

Poor Dad,

SECOND VOICE

grieves the Reverend Eli,

REVEREND ELI JENKINS

to die of drink and agriculture.

SECOND VOICE

Farmer Watkins in Salt Lake Farm hates his cattle on the hill as he ho's them in to milking.

UTAH WATKINS (*In a fury*)

Damn you, you damned dairies!

SECOND VOICE

A cow kisses him.

UTAH WATKINS

Bite her to death!

he shouts to his deaf dog who smiles and licks his hands.

Gore him, sit on him, Daisy!

he bawls to the cow who barbed him with her tongue, and she moos gentle words as he raves and dances among his summerbreathed slaves walking delicately to the farm. The coming of the end of the Spring day is already reflected in the lakes of their great eyes. Bessie Bighead greets them by the names she gave them when they were maidens.

Peg, Meg, Buttercup, Moll,
Fan from the Castle,
Theodosia and Daisy.

They bow their heads.

Look up Bessie Bighead in the White Book of Llareggub and you will find the few haggard rags and the one poor glittering thread of her history laid out in pages there with as much love and care as the lock of hair of a first lost love. Conceived in Milk Wood, born in a barn, wrapped in paper, left on a doorstep, big-headed and bass-voiced she grew in the dark until long-dead Gomer Owen kissed her when she wasn't looking because he was dared. Now in the light she'll work, sing, milk, say the cows' sweet names and sleep until the night sucks out her soul and spits it into the sky. In her life-long love light, holily Bessie milks the fond lake-eyed cows as dusk showers slowly down over byre, sea and town.

Utah Watkins curses through the farmyard on a carthorse.

UTAH WATKINS
Gallop, you bleeding cripple!

FIRST VOICE
and the huge horse neighs softly as though he had given it a lump of sugar.

Now the town is dusk. Each cobble, donkey, goose and gooseberry street is a thoroughfare of dusk; and dusk and ceremonial dust, and night's first darkening snow, and the sleep of birds, drift under and through the live dusk of this place of love. Llareggub is the capital of dusk.

Mrs Ogmore-Pritchard, at the first drop of the dusk-shower, seals all her sea-view doors, draws the germ-free blinds, sits, erect as a dry dream on a high-backed hygienic chair and wills herself to cold, quick sleep. At once, at twice, Mr Ogmore and Mr Pritchard, who all dead day long have been gossiping like ghosts in the woodshed, planning the loveless destruction of their glass widow, reluctantly sigh and sidle into her clean house.

MR PRITCHARD

You first, Mr Ogmore.

MR OGMORE

After you, Mr Pritchard.

MR PRITCHARD

No, no, Mr. Ogmore. You widowed her first.

FIRST VOICE

And in through the keyhole, with tears where their eyes once were, they ooze and grumble.

MRS OGMORE-PRITCHARD

Husbands,

FIRST VOICE

she says in her sleep. There is acid love in her voice for one of the two shambling phantoms. Mr Ogmore hopes that it is not for him. So does Mr Pritchard.

MRS OGMORE-PRITCHARD

I love you both.

MR OGMORE *(With terror)*

Oh, Mrs Ogmore.

MR PRITCHARD *(With horror)*

Oh, Mrs Pritchard.

MRS OGMORE-PRITCHARD

Soon it will be time to go to bed. Tell me your tasks in order.

MR OGMORE AND MR PRITCHARD

We must take our pyjamas from the drawer marked pyjamas.

MRS OGMORE-PRITCHARD (*Coldly*)

And then you must take them off.

SECOND VOICE

Down in the dusking town, Mae Rose Cottage, still lying in clover, listens to the nannygoats chew, draws circles of lipstick round her nipples.

MAE ROSE COTTAGE

I'm *fast*. I'm a bad lot. God will strike me dead. I'm seventeen. I'll go to hell,

SECOND VOICE

she tells the goats.

MAE ROSE COTTAGE

You just wait. I'll sin till I blow up!

SECOND VOICE

She lies deep, waiting for the worst to happen; the goats champ and sneer.

FIRST VOICE

And at the doorway of Bethesda House, the Reverend Jenkins recites to Llareggub Hill his sunset poem.

Every morning when I wake,
Dear Lord, a little prayer I make,
O please to keep Thy lovely eye
On all poor creatures born to die.

And every evening at sun-down
I ask a blessing on the town,
For whether we last the night or no
I'm sure is always touch-and-go.

We are not wholly bad or good
Who live our lives under Milk Wood,
And Thou, I know, wilt be the first
To see our best side, not our worst.

O let us see another day!
Bless us this night, I pray,
And to the sun we all will bow
And say, good-bye—but just for now!

FIRST VOICE

Jack Black prepares once more to meet his Satan
in the Wood. He grinds his night-teeth, closes his
eyes, climbs into his religious trousers, their flies sewn
up with cobbler's thread, and pads out, torched and
bibled, grimly, joyfully, into the already sinning dusk.

JACK BLACK

Off to Gomorrah!

And Lily Smalls is up to Nogood Boyo in the wash-house.

FIRST VOICE

And Cherry Owen, sober as Sunday as he is every day of the week, goes off happy as Saturday to get drunk as a deacon as he does every night.

CHERRY OWEN

I always say she's got two husbands,

FIRST VOICE

says Cherry Owen,

CHERRY OWEN

one drunk and one sober.

FIRST VOICE

And Mrs Cherry simply says

MRS CHERRY OWEN

And aren't I a lucky woman? Because I love them both.

SINBAD

Evening, Cherry.

CHERRY OWEN

Evening, Sinbad.

SINBAD

What'll you have?

Too much.

SINBAD

The Sailors Arms is always open . . .

FIRST VOICE

Sinbad suffers to himself, heartbroken,

SINBAD

. . . oh, Gossamer, open yours!

FIRST VOICE

Dusk is drowned for ever until to-morrow. It is all at once night now. The windy town is a hill of windows, and from the larrupped waves the lights of the lamps in the windows call back the day and the dead that have run away to sea. All over the calling dark, babies and old men are bribed and lullabied to sleep.

FIRST WOMAN'S VOICE

Hushabye, baby, the sandman is coming . . .

SECOND WOMAN'S VOICE (*Singing*)

Rockabye, grandpa, in the tree top,
When the wind blows the cradle will rock,
When the bough breaks the cradle will fall,
Down will come grandpa, whiskers and all.

FIRST VOICE

Or their daughters cover up the old unwinking men like parrots, and in their little dark in the lit and

89

bustling young kitchen corners, all night long they
watch, beady-eyed, the long night through in case
death catches them asleep.

SECOND VOICE

Unmarried girls, alone in their privately bridal
bedrooms, powder and curl for the Dance of the
World.

[*Accordion music: dim*

They make, in front of their looking-glasses,
haughty or come-hithering faces for the young men
in the street outside, at the lamplit leaning corners,
who wait in the all-at-once wind to wolve and whistle.

[*Accordion music louder, then fading under*

FIRST VOICE

The drinkers in the Sailors Arms drink to the
failure of the dance.

A DRINKER

Down with the waltzing and the skipping.

CHERRY OWEN

Dancing isn't natural,

FIRST VOICE

righteously says Cherry Owen who has just
downed seventeen pints of flat, warm, thin, Welsh,
bitter beer.

SECOND VOICE

A farmer's lantern glimmers, a spark on Llareggub
hillside.

[*Accordion music fades into silence*

90

Llareggub Hill, writes the Reverend Jenkins in his poem-room,

REVEREND ELI JENKINS

Llareggub Hill, that mystic tumulus, the memorial of peoples that dwelt in the region of Llareggub before the Celts left the Land of Summer and where the old wizards made themselves a wife out of flowers.

SECOND VOICE

Mr Waldo, in his corner of the Sailors Arms, sings:

MR WALDO

In Pembroke City when I was young
I lived by the Castle Keep
Sixpence a week was my wages
For working for the chimbley sweep.
Six cold pennies he gave me
Not a farthing more or less
And all the fare I could afford
Was parsnip gin and watercress.
I did not need a knife and fork
Or a bib up to my chin
To dine on a dish of watercress
And a jug of parsnip gin.
Did you ever hear a growing boy
To live so cruel cheap
On grub that has no flesh and bones
And liquor that makes you weep?
Sweep sweep chimbley sweep,

I wept through Pembroke City
Poor and barefoot in the snow
Till a kind young woman took pity.
Poor little chimbley sweep she said
Black as the ace of spades
O nobody's swept my chimbley
Since my husband went his ways.
Come and sweep my chimbley
Come and sweep my chimbley
She sighed to me with a blush
Come and sweep my chimbley
Come and sweep my chimbley
Bring along your chimbley brush!

FIRST VOICE

Blind Captain Cat climbs into his bunk. Like a
cat, he sees in the dark. Through the voyages of his
tears, he sails to see the dead.

CAPTAIN CAT

Dancing Williams!

FIRST DROWNED

Still dancing.

CAPTAIN CAT

Jonah Jarvis

THIRD DROWNED

Still.

FIRST DROWNED

Curly Bevan's skull.

Rosie, with God. She has forgotten dying.

FIRST VOICE
The dead come out in their Sunday best.

SECOND VOICE
Listen to the night breaking.

FIRST VOICE
Organ Morgan goes to chapel to play the organ.
He sees Bach lying on a tombstone.

ORGAN MORGAN
Johann Sebastian!

CHERRY OWEN *(Drunkenly)*
Who?

ORGAN MORGAN
Johann Sebastian mighty Bach. Oh, Bachfach.

CHERRY OWEN
To hell with you,

FIRST VOICE
says Cherry Owen who is resting on the tombstone on his way home.

Mr Mog Edwards and Miss Myfanwy Price happily apart from one another at the top and the sea end
of the town write their everynight letters of love and
desire. In the warm White Book of Llareggub you

will find the little maps of the islands of their contentment.

MYFANWY PRICE
Oh, my Mog, I am yours for ever.

FIRST VOICE
And she looks around with pleasure at her own neat neverdull room which Mr Mog Edwards will never enter.

MOG EDWARDS
Come to my arms, Myfanwy.

FIRST VOICE
And he hugs his lovely money to his *own* heart.
And Mr. Waldo drunk in the dusky wood hugs his lovely Polly Garter under the eyes and rattling tongues of the neighbours and the birds, and he does not care. He smacks his live red lips.

But it is not *his* name that Polly Garter whispers as she lies under the oak and loves him back. Six feet deep that name sings in the cold earth.

POLLY GARTER (*Sings*)
But I always think as we tumble into bed
Of little Willy Wee who is dead, dead, dead.

FIRST VOICE
The thin night darkens. A breeze from the creased water sighs the streets close under Milk waking Wood. The Wood, whose every tree-foot's cloven in the black glad sight of the hunters of lovers, that is a God-built

94

garden to Mary Ann Sailors, who knows there is Heaven on earth and the chosen people of His kind fire in Llareggub's land, that is the fairday farmhands' wantoning ignorant chapel of bridesbeds, and, to the Reverend Eli Jenkins, a greenleaved sermon on the innocence of men, the suddenly wind-shaken wood springs awake for the second dark time this one Spring day.

NOTES ON PRONUNCIATION

page   2: *Rhiannon*: strongly aspirated *r*, and accent on the second syllable. *Llareggub*: a voiceless *l* produced from the side of the mouth, accent on the second syllable, the third syllable rhyming with 'bib.' *Dai*: as 'dye.'

page   6: *Dowlais*: accent on the first syllable, the second syllable rhyming with 'ice.' *Maesgwyn*: mice-gwin, accent on the second syllable.

page   7: *Myfanwy*: accent on the second syllable, *f* as *v*, the first *y* an indeterminate sound, the second *y* as *ee*.

page   8: *Ach y fi*: the *ch* guttural, the *y* indeterminate, *f* as *v*, the whole pronounced as one word; an interjection expressing disgust.

page 13: *mwchins*: a compromise between the English 'mooching' and the Welsh dialect word 'mitching,' playing truant.

page 22: *Organ Morgan*: the *r*'s rolled, the *o*'s short. *Gippo*: gipsy.

page 23: *Eisteddfodau*: eye-steth-vod-eye, the *th* voiced, a strong accent on the third syllable. *Parchs*: the *ch* guttural; clergymen.

97

page 26: *Dewi*: de-wee; the first syllable, which has the accent, is short.

page 27: *Moel yr Wyddfa*: moil-er-ooithva, the *th* voiced. *Carnedd*: the *dd* a voiced *th*, the *r* rolled, accent on the first syllable. *Penmaen-mawr*: 'maen' rhymes with 'line,' 'mawr' with 'hour.'

page 28: *Sawddwy*: southay, the *th* voiced. *Edw*: aid-oo. *Llyfnant*: *y* indeterminate, *f* as *v*. *Claerwen, Cleddau, Dulais*: clire-wen; cleth-eye, the *th* voiced; dill-ice. *Ogwr*: ogoorr, accent on the first syllable. *Cennen*: the *c* hard.

page 42: *Gerwain*: gerr-wine, the *g* hard. *Ty*: as 'tee.'

page 45: *Gorslas*: gorse-lahss, with a strong accent on the second syllable.

page 54: *Twll*: tooll, the *oo* short, the *ll* as in 'Llareg-gub.'

page 66: *cawl*: as 'cowl'; a broth with leeks.

page 93: *fach*: an expression of endearment; *f* as *v*, and the *ch* guttural.

MUSIC FOR THE SONGS

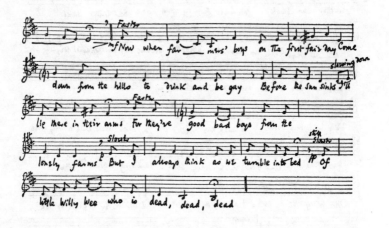

mf Now when farmers' boys on the first fair day Come down from the hills to drink and be gay Before the sun sinks i' th lie there in their arms For they're good bad boys from the lonely farms But I always think as we tumble into bed *pp* Of little Willy Wee who is dead, dead, dead

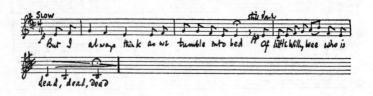

SLOW But I always think as we tumble into bed *pp* Of little Willy Wee who is dead, dead, dead

Up to his livver.... Quick quick Dirty Dick Beat him on the bum with a rhubarb stick Aiee Hush!....

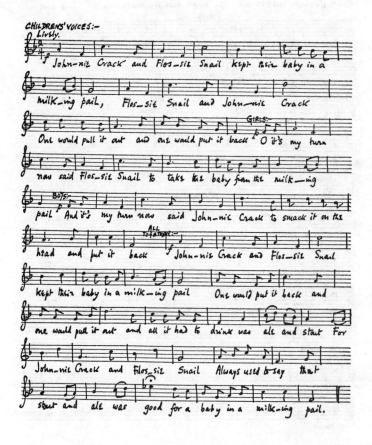

Livsly.

Johnnie Crack and Flossie Snail kept their baby in a milking pail, Flossie Snail and Johnnie Crack One would pull it out and one would put it back

GIRLS:

O it's my turn now said Flossie Snail to take the baby from the milking pail

BOYS:

And it's my turn now said Johnnie Crack to smack it on the head and put it back

ALL TOGETHER:—

Johnnie Crack and Flossie Snail kept their baby in a milking pail One would put it back and one would pull it out and all it had to drink was ale and stout For Johnnie Crack and Flossie Snail Always used to say that stout and ale was good for a baby in a milking pail.

103

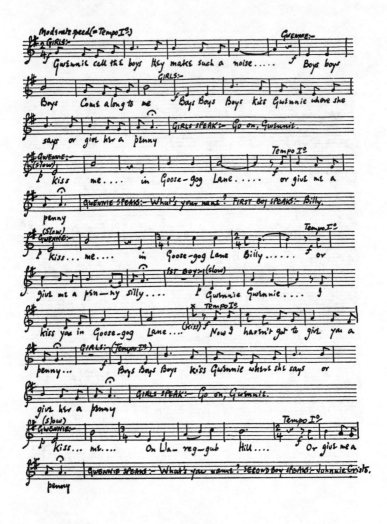

104

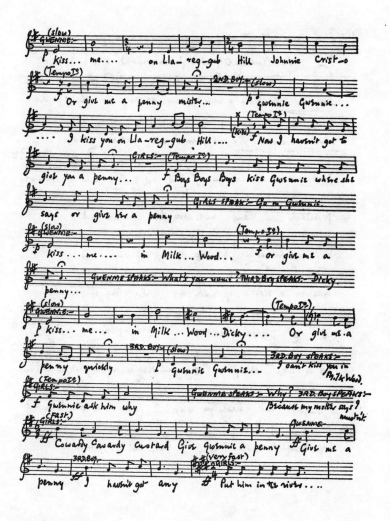

105

In Pembroke City when I was young I lived by the Castle Keep Six-pence a week was my wages For working for the chimbley sweep Six cold pennies he gave me Not a farthing more or less— And all the fare I— could afford was parsnip gin— and watercress I did not need a knife and fork or a bib up to my chin— To dine on a dish of watercress And a jug of parsnip gin. Did you ever hear a graving boy To live so cruel cheap On grub that has no— flesh and bones and liquor that makes you weep? Sweep Sweep chimbley sweep I wept through Pembroke City Poor— and barefoot in the

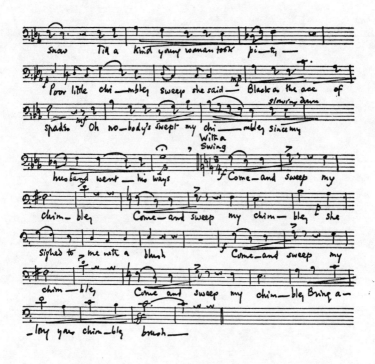

snow Till a kind young woman took pity —

Poor little chimbley sweep she said — Black as the ace of

spades Oh no-body's swept my chi — mbley since my

husband went — his ways f Come — and sweep my

chim — bley Come — and sweep my chim — bley she

sighed to me with a blush Come — and sweep my

chim — bley Come and sweep my chim — bley Bring a-

-long your chim — bley brush —

New Directions Paperbooks

Complete descriptive catalog available free on request from
New Directions, 333 Sixth Avenue, New York 10014. † Bilingual.

5-14

STEPHEN KING

A NOVEL

SCRIBNER

SCRIBNER
1230 Avenue of the Americas
New York, NY 10020

SCRIBNER and design are trademarks of Macmillan Library Reference USA, Inc.,
used under license by Simon & Schuster, the publisher of this work.

For information regarding special discounts for bulk purchases,
please contact Simon & Schuster Special Sales at 1-800-456-6798
or *business@simonandschuster.com*

DESIGNED BY ERICH HOBBING

Set in Garamond No. 3

Manufactured in the United States of America

1   3   5   7   9   10   8   6   4   2

Library of Congress Cataloging-in-Publication Data
King, Stephen, 1947–
From a Buick 8 : a novel / Stephen King.
p. cm.
1. Abandonmnent of automobiles—Fiction. 2. Police—Pennsylvania—Fiction.
3. Buick automobile—Fiction. 4. Pennsylvania—Fiction.
5. Teenage boys—Fiction. I. Title: From a Buick Eight. II. Title.

PS3561.I483 F76 2002
813'.54—dc21   2001055118

ISBN 0-7432-1137-5

This is for Surendra and Geeta Patel.

From 8
A Buick 8

Now: *Sandy*

Curt Wilcox's boy came around the barracks a lot the year after his father died, I mean a lot, but nobody ever told him get out the way or asked him what in *hail* he was doing there again. We understood what he was doing: trying to hold onto the memory of his father. Cops know a lot about the psychology of grief; most of us know more about it than we want to.

That was Ned Wilcox's senior year at Statler High. He must have quit off the football team; when it came time for choosing, he picked D Troop instead. Hard to imagine a kid doing that, choosing unpaid choring over all those Friday night games and Saturday night parties, but that's what he did. I don't think any of us talked to him about that choice, but we respected him for it. He had decided the time had come to put the games away, that's all. Grown men are frequently incapable of making such decisions; Ned made his at an age when he still couldn't buy a legal drink. Or a legal pack of smokes, for that matter. I think his Dad would have been proud. Know it, actually.

Given how much the boy was around, I suppose it was inevitable he'd see what was out in Shed B, and ask someone what it was and what it was doing there. I was the one he was most likely to ask, because I'd been his father's closest friend. Closest one that was still a Trooper, at least. I think maybe I wanted it to happen. Kill or cure, the oldtimers used to say. Give that curious cat a serious dose of satisfaction.

What happened to Curtis Wilcox was simple. A veteran county drunk, one Curt himself knew well and had arrested six or eight times, took his life. The drunk, Bradley Roach, didn't mean to hurt anyone; drunks so rarely do. That doesn't keep you from wanting to kick their numb asses all the way to Rocksburg, of course.

1

Toward the end of a hot July afternoon in the year oh-one, Curtis pulled over one of those big sixteen-wheelers, an interstate landcruiser that had left the fourlane because its driver was hoping for a home-cooked meal instead of just another dose of I-87 Burger King or Taco Bell. Curt was parked on the tarmac of the abandoned Jenny station at the intersection of Pennsylvania State Road 32 and the Humboldt Road—the very place, in other words, where that damned old Buick Roadmaster showed up in our part of the known universe all those years ago. You can call that a coincidence if you want to, but I'm a cop and don't believe in coincidences, only chains of event which grow longer and ever more fragile until either bad luck or plain old human mean-heartedness breaks them.

Ned's father took out after that semi because it had a flapper. When it went by he saw rubber spinning out from one of the rear tires like a big black pinwheel. A lot of independents run on recaps, with the price of diesel so high they just about have to, and sometimes the tread peels loose. You see curls and hunks of it on the interstate all the time, lying on the highway or pushed off into the breakdown lane like the shed skins of giant blacksnakes. It's dangerous to be behind a flapper, especially on a twolane like SR 32, a pretty but neglected stretch of state highway running between Rocksburg and Statler. A big enough chunk might break some unlucky follow-driver's windshield. Even if it didn't, it could startle the operator into the ditch, or a tree, or over the embankment and into Redfern Stream, which matches 32 twist for twist over a distance of nearly six miles.

Curt lit his bar lights, and the trucker pulled over like a good boy. Curt pulled over right behind him, first calling in his 20 and the nature of his stop and waiting for Shirley to acknowledge. With that done, he got out and walked toward the truck.

If he'd gone directly to where the driver was leaning out and looking back at him, he might still be on Planet Earth today. But he stopped to examine the flapper on the rear outside tire, even gave it a good yank to see if he could pull it off. The trucker saw all of it, and testified to it in court. Curt stopping to do that was the last link save one in the chain that brought his boy to Troop D and eventually made him a part of what we are. The very last link, I'd say, was Bradley Roach leaning over to get another brewski out of the six-pack sitting on the floor in the passenger footwell of his old Buick Regal (not *the* Buick, but *another* Buick, yes—it's funny how, when you look back on disasters and love affairs, things seem to line up like planets on an astrologer's chart). Less than a minute later, Ned Wilcox and his sisters were short a daddy and Michelle Wilcox was short a husband.

Not very long after the funeral, Curt's boy started showing up at the Troop D House. I'd come in for the three-to-eleven that fall (or maybe just to check on things; when you're the wheeldog, it's hard to stay away) and see the boy before I saw anyone else, like as not. While his friends were over at Floyd B. Clouse Field behind the high school, running plays and hitting the tackling dummies and giving each other high-fives, Ned would be out on the front lawn of the barracks by himself, bundled up in his green and gold high school jacket, making big piles of fallen leaves. He'd give me a wave and I'd return it: right back atcha, kid. Sometimes after I parked, I'd come out front and shoot the shit with him. He'd tell me about the foolishness his sisters were up to just lately, maybe, and laugh, but you could see his love for them even when he was laughing at them. Sometimes I'd just go in the back way and ask Shirley what was up. Law enforcement in western Pennsylvania would fall apart without Shirley Pasternak, and you can take that to the bank.

Come winter, Ned was apt to be around back in the parking lot, where the Troopers keep their personal vehicles, running the snowblower. The Dadier brothers, two local wide boys, are responsible for our lot, but Troop D sits in the Amish country on the edge of the Short Hills, and when there's a big storm the wind blows drifts across the lot again almost as soon as the plow leaves. Those drifts look to me like an enormous white ribcage. Ned was a match for them, though. There he'd be, even if it was only eight degrees and the wind still blowing a gale across the hills, dressed in a snowmobile suit with his green and gold jacket pulled over the top of it, leather-lined police-issue gloves on his hands and a ski-mask pulled down over his face. I'd wave. He'd give me a little right-back-atcha, then go on gobbling up the drifts with the snowblower. Later he might come in for coffee, or maybe a cup of hot chocolate. Folks would drift over and talk to him, ask him about school, ask him if he was keeping the twins in line (the girls were ten in the winter of oh-one, I think). They'd ask if his Mom needed anything. Sometimes that would include me, if no one was hollering too loud or if the paperwork wasn't too heavy. None of the talk was about his father; all of the talk was about his father. You understand.

Raking leaves and making sure the drifts didn't take hold out there in the parking lot was really Arky Arkanian's responsibility. Arky was the custodian. He was one of us as well, though, and he never got shirty or went territorial about his job. Hell, when it came to snowblowing the drifts, I'll bet Arky just about got down on his knees and thanked God for the kid. Arky was sixty by then, had to have been, and his own football-playing days were long behind him. So were the ones when he could spend an hour and a half outside in ten-degree temperatures (twenty-five below, if you factored in the wind chill) and hardly feel it.

And then the kid started in with Shirley, technically Police Communications Officer Pasternak. By the time spring rolled around, Ned was spending more and more time with her in her little dispatch cubicle with the phones, the TDD (telephonic device for the deaf), the Trooper Location Board (also known as the D-map), and the computer console that's the hot center of that high-pressure little world. She showed him the bank of phones (the most important is the red one, which is our end of 911). She explained about how the traceback equipment had to be tested once a week, and how it was done, and how you had to confirm the duty-roster daily, so you'd know who was out patrolling the roads of Statler, Lassburg, and Pogus City, and who was due in court or off-duty.

"My nightmare is losing an officer without knowing he's lost," I overheard her telling Ned one day.

"Has that ever happened?" Ned asked. "Just . . . losing a guy?"

"Once," she said. "Before my time. Look here, Ned, I made you a copy of the call-codes. We don't have to use them anymore, but all the Troopers still do. If you want to run dispatch, you have to know these."

Then she went back to the four basics of the job, running them past him yet again: know the location, know the nature of the incident, know what the injuries are, if any, and know the closest available unit. Location, incident, injuries, CAU, that was her mantra.

I thought: *He'll be running it next. She means to have him running it. Never mind that if Colonel Teague or someone from Scranton comes in and sees him doing it she'd lose her job, she means to have him running it.*

And by the good goddam, there he was a week later, sitting at PCO Pasternak's desk in the dispatch cubicle, at first only while she ran to the bathroom but then for longer and longer periods while she went across the room for coffee or even out back for a smoke.

The first time the boy saw me seeing him in there all alone, he jumped and then gave a great big guilty smile, like a kid who is surprised in the rumpus room by his mother while he's still got his hand on his girl-friend's tit. I gave him a nod and went right on about my beeswax. Never thought twice about it, either. Shirley had turned over the dispatch oper-ation of Statler Troop D to a kid who still only needed to shave three times a week, almost a dozen Troopers were out there at the other end of the gear in that cubicle, but I didn't even slow my stride. We were still talking about his father, you see. Shirley and Arky as well as me and the other uniforms Curtis Wilcox had served with for over twenty years. You don't always talk with your mouth. Sometimes what you say with your mouth hardly matters at all. You have to *signify*.

When I was out of his sightline, though, I stopped. Stood there. Lis-tened. Across the room, in front of the highway-side windows, Shirley Pasternak stood looking back at me with a Styrofoam cup of coffee in her hand. Next to her was Phil Candleton, who had just clocked off and was once more dressed in his civvies; he was also staring in my direction.

In the dispatch cubicle, the radio crackled. "Statler, this is 12," a voice said. Radio distorts, but I still knew all of my men. That was Eddie Jacubois.

"This is Statler, go ahead," Ned replied. Perfectly calm. If he was afraid of fucking up, he was keeping it out of his voice.

"Statler, I have a Volkswagen Jetta, tag is 14-0-7-3-9 Foxtrot, that's P-A, stopped County Road 99. I need a 10-28, come back?"

Shirley started across the floor, moving fast. A little coffee sloshed over the rim of the Styrofoam cup in her hand. I took her by the elbow, stopping her. Eddie Jacubois was out there on a county road, he'd just stopped a Jetta for some violation—speeding was the logical assumption—and he wanted to know if there were any red flags on the plate or the plateholder. He wanted to know because he was going to get out of his cruiser and approach the Jetta. He wanted to know because he was going to put his ass out on the line, same today as every day. Was the Jetta maybe stolen? Had it been involved in an accident at any time during the last six months? Had its owner been in court on charges of spousal abuse? Had he shot anyone? Robbed or raped anyone? Were there even outstanding parking tickets?

Eddie had a right to know these things, if they were in the database. But Eddie also had a right to know why it was a high school kid who had just told him *This is Statler, go ahead.* I thought it was Eddie's call. If he came back with *Where the hell is Shirley,* I'd let go of her arm. And if Eddie rolled with it, I wanted to see what the kid would do. *How* the kid would do.

"Unit 12, hold for reply." If Ned was popping a sweat, it still didn't show in his voice. He turned to the computer monitor and keyed in Uniscope, the search engine used by the Pennsylvania State Police. He hit the keys rapidly but cleanly, then punched ENTER.

There followed a moment of silence in which Shirley and I stood side by side, saying nothing and hoping in perfect unison. Hoping that the kid wouldn't freeze, hoping that he wouldn't suddenly push back the chair and bolt for the door, hoping most of all that he had sent the right code to the right place. It seemed like a long moment. I remember I heard a bird calling outside and, very distant, the drone of a plane. There was time to think about those chains of event some people insist on calling coincidence. One of those chains had broken when Ned's father died on Route 32; here was another, just beginning to form. Eddie Jacubois— never the sharpest knife in the drawer, I'm afraid—was now joined to Ned Wilcox. Beyond him, one link further down the new chain, was a Volkswagen Jetta. And whoever was driving it.

Then: "12, this is Statler."

"12."

"Jetta is registered to William Kirk Frady of Pittsburgh. He is previous . . . uh . . . wait . . ."

It was his only pause, and I could hear the hurried riffle of paper as he looked for the card Shirley had given him, the one with the call-codes on it. He found it, looked at it, tossed it aside with an impatient little grunt. Through all this, Eddie waited patiently in his cruiser twelve miles west. He would be looking at Amish buggies, maybe, or a farmhouse with the curtain in one of the front windows pulled aslant, indicating that the Amish family living inside included a daughter of marriageable age, or over the hazy hills to Ohio. Only he wouldn't really be seeing any of those things. The only thing Eddie was seeing at that moment—seeing clearly—was the Jetta parked on the shoulder in front of him, the driver nothing but a silhouette behind the wheel. And what was he, that driver? Rich man? Poor man? Beggarman? Thief?

Finally Ned just said it, which was exactly the right choice. "12, Frady is DUI times three, do you copy?"

Drunk man, that's what the Jetta's driver was. Maybe not right now, but if he had been speeding, the likelihood was high.

"Copy, Statler." Perfectly laconic. "Got a current laminate?" Wanting to know if Frady's license to drive was currently valid.

"Ah . . ." Ned peered frantically at the white letters on the blue screen. *Right in front of you, kiddo, don't you see it?* I held my breath.

Then: "Affirmative, 12, he got it back three months ago."

I let go of my breath. Beside me, Shirley let go of hers. This was good news for Eddie, too. Frady was legal, and thus less likely to be crazy. That was the rule of thumb, anyway.

"12 on approach," Eddie sent. "Copy that?"

"Copy, 12 on approach, standing by," Ned replied. I heard a click and then a large, unsteady sigh. I nodded to Shirley, who got moving again. Then I reached up and wiped my brow, not exactly surprised to find it was wet with sweat.

"How's everything going?" Shirley asked. Voice even and normal, saying that, as far as she was concerned, all was quiet on the western front.

"Eddie Jacubois called in," Ned told her. "He's 10-27." That's an operator check, in plain English. If you're a Trooper, you know that it also means citing the operator for some sort of violation, in nine cases out of ten. Now Ned's voice wasn't quite steady, but so what? Now it was all right for it to jig and and jag a little. "He's got a guy in a Jetta out on Highway 99. I handled it."

"Tell me how," Shirley said. "Go through your procedure. Every step, Ned. Quick's you can."

I went on my way. Phil Candleton intercepted me at the door to my office. He nodded toward the dispatch cubicle. "How'd the kid do?"

"Did all right," I said, and stepped past him into my own cubicle. I didn't realize my legs had gone rubbery until I sat down and felt them trembling.

His sisters, Joan and Janet, were identicals. They had each other, and their mother had a little bit of her gone man in them: Curtis's blue, slightly uptilted eyes, his blonde hair, his full lips (the nickname in Curt's yearbook, under his name, had been "Elvis"). Michelle had her man in her son, as well, where the resemblance was even more striking. Add a few crow's-feet around the eyes and Ned could have been his own father when Curtis first came on the cops.

That's what they had. What Ned had was us.

One day in April he came into the barracks with a great big sunny smile on his face. It made him look younger and sweeter. But, I remember thinking, we all of us look younger and sweeter when we smile our real smiles—the ones that come when we are genuinely happy and not just trying to play some dumb social game. It struck me fresh that day because Ned didn't smile much. Certainly not *big*. I don't think I realized it until that day because he was polite and responsive and quick-witted. A pleasure to have around, in other words. You didn't notice how grave he was until that rare day when you saw him brighten up and shine.

He came to the center of the room, and all the little conversations stopped. He had a paper in his hand. There was a complicated-looking gold seal at the top. "Pitt!" he said, holding the paper up in both hands like an Olympic judge's scorecard. "I got into Pitt, you guys! And they gave me a scholarship! Almost a full boat!"

Everyone applauded. Shirley kissed him smack on the mouth, and the kid blushed all the way down to his collar. Huddie Royer, who was off-duty that day and just hanging around, stewing about some case in which he had to testify, went out and came back with a bag of L'il Debbie cakes. Arky used his key to open the soda machine, and we had a party. Half an hour or so, no more, but it was good while it lasted. Everyone shook Ned's hand, the acceptance letter from Pitt made its way around the room (twice, I think), and a couple of cops who'd been at home dropped by just to talk to him and pass along their congrats.

Then, of course, the real world got back into the act. It's quiet over here in western Pennsylvania, but not dead. There was a farmhouse fire in Pogus City (which is a city about as much as I'm the Archduke Ferdinand), and an overturned Amish buggy on Highway 20. The Amish keep to themselves, but they'll gladly take a little outside help in a case like that. The horse was okay, which was the big thing. The worst buggy fuckups happen on Friday and Saturday nights, when the younger bucks in black have a tendency to get drunk out behind the barn. Sometimes they get a "worldly person" to buy them a bottle or a case of Iron City beer, and sometimes they drink their own stuff, a really murderous corn shine you wouldn't wish on your worst enemy. It's just part of the scene; it's our world, and mostly we like it, including the Amish with their big neat farms and the orange triangles on the backs of their small neat buggies.

And there's always paperwork, the usual stacks of duplicate and triplicate in my office. It gets worse every year. Why I ever wanted to be the guy in charge is beyond me now. I took the test that qualified me for Sergeant Commanding when Tony Schoondist suggested it, so I must have had a reason back then, but these days it seems to elude me.

Around six o'clock I went out back to have a smoke. We have a bench there facing the parking lot. Beyond it is a very pretty western view. Ned Wilcox was sitting on the bench with his acceptance letter from Pitt in one hand and tears rolling down his face. He glanced at me, then looked away, scrubbing his eyes with the palm of his hand.

I sat down beside him, thought about putting my arm around his shoulder, didn't do it. If you have to think about a thing like that, doing it usually feels phony. I guess, anyway. I have never married, and what I know about fathering you could write on the head of a pin with room left over for the Lord's Prayer. I lit a cigarette and smoked it awhile. "It's all right, Ned," I said eventually. It was the only thing I could think of, and I had no idea what it meant.

"I know," he replied at once in a muffled, trying-not-to-cry voice, and then, almost as if it was part of the same sentence, a continuation of the same thought: "No it ain't."

Hearing him use that word, that *ain't,* made me realize how bad he was hurt. Something had gored him in the stomach. It was the sort of word he would have trained himself out of long ago, just so he wouldn't be lumped with the rest of the Statler County hicks, the pickup-truck-n-snowmobile gomers from towns like Patchin and Pogus City. Even his sisters, eight years younger than he was, had probably given up *ain't* by then, and for much the same reasons. Don't say ain't or your mother will faint and your father will fall in a bucket of paint. Yeah, what father?

I smoked and said nothing. On the far side of the parking lot by one of the county roadsalt piles was a cluster of wooden buildings that needed either sprucing up or tearing down. They were the old Motor Pool buildings. Statler County had moved its plows, graders, 'dozers, and asphalt rollers a mile or so down the road ten years before, into a new brick facility that looked like a prison lockdown unit. All that remained here was the one big pile of salt (which we were using ourselves, little by little—once upon a time, that pile had been a mountain) and a few ram-shackle wooden buildings. One of them was Shed B. The black-paint letters over the door—one of those wide garage doors that run up on rails—were faded but still legible. Was I thinking about the Buick Roadmaster inside as I sat there next to the crying boy, wanting to put my arm around him and not knowing how? I don't know. I guess I might have been, but I don't think we know all the things we're thinking. Freud might have been full of shit about a lot of things, but not that one. I don't know about a subconscious, but there's a pulse in our heads, all right, same as there's one in our chests, and it carries unformed, no-language thoughts that most times we can't even read, and they are usually the important ones.

Ned rattled the letter. "*He's* the one I really want to show this to. *He's* the one who wanted to go to Pitt when he was a kid but couldn't afford it. He's the reason I *applied,* for God's sake." A pause; then, almost too low to hear: "This is fucked up, Sandy."

"What did your mother say when you showed her?"

That got a laugh, watery but genuine. "She didn't *say.* She screamed like a lady who just won a trip to Bermuda on a gameshow. Then she cried." Ned turned to me. His own tears had stopped, but his eyes were red and swollen. He looked a hell of a lot younger than eighteen just then. The sweet smile resurfaced for a moment. "Basically, she was great about it. Even the Little J's were great about it. Like you guys. Shirley kissing me . . . man, I got goosebumps."

I laughed, thinking that Shirley might have raised a few goose-bumps of her own. She liked him, he was a handsome kid, and the idea of playing Mrs. Robinson might have crossed her mind. Probably not, but it wasn't impossible. Her husband had been out of the picture almost twenty years by then.

Ned's smile faded. He rattled the acceptance letter again. "I knew this was yes as soon as I took it out of the mailbox. I could just tell, somehow. And I started missing him all over again. I mean *fierce.*"

"I know," I said, but of course I didn't. My own father was still alive, a hale and genially profane man of seventy-four. At seventy, my mother was all that and a bag of chips.

Ned sighed, looking off at the hills. "How he went out is just so *dumb,*" he said. "I can't even tell my kids, if I ever have any, that Grampy went down in a hail of bullets while foiling the bank robbers or the militia guys who were trying to put a bomb in the county courthouse. Nothing like that."

"No," I agreed, "nothing like that."

"I can't even say it was because he was careless. He was just . . . a drunk just came along and just . . ."

He bent over, wheezing like an old man with a cramp in his belly, and this time I at least put my hand on his back. He was trying so hard not to cry, that's what got to me. Trying so hard to be a man, whatever that means to an eighteen-year-old boy.

"Ned. It's all right."

He shook his head violently. "If there was a God, there'd be a reason," he said. He was looking down at the ground. My hand was still on his back, and I could feel it heaving up and down, like he'd just run a race. "If there was a God, there'd be some kind of thread running through it. But there isn't. Not that I can see."

"If you have kids, Ned, tell them their grandfather died in the line of duty. Then take them here and show them his name on the plaque, with all the others."

He didn't seem to hear me. "I have this dream. It's a bad one." He paused, thinking how to say it, then just plunged ahead. "I dream it was all a dream. Do you know what I'm saying?"

I nodded.

"I wake up crying, and I look around my room, and it's sunny. Birds are singing. It's morning. I can smell coffee downstairs and I think, 'He's okay. Jesus and thank you God, the old man's okay.' I don't hear him talking or anything, but I just know. And I think what a stupid idea it was, that he could be walking up the side of some guy's rig to give him a warning about a flapper and just get creamed by a drunk, the sort of idea you could only have in a stupid dream where everything seems so *real* . . . and I start to swing my legs out of bed . . . sometimes I see my ankles go into a patch of sun . . . it even feels warm . . . and then I wake up for real, and it's dark, and I've got the blankets pulled up around me but I'm still cold, shivering and cold, and I know that the *dream* was a dream."

"That's awful," I said, remembering that as a boy I'd had my own version of the same dream. It was about my dog. I thought to tell him that, then didn't. Grief is grief, but a dog is not a father.

"It wouldn't be so bad if I had it every night. Then I think I'd know, even while I was asleep, that there's no smell of coffee, that it's not even morning. But it doesn't come . . . doesn't come . . . and then when it finally does, I get fooled again. I'm so happy and relieved, I even think of something nice I'll do for him, like buy him that five-iron he wanted for his birthday . . . and then I wake up. I get fooled all over again."

Maybe it was the thought of his father's birthday, not celebrated this year and never to be celebrated again, that started fresh tears running down his cheeks. "I just hate getting fooled. It's like when Mr. Jones came down and got me out of World History class to tell me, but even worse. Because I'm alone when I wake up in the dark. Mr. Grenville—he's the guidance counselor at school—says time heals all wounds, but it's been almost a year and I'm still having that dream."

I nodded. I was remembering Ten-Pound, shot by a hunter one November, growing stiff in his own blood under a white sky when I found him. A white sky promising a winter's worth of snow. In *my* dream it was always another dog when I got close enough to see, not Ten-Pound at all, and I felt that same relief. Until I woke up, at least. And thinking of Ten-Pound made me think, for a moment, of our barracks mascot back in the old days. Mister Dillon, his name had been, after the TV sheriff played by James Arness. A good dog.

"I know that feeling, Ned."

"Do you?" He looked at me hopefully.

"Yes. And it gets better. Believe me, it does. But he was your Dad, not a schoolmate or a neighbor from down the road. You may still be having that dream next year at this time. You may even be having it ten years on, every once in awhile."

"That's horrible."

"No," I said. "That's memory."

"If there was a reason." He was looking at me earnestly. "A damn *reason*. Do you get that?"

"Of course I do."

"*Is* there one, do you think?"

I thought of telling him I didn't know about reasons, only about chains—how they form themselves, link by link, out of nothing; how they knit themselves into the world. Sometimes you can grab a chain and use it to pull yourself out of a dark place. Mostly, though, I think you get wrapped up in them. Just caught, if you're lucky. Fucking strangled, if you're not.

I found myself gazing across the parking lot at Shed B again. Looking at it, I thought that if I could get used to what was stored in its dark interior, Ned Wilcox could get used to living a fatherless life. People can get used to just about anything. That's the best of our lives, I guess. Of course, it's the horror of them, too.

"Sandy? What do you think?"

"I think that you're asking the wrong guy. I know about work, and hope, and putting a nut away for the GDR."

He grinned. In Troop D, everyone talked very seriously about the GDR, as though it were some complicated subdivision of law enforcement. It actually stood for "golden days of retirement." I think it might have been Huddie Royer who first started talking about the GDR.

"I also know about preserving the chain of evidence so no smart defense attorney can kick your legs out from under you in court and make you look like a fool. Beyond that, I'm just another confused American male."

"At least you're honest," he said.

But was I? Or was I begging the goddam question? I didn't *feel* particularly honest right then; I felt like a man who can't swim looking at a boy who is floundering in deep water. And once again Shed B caught my eye. *Is it cold in here?* this boy's father had asked, back in the once-upon-a-time, back in the day. *Is it cold in here, or is it just me?*

No, it hadn't been just him.

"What are you thinking about, Sandy?"

"Nothing worth repeating," I said. "What are you doing this summer?"

"Huh?"

"What are you doing this summer?" It wouldn't be golfing in Maine or boating on Lake Tahoe, that was for sure; scholarship or no scholarship, Ned was going to need all of the old folding green he could get.

"County Parks and Rec again, I suppose," he said with a marked lack of enthusiasm. "I worked there last summer until . . . you know."

Until his Dad. I nodded.

"I got a letter from Tom McClannahan last week, saying he was holding a place open for me. He mentioned coaching Little League, but that's just the carrot on the end of the stick. Mostly it'll be swinging a spade and setting out sprinklers, just like last year. I can swing a spade, and I'm not afraid of getting my hands dirty. But Tom . . ." He shrugged instead of finishing.

I knew what Ned was too discreet to say. There are two kinds of work-functional alcoholics, those who are just too fucking mean to fall down and those so sweet that other people go on covering for them way past the point of insanity. Tom was one of the mean ones, the last sprig on a family tree full of plump county hacks going back to the nineteenth century. The McClannahans had fielded a Senator, two members of the House of Representatives, half a dozen Pennsylvania Representatives, and Statler County trough-hogs beyond counting. Tom was, by all accounts, a mean boss with no ambition to climb the political totem pole. What he liked was telling kids like Ned, the ones who had been raised to be quiet and respectful, where to squat and push. And of course for Tom, they never squatted deep enough or pushed hard enough.

"Don't answer that letter yet," I said. "I want to make a call before you do."

I thought he'd be curious, but he only nodded his head. I looked at him sitting there, holding the letter on his lap, and thought that he looked like a boy who has been denied a place in the college of his choice instead of being offered a fat scholarship incentive to go there.

Then I thought again. Not just denied a place in college, maybe, but in life itself. That wasn't true—the letter he'd gotten from Pitt was only one of the things that proved it—but I've no doubt he felt that way just then. I don't know why success often leaves us feeling lower-spirited than failure, but I know it's true. And remember that he was just eighteen, a Hamlet age if there ever was one.

I looked across the parking lot again at Shed B, thinking about what was inside. Not that any of us really knew.

My call the following morning was to Colonel Teague in Butler, which is our regional headquarters. I explained the situation, and waited while *he* made a call, presumably to Scranton, where the big boys hang their hats. It didn't take long for Teague to get back to me, and the news was good. I then spoke to Shirley, although that was little more than a formality; she had liked the father well enough, but outright doted on the son.

When Ned came in that afternoon after school, I asked him if he'd like to spend the summer learning dispatch—and getting paid for it—instead of listening to Tom McClannahan bitch and moan down at Parks and Rec. For a moment he looked stunned . . . hammered, almost. Then he broke out in an enormous delighted grin. I thought he was going to hug me. If I'd actually put my arm around him the previous evening instead of just thinking about it, he probably would've. As it was, he settled for clenching his hands into fists, raising them to the sides of his face, and hissing *"Yesssss!"*

"Shirley's agreed to take you on as 'prentice, and you've got the official okay from Butler. It ain't swinging a shovel for McClannahan, of course, but—"

This time he *did* hug me, laughing as he did it, and I liked it just fine. I could get used to something like that.

When he turned around, Shirley was standing there with two Troopers flanking her: Huddie Royer and George Stankowski. All of them looking as serious as a heart attack in their gray uniforms. Huddie and George were wearing their lids, making them look approximately nine feet tall.

"You don't mind?" Ned asked Shirley. "Really?"

"I'll teach you everything I know," Shirley said.

"Yeah?" Huddie asked. "What's he going to do after the first week?"

Shirley threw him an elbow; it went in just above the butt of his Beretta and landed on target. Huddie gave an exaggerated *oof!* sound and staggered.

"Got something for you, kid," George said. He spoke quietly and gave Ned his best you-were-doing-sixty-in-a-hospital-zone stare. One hand was behind his back.

"What?" Ned asked, sounding a little nervous in spite of his obvious happiness. Behind George, Shirley, and Huddie, a bunch of other Troop D's had gathered.

"Don't you *ever* lose it," Huddie said. Also quietly and seriously.

"What, you guys, what?" More uneasy than ever.

From behind his back, George produced a small white box. He gave it to the boy. Ned looked at it, looked at the Troopers gathered around him, then opened the box. Inside was a big plastic star with the words DEPUTY DAWG printed on it.

"Welcome to Troop D, Ned," George said. He tried to hold onto his solemn face and couldn't. He started to guffaw, and pretty soon they were all laughing and crowding around to shake Ned's hand.

"Pretty funny, you guys," he said, "a real belly-buster." He was smiling, but I thought he was on the verge of tears again. It was nothing you could see, but it was there. I think Shirley Pasternak sensed it, too. And when the kid excused himself to go to the head, I guessed he was going there to regain his composure, or to assure himself he wasn't dreaming again, or both. Sometimes when things go wrong, we get more help than we ever expected. And sometimes it's still not enough.

It was great having Ned around that summer. Everyone liked him, and he liked being there. He particularly liked the hours he spent in dispatch with Shirley. Some of it was going over codes, but mostly it was learning the right responses and how to juggle multiple calls. He got good at it fast, shooting back requested information to the road units, playing the computer keys like it was a barrelhouse piano, liaising with other Troops when it was necessary, as it was after a series of violent thunderstorms whipped through western PA one evening toward the end of June. There were no tornadoes, thank God, but there were high winds, hail, and lightning.

The only time he came close to panic was a day or two later, when a guy taken before the Statler County magistrate suddenly went nuts and started running all over the place, pulling off his clothes and yelling about Jesus Penis. That's what the guy called him; I've got it in a report somewhere. About four different Troopers called in, a couple who were on-scene, a couple who were busting ass to get there. While Ned was trying to figure out how to deal with this, a Trooper from Butler called in, saying he was out on 99, in high-speed pursuit of . . . *blurk!* Transmission ceased. Ned presumed the guy had rolled his cruiser, and he presumed right (the Butler Troop, a rookie, came out all right, but his ride was totaled and the suspect he was chasing got away clean). Ned bawled for Shirley, backing away from the computer, the phones, and the mike as if they had suddenly gotten hot. She took over fast, but still took time to give him a quick hug and a kiss on the cheek before slipping into the seat he had vacated. Nobody was killed or even hurt badly, and Mr. Jesus Penis went to Statler Memorial for observation. It was the only time I saw Ned flustered, but he shook it off. And learned from it.

On the whole, I was impressed.

Shirley loved teaching him, too. That was no real surprise; she'd already demonstrated a willingness to risk her job by doing it without official sanction. She did know—we all did—that Ned had no intention of making police work his career, he never gave us so much as a hint of that, but it made no difference to Shirley. And he liked being around. We knew that, too. He liked the pressure and the tension, fed on it. There was that one lapse, true, but I was actually glad to see it. It was good to know it wasn't just a computer-game to him; he understood that he was moving real people around on his electronic chessboard. And if Pitt didn't work out, who knew? He was already better than Matt Babicki, Shirley's predecessor.

In early July—it could have been a year to the day since his father had been killed, for all I know—the kid came to me about Shed B. There was a rap on the side of my door, which I mostly leave open, and when I looked up he was standing there in a sleeveless Steelers T-shirt and old bluejeans, a cleaning rag dangling out of each rear pocket. I knew what it was about right away. Maybe it was the rags, or maybe it was something in his eyes.

"Thought it was your day off, Ned."

"Yeah," he said, then shrugged. "There were just some chores I'd been meaning to do. And . . . well . . . when you come out for a smoke, there's something I want to ask you about." Pretty excited, by the sound of him.

"No time like the present," I said, getting up.

"You sure? I mean, if you're busy—"

"I'm not busy," I said, though I was. "Let's go."

It was early afternoon on the sort of day that's common enough in the Short Hills Amish country during midsummer: overcast and hot, the heat magnified by a syrupy humidity that hazed the horizon and made our part of the world, which usually looks big and generous to me, appear small and faded instead, like an old snapshot that's lost most of its color. From the west came the sound of unfocused thunder. By suppertime there might be more storms—we'd been having them three days a week since the middle of June, it seemed—but now there was only the heat and the humidity, wringing the sweat from you as soon as you stepped out of the air conditioning.

Two rubber pails stood in front of the Shed B door, a bucket of suds and a bucket of rinse. Sticking out of one was the handle of a squeegee. Curt's boy was a neat worker. Phil Candleton was currently sitting on the smokers' bench, and he gave me a wise glance as we passed him and walked across the parking lot.

"I was doing the barracks windows," Ned was explaining, "and when I finished, I took the buckets over there to dump." He pointed at the waste ground between Shed B and Shed C, where there were a couple of rusting plow blades, a couple of old tractor tires, and a lot of weeds. "Then I decided what the heck, I'll give those shed windows a quick once-over before I toss the water. The ones on Shed C were filthy, but the ones on B were actually pretty clean."

That didn't surprise me. The small windows running across the front of Shed B had been looked through by two (perhaps even three) generations of Troopers, from Jackie O'Hara to Eddie Jacubois. I could remember guys standing at those roll-up doors like kids at some scary sideshow exhibit. Shirley had taken her turns, as had her predecessor, Matt Babicki; come close, darlings, and see the living crocodile. Observe his teeth, how they shine.

Ned's Dad had once gone inside with a rope around his waist. I'd been in there. Huddie, of course, and Tony Schoondist, the old Sergeant Commanding. Tony, whose last name no one could spell on account of the strange way it was pronounced (*Shane*-dinks), was four years in an "assisted living" institution by the time Ned officially came to work at the barracks. A lot of us had been in Shed B. Not because we wanted to but because from time to time we had to. Curtis Wilcox and Tony Schoondist became scholars (Roadmaster instead of Rhodes), and it was Curt who hung the round thermometer with the big numbers you could read from outside. To see it, all you had to do was lean your brow against one of the glass panes which ran along the roll-up door at a height of about five and a half feet, then cup your hands to the sides of your face to cut the glare. That was the only cleaning those windows would have gotten before Curt's boy showed up; the occasional polishing by the foreheads of those who had come to see the living crocodile. Or, if you want to be literal, the shrouded shape of something that almost looked like a Buick 8-cylinder. It was shrouded because we threw a tarpaulin over it, like a sheet over the body of a corpse. Only every now and then the tarp would slide off. There was no reason for that to happen, but from time to time it did. That was no corpse in there.

"Look at it!" Ned said when we got there. He ran the words all together, like an enthusiastic little kid. "What a neat old car, huh? Even better than my Dad's Bel Air! It's a Buick, I can tell that much by the portholes and the grille. Must be from the mid-fifties, wouldn't you say?"

Actually it was a '54, according to Tony Schoondist, Curtis Wilcox, and Ennis Rafferty. *Sort* of a '54. When you got right down to it, it wasn't a 1954 at all. Or a Buick. Or even a car. It was something else, as we used to say in the days of my misspent youth.

Meanwhile, Ned was going on, almost babbling.

"But it's in cherry condition, you can see that from here. It was so *weird,* Sandy! I looked in and at first all I saw was this hump. Because the tarp was on it. I started to wash the windows . . ." Only what he actually said was *warsh the windas,* because that's how we say it in this part of the world, where the Giant Eagle supermarket becomes *Jaunt Iggle.* ". . . and there was this sound, or two sounds, really, a *wisssshh* and then a thump. The tarp slid off the car while I was washing the windows! Like it wanted me to see it, or something! Now is that weird or is that weird?"

"That's pretty weird, all right," I said. I leaned my forehead against the glass (as I had done many times before) and cupped my hands to the sides of my face, eliminating what reflection there was on this dirty day. Yes, it looked like an old Buick, all right, but almost cherry, just as the kid had said. That distinctive fifties Buick grille, which looked to me like the mouth of a chrome crocodile. Whitewall tires. Fenderskirts in the back—*yow, baby,* we used to say, *too cool for school.* Looking into the gloom of Shed B, you probably would have called it black. It was actually midnight blue.

Buick did make a 1954 Roadmaster in midnight blue—Schoondist checked—but never one of that particular type. The paint had a kind of textured *flaky* look, like a kid's duded-up streetrod.

That's earthquake country in there, Curtis Wilcox said.

I jumped back. Dead a year or not, he spoke directly into my left ear. Or something did.

"What's wrong?" Ned asked. "You look like you saw a ghost."

Heard one, I almost said. What I *did* say was "Nothing."

"You sure? You jumped."

"Goose walked over my grave, I guess. I'm okay."

"So what's the story on the car? Who owns it?"

What a question *that* was. "I don't know," I said.

"Well, what's it doing just sitting there in the dark? Man, if I had a nice-looking street-custom like that—and vintage!—I'd never keep it sitting in a dirty old shed." Then an idea hit him. "Is it, like, some criminal's car? Evidence in a case?"

"Call it a repo, if you want. Theft of services." It's what *we'd* called it. Not much, but as Curtis himself had once said, you only need one nail to hang your hat on.

"What services?"

"Seven dollars' worth of gas." I couldn't quite bring myself to tell him who had pumped it.

"Seven *dollars?* That's all?"

"Well," I said, "you only need one nail to hang your hat on."

He looked at me, puzzled. I looked back at him, saying nothing.

"Can we go in?" he asked finally. "Take a closer look?"

I put my forehead back against the glass and read the thermometer hanging from the beam, as round and bland as the face of the moon. Tony Schoondist had bought it at the Tru-Value in Statler, paying for it out of his own pocket instead of Troop D petty cash. And Ned's father had hung it from the beam. Like a hat on a nail.

Although the temperature out where we were standing had to be at least eighty-five, and everyone knows heat builds up even higher in poorly ventilated sheds and barns, the thermometer's big red needle stood spang between the fives of 55.

"Not just now," I said.

"Why not?" And then, as if he realized that sounded impolite, perhaps even impudent: "What's wrong with it?"

"Right now it's not safe."

He studied me for several seconds. The interest and lively curiosity drained out of his face as he did, and he once more became the boy I had seen so often since he started coming by the barracks, the one I'd seen most clearly on the day he'd been accepted at Pitt. The boy sitting on the smokers' bench with tears rolling down his cheeks, wanting to know what every kid in history wants to know when someone they love is suddenly yanked off the stage: why does it happen, why did it happen to me, is there a reason or is it all just some crazy roulette wheel? If it means something, what do I do about it? And if it means nothing, how do I bear it?

"Is this about my father?" he asked. "Was that my Dad's car?"

His intuition was scary. No, it hadn't been his father's car . . . how could it be, when it wasn't really a car at all? Yes, it *had* been his father's car. And mine . . . Huddie Royer's . . . Tony Schoondist's . . . Ennis Rafferty's. Ennis's most of all, maybe. Ennis's in a way the rest of us could never equal. Never *wanted* to equal. Ned had asked who the car belonged to, and I supposed the real answer was Troop D, Pennsylvania State Police. It belonged to all the Troopers, past and present, who had ever known what we were keeping out in Shed B. But for most of the years it had spent in our custody, the Buick had been the special property of Tony and Ned's Dad. They were its curators, its Roadmaster Scholars.

"Not exactly your Dad's," I said, knowing I'd hesitated too long. "But he knew about it."

"What's to know? And did my Mom know, too?"

"Nobody knows these days except for us," I said.

"Troop D, you mean."

"Yes. And that's how it's going to stay." There was a cigarette in my hand that I barely remembered lighting. I dropped it to the macadam and crushed it out. "It's our business."

I took a deep breath.

"But if you really want to know, I'll tell you. You're one of us now . . . close enough for government work, anyway." His father used to say that, too—all the time, and things like that have a way of sticking. "You can even go in there and look."

"When?"

"When the temperature goes up."

"I don't get you. What's the temperature in there got to do with anything?"

"I get off at three today," I said, and pointed at the bench. "Meet me there, if the rain holds off. If it doesn't, we'll go upstairs or down to the Country Way Diner, if you're hungry. I expect your father would want you to know."

Was that true? I actually had no idea. Yet my impulse to tell him seemed strong enough to qualify as an intuition, maybe even a direct order from beyond. I'm not a religious man, but I sort of believe in such things. And I thought about the oldtimers saying kill or cure, give that curious cat a dose of satisfaction.

Does knowing really satisfy? Rarely, in my experience. But I didn't want Ned leaving for Pitt in September the way he was in July, with his usual sunny nature flickering on and off like a lightbulb that isn't screwed all the way in. I thought he had a right to some answers. Sometimes there are none, I know that, but I felt like trying. Felt I had to try, in spite of the risks.

Earthquake country, Curtis Wilcox said in my ear. *That's earthquake country in there, so be careful.*

"Goose walk over your grave again, Sandy?" the boy asked me.

"I guess it wasn't a goose, after all," I said. "But it was something."

The rain held off. When I went out to join Ned on the bench which faces Shed B across the parking lot, Arky Arkanian was there, smoking a cigarette and talking Pirate baseball with the kid. Arky made as if to leave when I showed up, but I told him to stay put. "I'm going to tell

Ned about the Buick we keep over there," I said, nodding toward the shed across the way. "If he decides to call for the men in the white coats because the Troop D Sergeant Commanding has lost his shit, you can back me up. After all, you were here."

Arky's smile faded. His iron-gray hair fluffed around his head in the limp, hot breeze that had sprung up. "You sure dat a good idear, Sarge?"

"Curiosity killed the cat," I said, "but—"

"—satisfaction brought him back," Shirley finished from behind me. "A great big dose of it, is what Trooper Curtis Wilcox used to say. Can I join you? Or is this the Boys' Club today?"

"No sex discrimination on the smokers' bench," I said. "Join us, please."

Like me, Shirley had just finished her shift and Steff Colucci had taken her place at dispatch.

She sat next to Ned, gave him a smile, and brought a pack of Parliaments out of her purse. It was two-double-oh-two, we all knew better, had for years, and we went right on killing ourselves. Amazing. Or maybe, considering we live in a world where drunks can crush State Troopers against the sides of eighteen-wheelers and where make-believe Buicks show up from time to time at real gas stations, not so amazing. Anyway, it was nothing to me right then.

Right then I had a story to tell.

Then

In 1979, the Jenny station at the intersection of SR 32 and the Humboldt Road was still open, but it was staggering badly; OPEC took all the little 'uns out in the end. The mechanic and owner was Herbert "Hugh" Bossey, and on that particular day he was over in Lassburg, getting his teeth looked after—a bear for his Snickers bars and RC Colas was Hugh Bossey. NO MECH ON DUTY BECAUSE OF TOOTH-AKE, said the sign taped in the window of the garage bay. The pump-jockey was a high school dropout named Bradley Roach, barely out of his teens. This fellow, twenty-two years and untold thousands of beers later, would come along and kill the father of a boy who was not then born, crushing him against the side of a Freuhof box, turning him like a spindle, unrolling him like a noisemaker, spinning him almost skinless into the weeds, and leaving his bloody clothes inside-out on the highway like a magic trick. But all that is in the yet-to-be. We are in the past now, in the magical land of Then.

At around ten o'clock on a morning in July, Brad Roach was sitting in the office of the Jenny station with his feet up, reading *Inside View*. On the front was a picture of a flying saucer hovering ominously over the White House.

The bell in the garage dinged as the tires of a vehicle rolled over the airhose on the tarmac. Brad looked up to see a car—the very one which would spend so many years in the darkness of Shed B—pull up to the second of the station's two pumps. That was the one labeled HI TEST. It was a beautiful midnight-blue Buick, old (it had the big chrome grille and the portholes running up the sides) but in mint condition. The paint sparkled, the windshield sparkled, the chrome side-strike sweeping along the body sparkled, and even before the driver opened the door and got out, Bradley Roach knew there was something wrong with it. He just couldn't put his finger on what it was.

He dropped his newspaper on the desk (he never would have been allowed to take it out of the desk drawer in the first place if the boss hadn't been overtown paying for his sweet tooth) and got up just as the Roadmaster's driver opened his door on the far side of the pumps and got out.

It had rained heavily the night before and the roads were still wet (hell, still *underwater* in some of the low places on the west side of Statler Township), but the sun had come out around eight o'clock and by ten the day was both bright and warm. Nevertheless, the man who got out of the car was dressed in a black trenchcoat and large black hat. "Looked like a spy in some old movie," Brad said to Ennis Rafferty an hour or so later, indulging in what was, for him, a flight of poetic fancy. The trenchcoat, in fact, was so long it nearly dragged on the puddly cement tarmac, and it billowed behind the Buick's driver as he strode toward the side of the station and the sound of Redfern Stream, which ran behind it. The stream had swelled wonderfully in the previous night's showers.

Brad, assuming that the man in the black coat and floppy black hat was headed for the seat of convenience, called: "Bathroom door's open, mister . . . how much of this jetfuel you want?"

"Fill 'er up," the customer said. He spoke in a voice Brad Roach didn't much like. What he told the responding officers later was that the guy sounded like he was talking through a mouthful of jelly. Brad was in a poetical mood for sure. Maybe Hugh being gone for the day had something to do with it.

"Check the earl?" Brad asked. By this time his customer had reached the corner of the little white station. Judging by how fast he was moving, Brad figured he had to offload some freight in a hurry.

The guy paused, though, and turned toward Brad a little. Just enough for Brad to see a pallid, almost waxy crescent of cheek, a dark, almond-shaped eye with no discernible white in it, and a curl of lank black hair falling beside one oddly made ear. Brad remembered the ear best, remembered it with great clarity. Something about it disturbed him deeply, but he couldn't explain just what it was. At this point, poesy failed him. *Melted, kinda, like he'd been in a fire* seemed to be the best he could do.

"Oil's fine!" the man in the black coat and hat said in his choked voice, and was gone around the corner in a final batlike swirl of dark cloth. In addition to the quality of the voice—that unpleasant, mucusy sound—the man had an accent that made Brad Roach think of the old *Rocky and Bullwinkle* show, Boris Badinoff telling Natasha *Ve must stop moose und squirrel!*

Brad went to the Buick, ambled down the side closest to the pumps (the driver had parked carelessly, leaving plenty of room between the car and the island), trailing one hand along the chrome swoop and the smooth paintjob as he went. That touch was more admiring than impudent, although it might have had a bit of harmless impudence in it; Bradley was then a young man, with a young man's high spirits. At the back, bending over the fuel hatch, he paused. The fuel hatch was there, but the rear license plate wasn't. There wasn't even a plate *holder,* or screw-holes where a plate would normally go.

This made Bradley realize what had struck him as wrong as soon as he heard the *ding-ding* of the bell and looked up at the car for the first time. There was no inspection sticker. Well, no business of his if there was no plate on the back deck and no inspection sticker on the windshield; either one of the local cops or a Statie from Troop D just up the road would see the guy and nail him for it . . . or they wouldn't. Either way, Brad Roach's job was to pump gas.

He twirled the crank on the side of the hi-test pump to turn back the numbers, stuck the nozzle in the hole, and set the automatic feed. The bell inside the pump started to bing and while it did, Brad walked up the driver's side of the Buick, completing the circuit. He looked through the leftside windows as he went, and the car's interior struck him as singularly stark for what had been almost a luxury car back in the fifties. The seat upholstery was wren-brown, and so was the fabric lining the inside of the roof. The back seat was empty, the front seat was empty, and there was nothing on the floor—not so much as a gum-wrapper, let alone a map or a crumpled cigarette pack. The steering wheel looked like inlaid wood. Bradley wondered if that was the way they had come on this model, or if it was some kind of special option. Looked ritzy. And why was it so *big?* If it had had spokes sticking out of it, you would have thought it belonged on a millionaire's yacht. You'd have to spread your arms almost as wide as your chest just to grip it. Had to be some sort of custom job, and Brad didn't think it would be comfortable to handle on a long drive. Not a bit comfortable.

Also, there was something funny about the dashboard. It looked like burled walnut and the chromed controls and little appliances—heater, radio, clock—looked all right . . . they were in the right *places,* anyway . . . and the ignition key was also in the right place (*trusting soul, ain't he?* Brad thought), yet there was something about the setup that was very much not right. Hard to say what, though.

Brad strolled back around to the front of the car again, admiring the sneering chrome grille (it was all Buick, that grille; that part, at least, was dead on the money) and verifying that there was no inspection sticker, not from PA or anyplace else. There were no stickers on the windshield at all. The Buick's owner was apparently not a member of Triple-A, the Elks, the Lions, or the Kiwanis. He did not support Pitt or Penn State (at least not to the extent of putting a decal on any of the Buick's windows), and his car wasn't protected by Mopar or good old Rusty Jones.

Pretty cool car just the same . . . although the boss would have told him that his job wasn't to admire the rolling stock but just to fill 'em fast.

The Buick drank seven dollars' worth of the good stuff before the feed cut off. That was a lot of gas in those days, when a gallon of hi-test could be purchased for seventy cents. Either the tank had been close to empty when the man in the black coat took the car out, or he'd driven it a far piece.

Then Bradley decided that second idea had to be bullshit. Because the roads were still wet, still brimming over in the dips, for God's sake, but there wasn't a single mudstreak or splatter on the Buick's smooth blue hide. Not so much as a smear on those fat and luxy whitewalls, either. And to Bradley Roach, that seemed flat-out impossible.

It was nothing to him one way or the other, of course, but he could point out the lack of a valid inspection sticker. Might get him a tip. Enough for a six-pack, maybe. He was still six or eight months from being able to buy legally, but there were ways and means if you were dedicated, and even then, in the early going, Bradley was dedicated.

He went back to the office, sat down, picked up his *Inside View,* and waited for the fellow in the black coat to come back. It was a damned hot day for a long coat like that, no doubt about it, but by then Brad thought he had that part figured out. The man was an SKA, just a little different from the ones around Statler. From a sect that allowed car-driving, it seemed. SKAs were what Bradley and his friends called the Amish. It stood for shitkicking assholes.

Fifteen minutes later, when Brad had finished reading "We *Have* Been Visited!" by UFO expert Richard T. Rumsfeld (U.S. Army Ret.) and had given close attention to a blonde Page Four Girl who appeared to be fly-fishing a mountain stream in her bra and panties, Brad realized he was *still* waiting. The guy hadn't gone to make any nickel-and-dime deposit, it seemed; that guy was clearly a shithouse millionaire.

Snickering, imagining the guy perched on the jakes under the rusty pipes, sitting there in the gloom (the single lightbulb had burned out a month ago and neither Bradley nor Hugh had gotten around to changing it yet) with his black coat puddled all around him and collecting mouse-turds, Brad picked up his newspaper again. He turned to the joke page, which was good for another ten minutes (some of the jokes were so comical Brad read them three and even four times). He dropped the paper back on the desk and looked at the clock over the door. Beyond it, at the pumps, the Buick Roadmaster sparkled in the sun. Almost half an hour had passed since its driver had cried "Oil's fine!" back over his shoulder in his strangly voice and then disappeared down the side of the building in a fine swirl of black cloth. *Was* he an SKA? Did *any* of them drive cars? Brad didn't think so. The SKAs thought anything with an engine was the work of Satan, didn't they?

Okay, so maybe he wasn't. But whatever he was, why wasn't he back?

All at once the image of that guy on the gloomy, discolored throne back there by the diesel pump didn't seem so funny. In his mind's eye, Brad could still see him sitting there with his coat puddled around him on the filthy linoleum and his pants down around his ankles, but now Brad saw him with his head down, his chin resting on his chest, his big hat (which didn't really look like an Amish hat at all) slewed forward over his eyes. Not moving. Not *breathing*. Not shitting but dead. Heart attack or brain trembolism or something like that. It was possible. If the goddam King of Rock and Roll could croak while doing Number Two, *anyone* could.

"Naw," Bradley Roach said softly. "Naw, that ain't . . . he wudd'n . . . *naw!*"

He picked up the paper, tried to read about the flying saucers that were keeping an eye on us, and couldn't convert the words into coherent thoughts. He put it down and looked out the door. The Buick was still there, shining in the sun.

No sign of the driver.

Half an hour . . . no, thirty-five minutes now. God*dang*. Another five minutes passed and he found himself tearing strips off the newspaper and drifting them down to the wastebasket, where they formed piles of nervous confetti.

"Fuggit," he said, and got to his feet. He went out the door and around the corner of the little white cinderblock cube where he'd worked since dropping out of high school. The restrooms were down at the back, on the east side. Brad hadn't made up his mind if he should play it straight—*Mister, are you all right?*—or humorous—*Hey Mister, I got a firecracker, if you need one.* As it turned out, he got to deliver neither of these carefully crafted phrases.

The men's room door had a loose latch and was apt to fly open in any strong puff of wind unless bolted shut from the inside, so Brad and Hugh always stuffed a piece of folded cardboard into the crack to keep the door shut when the restroom wasn't in use. If the man from the Buick had been inside the toilet, the fold of cardboard would either have been in there with him (probably left beside one of the sink's faucets while the man tended his business), or it would be lying on the small cement stoop at the foot of the door. This latter was usually the case, Brad later told Ennis Rafferty; he and Hugh were always putting that cardboard wedge back in its place after the customers left. They had to flush the toilet as well, more often than not. People were careless about that when they were away from home. People were as a rule downright *nasty* when they were away from home.

Right now, that cardboard wedge was poking out of the crack between the door and the jamb, just above the latch, exactly where it worked the best. All the same, Brad opened the door to check, catching the little cardboard wedge neatly as it fell—as neatly as he would learn to open a bottle of beer on the driver's-side handle of his own Buick in later years. The little cubicle was empty, just as he'd known in his heart it would be. No sign that the toilet had been used, and there had been no sound of a flush as Brad sat in the office reading his paper. No beads of water on the rust-stained sides of the basin, either.

It occurred to Brad then that the guy hadn't come around the side of the station to use the can but to take a look at Redfern Stream, which was pretty enough to warrant a peek (or even a snap of the old Kodak) from a passerby, running as it did with the Statler Bluffs on its north side and all those willows up on top, spreading out green like a mermaid's hair (there was a poet in the boy, all right, a regular Dylan McYeats). But around back there was no sign of the Buick's driver, either, only discarded auto parts and a couple of ancient tractor-axles lying in the weeds like rusty bones.

The stream was babbling at the top of its lungs, running broad and foamy. Its swelling would be a temporary condition, of course—floods in western PA are spring events, as a rule—but that day the normally sleepy Redfern was quite the torrent.

Seeing how high the water was gave rise to a horrifying possibility in Bradley Roach's mind. He measured the steep slope down to the water. The grass was still wet with rain and probably goddanged slippery, especially if an unsuspecting SKA came thee-ing and thou-ing along in shoes with slippery leather soles. As he considered this, the possibility hardened to a near certainty in his mind. Nothing else explained the unused shithouse and the car still waiting at the hi-test pump, all loaded and ready to go, key still in the ignition. Old Mr. Buick Roadmaster had gone around back for a peek at the Redfern, had foolishly dared the embankment slope to get an even better look . . . and then whoops, there goes your ballgame.

Bradley worked his own way down to the water's edge, slipping a couple of times in spite of his Georgia Giants but not falling, always keeping near some hunk of junk he could grab if he did lose his footing. There was no sign of the man at the water's edge, but when Brad looked downstream, he saw something caught in the lee of a fallen birch about two hundred yards from where he stood. Bobbing up and down. Black. It could have been Mr. Buick Roadmaster's coat.

"Aw, shit," he said, and hurried back to the office to call Troop D, which was at least two miles closer to his location than the local cop-shop. And that was how

Now: *Sandy*

"we got into it," I said. "Shirley's predecessor was a guy named Matt Babicki. He gave the call to Ennis Rafferty—"

"Why Ennis, Ned?" Shirley asked. "Quick as you can."

"CAU," he said at once. "Closest available unit." But his mind wasn't on that, and he never looked at her. His eyes were fixed on me.

"Ennis was fifty-five and looking forward to a retirement he never got to enjoy," I said.

"And my father was with him, wasn't he? They were partners."

"Yes," I said.

There was plenty more to tell, but first he needed to get past this first part. I was quiet, letting him get used to the idea that his father and Roach, the man who had killed him, had once stood face to face and conversed like normal human beings. There Curtis had been, listening to Bradley Roach talk, flipping open his notebook, starting to jot down a time-sequence. By then Ned knew the drill, how we work fresh cases.

I had an idea this was what would stick with the kid no matter what else I had to tell him, no matter how wild and woolly the narrative might get. The image of the manslaughterer and his victim standing together not four minutes' brisk walk from where their lives would again collide, this time with a mortal thud, twenty-two years later.

"How old was he?" Ned almost whispered. "My Dad, how old was he on the day you're telling me about?"

He could have figured it out for himself, I suppose, but he was just too stunned. "Twenty-four," I said. It was easy. Short lives make for simple mathematics. "He'd been in the Troop about a year. Same deal then as now, two Troopers per cruiser only on the eleven-to-seven, rookies the single exception to the rule. And your Dad was still a rookie. So he was paired with Ennis on days."

"Ned, are you all right?" Shirley asked. It was a fair question. All of the color had gradually drained out of the kid's face.

"Yes, ma'am," he said. He looked at her, then at Arky, then at Phil Candleton. The same look directed to all three, half-bewildered and half-accusing. "How much of this did you know?"

"All of it," Arky said. He had a little Nordic lilt in his voice that always made me think of Lawrence Welk going ah-one and ah-two, now here's da lovely Lennon Sisters, don't dey look swede. "It was no secret. Your Dad and Bradley Roach got on all right back den. Even later. Curtis arrested him tree-four times in the eighties—"

"Hell, five or six," Phil rumbled. "That was almost always his beat, you know. Five or six at least. One time he drove that dimwit direct to an AA meeting and made him stay, but it didn't do any good."

"Your Dad's job was bein a Statie," Arky said, "and by d'middle of d'eighties, Brad's job—his full-time job—was drinkin. Usually while he drove around d'back roads. He loved doin dat. So many of em do." Arky sighed. "Anyway, given dem two jobs, boy, dey was almos certain to bump heads from time to time."

"From time to time," Ned repeated, fascinated. It was as if the concept of time had gained a new dimension for him.

"But all dat was stric'ly business. Cep maybe for dat Buick. Dey had dat between em all d'years after." He nodded in the direction of Shed B. "Dat Buick hung between em like warsh on a close'line. No one's ever kep d'Buick a secret, eider—not edzactly, not on purpose—but I spec it's kinda one, anyway."

Shirley was nodding. She reached over and took Ned's hand, and he let it be taken.

"People ignore it, mostly," she said, "the way they always ignore things they don't understand . . . as long as they can, anyway."

"Sometimes we can't afford to ignore it," Phil said. "We knew that as soon as . . . well, let Sandy tell it." He looked back at me. They all did. Ned's gaze was the brightest.

I lit a cigarette and started talking again.

Then

Ennis Rafferty found his binoculars in his tackle box, which went with him from car to car during fishing season. Once he had them, he and Curt Wilcox went down to Redfern Stream for the same reason the bear went over the mountain: to see what they could see.

"Whaddya want *me* to do?" Brad asked as they walked away from him.

"Guard the car and think about your story," Ennis said.

"*Story?* Why would I need a *story?*" Sounding a little nervous about it. Neither Ennis nor Curt answered.

Easing down the weedy slope, each of them ready to grab the other if he slipped, Ennis said: "That car isn't right. Even Bradley Roach knows that, and he's pretty short in the IQ department."

Curt was nodding even before the older man had finished. "It's like a picture in this activity book I had when I was a kid. FIND TEN THINGS WRONG WITH THIS PICTURE."

"By God, it is!" Ennis was struck by this idea. He liked the young man he was partnered with, and thought he was going to make a good Trooper once he got a little salt on his skin.

They had reached the edge of the stream by then. Ennis went for his binocs, which he had hung over his neck by the strap. "No inspection sticker. No damn *license plates.* And the wheel! Curtis, did you see how big that thing is?"

Curt nodded.

"No antenna for the radio," Ennis continued, "and no mud on the body. How'd it get up Route 32 without getting some mud on it? *We* were splashing up puddles everywhere. There's even crud on the windshield."

"I don't know. Did you see the portholes?"

"Huh? Sure, but all old Buicks have portholes."

"Yeah, but these are wrong. There's four on the passenger side and only three on the driver's side. Do you think Buick ever rolled a model off the line with a different number of portholes on the sides? Cause I don't."

Ennis gave his partner a nonplussed look, then raised his binoculars and looked downstream. He quickly found and focused on the black bobbing thing that had sent Brad hurrying to the telephone.

"What is it? Is it a coat?" Curt was shading his eyes, which were considerably better than Bradley Roach's. "It's not, is it?"

"Nope," Ennis said, still peering. "It looks like . . . a garbage can. One of those black plastic garbage cans like they sell down at the Tru-Value in town. Or maybe I'm full of shit. Here. You take a look."

He handed the binoculars over, and no, he wasn't full of shit. What Curtis saw was indeed a black plastic garbage can, probably washed down from the trailer park on the Bluffs at the height of the previous night's cloudburst. It wasn't a black coat and no black coat was ever found, nor the black hat, nor the man with the white face and the curl of lank black hair beside one strangely made ear. The Troopers might have doubted that there ever *was* such a man—Ennis Rafferty had not failed to notice the copy of *Inside View* on the desk when he took Mr. Roach into the office to question him further—but there *was* the Buick. That odd Buick was irrefutable. It was part of the goddam scenery, sitting right there at the pumps. Except by the time the county tow showed up to haul it away, neither Ennis Rafferty nor Curtis Wilcox believed it was a Buick at all.

By then, they didn't know *what* it was.

Older cops are entitled to their hunches, and Ennis had one as he and his young partner walked back to Brad Roach. Brad was standing beside the Roadmaster with the three nicely chromed portholes on one side and the four on the other. Ennis's hunch was that the oddities they had so far noticed were only the whipped cream on the sundae. If so, the less Mr. Roach saw now, the less he could talk about later. Which was why, although Ennis was extremely curious about the abandoned car and longed for a big dose of satisfaction, he turned it over to Curt while he himself escorted Bradley into the office. Once they were there, Ennis called for a wrecker to haul the Buick up to Troop D, where they could put it in the parking lot out back, at least for the time being. He also wanted to question Bradley while his recollections were relatively fresh. Ennis expected to get his own chance to look over their odd catch, and at his leisure, later on.

"Someone modified it a little, I expect that's all" was what he said to Curt before taking Bradley into the office. Curt looked skeptical. Modifying was one thing, but this was just nuts. Removing one of the portholes, then refinishing the surface so expertly that the scar didn't even show? Replacing the usual Buick steering wheel with something that looked like it belonged in a cabin cruiser? Those were modifications?

"Aw, just look it over while I do some business," Ennis said.

"Can I check the mill?"

"Be my guest. Only, keep your mitts off the steering wheel, so we can get some prints if we need them. And use good sense. Try not to leave your own dabs anywhere."

They had reached the pumps again. Brad Roach looked eagerly at the two cops, the one he would kill in the twenty-first century and the one who would be gone without a trace that very evening.

"What do you think?" Brad asked. "Is he dead down there in the stream? Drownded? He is, isn't he?"

"Not unless he crawled into the garbage can floating around in the crotch of that fallen tree and drowned there," Ennis said.

Brad's face fell. "Aw, shit. Is that all it is?"

"'Fraid so. And it would be a tight fit for a grown man. Trooper Wilcox? Any questions for this young man?"

Because he was still learning and Ennis was still teaching, Curtis did ask a few, mostly to make sure Bradley wasn't drunk and that he was in his right mind. Then he nodded to Ennis, who clapped Bradley on the shoulder as if they were old buddies.

"Step inside with me, what do you say?" Ennis suggested. "Pour me a slug of mud and we'll see if we can figure this thing out." And he led Brad away. The friendly arm slung around Bradley Roach's shoulder was very strong, and it just kept hustling Brad along toward the office, Trooper Rafferty talking a mile a minute the whole time.

As for Trooper Wilcox, he got about three-quarters of an hour with that Buick before the county tow showed up with its orange light flashing. Forty-five minutes isn't much time, but it was enough to turn Curtis into a lifetime Roadmaster Scholar. True love always happens in a flash, they say.

Ennis drove as they headed back to Troop D behind the tow-truck and the Buick, which rode on the clamp with its nose up and its rear bumper almost dragging on the road. Curt rode shotgun, in his excitement squirming like a little kid who needs to make water. Between them, the Motorola police radio, scuffed and beat-up, the victim of God knew how many coffee- and cola-dousings but still as tough as nails, blatted away on channel 23, Matt Babicki and the Troopers in the field going through the call-and-response that was the constant background soundtrack of their working lives. It was there, but neither Ennis nor Curt heard it any-more unless their own number came up.

"The first thing's the engine," Curt said. "No, I suppose the first thing's the hood-latch. It's way over on the driver's side, and you push it in rather than pulling it out—"

"Never heard of that before," Ennis grunted.

"You wait, you wait," his young partner said. "I found it, anyway, and lifted the hood. The engine . . . man, that *engine* . . ."

Ennis glanced at him with the expression of a man who's just had an idea that's too horribly plausible to deny. The orange glow from the revolving light on the tow-truck's cab pulsed on his face like jaundice. "Don't you dare tell me it doesn't have one," he said. "Don't dare tell me it doesn't have anything but a radioactive crystal or some damn thing like in dumbwit's flying saucers."

Curtis laughed. The sound was both cheerful and wild. "No, no, there's an engine, but it's all wrong. It says BUICK 8 on both sides of the engine block in big chrome letters, as if whoever made it was afraid of forgetting what the damn thing was. There are eight plugs, four on each side, and *that's* right—eight cylinders, eight sparkplugs—but there's no distributor cap and no distributor, not that I can see. No generator or alternator, either."

"Get out!"

"Ennis, if I'm lyin I'm dyin."

"Where do the sparkplug wires go?"

"Each one makes a big loop and goes right back into the engine block, so far as I can tell."

"That's nuts!"

"Yes! But listen, Ennis, just listen!" Stop interrupting and let me talk, in other words. Curtis Wilcox squirming in his seat but never taking his eyes off the Buick being towed along in front of him.

"All right, Curt. I'm listening."

"It's got a radiator, but so far as I can tell, there's nothing inside it. No water and no antifreeze. There's no fanbelt, which sort of makes sense, because there's no fan."

"Oil?"

"There's a crankcase and a dipstick, but there's no markings on the stick. There's a battery, a Delco, but Ennis, dig this, *it's not hooked up to anything.* There are no battery cables."

"You're describing a car that couldn't possibly run," Ennis said flatly.

"Tell me about it. I took the key out of the ignition. It's on an ordinary chain, but the chain's all there is. No fob with initials or anything."

"Other keys?"

"No. And the ignition key's not really a key. It's just a slot of metal, about so long." Curt held his thumb and forefinger a key's length apart.

"A blank, is that what you're talking about? Like a keymaker's blank?"

"*No.* It's nothing like a key at all. It's just a little steel stick."

"Did you try it?"

Curt, who had been talking almost compulsively, didn't answer that at once.

"Go on," Ennis said. "I'm your partner, for Christ's sake. I'm not going to bite you."

"All right, yeah, I tried it. I wanted to see if that crazy engine worked."

"Of course it works. Someone drove it in, right?"

"Roach says so, but when I got a good look under that hood, I had to wonder if he was lying or maybe hypnotized. Anyway, it's still an open question. The key-thing won't turn. It's like the ignition's locked."

"Where's the key now?"

"I put it back in the ignition."

Ennis nodded. "Good. When you opened the door, did the dome light come on? Or isn't there one?"

Curtis paused, thinking back. "Yeah. There was a dome light, and it came on. I should have noticed that. How could it come on, though? How could it, when the battery's not hooked up?"

"There could be a couple of C-cells powering the dome light, for all we know." But his lack of belief was clear in his voice. "What else?"

"I saved the best for last," Curtis told him. "I had to do some touching inside, but I used a hanky, and I know where I touched, so don't bust my balls."

Ennis said nothing out loud, but gave the kid a look that said he'd bust Curt's balls if they needed busting.

"The dashboard controls are all fake, just stuck on there for show. The radio knobs don't turn and neither does the heater control knob. The lever you slide to switch on the defroster doesn't move. Feels like a post set in concrete."

Ennis followed the tow-truck into the driveway that ran around to the back of Troop D. "What else? Anything?"

"More like *everything*. It's fucked to the sky." This impressed Ennis, because Curtis wasn't ordinarily a profane man. "You know that great big steering wheel? I think that's probably fake, too. I shimmied it—just with the sides of my hands, don't have a hemorrhage—and it turns a little bit, left and right, but only a little bit. Maybe it's just locked, like the ignition, but . . ."

"But you don't think so."

"No. I don't."

The tow-truck parked in front of Shed B. There was a hydraulic whine and the Buick came out of its snout-up, tail-down posture, settling back on its whitewalls. The tow driver, old Johnny Parker, came around to unhook it, wheezing around the Pall Mall stuck in his gob. Ennis and Curt sat in Cruiser D-19 meanwhile, looking at each other.

"What the hell we got here?" Ennis asked finally. "A car that can't drive and can't steer cruises into the Jenny station out on Route 32 and right up to the hi-test pump. No tags. No sticker . . ." An idea struck him. "Registration? You check for that?"

"Not on the steering post," Curt said, opening his door, impatient to get out. The young are always impatient. "Not in the glove compartment, either, because there is no glove compartment. There's a handle for one, and there's a latch-button, but the button doesn't push, the handle doesn't pull, and the little door doesn't open. It's just stage-dressing, like everything else on the dashboard. The dashboard itself is bullshit. Cars didn't come with wooden dashboards in the fifties. Not American ones, at least."

They got out and stood looking at the orphan Buick's back deck. "Trunk?" Ennis asked. "Does *that* open?"

"Yeah. It's not locked. Push the button and it pops open like the trunk of any other car. But it smells lousy."

"Lousy how?"

"Swampy."

"Any dead bodies in there?"

"No bodies, no nothing."

"No spare tire? Not even a jack?"

Curtis shook his head. Johnny Parker came over, pulling off his work gloves. "Be anything else, men?"

Ennis and Curt shook their heads.

Johnny started away, then stopped. "What the hell is that, anyway? Someone's idea of a joke?"

"We don't know yet," Ennis told him.

Johnny nodded. "Well, if you find out, let me know. Curiosity killed the cat, satisfaction brought him back. You know?"

"Whole lot of satisfaction," Curt said automatically. The business about curiosity and the cat was a part of Troop D life, not quite an in-joke, just something that had crept into the day-to-day diction of the job.

Ennis and Curt watched the old man go. "Anything else you want to pass on before we talk to Sergeant Schoondist?" Ennis asked.

"Yeah," Curtis said. "It's earthquake country in there."

"Earthquake country? Just what in the hell does *that* mean?"

So Curtis told Ennis about a show he'd seen on the PBS station out of Pittsburgh just the week before. By then a number of people had drifted over. Among them were Phil Candleton, Arky Arkanian, Sandy Dearborn, and Sergeant Schoondist himself.

The program had been about predicting earthquakes. Scientists were a long way from developing a sure-fire way of doing that, Curtis said, but most of them believed it *could* be done, in time. Because there were fore-warnings. Precursors. Animals felt them, and quite often people did, too. Dogs got restless and barked to be let outside. Cattle ran around in their stalls or knocked down the fences of their pastures. Caged chickens some-times flapped so frantically they broke their wings. Some people claimed to hear a high humming sound from the earth fifteen or twenty minutes before a big temblor (and if some *people* could hear that sound, it stood to reason that most animals would hear it even more clearly). Also, it got cold. Not everyone felt these odd pre-earthquake cold pockets, but a great many people did. There was even some meteorological data to sup-port the subjective reports.

"Are you shitting me?" Tony Schoondist asked.

No indeed, Curt replied. Two hours before the big quake of 1906, temperatures in San Francisco had dropped a full seven degrees; that was a recorded fact. This although all other weather conditions had remained constant.

"Fascinating," Ennis said, "but what's it got to do with the Buick?"

By then there were enough Troopers present to form a little circle of listeners. Curtis looked around at them, knowing he might spend the next six months or so tagged the Earthquake Kid on radio calls, but too jazzed to care. He said that while Ennis was in the gas station office ques-tioning Bradley Roach, he himself had been sitting behind that strange oversized steering wheel, still being careful not to touch anything except with the sides of his hands. And as he sat there, he started to hear a hum-ming sound, very high. He told them he had *felt* it, as well.

"It came out of nowhere, this high, steady hum. I could feel it buzzing in my fillings. I think if it had been much stronger, it would've actually jingled the change in my pocket. There's a word for that, we learned it in physics, I think, but I can't for the life of me remember what it is."

"A harmonic," Tony said. "That's when two things start to vibrate together, like tuning-forks or wine-glasses."

Curtis was nodding. "Yeah, that's it. I don't know what could be caus-ing it, but it's very powerful. It seemed to settle right in the middle of my head, the way the sound of the powerlines up on the Bluff does when you're standing right underneath them. This is going to sound crazy, but after a minute or so, that hum almost sounded like *talking*."

"I laid a girl up dere on d'Bluffs once," Arky said sentimentally, sounding more like Lawrence Welk than ever. "And it was pretty har-monic, all right. Buzz, buzz, buzz."

"Save it for your memoirs, bub," Tony said. "Go on, Curtis."

"I thought at first it was the radio," Curt said, "because it sounded a little bit like that, too: an old vacuum-tube radio that's on and tuned to music coming from a long way off. So I took my hanky and reached over to kill the power. That's when I found out the knobs don't move, either of them. It's no more a real radio than . . . well, than Phil Candleton's a real State Trooper."

"That's funny, kid," Phil said. "At least as funny as a rubber chicken, I guess, or—"

"Shut up, I want to hear this," Tony said. "Go on, Curtis. And leave out the comedy."

"Yes, sir. By the time I tried the radio knobs, I realized it was cold in there. It's a warm day and the car was sitting in the sun, but it was cold inside. Sort of clammy, too. That's when I thought of the show about earthquakes." Curt shook his head slowly back and forth. "I got a feel-ing that I should get out of that car, and fast. By then the hum was qui-eting down, but it was colder than ever. Like an icebox."

Tony Schoondist, then Troop D's Sergeant Commanding, walked over to the Buick. He didn't touch it, just leaned in the window. He stayed like that for the best part of a minute, leaning into the dark blue car, back inclined but perfectly straight, hands clasped behind his back. Ennis stood behind him. The rest of the Troopers clustered around Curtis, waiting for Tony to finish with whatever it was he was doing. For most of them, Tony Schoondist was the best SC they'd ever have while wearing the Pennsylvania gray. He was tough; brave; fairminded; crafty when he had to be. By the time a Trooper reached the rank of Sergeant Commanding, the politics kicked in. The monthly meetings. The calls from Scranton. Sergeant Commanding was a long way from the top of the ladder, but it was high enough for the bureaucratic bullshit to hit high gear. Schoondist played the game well enough to keep his seat, but he knew and his men knew he'd never rise higher. Or want to. Because with Tony, his men always came first . . . and when Shirley replaced Matt Babicki, it was his men and his woman. His Troop, in other words. Troop D. They knew this not because he said anything, but because he walked the walk.

At last he came back to where his men were standing. He took off his hat, ran his hand through the bristles of his crewcut, then put the hat back on. Strap in the back, as per summer regulations. In winter, the strap went under the point of the chin. That was the tradition, and as in any organization that's been around for a long time, there was a lot of tradition in the PSP. Until 1962, for instance, Troopers needed permission from the Sergeant Commanding to get married (and the SCs used that power to weed out any number of rookies and young Troopers they felt were unqualified for the job).

"No hum," Tony said. "Also, I'd say the temperature inside is about what it should be. Maybe a little cooler than the outside air, but . . ." He shrugged.

Curtis flushed a deep pink. "Sarge, I swear—"

"I'm not doubting you," Tony said. "If you say the thing was humming like a tuning-fork, I believe you. Where would you say this humming sound was coming from? The engine?"

Curtis shook his head.

"The trunk area?"

Another shake.

"Underneath?"

A third shake of the head, and now instead of pink, Curt's cheeks, neck, and forehead were bright red.

"Where, then?"

"Out of the air," Curt said reluctantly. "I know it sounds crazy, but . . . yeah. Right out of the air." He looked around, as if expecting the others to laugh. None of them did.

Just about then Orville Garrett joined the group. He'd been over by the county line, at a building site where several pieces of heavy equipment had been vandalized the night before. Ambling along behind him came Mister Dillon, the Troop D mascot. He was a German shepherd with maybe a little taste of collie thrown in. Orville and Huddie Royer had found him as a pup, paddling around in the shallow well of an abandoned farm out on Sawmill Road. The dog might have fallen in by accident, but probably not.

Mister D was no K-9 specialty dog, but only because no one had trained him that way. He was plenty smart, and protective, as well. If a bad boy raised his voice and started shaking his finger at a Troop D guy while Mister Dillon was around, that fellow ran the risk of picking his nose with the tip of a pencil for the rest of his life.

"What's doin, boys?" Orville asked, but before anyone could answer him, Mister Dillon began to howl. Sandy Dearborn, who happened to be standing right beside the dog, had never heard anything quite like that howl in his entire life. Mister D backed up a pace and then hunkered, facing the Buick. His head was up and his hindquarters were down. He looked like a dog does when he's taking a crap, except for his fur. It was bushed out all over his body, every hair standing on end. Sandy's skin went cold.

"Holy God, what's wrong with him?" Phil asked in a low, awed voice, and then Mister D let loose with another long, quavering howl. He took three or four stalk-steps toward the Buick, never coming out of that hunched-over, cramped-up, taking-a-crap stoop, all the time with his muzzle pointing at the sky. It was awful to watch. He made two or three more of those awkward movements, then dropped flat on the macadam, panting and whining.

"What the *hell?*" Orv said.

"Put a leash on him," Tony said. "Get him inside."

Orv did as Tony said, actually running to get Mister Dillon's leash. Phil Candleton, who had always been especially partial to the dog, went with Orv once the leash was on him, walking next to Mister D, occasionally bending down to give him a comforting stroke and a soothing word. Later, he told the others that the dog had been shivering all over.

Nobody said anything. Nobody had to. They were all thinking the same thing, that Mister Dillon had pretty well proved Curt's point. The ground wasn't shaking and Tony hadn't heard anything when he stuck his head in through the Buick's window, but something was wrong with it, all right. A lot more wrong than the size of its steering wheel or its strange notchless ignition key. Something worse.

In the seventies and eighties, Pennsylvania State Police forensics investigators were rolling stones, travelling around to the various Troops in a given area from District HQ. In the case of Troop D, HQ was Butler. There were no forensics vans; such big-city luxuries were dreamed of, but wouldn't actually arrive in rural Pennsylvania until almost the end of the century. The forensics guys rode in unmarked police cars, carrying their equipment in trunks and back seats, toting it to various crime scenes in big canvas shoulder-bags with the PSP keystone logo on the sides. There were three guys in most forensics crews: the chief and two technicians. Sometimes there was also a trainee. Most of these looked too young to buy a legal drink.

One such team appeared at Troop D that afternoon. They had ridden over from Shippenville, at Tony Schoondist's personal request. It was a funny informal visit, a vehicle exam not quite in the line of duty. The crew chief was Bibi Roth, one of the oldtimers (men joked that Bibi had learned his trade at the knee of Sherlock Holmes and Dr. Watson). He and Tony Schoondist got along well, and Bibi didn't mind doing a solid for the Troop D SC. Not as long as it stayed quiet, that was.

Now: *Sandy*

Ned stopped me at this point to ask why the forensic examination of the Buick was conducted in such an odd (to him, at least) off-the-cuff manner.

"Because," I told him, "the only criminal complaint in the matter that any of us could think of was theft of services—seven dollars' worth of hi-test gasoline. That's a misdemeanor, not worth a forensic crew's time."

"Dey woulda burned almost dat much gas gettin over here from Shippenville," Arky pointed out.

"Not to mention the man-hours," Phil added.

I said, "Tony didn't want to start a paper trail. Remember that there wasn't one at that point. All he had was a car. A very weird car, granted, one with no license plates, no registration, and—Bibi Roth confirmed this—no VIN number, either."

"But Roach had reason to believe the owner drowned in the stream behind the gas station!"

"Pooh," Shirley said. "The driver's overcoat turned out to be a plastic garbage can. So much for Bradley Roach's ideas."

"Plus," Phil put in, "Ennis and your Dad observed no tracks going down the slope behind the station, and the grass was still wet. If the guy *had* gone down there, he would have left a sign."

"Mostly, Tony wanted to keep it in-house," Shirley said. "Would you say that's a fair way to put it, Sandy?"

"Yes. The Buick itself was strange, but our way of dealing with it wasn't much different from the way we'd deal with anything out of the ordinary: a Trooper down—like your father, last year—or one who's used his weapon, or an accident, like when George Morgan was in hot pursuit of that crazy asshole who snatched his kids."

We were all silent for a moment. Cops have nightmares, any Trooper's

47

wife will tell you that, and in the bad-dream department George Morgan was one of the worst. He'd been doing ninety, closing in on the crazy asshole, who had a habit of beating the kids he had snatched and claimed to love, when it happened.

George is almost on top of him and all at once here's this senior citizen crossing the road, seventy years old, slower than creeping bullfrog Jesus, and legally blind. The asshole would have been the one to hit her if she'd started across three seconds earlier, but she didn't. No, the asshole blew right by her, the rearview mirror on the passenger side of his vehicle so close it almost took off her nose. Next comes George, and kapow. He had twelve blameless years on the State Police, two citations for bravery, community service awards without number. He was a good father to his own children, a good husband to his wife, and all of that ended when a woman from Lassburg Cut tried to cross the street at the wrong moment and he killed her with PSP cruiser D-27. George was exonerated by the State Board of Review and came back to a desk job on the Troop, rated PLD—permanent light duty—at his own request. He could have gone back full-time as far as the brass was concerned, but there was a problem: George Morgan could no longer drive. Not even the family car to the market. He got the shakes every time he slid behind the wheel. His eyes teared up until he was suffering from a kind of hysterical blindness. That summer he worked nights, on dispatch. In the afternoons he coached the Troop D–sponsored Little League team all the way to the state tournament. When that was over, he gave the kids their trophy and their pins, told them how proud of them he was, then went home (a player's mother drove him), drank two beers, and blew his brains out in the garage. He didn't leave a note; cops rarely do. I wrote a press release in the wake of that. Reading it, you never would have guessed it was written with tears on my face. And it suddenly seemed very important that I communicate some of the reason why to Curtis Wilcox's son.

"We're a family," I said. "I know that sounds corny, but it's true. Even Mister Dillon knew that much, and you do, too. Don't you?"

The kid nodded his head. Of course he did. In the year after his father died, we were the family that mattered to him most, the one he sought out and the one that gave him what he needed to get on with his life. His mother and sisters loved him, and he loved them, but they were going on with their lives in a way that Ned could not . . . at least not yet. Some of it was being male instead of female. Some of it was being eighteen. Some of it was all those questions of *why* that wouldn't go away.

I said, "What families say and how families act when they're in their houses with the doors shut and how they talk and behave when they're out on their lawns and the doors are open . . . those can be very different things. Ennis knew the Buick was wrong, your Dad did, Tony did, I did. Mister D most certainly did. The way that dog howled . . ."

I fell silent for a moment. I've heard that howl in my dreams. Then I pushed on.

"But legally, it was just an object—a *res,* as the lawyers say—with no blame held against it. We couldn't very well hold the *Buick* for theft of services, could we? And the man who ordered the gas that went into its tank was long gone and hard to find. The best we could do was to think of it as an impoundment."

Ned wore the frown of someone who doesn't understand what he's hearing. I could understand that. I hadn't been as clear as I wanted to be. Or maybe I was just playing that famous old game, the one called It Wasn't Our Fault.

"Listen," Shirley said. "Suppose a woman stopped to use the restroom at that station and left her diamond engagement ring on the washstand and Bradley Roach found it there. Okay?"

"Okay . . ." Ned said. Still frowning.

"And let's say Roach brought it to us instead of just putting it in his pocket and then taking it to a pawnshop in Butler. We'd make a report, maybe put out the make and model of the woman's car to the Troopers in the field, if Roach could give them to us . . . but we wouldn't take the ring. Would we, Sandy?"

"No," I said. "We'd advise Roach to put an ad in the paper—*Found, a woman's ring, if you think it may be yours, call this number and describe.* At which point Roach would get pissing and moaning about the cost of putting an ad in the paper—a whole three bucks."

"And then *we'd* remind him that folks who find valuable property often get rewards," Phil said, "and he'd decide maybe he could find three bucks, after all."

"But if the woman never called or came back," I said, "that ring would become Roach's property. It's the oldest law in history: finders-keepers."

"So Ennis and my Dad took the Buick."

"No," I said. "The *Troop* took it."

"What about theft of services? Did that ever get filed?"

"Oh, well," I said with an uncomfortable little grin. "Seven bucks was hardly worth the paperwork. Was it, Phil?"

"Nah," Phil said. "But we squared it up with Hugh Bossey."

A light was dawning on Ned's face. "You paid for the gas out of petty cash."

Phil looked both shocked and amused. "Never in your life, boy! Petty cash is the taxpayers' money, too."

"We passed the hat," I said. "Everybody that was there gave a little. It was easy."

"If Roach found a ring and nobody claimed it, it would be his," Ned said. "So wouldn't the Buick be his?"

"Maybe if he'd kept it," I said. "But he turned it over to us, didn't he? And as far as he was concerned, that was the end of it."

Arky tapped his forehead and gave Ned a wise look. "Nuttin upstairs, dat one," he said.

For a moment I thought Ned would turn to brooding on the young man who had grown up to kill his father, but he shook that off. I could almost see him do it.

"Go on," he said to me. "What happened next?"

Oh boy. Who can resist that?

Then

It took Bibi Roth and his children (that's what he called them) only forty-five minutes to go over the Buick from stem to stern, the young people dusting and brushing and snapping pictures, Bibi with a clipboard, walking around and sometimes pointing wordlessly at something with his ballpoint pen.

About twenty minutes into it, Orv Garrett came out with Mister Dillon. The dog was on his leash, which was a rarity around the barracks. Sandy walked over to them. The dog wasn't howling, had quit trembling, and was sitting with his brush of tail curled neatly over his paws, but his dark brown eyes were fixed on the Buick and never moved. From deep in his chest, almost too low to hear, came a steady growl like the rumble of a powerful motor.

"For chrissake, Orvie, take him back inside," Sandy Dearborn said.

"Okay. I just thought he might be over it by now." He paused, then said: "I've heard bloodhounds act that way sometimes, when they've found a body. I know there's no body, but do you think someone might have died in there?"

"Not that we know of." Sandy was watching Tony Schoondist come out of the barracks' side door and amble over to Bibi Roth. Ennis was with him. Curt Wilcox was out on patrol again, much against his wishes. Sandy doubted that even pretty girls would be able to talk him into giving them warnings instead of tickets that afternoon. Curt wanted to be at the barracks, watching Bibi and his crew at work, not out on the road; if he couldn't be, lawbreakers in western Pennsylvania would pay.

Mister Dillon opened his mouth and let loose a long, low whine, as if something in him hurt. Sandy supposed something did. Orville took him

51

inside. Five minutes later Sandy himself was rolling again, along with Steve Devoe, to the scene of a two-car collision out on Highway 6.

Bibi Roth made his report to Tony and Ennis as the members of his crew (there were three of them that day) sat at a picnic table in the shade of Shed B, eating sandwiches and drinking the iced tea Matt Babicki had run out to them.

"I appreciate you taking the time to do this," Tony said.

"Your appreciation is appreciated," Bibi said, "and I hope it ends there. I don't want to submit any paperwork on this one, Tony. No one would ever trust me again." He looked at his crew and clapped his hands like Miss Frances on *Ding-Dong School.* "Do we want paperwork on this job, children?" One of the children who helped that day was appointed Pennsylvania's Chief Medical Examiner in 1993.

They looked at him, two young men and a young woman of extraordinary beauty. Their sandwiches were raised, their brows creased. None of them was sure what response was required.

"No, Bibi!" he prompted them.

"No, Bibi," they chorused dutifully.

"No what?" Bibi asked.

"No paperwork," said young man number one.

"No file copies," said young man number two.

"No duplicate or triplicate," said the young woman of extraordinary beauty. "Not even any singlicate."

"Good!" he said. "And with whom are we going to discuss this, *Kinder?*"

This time they needed no prompting. "No one, Bibi!"

"Exactly," Bibi agreed. "I'm proud of you."

"Got to be a joke, anyway," said one of the young men. "Someone's trickin on you, Sarge."

"I'm keeping that possibility in mind," Tony said, wondering what any of them would have thought if they had seen Mister Dillon howling and hunching forward like a crippled thing. Mister D hadn't been trickin on nobody.

The children went back to munching and slurping and talking

among themselves. Bibi, meanwhile, was looking at Tony and Ennis Rafferty with a slanted little smile.

"They see what they look at with youth's wonderful twenty-twenty vision and don't see it at the same time," he said. "Young people are such wonderful idiots. What *is* that thing, Tony? Do you have any idea? From witnesses, perhaps?"

"No."

Bibi turned his attention to Ennis, who perhaps thought briefly about telling the man what he knew of the Buick's story and then decided not to. Bibi was a good man . . . but he didn't wear the gray.

"It's not an automobile, that's for sure," Bibi said. "But a joke? No, I don't think it's that, either."

"Is there blood?" Tony asked, not knowing if he wanted there to be or not.

"Only more microscopic examination of the samples we took can determine that for sure, but I think not. Certainly no more than trace amounts, if there is."

"What did you see?"

"In a word, nothing. We took no samples from the tire treads because there's no dirt or mud or pebbles or glass or grass or anything else in them. I would have said that was impossible. Henry there"—he pointed to young man number one—"kept trying to wedge a pebble between two of them and it kept falling out. Now what is that? *Why* is that? And could you patent such a thing? If you could, Tony, you could take early retirement."

Tony was rubbing his cheek with the tips of his fingers, the gesture of a perplexed man.

"Listen to this," Bibi said. "We're talking floormats here. Great little dirtcatchers, as a rule. Every one a geological survey. Usually. Not here, though. A few smudges of dirt, a dandelion stalk. That's all." He looked at Ennis. "From your partner's shoes, I expect. You say he got behind the wheel?"

"Yes."

"Driver's-side footwell. And that's where these few artifacts were found." Bibi patted his palms together, as if to say QED.

"Are there prints?" Tony asked.

"Three sets. I'll want comparison prints from your two officers and the pump-jockey. The prints we lifted from the gas-hatch will almost certainly belong to the pump-jockey. You agree?"

"Most likely," Tony said. "You'd run the prints on your own time?"

"Absolutely, my pleasure. The fiber samples, as well. Don't annoy me by asking for anything involving the gas chromatograph in Pittsburgh, there's a good fellow. I will pursue this as far as the equipment in my basement permits. That will be quite far."

"You're a good guy, Bibi."

"Yes, and even the best guy will take a free dinner from time to time, if a friend offers."

"He'll offer. Meantime, is there anything else?"

"The glass is glass. The wood is wood . . . but a wooden dashboard in a car of this vintage—this *purported* vintage—is completely wrong. My older brother had a Buick from the late fifties, a Limited. I learned to drive on it and I remember it well. With fear and affection. The dashboard was padded vinyl. I would say the seatcovers in this one are vinyl, which would be right for this make and model; I will be checking with General Motors to make sure. The odometer . . . very amusing. Did you notice the odometer?"

Ennis shook his head. He looked hypnotized.

"All zeros. Which is fitting, I suppose. That car—that *purported* car—would never drive." His eyes moved from Ennis to Tony and then back to Ennis again. "Tell me you haven't seen it drive. That you haven't seen it move a single inch under its own power."

"Actually, I haven't," Ennis said. Which was true. There was no need to add that Bradley Roach claimed to have seen it moving under its own power, and that Ennis, a veteran of many interrogations, believed him.

"Good." Bibi looked relieved. He clapped his hands, once more being Miss Frances. "Time to go, children! Voice your thanks!"

"Thanks, Sergeant," they chorused. The young woman of extraordinary beauty finished her iced tea, belched, and followed her white-coated colleagues back to the car in which they had come. Tony was fascinated to note that not one of the three gave the Buick a look. To them it was now a closed case, and new cases lay ahead. To them the Buick was just an old car, getting older by the minute in the summer sun. So what if pebbles fell out when placed between the knuckles of the tread, even when placed so far up along the curve of the tire that gravity should have held them in? So what if there were three portholes on one side instead of four?

They see it and don't see it at the same time, Bibi had said. *Young people are such wonderful idiots.*

Bibi followed his wonderful idiots toward his own car (Bibi liked to ride to crime scenes in solitary splendor, whenever possible), then stopped. "I said the wood is wood, the vinyl is vinyl, and the glass is glass. You heard me say that?"

Tony and Ennis nodded.

"It appears to me that this purported car's exhaust system is also made of glass. Of course, I was only peering under from one side, but I had a flashlight. Quite a powerful one." For a few moments he just stood there, staring at the Buick parked in front of Shed B, hands in his pockets, rocking back and forth on the balls of his feet. "I have never heard of a car with a glass exhaust system," he said finally, and then walked toward his car. A moment later, he and his children were gone.

Tony was uncomfortable with the car out where it was, not just because of possible storms but because anyone who happened to walk out back could see it. Visitors were what he was thinking of, Mr. and Mrs. John Q. Public. The State Police served John Q and his family as well as they could, in some cases at the cost of their lives. They did not, however, completely trust them. John Q's family was not Troop D's family. The prospect of word getting around—worse, of *rumor* getting around—made Sergeant Schoondist squirm.

He strolled to Johnny Parker's little office (the County Motor Pool was still next door in those days) around quarter to three and sweet-talked Johnny into moving one of the plows out of Shed B and putting the Buick inside. A pint of whiskey sealed the deal, and the Buick was towed into the oil-smelling darkness that became its home. Shed B had garage doors at either end, and Johnny brought the Buick in through the back one. As a result, it faced the Troop D barracks from out there for all the years of its stay. It was something most of the Troopers became aware of as time passed. Not a forebrain thing, nothing like an organized thought, but something that floated at the back of the mind, never quite formed and never quite gone: the pressure of its chrome grin.

There were eighteen Troopers assigned to Troop D in 1979, rotating through the usual shifts: seven to three, three to eleven, and the grave-yard shift, when they rode two to a cruiser. On Fridays and Saturdays, the eleven-to-seven shift was commonly called Puke Patrol.

By four o'clock on the afternoon the Buick arrived, most of the off-duty Troopers had heard about it and dropped by for a look. Sandy Dearborn, back from the accident on Highway 6 and typing up the paperwork, saw them going out there in murmuring threes and fours, almost like tour groups. Curt Wilcox was off-duty by then and he con-ducted a good many of the tours himself, pointing out the mismatched portholes and big steering wheel, lifting the hood so they could marvel over the whacked-out mill with BUICK 8 printed on both sides of the engine block.

Orv Garrett conducted other tours, telling the story of Mister D's reaction over and over again. Sergeant Schoondist, already fascinated by the thing (a fascination that would never completely leave him until Alzheimer's erased his mind), came out as often as he could. Sandy remembered him standing just outside the open Shed B door at one point, foot up on the boards behind him, arms crossed. Ennis was beside him, smoking one of those little Tiparillos he liked and talking while Tony nodded. It was after three, and Ennis had changed into jeans and a plain white shirt. After three, and that was the best Sandy could say later on. He wished he could do better, but he couldn't.

The cops came, they looked at the engine (the hood permanently up by that point, gaping like a mouth), they squatted down to look at the exotic glass exhaust system. They looked at everything, they touched nothing. John Q and his family wouldn't have known to keep their mitts off, but these were cops. They understood that while the Buick might not be an evidential *res* as of right then, later on that might change. Especially if the man who had left it at the Jenny station should happen to turn up dead.

"Unless that happens or something else pops, I intend to keep the car here," Tony told Matt Babicki and Phil Candleton at one point. It was five o'clock or so by then, all three of them had been officially off-duty for a couple of hours, and Tony was finally thinking about going home. Sandy himself had left around four, wanting to mow the grass before sitting down to dinner.

"Why here?" Matt asked. "What's the big deal, Sarge?"

Tony asked Matt and Phil if they knew about the Cardiff Giant. They said they didn't, and so Tony told them the story. The Giant had been "discovered" in upstate New York's Onondaga Valley. It was supposed to be the fossilized corpse of a gigantic humanoid, maybe something from another world or the missing link between men and apes. It turned out to be nothing but a hoax perpetrated by a Binghamton cigar-maker named George Hull.

"But before Hull fessed up," Tony said, "just about everyone in the whole round world—including P. T. Barnum—dropped by for a look. The crops on the surrounding farms were trampled to mush. Houses were broken into. There was a forest fire started by asshole John Q's camping in the woods. Even after Hull confessed to having the 'petrified man' carved in Chicago and shipped Railway Express to upstate New York, people kept coming. They refused to believe the thing wasn't real. You've heard the saying 'There's a sucker born every minute'? That was coined in 1869, in reference to the Cardiff Giant."

"What's your point?" Phil asked.

Tony gave him an impatient look. "The point? The point is that I'm not having any Cardiff Fucking Giant on my watch. Not if I can help it. Or the goddam Buick of Turin, for that matter."

As they moved back toward the barracks, Huddie Royer joined them (with Mister Dillon at his side, now heeling as neatly as a pooch in a dog-show). Huddie caught the Buick of Turin line and snickered. Tony gave him a dour look.

"No Cardiff Giant in western PA; you boys mark what I say and pass the word. Because word of mouth's how it's gonna be done—I'm not tacking any memo up on the bulletin board. I know there'll be some gossip, but it'll die down. I will *not* have a dozen Amish farms overrun by lookie-loos in the middle of the growing season, is that understood?"

It was understood.

By seven o'clock that evening, things had returned to something like normal. Sandy Dearborn knew that for himself, because he'd come back after dinner for his own encore look at the car. He found only three Troopers—two off-duty and one in uniform—strolling around the Buick. Buck Flanders, one of the off-duties, was snapping pictures with his Kodak. That made Sandy a bit uneasy, but what would they show? A Buick, that was all, one not yet old enough to be an official antique.

Sandy got down on his hands and knees and peered under the car, using a flashlight that had been left nearby (and probably for just that purpose). He took a good gander at the exhaust system. To him it looked like Pyrex glass. He leaned in the driver's window for awhile (no hum, no chill), then went back to the barracks to shoot the shit with Brian Cole, who was in the SC chair that shift. The two of them started on the Buick, moved on to their families, and had just gotten to baseball when Orville Garrett stuck his head in the door.

"Either you guys seen Ennis? The Dragon's on the phone, and she's not a happy lady."

The Dragon was Edith Hyams, Ennis's sister. She was eight or nine years older than Ennis, a longtime widow-lady. There were those in Troop D who opined that she had murdered her husband, simply nagged him into his grave. "That's not a tongue in her mouth, that's a Ginsu knife," Dicky-Duck Eliot observed once. Curt, who saw the lady more than the rest of the Troop (Ennis was usually his partner; they got on well despite the difference in their ages), was of the opinion that Edith was the reason Trooper Rafferty had never married. "I think that deep down he's afraid they're all like her," he once told Sandy.

Coming back to work after your shift is through is never a good idea, Sandy thought after spending a long ten minutes on the phone with The Dragon. *Where is he, he promised he'd be home by six-thirty at the latest, I got the roast he wanted down at Pepper's, eighty-nine cents a pound, now it's cooked like an old boot, gray as wash-water* (only of course what the lady said was *warsh-warter*), *if he's down at The Country Way or The Tap you tell me right now, Sandy, so I can call and tell him what's what.* She also informed Sandy that she was out of her water-pills, and Ennis was supposed to have brought her a fresh batch. So where the hell was he? Pulling overtime? That would be all right, she reckoned, God knew they could use the money, only he should have called. Or was he drinking? Although she never came right out and said so, Sandy could tell that The Dragon voted for drinking.

Sandy was sitting at the dispatch desk, one hand cupped over his eyes, trying to get a word in edgeways, when Curtis Wilcox bopped in, dressed in his civvies and looking every inch the sport. Like Sandy, he'd come back for another peek at the Roadmaster.

"Hold on, Edith, hold on a second," Sandy said, and put the telephone against his chest. "Help me out here, rookie. Do you know where Ennis went after he left?"

"He left?"

"Yeah, but he apparently didn't go home." Sandy pointed to the phone, which was still held against his chest. "His sister's on the line."

"If he left, how come his car's still here?" Curt asked.

Sandy looked at him. Curtis looked back. And then, without a word spoken, the two of them jumped like Jack and Jill to the same conclusion.

Sandy got rid of Edith—told her he'd call her back, or have Ennis call her, if he was around. That taken care of, Sandy went out back with Curt.

There was no mistaking Ennis's car, the American Motors Gremlin they all made fun of. It stood not far from the plow Johnny Parker had moved out of Shed B to make room for the Buick. The shadows of both the car and the plow straggled long in the declining sun of a summer evening, printed on the earth like tattoos.

Sandy and Curt looked inside the Gremlin and saw nothing but the usual road-litter: hamburger wrappers, soda cans, Tiparillo boxes, a couple of maps, an extra uniform shirt hung from the hook in back, an extra citation book on the dusty dashboard, some bits of fishing gear. All that rickrack looked sort of comforting to them after the sterile emptiness of the Buick. The sight of Ennis sitting behind the wheel and snoozing with his old Pirates cap tilted over his eyes would have been even more comforting, but there was no sign of him.

Curt turned and started back toward the barracks. Sandy had to break into a trot in order to catch up and grab his arm. "Where do you think you're going?" he asked.

"To call Tony."

"Not yet," Sandy said. "Let him have his dinner. We'll call him later if we have to. I hope to God we don't."

Before checking anything else, even the upstairs common room, Curt and Sandy checked Shed B. They walked all around the car, looked inside the car, looked under the car. There was no sign of Ennis Rafferty in any of those places—at least, not that they could see. Of course, looking for signs in and around the Buick that evening was like looking for the track of one particular horse after a stampede has gone by. There was no sign of Ennis *specifically,* but . . .

"Is it cold in here, or is it just me?" Curt asked. They were about ready to return to the barracks. Curt had been down on his knees with his head cocked, taking a final look underneath the car. Now he stood up, brushing his knees. "I mean, I know it's not *freezing* or anything, but it's colder than it should be, wouldn't you say?"

Sandy actually felt too hot—sweat was running down his face—but that might have been nerves rather than room-temperature. He thought Curt's sense of cold was likely just a holdover from what he'd felt, or thought he'd felt, out at the Jenny station.

Curt read that on his face easily enough. "Maybe it is. Maybe it *is* just me. Fuck, *I* don't know. Let's check the barracks. Maybe he's downstairs in supply, coopin. Wouldn't be the first time."

The two men hadn't entered Shed B by either of the big roll-up doors but rather through the doorknob-operated, people-sized door that was set into the right side. Curt paused in it instead of going out, looking back over his shoulder at the Buick.

His gaze as he stood beside the wall of pegged hammers, clippers, rakes, shovels, and one posthole digger (the red AA on the handle stood not for Alcoholics Anonymous but for Arky Arkanian) was angry. Almost baleful. "It wasn't in my mind," he said, more to himself than to Sandy. "It was *cold*. It's not now, but it was."

Sandy said nothing.

"Tell you one thing," Curt said. "If that goddam car's going to be around long, I'm getting a thermometer for this place. I'll pay for it out of my own pocket, if I have to. And say! Someone left the damn trunk unlocked. I wonder who—"

He stopped. Their eyes met, and a single thought flashed between them: *Fine pair of cops* we *are.*

They had looked inside the Buick's cabin, and underneath, but had ignored the place that was—according to the movies, at least—the temporary body-disposal site of choice for murderers both amateur and professional.

The two of them walked over to the Buick and stood by the back deck, peering at the line of darkness where the trunk was unlatched.

"You do it, Sandy," Curt said. His voice was low, barely above a whisper.

Sandy didn't want to, but decided he had to—Curt was, after all, still a rookie. He took a deep breath and raised the trunk's lid. It went up much faster than he had expected. There was a clunk when it reached the top of its arc, loud enough to make both men jump. Curt grabbed Sandy with one hand, his fingers so cold that Sandy almost cried out.

The mind is a powerful and often unreliable machine. Sandy was so sure they were going to find Ennis Rafferty in the trunk of the Buick that for a moment he saw the body: a curled fetal shape in jeans and a white shirt, looking like something a Mafia hitman might leave in the trunk of a stolen Lincoln.

But it was only overlapped shadows that the two Troopers saw. The Buick's trunk was empty. There was nothing there but plain brown carpeting without a single tool or grease-stain on it. They stood in silence for a moment or two, and then Curt made a sound under his breath, either a snicker or an exasperated snort. "Come on," he said. "Let's get out of here. And shut the damn trunk tight this time. 'Bout scared the life out of me."

"Me too," Sandy said, and gave the trunk a good hard slam. He followed Curt to the door beside the wall with the pegged tools on it. Curtis was looking back again.

"Isn't that one hell of a thing," he said softly.

"Yes," Sandy agreed.

"It's fucked up, wouldn't you say?"

"I would, rook, I would indeed, but your partner isn't in it. Or anywhere in here. That much is for sure."

Curt didn't bridle at the word *rook*. Those days were almost over for him, and they both knew it. He was still looking at the car, so smooth and cool and *there*. His eyes were narrow, showing just two thin lines of blue. "It's almost like it's talking. I mean, I'm sure that's just my imagination—"

"Damn tooting it is."

"—but I can almost hear it. Mutter-mutter-mutter."

"Quit it before you give me the willies."

"You mean you don't already have them?"

Sandy chose not to reply to that. "Come on, all right?"

They went out, Curt taking one last look before closing the door.

The two of them checked upstairs in the barracks, where there was a living room and, behind a plain blue curtain, a dorm-style bedroom that contained four cots. Andy Colucci was watching a sitcom on television and a couple of Troopers who had the graveyard shift were snoozing; Sandy could hear the snores. He pulled back the curtain to check. Two guys, all right, one of them going *wheek-wheek* through his nose—polite—and the other going *ronk-ronk-ronk* through his open mouth—big and rude. Neither of them was Ennis. Sandy hadn't really expected to find him there; when Ennis cooped, he most commonly did it in the basement supply room, rocked back in the old swivel chair that went perfectly with the World War II–era metal desk down there, the old cracked radio on the shelf playing danceband music soft. He wasn't in the supply room that night, though. The radio was off and the swivel chair with the pillow on the seat was unoccupied. Nor was he in either of the storage cubicles, which were poorly lit and almost as spooky as cells in a dungeon.

There was a total of four toilets in the building, if you included the stainless steel lidless model in the Bad Boy Corner. Ennis wasn't hiding out in any of the three with doors. Not in the kitchenette, not in dispatch, not in the SC's office, which stood temporarily empty, with the doors open and the lights off.

By then, Huddie Royer had joined Sandy and Curt. Orville Garrett had gone home for the day (probably afraid that Ennis's sister would turn up in person), and had left Mister Dillon in Huddie's care, so the dog was there, too. Curt explained what they were doing and why. Huddie grasped the implications at once. He had a big, open Farmer John face, but Huddie was a long way from stupid. He led Mister D to Ennis's locker and let him smell inside, which the dog did with great interest. Andy Colucci joined them at this point, and a couple of other off-duty guys who had dropped by to sneak a peek at the Buick also joined the party. They went outside, split up into two groups, and walked around the building in opposing circles, calling Ennis's name. There was still plenty of good light, but the day had begun to redden.

Curt, Huddie, Mister D, and Sandy were in one group. Mister Dillon walked slowly, smelling at everything, but the only time he really perked and turned, the scent he'd caught took him on a beeline to Ennis's Gremlin. No help there.

At first yelling Ennis's name felt foolish, but by the time they gave up and went back inside the barracks, it no longer felt that way at all. That was the scary part, how fast yelling for him stopped feeling silly and started feeling serious.

"Let's take Mister D into the shed and see what he smells there," Curt proposed.

"No way," Huddie said. "He doesn't like the car."

"Come on, man, Ennie's my partner. Besides, maybe ole D will feel different about that car now."

But ole D felt just the same. He was okay outside the shed, in fact started to pull on his leash as the Troopers approached the side door. His head was down, his nose all but scraping the macadam. He was even more interested when they got to the door itself. The men had no doubt at all that he had caught Ennis's scent, good and strong.

Then Curtis opened the door, and Mister Dillon forgot all about whatever he had been smelling. He started to howl at once, and again hunched over as if struck by bad cramps. His fur bushed out like a peacock's finery, and he squirted urine over the doorstep and onto the shed's concrete floor. A moment later he was yanking at the leash Huddie was holding, still howling, still trying in a crazy, reluctant way to get inside. He hated it and feared it, that was in every line of his body—and in his wild eyes—but he was trying to get at it, just the same.

"Aw, never mind! Just get him out!" Curt shouted. Until then he had kept hold of himself very well, but it had been a long and stressful day for him and he was finally nearing the breaking point.

"It's not his fault," Huddie said, and before he could say more, Mister Dillon raised his snout and howled again . . . only to Sandy it sounded more like a scream than a howl. The dog took another crippled lurch forward, pulling Huddie's arm out straight like a flag in a high wind. He was inside now, howling and whining, lurching to get forward and pissing everywhere like a pup. Pissing in terror.

"I know it's not!" Curt said. "You were right to begin with, I'll give you a written apology if you want, just get him the fuck out!"

Huddie tried to reel Mister D back in, but he was a big dog, about ninety pounds, and he didn't want to come. Curt had to lay on with him in order to get D going in the right direction. In the end they dragged him out on his side, D fighting and howling and gnashing the air with his teeth the whole way. It was like pulling a sack of polecats, Sandy would say later.

When the dog was at last clear of the door, Curtis slammed it shut. The second he did, Mister Dillon relaxed and stopped fighting. It was as if a switch in his head had been flipped. He continued to lie on his side for a minute or two, getting his breath, then popped to his feet. He gave the Troopers a bewildered look that seemed to say, "What happened, boys? I was going along good, and then I kind of blanked out."

"Holy . . . fucking . . . *shit*," Huddie said in a low voice.

"Take him back to the barracks," Curt said. "I was wrong to ask you to let him inside there, but I'm awful worried about Ennis."

Huddie took the dog back to the barracks, Mister D once again as cool as a strawberry milkshake, just pausing to sniff at the shoes of the Troopers who had helped search the perimeter. These had been joined by others who had heard Mister D freaking out and had come to see what all the fuss was.

"Go on in, guys," Sandy said, then added what they always said to the lookie-loos who gathered at accident sites: "Show's over."

They went in. Curt and Sandy watched them, standing there by the closed shed door. After awhile Huddie came back without Mister D. Sandy watched Curt reach for the doorknob of the shed door and felt a sense of dread and tension rise in his head like a wave. It was the first time he felt that way about Shed B, but not the last. In the twenty-odd years that followed that day, he would go inside Shed B dozens of times, but never without the rise of that dark mental wave, never without the intuition of almost-glimpsed horrors, of abominations in the corner of the eye.

Not that all of the horrors went unglimpsed. In the end they glimpsed plenty.

The three of them walked in, their shoes gritting on the dirty cement. Sandy flipped on the light-switches by the door and in the glare of the naked bulbs the Buick stood like one prop left on a bare stage, or the single piece of art in a gallery that had been dressed like a garage for the showing. What would you call such a thing? Sandy wondered. *From a Buick 8* was what occurred to him, probably because there was a Bob Dylan song with a similar title. The chorus was in his head as they stood there, seeming to illuminate that feeling of dread: *Well, if I go down dyin', you know she bound to put a blanket on my bed.*

It sat there with its Buick headlights staring and its Buick grille sneering. It sat there on its fat and luxy whitewalls, and inside was a dashboard full of frozen fake controls and a wheel almost big enough to steer a privateer. Inside was something that made the barracks dog simultaneously howl in terror and yank forward as if in the grip of some ecstatic magnetism. If it had been cold in there before, it no longer was; Sandy could see sweat shining on the faces of the other two men and feel it on his own.

It was Huddie who finally said it out loud, and Sandy was glad. He felt it, but never could have put that feeling into words; it was too out-rageous.

"Fucking thing ate im," Huddie said with flat certainty. "I don't know how that could be, but I think he came in here by himself to take another look and it just . . . somehow . . . ate im."

Curt said, "It's watching us. Do you feel it?"

Sandy looked at the glassy headlight eyes. At the downturned, sneering mouth full of chrome teeth. The decorative swoops up the sides, which could almost have been sleek locks of slick hair. He felt *something,* all right. Perhaps it was nothing but childish awe of the unknown, the terror kids feel when standing in front of houses their hearts tell them are haunted. Or perhaps it was really what Curt said. Perhaps it was watching them. Gauging the distance.

They looked at it, hardly breathing. It sat there, as it would sit for all the years to come, while Presidents came and went, while records were replaced by CDs, while the stock market went up and a pair of sky-scrapers came down, while movie-stars lived and died and Troopers came and went in the D barracks. It sat there real as rocks and roses. And to some degree they all felt what Mister Dillon had felt: the *draw* of it. In the months that followed, the sight of cops standing there side by side in front of Shed B became common. They would stand with their hands cupped to the sides of their faces to block the light, peering in through the windows running across the front of the big garage door. They looked like sidewalk superintendents at a building site. Sometimes they went inside, too (never alone, though; when it came to Shed B, the buddy sys-tem ruled), and they always looked younger when they did, like kids creeping into the local graveyard on a dare.

Curt cleared his throat. The sound made the other two jump, then laugh nervously. "Let's go inside and call the Sarge," he said, and this time

Now: *Sandy*

". . . and that time I didn't say anything. Just went along like a good boy."

My throat was as dry as an old chip. I looked at my watch and wasn't exactly surprised to see that over an hour had gone by. Well, that was all right; I was off-duty. The day was murkier than ever, but the faint mutters of thunder had slid away south of us.

"Those old days," someone said, sounding both sad and amused at the same time—it's a trick only the Jews and the Irish seem to manage with any grace. "We thought we'd strut forever, didn't we?"

I glanced around and saw Huddie Royer, now dressed in civilian clothes, sitting on Ned's left. I don't know when he joined us. He had the same honest Farmer John face he'd worn through the world back in '79, but now there were lines bracketing the corners of his mouth, his hair was mostly gray, and it had gone out like the tide, revealing a long, bright expanse of brow. He was, I judged, about the same age Ennis Rafferty had been when Ennis pulled his Judge Crater act. Huddie's retirement plans involved a Winnebago and visits to his children and grandchildren. He had them everywhere, so far as I could make out, including the province of Manitoba. If you asked—or even if you didn't—he'd show you a U.S. map with all his proposed routes of travel marked in red.

"Yeah," I said. "I guess we did, at that. When did you arrive, Huddie?"

"Oh, I was passing by and heard you talking about Mister Dillon. He was a good old doggie, wasn't he? Remember how he'd roll over on his back if anyone said 'You're under arrest'?"

"Yeah," I said, and we smiled at each other, the way men do over love or history.

"What happened to him?" Ned asked.

67

"Punched his card," Huddie said. "Eddie Jacubois and I buried him right over there." He pointed toward the scrubby field that stretched up a hill north of the barracks. "Must be fifteen years ago. Would you say, Sandy?"

I nodded. It was actually fourteen years, almost to the day.

"I guess he was old, huh?" Ned asked.

Phil Candleton said, "Getting up there, yes, but—"

"He was poisoned," Huddie said in a rough, outraged voice, and then said no more.

"If you want to hear the rest of this story—" I began.

"I do," Ned replied at once.

"—then I need to wet my whistle."

I started to get up just as Shirley came out with a tray in her hands. On it was a plate of thick sandwiches—ham and cheese, roast beef, chicken—and a big pitcher of Red Zinger iced tea. "Sit back down, Sandy," she said. "I got you covered."

"What are you, a mind reader?"

She smiled as she set the tray down on the bench. "Nope. I just know that men get thirsty when they talk, and that men are always hungry. Even the ladies get hungry and thirsty from time to time, believe it or not. Eat up, you guys, and I expect you to put away at least two of these sandwiches yourself, Ned Wilcox. You're too damn thin."

Looking at the loaded tray made me think of Bibi Roth, talking with Tony and Ennis while his crew—his children, not much older than Ned was now—drank iced tea and gobbled sandwiches made in the same kitchenette, nothing different except for the color of the tiles on the floor and the microwave oven. Time is also held together by chains, I think.

"Yes, ma'am, okay."

He gave her a smile, but I thought it was dutiful rather than spontaneous; he kept looking over at Shed B. He was under the spell of the thing now, as so many men had been over the years. Not to mention one good dog. And as I drank my first glass of iced tea, cold and good going down my parched throat, loaded with real sugar rather than that unsatisfying artificial shit, I had time to wonder if I was doing Ned Wilcox any favors. Or if he'd even believe the rest of it. He might just get up, walk away all stiff-shouldered and angry, believing I'd been making a game of him and his grief. It wasn't impossible. Huddie, Arky, and Phil would back me up—so would Shirley, for that matter. She hadn't been around when the Buick came in, but she'd seen plenty—and *done* plenty—since taking the dispatch job in the mid-eighties. The kid still might not believe it, though. It was a lot to swallow.

Too late to back out now, though.

"What happened about Trooper Rafferty?" Ned asked.

"Nothing," Huddie said. "He didn't even get his ugly mug on the side of a milk carton."

Ned gazed at him uncertainly, not sure if Huddie was joking or not.

"Nothing happened," Huddie repeated, more quietly this time. "That's the insidious thing about disappearing, son. What happened to your Dad was terrible, and I'd never try to convince you any different. But at least you *know.* That's something, isn't it? There's a place where you can go and visit, where you can lay down flowers. Or take your college acceptance letter."

"That's just a grave you're talking about," Ned said. He spoke with a strange patience that made me uneasy. "There's a piece of ground, and there's a box under it, and there's something in the box that's dressed in my father's uniform, but it's not my father."

"But you know what happened to him," Huddie insisted. "With Ennis . . ." He spread his hands with the palms down, then turned them up, like a magician at the end of a good trick.

Arky had gone inside, probably to take a leak. Now he came back and sat down.

"All quiet?" I asked.

"Well, yes and no, Sarge. Steff tole me to tell you she's getting dose bursts of interference on d'radio again, dose li'l short ones. You know what I mean. Also, DSS is kaputnik. Jus' dat sign on the TV screen dat say STAND BY SEARCHING FOR SIGNAL."

Steff was Stephanie Colucci, Shirley's second-shift replacement in dispatch and old Andy Colucci's niece. The DSS was our little satellite dish, paid for out of our own pockets, like the exercise equipment in the corner upstairs (a year or two ago someone tacked a poster to the wall beside the free weights, showing buff biker types working out in the prison yard up at Shabene—THEY NEVER TAKE A DAY OFF is the punchline beneath).

Arky and I exchanged a glance, then looked over at Shed B. If the microwave oven in the kitchenette wasn't on the fritz now, it soon would be. We might lose the lights and the phone, too, although it had been awhile since that had happened.

"We took up a collection for that rotten old bitch he was married to," Huddie said. "That was mighty big of Troop D, in my view."

"I thought it was to shut her up," Phil said.

"Wasn't *nothing* going to shut that one up," Huddie said. "She meant to have her say. Anyone who ever met her knew that."

"It wasn't exactly a collection and he wasn't married to her," I said. "The woman was his sister. I thought I made that clear."

"He was married to her," Huddie insisted. "They were like any old couple, with all the yaps and grumps and sore places. They did everything married folks do except for the old in-out, and for all I know—"

"Snip, snip, bite your lip," Shirley said mildly.

"Yeah," Huddie said. "I s'pose."

"Tony passed the hat, and we all tossed in as much as we could," I told Ned. "Then Buck Flanders's brother—he's a stockbroker in Pittsburgh—invested it for her. It was Tony's idea to do it that way rather than just hand her a check."

Huddie was nodding. "He brought it up at that meeting he called, the one in the back room at The Country Way. Taking care of The Dragon was just about the last item on the agenda."

Huddie turned directly to Ned.

"By then we knew nobody was going to find Ennis, and that Ennis wasn't just going to walk into a police station somewhere in Bakersfield, California, or Nome, Alaska, with a case of amnesia from a knock on the head. He was gone. Maybe to the same place the fella in the black coat and hat went off to, maybe to some other place, but gone either way. There was no body, no signs of violence, not even any *clothes,* but Ennie was gone." Huddie laughed. It was a sour sound. "Oh, that bad-natured bitch he lived with was so *wild.* Of course she was half-crazy to begin with—"

"More dan half," Arky said complacently, and helped himself to a ham and cheese sandwich. "She call all d'time, tree-four times a day, made Matt Babicki in dispatch jus' about tear his hair out. You should count your blessins she's gone, Shirley. Edit' Hyams! What a piece of work!"

"What did she think had happened?" Ned asked.

"Who knows?" I said. "That we killed him over poker debts, maybe, and buried him in the cellar."

"You played *poker* in the barracks back then?" Ned looked both fascinated and horrified. "Did my father play?"

"Oh please," I said. "Tony would have scalped anyone he caught playing poker in the barracks, even for matches. And I'd do exactly the same. I was joking."

"We're not *firemen*, boy," Huddie said with such disdain that I had to laugh. Then he returned to the subject at hand. "That old woman believed we had something to do with it because she hated us. She would have hated anyone that distracted Ennis's attention from her. Is hate too strong a word, Sarge?"

"No," I said.

Huddie once more turned to Ned. "We took his time and we took his energy. And I think the part of Ennis's life that was the best for him was the part he spent here, or in his cruiser. She knew that, and she hated it—'The job, the job, the job,' she'd say. 'That's all he cares about, his damned *job*.' As far as she was concerned, we *must* have taken his life. Didn't we take everything else?"

Ned looked bewildered, perhaps because hate of the job had never been a part of his own home life. Not that he'd seen, anyway. Shirley laid a gentle hand on his knee. "She had to hate *somebody*, don't you see? She had to blame somebody."

I said, "Edith called, Edith hectored us, Edith wrote letters to her Congressman and to the State Attorney General, demanding a full investigation. I think Tony knew all that was in the offing, but he went right ahead with the meeting we had a few nights later, and laid out his proposal to take care of her. If we didn't, he said, no one would. Ennis hadn't left much, and without our help she'd be next door to destitute. Ennis had insurance and was eligible for his pension—probably eighty per cent of full by then—but she wouldn't see a penny of either one for a long time. Because—"

"—he just disappeared," Ned said.

"Right. So we got up a subscription for The Dragon. A couple of thousand dollars, all told, with Troopers from Lawrence, Beaver, and Mercer also chipping in. Buck Flanders's brother put it in computer stocks, which were brand-new then, and she ended up making a small fortune.

"As for Ennis, a story started going around the various Troops over here in western PA that he'd run off to Mexico. He was always talking about Mexico, and reading magazine stories about it. Pretty soon it was being taken as gospel: Ennis had run away from his sister before she could finish the job of cutting him up with that Ginsu knife tongue of hers. Even guys who knew better—or should have—started telling that story after awhile, guys who were in the back room of The Country Way when Tony Schoondist said right out loud that he believed the Buick in Shed B had something to do with Ennie's disappearance."

"Stopped just short of calling it a transporter unit from Planet X," Huddie said.

"Sarge was very forceful dat night," Arky said, sounding so much like Lawrence Welk—*Now here's da lovely Alice-uh Lon*—that I had to raise my hand to cover a smile.

"When she wrote her Congressman, I guess she didn't talk about what you guys had over there in the Twilight Zone, did she?" Ned asked.

"How could she?" I asked. "She didn't know. That was the main reason Sergeant Schoondist called the meeting. Basically it was to remind us that loose lips sink sh—"

"What's that?" Ned asked, half-rising from the bench. I didn't even have to look to know what he was seeing, but of course I looked anyway. So did Shirley, Arky, and Huddie. You couldn't not look, couldn't not be fascinated. None of us had ever pissed and howled over the Roadmaster like poor old Mister D, but on at least two occasions I had screamed. Oh yes. I had damned near screamed my guts out. And the nightmares afterward. Man oh man.

The storm had gone away to the south of us, except in a way it hadn't.

In a way it had been caged up inside of Shed B. From where we sat on the smokers' bench we could see bright, soundless explosions of light going off inside. The row of windows in the roll-up door would be as black as pitch, and then they'd turn blue-white. And with each flash, I knew, the radio in dispatch would give out another bray of static. Instead of showing *5:18 PM*, the clock on the microwave would be reading *ERROR*.

But on the whole, this wasn't a bad one. The flashes of light left after-images—greenish squares that floated in front of your eyes—but you could look. The first three or four times that pocket storm happened, looking was impossible—it would have fried the eyes right out of your head.

"Holy God," Ned whispered. His face was long with surprise—

No, that's too timid. It was shock I saw on his face that afternoon. Nor was shock the end of it. When his eyes cleared a little, I saw the same look of fascination I had seen on his father's face. On Tony's. Huddie's. Matt Babicki's and Phil Candleton's. And hadn't I felt it on my own face? It's how we most often appear when we confront the deep and authentic unknown, I think—when we glimpse that place where our familiar universe stops and the real blackness begins.

Ned turned to me. "Sandy, Jesus Christ, what is it? *What is it?*"

"If you have to call it something, call it a lightquake. A mild one. These days, most of them are mild. Want a closer look?"

He didn't ask if it was safe, didn't ask if it was going to explode in his face or bake the old sperm-factory down below. He just said, *"Yeah!"* Which didn't surprise me in the least.

We walked over, Ned and I in the lead, the others not far behind. The irregular flashes were very clear in the gloom of the late day, but they registered on the eye even in full sunshine. And when we first took possession (that was right around the time Three-Mile Island almost blew, now that I think about it), the Buick Roadmaster in one of its throes literally outshone the sun.

"Do I need shades?" Ned asked as we approached the shed door. I could now hear the humming from inside—the same hum Ned's father had noticed as he sat behind the Buick's oversized wheel out at the Jenny station.

"Nah, just squint," Huddie said. "You would have needed shades in '79, though, I can tell you that."

"You bet your Swede ass," Arky said as Ned put his face to one of the windows, squinting and peering in.

I slotted myself in next to Ned, fascinated as always. Step right up, see the living crocodile.

The Roadmaster stood entirely revealed, the tarp it had somehow shrugged off lying crumpled in a tan drift on the driver's side. To me, it looked more like an *objet d'art* than ever—that big old automotive dinosaur with its curvy lines and hardtop styling, its big wheels and sneer-mouth grille. Welcome, ladies and gentlemen! Welcome to this evening's viewing of *From a Buick 8!* Just keep a respectful distance, because this is the art that bites!

It sat there moveless and dead . . . moveless and dead . . . and then the cabin lit up a brilliant flashbulb purple. The oversized steering wheel and the rearview mirror stood out with absolute dark clarity, like objects on the horizon during an artillery barrage. Ned gasped and put up a hand to shield his face.

It flashed again and again, each silent detonation printing its leaping shadow across the cement floor and up the board wall, where a few tools still hung from the pegs. Now the humming was very clear. I directed my gaze toward the circular thermometer hanging from the beam which ran above the Buick's hood, and when the light bloomed again, I was able to read the temperature easily: fifty-four degrees Fahrenheit. Not great, but not terrible, either. It was mostly when the temperature in Shed B dropped below fifty that you had to worry; fifty-four wasn't a bad number at all. Still, it was best to play it safe. We had drawn a few con-clusions about the Buick over the years—established a few rules—but we knew better than to trust any of them very far.

Another of those bright soundless flashes went off inside the Buick, and then there was nothing for almost a full minute. Ned never budged. I'm not sure he even breathed.

"Is it over?" he asked at last.

"Wait," I said.

We gave it another two minutes and when there was still nothing, I opened my mouth to say we might as well go back and sit down, the Buick had exhausted its supply of fireworks for tonight. Before I could speak, there was a final monstrous flash. A wavering tendril of light, like a spark from some gigantic cyclotron, shot outward and upward from the Buick's rear passenger window. It rose on a jagged diagonal to the back corner of the shed, where there was a high shelf loaded with old boxes, most filled with hardware oddments. These lit up a pallid, somehow eldritch yellow, as if the boxes were filled with lighted candles instead of orphan nuts, bolts, screws, and springs. The hum grew louder, rattling my teeth and actually seeming to vibrate along the bridge of my nose. Then it quit. So did the light. To our dazzled eyes, the interior of the shed now looked pitch-black instead of just gloomy. The Buick was only a hulk with rounded corners and furtive gleams which marked the chrome facings around its headlights.

Shirley let out her breath in a long sigh and stepped back from the window where she had been watching. She was trembling. Arky slipped an arm around her shoulders and gave her a comforting hug.

Phil, who had taken the window to my right, said: "No matter how many times I see it, boss, I never get used to it."

"What is it?" Ned asked. His awe seemed to have wound ten or twelve years off his face and turned him into a child younger than his sisters. "Why does it happen?"

"We don't know," I said.

"Who else knows about it?"

"Every Trooper who's worked out of Troop D over the last twenty-plus years. Some of the Motor Pool guys know. The County Road Commissioner, I think—"

"Jamieson?" Huddie said. "Yeah, he knows."

"—and the Statler Township Chief of Police, Sid Brownell. Beyond that, not many."

We were walking back to the bench now, most of us lighting up. Ned looked like he could use a cigarette himself. Or something. A big knock of whiskey, maybe. Inside the barracks, things would be going back to normal. Steff Colucci would already be noting an improvement in her radio reception, and soon the DSS dish on the roof would be receiving again—all the scores, all the wars, and six Home Shopping stations. If that wouldn't make you forget about the hole in the ozone layer, by God, nothing would.

"How could folks not know?" Ned asked. "Something as big as this, how could it not get out?"

"It's not so big," Phil said. "I mean, it's a *Buick,* son. A Cadillac, now . . . *that* would be big."

"Some families can't keep secrets and some families can," I said. "Ours can. Tony Schoondist called that meeting in the The Country Way, two nights after the Buick came in and Ennis disappeared, mostly to make sure we would. Tony briefed us on any number of things that night. Ennis's sister, of course—how we were going to take care of her and how we were supposed to respond to her until she cooled down—"

"If she ever did, I wasn't aware of it," Huddie said.

"—and how we were to handle any reporters if she went to the press."

There had been a dozen Troopers there that night, and with the help of Huddie and Phil, I managed to name most of them. Ned wouldn't have met all of them face-to-face, but he'd probably heard the names at his dinner table, if his Dad talked shop from time to time. Most Troopers do. Not the ugly stuff, of course, not to their families—the spitting and cursing and the bloody messes on the highway—but there's funny stuff, too, like the time we got called out because this Amish kid was roller-skating through downtown Statler, holding onto the tail of a galloping horse and laughing like a loon. Or the time we had to talk to the guy out on the Culverton Road who'd done a snow-sculpture of a naked man and woman in a sexually explicit position. *But it's art!* he kept yelling. We tried to explain that it wasn't art to the neighbors; they were scandalized. If not for a warm spell and a storm of rain, we probably would have wound up in court on that one.

I told Ned about how we'd dragged the tables into a big hollow square without having to be asked, and how Brian Cole and Dicky-Duck Eliot escorted the waitresses out and closed the doors behind them. We served ourselves from the steam tables which had been set up at the front of the room. Later there was beer, the off-duty Troopers pulling their own suds and running their own tabs, and a fug of blue cigarette smoke rising to the ceiling. Peter Quinland, who owned the restaurant in those days, loved The Chairman of the Board, and a steady stream of Frank Sinatra songs rained down on us from the overhead speakers as we ate and drank and smoked and talked: "Luck Be a Lady," "Summer Wind," "New York, New York," and of course "My Way," maybe the dumbest pop song of the twentieth century. To this day I can't listen to it—or any Sinatra song, really—without thinking of The Country Way and the Buick out in Shed B.

Concerning the Buick's missing driver, we were to say we had no name, no description, and no reason to believe the fellow in question had done anything against the law. Nothing about theft of services, in other words. Queries about Ennis were to be taken seriously and treated honestly—up to a point, anyway. Yes, we were all puzzled. Yes, we were all worried. Yes, we had put out watch-and-want bulletins—what we called W2's. Yes, it was possible that Ennis had just pulled up stakes and moved on. Really, we were instructed to say, *anything* was possible, and Troop D was doing its best to take care of Trooper Rafferty's sister, a dear lady who was so deeply upset she might say anything.

"As for the Buick itself, if anyone asks about it at all, tell them it's an impound," Tony had said. "No more than that. If anyone does say more than that, I'll find out who and smoke him out like a cigar." He looked around the room; his men looked back at him, and no one was stupid enough to smile. They'd been around the Sarge long enough to know that when he looked the way he did just then, he was *not* joking. "Are we clear on this? Everyone got the scoop?"

A general rumble of agreement had temporarily blotted out The Chairman singing "It Was a Very Good Year." We had the scoop, all right.

Ned held up a hand, and I stopped talking, which was actually a pleasure. I hadn't much wanted to revisit that long-gone meeting in the first place.

"What about the tests that guy Bibi Roth did?"

"All inconclusive," I said. "The stuff that looked like vinyl wasn't *exactly* vinyl—close, but that was all. The paint-chips didn't match up to any of the automotive paints Bibi had samples of. The wood was wood. 'Likely oak,' Bibi said, but that was all he *would* say, no matter how much Tony pressed him. Something about it bothered him, but he wouldn't say what."

"Maybe he couldn't," Shirley said. "Maybe he didn't know."

I nodded. "The glass in the windows and windshield is plain old sandwich safety glass, but not trademarked. Not installed on any Detroit assembly line, in other words."

"The fingerprints?"

I ticked them off on my own fingers. "Ennis. Your father. Bradley Roach. End of story. No prints from the man in the black trenchcoat."

"He must have been wearing gloves," Ned said.

"You'd think so, yes. Brad couldn't say for sure, but he *thought* he remembered seeing the guy's hands and thinking they were as white as his face."

"People sometimes make up details like that afterwards, though," Huddie commented. "Eyewitnesses aren't as reliable as we'd like them to be."

"You done philosophizing?" I asked.

Huddie gave me a grand wave of the hand. "Continue."

"Bibi found no traces of blood in the car, but fabric samples taken from the interior of the trunk showed microscopic traces of organic matter. Bibi wasn't able to identify any of it, and the stuff—he called it 'soap-scum'—disintegrated. Every slide he took was clear of the stuff in a week. Nothing left but the staining agent he used."

Huddie raised his hand like a kid in school. I nodded to him.

"A week later you couldn't see the places where those guys chipped the dashboard and the wheel to get their samples. The wood grew back like skin over a grape. Same with the lining in the trunk. If you scratched a fender with a penknife or a key, six or seven hours later the scratch would be gone."

"It *heals* itself?" Ned said. "It can do that?"

"Yes," Shirley said. She'd lit another Parliament and was smoking it in quick, nervous little puffs. "Your father dragooned me into one of his experiments once—got me to run the video camera. He put a long scratch down the driver's-side door, right under the chrome swoop, and we just let the camera run, came back together every fifteen minutes. It wasn't anything dramatic, like something in a movie, but it was pretty damned amazing. The scratch got shallower and started to darken around the edges, like it was working to match the paintjob. And finally it was just gone. All sign of it."

"And the tires," Phil Candleton said, taking a turn. "You shoved a screwdriver into one of em, the air'd start to whoosh out just like you'd expect. Only then the whoosh'd thin to a whistle and a few seconds later that would stop, too. Then out comes the screwdriver." Phil pursed his lips and made a *thpp* sound. "Like spitting out a watermelon seed."

"Is it alive?" Ned asked me. His voice was so low I could hardly hear it. "I mean, if it can *heal* itself—"

"Tony always said it wasn't," I said. "He was vehement on the subject. 'Just a gadget,' he used to say. 'Just some kind of goddam thinga-majig we don't understand. Your Dad thought just the opposite, and by the end he was just as vehement as Tony had ever been. If Curtis had lived—"

"What? If he'd lived, what?"

"I don't know," I said. All at once I felt dull and sad. There was a lot more to tell, but suddenly I didn't want to tell it. I didn't feel up to it and my heart was heavy with the prospect of it, the way your heart can grow heavy at the prospect of toil which is necessary but hard and stu-pid—stumps to pull before sundown, hay to bundle into the barn before afternoon rain. "I don't know what would have happened if he'd lived, and that's the God's honest truth."

Huddie came to my rescue. "Your Dad was bullshit about the car, Ned. I mean bug-eyed bullshit. He was out there every spare minute, walking around it, taking pictures of it . . . touching it. That was what he mostly did. Just touching and touching, like to make sure it was real."

"Sarge d'same way," Arky put in.

Not exactly, I thought but didn't say. It had been different for Curt. In the end the Buick had been his in a way it had never been Tony's. And Tony had known it.

"But what about Trooper Rafferty, Sandy? Do you think the Buick—?"

"Ate im," Huddie said. He spoke with dead-flat certainty. "That's what I thought then and it's what I think now. It's what your Dad thought, too."

"Did he?" Ned asked me.

"Well, yes. Ate him or took him away to someplace else." Again the image of stupid work came to me—rows of beds to be made, stacks of dishes to be washed, acres of hay to be scythed and carried.

"But you're telling me," Ned said, "that no scientist has ever been allowed to study that thing since Trooper Rafferty and my father found it? *Ever?* No physicists, no chemists? No one's ever run a spectrographic analysis?"

"Bibi was back at least once, I think," Phil said, sounding just the tiniest bit defensive. "By himself, though, without those kids he used to travel around with. He and Tony and your father wheeled some big machine in there . . . maybe it *was* a spectrograph, but I don't know what it showed. Do you, Sandy?"

I shook my head. There was no one left to answer that question. Or a lot of others. Bibi Roth died of cancer in 1998. Curtis Wilcox, who often walked around the Buick with a Spiral notebook in his hands, writing things down (and sometimes sketching), was also dead. Tony Schoondist, alias the old Sarge, was still alive but now in his late seventies, lost in that confused twilit purgatory reserved for people with Alzheimer's disease. I remembered going to see him, along with Arky Arkanian, at the nursing home where he now lives. Just before Christmas, this was. Arky and I brought him a gold St. Christopher's medal, which a bunch of us older fellows had chipped in to buy. It had seemed to me that the old Sarge was having one of his good days. He opened the package without much trouble and seemed delighted by the medallion. Even undid the clasp himself, although Arky had to help him do it up again after he'd slipped it on. When that was finally accomplished, Tony had looked at me closely with his brows knit together, his bleary eyes projecting a parody of his old piercing glare. It was a moment when he really seemed himself. Then his eyes filled with tears, and the illusion was gone. "Who are you boys?" he'd asked. "I can almost remember." Then, as matter-of-factly as someone reporting the weather: "I'm in hell, you know. This is hell."

"Ned, listen," I said. "What that meeting in The Country Way really boiled down to was just one thing. The cops in California have it written on the sides of some of their cruisers, maybe because their memory is a little bit faulty and they have to write it down. We don't. Do you know what I'm talking about?"

"To serve and protect," Ned said.

"You got it. Tony thought that thing had come into our hands almost as a result of God's will. He didn't say it that flat-out, but we understood. And your father felt the same way."

I was telling Ned Wilcox what I thought he needed to hear. What I didn't tell him about was the light in Tony's eyes, and in the eyes of Ned's father. Tony could sermonize about our commitment to serve and protect; he could tell us about how the men of Troop D were the ones best equipped to take care of such a dangerous *res;* he could even allow as how later on we might turn the thing over to a carefully chosen team of scientists, perhaps one led by Bibi Roth. He could spin all those tales, and did. None of it meant jack shit. Tony and Curt wanted the Buick because they just couldn't bear to let it go. That was the cake, and all the rest of it was just icing. The Roadmaster was strange and exotic, unique, and it was *theirs.* They couldn't bear to surrender it.

"Ned," I asked, "would you know if your Dad left any notebooks? Spirals, they would have been, like the kind kids take to school."

Ned's mouth pinched at that. He dropped his head and spoke to a spot somewhere between his knees. "Yeah, all kinds of them, actually. My Mom said they were probably diaries. Anyway, in his will, he asked that Mom burn all his private papers, and she did."

"I guess that makes sense," Huddie said. "It jibes with what I know about Curt and the old Sarge, at least."

Ned looked up at him.

Huddie elaborated. "Those two guys distrusted scientists. You know what Tony called them? Death's cropdusters. He said their big mission in life was to spread poison everywhere, telling people to go ahead and eat all they wanted, that it was knowledge and it wouldn't hurt them— that it would set them free." He paused. "There was another issue, too."

"What issue?" Ned asked.

"Discretion," Huddie said. "Cops can keep secrets, but Curt and Tony didn't believe scientists could. 'Look how fast those idiots cropdusted the atomic bomb all around the world,' I heard Tony say once. 'We fried the Rosenbergs for it, but anyone with half a brain knows the Russians would have had the bomb in two years, anyway. Why? Because scientists like to chat. That thing we've got out in Shed B may not be the equivalent of the A-bomb, but then again it might. One thing's for sure, it isn't *anybody's* A-bomb as long as it's sitting out back under a piece of canvas.'"

I thought that was just part of the truth. I've wondered from time to time if Tony and Ned's father ever really needed to talk about it—I mean on some late weekday evening when things at the barracks were at their slowest, guys cooping upstairs, other guys watching a movie on the VCR and eating microwave popcorn, just the two of them downstairs from all that, in Tony's office with the door shut. I'm not talking about maybe or kinda or sorta. I mean whether or not they ever spoke the flat-out truth: *There's not anything like this anywhere, and we're keeping it.* I don't think so. Because really, all they would have needed to do was to look into each other's eyes. To see that same eagerness—the desire to touch it and pry into it. Hell, just to walk around it. It was a secret thing, a mystery, a marvel. But I didn't know if the boy could accept that. I knew he wasn't just missing his father; he was angry at him for dying. In that mood, he might have seen what they did as stealing, and that wasn't the truth, either. At least not the whole truth.

"By then we knew about the lightquakes," I said. "Tony called them 'dispersal events.' He thought the Buick was getting rid of something, discharging it like static electricity. Issues of discretion and caretaking aside, by the end of the seventies people in Pennsylvania—and not just us but everyone—had one very big reason not to trust the scientists and the techies."

"Three-Mile," Ned said.

"Yes. Plus, there's more to that car than self-healing scratches and dust-repellent. Quite a bit more."

I stopped. It seemed too hard, too much.

"Go on, tell him," Arky said. He sounded almost angry, a pissed-off bandleader in the gloaming. "You told him all dis dat don't mean shit, now you tell im da rest." He looked at Huddie, then Shirley. "Even 1988. Yeah, even dat part." He paused, sighed, looked at Shed B. "Too late to stop now, Sarge."

I got up and started across the parking lot. Behind me, I heard Phil say: "No, hunh-unh. Let him go, kid, he'll be back."

That's one thing about sitting in the big chair; people can say that and almost always be right. Barring strokes, heart attacks, and drunk drivers, I guess. Barring acts of what we mortals hope is God. People who sit in the big chair—who have worked to get there and work to stay there— never say oh fuck it and go fishing. No. Us big-chair folks continue making the beds, washing the dishes, and baling the hay, doing it the best we can. *Ah, man, what would we do without you?* people say. The answer is that most of them would go on doing whatever the hell they want, same as always. Going to hell in the same old handbasket.

I stood at the roll-up door of Shed B, looking through one of the windows at the thermometer. It was down to fifty-two. Still not bad—not *terrible,* anyway—but cold enough for me to think the Buick was going to give another shake or two before settling down for the night. No sense spreading the tarp back over it yet, then; we'd likely just have to do it again later on.

It's winding down: that was the received wisdom concerning the Roadmaster, the gospel according to Schoondist and Wilcox. Slowing like an unwound clock, wobbling like an exhausted top, beeping like a smoke detector that can no longer tell what's hot. Pick your favorite metaphor from the bargain bin. And maybe it was true. Then again, maybe it wasn't. We knew nothing about it, not really. Telling ourselves we did was just a strategy we used so we could continue living next door to it without too many bad dreams.

I walked back to the bench, lighting another cigarette, and sat down between Shirley and Ned. I said, "Do you want to hear about the first time we saw what we saw tonight?"

The eagerness I saw on his face made it a little easier to go on.

Then

Sandy was there when it started, the only one who was. In later years he would say—half-joking—that it was his one claim to fame. The others arrived on the scene soon enough, but to begin with it was only Sander Freemont Dearborn, standing by the gas-pump with his mouth hung open and his eyes squinched shut, sure that in another few seconds the whole bunch of them, not to mention the Amish and few non-Amish farmers in the area, would be so much radioactive dust in the wind.

It happened a couple of weeks after the Buick came into Troop D's possession, around the first of August in the year 1979. By then the newspaper coverage of Ennis Rafferty's disappearance was dying down. Most of the stories about the missing State Trooper appeared in the Statler County *American,* but the *Pittsburgh Post-Gazette* ran a feature piece on the front page of its Sunday edition at the end of July. **MISS-ING TROOPER'S SISTER LEFT WITH MANY QUESTIONS,** the headline read, and beneath that: **EDITH HYAMS CALLS FOR FULL INVESTIGATION.**

Overall, the story played out exactly as Tony Schoondist had hoped it would. Edith believed the men in D Troop knew more than they were telling about her brother's disappearance; she was quoted on that in both papers. What was left between the lines was that the poor woman was half out of her mind with grief (not to mention anger), and looking for someone to blame for what might have been her own fault. None of the Troopers said anything about her sharp tongue and nearly constant fault-finding, but Ennis and Edith had neighbors who weren't so dis-creet. The reporters from both papers also mentioned that, accusations or no, the men in Ennis's Troop were going ahead with plans to provide the woman with some modest financial support.

The harsh black-and-white photo of Edith in the *Post-Gazette* didn't help her case; it made her look like Lizzie Borden about fifteen minutes before she grabbed the hatchet.

The first lightquake happened at dusk. Sandy had come off patrol around six that evening in order to have a little chat with Mike Sanders, the County Attorney. They had a particularly nasty hit-and-run trial coming up, Sandy the prime witness for the prosecution, the victim a child who had been left a quadriplegic. Mike wanted to be very sure that the coke-snorting Mr. Businessman responsible went away. Five years was his goal, but ten wasn't out of the question. Tony Schoondist sat in on part of the meeting, which took place in a corner of the upstairs common room, then went down to his office while Mike and Sandy finished up. When the meeting was over, Sandy decided to top up the tank in his cruiser before hitting the road for another three hours or so.

As he walked past dispatch toward the back door, he heard Matt Babicki say in a low, just-talking-to-myself voice: "Oh, you fucking thing." This was followed by a whack. "Why don't you *behave?*"

Sandy peeped around the corner and asked if Matt was having that delicate time of the month.

Matt wasn't amused. "Listen to this," he said, and boosted the gain on his radio. The SQUELCH knob, Sandy saw, was already turned as far as it would go toward +.

Brian Cole checked in from Unit 7, Herb Avery from 5 out on the Sawmill Road, George Stankowski from God knew where. That one was almost entirely lost in a windy burst of static.

"If this gets any worse, I don't know how I'm going to keep track of the guys, let alone shoot them any information," Matt complained. He slapped the side of his radio again, as if for emphasis. "And what if someone calls in with a complaint? Is it getting ready to thunderstorm outside, Sandy?"

"It was clear as a bell when I came in," he said, then looked out the window. "Clear as a bell now, too . . . as you could see, if your neck had a swivel in it. I was born with one, see?" Sandy turned his head from side to side.

"Very funny. Haven't you got an innocent man to frame, or something?"

"Good one, Matt. That's a very snappy comeback."

As he went on his way, Sandy heard someone upstairs wanting to know if the damned TV antenna had fallen down, because the picture had all of a sudden gone to hell during a pretty good *Star Trek* rerun, the one about the Tribbles.

Sandy went out. It was a hot, hazy evening with thunder rumbling off in the distance but no wind and a clear sky overhead. The light was starting to drain away into the west, and a groundmist was rising from the grass; it had gotten to a height of maybe five feet.

He got in his cruiser (D-14 that shift, the one with the busted headrest), drove it across to the Amoco pump, got out, unscrewed the gas cap under the pull-down license plate, then stopped. He had suddenly become aware of how quiet it was—no crickets chirping in the grass, no birds singing anywhere around. The only noise was a low, steady humming, like the sound one hears if one is standing right under the county powerlines, or near an electrical substation.

Sandy started to turn around, and as he did, the whole world went purple-white. His first thought was that, clear sky overhead or no, he had been struck by lightning. Then he saw Shed B lit up like . . .

But there was no way to finish the simile. There *was* nothing like it, not in his experience.

If he had been looking at those first few flashes dead-on, he guessed he would have been blinded—maybe temporarily, maybe for good. Luckily for him, the shed's front roll-up door faced away from the gas-pump. Yet still the glare was enough to dazzle his eyes, and to turn that summer twilight as bright as noonday. And it made Shed B, a solid enough wooden structure, seem as insubstantial as a tent made out of gauze. Light shot through every crack and unoccupied nail-hole; it flashed out from beneath the eaves through a small cavity that might have been gnawed by a squirrel; it blazed at ground-level, where a board had fallen off, in a great brilliant bar. There was a ventilator stack on the roof, and it shot the glare skyward in irregular bursts, like smoke-signals made out of pure violet light. The flashes through the rows of windows on the roll-up doors, front and back, turned the rising groundmist into an eerie electric vapor.

Sandy was calm. Startled but calm. He thought: *This is it, motherfucker's blowing, we're all dead.* The thought of running or jumping into his cruiser never entered his head. Run where? Drive where? It was a joke.

What he wanted was crazy: to get closer. It *drew* him. He wasn't terrified of it, as Mister D had been; he felt the fascination but not the fear. Crazy or not, he wanted to get closer. Could almost hear it *calling* him closer.

Feeling like a man in a dream (it crossed his mind that dreaming was a serious possibility), he walked back to the driver's side of D-14, leaned in through the open window, and plucked his sunglasses off the dashboard. He put them on and started walking toward the shed. It was a little better with the sunglasses, but not much. He walked with his hand raised in front of him and his eyes narrowed down to stringent slits. The world boomed silent light all around and throbbed with purple fire. Sandy could see his shadow jumping out from his feet, disappearing, and then jumping out again. He could see the light leaping from the windows in the roll-up door and glaring off the back of the barracks. He could see Troopers starting to spill out, pushing aside Matt Babicki from dispatch, who had been closest and who got outside first. In the flashes from the shed, everyone moved herky-jerky, like actors in a silent film. Those who had sunglasses in their pockets reached to put them on. Some of those who didn't turned and stumbled back in to get them. One Trooper even drew his gun, looked down at it as if to say *What the fuck'm I gonna do with this?* and put it back in his holster. Two of the Troopers without sunglasses groped gamely on toward the shed nevertheless, heads down and eyes shut and hands held out before them like the hands of sleepwalkers, drawn as Sandy had been toward the stuttery flashes and that low, maddening hum. Like bugs to a buglight.

Then Tony Schoondist ran through them, slapping them, shoving them, telling them to get the hell back, to return to the barracks and that was an order. He was trying to get his own sunglasses on and kept missing his face with them. He got them where they belonged only after poking one bow into his mouth and the other into his left eyebrow.

Sandy saw and heard none of that. What he heard was the hum. What he saw were the flashes, turning the groundmist smoke into electric drag- ons. What he saw was the column of stuttery purple light rising from the conical roof-vent, stabbing up into the darkening air.

Tony grabbed him, shook him. Another silent gunshell of light went off in the shed, turning the lenses of Tony's sunglasses into small blue fire- balls. He was shouting, although there was no need to; Sandy could hear him perfectly. There was the humming sound, and *someone* murmuring *Good God almighty,* and that was all.

"Sandy! Were you here when this started?"

"Yes!" He found himself shouting back in spite of himself. The situ- ation somehow demanded that they shout. The light flared and glared, mute lightning. Each time it went off, the barracks seemed to jump forward like something that was alive, the shadows of the Troopers running up its board side.

"What started it? What set it off?"

"I don't know!"

"Get inside! Call Curtis! Tell him what's happening! Tell him to get his ass over here *now!*"

Sandy resisted the urge to tell his SC that he wanted to stay and see what happened next. In a very elementary way the idea was stupid to begin with: you couldn't actually see anything. It was too bright. Even with sunglasses it was too bright. Besides, he knew an order when he heard it.

He went inside, stumbling over the steps (it was impossible to judge depth or distance in those brilliant stutterflashes), and shuffled his way to dispatch, waving his arms in front of him. In his swimming, dazzled eyesight, the barracks was nothing but overlaid shadows. The only visual reality for him at that moment was the great purple flashes float- ing in front of him.

Matt Babicki's radio was an endless blare of static with a few voices sticking out of it like the feet or fingers of buried men. Sandy picked up the regular telephone beside the dedicated 911 line, thinking that would be out, too—sure it would—but it was fine. He dialed Curt's number from the list tacked to the bulletin board. Even the telephone seemed to jump with fright each time one of those purple-white flashes lit the room.

Michelle answered the phone and said Curt was out back, mowing the grass before it got dark. She didn't want to call him in, that was clear in her voice. But when Sandy asked her a second time, she said, "All right, just a minute, don't you guys ever give it a rest?"

The wait seemed interminable to Sandy. The thing in Shed B kept flashing like some crazy neon apocalypse, and the room seemed to waver into a slightly different perspective every time it did. Sandy found it nearly impossible to believe something generating such brilliance could be anything but destructive, yet he was still alive and breathing. He touched his cheeks with the hand not holding the telephone, checking for burns or swelling. There was neither.

For the time being, at least, he told himself. He kept waiting for the cops outside to begin screaming as the thing in the old garage exploded or melted or let something out—something unimaginable with burning electric eyes. Such ideas were a million miles from the usual run of cop-thoughts, but Sandy Dearborn had never felt less like a cop and more like a scared little boy. At last Curt picked up the telephone, sounding both curious and out of breath.

"You have to come right now," Sandy told him. "Sarge says so."

Curt knew what it was about immediately. "What's it doing, Sandy?"

"Shooting off fireworks. Flashes and sparks. You can't even look at Shed B."

"Is the building on fire?"

"Don't think so, but there's no way to tell for sure. You can't see inside. It's too bright. Get over here."

The phone at Curt's end crashed down without another word spoken and Sandy went back outside. If they were going to be nuked, he decided, he wanted to be with his friends when it happened.

Curt came roaring up the driveway marked TROOPERS ONLY ten minutes later, behind the wheel of his lovingly restored Bel Air, the one his son would inherit twenty-two years later. When he came around the corner he was still moving fast, and Sandy had one horrible moment when he thought Curtis was going to clean out about five guys with his bumper. But Curt was quick on the brake (he still had a kid's reflexes), and brought the Chevy to a nose-dipping halt.

He got out of his car, remembering to turn off the engine but not the headlights, tripping over his own eager feet and almost sprawling on the macadam. He caught his balance and went running toward the shed. Sandy had just time to see what was dangling from one hand: a pair of welder's goggles on an elastic strap. Sandy had seen excited men in his time—sure, plenty, almost every guy you stopped for speeding was excited in one way or another—but he had never seen anyone as burning with it as Curt was then. His eyes seemed to be bulging right out of his face, and his hair appeared to be standing on end . . . although that might have been an illusion caused by how fast he was running.

Tony reached out and grabbed him on the way by, almost spilling him again. Sandy saw Curt's free hand close into a fist and start to rise. Then it relaxed. Sandy didn't know how close the rookie had come to striking his sergeant and didn't want to know. What mattered was that he recognized Tony (and Tony's authority over him) and stood down.

Tony reached for the goggles.

Curt shook his head.

Tony said something to him.

Curt replied, shaking his head vehemently.

In the still-bright flashes, Sandy saw Tony Schoondist undergo his own brief struggle, wanting to simply order Curt to hand the goggles over. Instead, he swung around and looked at his gathered Troopers. In his haste and excitement, the SC had given them what could have been construed as two orders: to get back and to return to the barracks. Most had chosen to obey the first and ignore the second. Tony took a deep breath, let it out, then spoke to Dicky-Duck Eliot, who listened, nodded, and went back into the barracks.

The rest of them watched Curt run toward Shed B, dropping his baseball cap on the pavement as he went and slipping the goggles over his eyes. Much as Sandy liked and respected the newest member of Troop D, he did not see anything heroic in this advance, not even while it was happening. Heroism is the act of going forward in the face of fear. Curt

Wilcox felt no fear that night, not the slightest twinge of it. He was simply bugshit with excitement and a curiosity so deep it was a compulsion. Much later, Sandy would decide the old Sarge had let Curtis go because he saw there was no chance of holding him back.

Curt stopped about ten feet in front of the roll-up door, raising his hands to block his eyes as a particularly brilliant flash erupted from inside the shed. Sandy saw the light shining through Curt's fingers in purple-white spokes. At the same time, Curt's shadow appeared on the mist like the figure of a giant. Then the light died and through a blot of after-image, Sandy saw Curt advance again. He reached the door and looked inside. He stood that way until the next flash came. He recoiled when it did, then at once went back to the window.

Meanwhile, here came Dicky-Duck Eliot back from his errand, whatever it had been. Sandy saw what he was holding as Dicky-Duck went past. The Sarge insisted that all of his D-cars should go out equipped with Polaroid cameras, and Dicky-Duck had run to fetch one of them. He handed it to Tony, cringing involuntarily as the shed lit up in another silent fusillade of light.

Tony took the camera and jogged across to Curtis, who was still peering into the shed and recoiling at each new flash (or series of them). Even the welder's goggles weren't enough protection from what was going on in there, it seemed.

Something nuzzled Sandy's hand and he almost screamed before looking down and seeing the barracks dog. Mister Dillon had likely slept through the whole thing until then, snoring on the linoleum between the sink and the stove, his favorite spot. Now he'd emerged to see what all the excitement was about. It was clear to Sandy from the brilliance of his eyes, the peak of his ears, and the high set of his head that he knew *something* was going on, but his previous terror wasn't in evidence. The flashing lights didn't seem to bother him in the slightest.

Curtis tried to grab the Polaroid, but Tony wouldn't let it go. They stood there in front of the Shed B door, turned into flinching silhouettes by each new flash from the shed. Arguing? Sandy didn't think so. Not quite, anyway. It looked to him like they were having the sort of heated discussion any two scientists might have while observing some new phenomenon. *Or maybe it's not a phenomenon at all,* Sandy thought. *Maybe it's an experiment, and we're the guinea pigs.*

He began to measure the length of the dark intervals as he and the others stood watching the two men in front of the shed, one wearing an oversized pair of goggles and the other holding a boxy Polaroid camera, both of them outlined like figures on a laser-lit dancefloor. The flashes had been like chain lightning when they began, but now there were significant pauses. Sandy counted six seconds between . . . ten seconds . . . seven . . . fourteen . . . twenty.

Beside him, Buck Flanders said: "I think it's ending."

Mister D barked and made as if to start forward. Sandy grabbed him by the collar and held him back. Maybe the dog just wanted to go to Curt and Tony, but maybe it was the thing in the shed he wanted to go to. Maybe it was calling him again. Sandy didn't care which; he liked Mister Dillon right where he was.

Tony and Curt went around to the walk-in door. There they engaged in another warm discussion. At last Tony nodded—reluctantly, Sandy thought—and handed over the camera. Curt opened the door, and as he did the thing flashed out again, burying him in a glare of brilliant light. Sandy fully expected him to be gone when it died out, disintegrated or perhaps teleported to a galaxy far, far away, where he'd spend the rest of his life lubing X-wing fighters or maybe polishing Darth Vader's shiny black ass.

He had just time to register Curt still standing there, one hand upraised to shield his goggled eyes. To his right and slightly behind him, Tony Schoondist was caught in the act of turning away from the glare, hands upraised to shield his face. Sunglasses were simply no protection; Sandy was wearing his own and knew that. When he could see again, Curt had gone into the shed.

At that moment, all of Sandy's attention switched to Mister Dillon, who was lunging forward in spite of the hold Sandy had on his collar. The dog's former calm was gone. He was growling and whining, ears flat against his skull, muzzle wrinkled back to show the white wink of teeth.

"Help me, help me out here!" Sandy shouted.

93

Buck Flanders and Phil Candleton also grabbed Mister D's collar, but at first it made no difference. The dog went motoring on, coughing and dripping slobber on the pavement, eyes fixed on the side door. He was ordinarily the sweetest mutt in creation, but right then Sandy wished for a leash and a muzzle. If D turned to bite, one of them was apt to wind up a finger or two shy.

"Shut the door!" Sandy bawled at the Sergeant. "If you don't want D in there with him, *shut the damn door!*"

Tony looked startled, then saw what was wrong and closed the door. Almost at once Mister Dillon relaxed. The growling stopped, then the whining. He gave out a couple of puzzled barks, as if he couldn't remember exactly what had been bugging him. Sandy wondered if it was the hum, which was appreciably louder with the door open, or some smell. He thought the latter, but there was no way of telling for sure. The Buick wasn't about what you knew but what you didn't.

Tony saw a couple of men moving forward and told them to stay back. Hearing his normal speaking voice so clearly was calming, but it still seemed wrong. Sandy couldn't help feeling there should have been whoops and screams in the background, movie-soundtrack explosions, perhaps rumbles from the outraged earth itself.

Tony turned back to the windows running along the roll-up door and peered in.

"What's he doing, Sarge?" Matt Babicki asked. "He all right?"

"He's fine," Tony said. "Walking around the car taking pictures. What are you doing out here, Matt? Get in on dispatch, for Christ's sake."

"The radio's FUBAR, boss. Static."

"Well, maybe it's getting better. Because *this* is getting better." To Sandy he sounded normal on top—like the Sergeant—but underneath, that excitement still throbbed in his voice. And as Matt turned away, Tony added: "Not a word about this goes out over the air, you hear me? Not in the clear, anyway. Now or ever. If you have to talk about the Buick, it's . . . it's Code D. You understand?"

"Yessir," Matt said, and went up the back steps with his shoulders slumped, as if he had been spanked.

"Sandy!" Tony called. "What's up with the dog?"

"Dog's fine. Now. What's up with the car?"

"The car also appears to be fine. Nothing's burning and there's no sign anything exploded. The thermometer says fifty-four degrees. It's cold in there, if anything."

"If the car's fine, why's he taking pictures of it?" Buck asked.

"Y's a crooked letter that can't be made straight," Sergeant Schoondist replied, as if this explained everything. He kept his eye on Curtis, who went on circling the car like a fashion photographer circling a model, snapping photos, tucking each Polaroid as it came out of the slot into the waistband of the old khaki shorts he was wearing. While this was going on, Tony allowed the rest of those present to approach by fours and take a look. When Sandy's turn came, he was struck by how Curtis's ankles lit up green each time the Buick flashed out. *Radiation!* he thought. *Jesus Christ, he's got radiation burns!* Then he remembered what Curt had been doing earlier and had to laugh. Michelle hadn't wanted to call him in to the phone because he was mowing the grass. And that was what was on his ankles—grass-stains.

"Come outta there," Phil muttered from Sandy's left. He still had the dog by the collar, although now Mister D seemed quite docile. "Come on out, don't be pressing your luck."

Curt started backing toward the door as if he'd heard Phil—or all of them—thinking that same thing. More likely he was just out of film.

As soon as he came through the door, Tony put an arm around his shoulders and pulled him aside. As they stood talking, a final weak pulse of purple light came. It was really no more than a twitch. Sandy looked at his watch. It was ten minutes of nine. The entire event had lasted not quite an hour.

Tony and Curt were looking at the Polaroids with an intensity Sandy couldn't understand. If, that was, Tony had been telling the truth when he said the Buick and the other stuff in the shed were unchanged. And to Sandy, all of it did look unchanged.

At last Tony nodded as if something was settled and walked back to the rest of the Troopers. Curt, meanwhile, went to the roll-up door for a final peek. The welder's goggles were pushed up on his forehead by then. Tony ordered everyone back into the barracks except for George

Stankowski and Herb Avery. Herb had come in from patrol while the lightshow was still going on, probably to take a dump. Herb would drive five miles out of his way to take a dump at the barracks; he was famous for it, and took all ribbing stoically. He said you could get diseases from strange toilet seats, and anyone who didn't believe that deserved what he got. Sandy thought Herb was simply partial to the magazines in the upstairs crapper. Trooper Avery, who would be killed in a rollover car crash ten years later, was an *American Heritage* man.

"You two have got the first watch," Tony said. "Sing out if you see anything peculiar. Even if you only *think* it's peculiar."

Herb groaned at getting sentry duty and started to protest.

"Put a sock in it," Tony said, pointing at him. "Not one more word."

Herb noted the red spots on his SC's cheeks and closed his mouth at once. Sandy thought that showed excellent sense.

Matt Babicki was talking on the radio as the rest of them crossed the ready-room behind Sergeant Schoondist. When Matt told Unit 6 to state his twenty, Andy Colucci's response was strong and perfectly clear. The static had cleared out again.

They filled the seats in the little living room upstairs, those last in line having to content themselves with grabbing patches of rug. The ready-room downstairs was bigger and had more chairs, but Sandy thought Tony's decision to bring the crew up here was a good one. This was family business, not police business.

Not *strictly* police business, at least.

Curtis Wilcox came last, holding his Polaroids in one hand, goggles still pushed up on his forehead, rubber flip-flops on his green feet. His T-shirt read HORLICKS UNIVERSITY ATHLETIC DEPARTMENT.

He went to the Sergeant and the two of them conferred in murmurs while the rest waited. Then Tony turned back to the others. "There was no explosion, and neither Curt nor I think there was any sort of radiation leak, either."

Big sighs of relief greeted this, but several of the Troopers still looked doubtful. Sandy didn't know how he looked, there was no mirror handy, but he still *felt* doubtful.

"Pass these around, if you want," Curt said, and handed out his stack of Polaroids by twos and threes. Some had been taken during the flashes and showed almost nothing: a glimmer of grillwork, a piece of the Buick's roof. Others were much clearer. The best had that odd, flat, declamatory quality which is the sole property of Polaroid photographs. *I see a world where there's only cause and effect,* they seem to say. *A world where every object is an avatar and no gods move behind the scenes.*

"Like conventional film, or the badges workers in radiation-intensive environments have to wear," Tony said, "Polaroid stock fogs when it's exposed to strong gamma radiation. Some of these photos are over-exposed, but none of them are fogged. We're not hot, in other words."

Phil Candleton said, "No offense to you, Sarge, but I'm not crazy about trusting my 'nads to the Polaroid Corporation of America."

"I'll go up to The Burg tomorrow, first thing, and buy a Geiger counter," Curt said. He spoke calmly and reasonably, but they could still hear the pulse of excitement in his voice. Under the cool will-you-please-step-out-of-your-car-sir voice, Curt Wilcox was close to blowing his top. "They sell them at the Army Surplus store on Grand. I think they go for around three hundred bucks. I'll take the money out of the con-tingency fund, if no one objects."

No one did.

"In the meantime," Tony said, "it's more important than ever that we keep this quiet. I believe that, either by luck or providence, that thing has fallen into the hands of men who can actually do that. Will you?"

There were murmurs of agreement.

Dicky-Duck was sitting cross-legged on the floor, stroking Mister Dillon's head. D was asleep with his muzzle on his paws. For the bar-racks mascot, the excitement was definitely over. "I'm all right with that as long as the needle on the old Geiger doesn't move out of the green," Dicky-Duck said. "If it does, I vote we call the feds."

"Do you think they can take care of it any better than we can?" Curt asked hotly. "Jesus Christ, Dicky! The Feebs can't get out of their own way, and—"

"Unless you have plans to lead-line Shed B out of the contingency fund—" someone else began.

"That's a pretty stupid—" Curt began, and then Tony put a hand on his shoulder, stilling the kid before he could go any further and maybe hurt himself.

"If it's hot," Tony promised them, "we'll get rid of it. That's a promise."

Curt gave him a betrayed look. Tony stared back calmly. *We know it's not radioactive,* that gaze said, *the film proves it, so why do you want to start chasing your own tail?*

"I sort of think we ought to turn it over to the government anyway," Buck said. "They might be able to help us . . . you know . . . or find stuff out . . . defense stuff . . ." His voice getting smaller and smaller as he sensed the silent disapproval all around him. PSP officers worked with the federal government in one form or another every day—FBI, IRS, DEA, OSHA, and, most of all, the Interstate Commerce Commission. It didn't take many years on the job to learn most of those federal boys were *not* smarter than the average bear. Sandy's opinion was that when the feds did show the occasional flash of intelligence, it tended to be self-serving and sometimes downright malicious. Mostly they were slaves to the grind, worshippers at the altar of Routine Procedure. Before joining the PSP, Sandy had seen the same sort of dull go-through-the-proper-channels thinking in the Army. Also, he wasn't much older than Curtis himself, which made him young enough to hate the idea of giving the Roadmaster up. Better to hand it over to scientists in the private sector, though, if it came to that—perhaps even a bunch from the college advertised on the front of Curtis's lawn-mowing shirt.

But best of all, the Troop. The gray family.

Buck had petered out into silence. "Not a good idea, I guess," he said.

"Don't worry," someone said. "You *do* win the *Grolier Encyclopedia,* and our exciting home game."

Tony waited for a few chuckles to ripple across the room and die away before going on. "I want everyone who works out of this barracks to know what went on tonight, so they'll know what to expect if it happens again. Spread the word. Spread the code for the Buick, as well—D as in dog. Just D. Right? And I'll let you all know what happens next, starting with the Geiger counter. That test will be made before second shift tomorrow, I guarantee it. We're not going to tell our wives or sisters or brothers or best friends off the force what we have here, gentlemen, but we are going to keep each other *exquisitely* well-informed. That's my promise to you. We're going to do it the old-fashioned way, by verbal report. There has been no paperwork directly concerning the vehicle out there—if it *is* a vehicle—and that's how it's going to stay. All understood?"

There was another murmur of agreement.

"I won't tolerate a blabbermouth in Troop D, gentlemen; no gossip and no pillow-talk. Is *that* understood?"

It seemed it was.

"Look at this one," Phil said suddenly, holding up one of the Polaroids. "The trunk's open."

Curt nodded. "Closed again now, though. It opened during one of the flashes, and I think it closed during the next one."

Sandy thought of Ennis and had an image, very brief but very clear, of the Buick's trunk-lid opening and closing like a hungry mouth. See the living crocodile, take a good look, but for God's sake don't stick your fingers in there.

Curt went on, "I also believe the windshield wipers ran briefly, although my eyes were too dazzled by then for me to be sure, and none of the pictures show it."

"Why?" Phil asked. "Why would stuff like that happen?"

"Electrical surge," Sandy guessed. "The same thing that screwed up the radio in dispatch."

"Maybe the wipers, but the trunk of a car doesn't run on electricity. When you want to open the trunk, you just push the button and lift the lid."

Sandy had no answer for that.

"The temperature in the shed has gone down another couple of degrees," Curt said. "That'll bear watching."

The meeting ended, and Sandy went back out on patrol. Every now and then, when radioing back to Base, he'd ask Matt Babicki if D was 5-by. The response was always *Roger, D is 5-by-5.* In later years, it would become a standard call-and-response in the Short Hills area surrounding Statler, Pogus City, and Patchin. A few other barracks eventually picked it up, even a couple over the Ohio state line. They took it to mean *Is everything cool back home?* This amused the men working out of Troop D, because that was what *Is D still 5-by?* did mean.

By the next morning, everyone in Troop D was indeed in the picture, but it was business as usual. Curt and Tony went to Pittsburgh to get a Geiger counter. Sandy was off-shift but stopped by two or three times to check on the Buick just the same. It was quiet in there, the car simply sitting on the concrete and looking like an art exhibit, but the needle on the big red thermometer hung from the beam continued to ease down. That struck everyone as extremely eerie, silent confirmation that something was going on in there. Something beyond the ability of mere State Troopers to understand, let alone control.

No one actually went inside the shed until Curt and Tony got back in Curt's Bel Air—SC's orders. Huddie Royer was looking through the shed windows at the Buick when the two of them turned up. He strolled over as Curt opened the carton sitting on the hood of his car and took the Geiger counter out. "Where's your *Andromeda Strain* suits?" Huddie asked.

Curt looked at him, not smiling. "That's a riot," he said.

Curt and the Sergeant spent an hour in there, running the Geiger counter all over the Buick's hull, cruising the pickup over the engine, taking it into the cabin, checking the seats and dashboard and weird oversized wheel. Curt went underneath on a crawly gator, and the Sergeant checked the trunk, being especially careful about that; they propped the lid up with one of the rakes on the wall. The counter's needle hardly stirred during any of this. The only time the steady cluck-cluck-cluck coming from its little speaker intensified was when Tony held the pickup close to the radium dial of his wristwatch, wanting to make sure the gadget was working. It was, but the Roadmaster had nothing to tell it.

They broke only once, to go inside and get sweaters. It was a hot day outside, but in Shed B, the needle of the thermometer had settled just a hair below 48. Sandy didn't like it, and when the two of them came out, he suggested that they roll up the doors and let in some of the day's heat.

Mister Dillon was snoozing in the kitchenette, Sandy said; they could close him in there.

"No," Tony said, and Sandy could see that Curtis went along with that call.

"Why not?"

"I don't know. Just a feeling."

By three that afternoon, while Sandy was dutifully printing his name in the duty-book under **2ⁿᵈ Shift/3P-11P** and getting ready to head out on patrol, the temperature in Shed B had dropped to 47. That was forty degrees colder than the summer day on the other side of those thin wooden walls.

It must have been around six o'clock, while Sandy was parked around the side of Jimmy's Diner on the old Statler Pike, drinking coffee and watching for speeders, that the Roadmaster gave birth for the first time.

Arky Arkanian was the first person to see the thing that came out of the Buick, although he didn't know what he was seeing. Things were quiet at the Troop D barracks. Not serene, exactly, but quiet. This was due in large measure to Curt and Tony's report of zero radiation emanating from Shed B. Arky had come in from his trailer in Dreamland Park on top of the Bluffs, wanting his own little off-duty peek at the impounded car. He had it to himself; Shed B was for the time being entirely deserted. Forty yards away, the barracks was midshift quiet, which was about as quiet as it ever got. Matt Babicki had clocked out for the night and one of the younger cops was running dispatch. The Sarge had gone home at five o'clock. Curt, who had given his wife some cock-and-bull story about his call-out the night before, was presumably back in his flip-flop sandals and finishing his lawn like a good boy.

At five minutes past seven, the Troop D custodian (by then very pale, very thoughtful, and very scared) went past the kid in the dispatch cubby and into the kitchenette, to see who he could find. He wanted someone who wasn't a rookie, someone who knew the score. He found Huddie Royer, just putting the finishing touches on a big pot of Kraft Macaroni and Cheese.

Now: *Arky*

"Well?" the kid ask, and there was so much of his Daddy in him just then—the way he sat there on the bench, the way his eyes stared into yours, the way his eyebrows quirk, most of all the headlong impatience. That impatience was his Dad all over. *"Well?"*

"This isn't my part of the story," Sandy tell him. "I wasn't there. These other two were, though."

So then, sure, the kid switch over from Sandy to me and Huddie.

"You do it, Hud," I say. "You're used to makin reports."

"Shit on that," he tell me right back, "you were there first. You saw it first. You start."

"Aw—"

"Well, *one* of you start!" the boy tell us, and wham! He hit his forehead with the butt of his palm, right between the eyes. I had to laugh at that.

"Go on, Arky," the Sarge tell me.

"Ah, nuts," I say. "I ain't never told it, you know, like a story. Don't know how it'll come out."

"Give it your best shot," Sarge say, and so I do. It was pretty hard going at first—seemed I could feel the kid's eyes boring into me like nails and I kept thinking, *He ain't gonna believe this, who would?* But it got easier after a little bit. If you talk about something that happened long ago, you find it open up to you all over again. It open up like a flower. That can be a good thing or a bad thing, I guess. Sitting there that night, talking to Curtis Wilcox's boy, it felt like both.

Huddie join in after awhile and started to help. He remembered all sorts of things, even the part about how it was Joan Baez on the radio. "Redemption's in the details," old Sarge used to say (usually when someone left something out of a report that should have been in). And all through it the kid sittin there on the bench, looking at us, his eyes gettin bigger and bigger as the evening darkened and give up its smells like it does in the summer and the bats flew overhead and thunder rumbled all the way in the south. It made me sad to see how much he looked like his father. I don't know why.

He only broke in once. Turned to Sandy, wanting to know if we still had the—

"Yes," Sandy tell him right off. "Oh yes. We certainly do. Plus tons of pictures. Polaroids, mostly. If there's one thing cops know about, kiddo, it's preserving the chain of evidence. Now be quiet. You wanted to know; let the man tell you."

I know by that he mean me, so I started talkin again.

Then

Arky had an old Ford pickup in those days, a standard three-shifter (*But I got four if you count d'reverse,* he used to joke) with a squeaky clutch. He parked it where he would still be parking twenty-three years later, although by then he would have traded up to a Dodge Ram with the automatic transmission *and* the four-wheel drive.

In 1979 there was an ancient Statler County schoolbus at the far end of the parking lot, a rust-rotten yellow barge that had been there since the Korean War at least, sinking deeper and deeper into the weeds and the dirt with each passing year. Why no one ever took it away was just another of life's mysteries. Arky nestled his truck in beside it, then crossed to Shed B and looked through one of the windows in the roll-up door, cupping his hands to block the light of the sun, which was on the wester.

There was a light on overhead and the Buick sat beneath it, looking to Arky like a display model, the kind of unit that shows up so pretty under the lights that anyone in his right mind would want to sign on the line and drive that honey home. Everything looked 5-by except for the trunk-lid. It was up again.

I ought to report that to the duty officer, Arky thought. He wasn't a cop, just a custodian, but in his case, Trooper gray rubed off. He stepped back from the window, then happened to glance up at the thermometer Curt had mounted from one of the overhead beams. The temperature in the shed had gone up again, and by quite a lot. Sixty-one degrees in there. It occurred to Arky that the Buick was like some sort of weird refrigerator coil that had now turned itself off (or perhaps burnt itself out during the fireworks show).

The sudden rise in temperature was something else no one knew, and Arky was excited. He started to swing away from the door, meaning to hurry directly across to the barracks. That was when he saw the thing in the corner of the shed.

Nothing but an old bunch of rags, he thought, but something else suggested . . . well, something else. He went back to the glass, once more cupping his hands to the sides of his face. And no, by God, that thing in the corner was *not* just a bunch of rags.

Arky felt a flu-like weakness in the joints of his knees and the muscles of his thighs. The feeling spread upward into his stomach, dropping it, and then to his heart, speeding it up. There was an alarming moment when he was almost certain he was going to drop to the ground in a faint.

Hey, y'big dumb Swede—why don't you try breathing again? See if that helps any.

Arky took two big dry gasps of air, not caring much for the sound of them. His old man had sounded like that when he was having his heart attack, lying on the sofa and waiting for the ambulance to come.

He stepped away from the roll-up door, patting the center of his chest with the side of a closed fist. "Come on, honey. Take up d'slack, now."

The sun, going down in a cauldron of blood, glared in his eyes. His stomach had continued to drop, making him feel on the verge of vomiting. The barracks all at once looked two, maybe even three miles away. He set off in that direction, reminding himself to breathe and concentrating on taking big, even steps. Part of him wanted to break into a run, and part of him understood that if he tried doing that, he really *might* faint.

"Guys'd never let you hear the end of *dat,* and you know it."

But it wasn't really teasing he was concerned about. Mostly he didn't want to go in looking all wild-eyed and pushing the panic-button like any John Q in off the road with a tale to tell.

And by the time he got inside, Arky actually did feel a little better. Still scared, but no longer like he was going to puke or just go bolting away from Shed B any old whichway. By then he'd also had an idea which had eased his mind a bit. Maybe it was just a trick. A prank. Troopers were always pulling stuff on him, and hadn't he told Orville Garrett he might come back that evening for a little lookie-see at that old Buick? He had. And maybe Orv had decided to give him the business. Bunch of comedians he worked with, someone was *always* giving him the business.

The thought served to calm him, but in his heart of hearts, Arky didn't believe it. Orv Garrett was a practical joker, all right, liked to have his fun just like the next guy, but he wouldn't make that thing in the shed part of a gag. None of them would. Not with Sergeant Schoondist so hopped up about it.

Ah, but the Sarge wasn't there. His door was shut and the frosted glass panel was dark. The light was on in the kitchenette, though, and music was coming out through the door: Joan Baez, singing about the night they drove old Dixie down. Arky went in and there was Huddie Royer, just dropping a monster chunk of oleo into a pot of noodles. *Your heart ain't gonna thank you for* dat *shit,* Arky thought. Huddie's radio—a little one on a strap that he took everyplace—was sitting on the counter next to the toaster.

"Hey, Arky!" he said. "What're you doing here? As if I didn't know."

"Is Orv around?" Arky asked.

"Nope. He's got three days off, starting tomorrow. Lucky sucker went fishing. You want a bowl of this?" Huddie held the pot out, took a really good look at him, and realized he was looking at a man who was scared just about to death. "Arky? What the hell's wrong with you?"

Arky sat down heavily in one of the kitchen chairs, hands dangling between his thighs. He looked up at Huddie and opened his mouth, but at first nothing came out.

"What is it?" Huddie slung the pot of macaroni onto the counter without a second look. "The Buick?"

"Youda d-o tonight, Hud?"

"Yeah. Until eleven."

"Who else here?"

"Couple of guys upstairs. Maybe. If you're thinking about the brass, you can stop. I'm the closest you're going to get tonight. So spill it."

"You come out back," Arky told him. "Take a look for yourself. And bring some binoculars."

107

*　　　　*　　　　*

Huddie snagged a pair of binocs from the supply room, but they turned out to be no help. The thing in the corner of Shed B was actually too close—in the glasses it was just a blur. After two or three minutes of fiddling with the focus-knob, Huddie gave up. "I'm going in there."

Arky gripped his wrist. "Cheesus, no! Call the Sarge! Let him decide!"

Huddie, who could be stubborn, shook his head. "Sarge is sleeping. His wife called and said so. You know what it means when she does that—no one hadn't ought to wake him up unless it's World War III."

"What if dat t'ing in dere *is* World War III?"

"I'm not worried," Huddie said. Which was, judging from his face, the lie of the decade, if not the century. He looked in again, hands cupped to the sides of his face, the useless binoculars standing on the pavement beside his left foot. "It's dead."

"Maybe," Arky said. "And maybe it's just playin possum."

Huddie looked around at him. "You don't mean that." A pause. "Do you?"

"I dunno what I mean and what I don't mean. I dunno if dat t'ing's over for good or just restin up. Neither do you. What if it *wants* someone t'go in dere? You t'ought about dat? What if it's waitin for you?"

Huddie thought it over, then said: "I guess in that case, it'll get what it wants."

He stepped back from the door, looking every bit as scared as Arky had looked when he came into the kitchen, but also looking set. Meaning it. Just a stubborn old Dutchman.

"Arky, listen to me."

"Yeah."

"Carl Brundage is upstairs in the common room. Also Mark Rushing—I think, anyway. Don't bother Loving in dispatch, I don't trust him. Too wet behind the ears. But you go on and tell the other two what's up. And get that look off your face. This is probably nothing, but a little backup wouldn't hurt."

"Just in case it ain't nothin."

"Right."

"Cause it might be *sumpin*."

Huddie nodded.

"You sure?"

"Uh-huh."

"Okay."

Huddie walked along the front of the roll-up door, turned the corner, and stood in front of the smaller door on the side. He took a deep breath, held it in for a five-count, let it out. Then he unsnapped the strap over the butt of his pistol—a .357 Ruger, back in those days.

"Huddie?"

Huddie jumped. If his finger had been on the trigger instead of outside the guard, he might have blown off his own foot. He spun around and saw Arky standing there at the corner of the shed, his big dark eyes swimming in his pinched face.

"Lord Jesus Christ!" Huddie cried. "Why the fuck're you creeping after me?"

"I wasn't creepin, Troop—just walkin like normal."

"Go inside! Get Carl and Mark, like I told you."

Arky shook his head. Scared or not, he had decided he wanted to be a part of what was going down. Huddie supposed he could understand. Trooper gray did have a way of rubbing off.

"All right, ya dumb Swede. Let's go."

Huddie opened the door and stepped into the shed, which was still cooler than the outside . . . although just *how* cool it might have been was impossible for either man to tell, because they were both sweating like pigs. Huddie was holding his gun up beside his right cheekbone. Arky grabbed a rake from the pegs close by the door. It clanged against a shovel and both of them jumped. To Arky, the look of their shadows on the wall was even worse than the sound: they seemed to *leap* from place to place, like the shadows of nimble goblins.

"Huddie—" he began.

"Shhh!"

"If it's dead, why you go shhh?"

"Don't be a smartass!" Huddie whispered back.

He started across the cement floor toward the Buick. Arky followed with the rake-handle gripped tight in his sweaty hands, his heart pounding. His mouth tasted dry and somehow burnt. He had never been so scared in his life, and the fact that he didn't know exactly what he was scared *of* only made it worse.

Huddie got to the rear of the Buick and peeped into the open trunk. His back was so broad Arky couldn't see around it. "What's in there, Hud?"

"Nothing. It's clean."

Huddie reached for the trunk-lid, hesitated, then shrugged and slammed it down. They both jumped at the sound and looked at the thing in the corner. It didn't stir. Huddie started toward it, gun once more held up by the side of his head. The sound of his feet shuffling on the concrete was very loud.

The thing was indeed dead, the two men became more and more sure of it as they approached, but that didn't make things better, because neither of them had ever seen anything like it. Not in the woods of western Pennsylvania, not in a zoo, not in a wildlife magazine. It was just *different*. So goddam *different*. Huddie found himself thinking of horror movies he'd seen, but the thing huddled up in the angle where the shed walls met wasn't really like something from those, either.

Goddam different was what he kept coming back to. What they both kept coming back to. Everything about it screamed that it wasn't from here, *here* meaning not just the Short Hills but all of Planet Earth. Maybe the entire universe, at least as C-students in science such as themselves understood that concept. It was as if some warning circuit buried deep in their heads had suddenly awakened and begun to wail.

Arky was thinking of spiders. Not because the thing in the corner *looked* like a spider, but because . . . well . . . spiders were different. All those legs—and you had no idea what they might be thinking, or how they could even exist. This thing was like that, only worse. It made him sick just to look at it, to try to make sense of what his eyes said they were seeing. His skin had gone clammy, his heart was missing beats, and his guts seemed to have gained weight. He wanted to run. To just turn tail and stampede out of there.

"Christ," Huddie said in a little moan of a voice. "Ohhhh, *Christ*." It was as if he were pleading for it to go away. His gun sagged downward and outward until the barrel was pointed at the floor. It was only three pounds, but his arm could no longer support even that paltry weight. The muscles of his face also sagged, pulling his eyes wide and dropping his jaw down until his mouth opened. Arky never forgot the way Huddie's teeth gleamed in the shadows. At the same time he began to shiver all over, and Arky became aware he was shivering, too.

The thing in the corner was the size of a very large bat, like the ones that roosted in Miracle Caves over in Lassburg or the so-called Wonder Cavern (guided tours three dollars a head, special family rates available) in Pogus City. Its wings hid most of its body. They weren't folded but lay in messy overlapping crumples, as if it had *tried* to fold them—and failed—before it died. The wings were either black or a very dark mottled green. What they could see of the creature's back was a lighter green. The stomach area was a cheesy whitish shade, like the gut of a rotted stump or the throat of a decaying swamp-lily. The triangular head was cocked to one side. A bony thing that might have been a nose or a beak jutted from the eyeless face. Below it, the creature's mouth hung open. A yellowish rope of tissue dangled from it, as if the thing had been regurgitating its last meal as it died. Huddie took one look and knew he wouldn't be eating any more macaroni and cheese for awhile.

Beneath the corpse, spread around its hindquarters, was a thin puddle of congealing black goo. The idea that any such substance could serve as blood made Huddie feel like crying out. He thought: *I won't touch it. I'd kill my own mother before I'd touch that thing.*

He was still thinking that when a long wooden rod slid into his peripheral vision. He gave a little shriek and flinched back. "Arky, don't!" he yelled, but it was too late.

Later on, Arky was unable to say just why he had prodded the thing in the corner—it was simply some strong urge to which he had given in before he was completely aware of what he was doing.

When the end of the rake-handle touched the place where the wings were crumpled across each other, there was a sound like rustling paper and a bad smell, like old stewed cabbage. The two of them barely noticed. The top of the thing's face seemed to peel back, revealing a dead and glassy eye that looked as big as a factory ball bearing.

Arky backed away, dropping the rake with a clatter and putting both hands over his mouth. Above the spread fingers, his eyes had begun to ooze terrified tears. Huddie simply stood where he was, locked in place.

"It was an eyelid," he said in a low, hoarse voice. "Just an eyelid, that's all. You joggled it with the rake, you goddam fool. You joggled it and it rolled back."

"Christ, Huddie!"

"It's dead."

"Christ, Jesus God—"

"It's *dead,* okay?"

"Ho . . . Ho-kay," Arky said in that crazy Swedish accent of his. It was thicker than it had ever been. "Less get oudda here."

"You're pretty smart for a janitor."

The two of them headed back for the door—slowly, backing up, not wanting to lose sight of the thing. Also because both of them knew they would lose control and bolt if they actually *saw* the door. The safety of the door. The promise of a sane world beyond the door. Getting there seemed to take forever.

Arky backed out first and began taking huge gasps of the fresh evening air. Huddie came out behind him and slammed the door. Then for a moment the two of them just looked at each other. Arky had gone past white and directly to yellow. To Huddie he looked like a cheese sandwich without the bread.

"What-choo laughin about?" Arky asked him. "What's so funny?"

"Nothing," Huddie said. "I'm just trying not to be hysterical."

"You gonna call Sergeant Schoondist now?"

Huddie nodded. He kept thinking about how the whole top half of the thing's head had seemed to peel back when Arky prodded it. He had an idea he'd be revisiting that moment in his dreams later on, and that turned out to be absolutely correct.

"What about Curtis?"

Huddie thought about it and shook his head. Curt had a young wife. Young wives liked to have their husbands home, and when they didn't get what they wanted for at least a few nights in a row, they were apt to get hurt feelings and ask questions. It was natural. As it was natural for young husbands to sometimes answer their questions, even when they knew they weren't supposed to.

"Just the Sarge, then?"

"No," Huddie said. "Let's get Sandy Dearborn in on this, too. Sandy's got a good head."

Sandy was still in the parking lot at Jimmy's Diner with his radar gun in his lap when his radio spoke up. "Unit 14, Unit 14."

"14." As always, Sandy had glanced at his watch when he heard his unit number. It was twenty past seven.

"Ah, could you return to base, 14? We have a D-code, say again a D-code, copy?"

"3?" Sandy asked. In most American police forces, 3 means emergency.

"No, negative, but we sure could use some help."

"Roger."

He got back about ten minutes before the Sarge arrived in his personal, which happened to be an International Harvester pickup even older than Arky's Ford. By then the word had already started to spread and Sandy saw a regular Trooper convention in front of Shed B—lots of guys at the windows, all of them peering in. Brundage and Rushing, Cole and Devoe, Huddie Royer. Arky Arkanian was pacing around in little circles behind them with his hands stuffed forearm-deep in his pants pockets and lines climbing his forehead like the rungs of a ladder. He wasn't waiting for a window, though. Arky had seen all he wanted to, at least for one night.

Huddie filled Sandy in on what had happened and then Sandy had his own good long look at the thing in the corner. He also tried to guess what the Sergeant might want when he arrived, and put the items in a cardboard box near the side door.

Tony pulled in, parked askew behind the old schoolbus, and came jogging across to Shed B. He elbowed Carl Brundage unceremoniously away from the window that was closest to the dead creature and stared at it while Huddie made his report. When Huddie was done, Tony called Arky over and listened to Arky's version of the story.

Sandy thought that Tony's methods of handling the Roadmaster were put to the test that evening and proved sound. All through his debriefing of Huddie and Arky, Troop D personnel were showing up. Most of the men were off-duty. Those few in uniform had been close enough to come in for a look-see when they heard Huddie give the code for the Buick. Yet there was no loud cross-talk, no jostling for position, no men getting in the way of Tony's investigation or gumming things up with a lot of stupid questions. Above all, there were no flaring tempers and no panic. If reporters had been there and experienced the atavistic power of that thing—a thing which remained awful and somehow threatening even though it was obviously dead—Sandy dreaded to think about what the consequences might have been. When he mentioned that to Schoondist the next day, the Sarge had laughed. "The Cardiff Giant in hell," he said. "*That* would have been your consequence, Sandy."

Both of them, the Sarge who was and the Sarge who would be, knew what the press called such information-management, at least when the managers were cops: fascism. That was a little heavy, no doubt, but neither of them actually questioned the fact that all sorts of abuses lay a turn or two down that road. ("You want to see cops out of control, look at L.A.," Tony said once. "For every three good ones, you've got two Hitler Youth dingbats on motorcycles.") The business of the Buick was a bona fide Special Case, however. Neither of them questioned that, either.

Huddie wanted to know if he'd been right not to call Curtis. He was worried Curt would feel left out, passed over. If the Sarge wanted, Huddie said, he could go in the barracks that very second and make a telephone call. Happy to do it.

"Curtis is fine right where he is," Tony said, "and when it's explained to him why he wasn't called, he'll understand. As for the rest of you fellows . . ."

Tony stepped away from the roll-up door. His posture was easy and relaxed, but his face was very pale. The sight of that thing in the corner had affected him, too, even through a pane of glass. Sandy felt the same way himself. But he could also sense Sergeant Schoondist's excitement, the balls-to-the-wall curiosity he shared with Curt. The throbbing undertone that said *Holy shit, do you fuckin BELIEVE it!* Sandy heard it and recognized it for what it was, although he felt none of it himself, not a single iota. He didn't think any of the others did, either. Certainly Huddie's curiosity—and Arky's—had faded quickly enough. "Gone the way of the blue suede shoe," as Curtis might have said.

"You men on duty listen up to me, now," Tony said. He was wearing his slanted little grin, but to Sandy it looked a bit forced that night. "There's fires in Statler, floods in Leesburg, and a rash of Piggly Wiggly robberies down in Pogus County; we suspect the Amish."

There was some laughter at this.

"So what are you waiting for?"

There was a general exodus of Troopers on duty followed by the sound of Chevrolet V-8 engines starting up. The off-duty fellows hung around for awhile, but nobody had to tell them to move along, move along, come on, boys, show's over. Sandy asked the Sarge if he should also saddle up and ride.

"No, Trooper," he said. "You're with me." And he started briskly toward the walk-in door, pausing only long enough to examine the items Sandy had put into the carton: one of the evidence-documenting Polaroids, extra film, a yardstick, an evidence-collection kit. Sandy had also grabbed a couple of green plastic garbage bags from the kitchenette.

"Good job, Sandy."

"Thanks, sir."

"Ready to go in?"

"Yes, sir."

"Scared?"

"Yes, sir."

"Scared as me, or not quite that scared?"

"I don't know."

"Me, either. But I'm scared, all right. If I faint, you catch me."

"Just fall in my direction, sir."

He laughed. "Come on. Step into my parlor, said the spider to the fly."

*   *   *

Scared or not, the two of them made a pretty thorough investigation. They collaborated on a diagram of the shed's interior, and when Curt later complimented Sandy on it, Sandy nodded and agreed that it had been a good one. Good enough to take into court, actually. Still, a lot of the lines on it were wavery. Their hands began to shake almost from the moment they entered the shed, and didn't stop until they were back out again.

They opened the trunk because it had been open when Arky first looked in, and although it was as empty as ever, they took Polaroids of it. They likewise photo'd the thermometer (which by then had gotten all the way up to seventy degrees), mostly because Tony thought Curt would want them to. And they took pictures of the corpse in the corner, took them from every angle they could think of. Every Polaroid showed that unspeakable single eye. It was shiny, like fresh tar. Seeing himself reflected in it made Sandy Dearborn feel like screaming. And every two or three seconds, one of them would look back over his shoulder at the Buick Roadmaster.

When they were done with the photos, some of which they took with the yardstick lying beside the corpse, Tony shook out one of the garbage bags. "Get a shovel," he said.

"Don't you want to leave it where it is until Curt—"

"Probationary Trooper Wilcox can look at it down in the supply closet," Tony said. His voice was oddly tight—strangled, almost—and Sandy realized he was working very hard not to be sick. Sandy's own stomach took a queasy little lurch, perhaps in sympathy. "He can look at it there to his heart's content. For once we don't have to worry about breaking the chain of evidence, because no district attorney is ever going to be involved. Meantime, we're scooping this shit *up*." He wasn't shouting, but a raw little edge had come into his voice.

Sandy took a shovel from where it hung on the wall and slid the blade beneath the dead creature. The wings made a papery and somehow terrible crackling sound. Then one of them fell back, revealing a black and hairless side. For the second time since the two of them had stepped in, Sandy felt like screaming. He could not have told why, exactly, but there was something deep down in his head begging not to be shown any more.

And all the time they were smelling it. That sour, cabbagey reek.

Sandy observed sweat standing out all over Tony Schoondist's forehead in fine little dots. Some of these had broken and run down his cheeks, leaving tracks like tears.

"Go on," he said, holding the bag open. "Go on, now, Sandy. Drop it in there before I lose my groceries."

Sandy tilted it into the bag and felt a little bit better when the weight slid off the shovel. After Tony had gotten a sack of the liquid-absorbing red sawdust they kept for oil-spills and sprinkled it over the gooey stain in the corner, both of them felt better. Tony twirled the top of the garbage bag with the creature inside, then knotted it. Once that was done, the two of them started backing toward the door.

Tony stopped just before they reached it. "Photo that," he said, pointing to a place high on the roll-up door behind the Buick—the door through which Johnny Parker had towed the car in the first place. To Tony Schoondist and Sandy Dearborn, that already seemed like a long time ago. "And that, and there, and over there."

At first Sandy didn't see what the Sarge was pointing at. He looked away, blinked his eyes once or twice, then looked back. And there it was, three or four dark green smudges that made Sandy think of the dust that rubs off a moth's wings. As kids they had solemnly assured each other that mothdust was deadly poison, it would blind you if you got some on your fingers and then rubbed your eyes.

"You see what happened, don't you?" Tony asked as Sandy raised the Polaroid and sighted in on the first mark. The camera seemed very heavy and his hands were still shivering, but he got it done.

"No, Sarge, I, ah . . . don't guess I do."

"Whatever that thing is—bird, bat, some kind of robot drone—it flew out of the trunk when the lid came open. It hit the back door, that's the first smudge, and then it started bouncing off the walls. Ever seen a bird that gets caught in a shed or a barn?"

Sandy nodded.

"Like that." Tony wiped sweat off his forehead and looked at Sandy. It was a look the younger man never forgot. He had never seen the Sarge's eyes so naked. It was, he thought, the look you sometimes saw on the

faces of small children when you came to break up a domestic disturbance.

"Man," Tony said heavily. *"Fuck."*

Sandy nodded.

Tony looked down at the bag. "You think it looks like a bat?"

"Yeah," Sandy said, then "No." After another pause he added, "Bullshit."

Tony barked a laugh that sounded somehow haggard. "That's very
definitive. If you were on the witness stand, no defense attorney could
peel *that* back."

"I don't know, Tony." What Sandy did know was that he wanted to
stop shooting the shit and get back out into the open air. "What do you
think?"

"Well, if I drew it, it'd look like a bat," Tony said. "The Polaroids we
took also make it look like a bat. But . . . I don't know exactly how to
say it, but . . ."

"It doesn't *feel* like a bat," Sandy said.

Tony smiled bleakly and pointed a finger at Sandy like a gun. "Very
Zen, Grasshoppah. But those marks on the wall suggest it at least *acted*
like a bat, or a trapped bird. Flew around in here until it dropped dead
in the corner. Shit, for all we know, it died of fright."

Sandy recalled the glaring dead eye, a thing almost too alien to look
at, and thought that for the first time in his life, he could really understand the concept Sergeant Schoondist had articulated. Die of fright? Yes,
it could be done. It really could. Then, because the Sarge seemed to be
waiting for something, he said: "Or maybe it hit the wall so hard it broke
its neck." Another idea came to him. "Or—listen, Tony—maybe the *air*
killed it."

"Say what?"

"Maybe—"

But Tony's eyes had lit up and he was nodding. "Sure," he said.
"Maybe the air on the other side of the Buick's trunk is different air.
Maybe it'd taste like poison gas to us . . . rupture our lungs . . ."

For Sandy, that was enough. "I have to get out of here, Tony, or *I'm*
gonna be the one who throws up." But what he really felt in danger of

was choking, not vomiting. All at once the normally broad avenue of his windpipe was down to a pinhole.

Once they were back outside (it was nearly dark by then and an incredibly sweet summer breeze had sprung up), Sandy felt better. He had an idea Tony did, too; certainly some of the color had come back into the Sarge's cheeks. Huddie and a few other Troopers came over to the two of them as Tony shut the walk-in side door, but nobody said anything. An outsider with no context upon which to draw might have looked at those faces and thought that the President had died or war had been declared.

"Sandy?" Tony asked. "Any better now?"

"Yeah." He nodded at the garbage bag, hanging like a dead pendulum with its strange weight at the bottom. "You really think it might have been our air that killed it?"

"It's possible. Or maybe just the shock of finding itself in our world. I don't think I could live for long in the world this thing came from, tell you that much. Even if I *could* breathe the—" Tony stopped, because all at once Sandy looked bad again. Terrible, in fact. "Sandy, what is it? What's wrong?"

Sandy wasn't sure he wanted to tell his SC what was wrong, wasn't even sure he could. What he'd thought of was Ennis Rafferty. The idea of the missing Trooper added to what they had just discovered in Shed B suggested a conclusion that Sandy didn't want to consider. Once it had come into his mind, though, it was hard to get it back out. If the Buick was a conduit to some other world and the bat-thing had gone through it in one direction, then Ennis Rafferty had almost certainly gone through in the other.

"Sandy, talk to me."

"Nothing wrong, boss," Sandy replied, then had to bend over and grip his shins in both hands. It was a good way to stop yourself from fainting, always assuming you had enough time to use it. The others stood around watching him, still saying nothing, still wearing those long faces that said the King is dead, long live the King.

At last the world steadied again, and Sandy straightened up. "I'm okay," he said. "Really."

Tony considered his face, then nodded. He lifted the green bag slightly. "This is going into the storage closet off the supply room, the little one where Andy Colucci keeps his stroke-books."

A few nervous titters greeted this.

"That room is going to be off-limits except for myself, Curtis Wilcox, and Sandy Dearborn. BPO, people, got it?"

They nodded. By permission only.

"Sandy, Curtis, and me—this is now our investigation, so designated." He stood straight in the gathering gloom, almost at attention, holding the garbage bag in one hand and the Polaroids in the other. "This stuff is evidence. Of what I have no current idea. If any of *you* come up with any ideas, bring them to me. If they seem like crazy ideas to you, bring them to me even quicker. It's a crazy situation. But, crazy or not, we *will* roll this case. Roll it as we would any other. Questions?"

There were no questions. Or, if you wanted to look at it the other way, Sandy reflected, there was nothing *but* questions.

"We ought to have a man on that shed as much as we can," Tony said.

"Guard duty, Sarge?" Steve Devoe asked.

"Let's call it surveillance," Tony said. "Come on, Sandy, stick with me until I get this thing stowed. I don't want to take it downstairs by myself, and that's the God's truth."

As they started across the parking lot, Sandy heard Arky Arkanian saying that Curt was gonna get mad he dint get called, wait and see, dat boy was gonna be madder'n a wet hen.

But Curtis was too excited to be mad, too busy trying to prioritize the things he wanted to do, too full of questions. He asked only one of those before pelting down to look at the corpse of the creature they'd found in Shed B: where had Mister Dillon been last evening? With Orville, he was told. Orville Garrett often took Mister D when he had a few days off.

Sandy Dearborn was the one who brought Curtis up to speed (with occasional help from Arky). Curt listened silently, brows lifting when Arky described how the whole top of the thing's head had appeared to roll back, disclosing the eye. They lifted again when Sandy told him about the smudges on the door and the walls, and how they had reminded him of mothdust. He asked his question about Mister D, got his answer, then grabbed a pair of surgical gloves out of an evidence kit and headed downstairs at what was nearly a run. Sandy went with him. That much seemed to be his duty, somehow, since Tony had appointed him a co-investigator, but he stayed in the supply room while Curt went into the closet where Tony had left the garbage bag. Sandy heard it rustling as Curt undid the knot in the top; his skin prickled and went cold at the sound.

Rustle, rustle, rustle. Pause. Another rustle. Then, very low: "Christ almighty."

A moment later Curt came running out with his hand over his mouth. There was a toilet halfway down the hall leading to the stairs. Trooper Wilcox made it just in time.

Sandy Dearborn sat at the cluttered worktable in the supply room, listening to him vomit and knowing that the vomiting probably meant nothing in the larger scheme of things. Curtis wasn't going to back off. The corpse of the bat-thing had revolted him as much as it had Arky or Huddie or any of them, but he'd come back to examine it more fully, revulsion or no revulsion. The Buick—and the things *of* the Buick—had become his passion. Even coming out of the storage closet with his throat working and his cheeks pale and his hand pressed to his mouth, Sandy had seen the helpless excitement in his eyes, dimmed only a little by his physical distress. Passion is the hardest taskmaster.

From down the hall came the sound of running water. It stopped, and then Curt came back into the supply room, blotting his mouth with a paper towel.

"Pretty awful, isn't it?" Sandy asked. "Even dead."

"Pretty awful," he agreed, but he was heading back in there even as he spoke. "I thought I understood, but it caught me by surprise."

Sandy got up and went to the doorway. Curt was looking into the bag again but not *reaching* in. Not yet, at least. That was a relief. Sandy didn't want to be around when the kid touched it, even wearing gloves. Didn't even want to *think* about him touching it.

"Was it a trade, do you think?" Curt asked.

"Huh?"

"A trade. Ennis for this thing."

For a moment Sandy didn't reply. *Couldn't* reply. Not because the idea was horrible (although it was), but because the kid had gotten to it so fast.

"I don't know."

Curt was rocking back and forth on the heels of his shoes and frowning down at the plastic garbage bag. "I don't think so," he said after awhile. "When you make a swap, you usually do the whole deal at the same time. Right?"

"Usually, yeah."

He closed the bag and (with obvious reluctance) reknotted the top. "I'm going to dissect it," he said.

"Curtis, no! *Christ!*"

"Yes." He turned to Sandy, his face drawn and white, his eyes brilliant. "*Someone* has to, and I can't very well take it up to the Biology Department at Horlicks. Sarge says we keep this strictly in-house, and that's the right call, but who does that leave to do this? Just me. Unless I'm missing something."

Sandy thought, *You wouldn't take it up to Horlicks even if Tony hadn't said a goddam word about keeping it in-house. You can bear to have us in on it, probably because nobody but Tony really wants anything to do with it, but share it with someone else? Someone who doesn't wear Pennsylvania gray and know when to shift the hat-strap from the back of the head to under the chin? Someone who might first get ahead of you and then take it away from you? I don't think so.*

Curt stripped off the gloves. "The problem is that I haven't cut anything up since Chauncey, my fetal pig in high school biology. That was nine years ago and I got a C in the course. I don't want to fuck this up, Sandy."

Then don't touch it in the first place.

Sandy thought it but didn't say it. There would have been no point in saying it.

"Oh well." The kid talking to himself now. Nobody but himself. "I'll bone up. Get ready. I've got time. No sense being impatient. Curiosity killed the cat, but satisfaction—"

"What if that's a lie?" Sandy asked. He was surprised at how tired of that little jingle-jangle he had grown. "What if there's no satisfaction? What if you're never able to solve for x?"

Curt looked up at him, almost shocked. Then he grinned. "What do you think Ennis would say? If we could ask him, that is?"

Sandy found the question both patronizing and insensitive. He opened his mouth to say so—to say *something,* anyway—and then didn't. Curtis Wilcox didn't mean any harm; he was just flying high on adrenaline and possibility, as hyped as any junkie. And he really *was* a kid. Even Sandy recognized that, although they were much of an age.

"Ennis would tell you to be careful," Sandy said. "I'm sure of that much."

"I will," Curt agreed, starting up the stairs. "Oh yeah, of course I will." But those were just words, like the doxology you rush through in order to get free of church on Sunday morning. Sandy knew it even if Probationary Trooper Wilcox did not.

In the weeks that followed, it became obvious to Tony Schoondist (not to mention the rest of the Troop D personnel) that there wasn't enough manpower to institute twenty-four-hour surveillance of the Buick in the shed out back. Nor did the weather cooperate; the second half of that August was rainy and unseasonably cold.

Visitors added another headache. Troop D didn't live in a vacuum on top of its hill, after all; the Motor Pool was next door, the County Attorney (plus his staff) was just down the road, there were lawyers, there were perps cooling their heels in the Bad Boy Corner, the occasional Boy Scout tour, the steady trickle of folks who wanted to lodge complaints (against their neighbors, against their spouses, against Amish buggy-drivers taking too much of the road, against the State Troopers themselves), wives bringing forgotten lunches or sometimes boxes of fudge, and sometimes just interested John Q's who wanted a look at what their tax dollars were buying. These latter were usually surprised and disappointed by the calmness of the barracks, the ho-hum sense of bureaucracy at work. It didn't feel like their favorite TV shows.

One day toward the end of that month, Statler's member of the

United States House of Representatives dropped by, along with ten or twelve of his closest media friends, to do a meet-and-greet and to make a statement about the Police Aid, Science, and Infrastructure bill then pending before the House, a bill this fellow just happened to be co-sponsoring. Like many U.S. Representatives from rural districts, this fellow looked like a small-town barber who had a lucky day at the dog-track and hoped for a blowjob before bedtime. Standing beside one of the cruisers (Sandy thought it was the one with the busted headrest), he told his media friends how important the police were, especially the fine men and women of the Pennsylvania State Police, most especially the fine men and women of Troop D (that was a bit of information shortfall, there being no female Troopers or PCOs in D at that time, but none of the Troopers offered a correction, at least not while the cameras were rolling). They were, the Representative said, a thin gray line dividing Mr. and Mrs. John Q. Taxpayer from the evil of the Chaos Gang, and so on and so on, God bless America, may all your children grow up to play the violin. Captain Diment came down from Butler, presumably because someone felt his stripes would lend a little extra tone to the event, and he later told Tony Schoondist in a low growl: "That toupee-wearing touchhole asked me to fix his wife's speeding ticket."

And all the time the Representative was blathering and the entourage was touring and the reporters were reporting and the cameras were rolling, the Buick Roadmaster was sitting just fifty yards away, blue as deep dusk on its fat and luxy whitewalls. It sat under the big round thermometer Curt had mounted on one of the beams. It sat there with its zeroed odometer and dirt wouldn't stick to it. To the Troopers who knew about it, the damned thing felt like an itch between the shoulderblades, the one place you can't . . . quite . . . reach.

There was bad weather to contend with, there were all kinds of John Q's to contend with—many who came to praise the family but who weren't *of* the family—and there were also visiting police officers and Troopers from other barracks. These last were in some ways the most dangerous, because cops had sharp eyes and nosy minds. What might they have thought if they'd seen a Trooper in a rain-slicker (or a certain janitor with a Swedish accent) standing out there by Shed B like one of those tall-hat soldiers guarding the gate at Buckingham Palace? Occasionally walking over to the roll-up door and peering inside? Might a visiting policeman seeing this have been curious about what was in there? Does a bear shit in the woods?

Curt solved this as well as it could be solved. He sent Tony a memo that said it was a shame the way the raccoons kept getting into our garbage and scattering it around, and that Phil Candleton and Brian Cole had agreed to build a little hutch to store the garbage cans in. Curt thought that out behind Shed B would be a good place for it, if the SC agreed. SC Schoondist wrote OK across the top of the memo, and that one did get filed. What the memo neglected to mention was that the Troop hadn't had any real problems with coons since Arky bought a couple of plastic garbage cans from Sears, the kind with the snap-down tops.

The hutch was built, painted (PSP gray, of course), and ready for action three days after the memo landed in Tony's in-basket. Prefab and purely functional, it was just big enough for two garbage cans, three shelves, and one State Trooper sitting on a kitchen chair. It served the dual purpose of keeping the Trooper on watch (a) out of the weather and (b) out of sight. Every ten or fifteen minutes the man on duty would get up, leave the hutch, and look through one of the windows in Shed B's rear roll-up door. The hutch was stocked with soda, munchies, magazines, and a galvanized pail. The pail had a paper strip reading I COULD NOT HOLD IT ANY LONGER taped to the side. That was Jackie O'Hara's touch. The others called him The Irish Wonder Boy, and he never failed to make them laugh. He was making them laugh even three years later as he lay in his bedroom, dying of esophogeal cancer, eyes glassy with morphine, telling stories about Padeen the bogtrotter in a hoarse whisper while his old mates visited and sometimes held his hand when the pain was especially bad.

Later on, there would be plenty of video cameras at Troop D—at all the PSP barracks—because by the nineties, all the cruisers were equipped with dashboard-mounted Panasonic Eyewitness models. These were made specially for law enforcement organizations, and came without mikes. Video of road-stops was legal; because of existing wiretap laws, audio was not. But all of that was later. In the late summer of 1979, they had to make do with a videocam Huddie Royer had gotten for his birthday. They kept it on one of the shelves out in the hutch, stored in its box and wrapped in plastic to make sure it stayed dry. Another box contained extra batteries and a dozen blank tapes with the cellophane stripped off so they'd be ready to go. There was also a slate with a number chalked on it: the current temperature inside the shed. If the person on duty noticed a change, he erased the last observation, wrote in the current one, and added a chalk arrow pointing either up or down. It was the closest thing to a written record Sergeant Schoondist would allow.

Tony seemed delighted with this jury-rig. Curt tried to emulate him, but sometimes his worry and frustration broke through. "There won't be anyone on watch the next time something happens," he said. "You wait and see if I'm not right—it's always the way. Nobody'll volunteer for midnight to four some night, and whoever comes on next will look in and see the trunk-lid up and another dead bat on the floor. You wait and see."

Curt tried persuading Tony to at least keep a surveillance sign-up sheet. There was no shortage of volunteers, he argued; what they were short on was organization and scheduling, things that would be easy to change. Tony remained adamant: no paper trail. When Curt volunteered to take over more of the sentry duty himself (many of the Troopers took to calling it Hutch Patrol), Tony refused and told him to ease off. "You've got other responsibilities," he said. "Not the least of them is your wife."

Curt had the good sense to keep quiet while in the SC's office. Later, however, he unburdened himself to Sandy, speaking with surprising bitterness as the two of them stood outside at the far corner of the barracks. "If I'd wanted a marriage counselor, I would have consulted the goddam Yellow Pages," he said.

Sandy offered him a smile, one without much humor in it. "I think you better start listening for the pop," he said.

"What are you talking about?"

"The pop. Very distinctive sound. You hear it when your head finally comes out of your ass."

Curtis stared at him, hard little roses of color burning high up on his cheekbones. "Am I missing something here, Sandy?"

"Yes."

"What? For God's sake, *what?*"

"Your job and your life," Sandy said. "Not necessarily in that order. You are experiencing a problem of perspective. That Buick is starting to look too big to you."

"Too . . . !" Curt hit his forehead with the palm of his hand in that way he had. Then he turned and looked out at the Short Hills. At last he swung back to Sandy. "It's something from another world, Sandy—*from another world.* How *can* a thing like that look too big?"

"That's exactly your problem," Sandy replied. "Your problem of perspective."

He had an idea that the next thing Curtis said would be the beginning of an argument, possibly a bitter one. So before Curt could say anything, Sandy went inside. And perhaps that talk did some good, because as August gave way to September, Curt's all but constant requests for more surveillance time stopped. Sandy Dearborn never tried to tell himself that the kid had seen the light, but he did seem to understand that he'd gone as far as he could, at least for the time being. Which was good, but maybe not quite good enough. Sandy thought that the Buick was always going to look too big to Curtis. But then, there have always been two sorts of people in the world. Curt was of the sort who believed satisfaction actually did bring felines back from the other side of the great divide.

He began to show up at the barracks with biology books instead of *Field and Stream.* The one most commonly observed under his arm or lying on the toilet tank in the crapper was Dr. John H. Maturin's *Twenty Elementary Dissections,* Harvard University Press, 1968. When Buck Flanders and his wife went over to Curt's for dinner one evening, Michelle Wilcox complained about her husband's "gross new hobby." He had started getting specimens from a medical supply house, she said, and the area of the basement which he had designated as his darkroom-to-be only the year before now smelled of mortuary chemicals.

Curt started with mice and a guinea pig, then moved on to birds, eventually working his way up to a horned owl. Sometimes he brought specimens to work. "You haven't really lived," Matt Babicki told Orville Garrett and Steve Devoe one day, "until you go downstairs for a fresh box of ballpoint pens and find a jar of formaldehyde with an owl-eye in it sitting on top of the Xerox machine. Man, that wakes you up."

Once the owl had been conquered, Curtis moved on to bats. He did eight or nine of those, each specimen from a different species. A couple he caught himself in his back yard; the rest he ordered from a biological supply house in The Burg. Sandy never forgot the day Curtis showed him a South American vampire bat pinned to a board. The thing was furry, brownish on the belly, and velvet-black on the membranous wings. Its tiny pointed teeth were bared in a psychotic smile. Its guts were laid open in a teardrop shape by Curt's increasingly skilled technique. Sandy believed Curt's high school biology teacher—the one who had given him the C—would have been surprised at how fast his old student was learning.

Of course when desire drives, any fool can be a professor.

It was while Curt Wilcox was learning the fine art of dissection from Dr. Maturin that Jimmy and Rosalynn took up residence in the Buick 8. They were Tony's brainstorm. He had it one day at the Tri-Town Mall, while his wife tried on clothes in Country Casuals. An improbable sign in the window of My Pet caught his eye: **COME ON IN AND JOIN OUR GERBIL RIOT!**

Tony didn't join the gerbil riot just then—his wife would have had a thousand questions—but he sent big George Stankowski back the very next day with more cash from the contingency fund and orders to buy a pair of gerbils. Also a plastic habitat for them to live in.

"Should I get them some food, too?" George asked.

"No," Tony answered. "Absolutely not. We're going to buy a couple of gerbils and then let them starve to death out in the shed."

"Really? That seems sort of mean to—"

Tony sighed. "Get them food, George, yes. By all means get them food."

The only specification Tony made concerning the habitat was that it fit comfortably on the Buick's front seat. George got a nice one, not top-of-the-line but almost. It was made of a yellow see-through plastic and consisted of a long corridor with a boxy room at either end. One was the gerbil dining room and the other was the gerbil version of Gold's Gym. The dining room had a food-trough and a water-bottle clipped to the side; the gym had an exercise wheel.

"They live better than some people," Orvie Garrett said.

Phil, who was watching Rosalynn take a shit in the food-trough, said: "Speak for yourself."

Dicky-Duck Eliot, perhaps not the swiftest horse ever to canter around life's great racetrack, wanted to know why we were keeping gerbils in the Buick. Wasn't that sort of dangerous?

"Well, we'll see about that, won't we?" Tony asked in an oddly gentle voice. "We'll just see if it is or not."

On a day not long after Troop D acquired Jimmy and Rosalynn, Tony Schoondist crossed his own personal Rubicon and lied to the press.

Not that the representative of the Fourth Estate in this case was very impressive, just a weedy redheaded boy of twenty or so, a summer intern at the County *American* who would be going back to Ohio State in another week or so. He had a way of listening to you with his mouth hung partway open that made him look, in Arky's words, like a stark raving natural-born fool. But he *wasn't* a fool, and he'd spent most of one golden September afternoon listening to Mr. Bradley Roach. Brad gave the young reporter quite an earful about the man with the Russian accent (by this time Brad was positive the guy had been Russian) and the car the man had left behind. The weedy redhead, Homer Oosler by name, wanted to do a feature story on all of this and go back to college with a bang. Sandy thought the young man could imagine a front-page headline with the words **MYSTERY CAR** in it. Perhaps even **RUSSIAN SPY'S MYSTERY CAR**.

Tony never hesitated, just went ahead and lied. He undoubtedly would have done the same thing even if the reporter presenting himself that day had been case-hardened old Trevor Ronnick, who owned the County *American* and had forgotten more stories than the redhead would ever write.

"Car's gone," Tony said, and there it was: lie told, Rubicon crossed.

"Gone?" Homer Oosler asked, clearly disappointed. He had a big old Minolta camera on his lap. PROPERTY OF COUNTY AMERICAN was Dymo-taped across the back of the case. "Gone where?"

"State Impound Bureau," Tony said, creating this impressive-sounding organization on the spot. "In Philly."

"Why?"

"They auction unclaimed rolling iron. After they search em for drugs, of course."

"Course. Do you have any paperwork on it?"

"Must have," Tony said. "Got it on everything else. I'll look for it, give you a ring."

"How long do you think that'll take, Sergeant Schoondist?"

"Awhile, son." Tony waved his hand at his in/out basket, which was stacked high with papers. Oosler didn't need to know that most of them were the week's junkalogue from Scranton—everything from updates on retirement benefits to the schedule for autumn softball—and would be in the wastebasket before the Sarge went home. That weary wave of the hand suggested that there were similar piles of paper everywhere. "Hard keeping up with all this stuff, you know. They say things'll change when we start getting computerized, but that won't be this year."

"I go back to school next week."

Tony leaned forward in his chair and looked at Oosler keenly. "And I hope you work hard," he said. "It's a tough world out there, son, but if you work hard you can make it."

A couple of days after Homer Oosler's visit, the Buick fired up another of its lightstorms. This time it happened on a day that was filled with bright sun, but it was still pretty spectacular. And all Curtis's worries about missing the next manifestation proved groundless.

The shed's temperature made it clear the Buick was building up to something again, dropping from the mid-seventies to the upper fifties over a course of five days. Everyone became anxious to take a turn out in the hutch; everyone wanted to be the one on duty when it happened, whatever "it" turned out to be this time.

Brian Cole won the lottery, but all the Troopers at the barracks shared the experience at least to some extent. Brian went into Shed B at around two P.M. to check on Jimmy and Rosalynn. They were fine as paint, Rosalynn in the habitat's dining room and Jimmy busting heavies on the exercise wheel in the gym. But as Brian leaned farther into the Buick to check the water reservoir, he heard a humming noise. It was deep and steady, the kind of sound that vibrates your eyes in their sockets and rattles your fillings. Below it (or entwined with it) was something a lot more disturbing, a kind of scaly, wordless whispering. A purple glow, very dim, was spreading slowly across the dashboard and the steering wheel.

Mindful of Ennis Rafferty, gone no forwarding for well over a month by then, Trooper Cole vacated the Buick's vicinity in a hurry. He proceeded without panic, however, taking the video camera from the hutch, screwing it onto its tripod, loading in a fresh tape, checking the time-code (it was correct) and the battery level (all the way in the green). He turned on the overheads before going back out, then placed the tripod in front of one of the windows, hit the RECORD button, and double-checked to make sure the Buick was centered in the viewfinder. It was. He started toward the barracks, then snapped his fingers and went back to the hutch. There was a little bag filled with camera accessories in there. One of them was a brightness filter. Brian attached this to the video camera's lens without bothering to hit the PAUSE button (for one moment the big dark shapes of his hands blot out the image of the Buick, and when they leave the frame again the Buick reappears as if in a deep twilight). If there had been anyone there watching him go about his business—one of those visiting John Q's curious about how his tax dollars were spent, perhaps—he never would have guessed how fast Trooper Cole's heart was beating. He was afraid as well as excited, but he did okay. When it comes to dealing with the unknown, there's a great deal to be said for a good shot of police training. All in all, he forgot only one thing.

He poked his head into Tony's office at about seven minutes past two and said, "Sarge, I'm pretty sure something's happening with the Buick."

Tony looked up from his yellow legal pad, where he was scribbling the first draft of a speech he was supposed to give at a law enforcement symposium that fall, and said: "What's that in your hand, Bri?"

Brian looked down and saw he was holding the gerbils' water reservoir. "Ah, what the hell," he said. "They may not need it anymore, anyway."

By twenty after two, Troopers in the barracks could hear the humming clearly. Not that there were many in there; most were lined up at the windows in Shed B's two roll-up doors, hip to hip and shoulder to shoulder. Tony saw this, debated whether or not to order them away, and finally decided to let them stay where they were. With one exception.

"Arky."

"Yessir, Sarge?"

"I want you to go on out front and mow the lawn."

"I just mow it on Monday!"

"I know. Seemed like you spent the last hour doing the part under my office window. I want you to do it again just the same. With this in your back pocket." He handed Arky a walkie-talkie. "And if anyone comes calling who shouldn't see ten Pennsylvania State Troopers lined up in front of that shed like there was a big-money cockfight going on inside, shoot me the word. Got it?"

"Yeah, you betcha."

"Good. Matt! Matt Babicki, front and center!"

Matt rushed up, puffing and red-faced with excitement. Tony asked him where Curt was. Matt said he was on patrol.

"Tell him to return to base, code D and ride quiet, got that?"

"Code D and ride quiet, roger."

To ride quiet is to travel *sans* flashers and siren. Curt presumably obeyed this injunction, but he was still back at the barracks by quarter to three. No one dared ask him how far he'd come in half an hour. However many miles it might have been, he arrived alive and before the silent fireworks started up again. The first thing he did was to remove the videocam from the tripod. Until the fireworks were over, the visual record would be Curtis Wilcox's baby.

The tape (one of many squirreled away in the storage closet) preserves what there was to see and hear. The Buick's hum is very audible, sounding like a loose wire in a stereo speaker, and it gets appreciably louder as

132

time passes. Curt got footage of the big thermometer with its red needle standing at just a hair past 54. There's Curt's voice, asking permission to go in and check on Jimmy and Rosalynn, and Sergeant Schoondist's voice coming back with "Permission denied" almost at once, brisk and sure, brooking no argument.

At 3:08:41P, according to the time-code on the bottom of the screen, a blush like a violet sunrise begins to rise on the Buick's windshield. At first a viewer might pass this phenomenon off as a technical glitch or an optical illusion or perhaps some sort of reflection.

Andy Colucci: "What's that?"

Unknown speaker: "A power surge or a—"

Curtis Wilcox: "Those of you with goggles better put them on. Those of you without them, this is risky, I'd back the hell off. We have—"

Jackie O'Hara (probably): "Who took—"

Phil Candleton (probably): "My *God!*"

Huddie Royer: "I don't think we should—"

Sergeant Commanding Schoondist, sounding as calm as an Audubon guide on a nature hike: "Get those goggles down, fellas, I would. Chop-chop."

At 3:09:24, that violet light took an auroral leap in all the Buick's windows, turning them into brilliant purple mirrors. If one slows the tape down and then advances it frame by frame, one can see actual reflections appearing in the formerly clear window-glass: the tools hung on their pegs, the orange plow-blade stored against one wall, the men outside, peering in. Most are wearing goggles and look like aliens in a cheap science fiction movie. One can isolate Curt because of the video camera blocking the left side of his face. The hum gets louder and louder. Then, about five seconds before the Buick starts shooting off those flashes, the sound stops. A viewer of this tape can hear an excited babble of voices, none identifiable, all seeming to ask questions.

Then the image disappears for the first time. The Buick and the shed are both gone, lost in the white.

"Jesus Christ, did you guys see that?" Huddie Royer screams.

There are cries of *Get back, Holy fuck,* and everyone's favorite in times of trouble, *Oh shit*. Someone says *Don't look at it* and someone else says *It's pissing lightning* in that weirdly matter-of-fact tone one can sometimes hear on cockpit flight recorders, a pilot who's talking without realizing it, who only knows that he's down to the last ten or twelve seconds of his life.

Then the Buick returns from the land of overexposure, looking first like a meaningless clot, then taking back its actual form. Three seconds later it flashes out again. The glare shoots thick rays from every window and then whites out the image once more. During this one Curt says *We need a better filter* and Tony replies *Maybe next time*.

The phenomenon continues for the next forty-six minutes, every bit of it captured on tape. At first the Buick whites out and disappears with every flash. Then, as the phenomenon starts to weaken, the viewer can see a vague car-shape sunk deep in soundless lightbursts that are more purple than white. Sometimes the image joggles and there's a fast, blurry pan of human faces as Curtis hurries to a different observation point, hoping for a revelation (or perhaps just a better view).

At 3:28:17, one can observe a jagged line of fire burst up from (or maybe it's through) the Buick's closed trunk. It shoots all the way to the ceiling, where it seems to splash outward like water from a fountain.

Unidentified voice: "Holy shit, high voltage, high voltage!"

Tony: "The hell it is." Then, presumably to Curt: "Keep taping."

Curt: "Oh yeah. You better believe it."

There are several more of the lightning bolts, some shooting out of the Buick's windows, some rising from the roof or the trunk. One leaps out from beneath the car and fires itself directly at the rear roll-up door. There are surprised yells as the men back away from that one, but the camera stays steady. Curt was basically too excited to be afraid.

At 3:55:03 there's a final weak blip—it comes from the back seat, behind the driver's position—and then there's no more. You can hear Tony Schoondist say, "Why don't you save the battery, Curt? The show seems to be over." At that point the tape goes momentarily black.

When the picture resumes at 4:08:16, Curt is onscreen. There's something yellow wrapped around his midsection. He waves jauntily and says, "I'll be right back."

Tony Schoondist—he's the one running the camera at that point—replies, "You better be." And he doesn't sound jaunty in the least.

Curt wanted to go in and check on the gerbils—to see how they were, assuming they were still there at all. Tony refused permission adamantly and at once. No one was going in Shed B for quite awhile, he said, not until they were sure it was safe to do so. He hesitated, maybe replaying that remark in his head and realizing the absurdity of it—as long as the Buick Roadmaster was in Shed B it was never going to be safe—and changed it to: "Everyone stays out until the temperature's back over sixty-five."

"Someone's *gotta* go," Brian Cole said. He spoke patiently, as if discussing a simple addition problem with a person of limited intelligence.

"I fail to see why, Trooper," Tony said.

Brian reached into his pocket and pulled out Jimmy and Rosalynn's water reservoir. "They got plenty of those pellets they eat, but without this, they'll die of thirst."

"No, they won't. Not right away."

"It might be a couple of *days* before the temperature in there goes up to sixty-five, Sarge. Would you want to go forty-eight hours without a drink?"

"I know *I* wouldn't," Curt said. Trying not to smile (and smiling a little anyway), he took the calibrated plastic tube from Brian. Then Tony took it from *him* before it could start to feel at home in Curt's hand. The SC did not look at his fellow scholar as he did this; he kept his eyes fixed on Trooper Brian Cole.

"I'm supposed to allow one of the men under my command to risk his life in order to bring water to a pair of pedigreed mice. Is that what you're telling me, Trooper? I just want to be clear on this."

If he expected Brian to blush or scuffle, he was disappointed. Brian just kept looking at him in that patient way, as if to say *Yes, yes, get it out of your system, boss—the sooner you get it out of your system, the sooner you'll be able to relax and do the right thing.*

"I can't believe it," Tony said. "One of us has lost his mind. Probably it's me."

"They're just little guys," Brian said. His voice was as patient as his face. "And we're the ones who put them in there, Sarge, they didn't exactly volunteer. We're responsible. Now, I'll do it if you want, I'm the one who forgot—"

Tony raised his hands to the sky, as if to ask for divine intervention, then dropped them back to his sides. Red was creeping out of his collar, up his neck, and over his jaw. It met the red patches on his cheeks: howdy-do, neighbor. "*Hair* pie!" he muttered.

The men had heard him say this before, and knew better than to crack a smile. It is at this point that many people—perhaps even a majority—would be apt to yell, "Oh, screw it! Do what you want!" and stamp away. But when you're in the big chair, getting the big bucks for making the big decisions, you can't do that. The D Troopers gathered in front of the shed knew this, and so, of course, did Tony. He stood there, looking down at his shoes. From out front of the barracks came the steady blat of Arky's old red Briggs & Stratton mower.

"Sarge—" Curtis began.

"Kid, do us all a favor and shut up."

Curt shut up.

After a moment, Tony raised his head. "The rope I asked you to pick up—did you get it?"

"Yes, sir. It's the good stuff. You could take it mountain-climbing. At least that's what the guy at Calling All Sports said."

"Is it in there?" Tony nodded at the shed.

"No, in the trunk of my car."

"Well, thank God for small favors. Bring it over here. And I hope we never have to find out how good it is." He looked at Brian Cole. "Maybe you'd like to go down to The Agway or The Giant Eagle, Trooper Cole. Get those mice a few bottles of Evian or Poland Spring Water. Hell, Perrier! How about some Perrier?"

Brian said nothing, just gave the Sergeant a little more of that patient look. Tony couldn't stand it and looked away. "Mice with pedigrees! *Hair* pie!"

*   *   *

Curt brought the rope, a length of triple-braided yellow nylon at least a hundred feet long. He made a sliding loop, cinched it around his waist, then gave the coil to Huddie Royer, who weighed two-fifty and always anchored when D Troop played tug-of-war against the other PSP octets during the Fourth of July picnic.

"If I give you the word," Tony told Huddie, "you yank him back like he just caught fire. And don't worry about breaking his collarbone or his thick skull pulling him through the door. Do you understand that?"

"Yes, Sarge."

"If you see him fall down, or just start swaying on his feet like he's light-headed, don't wait for the word. Just yank. Got it?"

"Yes, Sarge."

"Good. I'm very glad that someone understands what's going on here. Fucking hair-pie summer-camp snipe-hunt is what it is." He ran his hand through the short bristles of his hair, then turned to Curt again. "Do I need to tell you to turn around and come out of there if you sense anything—*any slightest thing*—wrong?"

"No."

"And if the trunk of that car comes open, Curtis, you *fly*. Got it? Fly out of there like a bigass bird."

"I will."

"Give me the video camera."

Curtis held it out and Tony took it. Sandy wasn't there—missed the whole thing—but when Huddie later told him it was the only time he had ever seen the Sarge looking scared, Sandy was just as glad he spent that afternoon out on patrol. There were some things you just didn't want to see.

"You have one minute in the shed, Trooper Wilcox. After that I drag you out whether you're fainting, farting, or singing 'Columbia, the Gem of the Ocean.' "

"Ninety seconds."

"No. And if you try one more time to bargain with me, your time goes down to thirty seconds."

*   *   *

Curtis Wilcox is standing in the sun outside the walk-in door on the side of Shed B. The rope is tied around his waist. He looks young on the tape, younger with each passing year. He looked at that tape himself from time to time and probably felt the same, although he never said. And he doesn't look scared. Not a bit. Only excited. He waves to the camera and says, "I'll be right back."

"You better be," Tony replies.

Curt turns and goes into the shed. For a moment he looks ghostly, hardly there, then Tony moves the camera forward to get it out of the bright sun and you can see Curt clearly again. He crosses directly to the car and starts around to the back.

"No!" Tony shouts. "No, you dummy, you want to foul the rope? Check the gerbils, give em their goddam water, and get the hell out of there!"

Curt raises one hand without turning, giving him a thumbs-up. The picture jiggles as Tony uses the zoom to get in tighter on him.

Curtis looks in the driver's-side window, then stiffens and calls: "Holy *shit!*"

"Sarge, should I pull—" Huddie begins, and then Curt looks back over his shoulder. Tony's juggling the picture again—he doesn't have Curt's light touch with the camera and the image is going everywhere—but it's still easy enough to read the wide-eyed expression of shock on Curtis's face.

"Don't you pull me back!" Curt shouts. "Don't do it! I'm five-by-five!" And with that, he opens the door of the Roadmaster.

"Stay out of there!" Tony calls from behind the madly jiggling camera.

Curt ignores him and pulls the plastic gerbil condo out of the car, waggling it gently back and forth to get it past the big steering wheel. He uses his knee to shut the Buick's door and then comes back to the shed door with the habitat cradled in his arms. With a square room at either end, the thing looks like some strange sort of plastic dumbbell.

"Get it on tape!" Curt is shouting, all but *frying* with excitement. "Get it on tape!"

Tony did. The picture zooms in on the left end of the environment just as soon as Curt steps out of the shed and back into the sun. And here is Rosalynn, no longer eating but scurrying about cheerfully enough. She becomes aware of the men gathered around her and turns directly toward the camera, sniffing at the yellow plastic, whiskers quivering, eyes bright and interested. It was cute, but the Troopers from Statler Barracks D weren't interested in cute just then.

The camera makes a herky-jerky pan away from her, traveling along the empty corridor to the empty gerbil gym at the far end. Both of the environment's hatches are latched tight, and nothing bigger than a gnat could get through the hole for the water-tube, but Jimmy the gerbil is gone, just the same—just as gone as Ennis Rafferty or the man with the Boris Badinoff accent, who had driven the Buick Roadmaster into their lives to begin with.

Now: *Sandy*

I came to a stop and swallowed a glass of Shirley's iced tea in four long gulps. That planted an icepick in the center of my forehead, and I had to wait for it to melt.

At some point Eddie Jacubois had joined us. He was dressed in his civvies and sitting at the end of the bench, looking both sorry to be there and reluctant to leave. I had no such divided feelings; I was delighted to see him. He could tell his part. Huddie would help him along, if he needed helping; Shirley, too. By 1988 she'd been with us two years, Matt Babicki nothing but a memory refreshed by an occasional postcard showing palm trees in sunny Sarasota, where Matt and his wife own a learn-to-drive school. A very successful one, at least according to Matt.

"Sandy?" Ned asked. "Are you all right?"

"I'm fine. I was just thinking about how clumsy Tony was with that video camera," I said. "Your Dad was great, Ned, a regular Steven Spielberg, but—"

"Could I watch those tapes if I wanted to?" Ned asked.

I looked at Huddie . . . Arky . . . Phil . . . Eddie. In each set of eyes I saw the same thing: *It's your call.* As of course it was. When you sit in the big chair, you make all the big calls. And mostly I like that. Might as well tell the truth.

"Don't see why not," I said. "As long as it's here. I wouldn't be comfortable with you taking them out of the barracks—you'd have to call them Troop D property—but here? Sure. You can run em on the VCR in the upstairs lounge. You ought to take a Dramamine before you look at the stuff Tony shot, though. Right, Eddie?"

For a moment Eddie looked across the parking lot, but not toward where the Roadmaster was stored. His gaze seemed to rest on the place where Shed A had been until 1982 or thereabouts. "I dunno much about that," he said. "Don't remember much. Most of the big stuff was over by the time I got here, you know."

Even Ned must have known the man was lying; Eddie was spectacularly bad at it.

"I just came out to tell you I put in those three hours I owed from last May, Sarge—you know, when I took off to help my brother-in-law build his new studio?"

"Ah," I said.

Eddie bobbed his head up and down rapidly. "Uh-huh. I'm all clocked out, and I put the report on those marijuana plants we found in Robbie Rennerts's back field on your desk. So I'll just be heading on home, if it's all the same to you."

Heading down to The Tap was what he meant. His home away from home. Once he was out of uniform, Eddie J's life was a George Jones song. He started to get up and I put a hand on his wrist. "Actually, Eddie, it's not."

"Huh?"

"It's not all the same to me. I want you to stick around awhile."

"Boss, I really ought to—"

"Stick around," I repeated. "You might owe this kid a little something."

"I don't know what—"

"His father saved your life, remember?"

Eddie's shoulders came up in a kind of defensive hunch. "I don't know if I'd say he exactly—"

"Come on, get off it," Huddie said. "I was *there.*"

Suddenly Ned wasn't so interested in videotapes. "My father saved your life, Eddie? How?"

Eddie hesitated, then gave in. "Pulled me down behind a John Deere tractor. The O'Day brothers, they—"

"The spine-tingling saga of the O'Day brothers is a story for another time," I said. "The point is, Eddie, we're having us a little exhumation party here, and you know where one of the bodies is buried. And I mean quite literally."

"Huddie and Shirley were there, they can—"

"Yeah, they were. George Morgan was there, too, I think—"

"He was," Shirley said quietly.

"—but so what?" I still had my hand on Eddie's wrist, and had to fight a desire to squeeze it again. Hard. I liked Eddie, always had, and he could be brave, but he also had a yellow streak. I don't know how those two things can exist side by side in the same man, but they can; I've seen it more than once. Eddie froze back in '96, on the day Travis and Tracy O'Day started firing their fancy militia machine-guns out of their farm-house windows. Curt had to break cover and yank him to safety by the back of his jacket. And now here he was trying to squiggle out of his part in the other story, the one in which Ned's father had played such a key role. Not because he'd done anything wrong—he hadn't—but because the memories were painful and frightening.

"Sandy, I really ought to get toddling. I've got a lot of chores I've been putting off, and—"

"We've been telling this boy about his father," I said. "And what I think you ought to do, Eddie, is sit there quiet, maybe have a sandwich and a glass of iced tea, and wait until you have something to say."

He settled back on the end of the bench and looked at us. I know what he saw in the eyes of Curt's boy: puzzlement and curiosity. We'd become quite a little council of elders, though, surrounding the young fellow, singing him our warrior-songs of the past. And what about when the songs were done? If Ned had been a young Indian brave, he might have been sent out on some sort of dream quest—kill the right animal, have the right vision while the blood of the animal's heart was still smeared around his mouth, come back a man. If there could be some sort of test at the end of this, I reflected, some way in which Ned could demonstrate new maturity and understanding, things might have been a lot simpler. But that's not the way things work nowadays. At least not by and large. These days it's a lot more about how you feel than what you do. And I think that's wrong.

And what did Eddie see in our eyes? Resentment? A touch of contempt? Perhaps even the wish that it had been him who had flagged down the truck with the flapper rather than Curtis Wilcox, that it had been him who had gotten turned inside-out by Bradley Roach? Always-almost-overweight Eddie Jacubois, who drank too much and would probably be making a little trip to Scranton for a two-week stay in the Member Assistance Program if he didn't get a handle on his drinking soon? The guy who was always slow filing his reports and who almost never got the punchline of a joke unless it was explained to him? I hope he didn't see any of those things, because there was another side to him—a better side—but I can't say for sure he didn't see at least some of them. Maybe even all of them.

"—about the big picture?"

I turned to Ned, glad to be diverted from the uncomfortable run of my own thoughts. "Come again?"

"I asked if you ever talked about what the Buick really was, where it came from, what it meant. If you ever discussed, you know, the big picture."

"Well . . . there was the meeting at The Country Way," I said. I didn't quite see where he was going. "I told you about that—"

"Yeah, but that one sounded, you know, more administrative than anything else—"

"You do okay in college," Arky said, and patted him on the knee. "Any kid can say a word like dat, jus' roll it out, he bound t'do okay in college."

Ned grinned. "Administrative. Organizational. Bureaucratized. Compartmentalized."

"Quit showing off, kiddo," Huddie said. "You're giving me a headache."

"Anyway, the thing at The Country Way's not the kind of meeting I'm talking about. You guys must've . . . I mean, as time went on you *must* have . . ."

I knew what he was trying so say, and I knew something else at the same time: the boy would *never* quite understand the way it had really been. How *mundane* it had been, at least on most days. On most days we had just gone on. The way people go on after seeing a beautiful sunset, or tasting a wonderful champagne, or getting bad news from home. We had the miracle of the world out behind our workplace, but that didn't change the amount of paperwork we had to do or the way we brushed our teeth or how we made love to our spouses. It didn't lift us to new

144

realms of existence or planes of perception. Our asses still itched, and we still scratched them when they did.

"I imagine Tony and your father talked it over a lot," I said, "but at work, at least for the rest of us, the Buick gradually slipped into the background like any other inactive case. It—"

"*Inactive!*" He nearly shouted it, and sounded so much like his father it was frightening. It was another chain, I thought, this resemblance between father and son. The chain had been mangled, but it wasn't broken.

"For long periods of time, it was," I said. "Meantime, there were fender-benders and hit-and-runs and burglaries and dope and the occasional homicide."

The look of disappointment on Ned's face made me feel bad, as if I'd let him down. Ridiculous, I suppose, but true. Then something occurred to me. "I *can* remember one bull-session about it. It was at—"

"—the picnic," Phil Candleton finished. "Labor Day picnic. That's what you're thinking about, right?"

I nodded. 1979. The old Academy soccer field, down by Redfern Stream. We all liked the Labor Day picnic a lot better than the one on the Fourth of July, partly because it was a lot closer to home and the men who had families could bring them, but mostly because it was just us—just Troop D. The Labor Day picnic really *was* a picnic.

Phil put his head back against the boards of the barracks and laughed. "Man, I'd almost forgotten about it. We talked about that damn yonder Buick, kid, and just about nothing else. More we talked, the more we drank. My head ached for two days after."

Huddie said: "That picnic's always a good time. You were there last summer, weren't you, Ned?"

"Summer before last," Ned said. "Before Dad died." He was smiling. "That tire swing that goes out over the water? Paul Loving fell out of it and sprained his knee."

We all laughed at that, Eddie as loud as the rest of us.

"A lot of talk and not one single conclusion," I said. "But what conclusions could we draw? Only one, really: when the temperature goes down inside that shed, things happen. Except even that turned out not to be a hard-and-fast rule. Sometimes—especially as the years went by—the temperature would go down a little, then rebound. Sometimes that humming noise would start . . . and then it would stop again, just cut out as if someone had pulled the plug on a piece of electrical equipment. Ennis disappeared with no lightshow and Jimmy the gerbil disappeared after a *humongous* lightshow and Rosalynn didn't disappear at all."

"Did you put her back into the Buick?" Ned asked.

"Nah," Phil said. "This is America, kid—no double jeopardy."

"Rosalynn lived the rest of her life upstairs in the common room," I said. "She was three or four when she died. Tony said that was a fairly normal lifespan for a gerbil."

"Did more things come out of it? Out of the Buick?"

"Yes. But you couldn't correlate the appearance of those things with—"

"What sort of things? And what about the bat? Did my father ever get around to dissecting it? Can I see it? Are there pictures, at least? Was it—"

"Whoa, hold on," I said, raising my hand. "Eat a sandwich or something. Chill out."

He picked up a sandwich and began to nibble, his eyes looking at me over the top. For just a moment he made me think of Rosalynn the gerbil turning to look into the lens of the video camera, eyes bright and whiskers twitching.

"Things appeared from time to time," I said, "and from time to time things—living things—would disappear. Frogs. A butterfly. A tulip right out of the pot it was growing in. But you couldn't correlate the chill, the hum, or the lightshows with either the disappearances or what your Dad called the Buick's miscarriages. Nothing really correlates. The chill is pretty reliable, there's never been one of those fireworks displays without a preceding temperature-drop—but not every temperature-drop means a display. Do you see what I mean?"

"I think so," Ned said. "Clouds don't always mean rain, but you don't get rain without them."

"I couldn't have put it more neatly," I said.

Huddie tapped Ned on the knee. "You know how folks say, 'There's an exception to every rule'? Well, in the case of the Buick, we've got about one rule and a dozen exceptions. The driver himself is one—you know, the guy in the black coat and black hat. *He* disappeared, but not from the vicinity of the Buick."

"Can you say that for sure?" Ned asked.

It startled me. For a boy to look like his father is natural. To sound like his father, too. But for a moment there, Ned's voice and looks combined to make something more than a resemblance. Nor was I the only one who felt that. Shirley and Arky exchanged an uneasy glance.

"What do you mean?" I asked him.

"Roach was reading a newspaper, wasn't he? And from the way you described him, that probably took most of his concentration. So how do you know the guy didn't come back to his car?"

I'd had something like twenty years to think about that day and the consequences of that day. Twenty years, and the idea of the Roadmaster's driver coming back (perhaps even *sneaking* back) had never once occurred to me. Or, so far as I knew, to anyone else. Brad Roach said the guy hadn't returned, and we'd simply accepted that. Why? Because cops have built-in bullshit detectors, and in that case, none of the needles swung into the red. Never even twitched, really. Why would they? Brad Roach at least *thought* he was telling the truth. That didn't mean he knew what he was talking about, though.

"I guess that it's possible," I said.

Ned shrugged as if to say, *Well there you go.*

"We never had Sherlock Holmes or Lieutenant Columbo working out of D Troop," I said. I thought I sounded rather defensive. I *felt* rather defensive. "When you get right down to it, we're just the mechanics of the legal system. Blue-collar guys who actually wear gray collars and have a slightly better-than-average education. We can work the phones, compile evidence if there's evidence to compile, make the occasional deduction. On good days we can make fairly *brilliant* deductions. But with the Buick there was no consistency, hence no basis for deduction, brilliant or otherwise."

"Some of the guys thought it came from space," Huddie said. "That it was . . . oh, I don't know, a disguised scout-ship, or something. They had the idea Ennis was abducted by an E.T. disguised to look at least passably human in his—*its*—black coat and hat. This talk was at the picnic—the Labor Day picnic, okay?"

"Yeah," Ned said.

"That was one seriously weird get-together, kiddo," Huddie said. "It seems to me that everyone got a lot drunker'n usual, and a lot faster, but no one got rowdy, not even the usual suspects like Jackie O'Hara and Christian Soder. It was very quiet, especially once the shirts-and-skins touch football game was over.

"I remember sitting on a bench under an elm tree with a bunch of guys, all of us moderately toasted, listening to Brian Cole tell about these flying saucer sightings around the powerlines in New Hampshire—only a few years before, that was—and how some woman claimed to have been abducted and had all these probes stuck up inside her, entrance ramps and exit ramps both."

"Is that what my father believed? That aliens abducted his partner?"

"No," Shirley said. "Something happened here in 1988 that was so . . . so outrageous and beyond belief . . . so fucking *awful* . . ."

"What?" Ned asked. "For God's sake, *what?*"

Shirley ignored the question. I don't think she even heard it. "A few days afterward, I asked your father flat-out what he believed. He said it didn't matter."

Ned looked as if he hadn't heard her correctly. "It didn't *matter?*"

"That's what he said. He believed that, whatever the Buick was, it didn't matter in the great scheme of things. In that big picture you were talking about. I asked him if he thought someone was using it, maybe to watch us . . . if it was some sort of television . . . and he said, 'I think it's forgotten.' I still remember the flat, certain way he said it, as if he was talking about . . . I don't know . . . something as important as a king's treasure buried under the desert since before the time of Christ or something as *un*important as a postcard with the wrong address sitting in a Dead Letter file somewhere. 'Having a wonderful time, wish you were here,' and who cares, because all that was long, long ago. It comforted me and at the same time it chilled me to think anything so strange and awful could just be forgotten . . . misplaced . . . overlooked. I said that, and your Dad, he laughed. Then he flapped his arm at the western horizon and he said, 'Shirley, tell me something. How many nuclear weapons do you think this great nation of ours has got stored out there in various places between the Pennsylvania-Ohio line and the Pacific Ocean? And how many of them do you think will be left behind and forgotten over the next two or three centuries?' "

We were all silent for a moment, thinking about this.

"I was considering quitting the job," Shirley said at last. "I couldn't sleep. I kept thinking about poor old Mister Dillon, and in my mind quitting was almost a done deal. It was Curt who talked me into staying, and he did it without even knowing he was doing it. 'I think it's forgotten,' he said, and that was good enough for me. I stayed, and I've never been sorry, either. This is a good place, and most of the guys who work here are good Troops. That goes for the ones who are gone, too. Like Tony."

"I love you, Shirley, marry me," Huddie said. He put an arm around her and puckered his lips. Not a pretty sight, all in all.

She elbowed him. "You're married already, foolish."

Eddie J spoke up then. "If your Dad believed anything, it was that yonder machine came from some other dimension."

"Another *dimension?* You're kidding." He looked at Eddie closely. "No. You're *not* kidding."

"And he didn't think it was planned at all," Eddie went on. "Not, you know, like you'd plan to send a ship across the ocean or a satellite into space. In some ways, I'm not even sure he thought it was real."

"You lost me," the kid said.

"Me, too," Shirley agreed.

"He said . . ." Eddie shifted on the bench. He looked out again at the grassy place where Shed A had once stood. "This was at the O'Day farm, if you want to know the truth. That day. You hafta realize we were out there almost seven goddam hours, parked in the corn and waiting for those two dirtbags to come back. Cold. Couldn't run the engine, couldn't run the heater. We talked about everything—hunting, fishing, bowling, our wives, our plans. Curt said he was going to get out of the PSP in another five years—"

"He said that?" Ned was round-eyed.

149

Eddie gave him an indulgent look. "From time to time we all say that, kid. Just like all the junkies say they're going to quit the spike. I told him how I'd like to open my own security business in The Burg, also how I'd like to get me a brand-new Winnebago. He told me about how he wanted to take some science courses at Horlicks and how he was getting resistance from your Mom. She said it was their job to put the *kids* through school, not him. He caught a lot of flak from her but never blamed her. Because she didn't know why he wanted to take those courses, what had got him interested, and he couldn't tell her. That's how we got around to the Buick. And what he said—I remember this clear as the sky on a summer morning—was that we saw it as a Buick because we had to see it as *something*."

"Have to see it as something," Ned muttered. He was leaning forward and rubbing the center of his forehead with two fingers, like a man with a headache.

"You look as confused as I felt, but I did sort of understand what he meant. In here." Eddie tapped his chest, above his heart.

Ned turned back to me. "Sandy, that day at the picnic, did any of you talk about . . ." He trailed off without finishing.

"Talk about what?" I asked him.

He shook his head, looked down at the remains of his sandwich, and popped the last bite into his mouth. "Never mind. Isn't important. Did my Dad really dissect the bat-thing you guys found?"

"Yep. After the second lightshow but before the Labor Day picnic. He—"

"Tell the kid about the leaves," Phil said. "You forgot that part."

And I had. Hell, I hadn't even *thought* about the leaves in six or eight years. "*You* tell him," I said. "You're the one who had your hands on them."

Phil nodded, sat silent for a few moments, and then began to speak staccato, as if giving a report to a superior officer.

Now: *Phil*

"The second lightshow happened midafternoon. Okay? Curt goes into the shed with the rope on when it's over and brings out the gerbil whatchacallit. We see one of the critters is gone. There's some more talk. Some more picture-taking. Sergeant Schoondist says okay, okay, everyone as you were, who's on duty out in the hutch. Brian Cole says 'Me, Sarge.'

"The rest of us go back in the barracks. Okay? And I hear Curtis say to the Sarge, 'I'm gonna dissect that thing before it disappears like everything else. Will you help me?' And the Sarge says he will—that night, if Curt wants. Curt says, 'Why not right now?' and the Sarge says, 'Because you got a patrol to finish. Shift-and-a-half. John Q is depending on you, boy, and lawbreakers tremble at the sound of your engyne.' That's the way he talked, sometimes, like a piney-woods preacher. And he never said *engine,* always *engyne.*

"Curt, he don't argue. Knows better. Goes off. Around five o'clock Brian Cole comes in and gets me. Asks will I cover the shed for him while he goes to the can. I say sure. I go out there. Take a look inside. Situation normal, fi'-by. Thermometer's gone up a degree. I go into the hutch. Decide the hutch is too hot, okay? There's an L. L. Bean catalogue on the chair. I go to grab that. Just as I put my fingers on it, I hear this *creak-thump* sound. Only one sound like it, when you unlatch the trunk of your car and it springs up hard. I go rushing out of the hutch. Over to the shed windows. Buick's trunk's open. All this what I thought at first was paper, charred bits of paper, is whooshing up out of the trunk. Spinning around like they were caught in a cyclone. But the dust on the floor wasn't moving. Not at all. The only moving air was coming out of the trunk. And then I saw all the pieces of paper looked pretty much the same and I decided they were leaves. Turned out that was what they were."

151

I took my notebook out of my breast pocket. Clicked out the tip of my ballpoint and drew this:

"It looks sort of like a smile," the kid said.

"Like a goddam *grin*," I said. "Only there wasn't just one of them. Was hundreds. Hundreds of black grins swirling and spinning around. Some landed on the Buick's roof. Some dropped back into the trunk. Most of em went on the floor. I ran to get Tony. He came out with the video camera. He was all red in the face and muttering, 'What now, what next, what the hell, what now?' Like that. It was sort of funny, but only later on, okay? Wasn't funny at the time, believe me.

"We looked in the window. Saw the leaves scattered all across the cement floor. There were almost as many as you might have on your lawn after a big October windstorm blows through. Only by then they were curling up at the corners. Made em look a little less like grins and a little more like leaves. Thank God. And they weren't staying black. They were turning whitish-gray right in front of our eyes. And *thinning*. Sandy was there by then. Didn't make it in time for the lightshow, but turned up in time for the leafshow."

Sandy said, "Tony called me at home and asked if I could come in that evening around seven. He said that he and Curt were going to do something I might want to be in on. Anyway, I didn't wait for seven. I came in right away. I was curious."

"It killed the cat," Ned said, and sounded so much like his Pa that I almost shivered. Then he was looking at me. "Tell the rest."

"Not much to tell," I said. "The leaves were thinning. I might be wrong, but I think we could actually see it happening."

"You're not wrong," Sandy said.

"I was excited. Not thinking. Ran around to the side door of the shed. And Tony, man, Tony was on me like white on rice. He grabs me around the neck in a choke-hold. 'Hey,' I says. 'Leggo me, leggo me, police brutality!' And he tells me to save it for my gig at the Comedy Shop over in Statesboro. 'This is no joke, Phil,' he says. 'I have good reason to believe I've lost one officer to that goddamned thing. I'm not losing another.'

"I told him I'd wear the rope. I was hot to trot. Can't remember exactly why, but I was. He said he wasn't going back to get the goddam rope. I said *I'd* go back and get the goddam rope. He said, 'You can forget the goddam rope, permission denied.' So I says, 'Just hold my feet, Sarge. I want to get a few of those leaves. There's some not five feet from the door. Not even close to the car. What do you say?'

" 'I say you must have lost your friggin mind, *everything in there* is close to the car,' he says, but since that wasn't exactly no, I went ahead and opened the door. You could smell it right away. Something like peppermint, only not nice. Some smell underneath it, making the one on top even worse. That cabbagey smell. Made your stomach turn over, but I was almost too excited to notice. I was younger then, okay? I got down on my stomach. Wormed my way in. Sarge has got me by the calves, and when I'm just a little way inside the shed he says, 'That's far enough, Phil. If you can grab some, grab away. If you can't, get out.'

"There were all kinds that had turned white, and I got about a dozen of those. They were smooth and soft, but in a bad way. Made me think of how tomatoes get when they've gone rotten under the skin. A little farther away there was a couple that were still black. I stretched out and got hold of em, only the very second I touched em, they turned white like the others. There was this very faint stinging sensation in my fingertips. Got a stronger whiff of peppermint and I heard a sound. Think I did, anyway. A kind of sigh, like the sound a soda can makes when you break the seal on the poptop.

"I started wiggling out, and at first I was doing all right, but then I . . . something about the feel of those things in my hands . . . all sleek and smooth like they were . . ."

For a few seconds I couldn't go on. It was like I was feeling it all over again. But the kid was looking at me and I knew he wouldn't let it go, not for love or money, so I pushed ahead. Now just wanting to get it over with.

"I panicked. Okay? Started to push backward with my elbows and kick with my feet. Summer. Me in short sleeves. One of my elbows kind of winged out and touched one of the black leaves and it hissed like . . . like I don't know what. Just hissed, you know? And sent up a puff of that peppermint-cabbage stink. Turned white. Like me touching it had given it frostbite and killed it. Thought of that later. Right then I didn't think about anything except getting the righteous fuck out of there. Scuse me, Shirley."

"Not at all," Shirley said, and patted my arm. Good girl. Always was. Better in dispatch than Babicki—by a country mile—and a whole lot easier on the eyes. I put my hand over hers and gave a little squeeze. Then I went on, and it was easier than I thought it would be. Funny how things come back when you talk about them. How they get clearer and clearer as you go along.

"I looked up at that old Buick. And even though it was in the middle of the shed, had to be twelve feet away from me easy, all at once it seemed a lot closer than that. Big as Mount Everest. Shiny as the side of a diamond. I got the idea that the headlights were eyes and the eyes were looking at me. And I could hear it whispering. Don't look so surprised, kid. We've all heard it whispering. No idea what it's saying—if it's really saying anything—but sure, I could hear it. Only inside my head, going from the inside out. Like telepathy. Might have been imagination, but I don't think so. All of a sudden it was like I was six again. Scared of the thing under my bed. It meant to take me away, I was sure of it. Take me to wherever it had taken Ennis. So I panicked. I yelled, 'Pull me, pull me, hurry up!' and they sure did. The Sarge and some other guy—"

"The other guy was me," Sandy said. "You scared the living crap out of us, Phil. You seemed all right at first, then you started to yell and twist and buck. I sort of expected to see you bleeding somewhere, or turning blue in the face. But all you had was . . . well." And he made a little gesture at me to go on.

"I had the leaves. What was left of them, anyway. When I freaked out, I must have made fists, okay? Clenched down on them. And once I was back outside, I realized my hands were all wet. People were yelling *Are you all right?* and *What happened in there, Phil?* Me up on my knees, with most of my shirt around my neck and a damn floorburn on my gut from being dragged, and I'm thinking *My hands are bleeding. That's why they're wet.* Then I see this white goo. Looked like the kind of paste the teacher gives you in the first grade. It was all that was left of the leaves."

I stopped, thought about it.

"And now I'm gonna tell you the truth, okay? It didn't look like paste at all. It was like I had two fistfuls of warm bull-jizz. And the smell was awful. I don't know why. You could say *A little peppermint and cabbage, what's the big deal?* and you'd be right, but at the same time you'd be wrong. Because really that smell was like nothing on earth. Not that I ever smelled before, anyway.

"I wiped my hands on my pants and went back to the barracks. Went downstairs. Brian Cole is just coming out of the crapper down there. He thought he heard some yelling, wants to know what's going on. I pay him absolutely no mind. Almost knock him over getting into the can, matter of fact. I start washing my hands. I'm still washing away when all at once I think of how I looked with that cummy-white leaf-gunk dripping out of my fists and how it was so warm and soft and somehow *sleek* and how it made strings when I opened up my fingers. And that was it. Thinking of how it made strings between my palms and the tips of my fingers, I upchucked. It wasn't like having your guts send your supper back by Western Union, either. It was like my actual stomach making a personal appearance, coming right up my throat and tipping everything I'd swallowed down lately right back out my mouth. The way my Ma used to throw her dirty wash-water over the back porch railing. I don't mean to go on about it, but you need to know. It's another way of trying to understand. It wasn't like puking, it was like dying. Only other time I had anything like that was my first road fatality. I get there and the first thing I see is a loaf of Wonder bread on the yellow line of the old Statler Pike and the next thing I see is the top half of a kid. A little boy with blond hair. Next thing I see is there's a fly on the kid's tongue. Washing its legs. That set me off. I thought I was going to puke myself to death."

"It happened to me, too," Huddie said. "Nothing to be ashamed of."

"Not ashamed," I said. "Trying to make him see, is all. Okay?" I took in a deep breath, smelling the sweet air, and then it hit me that the kid's father was also a roadkill. I gave the kid a smile. "Oh well, thank God for small favors—the commode was right next to the basin, and I didn't get hardly any on my shoes or the floor."

"And in the end," Sandy said, "the leaves came to nothing. And I mean that literally. They melted like the witch in *The Wizard of Oz.* You could see traces of them in Shed B for awhile, but after a week there was nothing but some little stains on the concrete. Yellowish, very pale."

"Yeah, and for the next couple of months, I turned into one of those compulsive hand-washers," I said. "There were days when I couldn't bring myself to touch food. If my wife packed me sandwiches, I picked em up with a napkin and ate them that way, dropping the last piece out of the napkin and into my mouth so I never had to touch any of it with my fingers. If I was by myself in my cruiser, I was apt to eat with my gloves on. And I kept thinking I'd get sick just the same. What I kept imagining was that gum disease where all your teeth fall out. But I got over it." I looked at Ned and waited until he met my eyes. "I got over it, son."

He met my eyes, but there was nothing in them. It was funny. Like they were painted on, or something.

Okay?

Now: *Sandy*

Ned was looking at Phil. The boy's face was calm enough, but I sensed rejection in his gaze, and I think Phil sensed it, too. He sighed, folded his arms across his chest, and looked down as if to say he was done talking, his testimony was finished.

Ned turned to me. "What happened that night? When you dissected the bat?"

He kept calling it a bat and it *hadn't* been a bat. That was just a word I'd used, what Curtis would have called a nail to hang my hat on. And all at once I was mad at him. More than mad—pissed like a bear. And I was also angry at myself for feeling that way, for daring to feel that way. You see, mostly what I was angry at was the kid raising his head. Raising his eyes to mine. Asking his questions. Making his foolish assumptions, one of which happened to be that when I said bat I meant bat, and not some unspeakable, indescribable thing that crept out of a crack in the floor of the universe and then died. But mostly it was him raising his head and his eyes. I know that doesn't exactly make me out to be the prince of the world, but I'm not going to lie about it.

Up until then, what I'd mostly felt was sorry for him. Everything I'd done since he started showing up at the barracks had been based on that comfortable pity. Because all that time when he'd been washing windows and raking leaves and snowblowing his way through the drifts in the back parking lot, all that time he'd kept his head down. Meekly down. You didn't have to contend with his eyes. You didn't have to ask yourself any questions, because pity is comfortable. Isn't it? Pity puts you right up on top. Now he had lifted his head, he was using my own words back at me, and there was nothing meek in his eyes. He thought he had a right, and that made me mad. He thought I had a responsibility—that what was being said out here wasn't a gift being given but a debt being repaid—

and that made me madder. That he was right made me maddest of all. I felt like shoving the heel of my hand up into the shelf of his chin and knocking him spang off the bench. He thought he had a right and I wanted to make him sorry.

Our feelings toward the young never much change in this regard, I suppose. I don't have kids of my own, I've never been married—like Shirley, I guess I married Troop D. But I've got plenty of experience when it cames to the young, both inside and outside the barracks. I've had them in my face plenty of times. It seems to me that when we can no longer pity them, when they reject our pity (not with indignation but with impatience), we pity ourselves instead. We want to know where they went, our comfy little ones, our baby buntings. Didn't we give them piano lessons and show them how to throw the curveball? Didn't we read them *Where the Wild Things Are* and help them search for Waldo? How dare they raise their eyes to ours and ask their rash and stupid questions? How dare they want more than we want to give?

"Sandy? What happened when you guys dissected the—"

"Not what *you* want to hear," I said, and when his eyes widened a little at the coldness he heard in my voice, I was not exactly displeased. "Not what your father wanted to see. Or Tony, either. Not some answer. There never was an answer. Everything to do with the Buick was a shimmer-mirage, like the ones you see on I-87 when it's hot and bright. Except that's not quite true, either. If it had been, I think we could have dismissed the Buick eventually. The way you dismiss a murder when six months go by and you all just kind of realize you're not going to catch whoever did it, that the guy is going to slide. With the Buick and the things that came out of the Buick, there was always something you could catch hold of. Something you could touch or hear. Or something you could

Then

"Oi," Sandy Dearborn said. "That *smell*."

He put his hand up to his face but couldn't actually touch his skin because of the plastic breathing cup he was wearing over his mouth and nose—the kind dentists put on before going prospecting. Sandy didn't know how it was on germs, but the mask did nothing to stop the smell. It was that cabbagey aroma, and it choked the air of the storage closet as soon as Curt opened the stomach of the bat-thing.

"We'll get used to it," Curt said, his own breathing cup bobbing up and down on his face. His and Sandy's were blue; the Sergeant's was a rather cute shade of candy-pink. Curtis Wilcox was a smart guy, right about a lot of things, but he was wrong about the smell. They didn't get used to it. No one ever did.

Sandy couldn't fault Trooper Wilcox's preparation, however; it seemed perfect. Curt had swung home at the end of his shift and picked up his dissection kit. To this he had added a good microscope (borrowed from a friend at the university), several packets of surgical gloves, and a pair of extremely bright Tensor lamps. He told his wife he intended to examine a fox someone had shot behind the barracks.

"You be careful," she said. "They can have rabies."

Curt promised her he'd glove up, and it was a promise he meant to keep. Meant for all three of them to keep. Because the bat-thing might have something a lot worse than rabies, something which remained virulent long after its original host was dead. If Tony Schoondist and Sandy Dearborn had needed a reminder of this (they probably didn't), they got it when Curt first closed the door at the foot of the stairs and then bolted it.

"I'm in charge as long as that door's locked," Curt said. His voice was flat and absolutely sure of itself. It was mostly Tony he was speaking to,

159

because Tony was twice his age, and if anyone was his partner in this, it was the SC. Sandy was just along for the ride, and knew it. "Is that understood and agreed? Because if it isn't, we can stop right n—"

"It's understood," Tony said. "In here you're the general. Sandy and I are just a couple of buck privates. I have no problem with that. Just for chrissake let's get it over with."

Curt opened his kit, which was almost the size of an Army footlocker. The interior was packed with stainless steel instruments wrapped in chamois. On top of them were the dental masks, each in its own sealed plastic bag.

"You really think these are necessary?" Sandy asked.

Curt shrugged. "Better safe than sorry. Not that those things are worth much. We should probably be wearing respirators."

"I sort of wish we had Bibi Roth here," Tony said.

Curt made no verbal reply to that, but the flash of his eyes suggested that was the last thing in the world *he* wanted. The Buick belonged to the Troop. And anything that came out of it belonged to the Troop.

Curt opened the door of the storage closet and went in, pulling the chain that turned on the little room's green-shaded hanging lamp. Tony followed. There was a table not much bigger than a grade-schooler's desk under the light. Small as the closet was, there was barely room for two, let alone three. That was fine with Sandy; he never stepped over the threshold at all that night.

Shelves heaped with old files crowded in on three sides. Curt put his microscope on the little desk and plugged its light-source into the closet's one outlet. Sandy, meanwhile, was setting up Huddie Royer's videocam on its sticks. In the video of that peculiar postmortem, one can sometimes see a hand reach into the picture, holding out whatever instrument Curt has called for. It's Sandy Dearborn's hand. And one can hear the sound of vomiting at the end of the tape, loud and clear. That is also Sandy Dearborn.

"Let's see the leaves first," Curt said, snapping on a pair of the surgical gloves.

Tony had a bunch of them in a small evidence bag. He handed it over. Curt opened it and took out the remains of the leaves with a small pair of tongs. There was no way to get just one; by now they were all semi-transparent and stuck together like clumps of Saran Wrap. They were seeping little trickles of fluid, and the men could smell their aroma—that uneasy mix of cabbage and peppermint—immediately. It was not nice, but it was a long way from unbearable. Unbearable was at that point still ten minutes in the future.

Sandy used the zoom in order to get a good image of Curt separating a fragment of the mass from the whole, using the pincers deftly. He'd treated himself to a lot of practice over the last few weeks, and here was the payoff.

He transferred the fragment directly to the stage of the microscope, not attempting to make a slide. Phil Candleton's leaves were just the Coming Attractions reel. Curtis wanted to get to the feature presentation as soon as possible.

He bent over the twin eyepieces for a good long time nevertheless, then beckoned Tony for a look.

"What're the black things that look like threads?" Tony asked after several seconds of study. His voice was slightly muffled by his pink mask.

"I don't know," Curt said. "Sandy, give me that gadget that looks like a Viewmaster. It has a couple of cords wrapped around it and PROPERTY H.U. BIOLOGY DEPARTMENT Dymotaped on the side."

Sandy passed it to him over the top of the videocam, which was pretty much blocking the doorway. Curt plugged one of the cords into the wall and the other into the base of the microscope. He checked something, nodded, and pushed a button on the side of the Viewmaster-thing three times, presumably taking pictures of the leaf fragments on the microscope's stage.

"Those black things aren't moving," Tony said. He was still peering into the microscope.

"No."

Tony finally raised his head. His eyes had a dazed, slightly awed look. "Is it . . . could it be like, I don't know, DNA?"

Curt's mask bobbed slightly on his face as he smiled. "This is a great scope, Sarge, but we couldn't see DNA with it. Now, if you wanted to go up to Horlicks with me after midnight and pull a bag-job, they've got this really beautiful electron microscope in the Evelyn Silver Physics Building, never been driven except by a little old lady on her way to church and her weekly—"

"What's the white stuff?" Tony asked. "The stuff the black threads are floating in?"

"Nutrient, maybe."

"But you don't know."

"Of *course* I don't know."

"The black threads, the white goo, why the leaves are melting, what that smell is. We don't know dick about any of those things."

"No."

Tony gave him a level look. "We're crazy to be fucking with this, aren't we?"

"No," Curt said. "Curiosity killed the cat, satisfaction made him fat. You want to squeeze in and take a peek, Sandy?"

"You took photos, right?"

"I did if this thing worked the way it's s'posed to."

"Then I'll take a pass."

"Okay, let's move on to the main event," Curt said. "Maybe we'll actually find something."

The gobbet of leaves went back into the evidence bag and the evidence bag went back into a file cabinet in the corner. That battered green cabinet would become quite the repository of the weird and strange over the next two decades.

In another corner of the closet was an orange Eskimo cooler. Inside, under two of those blue chemical ice packets people sometimes take on camping trips, was a green garbage bag. Tony lifted it out and then waited while Curt finished getting ready. It didn't take long. The only real delay was finding an extension cord so they could plug in both of the Tensor lamps without disturbing the microscope or the attached still camera. Sandy went to get a cord from the cabinet of odds and ends at the far end of the hall. While he was doing that, Curt placed his borrowed microscope on a nearby shelf (of course in those close quarters, everything was nearby) and set up an easel on the desktop. On this he mounted a square of tan corkboard. Beneath it he placed a small metal trough of the sort found on the more elaborate barbecue setups, where they are used to catch drippings. Off to one side he put a jar-top filled with push-pins.

Sandy came back with the extension cord. Curt plugged in the lamps so they shone on the corkboard from either side, illuminating his work-surface with a fierce, even glow that eliminated every shadow. It was obvi-ous he'd thought all of this out, step by step. Sandy wondered how many nights he'd lain awake long after Michelle had gone to sleep beside him. Just lying there and looking up at the ceiling and going over the proce-dure in his mind. Reminding himself he'd just have the one shot. Or how many afternoons there had been, Curt parked a little way up some farmer's lane with the Genesis radar gun pointed at an empty stretch of highway, calculating how many practice bats he'd have to go through before he dared tackle the real thing.

"Sandy, are you getting glare from these lights?"

He checked the viewfinder. "No. With white I probably would, but tan is great."

"Okay."

Tony unwound the yellow tie holding the neck of the garbage bag shut. The moment he opened it, the smell got stronger. "Whew, Jesus!" he said, waving a gloved hand. Then he reached in and pulled out another evidence bag, this one a large.

Sandy was watching over the top of the camera. The thing in the bag looked like a shopworn freakshow monstrosity. One of the dark wings was folded over the lower body, the other pressed against the clear plastic of the evidence bag, making him think of a hand pressed against a pane of glass. Sometimes when you collared a drunk and shut him in the back of the cruiser he'd put his hands on the glass and look out at the world from between them, a dazed dark face framed by starfish. This was a little like that, somehow.

"Seal's open in the middle," Curt said, and nodded disapprovingly at the evidence bag. "That explains the smell."

Nothing explained it, in Sandy's opinion.

Curt opened the bag completely and reached inside. Sandy felt his stomach knot into a sick ball and wondered if he could have forced himself to do what Curt was doing. He didn't think so. Trooper Wilcox never hesitated, however. When his gloved fingers touched the corpse in the bag, Tony recoiled a little. His feet stayed put but his upper body swayed backward, as if to avoid a punch. And he made an involuntary sound of disgust behind his cute pink mask.

"You okay?" Curt asked.

"Yes," Tony said.

"Good. I'll mount it. You pin it."

"Okay."

"Are you sure you're all right?"

"Yes, goddammit."

"Because I feel queasy, too." Sandy could see sweat running down the side of Curt's face, dampening the elastic that held his mask.

"Let's save the sensitivity-training session for later and just get it done, what do you say?"

Curt lifted the bat-thing to the corkboard. Sandy could hear an odd and rather terrible sound as he did so. It might have been only the combination of overstrained ears and the quiet rustle of clothes and gloves, but Sandy didn't actually believe that. It was dead skin rubbing against dead skin, creating a sound that was somehow like words spoken very low in an alien tongue. It made Sandy want to cover his ears.

At the same time he became aware of that tenebrous rustling, his eyes seemed to sharpen. The world took on a preternatural clarity. He could see the rosy pink of Curtis's skin through the thin gloves he was wearing, and the matted whorls that were the hairs on the backs of his fingers. The glove's white was very bright against the creature's midsection, which had gone a matted, listless gray. The thing's mouth hung open. Its single black eye stared at nothing, its surface dull and glazed. To Sandy that eye looked as big as a teacup.

The smell was getting worse, but Sandy said nothing. Curt and the Sergeant were right in there with it, next to the source. He guessed if they could stand it, he could.

Curt peeled up the wing lying across the creature's middle, revealing sallow green fur and a small puckered cavity that might have held the thing's genitals. He held the wing against the corkboard. "Pin," he said.

164

Tony pinned the wing. It was dark gray and all membrane. There was no sign of bone or blood vessels that Sandy could see. Curt shifted his hand on the thing's midsection so he could raise the other wing. Sandy heard that liquid squelching sound again. It was getting hot in the supply room and had to be even worse in the closet. Those Tensor lamps.

"Pin, boss."

Tony pinned the other wing and now the creature hung on the board like something out of a Bela Lugosi film. Except, once you could see all of it, it didn't really look much like a bat at all, or a flying squirrel, or certainly any kind of bird. It didn't look like *anything*. That yellow prong sticking out from the center of its face, for instance—was it a bone? A beak? A nose? If it was a nose, where were the nostrils? To Sandy it looked more like a claw than a nose, and more like a thorn than a claw. And what about that single eye? Sandy tried to think of any earthly creature that had only one eye and couldn't. There had to be such a creature, didn't there? Somewhere? In the jungles of South America, or maybe at the bottom of the ocean?

And the thing had no feet; its body simply ended in a butt like a green-black thumb. Curt pinned this part of the specimen's anatomy to the board himself, pinching the furry hide away from its body and then impaling a loose fold. Tony finished the job by driving pins into the corkboard through the thing's armpits. *Or maybe you call them wingpits,* Sandy thought. This time it was Curtis who made an involuntary sound of disgust behind his mask, and he wiped his brow with his forearm. "I wish we'd thought to bring in the fan," he said. Sandy, whose head was beginning to swim, agreed. Either the stench was getting worse or it had a cumulative effect.

"Plug in one more thing and we'd probably trip the breaker," Tony said. "Then we could be in the dark with this ugly motherfucker. Also trapped, on account of Cecil B. DeMille's got his camera set up in the doorway. Go on, Curt. I'm okay if you are."

Curt stepped back, snatched a breath of slightly cleaner air, tried to compose himself, then stepped forward to the table again. "I'm not measuring," he said. "We got all that done out in the shed, right?"

"Yeah," Sandy replied. "Fourteen inches long. Thirty-six centimeters, if you like that better. Body's about a handspan across at the widest. Maybe a little less. Go on, for God's sake, so we can get out of here."

"Give me both scalpels, plus retractors."

"How many retractors?"

Curt gave him a look that said *Don't be a bozo.* "All of them." Another quick swipe of the forehead. And after Sandy had handed the stuff over the top of the camera and Curt had arranged it as best he could: "Watch through the viewfinder, okay? Zoom the shit out of the mother. Let's get the best record we can."

"People'd still say it's a fake," Tony told him. "You know that, don't you?"

Curtis then said something Sandy never forgot. He believed that Curtis, already under severe mental strain and in increasingly severe physical distress, spoke the truth of his mind in baldly simple terms people rarely dare to use, because they reveal too much about the speaker's real heart. "Fuck the John Q's," was what Curtis said. "This is for us."

"I've got a good tight shot," Sandy told him. "The smell may be bad, but the light's heavenly." The time-code at the bottom of the little interior TV screen read 7:49:01 P.

"Cutting now," Curt said, and slid his larger scalpel into the pinned creature's midsection. His hands didn't tremble; any stage-fright accompanying the arrival of the big moment must have come and gone quickly. There was a wet popping sound, like a bubble of some thick liquid breaking, and all at once drops of black goo began to patter into the trough under the easel.

"Oh man," Sandy said. "Oh, that really stinks."

"Fucking *foul,*" Tony added. His voice was thin and dismayed.

Curt took no notice. He opened the thing's abdomen and made the standard branching incisions up to the pinned wingpits, creating the Y-cut used in any human postmortem. He then used his pincers to pull back the hide over the thoracic area, more clearly revealing a spongy dark green mass beneath a narrow arch of bone.

"Jesus God, where's its *lungs?*" Tony asked. Sandy could hear him breathing in harsh little sips.

"This green thing could be a lung," Curt said.

"Looks more like a—"

"Like a brain, yeah, I know it does. A green brain. Let's take a look."

Curt turned his scalpel and used the blunt side to tap the white arch above the crenellated green organ. "If the green thing's a brain, then its particular evolution gave it a chastity belt for protection instead of a safety deposit box. Give me the shears, Sandy. The smaller pair."

Sandy handed them over, then bent back to the video camera's viewfinder. He was zoomed to the max, as per instructions, and had a nice clear picture.

"Cutting . . . now."

Curt slipped the lower blade of the shears under the arch of bone and snipped it as neatly as the cord on a package. It sprang back on both sides like a rib, and the moment it did, the surface of the green sponge in the thing's chest turned white and began to hiss like a radiator. A strong aroma of peppermint and clove filled the air. A bubbling sound joined the hissing. It was like the sound of a straw prospecting the bottom of a nearly empty milkshake glass.

"Think we should get out of here?" Tony asked.

"Too late." Curt was bent over the opened chest, where the spongy thing had now begun to sweat droplets and runnels of whitish-green liquid. He was more than interested; he was rapt. Looking at him, Sandy could understand about the fellow who deliberately infected himself with yellow fever or the Curie woman, who gave herself cancer fiddling around with radiation. "I am made the destroyer of worlds," Robert Oppenheimer muttered during the first successful detonation of an atomic bomb in the New Mexico desert, and then went on to start work on the H-bomb with hardly a pause for tea and scones. *Because stuff gets you,* Sandy thought. *And because, while curiosity is a provable fact, satisfaction is more like a rumor.*

"What's it doing?" Tony asked. Sandy thought that from what he could see above the pink mask, the Sarge already had a pretty good idea.

"Decomposing," Curt replied. "Getting a good picture, Sandy? My head not in your way?"

"It's fine, five-by," Sandy replied in a slightly strangled voice. At first the peppermint-clove variation had seemed almost refreshing, but now it sat in the back of his throat like the taste of machine-oil. And the cabbagey reek was creeping back. Sandy's head was swimming more strenuously than ever, and his guts had begun to slosh. "I wouldn't take too long about this, though, or we're going to choke in here."

"Open the door at the end of the hall," he said.

"You told me—"

"Go on, do what he says," Tony told him, and so Sandy did. When he came back, Tony was asking Curt if Curt thought snipping the bone arch had sped up the decomposition process.

"No," Curt said. "I think touching the spongy stuff with the tip of the shears is what did it. The things that come out of that car don't seem to get along with us very well, do they?"

Neither Tony nor Sandy had any wish to argue that. The green sponge didn't look like a brain or a lung or anything else recognizable by then; it was just a pustulant, decomposing sac in the corpse's open chest.

Curt glanced toward Sandy. "If that green thing was its brain, what do you suppose is in its head? Inquiring minds want to know." And before either of them completely realized what he was doing, Curt reached out with the smaller of his scalpels and poked the blade into the thing's glazed eye.

There was a sound like a man popping his finger in his cheek. The eye collapsed and slid out of its socket whole, like a hideous shed tear. Tony gave an involuntary shout of horror. Sandy uttered a low scream. The collapsed eye struck the thing's furry shoulder and then plopped into the drip-gutter. A moment later it began to hiss and turn white.

"Stop it," Sandy heard himself saying. "This is pointless. We're not going to learn anything from it, Curtis. There's nothing to learn."

Curtis, so far as Sandy could tell, didn't even hear him. "Holy shit," he was whispering. "Holy fucking shit."

Fibrous pink stuff began to bulge from the vacant eyesocket. It looked like cotton candy, or the insulation people use in their attics. It came out, formed an amorphous node, then turned white and began to liquefy, like the green thing.

"Was that shit alive?" Tony asked. "Was that shit alive when it—"

"No, that was only depressurization," Curt said. "I'm sure of it. It's no more alive than shaving cream when it comes out of the can. Did you get it on tape, Sandy?"

"Oh yeah. For what it's worth."

"Okay. Let's look in the lower gut and then we're done."

What came out next killed any real sleep for at least a month. Sandy was left with those short dozes from which one wakes, gasping, sure that something one can't quite see has been crouching on one's chest and stealing one's breath.

Curt retracted the hide from the abdominal area and asked Tony to pin it, first on the left and then on the right. Tony managed, although not without difficulty; the work had become very fine and both of them had their faces close to the incision. The reek in that close must have been tremendous, Sandy thought.

Without turning his head, Curt groped out, found one of the Tensor lamps, and turned it slightly, intensifying the light pouring into the incision. Sandy saw a folded rope of dark liverish red stuff—intestines—piled on top of a bluish-gray sac.

"Cutting," Curt murmured, and caressed the edge of his scalpel down the sac's lumpy, bulging surface. It split open and black ichor shot out directly into Curt's face, painting his cheeks and splashing his mask. More of it splattered Tony's gloves. Both men recoiled, crying out, while Sandy stood frozen behind the video camera with his jaw hung down. Pouring out of the rapidly deflating sac was a flood of rough black pellets, each of them wrapped in a swaddle of gray membrane. To Sandy they looked like spider-snacks which had been put up in cobweb shrouds. Then he saw that each pellet had an open glazed eye and that each eye seemed to be staring at *him*, marking him, and that was when his nerve broke. He backed away from the camera, screaming. The screams were replaced by a gagging sound. A moment later he vomited down the front of his shirt. Sandy himself remembered almost none of that; the five minutes or so following Curt's final incision were pretty much burned out of his memory, and he counted that a mercy.

The first thing he remembered on the other side of that cigarette-burn in the surface of his memory was Tony saying, "Go on, now, you hear?

You guys go on back upstairs. Everything here is under control." And, close to his left ear, Curt was murmuring another version of the same thing, telling Sandy he was all right, totally cool, fi'-by-fi'.

Five-by-five: that was what lured Sandy back from his brief vacation in the land of hysteria. But if everything was five-by, why was Curt breathing so fast? And why was the hand on Sandy's arm so cold? Even through the rubber membrane of the glove (which he had so far neglected to take off), Curt's hand was cold.

"I threw up," Sandy said, and felt the dull heat hit his cheeks as the blood rose there. He couldn't remember ever feeling so ashamed and demoralized. "Christ Jesus, I threw up all over myself."

"Yeah," Curt said, "you hurled like a hero. Don't worry about it."

Sandy took a breath and then grimaced as his stomach knotted and almost betrayed him again. They were in the corridor, but even out here that cabbagey reek was almost overpowering. At the same time he realized exactly where in the hallway he was: standing in front of the rick-rack cabinet from which he had scrounged the extension cord. The cabinet's door was open. Sandy wasn't sure, but he had an idea he'd fled down here from the supply room, perhaps with the idea of crawling into the cabinet, pulling the door shut behind him, and just curling up in the dark. This struck him funny and he voiced a single shrill chuckle.

"There, that's better," Curt said. He gave Sandy a pat and looked shocked when Sandy shrank away from his touch.

"Not you," Sandy said. "That mung . . . that goo—"

He couldn't finish; his throat had locked up. He pointed at Curt's hand, instead. The slime which had come out of the bat-thing's pregnant dead uterus was smeared all over Curt's gloves, and some of it was now on Sandy's arm as well. Curt's mask, pulled down so it hung against his neck, was also streaked and stained. There was a black crust like a scab on his cheek.

At the other end of the hall, past the open supply room door, Tony stood at the foot of the stairs, talking to four or five gawking, nervous State Troopers. He was making shooing gestures, trying to get them to go back up, but they weren't quite ready to do that.

Sandy walked back down the hall as far as the supply room door, stopping where they could all get a good look at him. "I'm okay, fellas—I'm okay, you're okay, everybody's okay. Go upstairs and chill out. After we get squared away, you can all look at the video."

"Will we want to?" Orville Garrett asked.

"Probably not," Sandy said.

The Troopers went upstairs. Tony, his cheeks as pale as glass, turned to Sandy and gave him a little nod. "Thanks."

"Least I could do. I panicked, boss. I'm sorry as hell."

Curtis clapped him on the shoulder this time instead of just patting. Sandy almost shrank away again before seeing that the kid had pulled off his stained gloves. So that was all right. Better, anyway.

"You weren't alone," Curt said. "Tony and I were right behind you. You were just too freaked to notice. We knocked over Huddie's videocam in the stampede. Hope it's okay. If it's not, I guess we'll be passing the hat to buy him a replacement. Come on, let's look."

The three of them returned to the supply room resolutely enough, but at first none of them was able to go inside. Part of it was the smell, like rotten soup. Most of it was just knowing the bat-thing was still in there, pinned to the corkboard, flayed open and needing to be cleaned up like the weekend road accidents where when you got there the smell of blood and busted guts and spilled gasoline and boiled rubber was like some hideous old acquaintance who would never move out of town; you smelled it and knew that somebody was dead or almost dead, that somebody else would be crying and screaming, that you were going to find a shoe—hopefully not a child's, but all too often it was—lying in the road. For Sandy it was like that. You found them in the road or on the side of the road with the bodies God gave them and said *Here, get through life with it just as best you can* tortured into new shapes: bones bursting out through pants and shirts, heads twisted halfway around the neck but still talking (and screaming), eyes hanging loose, a bleeding mother holding out a bleeding child like a broken doll and saying *Is she still alive? Please, would you check? I can't, I don't dare.* There was always blood on the seats in pools and fingerprints of blood on what remained of the windows. When the blood was on the road it was also in pools and it turned purple in the pulse of the red bubblegum lights and you needed to clean it up, the blood and the shit and the broken glass, oh yes, because John Q and his family didn't want to be looking at it on their way to church come Sunday morning. And John Q paid the bills.

"We have to take care of this," the Sarge said. "You boys know that."

They knew it. And still none of them moved.

What if some of them are still alive? That was what Sandy was thinking. It was a ridiculous idea, the bat-thing had been in a plastic evidence bag which had been in a sealed Eskimo cooler for six weeks or more, but knowing such an idea was ridiculous wasn't enough. Logic had lost its power, at least for awhile. When you were dealing with a one-eyed thing that had its brain (its *green* brain) in its chest, the very idea of logic seemed laughable. Sandy could all too easily imagine those black pellets in their gauzy over-wrappings starting to pulse and move about like lethargic jumping-beans on the little desk as the fierce glow from the Tensor lamps warmed them back to vitality. Sure, that was easy to imagine. And sounds coming from them. High little mewling noises. The sounds of baby birds or baby rats working to be born. But he had been the first one out, goddammit. He could be the first one back in, at least he could do that much.

"Come on," Sandy said, and stepped over the threshold. "Let's get this done. Then I'm going to spend the rest of the night in the shower."

"You'll have to wait in line," Tony said.

So they cleaned the mess up as they had cleaned up so many on the high-way. It took about an hour, all told, and although getting started was hard, they were almost themselves by the time the job was finished. The biggest help in getting back on an even keel was the fan. With the Tensor lamps turned off, they could run it with no worries about popping a breaker. Curt never said another word about keeping the supply room's door shut, either. Sandy guessed he'd figured any poor quarantine they might have managed had been breached to a faretheewell.

The fan couldn't clear that sallow stench of cabbage and bitter peppermint entirely, but it drove enough of it out into the hall so that their stomachs settled. Tony checked the videocam and said it appeared to be fine.

"I remember when Japanese stuff used to break," he said. "Curt, do you want to look at anything under the microscope? We can hang in a little longer if you do. Right, Sandy?"

Although not enthusiastic, Sandy nodded his head. He was still deeply ashamed of the way he had puked and run; felt he hadn't made up for that yet, not quite.

"No," Curt said. He sounded tired and dispirited. "The damn Gummi Bears that fell out of it were its litter. The black stuff was probably its blood. As for the rest? I wouldn't know what I was seeing."

Not just dispirit but something close to despair, although neither Tony nor Sandy would realize that until later. It came to Sandy on one of those sleepless nights he had just bought and paid for. Lying in the bedroom of his small home in East Statler Heights with his hands behind his head and the lamp on the nighttable burning and the radio on low, sleep a thousand miles away. Realizing what Curt had come face to face with for the first time since the Buick showed up, and maybe for the first time in his life: that he was almost certainly never going to know what he wanted to know. What he'd told himself he *needed* to know. His ambition had been to discover and uncover, but so what? Spit on that, Jack, as they used to say when they were kids. All over the United States there were scrambling shirttail grammar school kids who'd tell you their ambition was to play in the NBA. Their futures in almost all cases would turn out to be more mundane. There comes a time when most folks see the big picture and realize they're puckered up not to kiss smiling fate on the mouth but because life just slipped them a pill, and it tastes bitter. Wasn't that where Curtis Wilcox was now? Sandy thought yeah. His interest in the Buick was likely to continue, but with each passing year that interest would look more and more like what it really was—ordinary police work. Stakeout and surveillance, writing reports (in journals his wife would later burn), cleaning up the occasional mess when the Buick gave birth to another monstrosity which would struggle briefly and then die.

Oh, and living through the occasional sleepless night. But they came with the territory, didn't they?

Curt and Tony unpinned the monstrosity from the corkboard. They put it back in the evidence bag. All but two of the black pellets followed, swept into the evidence bag with a fingerprint brush. This time Curt made sure the seal on the bag was tight all the way across the top. "Is Arky still around?" he asked.

Tony said, "No. He wanted to stay, but I sent him home."

"Then would one of you go upstairs and ask Orv or Buck to start a fire in the incinerator out back? Also, someone needs to put a pot of water on the stove. A big one."

"I'll do it," Sandy said, and after ejecting the tape from Huddie's video-cam, he did.

While he was gone, Curt took swabs of the viscid black stuff which had come out of the thing's gut and uterus; he also swabbed the thinner white fluid from the chest organ. He covered each swab with Saran Wrap and put them into another evidence bag. The two remaining unborn creatures with their tiny wings wrapped around them (and their unset-tling one-eyed stares) went into a third evidence bag. Curt worked competently, but with no zest, much as he would have worked a cold crime-scene.

The specimens and the bat-thing's flayed body eventually wound up in the battered green cabinet, which George Morgan took to calling "the Troop D sideshow." Tony allowed two of the Troopers from upstairs to come down when the pot of water on the stove had reached a boil. The five men donned heavy rubber kitchen gloves and scrubbed down everything they could reach. The unwanted organic leftovers went into a plastic bag, along with the scrub-rags, surgical gloves, dental masks, and shirts. The bag went into the incinerator and the smoke went up to the sky, God the Father, ever and ever, amen.

Sandy, Curtis, and Tony took showers—long enough and hot enough to exhaust the tank downstairs not once but twice. After that, rosy-cheeked and freshly combed, dressed in clean clothes, they ended up on the smokers' bench.

"I'm so clean I almost squeak," Sandy said.

"Squeak this," Curt replied, but amiably enough.

They sat and just looked at the shed for awhile, not talking.

"A lot of that shit got on us," Tony said at last. "*Lot* of that shit." Over-head, a three-quarter moon hung in the sky like a polished rock. Sandy could feel a tremble in the air. He thought maybe it was the seasons getting ready to change. "If we get sick—"

"I think if we were going to get sick, we'd be sick already," Curt said. "We were lucky. *Damn* lucky. Did you boys get a good look at your peepers in the bathroom mirror?"

They had, of course. Their eyes were red-rimmed and bloodshot, the eyes of men who have spent a long day fighting a brushfire.

"I think that'll go away," Curt said, "but I believe wearing those masks was probably a damn good idea, after all. They're no protection against germs, but at least none of that black crap got in our mouths. I think the results of something like that might have been quite nasty."

He was right.

Now: *Sandy*

The sandwiches were gone. So was the iced tea. I told Arky to get ten bucks out of the contingency fund (which was kept in a jar in the upstairs closet) and go down to Finn's Cash and Carry. I thought two six-packs of Coke and one of root beer would probably carry us through to the end.

"I do dat, I miss d'part about d'fish," Arky said.

"Arky, you *know* the part about the fish. You know *all* the parts of this story. Go on and get us some cold drinks. Please."

He went, firing up his old truck and driving out of the parking lot too fast. A man driving that way was apt to get a ticket.

"Go on," Ned said. "What happened next?"

"Well," I said, "let's see. The old Sarge became a grandfather, that was one thing. It probably happened a lot sooner than he wanted it to, baby girl born out of wedlock, big hooraw in the family, but everyone eventually calmed down and that girl has gone on to Smith, which is not a bad place for a young lady to get her diploma, or so I understand. George Morgan's boy hit a home run in tee-ball and George went around just about busting his buttons, he was so proud. This was I think two years before he killed the woman in the road and then killed himself. Orvie Garrett's wife got blood poisoning in her foot and lost a couple of toes. Shirley Pasternak came to work with us in 1984—"

"1986," she murmured.

"'86 it was," I said, and patted her knee. "There was a bad fire in Lass-burg around that same time, kids playing with matches in the basement of an apartment house. Just goofing. No supervision. When someone says to me that the Amish are crazy to live like they do, I think about that fire in Lassburg. Nine people killed, including all but one of the kids in the basement. The one who got out probably wishes he hadn't. He'd be

177

sixteen now, right around the age boys are generally getting good and interested in girls, and this kid probably looks like the lead actor in a burn-ward production of *Beauty and the Beast*. It didn't make the national news—I have a theory that multiple-fatality apartment-house fires only make the news if they happen at Christmas—but it was bad enough for these parts, thank you very much, and Jackie O'Hara got some terrible burns on his hands, helping out. Oh, and we had a Trooper—James Dockery, his name was—"

"Docker-*ty*," Phil Candleton said. "*T.* But you're forgiven, Sarge, he wasn't here more than a month or two, then he transferred over to Lycoming."

I nodded. "Anyhow, this Dockerty won a third prize in the Betty Crocker Bakeoff for a recipe called Golden Sausage Puffs. He got ribbed like a motherfucker, but he took it well."

"*Very* well," Eddie J agreed. "He shoulda stayed. He woulda fit in here."

"We won the tug-of-war that year at the Fourth of July picnic, and—"

I saw the look on the kid's face and smiled at him.

"You think I'm teasing you, Ned, but I'm not. Honest. What I'm doing is trying to make you understand. The Buick was not the only thing happening around here, okay? *Not.* In fact, there were times when we forgot it entirely. Most of us, anyway. For long stretches of time it was easy to forget. For long stretches of time all it did was sit out back and be quiet. Cops came and went while it did. Dockerty stayed just long enough to get nicknamed Chef Prudhomme. Young Paul Loving, the one who sprained his knee last Labor Day, got transferred out and then got transferred back in three years later. This job isn't the revolving door that some jobs are, but the door turns, all right. There's probably been seventy Troopers through here since the summer of 1979—"

"Oh, that's way low," Huddie said. "Make it a hundred, counting the transfers and the Troops who are on duty here currently. Plus a few bad eggs."

"Yeah, a few bad eggs, but most of us did our jobs. And Ned, listen— your father and Tony Schoondist learned a lesson the night your father opened up that bat-thing. I did, too. Sometimes there's nothing to learn, or no way to learn it, or no reason to even try. I saw a movie once where this fellow explained why he lit a candle in church even though he wasn't a very good Catholic anymore. 'You don't fuck around with the infinite,' he said. Maybe that was the lesson we learned.

"Every now and then there was another lightquake in Shed B. Sometimes just a little temblor, sometimes a great-gosh-a'mighty. But people have a really amazing capacity to get used to stuff, even stuff they don't understand. A comet shows up in the sky and half the world goes around bawling about the Last Days and the Four Horsemen, but let the comet stay there six months and no one even notices. It's a big ho-hum. Same thing happened at the end of the twentieth century, remember? Everyone ran around screaming that the sky was falling and all the computers were going to freeze up; a week goes by and it's business as usual. What I'm doing is trying to keep things in perspective for you. To—"

"Tell me about the fish," he said, and I felt that anger again. He wasn't going to hear all I had to say, no matter how much I wanted him to or how hard I tried. He'd hear the parts he wanted to hear and call it good. Think of it as the Teenage Disease. And the light in his eyes was like the light in his father's when Curt bent over the bat-thing with his scalpel in his gloved hand. (*Cutting now:* I sometimes still hear Curtis Wilcox saying that in my dreams.) Not *exactly* like it, though. Because the boy wasn't just curious. He was angry, as well. Pissed like a bear.

My own anger rose out of his refusal to take everything I wanted to give, for having the gall to pick and choose. But where did his come from? What was its center? That his mother had been lied to, not just once but over and over as the years passed? That he himself had been lied to, if only by omission? Was he mad at his father for holding onto a secret? Mad at us? *Us?* Surely he didn't believe the Buick had killed his father, why would he? Bradley Roach was safely on the hook for that, Roach had unspooled him up the side of a pulled-over sixteen-wheeler, leaving a bloodsmear ten feet long and as tall as a State Trooper, about six-feet-two in the case of Curtis Wilcox, pulling his clothes not just off but inside out as well in the scream of brakes and all the while the radio playing WPND, which billed itself Western Pennsylvania's Country-

Fried Radio, what else would it be but country with a half-drunk low rider like Bradley? Daddy sang bass and Momma sang tenor as the coins were ripped out of Curt Wilcox's pants and his penis was torn off like a weed and his balls were reduced to strawberry jelly and his comb and wallet landed on the yellow line; Bradley Roach responsible for all that, or maybe you wanted to save some blame for Dicky's Convenience in Statler that sold him the beer, or maybe for the the beer company itself with its goodtime ads about cute talking frogs and funny ballpark beer-men instead of dead people lying by the highway with their guts hanging out, or maybe you want to blame it on Bradley's DNA, little twists of cellular rope that had been whispering *Drink more, drink more* ever since Bradley's first sip (because some people are just wired up that way, which is to say like suitcase bombs ready to explode, which is absolutely zero comfort to the dead and wounded). Or maybe God was to blame, God's always a popular whipping boy because He doesn't talk back and never writes a column for the Op-Ed page. Not the Buick, though. Right? He couldn't find the Buick in Curt's death no matter how he traced it out. The Buick had been sitting miles away in Shed B, fat and luxy and blameless on whitewall tires that wouldn't take dirt or even the slightest pebble in the treads but repudiated them each and every one, right down to (as far as we could tell) the finest grain of sand. It was just sitting there and minding its business when Trooper Wilcox bled out on the side of Pennsylvania State Road 32. And if it was sitting there all the while in the faintest baleful reek of cabbage, what of that? Did this boy think—

"Ned, it didn't reach out for him, if that's what you're thinking," I said. "It doesn't do that." I had to laugh at myself a little, sounding so sure. Sounding as if I knew that for a fact. Or anything else for a fact, when it came to the Roadmaster. "It has pull, maybe even a kind of voice, when it's in one of its . . . I don't know . . ."

"Active phases," Shirley suggested.

"Yes. When it's in one of its active phases. You can hear the hum, and sometimes you can hear it in your head, as well . . . kind of calling . . . but could it reach out all the way to Highway 32 by the old Jenny station? No way."

Shirley was looking at me as if I'd gone slightly loopy, and I *felt* slightly loopy. What, exactly, was I doing? Trying to talk myself out of being angry at this unlucky, father-lost boy?

"Sandy? I just want to hear about the fish."

I looked at Huddie, then Phil and Eddie. All three offered variations of the same rueful shrug. *Kids! What are you gonna do?*

Finish it. That was what I was going to do. Set aside my anger and finish it. I had spilled the beans (I hadn't known how many beans there were in the bag when I started, I'll grant you that much), and now I was going to clean them up.

"All right, Ned. I'll tell you what you want to hear. But will you at least bear in mind that this place stayed a barracks? Will you try to remember that, whether you believe it or not, whether you *like* it or not, the Buick eventually became just another part of our day, like writing reports or testifying in court or cleaning puke off the floormats of a cruiser or Steve Devoe's Polish jokes? Because it's important."

"Sure. Tell me about the fish."

I leaned back against the wall and raised my eyes to the moon. I wanted to give him his life back if I could. Or stars in a paper cup. All that poetry. All *he* wanted to hear about was the goddamned fish.

So fuck it, I told him.

Then

No paper trail: that was Tony Schoondist's decree, and it was followed. People still knew how matters pertaining to the Buick were to be handled, though, what the proper channels were. It wasn't tough. One either reported to Curt, the Sarge, or to Sandy Dearborn. They were the Buick guys. Sandy supposed he'd become part of that triumvirate simply by virtue of having been present at the infamous autopsy. Certainly it wasn't because he had any special curiosity about the thing.

Tony's no-paper edict notwithstanding, Sandy was quite sure that Curt kept his own records—notes and speculations—about the Buick. If so, he was discreet about it. Meanwhile, the temperature drops and the energy discharges—the lightquakes—seemed to be slowing down. The life was draining out of the thing.

Or so they all hoped.

Sandy kept no notes and could never have provided a reliable sequence of events. The videotapes made over the years would have helped do that (if it ever needed doing), but there would still be gaps and questions. Not every lightquake was taped, and so what if they had been? They were all pretty much the same. There were probably a dozen between 1979 and 1983. Most were small. A couple were as big as the first one, and one was even bigger. That big one—the all-time champ—came in 1983. Those who were there sometimes still called '83 The Year of the Fish, as if they were Chinese.

Curtis made a number of experiments between '79 and '83, leaving various plants and animals in and around the Buick when the temperature dropped, but all the results were essentially reruns of what happened with Jimmy and Rosalynn. Which is to say sometimes things disappeared, and sometimes they didn't. There was no way of predicting in advance; it all seemed as random as a coin-toss.

During one temperature drop, Curt left a guinea pig by the Roadmaster's left front tire. Put it in a plastic bucket. Twenty-four hours after the purple fireworks were over and the temperature in the shed had gone back to normal, the guinea pig was still in his bucket, hopping and reasonably happy. Before another lightshow, Curt put a cage with two frogs in it directly under the Buick. There were still two frogs in the cage after the lightshow ended. A day later, however, there was only *one* frog in the cage.

A day after that, the cage was empty.

Then there was the Famous Trunk Experiment of 1982. That one was Tony's idea. He and Curt put six cockroaches in a clear plastic box, then put the box in the Buick's trunk. This was directly after one of the fireworks shows had ended, and it was still cold enough in the Buick so that they could see vapor coming out of their mouths when they bent into the trunk. Three days went by, with one of them checking the trunk every day (always with a rope tied around the waist of the one doing the checking, and everyone wondering what good a damn rope would do against something that had been able to snatch Jimmy out of his gerbil-condo without opening either of the hatches . . . or the frogs out of their latched cage, for that matter). The roaches were fine the first day, and the second, and the third. Curt and Tony went out on the fourth day to retrieve them, another failed experiment, back to the old drawing board. Only, the roaches were gone, or so it seemed when they first opened the trunk.

"No, wait!" Curt yelled. "There they are! I see em! Running around like mad bastards!"

"How many?" Tony called back. He was standing outside the door on the side of the shed, holding the end of the rope. "Are they all there? How'd they get out of the damn *box,* Curtis?"

Curtis counted only four instead of six, but that didn't mean much. Cockroaches don't need a bewitched automobile to help them disappear; they are quite good at that on their own, as anybody who's ever chased one with a slipper knows. As for how they'd gotten out of the plastic box, that much was obvious. It was still latched shut, but now there was a small round hole in one side of it. The hole was three-quarters of an inch across. To Curt and the Sarge, it looked like a large-caliber bullet-hole. There were no cracks radiating out from around it, which might also indicate that something had punched through at an extremely high velocity. Or perhaps *burned* through. No answers. Only mirages. Same as it ever was. And then the fish came, in June of 1983.

It had been at least two and a half years since Troop D had kept a day-in-and-out watch on the Buick, because by late 1979 or early 1980 they had decided that, with reasonable precautions, there wasn't much to worry about. A loaded gun is dangerous, no argument, but you don't have to post an around-the-clock guard on one to make sure it won't shoot by itself. If you put it up on a high shelf and keep the kiddies away, that's usually enough to do the trick.

Tony bought a vehicle tarp so anyone who came out back and happened to look in the shed wouldn't see the car and ask questions (in '81 a new fellow from the Motor Pool, a Buick-fancier, had once offered to buy it). The video camera stayed out in the hutch, mounted on its tripod and with a plastic bag pulled over it to keep it free of moisture, and the chair was still there (plus a good high stack of magazines beneath it), but Arky began to use the place more and more as a gardening shed. Bags of peat and fertilizer, pallets of sod, and flower-planters first began to crowd the Buick-watching stuff and then to crowd it out. The only time the hutch reverted to its original purpose was just before, during, and after one of the lightquakes.

June in The Year of the Fish was one of the most beautiful early summer months in Sandy's memory—the grass lush, the birds all in tune, the air filled with a kind of delicate heat, like a teenage couple's first real kiss. Tony Schoondist was on vacation, visiting his daughter on the West Coast (she was the one whose baby had caused all that trouble). The Sarge and his wife were trying to mend a few fences before they got broken down entirely. Probably not a bad plan. Sandy Dearborn and Huddie Royer were in charge while he was gone, but Curtis Wilcox—no longer a rookie—was boss of the Buick, no doubt about that. And one day in that marvelous June, Buck Flanders came to see him in that capacity.

"Temp's down in Shed B," he said.

Curtis raised his eyebrows. "Not exactly the first time, is it?"

"No," Buck admitted, "but I've never seen it go down so fast. Ten degrees since this morning."

That got Curt out to the shed in a hurry, with the old excited light in his eyes. When he put his face to one of the windows in the roll-up front door, the first thing he noticed was the tarp Tony had bought. It was crumpled along the driver's side of the Buick like a scuffed-up rug. It wasn't the first time for that, either; it was as if the Buick sometimes trembled (or shrugged) and slid the nylon cover off like a lady shrugging off an evening wrap by lifting her shoulders. The needle on the round thermometer stood at 61.

"It's seventy-four out here," Buck said. He was standing at Curt's elbow. "I checked the thermometer over by the bird-feeder before coming in to see you."

"So it's actually gone down *thirteen* degrees, not ten."

"Well, it was sixty-four in there when I came to get you. That's how fast it's going down. Like a . . . a cold front setting in, or something. Want me to get Huddie?"

"Let's not bother him. Make up a watch-roster. Get Matt Babicki to help you. Mark it . . . um, 'Car Wash Detail.' Let's get two guys watching the Buick the rest of the day, and tonight, as well. Unless Huddie says no or the temp bounces back up."

"Okay," Buck said. "Do you want to be on the first stand?"

Curt did, and quite badly—he sensed something was going to happen—but he shook his head. "Can't. I have court, then there's that truck-trap over in Cambria." Tony would have screamed and clutched his head if he had heard Curt call the weigh-in on Highway 9 a truck-trap, but essentially that was what it was. Because someone was moving heroin and cocaine from New Jersey over that way, and the thinking was that it was moving in some of the independent truckers' loads. "Truth is, I'm busier'n a one-legged man in an ass-kicking contest. Damn!"

He struck his thigh with his fist, then cupped his hands to the sides of his face and peered in through the glass again. There was nothing to see but the Roadmaster, sitting in two bars of sunlight that criss-crossed on the long dark blue hood like the contending beams of spot-lights.

"Get Randy Santerre. And didn't I see Chris Soder mooning around?"

"Yeah. He's technically off-duty, but his wife's two sisters are still visiting from over Ohio and he came here to watch TV." Buck lowered his voice. "Don't want to tell you your business, Curt, but I think both those guys are jagoffs."

"They'll do for this. They'll have to. Tell them I want regular reports, too. Standard Code D. And I'll call in by landline before I leave court."

Curt took a final, almost anguished look at the Buick, then started back to the barracks, where he would shave and get ready for the witness stand. In the afternoon he'd be poking in the backs of trucks along with some boys from Troop G, looking for coke and hoping nobody decided to unlimber an automatic weapon. He would have found someone to swap with if there had been time, but there wasn't.

Soder and Santerre got Buick-watching duty instead, and they didn't mind. Jagoffs never do. They stood beside the hutch, smoking, shooting the shit, taking the occasional look in at the Buick (Santerre too young to know what to expect, and he never lasted long in the PSP, anyway), telling jokes and enjoying the day. It was a June day so simple and so simply beautiful that even a jagoff couldn't help but enjoy it. At some point Buck Flanders spelled Randy Santerre; a little later on, Orville Garrett spelled Chris Soder. Huddie came out for the occasional peek. At three o'clock, when Sandy came in to drop his ass in the SC's chair, Curtis Wilcox finally got back and spelled Buck out by Shed B. Far from rebounding, the shed's temperature had rolled off another ten degrees by then, and off-duty Troopers began to clog the lot out back with their personal vehicles. Word had spread. Code D.

Around four P.M., Matt Babicki stuck his head into the SC's office and told Sandy he was losing the radio. "Bad static, boss. Worst ever."

"Shit." Sandy closed his eyes, rubbed his knuckles against them, and wished for Tony. This was his first time as acting Sergeant Commanding, and while the temporary bump in his paycheck at the end of the month would no doubt be satisfying, this aggravation was not. "Trouble with that goddam car. Just what I wanted."

"Don't take it to heart," Matt said. "It'll shoot off a few sparks and then everything'll go back to normal. Including the radio. Isn't that the way it usually goes?"

Yes, that was the way it usually went. Sandy was not, in truth, especially worried about the Buick. But what if someone out on patrol found trouble while communications were FUBAR? Someone who had to call in a 33—*Help me quick*—or a 47—*Send an ambulance*—or worst of all, a 10-99: *Officer down.* Sandy had well over a dozen guys out there, and at that moment it felt as if every one of them was riding him piggyback.

"Listen to me, Matt. Get in my ride—it's Unit 17—and take it down to the bottom of the hill. You should be clear of interference there. Call every one of ours currently running the roads and tell them base dispatch is temporarily 17. Code D."

"Aw, Sandy, Jesus! Isn't that a little—"

"I don't have time to listen to your imitation of *Siskel and Ebert at the Movies* just now," Sandy said. He had never felt more impatient with Police Communications Officer Babicki's whiny brand of foot-dragging bullshit than he did then. "Just do it."

"But I won't be here to see—"

"No, probably you won't." Sandy's voice rising a little now. "That's one you'll absolutely have to put on your TS list before you send it to the chaplain."

Matt started to say something else, took a closer look at Sandy's face, and wisely decided to keep his mouth shut. Two minutes later, Sandy saw him headed down the hill, behind the wheel of Unit 17.

"Good," Sandy muttered. "Stay there awhile, you little backtalking pissant."

Sandy went out to Shed B, where there was quite a little crowd. Most of them were Troopers, but some were Motor Pool guys in the grease-stained green Dickies that were their unofficial uniform. After four years of living with the Buick, none of them were afraid, exactly, but they were a rather nervy group that day, just the same. When you saw twenty degrees roll off the thermometer on a warm summer day, in a room where the air conditioning consisted of an occasionally opened door, it was hard not to believe that something large was in the works.

Curt had been back long enough to set up a number of experiments—all he had time to arrange, Sandy guessed. On the Buick's front seat he'd placed a Nike sneaker box with some crickets in it. The frog cage was on the back seat. There was only one frog in it this time, but it was a whopper, one of those marsh bullfrogs with the bulgy yellow-black eyes. He had also taken the windowbox of flowers which had been outside Matt Babicki's office window and stuck them in the Buick's trunk. Last but not least, he took Mister Dillon for a promenade out there, toured him all around the car on his leash, the full three-sixty, just to see what would happen. Orvie Garrett didn't like that much, but Curt talked him into it. In most respects Curt was still a little rough around the edges and a little wet behind the ears, but when it came to the Buick, he could be as smooth as a riverboat gambler.

Nothing happened during D's walk—not that time—but it was clear the Troop mascot would rather have been just about anywhere else. He hung at the end of his leash so hard it choked him a little, and he walked with his head down and his tail lowered, giving the occasional dry cough. He looked at the Buick, but he looked at everything else out there as well, as if whatever it was he didn't like had spread out from the bogus car until it contaminated the whole shed.

When Curt brought him outside again and handed the leash back to Orville, he said, "There's something going on, he feels it and so do I. But it's not like before." He saw Sandy and repeated it: not like before.

"No," Sandy said, then nodded at Mister D. "At least he's not howling."

"Not yet," Orville said. "Come on, D, let's go back in the barracks. You did good. I'll give you a Bonz." What Orvie gave Curt was a final reproachful look. Mister Dillon trotted neatly at Trooper Garrett's right knee, no longer needing the leash to keep him at heel.

At four-twenty or so, the TV upstairs in the common room suddenly went goofy. By four-forty, the temperature in Shed B had dropped to forty-nine degrees. At four-fifty, Curtis Wilcox shouted: "It's starting! I hear it!"

Sandy had been inside to check on dispatch (and what a snafu it was by then, nothing but one big balls-to-the-wall roar of static), and when Curt yelled he was returning across the parking lot, where there were now so many personals you would have thought it was the Police Benefit Rummage Sale or the Muscular Dystrophy Kids' Carnival they put on each July. Sandy broke into a run, cutting through the knot of spectators craning to look in through the side door, which was still, unbelievably, standing wide open. And Curt was there, standing in it. Waves of cold were rolling out, but he seemed not to feel them. His eyes were huge, and when he turned to Sandy he was like a man dreaming. "Do you see it? Sandy, *do you see it?*"

Of course he did: a waxing violet glow that was spilling out of the car's windows and seeping up through the crack which outlined the trunk-lid and went spilling down the Buick's sides like some thin radioactive fluid. Inside the car Sandy could clearly see the shapes of the seats and the oversized steering wheel. They were outlines, silhouettes. The rest of the cabin was swallowed in a cold purple glare, brighter than any furnace. The hum was loud and getting louder. It made Sandy's skull ache, made his ears almost wish they were deaf. Not that being deaf would do any good, because you seemed to hear that sound not just with your ears but with your whole body.

Sandy yanked Curt out onto the pavement, then grabbed the knob, meaning to shut the door. Curt took hold of his wrist. "No, Sandy, no! I want to see it! I want—"

Sandy peeled his hand off, not gently. "Are you crazy? There's a procedure we follow on this, a goddam *procedure.* No one should know that better than you! You helped think it up, for God's sake!"

When Sandy slammed the door shut, cutting off any direct view of the Buick, Curt's eyelids fluttered and he twitched like a man waking out of a deep sleep. "Okay," he said. "Okay, boss. I'm sorry."

"It's all right." Not really believing it was. Because the damned fool would have stood right there in the doorway. No question about it in Sandy's mind. Would have stood there and been fried, if frying was on that thing's agenda.

"I need to get my goggles," Curt said. "They're in the trunk of my car. I have extras, and they're extra dark. A whole box of them. Do you want a pair?" Sandy still got the feeling that Curt wasn't fully awake, that he was only pretending, like you did when the telephone rang in the middle of the night.

"Sure, why not? But we're going to be cautious, right? Because this is looking like a bad one."

"Looking like a *great* one!" he said, and the exuberance in his voice, although slightly scary, made Sandy feel a little better. At least Curt didn't sound as if he was sleepwalking any longer. "But yes, Mother— we'll follow procedure and be as cautious as hell."

He ran for his car—not his cruiser but his personal, the restored Bel Air—and opened the trunk. He was still rummaging in the boxes of stuff he kept back there when the Buick exploded.

It did not literally explode, but there seemed to be no other word for what it *did* do. Those who were there that day never forgot it, but they talked about it remarkably little, even among themselves, because there seemed no way to express the terrifying magnificence of it. The *power* of it. The best they could say was that it darkened the June sun and seemed to turn the shed transparent, into a ghost of itself. It was impossible to comprehend how mere glass could stand between that light and the outside world. The throbbing brilliance poured through the boards of the shed like water through cheesecloth; the shapes of the nails stood out like the dots in a newspaper photograph or purple beads of blood on top of a fresh tattoo. Sandy heard Carl Brundage shout *She's gonna blow this time, she most surely will!* From behind him, in the barracks, he could hear Mister Dillon howling in terror.

"But he still wanted to get out and get at it," Orville told Sandy later. "I had im in the upstairs lounge, as far from that goddam shed as I could get him, but it didn't make any difference. He knew it was there. Heard it, I imagine—heard it humming. And then he saw the window. Holy Christ! If I hadn't been quick, hadn't grabbed him right off, I think he would have jumped right through it, second story or not. He pissed all over me and I never realized it until half an hour later, that's how scared *I* was."

Orville shook his head, his face heavy and thoughtful.

"Never seen a dog like that. *Never.* His fur was all bushed out, he was foamin at the mouth, and his eyeballs looked like they were poppin right out of his head. *Christ.*"

Curt, meanwhile, came running back with a dozen pairs of protective goggles. The Troopers put them on but there was still no way of looking in at the Buick; it was impossible to even approach the windows. And again there was that weird silence when they all felt they should have been standing at the center of a cacophony, hearing thunder and land-slides and erupting volcanoes. With the shed's doors shut, they (unlike Mister D) couldn't even hear the humming noise. There was the shuffle of feet and someone clearing his throat and Mister Dillon howling in the barracks and Orvie Garrett telling him to calm down and the sound of Matt Babicki's static-drowned radio from dispatch, where the window (now denuded of its flower box, thanks to Curt) had been left open. Nothing else.

Curt walked to the roll-up door, head bent and hands raised. Twice he tried to lift his face and look inside Shed B, but he couldn't. It was too bright. Sandy grabbed his shoulder.

"Quit trying to look. You can't do it. Not yet, anyway. It'll knock the eyes right out of your head."

"What is it, Sandy?" he whispered. "What in God's name is it?"

Sandy could only shake his head.

For the next half hour the Buick put on the lightshow to end all light-shows, turning Shed B into a kind of fireball, shooting parallel lines of brilliance through all the windows, flashing and flashing, a gaudy neon furnace without heat or sound. If anyone from John Q. Public's family had turned up during that time, God knew what they might have thought or who they would have told or how much those they told might have believed, but no outsiders *did* turn up. And by five-thirty, the D Troopers had started to see individual flashes of light again, as if the power-source driving the phenomenon had begun to wobble. It made Sandy think of the way a motorcycle will lurch and spurt when the gas-tank is almost dry.

Curt edged up to the windows again, and although he had to duck down each time one of those bolts of light shot out, he could take little peeks in between. Sandy joined him, ducking away from the brighter pulses (*We probably look like we're practicing some weird drill routine,* he thought), squinting, eyes dazzled in spite of the triple layer of polarized glass in the goggles.

The Buick was still perfectly intact and apparently unchanged. The tarp lay in its same draped dune, unsinged by any fire. Arky's tools hung undisturbed on their pegs, and the stacks of old County *American* newspapers were still in the far corner, bundled and tied with twine. A single kitchen match would have been enough to turn those dry piles of old news into pillars of flame, but all that brilliant purple light hadn't charred so much as a single corner of a single Bradlee's circular.

"Sandy—can you see any of the specimens?"

Sandy shook his head, stood back, and took off the goggles Curt had loaned him. He passed them on to Andy Colucci, who was wild for a look into the shed. Sandy himself headed back to the barracks. Shed B was not going to blow up after all, it seemed. And he was the acting SC, with a job to do.

On the back step, he paused and looked back. Even wearing goggles, Andy Colucci and the others were reluctant to approach the row of windows. There was only one exception, and that was Curtis Wilcox. He stood right there—big as Billy-be-damned, Sandy's mother might have said—as close as he could get and leaning forward to get even closer, goggles actually pressed to the glass, only turning his head aside slightly each time the thing flashed out an especially bright bolt, which it was still doing every twenty seconds or so.

Sandy thought, *He's apt to put his eyes out, or at least go snowblind from it.* Except he wouldn't. He seemed to have almost timed the flashes, to have gotten in rhythm with them. From where Sandy was, it looked as if Curtis was actually turning his face aside a second or two before each flash came. And when it did come he would for a moment become his own exclamatory shadow, an exotic frozen dancer caught against a great sheet of purple light. Looking at him that way was scary. To Sandy it was like watching something that was there and not there at the same time, real but not real, both solid and mirage. Sandy would later think that when it came to the Buick 8, Curt was oddly like Mister Dillon. He wasn't howling like the dog was, upstairs in the common room, but he seemed in touch with the thing just the same, in sync with it. *Dancing* with it: then and later, that was how it would come back to Sandy.

Dancing with it.

At ten minutes of six that evening, Sandy radioed down the hill to Matt and asked what was up. Matt said nothing (*Nothing, Gramma* was what Sandy heard in his tone), and Sandy told him to come on back to base. When he did, Sandy said he was free to step across the parking lot and have a look at Old 54, if he still wanted one. Matt was gone like a shot. When he came back a few minutes later, he looked disappointed.

"I've seen it do *that* before," he said, leaving Sandy to reflect on how dense and thankless human beings were, for the most part; how quickly their senses dulled, rendering the marvelous mundane. "All the guys said it really blew its stack an hour ago, but none of them could describe it." This was said with a contempt Sandy didn't find surprising. In the world of the police communications officer, *everything* is describable; the world's cartography must and can be laid out in ten-codes.

"Well, don't look at *me*," Sandy said. "I can tell you one thing, though. It was bright."

"Oh. Bright." Matt gave him a look that said *Not just a gramma but a loser gramma.* Then he went back inside.

By seven o'clock, Troop D's TV reception (always an important consideration when you were off the road) had returned to normal. Dispatch communications were back to normal. Mister Dillon had eaten his usual big bowl of Gravy Train and then hung out in the kitchen, trolling for scraps, so *he* was back to normal. And when Curt poked his head into the SC's office at seven forty-five to tell Sandy he wanted to go into the shed and check on his specimens, Sandy could think of no way to stop him. Sandy was in charge of Troop D that evening, no argument there, but when it came to the Buick, Curt had as much authority as he did, maybe even a little more. Also, Curt was already wearing the damn yellow rope around his waist. The rest was looped over his fore-arm in a coil.

"Not a good idea," Sandy told him. That was about as close to no as he could get.

"Bosh." It was Curtis's favorite word in 1983. Sandy hated it. He thought it was a snotty word.

He looked over Curt's shoulder and saw they were alone. "Curtis," he said, "you've got a wife at home, and the last time we talked about her, you said she might be pregnant. Has that changed?"

"No, but she hasn't been to the—"

"So you've got a wife for sure and a maybe baby. And if she's not preg this time, she probably will be next time. That's nice. It's just the way it should be. What I don't understand is why you'd put all that on the line for that goddam Buick."

"Come on, Sandy—I put it on the line every time I get into a cruiser and go out on the road. Every time I step out and approach. It's true of everyone who works the job."

"This is different and we both know it, so you can quit the high school debate crap. Don't you remember what happened to Ennis?"

"I remember," he said, and Sandy supposed he did, but Ennis Rafferty had been gone almost four years by then. He was, in a way, as out-of-date as the stacks of County *Americans* in Shed B. And as for more recent developments? Well, the frogs had just been frogs. Jimmy might have been named after a President, but he was really just a gerbil. And Curtis was wearing the rope. The rope was supposed to make everything all right. *Sure,* Sandy thought, *and no toddler wearing a pair of water-wings ever drowned in a swimming pool.* If he said that to Curt, would Curtis laugh? No. Because Sandy was sitting in the big chair that night, the acting SC, the visible symbol of the PSP. But Sandy thought he would see laughter in Curt's eyes, just the same. Curtis had forgotten the rope had never been tested, that if the force hiding inside the Buick decided it wanted him, there might be a single last flash of purple light and then nothing but a length of yellow line lying on the cement floor with an empty loop at the end of it; so long, partner, happy trails to you, one more curious cat off hunting satisfaction in the big nowhere. But Sandy couldn't order him to stand down as he'd ordered Matt Babicki to drive down the hill. All he could do was get into an argument with him, and it was no good arguing with a man who had that bright and twirly let's-play-Bingo look in his eyes. You could cause plenty of hard feelings, but you could never convince the other guy that you had the right side of the argument.

"You want me to hold the other end of the rope?" Sandy asked him. "You came in here wanting something, and it surely wasn't my opinion."

"Would you?" He grinned. "I'd like that."

Sandy went out with him, and he held the rope with most of the coil snubbed around his elbow and Dicky-Duck Eliot standing behind him, ready to grab his belt loops if something happened and Sandy started to slide. The acting SC, standing in the side doorway of Shed B, not braced but ready to brace if something funny happened, biting his lower lip and breathing just a little too fast. His pulse felt like maybe a hundred and twenty beats a minute. He could still feel the chill in the shed even though the thermometer was by then easing its way back up; in Shed B, early summer had been revoked and what one met at the door was the dank cold of a hunting camp when you arrive in November, the stove in the middle of the room as dead as an unchurched god. Time slowed to a crawl. Sandy opened his mouth to ask Curt if he was going to stay in there forever, then glanced down at his watch and saw only forty seconds had passed. He did tell Curt not to go around to the far side of the Buick. Too much chance of snagging the rope.

"And Curtis? When you open the trunk, stand clear!"

"Roger that." He sounded almost amused, indulgent, like a kid promising Mother and Dad that no, he *won't* speed, he *won't* take a drink at the party, he *will* watch out for the other guy, oh gosh yes, of course, you bet. Anything to keep them happy long enough to get the Christ out of the house, and then . . . *yeeeeeee-HAW!*

He opened the driver's door of the Buick and leaned in past the steering wheel. Sandy braced again for the pull he more than half-expected, the *yank.* He must have communicated the feeling backward, because he felt Dicky grab his belt loops. Curt reached, reached, and then stood up holding the shoebox with the crickets inside. He peered through the holes. "Looks like they're all still there," he said, sounding a little disappointed.

"You'd think they'd be roasted," Dicky-Duck said. "All that fire."

But there had been no fire, just light. There wasn't a single scorchmark on the shed's walls, they could see the thermometer's needle standing in the fifties, and electing not to believe that number wasn't much of an option, not with the shed's dank chill pushing into their faces. Still, Sandy knew how Dicky-Duck Eliot felt. When your head was still pounding from the dazzle and the last of the afterimages still seemed to be dancing in front of your eyes, it was hard to believe that a bunch of crickets sitting on ground zero could come through unscathed.

Yet they had. Every single one of them, as it turned out. So did the bullfrog, except its yellow-black eyes had gone cloudy and dull. It was present and accounted for, but when it hopped, it hopped right into the wall of its cage. It had gone blind.

Curt opened the trunk and moved back from it all in the same gesture, a move almost like ballet and one most policemen know. Sandy braced in the doorway again, hands fisted on the slack rope, ready for it to go taut. Dicky-Duck once more snagged a tight hold on his belt loops. And again there was nothing.

Curt leaned into the trunk.

"Cold in here," he called. His voice sounded hollow, oddly distant. "And I'm getting that smell—the cabbage smell. Also peppermint. And . . . wait . . ."

Sandy waited. When nothing came, he called Curt's name.

"I think it's salt," Curt said. "Like the ocean, almost. This is the center of it, the vortex, right here in the trunk. I'm sure of it."

"I don't care if it's the Lost Dutchman Mine," Sandy told him. "I want you out of there. Now."

"Just a second more." He leaned deep into the trunk. Sandy almost expected him to jerk forward as if something was pulling him, Curt Wilcox's idea of a knee-slapper. Perhaps he thought of it, but in the end he knew better. He simply got Matt Babicki's windowbox and pulled it out. He turned and held it up so Sandy and Dicky could see. The flowers looked fine and blooming. They were dead a couple of days later, but there was nothing very supernatural about that; they had been frozen in the trunk of the car as surely as they would have been if Curtis had put them in the freezer for awhile.

"Are you done yet?" Sandy was even starting to sound like Old Gammer Dearborn to himself, but he couldn't help it.

"Yeah. Guess so." Curtis sounding disappointed. Sandy jumped when he slammed the Buick's trunk-lid back down, and Dick's fingers tightened on the back of his pants. Sandy had an idea ole Dicky-Duck had come pretty close to yanking him right out the doorway and onto his ass in the parking lot. Curt, meantime, walked slowly toward them with the frog cage, the sneaker box, and the windowbox stacked up in his arms. Sandy kept coiling up the rope as he came so Curt wouldn't trip over it.

When they were all outside again, Dicky took the cage and looked wonderingly at the blind bullfrog. "That beats everything," he said.

Curt slipped out of the loop around his waist, then knelt on the macadam and opened the shoebox. Four or five other Troopers had gathered around by then. The crickets hopped out almost as soon as Curt took the lid off the box, but not before both Curtis and Sandy had a chance to take attendance. Eight, the number of cylinders in yonder Buick's useless engine. Eight, the same number of crickets that had gone in.

Curt looked disgusted and disappointed. "Nothing," he said. "In the end, that's what it always comes to. If there's a formula—some binomial theorem or quadratic equation or something like that—I don't see it."

"Then maybe you better give it a pass," Sandy said.

Curt lowered his head and watched the crickets go hopping across the parking lot, widening out from each other, going their separate ways, and no equation or theorem ever invented by any mathematician who ever breathed could predict where any single one of them might end up. They were Chaos Theory hopping. The goggles were still hung around Curt's neck on their elastic strap. He fingered them for a few moments, then glanced at Sandy. His mouth was set. The disappointed look had gone out of his eyes. The other one, the half-crazed let's-play-Bingo-until-the-money's-all-gone look, had come back to take its place.

"Don't think I'm ready to do that," he said. "There must be . . ."

Sandy gave him a chance, and when Curtis didn't finish, he asked: "There must be what?"

But Curtis only shook his head, as if he could not say. Or would not.

Three days went by. They waited for another bat-thing or another cyclone of leaves, but there was nothing immediate in the wake of the lightshow; the Buick just sat there. Troop D's piece of Pennsylvania was quiet, especially on the second shift, which suited Sandy Dearborn right down to the ground. One more day and he'd be off for two. Huddie's turn to run the show again. Then, when Sandy came back, Tony Schoondist would be in the big chair, where he belonged. The temperature in Shed B still hadn't equalized with the temperature of the outside world, but was getting there. It had risen into the low sixties, and Troop D had come to think of the sixties as safe territory.

For the first forty-eight hours after the monster lightquake, they'd kept someone out there around the clock. After twenty-four uneventful hours, some of the men had started grumbling about putting in the extra time, and Sandy couldn't much blame them. It was uncompensated time, of course. Had to be. How could they have sent Overtime Reports for Shed B–watching to Scranton? What would they have put in the space marked REASON FOR OVERTIME ACTIVITY (SPECIFY IN FULL)?

Curt Wilcox wasn't crazy about dropping the full-time surveillance, but he understood the realities of the situation. In a brief conference, they decided on a week's worth of spot checks, most to be performed by Troopers Dearborn and Wilcox. And if Tony didn't like that when he got back from sunny California, he could change it.

So now comes eight o'clock of a summer evening right around the time of the solstice, the sun not down but sitting red and bloated on the Short Hills, casting the last of its long and longing light. Sandy was in the office, beavering away at the weekend duty roster, that big chair fitting him pretty well just then. There were times when he could imagine himself sitting in it more or less permanently, and that summer evening was one of them. *I think I could do this job:* that was what was going through his mind as George Morgan rolled up the driveway in

199

Unit D-11. Sandy raised his hand to George and grinned when George ticked a little salute off the brim of his big hat in return: right-back-atcha.

George was on patrol that shift, but happened to be close by and so came in to gas up. By the nineties, Pennsylvania State Troopers would no longer have that option, but in 1983 you could still pump your go-juice at home and save the state a few pennies. He put the pump on slow automatic and strolled over to Shed B for a peek.

There was a light on inside (they always left it on) and there it was, the Troop D bonus baby, Old 54, sitting quiet with its chrome gleaming, looking as if it had never eaten a State Trooper, blinded a frog, or produced a freak bat. George, still a few years from his personal finish-line (two cans of beer and then the pistol in the mouth, jammed way up in back past the soft palate, not taking any chances, when a cop decides to do it he or she almost always gets it right), stood at the roll-up door as they all did from time to time, adopting the stance they all seemed to adopt, kind of loose and spraddle-legged like a sidewalk superintendent at a city building site, hands on hips (Pose A) or crossed on the chest (Pose B) or cupped to the sides of the face if the day was especially bright (Pose C). It's a stance that says the sidewalk superintendent in question is a man with more than a few of the answers, an expert gent with plenty of time to discuss taxes or politics or the haircuts of the young.

George had his look and was just about to turn away when all at once there was a thud from in there, toneless and heavy. This was followed by a pause (long enough, he told Sandy later, for him to think he'd imagined the sound in the first place) and then there was a second thud. George saw the Buick's trunk-lid move up and down in the middle, just once, quick. He started for the side door, meaning to go in and investigate. Then he recalled what he was dealing with, a car that sometimes ate people. He stopped, looked around for someone else—for backup—and saw no one. There's never a cop around when you need one. He considered going into the shed by himself anyway, thought of Ennis—four years and still not home for lunch—and ran for the barracks instead.

*   *   *

"Sandy, you better come." George standing in the doorway, looking scared and out of breath. "I think maybe one of these idiots may have locked some other idiot in the trunk of that fucking nuisance in Shed B. Like for a joke."

Sandy stared at him, thunderstruck. Unable (or perhaps unwilling) to believe that *anyone,* even that dope Santerre, could do such a thing. Except people could, he knew it. He knew something else, as well— incredible as it might seem, in many cases they meant no harm.

George mistook the acting SC's surprise for disbelief. "I might be wrong, but honest-to-God I'm not pulling your chain. Something's thumping the lid of the trunk. *From the inside.* Sounds like with his fist. I started to go in on my own, then changed my mind."

"That was the right call," Sandy said. "Come on."

They hurried out, stopping just long enough so Sandy could look in the kitchen and then bawl upstairs to the common room. No one. The barracks was never deserted, but it was deserted now, and why? Because there was never a cop around when you needed one, that was why. Herb Avery was running dispatch that night, at least that was one, and he joined them.

"Want me to call someone in off the road, Sandy? I can, if you want."

"No." Sandy was looking around, trying to remember where he'd last seen the coil of rope. In the hutch, probably. Unless some yo-yo had taken it home to haul something upstairs with, which would be just about par for the course. "Come on, George."

The two of them crossed the parking lot in the red sunset light, their trailing shadows all but infinite, going first to the roll-up door for a little look-see. The Buick sat there as it had ever since old Johnny Parker dragged it in behind his tow-truck (Johnny now retired and getting through his nights with an oxygen tank beside his bed—but still smoking). It cast its own shadow on the concrete floor.

Sandy started to turn away, meaning to check the hutch for the rope, and just as he did there came another thump. It was strong and flat and unemphatic. The trunk-lid shivered, dimpled up in the middle for a moment, then went back down. It looked to Sandy as if the Road-master actually rocked a little bit on its springs.

"There! You see?" George said. He started to add something else, and that was when the Buick's trunk came unlatched and the lid sprang up on its hinges and the fish fell out.

Of course, it was a fish no more than the bat-thing was a bat, but they both knew at once it was nothing made to live on land; it had not one gill on the side they could see but four of them in a line, parallel slashes in its skin, which was the color of dark tarnished silver. It had a ragged and membranous tail. It unfolded out of the trunk with a last convulsive, dying shiver. Its bottom half curved and flexed, and Sandy could see how it might have made that thumping sound. Yes, that was clear enough, but how a thing of such size could ever have fit into the closed trunk of the Buick in the first place was beyond both of them. What hit the concrete floor of Shed B with a flat wet slap was the size of a sofa.

George and Sandy clutched each other like children and screamed. For a moment they *were* children, with every adult thought driven out of their heads. Somewhere inside the barracks, Mister Dillon began to bark.

It lay there on the floor, no more a fish than a wolf is a housepet, although it may look quite a bit like a dog. And in any case, *this* fish was only a fish up to the purple slashes of its gills. Where a fish's head would have been—something that at least had the steadying sanity of eyes and a mouth—there was a knotted, naked mass of pink things, too thin and stiff to be tentacles, too thick to be hair. Each was tipped with a black node and Sandy's first coherent thought was *A shrimp, the top half of it's some kind of shrimp and those black things are its eyes.*

"What's wrong?" someone bawled. "What is it?"

Sandy turned and saw Herb Avery on the back step. His eyes were wild and he had his Ruger in his hand. Sandy opened his mouth and at first nothing came out but a phlegmy little wheeze. Beside him, George hadn't even turned; he was still looking through the window, mouth hanging slack in an idiot's gape.

Sandy took a deep breath and tried again. What was meant for a shout emerged as a faint punched-in-the-belly wheeze, but at least it was something. "Everything's okay, Herb—five-by-five. Go back inside."

"Then why did you—"

"Go inside!" *There, that's a little better,* Sandy thought. "Go on, now, Herb. And holster that piece."

Herb looked down at the gun as if unaware until then that he had drawn it. He put it back in his holster, looked at Sandy as if to ask was he sure. Sandy made little flapping gestures with his hands and thought, *Granny Dearborn says go back inside, dad-rattit!*

Herb went, yelling for Mister D to shut up that foolish barking as he did.

Sandy turned back to George, who had gone white. "It was breathing, Sandy—or trying to. The gills were moving and the side was going up and down. Now it's stopped." His eyes were huge, like the eyes of a child who has been in a car accident. "I think it's dead." His lips were quivering. "Man, I *hope* it's dead."

Sandy looked in. At first he was sure George was wrong: the thing was still alive. Still breathing, or trying to breathe. Then he realized what he was seeing and told George to get the videocam out of the hutch.

"What about the r—"

"We won't need the rope, because we're not going in there—not yet, we're not—but get the camera. Fast as you can."

George went around the side of the garage, not moving very well. Shock had made him gawky. Sandy looked back into the shed, cupping his eyes to the sides of his face to cut the red sunset glare. There was motion in the shed, all right, but not life's motion. It was mist rising from the thing's silver side and also from the purple slashes of its gills. The bat-thing hadn't decomposed, but the leaves had, and quickly. This thing was starting to rot like the leaves, and Sandy had the feeling that once the process really got going, it would go fast.

Even standing outside, with the closed door between him and it, he could smell it. An acrid, watery reek of mixed cabbage and cucumber and salt, the smell of a broth you might feed to someone if you wanted to make them sicker instead of well.

More mist was rising from its side; it dribbled up from the nest of tangled pink ropes that seemed to serve as its head, as well. Sandy thought he could hear a faint hissing noise, but knew he could just as well be imagining it. Then a black slit appeared in the grayish-silver scales, running north from the tattered nylon of its tail to the rearmost gill. Black fluid, probably the same stuff Huddie and Arky had found around the bat-thing's corpse, began to trickle out—listlessly at first, then with a little more spirit. Sandy could see an ominous bulge developing behind the split in the skin. It was no hallucination, and neither was the hissing sound. The fish was doing something more radical than decomposing; it was *giving in.* Yielding to the change in pressure or perhaps the change in everything, its whole environment. He thought of something he'd read once (or maybe seen in a *National Geographic* TV special), about how when some deep-sea creatures were brought up from their dwelling places, they simply exploded.

"George!" Bawling at the top of his lungs. *"Hurry the hell up!"*

George flew back around the corner of the shed, holding the tripod way up high, where the aluminum legs came together. The lens of the videocam glared above his fist, looking like a drunk's eyeball in the day's declining red light.

"I couldn't get it off the tripod," he panted. "There's some kind of latch or lock and if I'd had time to figure it out—or maybe I was trying to turn the Christly thing backward—"

"Never mind." Sandy snatched the videocam from him. There was no problem with the tripod, anyway; the legs had been adjusted to the height of the windows in the shed's two roll-up doors for years. The problem came when Sandy pushed the ON button and looked through the viewfinder. Instead of a picture, there were just red letters reading LO BAT.

"Judas-fucking-Iscariot on a chariot-driven crutch! Go back, George. Look on the shelf by the box of blank tapes, there's another battery there. Get it."

"But I want to see—"

"I don't care! Go on!"

He went, running hard. His hat had gone askew on his head, giving him a weirdly jaunty look. Sandy pushed the RECORD button on the side of the camera's housing, not knowing what he'd get but hoping for something. When he looked into the viewfinder again, however, even the letters reading LO BAT were fading.

Curt's going to kill me, he thought.

He looked back through the shed window just in time to catch the nightmare. The thing ruptured all the way up its side, spilling out that black ichor not in trickles but in a flood. It spread across the floor like backflow from a clogged drain. Following it came a noisome spew of guts: flabby bags of yellowish-red jelly. Most of them split and began to steam as soon as the air hit them.

Sandy turned, the back of his hand pressed hard against his mouth until he was sure he wasn't going to vomit, and then he yelled: "Herb! If you still want a look, now's your chance! Quick as you can!"

Why getting Herb Avery on-scene should have been the first thing he thought of, Sandy could not later say. At the time, however, it seemed perfectly reasonable. If he had called his dead mother's name, he would have been equally unsurprised. Sometimes one's mind simply passes beyond one's rational and logical control. Right then he wanted Herb. Dispatch is never to be left unattended, it's a rule anyone in rural law enforcement knows, the Fabled Automatic. But rules were made to be broken, and Herb would never see anything like this again in his life, none of them would, and if Sandy couldn't have videotape, he would at least have a witness. Two, if George got back in time.

Herb came out fast, as if he had been standing right inside the back door and watching through the screen all along, and sprinted across the nearly empty parking lot in the red light. His face was both scared and avid. Just as he arrived, George steamed back around the corner, waving a fresh battery for the video camera. He looked like a gameshow contestant who has just won the grand prize.

"Oh Mother, what's that smell?" Herb asked, clapping his hand over his mouth and nose so that everything after *Mother* came out muffled.

"The smell isn't the worst," Sandy said. "You better get a look while you still can."

They both looked, and uttered almost identical cries of revulsion. The fish was blown out all down its length by then, and deflating—sinking into the black liquor of its own strange blood. White billows rose from its body and the innards which had already spilled from that gaping flayment. The vapor was as thick as smoke rising from a pile of smoldering

205

damp mulch. It obscured the Buick from its open trunk forward until Old 54 was nothing but a ghost-car.

If there had been more to see, Sandy might actually have fumbled longer with the camera, perhaps getting the battery in wrongways on the first try or even knocking the whole works over and breaking it in his fumble-fingered haste. The fact that there was going to be damned little to tape no matter how fast he worked had a calming effect, and he snapped the battery home on the first try. When he looked into the viewfinder again, he had a clear, bright view of not much: a disappearing amphibious thing that might have been a fabulous landlocked sea monster or just a fishy version of the Cardiff Giant sitting on a concealed block of dry ice. On the tape one can see the pink tangle that served as the amphibian's head quite clearly for perhaps ten seconds, and a number of rapidly liquefying red lumps strewn along its length; one can see what appears to be filthy seafoam sweating out of the thing's tail and running across the concrete in a sluggish rill. Then the creature that convulsed its bulk out of the Roadmaster's trunk is mostly gone, no more than a shadow in the mist. The car itself is hardly there. Even in the mist, however, the open trunk is visible, and it looks like a gaping mouth. Come closer, all good little children, come closer, see the living crocodile.

George stepped away, gagging and shaking his head.

Sandy thought again of Curtis, who for a change had left as soon as his shift was over. He and Michelle had big plans—dinner at The Cracked Platter in Harrison, followed by a movie. The meal would be over by now and they'd be at the show. Which one? There were three within striking distance. If there had been kids instead of just a maybe baby, Sandy could have called the house and asked the sitter. But would he have made that call? Maybe not. Probably not, in fact. Curt had begun to settle a bit over the last eighteen months or so, and Sandy hoped that settling would continue. He had heard Tony say on more than one occasion that when it came to the PSP (or any law enforcement agency worth its salt), one could best assess a man's worth by the truthful answer to a single question: How are things at home? It wasn't just that the job was dangerous; it was also a *crazy* job, full of opportunities to see people at their absolute worst. To do it well over a long period of time, to do it *fairly,* a cop needed an anchor. Curt had Michelle, and now he had the baby (maybe). It would be better if he didn't go bolting off to the barracks unless he absolutely had to, especially when he had to lie about the reason. A wife could swallow only so many rabid fox-tales and unexpected changes in the duty roster. He'd be angry that he hadn't been called, angrier still when he saw the bitched-up videotape, but Sandy would deal with that. He'd have to. And Tony would be back. Tony would help him deal with it.

The following day was cool, with a fresh breeze. They rolled up Shed B's big doors and let the place air out for six hours or so. Then four Troopers, led by Sandy and a stony-faced Trooper Wilcox, went in with hoses. They cleaned off the concrete and washed the final decaying lumps of the fish out into the tall grass behind the shed. It was really the story of the bat all over again, only with more mess and less to show at the end of the day. In the end it was more about Curtis Wilcox and Sandy Dearborn than it was about the ruins of that great unknown fish.

Curt was indeed furious at not having been called, and the two law enforcement officers had an extremely lively discussion on that subject—and others—when they had gotten to a place where no one else on the roster could possibly overhear. This turned out to be the parking lot behind The Tap, where they had gone for a beer after the clean-up operation was finished. In the bar it was just talking, but once outside, their voices started to climb. Pretty soon they were both trying to talk at the same time, and of course that led to shouting. It almost always does.

Man, I can't believe you didn't call me.

You were off-duty, you were out with your wife, and besides, there was nothing to see.

I wish you'd let me decide—

There wasn't—

—decide that, Sandy—

—any time! It all happened—

Least you could have done was get some half-decent video for the file—

Whose file are we talking about, Curtis? Huh? Whose goddam file?

By then the two of them standing nose to nose, fists clenched, almost down to it. Yes, really on the verge of getting down to it. There are moments in a life that don't matter and moments that do and some—maybe a dozen—when everything is on a hinge. Standing there in the parking lot, wanting to sock the kid who was no longer a kid, the rookie who was no longer a rookie, Sandy realized he had come to one of those moments. He liked Curt, and Curt liked him. They had worked together well over the last years. But if this went any further, all that would change. It depended on what he said next.

"It smelled like a basket of minks." That was what he said. It was a remark that came from nowhere at all, at least nowhere he could pinpoint. "Even from the outside."

"How would you know what a basket of minks smelled like?" Curt starting to smile. Just a little.

"Call it poetic license." Sandy also starting to smile, but also only a little. They had turned in the right direction, but they weren't out of the woods.

Then Curtis asked: "Did it smell worse than that whore's shoes? The one from Rocksburg?"

Sandy started laughing. Curt joined him. And they were off the hinge, just like that.

"Come on in," Curt said. "I'll buy you another beer."

Sandy didn't want another beer, but he said okay. Because now it wasn't about beer; it was about putting the crap behind them.

Back inside, sitting in a corner booth, Curt said: "I've had my hands in that trunk, Sandy. I've knocked on the bottom of it."

"Me too."

"And I've been under it on a crawler. It's not a magician's trick, like a box with a false bottom."

"Even if it was, that was no white rabbit that came out of there yesterday."

Curtis said, "For things to disappear, they only have to be in the *vicinity.* But when things show up, they always come out of the trunk. Do you agree?"

Sandy thought it over. None of them had actually seen the bat-thing emerge from the Buick's trunk, but the trunk had been open, all right. As for the leaves, yes—Phil Candleton had seen them swirling out.

"Do you agree?" Impatient now, his voice saying Sandy *had* to agree, it was so goddam obvious.

"It seems likely, but I don't think we have enough evidence to be a hundred per cent sure yet," Sandy replied at last. He knew saying that made him hopelessly stodgy in Curtis's eyes, but it was what he believed. " 'One swallow doesn't make a summer.' Ever heard that one?"

Curt stuck out his lower lip and blew an exasperated breath up his face. " 'Plain as the nose on your face,' ever heard *that* one?"

"Curt—"

Curt raised his hands as if to say no, no, they didn't have to go back out into the parking lot and pick up where they had left off. "I see your point. Okay? I don't agree, but I see it."

"Okay."

"Just tell me one thing: when'll we have enough to draw some conclusions? Not about everything, mind you, but maybe a few of the bigger things. Like where the bat and the fish came from, for instance. If I had to settle for just one answer, it'd probably be that one."

"Probably never."

Curt raised his hands to the smoke-stained tin ceiling, then dropped them back to the table with a clump. "*Gahh!* I *knew* you'd say that! I could *strangle* you, Dearborn!"

They looked at each other across the table, across the tops of beers neither one of them wanted, and Curt started to laugh. Sandy smiled. And then he was laughing, too.

Now: *Sandy*

Ned stopped me there. He wanted to go inside and call his mother, he said. Tell her he was okay, just eating dinner at the barracks with Sandy and Shirley and a couple of the other guys. Tell her lies, in other words. As his father had before him.

"Don't you guys move," he said from the doorway. "Don't you move a red inch."

When he was gone, Huddie looked at me. His broad face was thoughtful. "You think telling him all this stuff is a good idea, Sarge?"

"He gonna want to see all dose ole tapes, nex' t'ing," Arky said dolefully. He was drinking a root beer. "Hell's own movie-show."

"I don't know if it's a good idea or a bad one," I said, rather peevishly. "I only know that it's a little late to back out now." Then I got up and went inside myself.

Ned was just hanging up the phone. "Where are *you* going?" he asked. His brows had drawn together, and I thought of standing nose to nose with his father outside The Tap, the scurgy little bar that had become Eddie J's home away from home. That night Curt's brows had drawn together in that exact same way.

"Just to the toilet," I said. "Take it easy, Ned, you'll get what you want. What there is to get, anyway. But you have to stop waiting for the punchline."

I went into the can and shut the door before he had a chance to reply. And the next fifteen seconds or so were pure relief. Like beer, iced tea is something you can't buy, only rent. When I got back outside, the smokers' bench was empty. They had stepped across to Shed B and were looking in, each with his own window in the roll-up door facing the rear of the barracks, each in that sidewalk superintendent posture I knew so well. Only now it's changed around in my mind. It's exactly backwards.

211

Whenever I pass men lined up at a board fence or at sawhorses blocking off an excavation hole, the first things I think of are Shed B and the Buick 8.

"You guys see anything in there you like better than yourselves?" I called across to them.

It seemed they didn't. Arky came back first, closely followed by Huddie and Shirley. Phil and Eddie lingered a bit longer, and Curt's boy returned last to the barracks side of the parking lot. Like father like son in this, too. Curtis had also always lingered longest at the window. If, that was, he had time to linger. He wouldn't *make* time, though, because the Buick never took precedence. If it had, he and I almost certainly *would* have come to blows that night at The Tap instead of finding a way to laugh and back off. We found a way because us getting into a scrape would have been bad for the Troop, and he kept the Troop ahead of everything—the Buick, his wife, his family when the family came. I once asked him what he was proudest of in his life. This was around 1986, and I imagined he'd say his son. His response was *The uniform.* I understood that and responded to it, but I'd be wrong not to add that the answer horrified me a little, as well. But it saved him, you know. His pride in the job he did and the uniform he wore held him steady when the Buick might otherwise have unbalanced him, driven him into an obsessional madness. Didn't the job also get him killed? I suppose. But there were years in between, a lot of good years. And now there was this kid, who was troubling because he didn't have the job to balance him. All he had was a lot of questions, and the naïve belief that, just because he felt he needed the answers, those answers would come. *Bosh,* his father might have said.

"Temp in there's gone down another tick," Huddie said as we all sat down again. "Probably nothing, but she might have another surprise or two left in her. We'd best watch out."

"What happened after you and my Dad almost got into that fight?" Ned asked. "And don't start telling me about calls and codes, either. I *know* about calls and codes. I'm learning dispatch, remember."

What *was* the kid learning, though? After spending a month of officially sanctioned time in the cubicle with the radio and the computers and the modems, what did he really know? The calls and codes, yes, he was a quick study and he sounded as professional as hell when he answered the red phone with *State Police Statler, Troop D, this is PCO Wilcox, how can I help?,* but did he know that each call and each code is a link in a chain? That there are chains everywhere, each link in each one a little bit stronger or weaker than the last? How could you expect a kid, even a smart one, to know that? These are the chains we forge in life, to mis-quote Jacob Marley. We make them, we wear them, and sometimes we share them. George Morgan didn't really shoot himself in his garage; he just got tangled in one of those chains and hanged himself. Not, however, until after he'd helped us dig Mister Dillon's grave on one brutally hot summer day after the tanker-truck blew over in Poteenville.

There was no call or code for Eddie Jacubois spending more and more of his time in The Tap; there was none for Andy Colucci cheating on his wife and getting caught at it and begging her for a second chance and not getting it; no code for Matt Babicki leaving; no call for Shirley Pasternak coming. There are just things you can't explain unless you admit a knowledge of those chains, some made of love and some of pure hap-penstance. Like Orville Garrett down on one knee at the foot of Mister Dillon's fresh grave, crying, putting D's collar on the earth and saying *Sorry, partner, sorry.*

And was all that important to my story? I thought so. The kid, obviously, thought different. I kept trying to give him a context and he kept repudiating it, just as the Buick's tires repudiated any invasion—yes, right down to the smallest sliver of a pebble that would simply not stay caught between the treads. You could put that sliver of pebble in, but five or ten or fifteen seconds later it would fall back out again. Tony had tried this experiment; I had tried it; this boy's father had tried it time and time and time again, often with videotape rolling. And now here sat the boy himself, dressed in civvies, no gray uniform to balance *his* interest in the Buick, here he sat repudiating even in the face of his father's undoubtedly dangerous eight-cylinder miracle, wanting to hear the story out of context and out of history, chainless and immaculate. He wanted what suited him. In his anger, he thought he had a right to that. I thought he was wrong, and I was sort of pissed at him myself, but I tell

213

you with all the truth in my heart that I loved him, too. He was so much like his father then, you see. Right down to the let's-play-Bingo-with-the-paycheck look in his eyes.

"I can't tell you this next part," I said. "I wasn't there."

I turned to Huddie, Shirley, Eddie J. None of them looked comfortable. Eddie wouldn't meet my gaze at all.

"What do you say, guys?" I asked them. "PCO Wilcox doesn't want any calls or codes, he just wants the story." I gave Ned a satiric look he either didn't understand or chose not to understand.

"Sandy, what—" Ned began, but I held up my palm like a traffic cop. I had opened the door to this. Probably opened it the first time I'd gotten to the barracks and seen him out mowing the lawn and hadn't sent him home. He wanted the story. Fine. Let him have it and be done.

"This boy is waiting. Which of you will help him out? And I want to have *all* of it. Eddie."

He jumped as if I'd goosed him, and gave me a nervous look.

"What was the guy's name? The guy with the cowboy boots and the Nazi necklace?"

Eddie blinked, shocked. His eyes asked if I was sure. No one talked about that guy. Not, at least, until now. Sometimes we talked about the day of the tanker-truck, laughed about how Herb and that other guy had tried to make up with Shirley by picking her a bouquet of flowers out back (just before the shit hit the fan, that was), but not about the guy in the cowboy boots. Not him. Never. But we were going to talk about him now, by God.

"Leppler? Lippman? Lippier? It was something like that, wasn't it?"

"His name was Brian Lippy," Eddie said at last. "Him and me, we went back a little."

"Did you?" I asked. "I didn't know that."

I began the next part, but Shirley Pasternak told quite a bit of the tale (once she came into it, that was), speaking warmly, eyes fixed on Ned's and one of her hands lying on top of his. It didn't surprise me that she should be the one, and it didn't surprise me when Huddie chimed in and began telling it with her, turn and turn about. What surprised me was when Eddie J began to add first sidelights . . . then footlights . . . and finally spotlights. I had told him to stick around until he had something to say, but it still surprised me when his time came and he started talking. His voice was low and tentative at first, but by the time he got to the part about discovering that asshole Lippy had kicked out the window, he was speaking strongly and steadily, his voice that of a man who remembers everything and has made up his mind to hide nothing. He spoke without looking at Ned or me or any of us. It was the shed he looked at, the one that sometimes gave birth to monsters.

Then: *Sandy*

By the summer of 1988, the Buick 8 had become an accepted part of Troop D's life, no more or less a part of it than any other. And why not? Given time and a fair amount of goodwill, any freak can become a part of any family. That was what had happened in the nine years since the disappearance of the man in the black coat ("Oil's fine!") and Ennis Rafferty.

The thing still put on its lightshows from time to time, and both Curt and Tony continued to run experiments from time to time. In 1984, Curtis tried a videocam which could be activated by remote control inside the Buick (nothing happened). In '85, Tony tried much the same thing with a top-of-the-line Wollensak audio recorder (he got a faint off-and-on humming and the distant calling of some crows, nothing more). There were a few other experiments with live test animals. A couple died, but none disappeared.

On the whole, things were settling down. When the lightshows *did* happen, they were nowhere near as powerful as the first few (and the whopper in '83, of course). Troop D's biggest problem in those days was caused by someone who knew absolutely nothing about the Buick. Edith Hyams (aka The Dragon) continued to talk to the press (whenever the press would listen, that was) about her brother's disappearance. She continued to insist it was no ordinary disappearance (which once caused Sandy and Curt to muse on just what an "ordinary disappearance" might be). She also continued to insist that Ennis's fellow officers Knew More Than They Were Telling. She was absolutely right on that score, of course. Curt Wilcox said on more than one occasion that if Troop D ever came to grief over the Buick, it would be that woman's doing. As a matter of public policy, however, Ennis's Troop-mates continued to support her. It was their best insurance, and they all knew it.

After one of her forays in the press Tony said, "Never mind, boys—time's on our side. Just remember that and keep smilin." And he was right. By the mid-eighties, the representatives of the press were for the most part no longer returning her calls. Even WKML, the tri-county indie station whose *Action News at Five* broadcasts frequently featured stories about sightings of Sasquatch in the Lassburg Forest and such thoughtful medical briefings as **CANCER IN THE WATER SUPPLY! IS YOUR TOWN NEXT?**, had begun to lose interest in Edith.

On three more occasions, things appeared in the Buick's trunk. Once it was half a dozen large green beetles which looked like no beetles anyone in Troop D had ever seen. Curt and Tony spent an afternoon at Horlicks University, looking through stacks of entomology texts, and there was nothing like those green bugs in the books, either. In fact, the very shade of green was like nothing anyone in Troop D had ever seen before, although none could have explained exactly how it was different. Carl Brundage dubbed it Headache Green. Because, he said, the bugs were the color of the migraines he sometimes got. They were dead when they showed up, the whole half-dozen. Tapping their carapaces with the barrel of a screwdriver produced the sort of noise you would have gotten by tapping a piece of metal on a block of wood.

"Do you want to try a dissection?" Tony asked Curt.

"Do *you* want to try one?" Curt replied.

"Not particularly, no."

Curt looked at the bugs in the trunk—most of them on their backs with their feet up—and sighed. "Neither do I. What would be the point?"

So, instead of being pinned to a piece of corkboard and dissected while the video camera ran, the bugs were bagged, tagged with the date (the line on the tag for NAME/RANK OF OIC was left blank, of course), and stored away downstairs in that battered green file-cabinet. Allowing the alien bugs to make their journey from the Buick's trunk to the green file-cabinet unexamined was another step down Curt's road to acceptance. Yet the old look of fascination still came into his eyes sometimes. Tony or Sandy would see him standing at the roll-up door, peering in, and that light would be there, more often than not. Sandy came to think of it as his Kurtis the Krazy Kat look, although he never told anyone that, not even the old Sarge. The rest of them lost interest in the Buick's misbegotten stillbirths, but Trooper Wilcox never did.

In Curtis, familiarity never bred contempt.

On a cold February day in 1984, five months or so after the appearance of the bugs, Brian Cole stuck his head into the SC's office. Tony Schoondist was in Scranton, trying to explain why he hadn't spent his entire budget appropriation for 1983 (there was nothing like one or two scrimpy SCs to make everyone else look bad), and Sandy Dearborn was holding down the big chair.

"Think you better take a little amble out to the back shed, boss," Brian said. "Code D."

"What kind of Code D we talking about, Bri?"

"Trunk's up."

"Are you sure it didn't just pop open? There haven't been any fireworks since just before Christmas. Usually—"

"Usually there's fireworks, I know. But the temperature's been too low in there for the last week. Besides, I can see something."

That got Sandy on his feet. He could feel the old dread stealing its fat fingers around his heart and starting to squeeze. Another mess to clean up, maybe. Probably. *Please God don't let it be another fish,* he thought. *Nothing that has to be hosed out of there by men wearing masks.*

"Do you think it might be alive?" Sandy asked. He thought he sounded calm enough, but he did not feel particularly calm. "The thing you saw, does it look—"

"It looks like some sort of uprooted plant," Brian said. "Part of it's hanging down over the back bumper. Tell you what, boss, it looks a little bit like an Easter lily."

"Have Matt call Curtis in off the road. His shift's almost over, anyway."

Curt rogered the Code D, told Matt he was out on Sawmill Road, and said he'd be back at base in fifteen minutes. That gave Sandy time to get the coil of yellow rope out of the hutch and to have a good long look into Shed B with the pair of cheap low-power binoculars that were also kept in the hutch. He agreed with Brian. The thing hanging out of the trunk, a draggled and membranous white shading to dark green, looked as much like an Easter lily as anything else. The kind you see about five days after the holiday, half-past drooping and going on dead.

Curt showed up, parked sloppily in front of the gas-pump, and came on the trot to where Sandy, Brian, Huddie, Arky Arkanian, and a few others were standing at the shed windows in those sidewalk superintendent poses. Sandy held the binoculars out and Curt took them. He stood for nearly a full minute, at first making tiny adjustments to the focus-knob, then just looking.

"Well?" Sandy asked when he was finally finished.

"I'm going in," Curt replied, a response that didn't surprise Sandy in the slightest; why else had he bothered to get the rope? "And if it doesn't rare up and try to bite me, I'll photograph it, video it, and bag it. Just give me five minutes to get ready."

It didn't take him even that. He came out of the barracks wearing surgical gloves—what were already coming to be known in the PSP as "AIDS mittens"—a barber's smock, rubber galoshes, and a bathing cap over his hair. Hung around his neck was a Puff-Pak, a little plastic breathing mask with its own air supply that was good for about five minutes. In one of his gloved hands he had a Polaroid camera. There was a green plastic garbage bag tucked into his belt.

Huddie had unlimbered the videocam and now he trained it on Curt, who looked *très fantastique* as he strode manfully across the parking lot in his blue bathing cap and red galoshes (and even more so when Sandy had knotted the yellow rope around his middle).

"You're beautiful!" Huddie cried, peering through the video camera. "Wave to your adoring fans!"

Curtis Wilcox waved dutifully. Some of his fans would look at this tape in the days after his sudden death seventeen years later, trying not to cry even as they laughed at the foolish, amiable look of him.

From the open dispatch window, Matt sang after him in a surprisingly strong tenor voice: *"Hug me . . . you sexy thing! Kiss me . . . you sexy thing!"*

Curt took all the ribbing well, but it was secondary to him, his mates' laughter like something overheard in another room. That light was in his eyes.

"This really isn't very bright," Sandy said as he cinched the loop of the rope snugly around Curt's waist. Not with any real hope of changing Curt's mind, however. "We should probably wait and see what develops. Make sure this is all, that there's nothing else coming through."

"I'll be okay," Curt said. His tone was absent; he was barely listening. Most of him was inside his own head, running over a checklist of things to do.

"Maybe," Sandy said, "and maybe we're starting to get a little careless with that thing." Not knowing if it was really true, but wanting to say it out loud, try it on for size. "We're starting to really believe that if nothing's happened to any of us so far, nothing ever will. That's how cops and lion-tamers get hurt."

"We're fine," Curt said, and then—appearing not to sense any contradiction—he told the other men to stand back. When they had, he took the video camera from Huddie, put it on the tripod, and told Arky to open the door. Arky pushed the remote clipped to his belt and the door rattled up on its tracks.

Curt let the Polaroid's strap slip to his elbow, so he could pick up the videocam tripod, and went into Shed B. He stood for a moment on the concrete halfway between the door and the Buick, one gloved hand touching the Puff-Pak's mask under his chin, ready to pull it up at once if the air was as foul as it had been on the day of the fish.

"Not bad," he said. "Just a little whiff of something sweet. Maybe it really *is* an Easter lily."

It wasn't. The trumpet-shaped flowers—three of them—were as pallid as the palms of a corpse, and almost translucent. Within each was a dab of dark blue stuff that looked like jelly. Hanging in the jelly were little pips. The stalks looked more like treebark than parts of a flowering plant, their green surfaces covered with a network of cracks and crenellations. There were brown spots that looked like some sort of fungoid growth, and these were spreading. The stems came together in a rooty clod of black soil. When he leaned toward this (none of them liked seeing Curt lean into the trunk that way, it was too much like watching a man stick his stupid head into a bear's mouth), Curt said he could smell that cabbagey aroma again. It was faint but unmistakable.

221

"And I tell you, Sandy, there's the smell of salt, as well. I know there is. I spent a lot of summers on Cape Cod, and you can't miss that smell."

"I don't care if it smells like truffles and caviar," Sandy replied. "Get the hell out of there."

Curt laughed—*Silly old Gramma Dearborn!*—but he pulled back. He set the video camera pointing down into the trunk from its tripod, got it running, then took some Polaroids for good measure.

"Come on in, Sandy—check it out."

Sandy thought it over. Bad idea, very bad idea. *Stupid* idea. No doubt about it. And once he had that clear in his head, Sandy handed the coil of rope to Huddie and went on in. He looked at the deflated flowers lying in the Buick's trunk (and the one hanging over the lip, the one Brian Cole had seen) and couldn't suppress a little shiver.

"I know," Curt said, lowering his voice so the Troopers outside wouldn't hear. "Hurts just to look, doesn't it? It's the visual equivalent of hearing someone scrape a blackboard with his fingernails."

Sandy nodded. Hole in one.

"But what triggers that reaction?" Curt asked. "I can't put my finger on any one thing. Can you?"

"No." Sandy licked his lips, which had gone dry. "And I think that's because it's everything together. A lot of it's the white."

"The white. The color."

"Yeah. Nasty. Like a toad's belly."

"Like cobwebs spun into flowers," Curt said.

They looked at each other for a moment, trying to smile and not doing a very good job of it. State Police poets, Trooper Frost and Trooper Sandburg. Next they'd be comparing the goddam thing to a summer's day. But you had to try doing that, because it seemed you could only grasp what you were seeing by an act of mental reflection that was like poetry.

Other similes, less coherent, were banging and swerving in Sandy's head. White like a Communion wafer in a dead woman's mouth. White like a thrush infection under your tongue. White like the foam of creation just beyond the edge of the universe, maybe.

"This stuff comes from a place we can't even begin to comprehend," Curt said. "Our senses can't grasp any of it, not really. Talking about it's a joke—you might as well try to describe a four-sided triangle. Look there, Sandy. Do you see?" He pointed the tip of a gloved finger at a dry brown patch just below one of the corpse-lily flowers.

"Yeah, I see it. Looks like a burn."

"And it's getting bigger. All the spots are. And look there on the flower." It was another brown patch, spreading as they looked at it, gobbling an ever-widening hole in the flower's fragile white skin. "That's decomposition. It's not going in quite the same way as the bat and the fish, but it's going, just the same. Isn't it?"

Sandy nodded.

"Pull the garbage bag out of my belt and open it, would you?"

Sandy did as he was asked. Curt reached into the trunk and grasped the plant just above its rooty bulb. When he did, a fresh whiff of that watery cabbage/spoiled cucumber stench drifted up to them. Sandy took a step back, hand pressed against his mouth, trying not to gag and gagging anyway.

"Hold that bag open, goddammit!" Curt cried in a choked voice. To Sandy he sounded like someone who has just taken a long hit off a primo blunt and wants to hold the smoke down as long as possible. "Jesus, it feels nasty! Even through the gloves!"

Sandy held the bag open and shook the top. "Hurry up, then!"

Curt dropped the decaying corpse-lily plant inside, and even the sound it made going down the bag's plastic throat was somehow wrong—like a harsh whispered cry, something being pressed relentlessly between two boards and almost silently choking. None of the similes was right, yet each seemed to flash a momentary light on what was basically unknowable. Sandy Dearborn could not express even to himself how fundamentally revolting and dismaying the corpse-lilies were. Them and all the Buick's miscarried children. If you thought about them too long, the chances were good that you really would go mad.

Curt made as if to wipe his gloved hands on his shirt, then thought better of it. He bent into the Buick's trunk instead, and rubbed them briskly on the brown trunk-mat. Then he stripped the gloves off, motioned for Sandy to open the plastic bag again, and threw them inside on top of the corpse-lily. That smell puffed out again and Sandy thought of once when his mother, eaten up by cancer and with less than a week to live, had belched in his face. His instinctive but feeble effort to block that memory before it could rise fully into his consciousness was useless.

Please don't let me be sick, Sandy thought. *Oh please, no.*

Curt checked to make sure the Polaroids he had taken were still tucked into his belt, then slammed the Buick's trunk. "Let's get out of here, Sandy. What do you say?"

"I say that's the best idea you've had all year."

Curt winked at him. It was the perfect wiseguy wink, spoiled only by his pallor and the sweat running down his cheeks and forehead. "Since it's only February, that's not saying much. Come on."

Fourteen months later, in April of 1985, the Buick threw a lightquake that was brief but extremely vicious—the biggest and brightest since The Year of the Fish. The force of the event mitigated against Curt and Tony's idea that the energy flowing from or through the Roadmaster was dissipating. The brevity of the event, on the other hand, seemed to argue *for* the idea. In the end, it was a case of you pays your money and you takes your choice. Same as it ever was, in other words.

Two days after the lightquake, with the temperature in Shed B standing at an even sixty degrees, the Buick's trunk flew open and a red stick came sailing up and out of it, as if driven by a jet of compressed air. Arky Arkanian was actually in the shed when this happened, putting his posthole digger back on its pegs, and it scared the hell out of him. The red stick clunked against one of the shed's overhead beams, came down on the Buick's roof with a bang, then rolled off and landed on the floor. Hello, stranger.

The new arrival was about nine inches long, irregular, the thickness of a man's wrist, with a couple of knotholes in one end. It was Andy Colucci, looking in at it through the binoculars five or ten minutes later, who determined that the knotholes were eyes, and what looked like grooves or cracks on one side of the thing was actually a leg, perhaps drawn up in its final death-agony. Not a stick, Andy thought, but some kind of red lizard. Like the fish, the bat, and the lily, it was a goner.

Tony Schoondist was the one to go in and collect the specimen that time, and that night at The Tap he told several Troopers he could barely bring himself to touch it. "The goddamned thing was staring at me," he said. "That's what it felt like, anyway. Dead or not." He poured himself a glass of beer and drank it down at a single draught. "I hope that's the end of it," he said. "I really, really do."

But of course it wasn't.

Shirley

It's funny how little things can mark a day in your mind. That Friday in 1988 was probably the most horrible one in my life—I didn't sleep well for six months after, and I lost twenty-five pounds because for awhile I couldn't eat—but the way I mark it in time is by something nice. That was the day Herb Avery and Justin Islington brought me the bouquet of field-flowers. Just before everything went crazy, that was.

They were in my bad books, those two. They'd ruined a brand-new linen skirt, horsing around in the kitchen. I was no part of it, just a gal minding her own business, getting a cup of coffee. Not paying attention, and isn't that mostly when they get you? Men, I mean. They'll be all right for awhile, so you relax, even get lulled into thinking they might be basically sane after all, and then they just break out. Herb and that Islington came galloping into the kitchen like a couple of horses, yelling about some bet. Justin is thumping Herb all around the head and shoulders and hollering *Pay up, you son of a buck, pay up!* and Herb is like *We were just kidding around, you know I don't bet when I play cards, let loose of me!* But laughing, both of them. Like loons. Justin was half up on Herb's back, hands around his neck, pretending to choke him. Herb was trying to shake him off, neither of them looking at me or even knowing I was there, standing by the Mr. Coffee in my brand-new skirt. Just PCO Pasternak, you know—part of the furniture.

"Look out, you two galoots!" I yelled, but it was too late. They ran smack into me before I could put my cup down and there went the coffee, all down my front. Getting it on the blouse didn't bother me, it was just an old thing, but the skirt was brand-new. And *nice*. I'd spent half an hour the night before, fixing the hem.

I gave a yell and they finally stopped pushing and thumping. Justin still had one leg around Herb's hip and his hands around his neck. Herb was looking at me with his mouth hung wide open. He was a nice enough fellow (about Islington I couldn't say one way or the other; he was transferred over to Troop K in Media before I really got to know him), but with his mouth hung open that way, Herb Avery looked as dumb as a bag of hammers.

"Shirley, oh jeez," he said. You know, he sounded like Arky, now that I think back—same accent, just not quite as thick. "I never sar' you dere."

"I'm not surprised," I said, "with that other one trying to ride you like you were a horse in the goddam Kentucky Derby."

"Are you burned?" Justin asked.

"You bet I'm burned," I said. "This skirt was thirty-five dollars at JC Penney and it's the first time I wore it to work and it's ruined. You want to believe I'm burned."

"Jeepers, calm down, we're sorry," Justin said. He even had the gall to sound offended. And that's also men as I've come to know them, pardon the philosophy. If they say they're sorry, you're supposed to go all mellow, because that takes care of everything. Doesn't matter if they broke a window, blew up the powerboat, or lost the kids' college fund playing blackjack in Atlantic City. It's like *Hey, I said I was sorry, do you have to make a federal case of it?*

"Shirley—" Herb started.

"Not now, honeychile, not now," I said. "Just get out of here. Right out of my sight."

Trooper Islington, meanwhile, had grabbed a handful of napkins off the counter and started mopping the front of my skirt.

"Stop that!" I said, grabbing his wrist. "What do you think this is, Free Feel Friday?"

"I just thought . . . if it hasn't set in yet . . ."

I asked him if his mother had any kids that lived and he started in with *Well Jesus, if* that's *the way you feel,* all huffy and offended.

"Do yourself a favor," I said, "and go right now. Before you end up wearing this goddam coffee pot for a necklace."

Out they went, more slinking than walking, and for quite awhile afterward they steered wide around me, Herb shamefaced and Justin Islington still wearing that puzzled, offended look—*I said I was sorry, what do you want, egg in your beer?*

Then, a week later—on the day the shit hit the fan, in other words—they showed up in dispatch at two in the afternoon, Justin first, with the bouquet, and Herb behind him. Almost *hiding* behind him, it looked like, in case I should decide to start hucking paperweights at them.

Thing is, I'm not much good at holding a grudge. Anyone who knows me will tell you that. I do all right with them for a day or two, and then they just kind of melt through my fingers. And the pair of them looked cute, like little boys who want to apologize to Teacher for cutting up dickens in the back of the room during social studies. That's another thing about men that gets you, how in almost the blink of a damned eye they can go from being loudmouth galoots who cut each other in the bars over the least little thing—*baseball scores,* for the love of God—to sweeties right out of a Norman Rockwell picture. And the next thing you know, they're in your pants or trying to get there.

Justin held out the bouquet. It was just stuff they'd picked in the field behind the barracks. Daisies, black-eyed Susans, things of that nature. Even a few dandelions, as I recall. But that was part of what made it so cute and disarming. If it had been hothouse roses they'd bought downtown instead of that kid's bouquet, I might have been able to stay mad a little longer. That was a *good* skirt, and I hate hemming the damned things, anyway.

Justin Islington out in front because he had those blue-eyed football-player good looks, complete with the one curl of dark hair tumbled over his forehead. Supposed to make me melt, and sort of did. Holding the flowers out. Shucks, oh gorsh, Teacher. There was even a little white envelope stuck in with the flowers.

"Shirley," Justin said—solemn enough, but with that cute little twinkle in his eyes—"we want to make up with you."

"That's right," Herb said. "I hate having you mad at us."

"I do, too," Justin said. I wasn't so sure that one meant it, but I thought Herb really did, and that was good enough for me.

"Okay," I said, and took the flowers. "But if you do it again—"

"We won't!" Herb said. "No way! Never!" Which is what they all say, of course. And don't accuse me of being a hardass, either. I'm just being realistic.

"If you do, I'll thump you crosseyed." I cocked an eyebrow at Islington. "Here's something your mother probably never told you, you being a pointer instead of a setter: sorry won't take a coffee stain out of a linen skirt."

"Be sure to look in the envelope," Justin said, still trying to slay me with those bright blue eyes of his.

I put the vase down on my desk and plucked the envelope out of the daisies. "This isn't going to puff sneezing powder in my face or anything like that, is it?" I asked Herb. I was joking, but he shook his head earnestly. Looking at him that way, you had to wonder how he could ever stop anyone and give them a ticket for speeding or reckless driving without getting a ration of grief. But Troopers are different on the highway, of course. They have to be.

I opened the envelope, expecting a little Hallmark card with another version of *I'm sorry* on it, this one written in flowery rhymes, but instead there was a folded piece of paper. I took it out, unfolded it, and saw it was a JC Penney gift certificate, made out to me in the amount of fifty dollars.

"Hey, no," I said. All at once I felt like crying. And while I'm at it, that's the other thing about men—just when you're at your most disgusted with them, they can lay you out with some gratuitous act of generosity and all at once, stupid but true, instead of being mad you feel ashamed of yourself for ever having had a mean and cynical thought about them. "Fellas, you didn't need to—"

"We did need to," Justin said. "That was double dumb, horsing around in the kitchen like that."

"*Triple* dumb," Herb said. He was bobbing his head up and down, never taking his eyes off me.

"But this is too much!"

Islington said, "Not according to our calculations. We had to figure in the annoyance factor, you see, as well as the pain and suffering—"

"I didn't get burned, that coffee was only luke—"

"You're taking it, Shirley," Herb said, very firmly. He hadn't gotten all the way back to being Mr. State Cop Marlboro Man, but he was well on his way. "It's a done deal."

I'm really glad they did that, and I'll never forget it. What happened later was so horrible, you see. It's nice to have something that can balance out a little bit of that horror, some act of ordinary kindness like two goofs paying not just for the skirt they spoiled but for the inconvenience and exasperation. And giving me flowers on top of that. When I remember the other part, I try to remember those guys, too. Especially the flowers they picked out back.

I thanked them and they headed upstairs, probably to play chess. There used to be a tournament here toward the end of every summer, with the winner getting this little bronze toilet seat called The Scranton Cup. All that kind of got left behind when Lieutenant Schoondist retired. The two of them left me with the look of men who've done their duty. I suppose that in a way they had. *I* felt that they had, anyway, and I could do my part by getting them a big box of chocolates or some winter hand-warmers with what was left over from the gift certificate after I'd bought a new skirt. Hand-warmers would be more practical, but maybe a little too domestic. I was their dispatcher, not their den mother, after all. They had wives to buy them hand-warmers.

Their silly little peace bouquet had been nicely arranged, there were even a few springs of green to give it that all-important town florist's feel, but they hadn't thought to add water. Arrange the flowers, then forget the water: it's a guy thing. I picked up the vase and started toward the kitchen and that was when George Stankowski came on the radio, coughing and sounding scared to death. Let me tell you something you can file away with whatever else you consider to be the great truths of life: only one thing scares a police communications officer more than hearing a Trooper in the field actually sounding scared on the radio, and that's one calling in a 29–99. Code 99 is *General response required.* Code 29 . . . you look in the book and you see only one word under 29. The word is *catastrophe.*

"Base, this is 14. Code 29–99, do you copy? Two-niner-niner-niner."

I put the vase with the wildflowers in it back down on my desk, very carefully. As I did, I had a very vivid memory: hearing on the radio that John Lennon had died. I was making breakfast for my Dad that day. I was going to serve him and then just dash, because I was late for school. I had a glass bowl with eggs in it curled against my stomach. I was beating them with a whisk. When the man on the radio said that Lennon had been shot in New York City, I set the glass bowl down in the same careful way I now set down the vase.

"Tony!" I called across the barracks, and at the sound of my voice (or the sound of what was *in* my voice), everyone stopped what they were doing. The talk stopped upstairs, as well. "Tony, George Stankowski is 29–99!" And without waiting, I scooped up the microphone and told George that I copied, five-by, and come on back.

"My 20 is County Road 46, Poteenville," he said. I could hear an uneven crackling sound behind his transmission. It sounded like fire. Tony was standing in my doorway by then, and Sandy Dearborn in his civvies, with his cop-shoes hung from the fingers of one hand. "A tanker-truck has collided with a schoolbus and is on fire. That's the *tanker* that's on fire, but the front half of the schoolbus is involved, copy that?"

"Copy," I said. I sounded okay, but my lips had gone numb.

"This is a chemical tanker, Norco West, copy?"

"I copy Norco West, 14." Writing it on the pad beside the red telephone in large capital letters. "Placks?" Short for *placards,* the little diamonds with icons for fire, gas, radiation, and a few other fun things.

"Ah, can't make out the placks, too much smoke, but there's white stuff coming out and it's catching fire as it runs down the ditch and across the highway, copy that?" George had started coughing into his mike again.

"Copy," I said. "Are you breathing fumes, 14? You don't sound so good, over?"

"Ah, roger that, roger fumes, but I'm okay. The problem—" But before he could finish, he started coughing again.

Tony took the mike from me. He patted my shoulder to say I'd been doing all right, he just couldn't bear to stand there listening anymore. Sandy was putting on his shoes. Everyone else was drifting toward dispatch. There were quite a few guys there, with the shift change coming up. Even Mister Dillon had come out of the kitchen to see what all the excitement was about.

"The problem's the *school*," George went on when he could. "Poteenville Grammar is only two hundred yards away."

"School's not in for almost another month, 14. You—"

"Break, break. Maybe not, but I see kids."

Behind me someone murmured, "August is Crafts Month out there. My sister's teaching pottery to nine- and ten-year-olds." I remember the terrible sinking feeling I got in my chest when I heard that.

"Whatever the spill is, I'm upwind of it," George went on when he could. "The school isn't, I repeat the school is not. Copy?"

"Copy, 14," Tony said. "Do you have FD support?"

"Negative, but I hear sirens." More coughing. "I was practically on top of this when it happened, close enough to hear the crash, so I got here first. Grass is on fire, fire's headed toward the school. I see kids on the playground, standing around and watching. I can hear the alarm inside, so I have to guess they've been evacked. Can't tell if the fumes have gotten that far, but if they haven't, they will. Send the works, boss. Send the farm. This is a legitimate 29."

Tony: "Are there casualties on the bus, 14? Do you see casualties, over?"

I looked at the clock. It was quarter till two. If we were lucky, the bus would've been coming, not going—arriving to take the kids home from making their pots and jars.

"Bus appears empty except for the driver. I can see him—or maybe it's her—slumped over the wheel. That's the half in the fire and I'd have to say the driver is DRT, copy?"

DRT is a slang abbreviation the PSP picked up in the ER's back in the seventies. It stands for "dead right there."

"Copy, 14," Tony said. "Can you get to where the kids are?"

Cough-cough-cough. He sounded bad. "Roger, base, there's an access road runs alongside the soccer field. Goes right to the building, over."

"Then get in gear," Tony said. He was the best I ever saw him that day, as decisive as a general on the field of battle. The fumes turned out not to be all that toxic after all, and most of the burning was leaking gasoline, but of course none of us knew that then. For all George Stankowski knew, Tony had just signed his death warrant. And sometimes that's the job, yes.

"Roger, base, rolling."

"If they're getting gassed, stuff them in your cruiser, sit them on the hood and the trunk, put them on the roof hanging onto the lightbars. Get as many as you can, copy that?"

"Copy, base, 14 out."

Click. That last click seemed very loud.

Tony looked around. "29–99, you all heard it. Assigned units, all rolling. Those of you waiting for switch-over rides at three, get Kojak lights out of the supply room and run your personals. Shirley, bend every duty-officer you can raise."

"Yes, sir. Should I start calling od's?"

"Not yet. Huddie Royer, where are you?"

"Here, Sarge."

"You're anchoring."

There were no movie-show protests about this from Huddie, nothing about how he wanted to be out there with the rest of the crew, fighting fire and poison gas, rescuing children. He just said yessir.

"Check Pogus County FD, find out what they're rolling, find out what Lassburg and Statler's rolling, call Pittsburgh OER, anyone else you can think of."

"How about Norco West?"

Tony didn't quite slap his forehead, but almost. "Oh you bet." Then he headed for the door, Curt beside him, the others right behind them, Mister Dillon bringing up the rear.

Huddie grabbed his collar. "Not today, boy. You're here with me and Shirley." Mister D sat down at once; he was well-trained. He watched the departing men with longing eyes, just the same.

All at once the place seemed very empty with just the two of us there—the three of us, if you counted D. Not that we had time to dwell on it; there was plenty to do. I might have noticed Mister Dillon getting up and going to the back door, sniffing at the screen and whining way back low in his throat. I think I did, actually, but maybe that's only hindsight at work. If I did notice, I probably put it down to disappointment at being left behind. What I think now is that he sensed something starting to happen out in Shed B. I think he might even have been trying to let us know.

I had no time to mess with the dog, though—not even time enough to get up and shut him in the kitchen, where he might have had a drink from his water bowl and then settled down. I wish I'd made time; poor old Mister D might have lived another few years. But of course I didn't know. All I knew right then was that I had to find out who was on the road and where. I had to bend them west, if I could and they could. And while I worked on that, Huddie was in the SC's office, hunched over the desk and talking into the phone with the intensity of a man who's making the biggest deal of his life.

I got all my active officers except for Unit 6, which was almost here ("20-base in a tick" had been my last word from them). George Morgan and Eddie Jacubois had a delivery to make before heading over to Poteenville. Except, of course, 6 never *did* get to Poteenville that day. No, Eddie and George never got to Poteenville at all.

Eddie

It's funny how a person's memory works. I didn't recognize the guy who got out of that custom Ford pickup, not to begin with. To me he was just a red-eyed punk with an inverted crucifix for an earring and a silver swastika hung around his neck on a chain. I remember the stickers. You learn to read the stickers people put on their rides; they can tell you a lot. Ask any motor patrol cop. I DO WHATEVER THE LITTLE VOICES TELL ME TO on the left side of this guy's back bumper, I EAT AMISH on the right. He was unsteady on his feet, and probably not just because he was wearing a pair of fancy-stitched cowboy boots with those stacked heels. The red eyes peeking out from under his scraggle of black hair suggested to me that he was high on something. The blood on his right hand and spattered on the right sleeve of his T-shirt suggested it might be something mean. Angel dust would have been my guess. It was big in our part of the world back then. Crank came next. Now it's ex, and I'd give that shit away myself, if they'd let me. At least it's mellow. I suppose it's also possible that he was gazzing—what the current crop of kids calls huffing. But I didn't think I knew him until he said, "Hey, I be goddam, it's Fat Eddie."

Bingo, just like that I knew. Brian Lippy. He and I went back to Statler High, where he'd been a year ahead of me. Already majoring in Dope Sales & Service. Now here he was again, standing on the edge of the highway and swaying on the high heels of his fancy cowboy boots, head-down Christ hanging from his ear, Nazi twisted cross around his neck, numb-fuck stickers on the bumper of his ride.

"Hi there, Brian, want to step away from the truck?" I said.

When I say the truck was a custom, I mean it was one of those big-foot jobs. It was parked on the soft shoulder of the Humboldt Road, not a mile and a half from the intersection where the Jenny station

237

stood . . . only by that summer, the Jenny'd been closed two or three years. In truth, the truck was almost in the ditch. My old pal Brian Lippy had swerved *way* over when George hit the lights, another sign that he wasn't exactly straight.

I was glad to have George Morgan with me that day. Mostly riding single is all right, but when you happen on a guy who's all over the road because he's whaling on the person sitting next to him in the cab of the truck he's driving, it's nice to have a partner. As for the punching, we could *see* it. First as Lippy drove past our 20 and then as we pulled out behind him, this silhouette driver pistoning out his right arm, his right fist connecting again and again with the side of the passenger's silhouette head, too busy-busy-busy to realize the fuzz was crawling right up his tailpipe until George hit the reds. Fuck me till I cry, I think, ain't that prime. Next thing my old pal Brian's over on the shoulder and half in the ditch like he's been expecting it all his life, which on some level he probably has been.

If it's pot or tranks, I don't worry as much. It's like ex. They go, "Hey, man, what's up? Did I do something wrong? I love you." But stuff like angel dust and PCP makes people crazy. Even glueheads can go bonkers. I've seen it. For another thing, there was the passenger. It was a woman, and that could make things a lot worse. He might have been punching the crap out of her, but that didn't mean she might not be dangerous if she saw us slapping the cuffs on her favorite Martian.

Meantime, my old pal Brian wasn't stepping away from the truck as he'd been asked. He was just standing there, grinning at me, and how in God's name I hadn't recognized him right off the bat was a mystery, because at Statler High he'd been one of those kids who makes your life hell if he notices you. Especially if you're a little pudgy or pimply, and I was both. The Army took the weight off—it's the only diet program I know where they pay you to participate—and the pimples took care of themselves in time like they almost always do, but in SHS I'd been this guy's afternoon snack any day he wanted. That was another reason to be happy George was with me. If I'd been alone, my old pal Bri might have gotten the idea that if he put the evil eye on me, I'd still shrivel. The more stoned he was, the more apt he was to think that.

"Step away from the truck, sir," George said in his flat and colorless Trooper voice. You'd never believe, hearing him talk to some John Q at the side of the road, that he could scream himself hoarse on the Little League field, yelling at kids to bunt the damn ball and to keep their heads down while they were running the bases. Or kidding with them on the bench before their games to loosen them up.

Lippy had never torn the Fruit Loops off any of *George's* shirts in study hall period four, and maybe that's why he stepped away from the truck when George told him to. Looking down at his boots as he did it, losing the grin. When guys like Brian Lippy lose the grin, what comes in to take its place is this kind of dopey sullenness.

"Are you going to be trouble, sir?" George asked. He hadn't drawn his gun, but his hand was on the butt of it. "If you are, tell me now. Save us both some grief."

Lippy didn't say anything. Just looked down at his boots.

"His name is Brian?" George asked me.

"Brian Lippy." I was looking at the truck. Through the back window I could see the passenger, still sitting in the middle, not looking at us. Head dropped. I thought maybe he'd beaten her unconscious. Then one hand went up to her mouth and out of the mouth came a plume of cigarette smoke.

"Brian, I want to know if we're going to have trouble. Answer up so I can hear you, now, just like a big boy."

"Depends," Brian said, lifting his upper lip to get a good sneer on the word. I started toward the truck to do my share of the job. When my shadow passed over the toes of his boots, Brian kind of recoiled and took a step backward, as if it had been a snake instead of a shadow. He was high, all right, and to me it was seeming more like PCP or angel dust all the time.

"Let me have your driver's license and registration," George said.

Brian paid no immediate attention. He was looking at me again. "ED-die JACK-you-BOYS," he said, chanting it the way he and his friends always had back in high school, making a joke out of it. He hadn't worn any head-down Christs or Nazi swastikas back at Statler High, though; they would have sent him home if he'd tried that shit. Anyway, him saying my name like that got to me. It was like he'd found an old electrical switch, dusty and forgotten behind a door but still wired up. Still hot.

He knew it, too. Saw it and started grinning. "Fat Eddie JACK-you-BOYS. How many boys *did* you jack, Eddie? How many boys did you jack in the shower room? Or did you just get right down on your knees and suck em off? Straight to the main event. Mister Takin Care of Business."

"Want to close your mouth, Brian?" George asked. "You'll catch a fly." He took his handcuffs off his belt.

Brian Lippy saw them and started to lose the grin again. "What you think you gonna do with those?"

"If you don't hand me your operating papers right now, I'm going to put them on you, Brian. And if you resist, I can guarantee you two things: a broken nose and eighteen months in Castlemora for resisting arrest. Could be more, depending on which judge you draw. Now what do you think?"

Brian took his wallet out of his back pocket. It was a greasy old thing with the logo of some rock group—Judas Priest, I think—inexpertly burned into it. Probably with the tip of a soldering iron. He started thumbing through the various compartments.

"Brian," I said.

He looked up.

"The name is Jacubois, Brian. Nice French name. And I haven't been fat for quite awhile now."

"You'll gain it back," he said, "fat boys always do."

I burst out laughing. I couldn't help it. He sounded like some half-baked guest on a talkshow. He glowered at me, but there was something uncertain in it. He'd lost the advantage and he knew it.

"Little secret," I said. "High school's over, my friend. This is your actual, real life. I know that's hard for you to believe, but you better get used to it. It's not just detention anymore. This *actually counts.*"

What I got was a kind of stupid gape. He wasn't getting it. They so rarely do.

"Brian, I want to see your paperwork with no more delay," George said. "You put it right in my hand." And he held his hand out, palm up.

Not very wise, you might say, but George Morgan had been a State Trooper for a long time, and in his judgment, this situation was now going in the right direction. Right enough, anyway, for him to decide he didn't need to put the cuffs on my old friend Brian just to show him who was in charge.

I went over to the truck, glancing at my watch as I did. It was just about one-thirty in the afternoon. Hot. Crickets singing dry songs in the roadside grass. The occasional car passing by, the drivers slowing down for a good look. It's always nice when the cops have someone pulled over and it's not you. That's a real daymaker.

The woman in the truck was sitting with her left knee pressed against the chrome post of Brian's Hurst shifter. Guys like Brian put them in just so they can stick a Hurst decal in the window, that's what I think. Next to the ones saying Fram and Pennzoil. She looked about twenty years old with long ironed brownette hair, not particularly clean, hanging to her shoulders. Jeans and a white tank top. No bra. Fat red pimples on her shoulders. A tat on one arm that said **AC/DC** and one on the other saying BRIAN MY LUV. Nails painted candycane pink but all bitten down and ragged. And yes, there was blood. Blood and snot hanging out of her nose. More blood spattered up her cheeks like little birthmarks. Still more on her split lips and chin and tank top. Head down so the wings of her hair hid some of her face. Cigarette going up and down, tick-tock, either a Marlboro or a Winston, in those days before the prices went up and all the fringe people went to the cheap brands, you could count on it. And if it's Marlboro, it's always the hard pack. I have seen so many of them. Sometimes there's a baby and it straightens the guy up, but usually it's just bad luck for the baby.

"Here," she said, and lifted her right thigh a little. Under it was a slip of paper, canary yellow. "The registration. I tell him to keep his ticket in his wallet or the glove compartment, but it's always flopping around in here someplace with the Mickey Dee wrappers and the rest of the trash."

She didn't sound stoned and there were no beer cans or liquor bottles floating around in the cab of the truck. That didn't make her sober, of course, but it was a step in the right direction. She also didn't seem like she was going to turn abusive, but of course that can change. In a hurry.

"What's your name, ma'am?"

"Sandra?"

"Sandra what?"

"McCracken?"

"Do you have any ID, Ms. McCracken?"

"Yeah."

"Show me, please."

There was a little Leatherette clutch purse on the seat beside her. She opened it and started pawing through it. She worked slowly, and with her head bent over her purse, her face disappeared completely. You could still see the blood on her tank top but not on her face; you couldn't see the swollen lips that turned her mouth into a cut plum, or the old mouse fading around one eye.

And from behind me: "Fuck no, I ain't getting in there. What makes you think you got a right to put me in there?"

I looked around. George was holding the back door of the cruiser open. A limo driver couldn't have done it more courteously. Except the back seat of a limo doesn't have doors you can't open and windows you can't unroll from the inside, or mesh between the front and the back. Plus, of course, that faint smell of puke. I've never driven a cruiser—well, except for a week or so after we got the new Caprices—that didn't have that smell.

"What makes me think I have the right is you're *busted*, Brian. Did you just hear me read you your rights?"

"The fuck *for*, man? I wasn't speedin!"

"That's true, you were too busy tuning up on your girlfriend to really get the pedal to the metal, but you were driving recklessly, driving to endanger. Plus assault. Let's not forget that. So get in."

"Man, you can't—"

"Get in, Brian, or I'll put you up against the car and cuff you. Hard, so it hurts."

"Like to see you try it."

"Would you?" George asked, his voice almost too low to hear even in that dozy afternoon quiet.

Brian Lippy saw two things. The first was that George could do it. The second was that George sort of *wanted* to do it. And Sandra McCracken would see it happen. Not a good thing, letting your bitch see you get cuffed. Bad enough she saw you getting busted.

"You'll be hearing from my lawyer," said Brian Lippy, and got into the back of the cruiser.

George slammed the door and looked at me. "We're gonna hear from his lawyer."

"Don't you hate that," I said.

The woman poked my arm with something. I turned and saw it was the corner of her driver's license laminate. "Here," she said. She was looking at me. It was only a moment before she turned away and began rummaging in her bag again, this time coming out with a couple of tissues, but it was long enough for me to decide she really was straight. Dead inside, but straight.

"Trooper Jacubois, the vehicle operator states his registration is in his truck," George said.

"Yeah, I have it."

George and I met at the pickup's ridiculous jacked rear bumper—I DO WHATEVER THE LITTLE VOICES TELL ME TO, I EAT AMISH—and I handed him the registration.

"Will she?" he asked in a low voice.

"No," I said.

"Sure?"

"Pretty."

"Try," George said, and went back to the cruiser. My old schoolmate started yelling at him the second George leaned through the driver's-side window to snag the mike. George ignored him and stretched the cord to its full length, so he could stand in the sun. "Base, this is 6, copy-back?"

I returned to the open door of the pickup. The woman had snubbed her cigarette out in the overflowing ashtray and lit a fresh one. Up and down went the fresh cigarette. Out from between the mostly closed wings of her hair came the plumes of used smoke.

"Ms. McCracken, we're going to take Mr. Lippy to our barracks— Troop D, on the hill? Like you to follow us."

She shook her head and began to work with the Kleenex. Bending her head to it rather than raising the tissue to her face, closing the curtains of her hair even farther. The hand with the cigarette in it now resting on the leg of her jeans, the smoke rising straight up.

"Like you to follow us, Ms. McCracken." Speaking just as softly as I could. Trying to make it caring and knowing and just between us. That's how the shrinks and family therapists say to handle it, but what do they know? I kind of hate those SOBs, that's the ugly truth. They come out of the middle class smelling of hairspray and deodorant and they talk to us about spousal abuse and low self-esteem, but they don't have a clue about places like Lassburg County, which played out once when the coal finished up and then again when big steel went away to Japan and China. Does a woman like Sandra McCracken even hear soft and caring and nonthreatening? Once upon a time, maybe. I didn't think anymore. If, on the other hand, I'd grabbed all that hair out of her face so she had to look at me and then shouted, "YOU'RE COMING! YOU'RE COMING AND YOU'RE GOING TO MAKE AN ASSAULT CHARGE AGAINST HIM! YOU'RE COMING, YOU DUMB BEATEN BITCH! YOU ALLOWING CUNT! YOU ARE! *YOU FUCKING WELL ARE!,*" that might have made a difference. That might have worked. You have to speak their language. The shrinks and the therapists, they don't want to hear that. They don't want to believe there's a language that's not their language.

She shook her head again. Not looking at me. Smoking and not looking at me.

"Like you to come on up and swear out an assault complaint on Mr. Lippy there. You pretty much have to, you know. I mean, we saw him hitting you, my partner and I were right behind you, and we got a real good look."

"I *don't* have to," she said, "and you can't make me." She was still using that clumpy, greasy old mop of brownette to hide her face, but she spoke with a certain quiet authority, all the same. She knew we couldn't force her to press charges because she'd been down this road before.

"So how long do you want to take it?" I asked her.

Nothing. The head down. The face hidden. The way she'd lowered her head and hidden her face at twelve when her teacher asked her a hard question in class or when the other girls made fun of her because she was getting tits before they did and that made her a chunky-fuck. That's what girls like her grow that hair for, to hide behind. But knowing didn't give me any more patience with her. Less, if anything. Because, see, you have to take care of yourself in this world. Especially if you ain't purty.

"Sandra."

A little movement of her shoulders when I switched over to her first name. No more than that. And boy, they make me mad. It's how easy they give up. They're like birds on the ground.

"Sandra, look at me."

She didn't want to, but she would. She was used to doing what men said. Doing what men said had pretty much become her life's work.

"Turn your head and look at me."

She turned her head but kept her eyes down. Most of the blood was still on her face. It wasn't a bad face. She probably *was* a little bit purty when someone wasn't tuning up on her. Nor did she look as stupid as you'd think she must be. As stupid as she wanted to be.

"I'd like to go home," she said in a faint child's voice. "I had a nosebleed and I need to clean up."

"Yeah, I know you do. Why? You run into a door? I bet that was it, wasn't it?"

"That's right. A door." There wasn't even defiance in her face. No trace of her boyfriend's I EAT AMISH 'tude. She was just waiting for it to be over. This roadside chatter wasn't real life. Getting hit, that was real life. Hawking back the snot and the blood and the tears all together and swallowing it like cough syrup. "I was comin down the hall to use the bat'-room, and Bri, I dittun know he was in there and he come out all at once, fast, and the door—"

"How long, Sandra?"

"How long what?"

"How long you going to go on eating his shit?"

Her eyes widened a little. That was all.

"Until he knocks all your teeth out?"

"I'd like to go home."

"If I check at Statler Memorial, how many times am I going to find your name? Cause you run into a lot of doors, don't you?"

"Why don't you leave me alone? I ain't bothering you."

"Until he fractures your skull? Until he kills your ass?"

"I want to go home, Officer."

I want to say *That was when I knew I'd lost her* but it would be a lie because you can't lose what you never had. She'd sit there until hell froze over or until I got pissed enough to do something that would get me in trouble later. Like hit her. Because I wanted to hit her. If I hit her, at least she'd know I was there.

I keep a card case in my back pocket. I took it out, riffled through the cards, and found the one I wanted. "This woman's in Statler Village. She's talked to hundreds of young women like you, and helped a lot of them. If you need pro bono, which means free counselling, that'll happen. She'll work it out with you. Okay?"

I held the card in front of her face, between the first two fingers of my right hand. When she didn't take it, I dropped it onto the seat. Then I went back to the cruiser to get the registration. Brian Lippy was sitting in the middle of the back seat with his chin lowered to the neck of his T-shirt, staring up at me from under his brows. He looked like some fucked-up hotrod Napoleon.

"Any luck?" George asked.

"Nah," I said. "She ain't had enough fun yet."

I took the registration back to the truck. She'd moved over behind the wheel. The truck's big V-8 was rumbling. She had pushed the clutch in, and her right hand was on the shifter-knob. Bitten pink nails against chrome. If places like rural Pennsylvania had flags, you could put that on it. Or maybe a six-pack of Iron City Beer and a pack of Winstons.

"Drive safely, Ms. McCracken," I said, handing her the yellow.

"Yeah," she said, and pulled out. Wanting to give me some lip and not daring because she was well-trained. The truck did some jerking at first—she wasn't as good with his manual transmission as she maybe thought she was—and she jerked with it. Back and forth, hair flying. All at once I could see it again, him all over the road, driving his one piece of property with his one hand and punching the piss out of his other piece of property with the other one, and I felt sick to my stomach. Just before she finally achieved second gear, something white fluttered out of the driver's-side window. It was the card I'd given her.

I went back to the cruiser. Brian was still sitting with his chin down on his chest, giving me his fucked-up Napoleon look from beneath his brows. Or maybe it was Rasputin. I got in on the passenger side, feeling very hot and tired. Just to make things complete, Brian started chanting from behind me. "Fat ED-die JACK-you-BOYS. How many boys—"

"Oh shut up," I said.

"Come on back here and shut me up, Fat Eddie. Why don't you come on back here and try it?"

Just another wonderful day in the PSP, in other words. This guy was going to be back in whatever shithole he called home by seven o'clock, drinking a beer while Vanna spun the Wheel of Fortune. I glanced at my watch—1:44 P.M.—and then picked up the microphone. "Base, this is 6."

"Copy, 6." Shirley right back at me, calm as a cool breeze. Shirley just about to get her flowers from Islington and Avery. Out on C.R. 46 in Poteenville, about twenty miles from our 20, a Norco West tanker had just collided with a schoolbus, killing the schoolbus's driver, Mrs. Esther Mayhew. George Stankowski had been close enough to hear the bang of the collision, so who says there's never a cop around when you need one?

"We are Code 15 and 17-base, copy?" Asshole in custody and headed home, in other words.

"Roger, 6, you have one subject in custody or what, over?"

"One subject, roger."

"This is Fat Fuck One, over and out," Brian said from the back seat. He began to laugh—the high, chortling laugh of the veteran stoner. He also began to stomp his cowboy boots up and down. We'd be half an hour getting back to the barracks. I had an idea it was going to be a long ride.

Huddie

I dropped the SC's phone into the cradle and almost trotted across to dispatch, where Shirley was still working hard, bending active Troopers west. "Norco says it's chlorine liquid," I told her. "That's a break. Chlorine's nasty, but it's not usually fatal."

"Are they sure that's what it is?" Shirley asked.

"Ninety per cent. It's what they have out that way. You see those trucks headed up to the water-treatment plant all the time. Pass it on, starting with George S. And what in the name of God's wrong with the dog?"

Mister Dillon was at the back door, nose down to the base of the screen, going back and forth. Almost *bouncing* back and forth, and whining way down in his throat. His ears were laid back. While I was watching, he bumped the screen with his muzzle hard enough to bell it out. Then gave a kind of yelp, as if to say *Man, that hurts.*

"No idea," Shirley said in a voice that told me she had no time for Mister Dillon. Neither, strictly speaking, did I. Yet I looked at him a moment longer. I'd seen hunting dogs behave that way when they ran across the scent of something big in the woods nearby—a bear, or maybe a timberwolf. But there hadn't been any wolves in the Short Hills since before Vietnam, and precious few bears. There was nothing beyond that screen but the parking lot. And Shed B, of course. I looked up at the clock over the kitchen door. It was 2:12 P.M. I couldn't remember ever having been in the barracks when the barracks was so empty.

"Unit 14, Unit 14, this is base, copy?"

George came back to her, still coughing. "Unit 14."

"It's chlorine, 14, Norco West says it's pretty confident of that. Chlorine liquid." She looked at me and I gave her a thumb up. "Irritating but not—"

"Break, break." And cough, cough.

"Standing by, 14."

"Maybe it's chlorine, maybe it's not, base. It's on fire, whatever it is, and there are big white clouds of it rolling this way. My 20 is at the end of the access road, the one by the soccer field. Those kids're coughing worse'n me and I see several people down, including one adult female. There are two schoolbuses parked off to the side. I'm gonna try and take those folks out in one. Over."

I took the mike from Shirley. "George, this is Huddie. Norco says the fire's probably just fuel running out on top of the chlorine. You ought to be safe moving the kids on foot, over?"

What came next was a classic George S response, solid and stolid. Eventually he got one of those above-and-beyond-the-call-of-duty citations for his day's work—from the governor, I think—and his picture was in the paper. His wife framed the citation and hung it on the wall of the rumpus room. I'm not sure George ever understood what the fuss was about. In his mind he was just doing what seemed prudent and reasonable. If there was ever such a thing as the right man at the right place, it was George Stankowski that day at Poteenville Grammar School.

"Bus'd be better," he said. "Faster. This is 14, I'm 7."

Shortly, Shirley and I would forget all about Poteenville for awhile; we had our own oats to roll. If you're curious, Trooper George Stankowski got into one of the buses he'd seen by busting a folding door with a rock. He started the forty-passenger Blue Bird with a spare key he found taped to the back of the driver's sunvisor, and eventually packed twenty-four coughing, weeping, red-eyed children and two teachers inside. Many of the children were still clutching the misshapen pots, blots, and ceramic ashtrays they'd made that afternoon. Three of the kids were unconscious, one from an allergic reaction to chlorine fumes. The other two were simple fainting victims, OD'd on terror and excitement. One of the crafts teachers, Rosellen Nevers, was in more serious straits—George saw her on the sidewalk, lying on her side, gasping and semiconscious, digging at her swelled throat with weakening fingers. Her eyes bulged from their sockets like the yolks of poached eggs.

"That's my Mommy," one of the little girls said. Tears were welling steadily from her huge brown eyes, but she never lost hold of the clay vase she was holding, or tilted it so the black-eyed Susan she'd put in it fell out. "She has the azmar."

George was kneeling beside the woman by then with her head back over his forearm to keep her airway as wide-open as possible. Her hair hung down on the concrete. "Does she take something for her asthma, honey, when it's bad like this?"

"In her pocket," the little girl with the vase said. "Is my Mommy going to die?"

"Nah," George said. He got the Flovent inhaler out of Mrs. Nevers's pocket and shot a good blast down her throat. She gasped, shivered, and sat up.

George carried her onto the bus in his arms, walking behind the coughing, crying children. He plopped Rosellen in a seat next to her daughter, then slipped behind the steering wheel. He put the bus in gear and bumped it across the soccer field, past his cruiser, and onto the access road. By the time he nosed the Blue Bird back onto County Road 46, the kids were singing "Row, Row, Row Your Boat." And that's how Trooper George Stankowski became an authentic hero while the few of us left behind were just trying to hold onto our sanity.

And our lives.

Shirley

George's last communication to dispatch was *14, I'm 7*—this is Unit 14, I'm out of service. I logged it, looking up at the clock to note the time. It was 2:23 P.M. I remember that well, just as I remember Huddie standing beside me, giving my shoulder a little squeeze—trying to tell me George and the kids would be all right without coming right out and saying it, I suppose. 2:23 P.M., that's when all hell broke loose. And I mean that as literally as anyone ever has.

Mister Dillon started barking. Not his deep-throated bark, the one he usually saved for deer who scouted our back field or the raccoons that dared come sniffing around the stoop, but a series of high, yarking yips I had never heard before. It was as if he'd run himself onto something sharp and couldn't get free.

"What the *hell?*" Huddie said.

D took five or six stiff, backing steps away from the screen door, looking sort of like a rodeo horse in a calf-roping event. I think I knew what was going to happen next, and I think Huddie did, too, but neither of us could believe it. Even if we *had* believed it, we couldn't have stopped him. Sweet as he was, I think Mister Dillon would have bitten us if we'd tried. He was still letting out those yipping, hurt little barks, and foam had started to splatter from the corners of his mouth.

I remember reflected light dazzling into my eyes just then. I blinked and the light ran away from me down the length of the wall. That was Unit 6, Eddie and George coming in with their suspect, but I hardly registered that at all. I was looking at Mister Dillon.

He ran at the screen door, and once he was rolling he never hesitated. Never even slowed. Just dropped his head and broke on through to the other side, tearing the door out of its latch and pulling it after him even as he went through, still voicing barks that were almost like screams. At

253

the same time I smelled something, very strong: seawater and decayed vegetable matter. There came a howl of brakes and rubber, the blast of a horn, and someone yelling, *"Watch out! Watch out!"* Huddie ran for the door and I followed him.

Eddie

We were wrecking his day by taking him to the barracks. We'd stopped him, at least temporarily, from beating up his girlfriend. He had to sit in the back seat with the springs digging into his ass and his fancy boots planted on our special puke-resistant plastic floormats. But Brian was making us pay. Me in particular, but of course George had to listen to him, too.

He'd chant his version of my name and then stomp down rhythmically with the big old stacked heels of his shitkickers just as hard as he could. The overall effect was something like a football cheer. And all the time he was staring through the mesh at me with his head down and his little stoned eyes gleaming—I could see him in the mirror clipped to the sunvisor.

"JACK-you-BOYS!" *Clump-clumpclump!* "JACK-you-BOYS!" *Clump-clumpclump!*

"Want to quit that, Brian?" George asked. We were nearing the barracks. The pretty nearly empty barracks; by then we knew what was going on out in Poteenville. Shirley had given us some of it, and the rest we'd picked up from the chatter of the converging units. "You're giving me an earache."

It was all the encouragement Brian needed.

"JACK-you-BOYS!" CLUMP-CLUMPCLUMP!

If he stomped much harder he was apt to put his feet right through the floorboards, but George didn't bother asking him to stop again. When they're buttoned up in the back of your cruiser, getting under your skin is just about all they can try. I'd experienced it before, but hearing this dumbbell, who once knocked the books out of my arms in the high school caff and tore the loops off the backs of my shirts in study hall,

255

chanting that old hateful version of my name . . . man, that was spooky. Like a trip in Professor Peabody's Wayback Machine.

I didn't say anything, but I'm pretty sure George knew. And when he picked up the mike and called in—"20-base in a tick" was what he said—I knew he was talking to me more than Shirley. We'd chain Brian to the chair in the Bad Boy Corner, turn on the TV for him if he wanted it, and take a preliminary pass at the paperwork. Then we'd head for Poteenville, unless the situation out there changed suddenly for the better. Shirley could call Statler County Jail and tell them we had one of their favorite troublemakers coming their way. In the meantime, however—

"JACK-you-BOYS!" *Clump-clumpclump!* "JACK-you-BOYS!"

Now screaming so loud his cheeks were red and the cords stood out on the sides of his neck. He wasn't just playing me anymore; Brian had moved on to an authentic shit fit. What a pleasure getting rid of him was going to be.

We went up Bookin's Hill, George driving a little faster than was strictly necessary, headed for Troop D at the top. George signaled and turned in, perhaps still moving a little faster than he strictly should have been. Lippy, understanding that his time to annoy us had grown short, began shaking the mesh between us and him as well as thumping down with those John Wayne boots of his.

"JACK-you-BOYS!" *Clump-clumpclump! Shake-shakeshake!*

Up the driveway we went, toward the parking lot at the back. George turned tight to the left around the corner of the building, meaning to park with the rear half of Unit 6 by the back steps of the barracks, so we could take good old Bri right up and right in with no fuss, muss, or bother.

And as George came around the corner, there was Mister Dillon, right in front of us.

"Watch out, watch out!" George shouted, whether to me or to the dog or possibly to himself I have no way of knowing. And remembering all this, it strikes me how much it was like the day he hit the woman in Lassburg. So close it was almost a dress rehearsal, but with one very large difference. I wonder if in the last few weeks before he sucked the barrel of

his gun he didn't find himself thinking *I missed the dog and hit the woman* over and over again. Maybe not, but I know I would've, if it had been me. *Missed the dog and hit the woman. How can you believe in a God when it's that way around instead of the other?*

George slammed on the brakes with both feet and drove the heel of his left hand down on the horn. I was thrown forward. My shoulder-harness locked. There were lap belts in the back but our prisoner hadn't troubled to put one on—he'd been too busy doing the Jacubois Cheer for that—and his face shot forward into the mesh, which he'd been gripping. I heard something snap, like when you crack your knuckles. I heard something else crunch. The snap was probably one of his fingers. The crunch was undoubtedly his nose. I have heard them go before, and it always sounds the same, like breaking chicken bones. He gave a muffled, surprised scream. A big squirt of blood, hot as the skin of a hot-water bottle, landed on the shoulder of my uniform.

Mister Dillon probably came within half a foot of dying right there, maybe only two inches, but he ran on without a single look at us, ears laid back tight against his skull, yelping and barking, headed straight for Shed B. His shadow ran beside him on the hottop, black and sharp.

"Ah Grise, I'be hurd!" Brian screamed through his plugged nose. *"I'be bleedin all fuggin over!"* And then he began yelling about police brutality.

George opened the driver's-side door. I just sat where I was for a moment, watching D, expecting him to stop when he got to the shed. He never did. He ran full-tilt into the roll-up door, braining himself. He fell over on his side and let out a scream. Until that day I didn't know dogs could scream, but they can. To me it didn't sound like pain but frustration. My arms broke out in gooseflesh. D got up and turned in a circle, as if chasing his tail. He did that twice, shook his head as if to clear it, and ran straight at the roll-up door again.

"D, no!" Huddie shouted from the back stoop. Shirley was standing right beside him, her hand up to shade her eyes. *"Stop it, D, you mind me, now!"*

Mister D paid zero attention to them. I don't think he would have paid any attention to Orville Garrett, had Orville been there that day, and Orv was the closest thing to an alpha male that D had. He threw himself into the roll-up door again and again, barking crazily, uttering another of those awful frustrated screams each time he struck the solid surface. The third time he did it, he left a bloody noseprint on the white-painted wood.

During all of this, my old pal Brian was yelling his foolish head off. *"Help me, Jacubois, I'be bleedin like a stuck fuggin pig, where'd your dumbdick friend learn to drive, Sears and fuckin Roebuck? Ged me outta here, my fuggin dose!"*

I ignored him and got out of the cruiser, meaning to ask George if he thought D might be rabid, but before I could open my mouth the stink hit me: that smell of seawater and old cabbage and something else, something a whole lot worse.

Mister D suddenly turned and raced to his right, toward the corner of the shed.

"No, D, no!" Shirley screamed. She saw what I saw a second after her— the door on the side, the one you opened with a regular knob instead of rolling up on tracks, was standing a few inches open. I have no idea if someone—Arky, maybe—left it that way

Arky

It wasn't me, I always close dat door. If I forgot, old Sarge woulda torn me a new asshole. Maybe Curt, too. Dey wanted dat place closed up *tight.*
   Dey was *strong* on dat.

Eddie

or maybe something from inside opened it. Some force originating in the Buick, I suppose that's what I'm talking about. I don't know if that's the case or not; I only know that the door *was* open. That was where the worst of the stench was coming from, and that was where Mister Dillon was going.

Shirley ran down the steps, Huddie right behind her, both of them yelling for Mister D to come back. They passed us. George ran after them, and I ran after George.

There had been a lightshow from the Buick two or three days before. I hadn't been there, but someone had told me about it, and the temperature had been down in Shed B for almost a week. Not a lot, only four or five degrees. There were a few signs, in other words, but nothing really spectacular. Nothing you'd get up in the middle of the night and write home to Mother about. Nothing that would have led us to suspect what we found when we got inside.

Shirley was first, screaming D's name . . . and then just *screaming*. A second later and Huddie was screaming, too. Mister Dillon was barking in a lower register by then, only it was barking and growling all mixed together. It's the sound a dog makes when he's got something treed or at bay. George Morgan yelled out, "Oh my Lord! Oh my dear Jesus Christ! What is it?"

I went into the shed, but not very far. Shirley and Huddie were standing shoulder to shoulder and George was right behind them. They had the way pretty well blocked up. The smell was rank—it made your eyes water and your throat close—but I hardly noticed it.

The Buick's trunk was open again. Beyond the car, in the far corner of the shed, stood a thin and wrinkled yellow nightmare with a head that wasn't really a head at all but a loose tangle of pink cords, all of them twitching and squirming. Under them you could see more of the yellow, wrinkled flesh. It was very tall, seven feet at least. Some of those pink cords lashed at one of the overhead beams as it stood there. The sound they made was fluttery, like moths striking window-glass at night, trying to get at the light they see or sense behind it. I can still hear that sound. Sometimes I hear it in my dreams.

Within the thicket made by those wavering, convulsing pink things, something kept opening and closing in the yellow flesh. Something black and round. It might have been a mouth. It might have been trying to scream. I can't describe what it was standing on. It's like my brain couldn't make any sense of what my eyes were seeing. Not legs, I'm sure of that much, and I think there might have been three instead of two. They ended in black, curved talons. The talons had bunches of wiry hair growing out of them—I think it was hair, and I think there were bugs hopping in the tufts, little bugs like nits or fleas. From the thing's chest there hung a twitching gray hose of flesh covered with shiny black circles of flesh. Maybe they were blisters. Or maybe, God help me, those things were its eyes.

Standing in front of it, barking and snarling and spraying curds of foam from his muzzle, was our dog. He made as if to lunge forward and the thing shrieked at him from the black hole. The gray hose twitched like a boneless arm or a frog's leg when you shoot electricity into it. Drops of something flew from the end and hit the shed's floor. Smoke began to rise from those spots at once, and I could see them eating into the concrete.

Mister D drew back a little when it shrieked at him but kept on barking and snarling, ears laid back against his skull, eyes bulging out of their sockets. It shrieked again. Shirley screamed and put her hands over her ears. I could understand the urge to do that, but I didn't think it would help much. The shrieks didn't seem to go into your head through your ears but rather just the other way around: they seemed to start in your head and then go *out* through your ears, escaping like steam. I felt like telling Shirley not to do that, not to block her ears, she'd give herself an embolism or something if she held that awful shrieking inside, and then she dropped her hands on her own.

Huddie put his arm around Shirley and she

Shirley

I felt Huddie put his arm around me and I took his hand. I had to. I had to have something human to hold onto. The way Eddie tells it, the Buick's first livebirth sounds too close to human: it had a mouth inside all those writhing pink things, it had a chest, it had something that served it for eyes. I'm not saying any of that's wrong, but I can't say it's right, either. I'm not sure we ever saw it at all, certainly not the way police officers are trained to look and see. That thing was too strange, too far outside not just our experience but our combined frame of reference. Was it humanoid? A little—at least we perceived it that way. Was it *human?* Not in the least, don't you believe it. Was it intelligent, aware? There's no way to tell for sure, but yes, I think it probably was. Not that it mattered. We were more than horrified by its strangeness. Beyond the horror (or perhaps inside it is what I mean, like a nut inside a shell) there was hate. Part of me wanted to bark and snarl at it just as Mister Dillon was. It woke an anger in me, an *enmity,* as well as fright and revulsion. The other things had been dead on arrival. This one wasn't, but we *wanted* it dead. Oh boy, did we ever!

The second time it shrieked, it seemed to be looking right at us. The hose in its middle lifted like an outstretched arm that's perhaps trying to signal *Help me, call this barking monstrosity off.*

Mister Dillon lunged again. The thing in the corner shrieked a third time and drew back. More liquid splattered from its trunk or arm or penis or whatever it was. A couple of drops struck D and his fur began to smoke at once. He gave a series of hurt, yipping cries. Then, instead of backing off, he leaped at it.

It moved with eerie, gliding speed. Mister Dillon snatched his teeth into one fold of its wrinkled, baggy skin and then it was gone, lurching along the wall on the far side of the Buick, shrieking from that hole in

263

its yellow skin, the hose wagging back and forth. Black goop, like the stuff that had come out of the bat and the fish, was dribbling from where D had nicked it.

It struck the roll-up door and screeched in pain or frustration or both. And then Mister Dillon was on it from behind. He leaped up and seized it by the loose folds hanging from what I suppose you'd call its back. The flesh tore with sickening ease. Mister Dillon dropped to the shed floor with his jaws clenched. More of the thing's skin tore loose and unrolled like loose wallpaper. Black slime . . . blood . . . whatever it was . . . poured over D's upturned face. He howled at the touch of it but held onto what he had, even shaking his head from side to side to tear more of it loose, shaking his head the way a terrier does when it has hold of a rat.

The thing screamed and then made a gibbering sound that was almost words. And yes, the screams and the wordlike sounds all seemed to start in the middle of your head, almost to *hatch* there. The thing beat at the roll-up door with its trunk, as if demanding to be let out, but there was no strength in it.

Huddie had drawn his gun. He had a momentarily clear shot at the pink threads and the yellow knob under them, but then the thing whirled around, still wailing out of that black hole, and it fell on top of Mister D. The gray thing growing from its chest wrapped itself around D's throat and D began to yip and howl with pain. I saw smoke starting to rise up from where the thing had him, and a moment later I could smell burning fur as well as rotting vegetables and seawater. The intruder was sprawled on top of our dog, squealing and thrashing, its legs (if they *were* legs) thumping against the roll-up door and leaving smudges that looked like nicotine stains. And Mister Dillon let out howl after long, agonized howl.

Huddie leveled his gun. I grabbed his wrist and forced it down. *"No! You'll hit D!"* And then Eddie shoved past me, almost knocking me down. He'd found a pair of rubber gloves on some bags by the door and snapped them on.

Eddie

You have to understand that I don't remember any of this the way people ordinarily remember things. For me this is more like remembering the bitter end of a bad drunk. It wasn't Eddie Jacubois who took that pair of rubber gloves from the pile of them on top of the lawn-food bags by the door. It was someone *dreaming* that he was Eddie Jacubois. That's how it seems now, anyway. I think it seemed that way then.

Was Mister Dillon on my mind? Kid, I'd like to think so. And that's the best I can say. Because I can't really remember. I think it's more likely that I just wanted to shut that shrieking yellow thing up, get it out of the middle of my head. I hated it in there. Loathed it. Having it in there was like being raped.

But I must have been thinking, you know it? On some level I really must have been, because I put the rubber gloves on before I took the pickaxe down from the wall. I remember the gloves were blue. There were at least a dozen pairs stacked on those bags, all the colors of the rainbow, but the ones I took were blue. I put them on fast—as fast as the doctors on that *ER* show. Then I took the pickaxe off its pegs. I pushed past Shirley so hard I almost knocked her down. I *would* have knocked her down, I think, only Huddie grabbed her before she could fall.

George shouted something. I think it was "Be careful of the acid." I don't remember feeling scared and I certainly don't remember feeling brave. I remember feeling outrage and revulsion. It was the way you'd feel if you woke up with a leech in your mouth, sucking the blood out of your tongue. I said that once to Curtis and he used a phrase I never forgot: *the horror of trespass.* That's what it was, the horror of trespass.

Mister D, howling and thrashing and snarling, trying to get away; the thing lying on him, the pink threads growing out of its top thrashing around like kelp in a wave; the smell of burning fur; the stench of salt and cabbage; the black stuff pouring out of the thing's dog-bit, furrowed back, running down the wrinkles in its yellow skin like sludge and then pattering on the floor; my need to kill it, erase it, make it gone from the world: all these things were whirling in my mind—*whirling,* I tell you, as if the shock of what we'd found in Shed B had whipped my brains, pureed them, and then stirred them into a cyclone that had nothing to do with sanity or lunacy or police work or vigilante work or Eddie Jacubois. Like I say, I remember it, but not the way you remember ordinary things. More like a dream. And I'm glad. To remember it at all is bad enough. And you can't not remember. Even drinking doesn't stop that, only pushes it away a little bit, and when you stop, it all comes rushing back. Like waking up with a bloodsucker in your mouth.

I got to it and I swung the pickaxe and the pointed end of it went into the middle of it. The thing screamed and threw itself backward against the roll-up door. Mister Dillon got loose and backed away, creeping with his belly low to the floor. He was barking with anger and howling with pain, the sounds mixed together. There was a charred trench in his fur behind his collar. Half his muzzle had been singed black, as if he'd stuck it in a campfire. Little tendrils of smoke were rising from it.

The thing lying against the roll-up door lifted that gray hose in its chest and those *were* eyes embedded in it, all right. They were looking at me and I couldn't bear it. I turned the pickaxe in my hands and brought the axe side of it down. There was a thick *chumping* sound, and part of the hose rolled away on the concrete. I'd also caved in the chest area. Clouds of stuff like pink shaving cream came out of the hole, billowing, like it was under pressure. Along the length of the gray trunk—the severed piece is what I'm talking about—those eyes rolled spastically, seeming to look in all different directions at once. Clear drops of liquid, its venom, I guess, dribbed out and scorched the concrete.

Then George was beside me. He had a shovel. He drove the blade of it down into the middle of the tendrils on the creature's head. Buried it in the thing's yellow flesh all the way up to the ashwood shaft. The thing screamed. I heard it so loud in my mind that it seemed to push my eyes out in their sockets, the way a frog's eyes will bulge when you wrap your hand around its flabby body and squeeze.

Huddie

I put on a pair of gloves myself and grabbed one of the other tools—I think it was a hard rake, but I'm not entirely sure. Whatever it was, I grabbed it, then joined Eddie and George. A few seconds later (or maybe it was a minute, I don't know, time stopped meaning anything) I looked around and Shirley was there, too. She'd put on her own pair of gloves, then grabbed Arky's posthole digger. Her hair had come loose and was hanging down all around her face. She looked to me like Sheena, Queen of the Jungle.

We all remembered to put on gloves, but we were all crazy. Completely nuts. The look of it, the gibbering keening screeching *sound* of it, even the way Mister D was howling and whining—all of that *made* us crazy. I'd forgotten about the overturned tanker, and George Stankowski trying to get the kids into the schoolbus and drive them to safety, and the angry young man Eddie and George Morgan had brought in. I think I forgot there was any world at all outside that stinking little shed. I was screaming as I swung the rake, plunging the tines into the thing on the floor again and again and again. The others were screaming, too. We stood around it in a circle, beating and bludgeoning and cutting it to pieces; we were screaming at it to die and it *wouldn't* die, it seemed as if it would never die.

If I could forget anything, any part of it, I'd forget this: at the very end, just before it finally did die, it raised the stump of the thing in its chest. The stump was trembling like an old man's hand. There were eyes in the stump, some of them hanging from shiny threads of gristle by then. Maybe those threads were optic nerves. I don't know. Anyway, the stump rose up and for just a moment, in the center of my head, *I saw myself.* I saw all of us standing around in a circle and looking down, looking like murderers at the grave of their victim, and I saw how strange and alien we were. How *horrible* we were. In that moment I felt its awful confusion. Not its fear, because it wasn't afraid. Not its innocence, because it wasn't innocent. Or guilty, for that matter. What it was was confused. Did it know *where* it was? I don't think so. Did it know why Mister Dillon had attacked it and we were killing it? Yes, it knew that much. We were doing it because we were so different, so different and so horrible that its many eyes could hardly see us, could hardly hold onto our images as we surrounded it screaming and chopping and cutting and hitting. And then it finally stopped moving. The stub of the trunk-thing in its chest dropped back down again. The eyes stopped twitching and just stared.

We stood there, Eddie and George side by side, panting. Shirley and I were across from them—on the other side of that thing—and Mister D was behind us, panting and whining. Shirley dropped the posthole digger and when it hit the concrete, I saw a plug of the dead thing's yellow flesh caught in it like a piece of diseased dirt. Her face was bone-white except for two wild bright patches of red in her cheeks and another blooming on her throat like a birthmark.

"Huddie," she whispered.

"What?" I asked. I could hardly talk, my throat was that dry.

"Huddie!"

"*What,* goddammit?"

"It could *think,*" she whispered. Her eyes were big and horrified, swimming with tears. "We killed a *thinking being.* That's murder."

"Bullshit's what that is," George said. "Even if it's not, what damn good does it do to go on about it?"

Whining—but not in the same urgent way as before—Mister Dillon pushed in between me and Shirley. There were big bald patches in the fur on his neck and back and chest, as if he had the mange. The tip of one ear seemed to be singed clean off. He stretched out his neck and sniffed the corpse of the thing lying beside the roll-up door.

"Grab him outta there," George said.

"No, he's all right," I said.

As D scented at the limp and now unmoving tangle of pink tendrils on the thing's head, he whined again. Then he lifted his leg and pissed on the severed piece of trunk or horn or whatever it was. With that done he backed away, still whining.

I could hear a faint hiss. The smell of cabbage was getting stronger, and the yellow color was fading from the creature's flesh. It was turning white. Tiny, almost invisible ribbons of steam were starting to drift up. That's where the worst of the stench was, in that rising vapor. The thing had started to decompose, like the rest of the stuff that had come through.

"Shirley, go back inside," I said. "You've got a 99 to handle."

She blinked rapidly, like someone who is just coming to. "The tanker," she said. "George S. Oh Lord, I forgot."

"Take the dog with you," I said.

"Yes. All right." She paused. "What about—?" She gestured at the tools scattered on the concrete, the ones we'd used to kill the creature as it lay against the door, mangled and screaming. Screaming what? For mercy? Would it (or its kind) have accorded mercy to one of us, had our positions been reversed? I don't think so . . . but of course I wouldn't, would I? Because you have to get through first one night and then another and then a year of nights and then ten. You have to be able to turn off the lights and lie there in the dark. You have to believe you only did what would have been done to you. You have to arrange your thoughts because you know you can only live with the lights on so much of the time.

"I don't know, Shirley," I said. I felt very tired, and the smell of the rotting cabbage was making me sick to my stomach. "What the fuck does it matter, it's not like there's going to be a trial or an inquest or anything official. Go on inside. You're the police communications officer. So communicate."

She nodded jerkily. "Come on, Mister Dillon."

I wasn't sure D would go with her but he did, walking neatly behind one of Shirley's brown low-heeled shoes. He kept whining, though, and just before they went out the side door he kind of shivered all over, as if he'd caught a chill.

"*We* oughtta get out, too," George said to Eddie. He started to rub at his eyes, realized he was still wearing gloves, and stripped them off. "We've got a prisoner to take care of."

Eddie looked as surprised as Shirley had when I reminded her that she had business to deal with over in Poteenville. "Forgot all about the loudmouth sonofabitch," he said. "He broke his nose, George—I heard it."

"Yeah?" George said. "Oh what a shame."

Eddie grinned. You could see him trying to pull it back. It widened, instead. They have a way of doing that, even under the worst of circumstances. *Especially* under the worst of circumstances.

"Go on," I said. "Take care of him."

"Come with us," Eddie said. "You shouldn't be in here alone."

"Why not? It's dead, isn't it?"

"That's not." Eddie lifted his chin in the Buick's direction. "Goddam fake car's hinky, still hinky, and I mean to the max. Don't you feel it?"

"I feel something," George said. "Probably just reaction from dealing with that"—he gestured at the dead creature—"that whatever-it-was."

"No," Eddie said. "What you feel's coming from the goddam Buick, not that dead thing. It *breathes,* that's what I think. Whatever that car really is, it breathes. I don't think it's safe to be in here, Hud. Not for any of us."

"You're overreacting."

"The hell I am. *It breathes.* It blew that pink-headed thing out on the exhale, the way you can blow a booger out of your nose when you sneeze. Now it's getting ready to suck back in. I tell you I can feel it."

"Look," I said, "I just want one quick look around, okay? Then I'm going to grab the tarp and cover up . . . that." I jerked my thumb at what we'd killed. "Anything more complicated can wait for Tony and Curt. They're the experts."

But calming him down was impossible. He was working himself into a state.

"You can't let them near that fake car until after it sucks in again." Eddie looked balefully at the Buick. "And you better be ready for an argument on the subject. The Sarge'll want to come in and Curt will want to come in even more, but you can't let them. Because—"

272

"I know," I said. "It's getting ready to suck back in, you can feel it. We ought to get you your own eight-hundred number, Eddie. You could make your fortune reading palms over the phone."

"Yeah, go ahead, laugh. You think Ennis Rafferty's laughing, wherever he is? I'm telling you what I know, whether you like it or not. It's breathing. It's what it's been doing all along. This time when it sucks back, it's going to be hard. Tell you what. Let me and George help you with the tarp. We'll cover the thing up together and then we'll all go out together."

That seemed like a bad idea to me, although I didn't know exactly why. "Eddie, I can handle this. Swear to God. Also, I want to take a few pictures of Mr. E.T. before he rots away to nothing but stone-crab soup."

"Quit it," George said. He was looking a little green.

"Sorry. I'll be out in two shakes of a lamb's tail. Go on, now, you guys, take care of your subject."

Eddie was staring at the Buick, standing there on its big smooth whitewall tires, its trunk open so its ass end looked like the front end of a crocodile. "I hate that thing," he said. "For two cents—"

George was heading for the door by then, and Eddie followed without finishing what he'd do for two cents. It wasn't that hard to figure out, anyway.

The smell of the decaying creature was getting worse by the minute, and I remembered the Puff-Pak Curtis had worn when he'd come in here to investigate the plant that looked like a lily. I thought it was still in the hutch. There was a Polaroid camera, too, or had been the last time I looked.

Very faint, from the parking lot, I heard George calling to Shirley, asking her if she was all right. She called back and said she was. A second or two later, Eddie yelled *FUCK!* at the top of his voice. Another country heard from. He sounded pissed like a bear. I figured his prisoner, probably high on drugs and with a broken nose to boot, had upchucked in the back of Unit 6. Well, so what? There are worse things than having a prisoner blow chunks in your ride. Once, while I was assisting at the scene of a three-car collision over in Patchin, I stashed the drunk driver who'd

273

caused it all in the back of my unit for safekeeping while I set out some road flares. When I returned, I discovered that my subject had taken off his shirt and taken a shit in it. He then used one of the sleeves as a squeeze-tube—you have to imagine a baker decorating a cake to get what I'm trying to describe here—and wrote his name on both side windows in the back. He was trying to do the rear window, too, only he ran out of his special brown icing. When I asked him why he'd want to do such a nasty goddam thing, he looked at me with that cockeyed hauteur only a longtime drunk can manage and said, "It's a nasty goddam world, Trooper."

Anyway, I didn't think Eddie yelling was important, and I went out back to the hutch where we kept our supplies without bothering to check on him. I was more than half-convinced the Puff-Pak would be gone, but it was still on the shelf, wedged between the box of blank videotapes and a pile of *Field & Stream* magazines. Some tidy soul had even tucked it into a plastic evidence bag to keep the dust off. Taking it down, I remembered how crazy Curt had looked on the day I first saw him wearing this gadget, Curt also wearing a plastic barber's smock and a blue bathing cap and red galoshes. *You're beautiful, wave to your adoring fans,* I'd told him.

I put the mask to my mouth and nose, almost sure that what came out of it would be unbreathable, but it was air, all right—stale as week-old bread but not actually moldy, if you know what I mean. Better than the stench in the shed, certainly. I grabbed the battered old Polaroid One-Shot from the nail where it was hanging by the strap. I backed out of the hutch, and—this could be nothing but hindsight, I'll be the first to admit it—I think I saw movement. Just a flash of movement. Not from the vicinity of the shed, though, because I was looking right at that and this was more a corner-of-the-eye phenomenon. Something in our back field. In the high grass. I probably thought it was Mister Dillon, maybe rolling around and trying to get that thing's smell off. Well, it wasn't. Mister Dillon wasn't up to any rolling around by then. By then poor old D was busy dying.

I went back into the shed, breathing through the mask. And although I hadn't felt what Eddie was talking about before, this time it came through loud and clear. It was like being outside the shed for a few

274

moments had freshened me for it, or attuned me to it. The Buick wasn't flashing purple lightning or glowing or humming, it was only sitting there, but there was a sense of *liveliness* to it that was unmistakable. You could feel it hovering just over your skin, like the lightest touch of a breeze huffing at the hairs on your forearms. And I thought . . . this is crazy, but I thought, *What if the Buick's nothing but another version of what I'm wearing on my face right now? What if it's nothing but a Puff-Pak? What if the thing wearing it has exhaled and now its chest is lying flat but in a second or two—*

Even with the Puff-Pak, the smell of the dead creature was enough to make my eyes water. Brian Cole and Jackie O'Hara, two of the handier build-em-and-fix-em fellows on the roster back then, had installed an overhead fan the year before, and I flipped the switch as I passed it.

I took three pictures, and then the One-Shot was out of film—I'd never even checked the load. Stupid. I tucked the photos into my back pocket, put the camera down on the floor, then went to get the tarp. As I bent and grabbed it, I realized that I'd taken the camera but walked out of the hutch right past the looped length of bright yellow rope. I should have taken it and cinched the loop in the end of it around my waist. Tied the other end to the big old hook Curtis had mounted to the left of Shed B's side door for just that purpose. But I didn't do that. The rope was too goddam bright to miss, but I missed it anyway. Funny, huh? And there I was where I had no business to be on my own, but I *was* on my own. I wasn't wearing a security line, either. Had walked right past it, maybe because something *wanted* me to walk right past it. There was a dead E.T. on the floor and the air was full of a lively, chilly, *gathering* feeling. I think it crossed my mind that if I disappeared, my wife and Ennis Rafferty's sister could join up forces. I think I might have laughed out loud at that. I can't remember for sure, but I do remember being struck humorous by something. The global absurdity of the situation, maybe.

The thing we'd killed had turned entirely white. It was steaming like dry ice. The eyes on the severed piece still seemed to be staring at me, even though by then they'd started to melt and run. I was as afraid as I've ever been in my life, afraid the way you are when you're in a situation where you could really die and you know it. That sense of something about to breathe, to *suck in,* was so strong it made my skin crawl. But I was grinning, too. Big old grin. Not quite laughing, but almost. Feeling humorous. I tossed the tarp over Mr. E.T. and started backing out of the shed. Forgot the Polaroid entirely. Left it sitting there on the concrete.

I was almost at the door when I looked at the Buick. And some force pulled me toward it. Am I sure it was *its* force? Actually, I'm not. It might just have been the fascination deadly things have for us: the edge and the drop, how the muzzle of a gun looks back at us like an eye if we turn it this way and that. Even the point of a knife starts to look different if the hour's late and everyone else in the house has gone to sleep.

All this was below the level of thinking, though. On the level of thinking I just decided I couldn't go out and leave the Buick with its trunk open. It just looked too . . . I don't know, too getting ready to breathe. Something like that. I was still smiling. Might even have laughed a little.

I took eight steps—or maybe it was a dozen, I guess it could have been as many as a dozen. I was telling myself there was nothing foolish about what I was doing, Eddie J was nothing but an old lady mistaking feelings for facts. I reached for the trunk-lid. I meant to just slam it and scat (or so I told myself), but then I looked inside and I said one of those things you say when you're surprised, I can't remember which one, it might have been *Well, I be dog* or *I'll be switched.* Because there was something in there, lying on the trunk's plain brown carpeting. It looked like a transistor radio from the late fifties or early sixties. There was even a shiny stub of what could have been an antenna sticking up from it.

I reached into the trunk and picked the gizmo up. Had a good laugh over it, too. I felt like I was in a dream, or tripping on some chemical. And all the time I knew it was closing in on me, getting ready to take me. I didn't know if it got Ennis the same way, but probably, yeah. I was standing in front of that open trunk, no rope on me and no one to pull me back, and something was getting ready to pull me in, to breathe me like cigarette smoke. And I didn't give Shit One. All I cared about was what I'd found in the trunk.

It might have been some sort of communication device—that's what it looked like—but it might have been something else entirely: where the monster kept its prescription drugs, some sort of musical instrument, maybe even a weapon. It was the size of a cigarette-pack but a lot heavier. Heavier than a transistor radio or a Walkman, too. There were no dials or knobs or levers on it. The stuff it was made of didn't look or feel like either metal or plastic. It had a fine-grained texture, not exactly unpleasant but organic, like cured cowhide. I touched the rod sticking out of it and it retracted into a hole on top. I touched the hole and the rod came back out. Touched the rod again and this time nothing happened. Not then, not ever. Although *ever* for what we called "the radio" wasn't very long; after a week or so, the surface of it began to pit and corrode. It was in an evidence bag with a Ziploc top, but that didn't matter. A month later the "radio" looked like something that's been left out in the wind and rain for about eighty years. And by the following spring it was nothing but a bunch of gray fragments lying at the bottom of a Baggie. The antenna, if that's what it was, never moved again. Not so much as a silly millimeter.

I thought of Shirley saying *We killed a thinking being* and George saying that was bullshit. Except it wasn't bullshit. The bat and the fish hadn't come equipped with things that looked like transistor radios because they had been animals. Today's visitor—which we'd hacked to pieces with tools we'd taken from the pegboard—had been something quite different. However loathsome it had seemed to us, no matter how instinctively we'd—what was that word?—we'd repudiated it, Shirley was right: it had been a thinking being. We'd killed it nevertheless, hacked it to pieces even as it lay on the concrete, holding out the severed stump of its trunk in surrender and screaming for the mercy it must have known we'd never give it. *Couldn't* give it. And that didn't horrify me. What did was a vision of the shoe on the other foot. Of Ennis Rafferty falling into the midst of other creatures like this, things with yellow knobs for heads under tangled masses of pink ropes that might have been hair. I saw him dying beneath their flailing, acid-lined trunks and hooking talons, trying to scream for mercy and choking on air he could barely breathe, and when he lay dead before them, dead and already beginning to rot, had one of them worked his weapon out of its holster? Had they stood there looking at it under an alien sky of some unimaginable color? As puzzled by the gun as I had been by the "radio"? Had one of them said *We just killed a thinking being,* to which another had responded *That's bullshit*? And as I thought these things, I also thought I ought to get out of there right away. Unless I wanted to investigate such questions in person, that was. So what happened next? I've never told anyone that, but I might as well tell now; seems foolish to come this far and then hold back.

I decided to get in the trunk.

I could see myself doing it. There would be plenty of space; you know how big the trunks of those old cars were. When I was a kid we used to joke that Buicks and Cadillacs and Chryslers were mob cars because there was room enough for either two polacks or three guineas in the trunk. Plenty of space. Old Huddie Royer would get in, and lie on his side, and reach up, and pull the trunk closed. Softly. So it made just the faintest click. Then he'd lie there in the dark, breathing stale air from the Puff-Pak and holding the "radio" to his chest. There wouldn't be much air left in the little tank, but there'd be enough. Old Huddie would just curl up and lie there and keep smilin and then . . . pretty soon . . .

Something interesting would happen.

I haven't thought of this in years, unless it was in the kind of dreams you can't remember when you wake up, the ones you just know were bad because your heart is pounding and your mouth is dry and your tongue tastes like a burnt fuse. The last time I thought consciously about standing there in front of the Buick Roadmaster's trunk was when I heard George Morgan had taken his own life. I thought of him out there in his garage, sitting down on the floor, maybe listening to the kids playing baseball under the lights over on McClurg Field around the other side of the block and then with his can of beer finished taking up the gun and looking at it. We might have switched over to the Beretta by then, but George kept his Ruger. Said it just felt right in his hand. I thought of him turning it this way and that, looking into its eye. Every gun has an eye. Anyone who's ever looked into one knows that. I thought of him putting the barrel between his teeth and feeling the hard little bump of the gunsight against the roof of his mouth. Tasting the oil. Maybe even poking into the muzzle with the tip of his tongue, the way you might tongue the mouthpiece of a trumpet when you're getting ready to blow. Sitting there in the corner of the garage, still tasting that last can of beer, also tasting the gun-oil and the steel, licking the hole in the muzzle, the eye the slug comes out of at twice the speed of sound, riding a pad of hot expanding gases. Sitting there smelling the grass caked under the Lawnboy and a little spilled gasoline. Hearing kids cheer across the block. Thinking of how it felt to hit a woman with two tons of police cruiser, the thud and slew of it, seeing drops of blood appear on the windshield like the debut of a biblical curse and hearing the dry gourdlike rattle of something caught in one of the wheelwells, what turned out to be one of her sneakers. I thought of all that and I think it was how it was for him because I know it's how it was for me. I knew it was going to be horrible but I didn't care because it would be kind of funny, too. That's why I was smiling. I didn't want to get away. I don't think George did, either. In the end, when you really decide to do it, it's like falling in love. It's like your wedding night. And I had decided to do it.

Saved by the bell, that's the saying, but I was saved by a scream: Shirley's. At first it was just a high shriek, and then there were words. *"Help! Please! Help me! Please, please help me!"*

It was like being slapped out of a trance. I took two big steps away from the Buick's trunk, wavering like a drunk, hardly able to believe what I'd been on the verge of. Then Shirley screamed again and I heard Eddie yell: *"What's wrong with him, George? What's happening to him?"*

I turned and ran out the shed door.

Yeah, saved by the scream. That's me.

Eddie

It was better outside, so much better I almost felt, as I hurried along after George, that the whole thing in Shed B had been a dream. Surely there were no monsters with pink strings growing out of their heads and trunks with eyes in them and talons with hair growing out of them. Reality was our subject in the back seat of Unit 6, that debonair, girlfriend-punching puke, ladies and gentlemen, let's give him a great big hand, Brian Lippy. I was still afraid of the Buick—afraid as I'd never been before or have been since—and I was sure there was a perfectly good reason to feel that way, but I could no longer remember what it was. Which was a relief.

I trotted to catch up with George. "Hey, man, I might have gotten a little carried away in there. If I did—"

"Shit," he said in a flat, disgusted voice, stopping so quick I almost ran into his back. He was standing at the edge of the parking lot with his hands curled into fists that were planted on his hips. "Look at that." Then he called, "Shirley! You all right?"

"Fine," she called back. "But Mister D . . . aw sugar, there goes the radio. I have to get that."

"Doesn't this *bite,*" George said in a low voice.

I stepped up beside him and saw why he was upset. 6's right rear window had been broken clean out to the doorframe, undoubtedly by a pair of cowboy boots with stacked heels. Two or three kicks wouldn't have done that, maybe not even a dozen, but we'd given my old school chum Brian plenty of time to go to town. Rowdy-dow and a hot-cha-cha, as my old mother used to say. The sun was reflecting fire off a thousand crumbles of glass lying heaped on the hottop. Of Monsieur Brian Lippy himself, there was no sign. *"FUCK!"* I shouted, and actually shook my fists at Unit 6.

We had a burning chemical tanker over in Pogus County, we had a dead monster rotting in our back shed, and now we also had one escaped neo-Nazi asshole. Plus a broken cruiser window. You might think that's not much compared to the rest, kid, but that's because you've never had to fill out the forms, beginning with 24-A-24, Damaged Property, PSP, and ending with Complete Incident Report, Fill Out All Appropriate Fields. One thing I'd like to know is why you never have a series of good days in which one thing goes wrong. Because it's not that way, at least not in my experience. In my experience the bad shit gets saved up until you have a day when everything comes due at once. That was one of those days. The granddaddy of them all.

George started walking toward 6. I walked beside him. He hunkered down, took the walkie out of its holster on his hip, and stirred through the strew of broken Saf-T-Glas with the rubber antenna. Then he picked something up. It was our pal's crucifix earring. He must have lost it when he climbed through the broken window.

"Fuck," I said again, but in a lower voice. "Where do you think he went?"

"Well, he's not in with Shirley. Which is good. Otherwise? Down the road, up the road, across the road, across the back field and into the woods. One of those. Take your pick." He got up and looked into the empty back seat. "This could be bad, Eddie. This could be a real fuckarow. You know that, don't you?"

Losing a prisoner was never good, but Brian Lippy wasn't exactly John Dillinger, and I said so.

George shook his head as if I didn't get it. "We don't know what he *saw.* Do we?"

"Huh?"

"Maybe nothing," he went on, and dragged a shoe through the broken glass. The little pieces clicked and scritched. There were droplets of blood on some of them. "Maybe he hightailed it *away* from the shed. But of course going that way'd take him to the road, and even if he was as high as an elephant's eye, he might not've wanted to go that way, in case some cop 20-base should see him—a guy covered with blood, busted glass in his hair—and arrest him all over again."

I was slow that day and I admit it. Or maybe I was still in shock. "I don't see what you're—"

George was standing with his head down and his arms folded across his chest. He was still dragging his foot back and forth, stirring that broken glass like stew. "Me, I'd head for the back field. I'd want to hook around to the highway through the woods, maybe wash up in one of the streams back there, then try to hitch a ride. Only what if I get distracted while I'm making my escape? What if I hear a lot of screaming and thrashing coming from inside that shed?"

"Oh," I said. "Oh my God. You don't think he'd really stop what *he* was doing to check on what *we* were doing, do you?"

"Probably not. But is it possible? Hell, yes. Curiosity's a powerful thing."

That made me think of what Curt liked to say about the curious cat. "Yeah, but who on God's earth would ever believe him?"

"If it ever got into the *American,*" George said heavily, "Ennis's sister might. And that would be a start. Wouldn't it?"

"Shit," I said. I thought it over. "We better have Shirley put out an all-points on Brian Lippy."

"First let's let folks get the mess in Poteenville picked up a little. Then, when he gets here, we'll tell the Sarge everything—including what Lippy might have seen—and show him what's left in Shed B. If Huddie gets some half-decent pictures . . ." He glanced back over his shoulder. "Say, where *is* Huddie? He should've been out of there by now. Christ, I hope—"

He got that far and then Shirley started screaming. *"Help! Please! Help me! Please, please help me!"*

Before either of us could take a step toward the barracks, Mister Dillon came out through the hole he'd already put in the screen door. He was staggering from side to side like a drunk, and his head was down. Smoke was rising from his fur. More seemed to be coming out of his head, although at first I couldn't see where it was coming from; *everywhere* was my first impression. He got his forepaws on the first of the three steps going down from the back stoop to the parking lot, then lost his balance and fell on his side. When he did, he twisted his head in a series of jerks.

It was the way people move in those oldtime silent movies. I saw smoke coming out of his nostrils in twin streams. It made me think of the woman sitting there in Lippy's bigfoot truck, the smoke from her cigarette rising in a ribbon that seemed to disappear before it got to the roof. More smoke was coming from his eyes, which had gone a strange, knitted white. He vomited out a spew of smoky blood, half-dissolved tissue, and triangular white things. After a moment or two I realized they were his teeth.

Shirley

There was a great confused clatter of radio traffic, but none of it was directed to base. Why would it be, when all the action was either out at Poteenville Grammar School or headed that way? George Stankowski had gotten the kids away from the smoke, at least, I got that. Poteenville Volunteer One, aided by pumpers from Statler County, were controlling the grassfires around the school. Those fires had indeed been touched off by burning diesel and not some flammable chemical. It was chlorine liquid in the tanker, that was now confirmed. Not good, but nowhere near as bad as it might have been.

George called to me from outside, wanting to know if I was all right. Thinking that was rather sweet, I called back and told him I was. A second or two later, Eddie called out the f-word, angry. During all this I felt strange, not myself, like someone going through ordinary chores and routines in the wake of some vast change.

Mister D was standing in the door to dispatch with his head down, whining at me. I thought the burned patches in his fur were probably paining him. There were more burned places, dottings of them, on both sides of his muzzle. I reminded myself that someone—Orv Garrett was the logical choice—should take him to the vet when things finally settled back down. That would mean making up some sort of story about how he got burned, probably a real whopper.

"Want some water, big boy?" I asked. "Bet you do, don't you?"

He whined again, as if to say water was a very good idea. I went into the kitchenette, got his bowl, filled it at the sink. I could hear him clicking along on the lino behind me but I never turned around until I had the bowl full.

"Here you a—"

I got that far, then took a good look at him and dropped the bowl on the floor, splashing my ankles. He was shivering all over—not like he was cold but like someone was passing an electric current through him. And foam was dripping out from both sides of his muzzle.

He's rabid, I thought. *Whatever that thing had, it's turned D rabid.*

He didn't look rabid, though, only confused and in misery. His eyes seemed to be asking me to fix whatever was wrong. I was the human, I was in charge, I should be able to fix it.

"D?" I said. I dropped down on one knee and held my hand out to him. I know that sounds stupid—dangerous—but at the time it seemed like the right thing. "D, what is it? What's wrong? Poor old thing, what's wrong?"

He came to me, but very slowly, whining and shivering with every step. When he got close I saw a terrible thing: little tendrils of smoke were coming from the birdshot-spatter of holes on his muzzle. More was coming from the burned patches on his fur, and from the corners of his eyes, as well. I could see his eyes starting to lighten, as if a mist was covering them from the inside.

I reached out and touched the top of his head. When I felt how hot it was, I gave a little yell and yanked my hand back, the way you do when you touch a stove burner you thought was off but isn't. Mister D made as if to snap at me, but I don't think he meant anything by it; he just couldn't think what else to do. Then he turned and blundered his way out of the kitchen.

I got up, and for a moment the whole world swam in front of my eyes. If I hadn't grabbed the counter, I think I would have fallen. Then I went after him (staggering a little myself) and said, "D? Come back, honey-bunch."

He was halfway across the duty room. He turned once to look back at me—toward the sound of my voice—and I saw . . . oh, I saw smoke coming out of his mouth and nose, out of his ears, too. The sides of his mouth drew back and for a second it seemed like he was trying to grin at me, the way dogs will do when they're happy. Then he vomited. Most of what came out wasn't food but his own insides. And they were smoking.

That was when I screamed. *"Help! Please! Help me! Please, please help me!"*

Mister D turned away as if all that screaming was hurting his poor hot ears, and went on staggering across the floor. He must have seen the hole in the screen, he must have had enough eyesight left for that, because he set sail for it and slipped out through it.

I went after him, still screaming.

Eddie

"What's wrong with him, George?" I shouted. Mister Dillon had managed to get on his feet again. He was turning slowly around, the smoke rising from his fur and coming out of his mouth in gray billows. *"What's happening to him?"*

Shirley came out, her cheeks wet with tears. "Help him!" she shouted. "He's burning up!"

Huddie joined us then, panting as if he'd run a race. "What the hell is it?"

Then he saw. Mister Dillon had collapsed again. We walked cautiously toward him from one side. From the other, Shirley came down steps from the stoop. She was closer and reached him first.

"Don't touch him!" George said.

Shirley ignored him and put a hand on D's neck, but she couldn't hold it there. She looked at us, her eyes swimming with tears. "He's on fire inside," she said.

Whining, Mister Dillon tried to get on his feet again. He made it halfway, the front half, and began to move slowly toward the far side of the parking lot, where Curt's Bel Air was parked next to Dicky-Duck Eliot's Toyota. By then he *had* to have been blind; his eyes were nothing but boiling jelly in their sockets. He kind of paddled along, pulling himself with his front paws, dragging his rump.

"Christ," Huddie said.

By then tears were pouring down Shirley's face and her voice was so choked it was hard to make out what she was saying. "Please, for the love of God, can't one of you help him?"

I had an image then, very bright and clear. I saw myself getting the hose, which Arky always kept coiled under the faucet-bib on the side of the building. I saw myself turning on the spigot, then running to Mister D and slamming the cold brass nozzle of the hose into his mouth, feeding water down the chimney that was his throat. I saw myself putting him out.

But George was already walking toward the dying ruin that had been our barracks dog, taking his gun out of his holster as he went. D, meanwhile, was still paddling mindlessly along toward a spot of nothing much between Curt's Bel Air and Dicky-Duck's Toyota, moving in a cloud of thickening smoke. How long, I wondered, before the fire inside broke through and he went up in flames like one of those suicidal Buddhist monks you used to see on television during the Vietnam War?

George stopped and held his gun up so Shirley could see it. "It's the only thing, darlin. Don't you think?"

"Yes, hurry," she said, speaking very rapidly.

Now: *Shirley*

I turned to Ned, who was sitting there with his head down and his hair hanging on his brow. I put my hand on his chin and tilted it up so he'd have to look at me. "There was nothing else we could do," I said. "You see that, don't you?"

For a moment he said nothing and I was afraid. Then he nodded.

I looked at Sandy Dearborn, but he wasn't looking at me. He was looking at Curtis's boy, and I've rarely seen him with such a troubled expression.

Then Eddie started talking again and I sat back to listen. It's funny how close the past is, sometimes. Sometimes it seems as if you could almost reach out and touch it. Only . . .

Only who really wants to?

Then: *Eddie*

In the end there was no more melodrama, just a Trooper in a gray uniform with the shadow of his big hat shielding his eyes bending and reaching out like you might reach out your hand to a crying child to comfort him. He touched the muzzle of his Ruger to the dog's smoking ear and pulled the trigger. There was a loud *Pow!* and D fell dead on his side. The smoke was still coming out of his fur in little ribbons.

George holstered his weapon and stood back. Then he put his hands over his face and cried something out. I don't know what it was. It was too muffled to tell. Huddie and I walked to where he was. Shirley did, too. We put our arms around him, all of us. We were standing in the middle of the parking lot with Unit 6 behind us and Shed B to our right and our nice barracks dog who never made any trouble for anybody lying dead in front of us. We could smell him cooking, and without a word we all moved farther to our right, upwind, shuffling rather than walking because we weren't quite ready to lose hold of one another. We didn't talk. We waited to see if he'd actually catch on fire like we thought he might, but it seemed that the fire didn't want him or maybe couldn't use him now that he was dead. He swelled some, and there was a gruesome little sound from inside him, almost like the one you get when you pop a paper lunchsack. It might have been one of his lungs. Anyway, once that happened, the smoke started to thin.

"That thing from the Buick poisoned him, didn't it?" Huddie asked. "It poisoned him when he bit into it."

"Poisoned him, my ass," I said. "That pink-hair motherfucker *firebombed* him." Then I remembered that Shirley was there, and she never had appreciated that kind of talk. "Sorry," I said.

She seemed not to have heard me. She was still looking fixedly down at Mister D. "What do we do now?" she asked. "Does anyone have any ideas?"

"I don't," I said. "This situation is totally out of control."

"Maybe not," George said. "Did you cover up the thing in there, Hud?"

"Yeah."

"All right, that's a start. And how does it look out in Poteenville, Shirl?"

"The kids are out of danger. They've got a dead bus driver, but considering how bad things looked at first, I'd say . . ." She stopped, lips pressed together so tight they were almost gone, her throat working. Then she said, "Excuse me, fellas."

She walked stiff-legged around the corner of the barracks with the back of her hand pressed against her mouth. She held on until she was out of sight—nothing showing but her shadow—and then there came three big wet whooping sounds. The three of us stood over the smoking corpse of the dog without saying anything, and after a few minutes she came back, dead white and wiping her mouth with a Kleenex. And picked up right where she'd left off. It was as if she'd paused just long enough to clear her throat or swat a fly. "I'd say that was a pretty low score. The question is, what's the score here?"

"Get either Curt or the Sarge on the radio," George said. "Curt will do but Tony's better because he's more level-headed when it comes to the Buick. You guys buy that?"

Huddie and I nodded. So did Shirley. "Tell him you have a Code D and we want him here as soon as he can get here. He should know it's not an emergency, but he should also know it's damn *close* to an emergency. Also, tell him we may have a Kubrick." This was another piece of slang peculiar (so far as I know) to our barracks. A Kubrick is a 2001, and 2001 is PSP code for "escaped prisoner." I had heard it talked about, but never actually called.

"Kubrick, copy," Shirley said. She seemed steadier now that she had orders. "Do you—"

There was a loud bang. Shirley gave a small scream and all three of us turned toward the shed, reaching for our weapons as we did. Then Huddie laughed. The breeze had blown the shed door closed.

"Go on, Shirley," George said. "Get the Sarge. Let's make this happen."

"And Brian Lippy?" I asked. "No APB?"

Huddie sighed. Took off his hat. Rubbed the nape of his neck. Looked up at the sky. Put his hat back on. "I don't know," he said. "But if one *does* go out, it won't be any of us who *puts* it out. That's the Sarge's call. It's why they pay him the big bucks."

"Good point," George said. Now that he saw that the responsibility was going to travel on, he looked a little more relaxed.

Shirley turned to go into the barracks, then looked back over her shoulder. "Cover him up, would you?" she said. "Poor old Mister D. Put something over him. Looking at him that way hurts my heart."

"Okay," I said, and started toward the shed.

"Eddie?" Huddie said.

"Yeah?"

"There's a piece of tarp big enough to do the job in the hutch. Use that. Don't go into the shed."

"Why not?"

"Because something's still going on with that Buick. Hard to tell exactly what, but if you go in there, you might not come back out."

"All right," I said. "You don't have to twist my arm."

I got the piece of tarp out of the hutch—just a flimsy blue thing, but it would do. On the way back to cover D's body, I stopped at the roll-up door and took a look into the shed, cupping one hand to the side of my face to cut the glare. I wanted a look at the thermometer; I also wanted to make sure my old school chum Brian wasn't skulk-assing around in there. He wasn't, and the temperature appeared to have gone up a degree or two. Only one thing in the landscape had changed. The trunk was shut.

The crocodile had closed its mouth.

Now: *Sandy*

Shirley, Huddie, Eddie: the sound of their entwined voices was oddly beautiful to me, like the voices of characters speaking lines in some strange play. Eddie said the crocodile had closed its mouth and then his voice ceased and I waited for one of the other voices to come in and when none did and Eddie himself didn't resume, I knew it was over. I knew but Ned Wilcox didn't. Or maybe he did and just didn't want to admit it.

"Well?" he said, and that barely disguised impatience was back in his voice.

What happened when you dissected the bat-thing? Tell me about the fish. Tell me everything. But—this is important—tell me a story, *one that has a beginning and a middle and an end where everything is explained. Because I deserve that. Don't shake the rattle of your ambiguity in my face. I deny its place. I repudiate its claim. I want a* story.

He was young and that explained part of it, he was faced with something that was, as they say, not of this Earth, and that explained more of it . . . but there was something else, too, and it wasn't pretty. A kind of selfish, single-minded grubbing. And he thought he had a right. We spoil the grief-stricken, have you ever noticed that? And they become used to the treatment.

"Well what?" I asked. I spoke in my least encouraging voice. Not that it would help.

"What happened when Sergeant Schoondist and my father got back? Did you catch Brian Lippy? Did he see? Did he *tell?* Jesus, you guys can't stop there!"

He was wrong, we could stop anyplace we chose to, but I kept that fact to myself (at least for the time being) and told him that no, we never did catch Brian Lippy; Brian Lippy remained Code Kubrick to this very day.

"Who wrote the report?" Ned asked. "Did you, Eddie? Or was it Trooper Morgan?"

"George," he said with a trace of a grin. "He was always better at stuff like that. Took Creative Writing in college. He used to say any state cop worth his salt needed to know the basics of creative writing. When we started to fall apart that day, George was the one who pulled us together. Didn't he, Huddie?"

Huddie nodded.

Eddie got up, put his hands in the small of his back, and stretched until we could hear the bones crackle. "Gotta go home, fellas. Might stop for a beer at The Tap on the way. Maybe even two. After all this talking, I'm pretty dry, and soda pop just don't cut it."

Ned looked at him with surprise, anger, and reproach. "You can't leave just like that!" he exclaimed. "I want to hear the whole thing!"

And Eddie, who was slowly losing the struggle not to return to being Fat Eddie, said what I knew, what we all knew. He said it while looking at Ned with eyes which were not exactly friendly. "You did, kid. You just don't know it."

Ned watched him walk away, then turned to the rest of us. Only Shirley looked back with real sympathy, and I think that hers was tempered with sadness for the boy.

"What does he mean, I heard it all?"

"There's nothing left but a few anecdotes," I said, "and those are only variations on the same theme. About as interesting as the kernels at the bottom of the popcorn bowl.

"As for Brian Lippy, the report George wrote said 'Troopers Morgan and Jacubois spoke to the subject and ascertained he was sober. Subject denied assaulting his girlfriend and Trooper Jacubois ascertained that the girlfriend supported him in this. Subject was then released.' "

"But Lippy kicked out their cruiser window!"

"Right, and under the circumstances, George and Eddie couldn't very well put in a claim for the damages."

"So?"

"So the money to replace it probably came out of the contingency fund. The Buick 8 contingency fund, if you want me to cross the *t*'s.

We keep it the same place now we did then, a coffee can in the kitchen."

"Yar, dat's where it come from," Arky said. "Poor ole coffee can's taken a fair number of hits over d'years." He stood up and also stretched his back. "Gotta go, boys n girls. Unlike some of you, I got friends—what dey call a personal life on d'daytime talkshows. But before I leave, you want to know sup'm else, Neddie? About dat day?"

"Anything you want to tell me."

"Dey buried D." He said the verb the old way, so it rhymes with *scurried*. "An right nex' to im dey buried d'tools dey use on dat t'ing poisoned im. One of em was my pos'hole digger, an I din' get no coffee-can compensation for *dat!*"

"You didn't fill out a T.S. 1, that's why," Shirley said. "I know the paperwork's a pain in the fanny, but . . ." She shrugged as if to say *That's the way of the world.*

Arky was frowning suspiciously at her. "T.S. 1? What kind of form is dat?"

"It's your tough-shit list," Shirley told him, perfectly straight-faced. "The one you fill out every month and send to the chaplain. Goodness, I never saw such a Swedish squarehead. Didn't they teach you *anything* in the Army?"

Arky flapped his hands at her, but he was smiling. He'd taken plenty of ribbing over the years, believe me—that accent of his attracted it. "Geddout witcha!"

"Walked right into it, Arky," I said. I was also smiling. Ned wasn't. Ned looked as if the joking and teasing—our way of winding things back down to normal—had gone right past him.

"Where were you, Arky?" he asked. "Where were you when all this was going on?" Across from us, Eddie Jacubois started his pickup truck and the headlights came on.

"Vacation," Arky said. "On my brudder's farm in Wisconsin. So dat was one mess someone else got to clean up." He said this last with great satisfaction.

Eddie drove past, giving us a wave. We gave him a little right-back-atcha, Ned along with the rest of us. But he continued to look troubled.

"I gotta get it in gear, too," Phil said. He disposed of his cigarette butt, got on his feet, hitched up his belt. "Kiddo, leave it at this: your Dad was an excellent officer and a credit to Troop D, Statler Barracks."

"But I want to know—"

"It don't *matter* what you want to know," Phil told him gently. "He's dead, you're not. Those are the facts, as Joe Friday used to say. G'night, Sarge."

"Night," I said, and watched the two of them, Arky and Phil, walk away together across the parking lot. There was good moonlight by then, enough for me to see that neither man so much as turned his head in the direction of Shed B.

That left Huddie, Shirley, and me. Plus the boy, of course. Curtis Wilcox's boy, who had come and mowed the grass and raked the leaves and erased the snowdrifts when it was too cold for Arky to be outside; Curt's boy, who had quit off the football team and come here instead to try and keep his father alive a little longer. I remembered him holding up his college acceptance letter like a judge holding up a score at the Olympics, and I was ashamed to feel angry with him, considering all that he'd been through and how much he'd lost. But he wasn't the only boy in the history of the world to lose his Dad, and at least there'd been a funeral, and his father's name was on the marble memorial out front of the barracks, along with those of Corporal Brady Paul, Trooper Albert Rizzo, and Trooper Samuel Stamson, who died in the seventies and is sometimes known in the PSP as the Shotgun Trooper. Until Stamson's death, we carried our shotguns in roof-racks—if you needed the gun, you just had to reach up over your shoulder and grab it. Trooper Stamson was rear-ended while parked in the turnpike breakdown lane, writing up a traffic stop. The guy who hit him was drunk and doing about a hundred and five at the moment of impact. The cruiser accordioned forward. The gas tank didn't blow, but Trooper Stamson was decapitated by his own shotgun rack. Since 1974 we keep our shotguns clipped under the dash, and since 1973 Sam Stamson's name has been on the memorial. "On the rock," we say. Ennis Rafferty is on the books as a disappearance, so he's not on the rock. The official story on Trooper George Morgan is that he died while cleaning his gun (the same Ruger that ended Mister

Dillon's misery), and since he didn't die on the job, his name isn't on the rock, either. You don't get on the rock for dying *as a result of* the job; it was Tony Schoondist who pointed that out to me one day when he saw me looking at the names. "Probably just as well," he said. "We'd have a dozen of those things out here."

Currently, the last name on the stone is Curtis K. Wilcox. July, 2001. Line of duty. It wasn't nice to have your father's name carved in granite when what you wanted—*needed*—was the father, but it was something. Ennis's name should have been carved there, too, so his bitch of a sister could come and look at it if she wanted to, but it wasn't. And what *did* she have? A reputation as a nasty old lady, that's what, the kind of person who if she saw you on fire in the street wouldn't piss on you to put you out. She'd been a thorn in our side for years and liking her was impossible but feeling sorry for her was not. She'd ended up with even less than this boy, who at least knew for sure that his father was over, that he was never going to come back in someday with a shamefaced grin and some wild story to explain his empty pockets and how come he had that Tijuana tan and why it hurt like hell each time he had to pass a little water.

I had no good feeling about the night's work. I'd hoped the truth might make things better (it'll set you free, someone said, probably a fool), but I had an idea it had made things worse instead. Satisfaction might have brought the curious cat back, but I could make out zero satisfaction on Ned Wilcox's face. All I saw there was a kind of stubborn, tired curiosity. I'd seen the same look on Curtis's face from time to time, most often when he was standing at one of Shed B's roll-up doors in that sidewalk superintendent's stance—legs apart, forehead to the glass, eyes squinted a little, mouth thoughtful. But what's passed down in the blood is the strongest chain of all, isn't it? What's mailed along, one generation to the next, good news here, bad news there, complete disaster over yonder.

I said, "As far as anyone knows, Brian Lippy just took off for greener pastures. It might even be the truth; none of us can say different for certain. And it's an ill wind that doesn't blow somebody some good; him disappearing that way might have saved his girlfriend's life."

"I doubt it," Huddie rumbled. "I bet her next one was just Brian Lippy with different-colored hair. They pick up guys who beat them until they go through the change. It's like they define themselves through the bruises on their faces and arms."

"She never filed a missing-persons on him, tell you that," Shirley said. "Not one that came across my desk, anyway, and I see the town and county reports as well as our own. No one in his family did, either. I don't know what happened to her, but he was an authentic case of good riddance to bad rubbish."

"*You* don't believe he just slipped out through that broken window and ran away, do you?" Ned asked Huddie. "I mean, you were *there*."

"No," Huddie said, "as a matter of fact I don't. But what I think doesn't matter. The point's the same as the one Sarge has been trying to drum into your thick head all night long: *we don't know.*"

It was as if the kid didn't hear him. He turned back to me. "What about my Dad, Sandy? When it came to Brian Lippy, what did *he* believe?"

"He and Tony believed that Brian wound up in the same place as Ennis Rafferty and Jimmy the Gerbil. As for the corpse of the thing they killed that day—"

"Son of a bitch rotted quick," Shirley said in a brisk that-ends-it voice. "There are pictures and you can look at them all you want, but for the most part they're photos of something that could be anything, including a complete hoax. They don't show you how it looked when it was trying to get away from Mister D—how fast it moved or how loud it shrieked. They don't show you anything, really. Nor can we tell you so you'll understand. That's all over your face. Do you know why the past is the past, darling?"

Ned shook his head.

"Because it doesn't work." She looked into her pack of cigarettes, and whatever she saw there must have satisfied her because she nodded, put them into her purse, and stood up. "I'm going home. I have two cats that should have been fed three hours ago."

That was Shirley, all right—Shirley the All-American Girlie, Curt used to call her when he felt like getting under her skin a bit. No husband (there'd been one once, when she was barely out of high school), no kids, two cats, roughly 10,000 Beanie Babies. Like me, she was married to Troop D. A walking cliché, in other words, and if you didn't like it, you could stick it.

"Shirl?"

She turned to the plaintive sound in Ned's voice. "What, hon?"

"Did you like my father?"

She put her hands on his shoulders, bent down, and planted a kiss on Ned's forehead. "Loved him, kid. And I love you. We've told you all we can, and it wasn't easy. I hope it helps." She paused. "I hope it's enough."

"I hope so, too," he said.

Shirley tightened her grip on his shoulders for a moment, giving him a squeeze. Then she let go and stood up. "Hudson Royer—would you see a lady to her car?"

"My pleasure," he said, and took her arm. "See you tomorrow, Sandy? You still on days?"

"Bright and early," I said. "We'll do it all again."

"You better go home and get some sleep, then."

"I will."

He and Shirley left. Ned and I sat on the bench and watched them go. We raised our hands as they drove past in their cars—Huddie's big old New Yorker, Shirley in her little Subaru with the bumper sticker reading MY KARMA RAN OVER MY DOGMA. When their taillights had disappeared around the corner of the barracks, I took out my cigarettes and had my own peek into the pack. One left. I'd smoke it and then quit. I'd been telling myself this charming fable for at least ten years.

"There's really no more you can tell me?" Ned asked in a small, disillusioned voice.

"No. It'd never make a play, would it? There's no third act. Tony and your Dad ran a few more experiments over the next five years, and finally brought Bibi Roth in on it. That would've been your father persuading Tony and me getting caught in the middle, as usual. And I have to tell you the truth: after Brian Lippy disappeared and Mister Dillon died, I was against doing anything with the Buick beyond keeping an eye on it and offering up the occasional prayer that it would either fall apart or disappear back to where it came from. Oh, and killing anything that came out of the trunk still lively enough to stand up and maybe run around the shed looking for a way out."

"Did that ever happen?"

"You mean another pink-headed E.T.? No."

"And Bibi? What did he say?"

"He listened to Tony and your Dad, he took another look, and then he walked away. He said he was too old to deal with anything so far outside his understanding of the world and how it works. He told them he intended to erase the Buick from his memory and urged Tony and Curt to do the same."

"Oh, for God's sake! This guy was a scientist? Jesus, he should have been *fascinated!*"

"Your *father* was the scientist," I said. "An amateur one, yeah, but a good one. The things that came out of the Buick and his curiosity about the Buick itself, those were the things that *made* him a scientist. His dissection of the bat-thing, for instance. Crazy as that was, there was something noble about it, too, like the Wright Brothers going up in their little glue-and-paste airplane. Bibi Roth, on the other hand . . . Bibi was a microscope mechanic. He sometimes called himself that, and with absolute pride. He was a person who had carefully and consciously narrowed his vision to a single strip of knowledge, casting a blaze of light over a small area. Mechanics hate mysteries. Scientists—especially *amateur* scientists—embrace them. Your father was two people at the same time. As a cop, he was a mystery-hater. As a Roadmaster Scholar . . . well, let's just say that when your father was that person, he was very different."

"Which version did you like better?"

I thought it over. "That's like a kid asking his parents who they love best, him or his sister. Not a fair question. But the amateur Curt used to scare me. Used to scare Tony a little, too."

The kid sat pondering this.

"A few more things appeared," I said. "In 1991, there was a bird with four wings."

"*Four—!*"

"That's right. It flew a little bit, hit one of the walls, and dropped dead. In the fall of 1993, the trunk popped open after one of those lightquakes and it was half-filled with dirt. Curt wanted to leave it there and see what would happen and Tony agreed at first, but then it began to stink. I didn't know dirt could decompose, but I guess it can if it's dirt from the right place. And so . . . this is crazy, but we buried the dirt. Can you believe it?"

He nodded. "And did my Dad keep an eye on the place where it was buried? Sure he did. Just to see what would grow."

"I think he was hoping for a few of those weird lilies."

"Any luck?"

"I guess that depends on what you think of as luck. Nothing sprouted, I'll tell you that much. The dirt from the trunk went into the ground not far from where we buried Mister D and the tools. As for the monster, what didn't turn to goo we burned in the incinerator. The ground where the dirt went is still bare. A few things try to straggle up every spring, but so far they always die. Eventually, I suppose, that'll change."

I put the last cigarette in my mouth and lit it.

"A year and a half or so after the dirt-delivery, we got another red-stick lizard. Dead. That's been the last. It's still earthquake country in there, but the earth never shakes as hard these days. It wouldn't do to be careless around the Buick any more than it would to be careless around an old rifle just because it's rusty and the barrel's plugged with dirt, but with reasonable precautions it's probably safe enough. And someday—your Dad believed it, Tony believed it, and I do too—that old car really *will* fall apart. All at once, just like the wonderful one-hoss shay in the poem."

He looked at me vaguely, and I realized he had no idea what poem I was talking about. We live in degenerate times. Then he said, "I can feel it."

Something in his tone startled me badly, and I gave him a hard stare. He still looked younger than his eighteen years, I thought. Just a boy, no more than that, sitting with his sneakered feet crossed and his face painted with starlight. "Can you?" I asked.

"Yes. Can't you?"

All the Troopers who'd passed through D over the years had felt the pull of it, I guessed. Felt it the way people who live on the coast come to feel the motions of the sea, the tides a clock their hearts beat to. On most days and nights we noticed it no more than you consciously notice your nose, a shape sitting at the bottom of all you see. Sometimes, though, the pull was stronger, and then it made you ache, somehow.

"All right," I said, "let's say I do. Huddie sure did—what do you think would have happened to him that day if Shirley hadn't screamed when she did? What do you think would have happened to him if he'd crawled into the trunk like he said he had a mind to do?"

"You really never heard that story before tonight, Sandy?"

I shook my head.

"You didn't look all that surprised, even so."

"Nothing about that Buick surprises me anymore."

"Do you think he really meant to do it? To crawl in and shut the lid behind him?"

"Yes. Only I don't think *he* had anything to do with it. It's that pull—that attraction it has. It was stronger then, but it's still there."

He made no reply to that. Just sat looking across at Shed B.

"You didn't answer my question, Ned. What do you think would have happened to him if he'd crawled in there?"

"I don't know."

A reasonable enough answer, I suppose—a kid's answer, certainly, they say it a dozen times a day—but I hated it just the same. He'd quit off the football team, but it seemed he hadn't forgotten all he'd learned there about bobbing and weaving. I drew in smoke that tasted like hot hay, then blew it back out. "You don't."

"No."

"After Ennis and Jimmy and—probably—Brian Lippy, you don't."

"Not everything goes on to somewhere else, Sandy. Take the other gerbil, for instance. Rosalie or Rosalynn or whatever her name was."

I sighed. "Have it your way. I'm going down to The Country Way to bite a cheeseburger. You're welcome to join me, but only if we can let this go and talk about something else."

He thought it over, then shook his head. "Think I'll head home. Do some thinking."

"Okay, but don't be sharing any of your thinking with your mother."

He looked almost comically shocked. "God, no!"

I laughed and clapped him on the shoulder. The shadows had gone out of his face and suddenly it was possible to like him again. As for his questions and his childish insistence that the story must have an ending and the ending must hold some kind of answer, time might take care of it. Maybe I'd been expecting too many of my own answers. The imitation lives we see on TV and in the movies whisper the idea that human existence consists of revelations and abrupt changes of heart; by the time we've reached full adulthood, I think, this is an idea we have on some level come to accept. Such things may happen from time to time, but I think that for the most part it's a lie. Life's changes come slowly. They come the way my youngest nephew breathes in his deepest sleep; sometimes I feel the urge to put a hand on his chest just to assure myself he's still alive. Seen in that light, the whole idea of curious cats attaining satisfaction seemed slightly absurd. The world rarely finishes its conversations. If twenty-three years of living with the Buick 8 had taught me nothing else, it should have taught me that. At this moment Curt's boy looked as if he might have taken a step toward getting better. Maybe even two. And if I couldn't let that be enough for one night, I had my own problems.

"You're in tomorrow, right?" I asked.

"Bright and early, Sarge. We'll do it all again."

"Then maybe you ought to postpone your thinking and do a little sleeping instead."

"I guess I can give it a try." He touched my hand briefly. "Thanks, Sandy."

"No problem."

"If I was a pisshead about any of it—"

"You weren't," I said. He *had* been a pisshead about some of it, but I didn't think he'd been able to help it. And at his age I likely would have been pissier by far. I watched him walk toward the restored Bel Air his father had left behind, a car of roughly the same vintage as the one in our shed but a good deal less *lively*. Halfway across the parking lot he paused, looking at Shed B, and I paused with the smoldering stub of my cigarette poised before my lips, watching to see what he'd do.

He moved on instead of going over. Good. I took a final puff on my delightful tube of death, thought about crushing it on the hottop, and found a place for it in the butt-can instead, where roughly two hundred previous butts had been buried standing up. The others could crush out their smokes on the pavement if they wanted to—Arky would sweep them up without complaint—but it was better if I didn't do that. I was the Sarge, after all, the guy who sat in the big chair.

I went into the barracks. Stephanie Colucci was in dispatch, drinking a Coke and reading a magazine. She put the Coke down and smoothed her skirt over her knees when she saw me.

"What's up, sweetheart?" I asked.

"Nothing much. Communications are clearing up, though not as fast as they usually do after . . . one of those. I've got enough to keep track of things."

"What things?"

"9 is responding to a car-fire on the I-87 Exit 9 ramp, Mac says the driver's a salesman headed for Cleveland, lit up like a neon sign and refusing the field sobriety test. 16 with a possible break-in at Statler Ford. Jeff Cutler with vandalism over at Statler Middle School, but he's just assisting, the local police have got that one."

"That it?"

"Paul Loving is 10-98 for home in his cruiser, his son's having an asthma attack."

"You might forget to put that on the report."

Steffie gave me a reproachful look, as if she hardly needed me to tell her that. "What's going on out in Shed B?"

"Nothing," I said. "Well, nothing much. Normalizing. I'm out of here. If anything comes up, just—" I stopped, sort of horrified.

"Sandy?" she asked. "Is something wrong?"

If anything comes up, just call Tony Schoondist, I'd been about to say, as if twenty years hadn't slipped under the bridge and the old Sarge wasn't dribbling mindlessly in front of Nick at Nite in a Statler nursing home. "Nothing wrong," I said. "If anything comes up, call Frank Soderberg. It's his turn in the barrel."

"Very good, sir. Have a nice night."

"Thanks, Steff, right back atcha."

As I stepped out, the Bel Air rolled slowly toward the driveway with one of the groups Ned likes—Wilco, or maybe The Jayhawks—blaring from the custom speakers. I lifted a hand and he returned the wave. With a smile. A sweet one. Once more I found it hard to believe I'd been so angry with him.

I stepped over to the shed and assumed the position, that feet-apart, sidewalk superintendent stance that makes everyone feel like a Republican somehow, ready to heap contempt on welfare slackers at home and flag-burning foreigners abroad. I looked in. There it sat, silent under the overhead lights, casting a shadow just as though it were sane, fat and luxy on its whitewall tires. A steering wheel that was far too big. A hide that rejected dirt and healed scratches—that happened more slowly now, but it did still happen. *Oil's fine* was what the man said before he went around the corner, those were his last words on the matter, and here it still was, like an *objet d'art* somehow left behind in a closed-down gallery. My arms broke out in gooseflesh and I could feel my balls tightening. My mouth had that dry-lint taste it gets when I know I'm in deep shit. Ha'past trouble and goin on a jackpot, Ennis Rafferty used to say. It wasn't humming and it wasn't glowing, the temperature was up above sixty again, but I could feel it pulling at me, whispering for me to come in and look. It could show me things, it whispered, especially now that we were alone. Looking at it like this made one thing clear: I'd been angry at Ned because I'd been scared for him. Of course. Looking at it like this, feeling its tidal pull way down in the middle of my head—beating in my guts and my groin, as well—made everything easier to understand. The Buick bred monsters. Yes. But sometimes you still wanted to go to it, the way you sometimes wanted to look over the edge when you were on a high place or peer into the muzzle of your gun and see the hole at the end of the barrel turn into an eye. One that was watching you, just you and only you. There was no sense trying to reason your way through such moments, or trying to understand that neurotic attraction; best to just step back from the drop, put the gun back in its holster, drive away from the barracks. Away from Shed B. Until you got beyond the range of that subtle whispering voice. Sometimes running away is a perfectly acceptable response.

I stood there a moment longer, though, feeling that distant beat-beat-beat in my head and around my heart, looking in at the midnight-blue Buick Roadmaster. Then I stepped back, drew a deep breath of night air, and looked up at the moon until I felt entirely myself again. When I did, I went to my own car and got in and drove away.

The Country Way wasn't crowded. It never is these days, not even on Friday and Saturday nights. The restaurants out by Wal-Mart and the new Statler Mall are killing the downtown eateries just as surely as the new cineplex out on 32 killed off the old Gem Theater downtown.

As always, people glanced at me when I walked in. Only it's the uniform they're really looking at, of course. A couple of guys—one a deputy sheriff, the other a county attorney—said hello and shook my hand. The attorney asked if I wouldn't join him and his wife and I said no thanks, I might be meeting someone. The idea of being with people, of having to do any more talking that night (even small-talking), made me feel sick in my stomach.

I sat in one of the little booths at the back of the main room, and Cynthia Garris came over to take my order. She was a pretty blonde thing with big, beautiful eyes. I'd noticed her making someone a sundae when I came in, and was touched to see that between delivering the ice cream and bringing me a menu, she'd undone the top button on her uniform so that the little silver heart she wore at the base of her throat showed. I didn't know if that was for me or just another response to the uniform. I hoped it was for me.

"Hey, Sandy, where you been lately? Olive Garden? Outback? Macaroni Grille? One of those?" She sniffed with mock disdain.

"Nope, just been eatin in. What you got on special?"

"Chicken and gravy, stuffed shells with meat sauce—both of em a little heavy on a night like this, in my humble opinion—and fried haddock. All you can eat's a dollar more. You know the deal."

"Think I'll just have a cheeseburger and an Iron City to wash it down with."

She jotted on her pad, then gave me a real stare. "Are you all right? You look tired."

"I *am* tired. Otherwise fine. Seen anyone from Troop D tonight?"

"George Stankowski was in earlier. Otherwise, you're it, darlin. Cop-wise, I mean. Well, those guys out there, but . . ." She shrugged as if to say those guys weren't real cops. As it happened, I agreed with her.

"Well, if the robbers come in, I'll stop em single-handed."

"If they tip fifteen per cent, Hero, let em rob," she said. "I'll get your beer." Off she went, pert little tail switching under white nylon.

Pete Quinland, the grease-pit's original owner, was long gone, but the mini-jukeboxes he'd installed were still on the walls of the booths. The selections were in a kind of display-book, and there were little chrome levers on top to turn the pages. These antique gadgets no longer worked, but it was hard to resist twiddling the levers, turning the pages, and reading the songs on the little pink labels. About half of them were by Pete's beloved Chairman of the Board, hepcat fingersnappers like "Witchcraft" and "Luck Be a Lady Tonight." **FRANK SINATRA**, said the little pink labels, and beneath, in smaller letters: **THE NELSON RIDDLE ORCH**. The others were those old rock and roll songs you never think about anymore once they leave the charts; the ones they never seem to play on the oldies stations, although you'd think there'd be room; after all, how many times can you listen to "Brandy (You're a Fine Girl)" before beginning to scream? I flipped through the jukebox pages, looking at tunes a dropped quarter would no longer call forth; time marches on. If you're quiet you can hear its shuffling, rueful tread.

If anyone asks about that Buick 8, just tell em it's an impound. That's what the old Sarge had said on the night we met out here in the back room. By then the waitresses had been sent away and we were pulling our own beers, running our own tab, and keeping our accounts straight down to the very last penny. Honor system, and why not? We were honorable men, doing our duty as we saw it. Still are. We're the Pennsylvania State Police, do you see? The *real* road warriors. As Eddie used to say—when he was younger as well as thinner—it's not just a job, it's a fuckin adventure.

I turned a page. Here was "Heart of Glass," by **BLONDIE**.

On this subject you can't get far enough off the record. More words of wisdom from Tony Schoondist, spoken while the blue clouds of cigarette smoke rose to the ceiling. Back then *everybody* smoked, except maybe for

Curt, and look what happened to *him*. Sinatra sang "One for My Baby" from the overhead speakers, and from the steam tables had come the sweet smell of barbecued pork. The old Sarge had been a believer in that off-the-record stuff, at least as regarded the Buick, until his mind had taken French leave, first just infantry squads of brain-cells stealing away in the night, then platoons, then whole regiments in broad daylight. *What's not on the record can't hurt you,* he'd told me once—this was around the time when it became clear it would be me who'd step into Tony's shoes and sit in Tony's office, ooh grampa, what a big chair you have. Only I'd gone on the record tonight, hadn't I? Yeah, whole hog. Opened my mouth and spilled the whole tale. With a little help from my friends, as the song says. We'd spilled it to a boy who was still lost in the fun-house of grief. Who was agog with quite natural curiosity in spite of that grief. A lost boy? Perhaps. On TV, such tales as Ned's end happily, but I can tell you that life in Statler, Pennsylvania, bears Christing little resemblance to *The Hallmark Hall of Fame.* I'd told myself I knew the risks, but now I found myself wondering if that was really true. Because we never go forward believing we will fail, do we? No. We do it because we think we're going to save the goddam day and six times out of ten we step on the business end of a rake hidden in the high grass and up comes the handle and whammo, right between the eyes.

Tell me what happened when you dissected the bat. Tell me about the fish.

Here was "Pledging My Love," by **JOHNNY ACE**.

Brushing aside every effort I made—that any of us made—to suggest this lesson was not in the learning but in the letting go. Just bulling onward. Sort of a surprise he hadn't read us the Miranda, because hadn't it been an interrogation as much as it had been stories of the old days when his old man had still been alive? *Young* and alive?

I still felt sick in my stomach. I could drink the beer Cynthia was bringing, the bubbles might even help, but eat a cheeseburger? I didn't think so. It had been years since the night Curtis dissected the bat-thing, but I was thinking about it now. How he'd said *Inquiring minds want to know* and then poked his scalpel into its eye. The eye had made a popping sound and then collapsed, dribbling out of its socket like a black tear. Tony and I had screamed, and how was I supposed to eat a cheeseburger now, remembering that? *Stop it, this is pointless,* I'd said, but he hadn't stopped. The father had been as insistent as the son. *Let's look in the lower gut and then we're done,* he had said, only he had *never* been done. He had poked, he had prodded, he had investigated, and the Buick had killed him for his pains.

I wondered if the boy knew it. I wondered if he understood the Buick Roadmaster 8 had killed his father as surely as Huddie, George, Eddie, Shirley, and Mister Dillon had killed the shrieking monstrosity that had come out of the car's trunk in 1988.

Here was "Billy Don't Be a Hero," by **BO DONALDSON AND THE HEYWOODS**. Gone from the charts *and* our hearts.

Tell me about the bat, tell me about the fish, tell me about the E.T. with the pink cords for hair, the thing that could think, the thing that showed up with something like a radio. Tell me about my father, too, because I have to come to terms with him. Of course I do, I see his life in my face and his ghost in my eyes every time I stand at the mirror to shave. Tell me everything . . . but don't tell me there's no answer. Don't you dare. I reject that. I repudiate it.

"Oil's fine," I murmured, and turned the steel levers on top of the booth's minijuke a little faster. There was sweat on my forehead. My stomach felt worse than ever. I wished I could believe it was the flu, or maybe food poisoning, but it wasn't either one and I knew it. "Oil's just fuckin ducky."

Here was "Indiana Wants Me" and "Green-Eyed Lady" and "Love Is Blue." Songs that had somehow slipped between the cracks. "Surfer Joe," by The Surfaris.

Tell me everything, tell me the answers, tell me the one answer.

The kid had been clear about the things he wanted, you had to give him that. He'd asked for it with the pure untinctured selfishness of the lost and the grief-stricken.

Except once.

He'd started to ask for one piece of the past . . . and then changed his mind. What piece had that been? I reached for it, fumbled at it, felt it shrink slyly from my touch. When that happens, it's no good to chase. You have to back off and let the recollection come back to you of its own free will.

I thumbed the pages of the useless jukebox back and forth. Little pink stickers like tongues.

"Polk Salad Annie," by **TONY JOE WHITE** and *Tell me about The Year of the Fish.*

"When," by **THE KALIN TWINS** and *Tell me about the meeting you had, tell me everything, tell me everything but the one thing that might pop up a red flag in your suspicious cop's mind—*

"Here's your beer—" Cynthia Garris began, and then there was a light gasp.

I looked up from twiddling the metal levers (the pages flipping back and forth under the glass had half-hypnotized me by then). She was looking at me with fascinated horror. "Sandy—you got a fever, hon? Because you're just *running* with sweat."

And that was when it came to me. Telling him about the Labor Day picnic of 1979. *The more we talked, the more we drank,* Phil Candleton had said. *My head ached for two days after.*

"Sandy?" Cynthia standing there with a bottle of I.C. and a glass. Cynthia with the top button of her uniform undone so she could show me her heart. So to speak. She was there but she wasn't. She was years from where I was at that moment.

All that talk and not one single conclusion, I'd said, and the talk had moved on—to the O'Day farm, among other things—and then all at once the boy had asked . . . had *begun* to ask . . .

Sandy, that day at the picnic, did any of you talk about . . .

And then he had trailed off.

"Did any of you talk about destroying it," I said. "That's the question he didn't finish." I looked into Cynthia Garris's frightened, concerned face. "He started to ask and then he stopped."

Had I thought storytime was over and Curt's boy was heading home? That he'd let go that easily? A mile or so down the road, headlights had passed me going the other way. Going back toward the barracks at a good but not quite illegal clip. Had Curt Wilcox's Bel Air been behind those lights, and Curt Wilcox's son behind the wheel? Had he gone back just as soon as he could be sure we were gone?

I thought yes.

314

I took the bottle of Iron City from Cynthia's tray, watching my arm stretch out and my hand grasp the neck the way you watch yourself do things in dreams. I felt the cold ring of the bottle's neck slip between my teeth and thought of George Morgan in his garage, sitting on the floor and smelling cut grass under the mower. That good green smell. I drank the beer, all of it. Then I stood up and put a ten on Cynthia's tray.

"Sandy?"

"I can't stay and eat," I said. "I forgot something back at the barracks."

I kept a battery-powered Kojak light in the glove compartment of my personal and put it on the roof as soon as I was out of town, running my car up to eighty and trusting the red flasher to get anyone ahead of me out of my way. There weren't many. Western Pennsylvania folks roll up the sidewalks early on most weeknights. It was only four miles back to the barracks, but the run seemed to take an hour. I kept thinking about how my heart sank each time Ennis's sister—The Dragon—walked into the barracks under the haystack heap of her outrageous henna hair. I kept thinking, *Get out of here, you're too close.* And I didn't even like her. How much worse would it be to have to face Michelle Wilcox, especially if she had the twins, the Little J's, with her?

I drove up the driveway too fast, just as Eddie and George had done a dozen or so years before, wanting to be rid of their unpleasant prisoner so they could go over to Poteenville, where it must have seemed half the world was going up in smoke. The names of old songs—"I Met Him on a Sunday," "Ballroom Blitz," "Sugar Sugar"—jigged senselessly up and down in my head. Foolish, but better than asking myself what I'd do if the Bel Air was back but empty; what I'd do if Ned Wilcox was gone off the face of the earth.

The Bel Air *was* back, as I'd known it would be. He'd parked it where Arky's truck had been earlier. And it was empty. I could see that in the first splash of my headlights. The song titles dropped out of my head. What replaced them was a cold readiness, the kind that comes by itself, empty-handed and without plans, ready to improvise.

The Buick had taken hold of Curt's boy. Even while we'd been sitting

315

with him, conducting our own peculiar kind of wake for his Dad and trying to be his friend, it had reached out and taken hold of him. If there was still a chance to take him back, I'd do well not to bitch it up by thinking too much.

Steff, probably worried at the sight of a single Kojak instead of a rack of roof-lights, poked her head out the back door. "Who's that? Who's there?"

"It's me, Steff." I got out of the car, leaving it parked where it was with the red bubble flashing on the roof over the driver's seat. If anyone came hauling in behind me, it would at least keep them from rear-ending my car. "Go back inside."

"What's wrong?"

"Nothing."

"That's what *he* said." She pointed at the Bel Air, then stalked back inside.

I ran for the roll-up door of Shed B in the stutter-pulse of the light— so many stressful moments of my life have been lit by flashers. A John Q stopped or overtaken by flashers is always frightened. They have no idea what those same lights sometimes do to us. And what we have seen by their glow.

We always left a light on in the shed, but it was brighter than a single night-light in there now, and the side door was standing open. I thought about diverting to it, then kept on as I was. I wanted a look at the playing-field before anything else.

What I'd been most afraid of seeing was nothing but the Buick. Looking in, I discovered something scarier. The boy was sitting behind the Roadmaster's oversized steering wheel with his chest smashed in. There was nothing where his shirt had been except a bright bloody ruin. My legs started to unbuckle at the knees, and then I realized it wasn't blood I was looking at, after all. *Maybe* not blood. The shape was too regular. There was a straight red line running just below the round neck of his blue T-shirt . . . and corners . . . neat right-angled corners . . .

No, not blood.

The gas-can Arky kept for the mower.

Ned shifted behind the wheel and one of his hands came into view. It moved slowly, dreamily. There was a Beretta in it. Had he been driving around with his father's sidearm in the trunk of the Bel Air? Perhaps even in the glove compartment?

I decided it didn't matter. He was sitting in that deathtrap with gas and a gun. Kill or cure, I'd thought. It had never crossed my mind to think he might try doing both at the same time.

He didn't see me. He should've—my white, scared face filling one of those dark windows should have been perfectly visible to him from where he sat—and he should've seen the red pulse from the light I'd stuck on the roof of my car. He saw neither. He was as hypnotized as Huddie Royer had been when Huddie decided to crawl into the Roadmaster's trunk and pull the lid shut behind him. I could feel it even from outside. That tidal pulse. That *liveliness.* There were even words in it. I suppose I might have made them up to suit myself, but it almost doesn't matter because it was the pulse that called them forth, the throb all of us had felt around the Buick from the very start. It was a throb some of us—this boy's father, for one—had felt more strongly than others.

Come in or stay out, the voice in my head told me, and it spoke with perfect chilling indifference. *I'll take one or two, then sleep. That much more mischief before I'm done for good. One or two, I don't care which.*

I looked up at the round thermometer mounted on the beam. The red needle had stood at sixty-one before I went down to The Country Way, but now it had dropped back to fifty-seven. I could almost see it slumping to even colder levels as I watched, and all at once I was struck by a memory so vivid it was frightening.

On the smokers' bench, this had been. I had been smoking and Curt had just been sitting. The smokers' bench had assumed odd importance in the six years since the barracks itself was declared a smoke-free zone. It's where we went to compare notes on the cases we were rolling, to work out scheduling conflicts, to mull over retirement plans and insurance plans and the GDR. It was on the smokers' bench that Carl Brundage told me his wife was leaving him and taking the kids. His voice hadn't quavered but tears had gone rolling down his cheeks as he talked. Tony had been sitting on the bench with me on one side and Curt on the other ("Christ and the two thieves," he'd said with a sardonic smile) when he told us he was putting me up for the SC post his own retirement would leave vacant. If I wanted it, that was. The little gleam in his eyes saying he knew goddam well I wanted it. Curtis and I had both nodded, not saying much. And it was on the smokers' bench that Curt and I had our final discussion about the Buick 8. How soon before his death had that been? I realized with a nasty chill that it might well have been on the very day. Certainly that would explain why the vividness of the memory seemed so terrible to me.

Does it think? Curt had asked. I could remember strong morning sun on his face and—I think—a paper cup of coffee in his hand. *Does it watch and think, wait for its chances, pick its moments?*

I'm almost sure not, I had replied, but I'd been troubled. Because *almost* covers a lot of territory, doesn't it? Maybe the only word in the language that covers more is *if.*

But it saved its biggest horror show for a time when this place was almost entirely deserted, Ned's father had said. Thoughtful. Setting his coffee aside so he could turn his Stetson over and over in his hands, an old habit of his. If I was right about the day, that hat was less than five hours from being knocked from his head and cast bloody into the weeds, where it would later be found among the McDonald's wrappers and empty Coke cans. *As if it knew. As if it can think. Watch. Wait.*

I had laughed. It was one of those gruff little ha-ha laughs that don't really have much amusement in them. I told him he was cuckoo on the subject. I said, *Next thing you'll be telling me it sent out a ray or something to make that Norco tanker crash into the schoolbus that day.*

He made no verbal reply, but his eyes had looked a question at me. *How do you know it didn't?*

And then I had asked the boy's question. I had asked—

A warning bell went off inside my head, very dim and deep. I stepped back from the window and raised my hands to my face, as if I thought I could block off that tidal ache simply by blocking off sight of the Buick. And the sight of Ned, looking so white and lost behind the oversized steering wheel. It had taken hold of him and just now, briefly, it had taken hold of me. Had tried to sidetrack me with a lot of old useless memories. Whether or not it had consciously waited for its chance to get at Ned didn't matter. What mattered was that the temperature in there was going down fast, almost *diving,* and if I intended doing something, now was the time.

Maybe you ought to get some backup in on this, the voice in my head whispered. It sounded like my own voice, but it wasn't. *Might be someone in the barracks. I'd check, if I were you. Not that it matters to me. Doing one more piece of mischief before I sleep, that's what matters to me. Pretty much* all *that matters to me. And why? Because I can, boss—just because I can.*

Backup seemed like a good idea. God knows I was terrified at the idea of going into Shed B on my own and approaching the Buick in its current state. What got me going was the knowledge that I had caused this. I was the one who had opened Pandora's box.

I ran around to the hutch, not pausing at the side door although I registered the smell of gasoline, heavy and rich. I knew what he'd done. The only question was how much gas he'd poured under the car and how much he'd saved back in the can.

The door to the hutch was secured with a padlock. For years it had been left open, the curved steel arm just poked through the hasp to keep the door from swinging open in a breeze. The lock was open that night, too. I swear that's the truth. It wasn't noontime bright out there, but there was enough glow from the open side door to see the lock clearly. Then, as I reached for it, the steel post slid down into the hole on the body of the lock with a tiny audible *click.* I saw that happen . . . and I felt it, too. For just a moment the pulse in my head sharpened and focused. It was like a gasp of effort.

I keep two keyrings: cop-keys and personals. There were about twenty on the "official" ring, and I used a trick I'd learned a long time before, from Tony Schoondist. I let the keys fall on my palm as they would, like pickup sticks, then simply felt among them without looking. It doesn't always work but this time it did, likely because the key to the hutch padlock was smaller than all the others except the one to my locker downstairs, and the locker key has a square head.

Now, faintly, I heard the humming begin. It was faint, like the sound of a motor buried in the earth, but it was there.

I took the key my fingers had found and rammed it into the padlock. The steel arm popped up again. I yanked the lock out of the hasp and dropped it on the ground. Then I opened the door to the hutch and stepped inside.

The little storage space held the still and explosive heat which belongs only to attics and sheds and cubbyholes that have been closed up for a long time in hot weather. No one came out here much anymore, but the things which had accumulated over the years (except for the paint and the paint thinner, flammable items that had been prudently removed) were still here; I could see them in the faint wash of light. Stacks of magazines, the kind men read, for the most part (women think we like to look at naked women but mostly I think we like tools). The kitchen chair with the tape-mended seat. The cheap police-band radio from Radio Shack. The videocam, its battery undoubtedly dead, on its shelf next to the old box of blank tapes. A bumper sticker was pasted to one wall: SUPPORT THE MENTALLY HANDICAPPED, TAKE AN FBI AGENT TO LUNCH. I could smell dust. In my head the pulse that was the Buick's voice was getting stronger and stronger.

There was a hanging lightbulb and a switch on the wall, but I didn't even try it. I had an idea the bulb would be dead, or the switch would be live enough to give me a real walloper of a shock.

The door swung shut behind me, cutting off the moonlight. That was impossible, because when it was left to its own devices, the door always swung the other way, outward. We all knew it. It was why we left the padlock threaded through the hasp. Tonight, however, the impossible was selling cheap. The force inhabiting the Buick wanted me in the dark. Maybe it thought being in the dark would slow me down.

It didn't. I'd already seen what I needed: the coil of yellow rope, still hanging on the wall below the joke sticker and next to a forgotten set of jumper cables. I saw something else, too. Something Curt Wilcox had put up on the shelf near the videocam not long after the E.T. with the lashing pink ropes had made its appearance.

I took this item, stuck it in my back pocket, and grabbed the coil of rope from the wall. Then I banged out again. A dark form loomed up in front of me and I almost screamed. For one mad moment I was sure it was the man in the dark coat and hat, the one with the malformed ear and the Boris Badinoff accent. When the boogeyman spoke up, however, the accent was pure Lawrence Welk.

"Dat damn kid came back," Arky whispered. "I got halfway home and Yudas Pries' I jus' turned around. I knew it, somehow. I jus'——"

I interrupted then, told him to stay clear, and ran back around the corner of Shed B with the rope looped over my arm.

"Don' go in dere, Sarge!" Arky said. I think he might've been trying to shout, but he was too scared to get much in the way of volume. "He's t'rown down gas an' he got a gun, I seen it."

I stopped beside the door, slipped the rope off my arm, started to tie one end to the stout hook mounted there, then gave the coil of rope to Arky instead.

"Sandy, can you feel it?" he asked. "An' the radio gone all blooey again, nuttin but static, I heard Steff cussin at it t'rough d'window."

"Never mind. Tie the end of the rope off. Use the hook."

"Huh?"

"You heard me."

I'd held onto the loop in the end of the rope and now I stepped into it, yanked it up to my waist, and ran it tight. It was a hangman's knot, tied by Curt himself, and it ran shut easily.

"Sarge, you can't do dis." Arky made as if to grab my shoulder, but without any real force.

"Tie it off and then hold on," I said. "Don't go in, no matter what. If we . . ." I wasn't going to say *If we disappear,* though—didn't want to hear those words come out of my mouth. "If anything happens, tell Steff to put out a Code D as soon as the static clears."

"Jesus!" Only from Arky it sounded more like *Yeesus.* "What are you, crazy? Can't you feel it?"

"I feel it," I said, and went inside. I shook the rope continually as I went to keep it from snagging. I felt like a diver starting down to some untried depth, minding his airhose not because he really thinks minding it will help, but because it's at least something to do, something to keep your mind off the things that may be swimming around in the blackness just beyond the reach of your light.

*　　　*　　　*

The Buick 8 sat fat and luxy on its whitewalls, our little secret, humming deep down in the hollows of itself. The pulse was stronger than the humming, and now that I was actually inside I felt it stop its halfhearted efforts to keep me out. Instead of pushing with its invisible hand, it pulled.

The boy sat behind the wheel with the gas can in his lap, his cheeks and forehead white, the skin there taut and shiny. As I came toward him, his head turned with robotic slowness on his neck and he looked at me. His gaze was wide and dark. In it was the stupidly serene look of the deeply drugged or the cataclysmically wounded. The only emotion that remained in his eyes was a terrible weary stubbornness, that adolescent insistence that there must be an answer and he must know the answer. He had a right. And that was what the Buick had used, of course. What it had used against him.

"Ned."

"I'd get out of here if I were you, Sarge." Speaking in slow, perfectly articulated syllables. "There's not much time. It's coming. It sounds like footsteps."

And he was right. I felt a sudden surge of horror. The hum was some sort of machinery, perhaps. The pulse was almost certainly a kind of telepathy. This was something else, though, a third thing.

Something was coming.

"Ned, please. You can't understand what this thing is and you certainly can't kill it. All you can do is get yourself sucked up like dirt in a vacuum cleaner. And that'll leave your mother and your sisters on their own. Is that what you want, to leave them alone with a thousand questions no one can answer? It's hard for me to believe that the boy who came here looking so hard for his father could be so selfish."

Something flickered in his eyes at that. It was the way a man's eyes may flicker when, deep in concentration, he hears a loud noise on the next block. Then the eyes grew serene again. "This goddamned car killed my Dad," he said. Spoken calmly. Even patiently.

I certainly wasn't going to argue that. "All right, maybe it did. Maybe in some way it was as much to blame for what happened to your Dad as Bradley Roach was. Does that mean it can kill you, too? What is this, Ned? Buy one, get one free?"

"I'm going to kill *it,*" he said, and at last something rose in his eyes, disturbing the surface serenity. It was more than anger. To me it looked like a kind of madness. He raised his hands. In one was the gun. In the other he now held a butane match. "Before it sucks me through, I'm going to light its damned transporter on fire. That'll shut the door to this side forever. That's step one." Spoken with the scary, unconscious arrogance of youth, positive that this idea has occurred to no one before it has occurred to him. "And if I live through *that* experience, I'm going to kill whatever's waiting on the other side. That's step two."

"Whatever's *waiting?*" I realized the enormity of his assumptions and was staggered by them. "Oh, Ned! Oh, Christ!"

The pulse was stronger now. So was the hum. I could feel the unnatural cold that marked the Buick's periods of activity settling against my skin. And saw purple light first blooming in the air just above the oversized steering wheel and then starting to skate across its surface. Coming. It was coming. Ten years ago it would have been here already. Maybe even five. Now it took a little longer.

"Do you think there's going to be a welcoming party, Ned? Are you expecting them to send the Exalted President of the Yellow-Skin Pink-Hair People or maybe the Emperor of the Alternate Universe to say howdy and give you the key to the city? Do you think they'd take the trouble? For what? A kid who can't accept the fact that his father is dead and get on with his own life?"

"Shut up!"

"Know what I think?"

"I don't care what you think!"

"I think the last thing you see is going to be a whole lot of nothing much before you choke to death on whatever they breathe over there."

The uncertainty flickered in his eyes again. Part of him wanted to do a George Morgan and just finish it. But there was another part of him as well, one that might not care so much about Pitt anymore but still wanted to go on living. And above both, above and under and around, binding everything, was the pulse and the quietly calling voice. It wasn't even seductive. It just *pulled* at you.

"Sarge, come outta dere!" Arky called.

I ignored him and kept my eyes on Curt's boy. "Ned, use the brains that got you this far. *Please.*" Not shouting at him, but raising my voice to get it over the strengthening hum. And at the same time I touched the thing I'd put in my back pocket.

"This *res* you're sitting in may be alive, but that still doesn't make it worth your time. It's not much different from a Venus flytrap or a pitcher plant, don't you see that? You can't get revenge out of this thing, not even a nickel's worth. It's brainless."

His mouth began to tremble. That was a start, but I wished to God he'd let go of the gun or at least lower it. And there was the butane match. Not as dangerous as the automatic, but bad enough; my shoes were in gasoline as I stood near the driver's door of the Buick, and the fumes were strong enough to make my eyes water. Now the purple glow had begun to spin lazy lines of light across the bogus dashboard controls and to fill up the speedometer dial, making it look like the bubble in a carpenter's level.

"*It killed my Daddy!*" he shouted in a child's voice, but it wasn't me he was shouting at. He couldn't find whatever it was he wanted to shout at, and that was precisely what was killing him.

"No, Ned. Listen, if this thing could laugh, it'd be laughing now. It didn't get the father the way it wanted to—not the way it got Ennis and Brian Lippy—but now it's got a damned fine chance at the son. If Curt knows, if he sees, he must be screaming in his grave. Everything he feared, everything he fought to prevent. All of it happening again. To his own son."

"*Stop it, stop it!*" Tears were spilling over his eyelids.

I bent down, bringing my face into that growing purple glow, into the welling coldness. I brought my face down to Ned's face, where the resistance was finally crumbling. One more blow would do it. I pulled the can I'd taken from the hutch out of my back pocket and held it against my leg and said, "He must be hearing it laugh, Ned, he must know it's too late—"

"*No!*"

"—that there's nothing he can do. Nothing at all."

He raised his hands to cover his ears, the gun in the left, the butane match in the right, the gas-can balanced on his thighs, his legs dimming out to lavender mist below his shins, that glow rising like water in a well, and it wasn't great—I hadn't knocked him as completely off-balance as I would have liked—but it would have to be good enough. I pushed the cap off the aerosol can with my thumb, had just one fraction of a second to wonder if there was any pressure left in the damned thing after all the years it had stood unused on the shelf in the hutch, and then I Maced him.

Ned howled with surprise and pain as the spray hit his eyes and nose. His finger squeezed the trigger of his Dad's Beretta. The report was deafening in the shed.

"Gah-*DAM!*" I heard Arky shout through the ringing in my ears.

I grabbed the doorhandle, and as I did the little locking post went down by itself, just like the arm of the padlock on the hutch door. I reached through the open window, made a fist, and punched the side of the gas-can. It flew off the convulsing boy's lap, tumbled into the misty lavender light rising up from the floor of the car, and disappeared. I had a momentary sense of it *tumbling,* the way things do when you drop them off a high place. The gun went off again and I felt the wind of the slug. It wasn't really close—he was still firing blind into the Buick's roof, probably unaware that he was shooting at all—but whenever you can feel the air stir with a bullet's passage, it's too damned close.

I fumbled down inside the Buick's door, finally found the inside handle, and pulled. If it didn't come up I wasn't sure what I'd do next—he was too big and too heavy to yank through the window—but it did come up and the door opened. As it did, a brilliant purple flash rose up from where the Roadmaster's floorboards had been, the trunk banged open, and the real pulling began. *Sucked up like dirt in a vacuum cleaner,* I'd said, but I hadn't known the half of it. That tidal beat suddenly sped up to a ferocious, arrhythmic pounding, like precursor waves before the tsunami that will destroy everything. There was a sense of an inside-out wind that seemed to pull instead of push, that wanted to suck your eyeballs from their sockets and then peel the skin right off your face, and yet not a hair on my head stirred.

Ned screamed. His hands dropped suddenly, as if invisible ropes had been tied around his wrists and now someone below him was yanking on them. He started to sink in his seat, only the seat was no longer precisely there. It was vanishing, dissolving into that stormy bubble of rising violet light. I grabbed him under the arms, yanked, stumbled backward first one step and then two. Fighting the incredible traction of the force trying to pull me into the descending purple throat that had been the Buick's interior. I fell over backward with Ned on top of me. Gasoline soaked through the legs of my pants.

"Pull us!" I screamed at Arky. I paddled with my feet, trying to slide away from the Buick and the light pouring out of it. My feet could find no good purchase. They kept slipping in the gasoline.

Ned was *yanked,* pulled toward the open driver's door so hard he was almost torn out of my grip. At the same time I felt the rope tighten around my waist. We were tugged sharply backward as I resettled my grip around Ned's chest. He was still holding the gun, but as I watched, his arm shot out straight in front of him and the gun flew from his hand. The throbbing purple light in the cabin of the car swallowed it up, and I thought I heard it fire twice more, all by itself, as it disappeared. At the same time the pull around *us* seemed to weaken a little. Maybe enough to make our escape if we went now, just exited stage left with no hesitation.

"Pull!" I screamed at Arky.

"Boss, I'm pullin as hard as I—"

"Pull *harder!"*

There was another furious yank, one that cut my breath off as Curtis's hangman's noose pulled tight around my midsection. Then I was scrambling to my feet and stumbling backward at the same time with the boy still clasped in front of me. He was gasping, his eyes puffed shut like the eyes of a fighter who's had the worst of it for twelve rounds. I don't think he saw what happened next.

The inside of the Buick was gone, cored out by purple light. Some unspeakable, unknowable conduit had opened. I was looking down an infected gullet and into another world. I might have frozen in place long enough for the suction to renew its hold on me and pull me in—to pull both of us in—but then Arky was screaming, high and shrill: "Help me,

Steff! God's sake! Muckle on here and help me!" She must have done it, too, because a second or so later, Ned and I were yanked backward like a couple of well-hooked fish.

I went down again and banged my head, aware that the pulse and the hum had merged, had turned into a howl that seemed to be drilling a hole in my brains. The Buick had begun flashing like a neon sign, and a flood of green-backed beetles came tumbling out of the blazing trunk. They struck the floor, scuttered, died. The suction took hold yet again, and we started moving back toward the Buick. It was like being caught in a hideously strong undertow. Back and forth, back and forth.

"Help me!" I shouted in Ned's ear. *"You have to help me or we're going in!"* What I was thinking by that time was that we were probably going in whether he helped me or not.

He was blind but not deaf and had decided he wanted to live. He put his sneakered feet down on the cement floor and shoved backward just as hard as he could, his skidding heels splashing up little flurries of spilled gasoline. At the same time, Arky and Stephanie Colucci gave the rope another hard tug. We shot backward almost five feet toward the door, but then the undertow grabbed hold again. I was able to wrap a bight of slack rope around Ned's chest, binding him to me for better or worse. Then we were off again, the Buick taking back all the ground we'd gained and more. It moved us slowly but with a terrible relentlessness. There was a breathless, claustrophobic pressure in my chest. Part of it was being wrapped in the rope. Part of it was the sense of being pinched and petted and jerked by a huge invisible hand. I didn't want to go into the place I'd seen, but if we got much closer to the car, I would. We both would. The closer we got, the more the force pulling us stacked up. Soon it would snap the yellow nylon rope. The two of us would fly away, still bound together. Into that sick purple throat we'd go and into whatever lay beyond it.

"Last chance!" I screamed. *"Pull on three! One . . . two . . . THREE!"*

Arky and Stephanie, standing shoulder to shoulder just outside the door, gave it all they had. Ned and I pushed with our feet. We flew backward, this time all the way to the door before that force seized us yet again, pulling as inexorably as a magnet pulls iron filings.

I rolled over on my side. "Ned, the doorframe! *Grab the doorframe!*"

He reached blindly out, extending his left arm fully. His hand groped.

"To your right, kid!" Steff screamed. "Your *right!*"

He found the doorjamb and gripped. Behind us there was another monstrous purple flash from the Buick, and I could feel the pull of the thing ratchet up another notch. It was like some hideous new gravity. The rope around my chest had turned into a steel band and I couldn't get a single inch of fresh breath. I could feel my eyes bulging and my teeth throbbing in their gums. My guts felt all in a plug at the base of my throat. The pulse was filling up my brain, burning out conscious thought. I began slipping toward the Buick again, the heels of my shoes skidding on the cement. In another moment I would be sliding, and a moment after that I'd be *flying,* like a bird sucked into a jet turbine engine. And when I went the boy would go with me, likely with splinters of the doorjamb sticking out from under his fingernails. He would *have* to come with me. My metaphor about chains had become literal reality.

"Sandy, grab my hand!"

I craned my neck to look and wasn't exactly surprised to see Huddie Royer—and behind him, Eddie. They'd come back. It had taken them a little longer than it had taken Arky, but they'd come. And not because Steff had radioed them a Code D, either; they'd been in their personals, and radio communications out of our barracks were FUBAR, for the time being, anyway. No, they had just . . . come.

Huddie was kneeling in the doorway, holding on with one hand to keep from being sucked in. His hair didn't move around his head and his shirt didn't ripple, but he swayed back and forth like a man in a high wind just the same. Eddie was behind him, crouching, looking over Huddie's left shoulder. Probably holding onto Huddie's belt, although I couldn't see that. Huddie's free hand was held out to me, and I seized it like a drowning man. I *felt* like a drowning man.

"Now *pull,* goddammit," Huddie growled at Arky and Eddie and Steff Colucci. The Buick's purple light was flashing in his eyes. "Pull your *guts* out."

They might not have gone quite that far, but they pulled hard and we tumbled out the door like a cork coming out of a bottle, landing in a pigpile with Huddie on the bottom. Ned was panting, his face turned sideways against my neck, the skin of his cheek and forehead burning against me like embers. I could feel the wetness of his tears.

"Ow, Sarge, Christ, get your elbow outta my *nose!*" Huddie yelled in a muffled, furious voice.

"Shut the door!" Steff cried. "Hurry, before something bad gets out!"

There was nothing but a few harmless bugs with green backs, but she was right, just the same. Because the light was bad enough. That flashing, stuttery purple light.

We were still tangled together on the pavement, arms pinned by knees, feet caught under torsos, Eddie now somehow tangled in the rope as well as Ned, yelling at Arky that it was around his neck, it was choking him, and Steff kneeling beside him, trying to get her fingers under one of the bright yellow loops while Ned gasped and flailed against me. There was no one to shut the door but it *did* slam shut and I craned my head at an angle only raw panic would permit, suddenly sure it was one of *them,* it had come through unseen and now it was out and maybe wanting a little payback for the one that had been slaughtered all those years ago. And I *saw* it, a shadow against the shed's white-painted side. Then it shifted and the shadow's owner came forward and I could see the curves of a woman's breast and hip in the dim light.

"Halfway home and I get this feeling," Shirley said in an unsteady voice. "This really bad feeling. I decided the cats could wait a little longer. Stop thrashing, Ned, you're making everything worse."

Ned stilled at once. She bent down and with a single deft gesture freed Eddie from the loop around his neck. "There, ya baby," she said, and then her legs gave out. Shirley Pasternak sprawled on the hottop and began to cry.

We got Ned into the barracks and flushed his eyes in the kitchen. The skin around them was puffed and red, the whites badly bloodshot, but he said his vision was basically okay. When Huddie held up two fingers, that was what the kid reported. Ditto four.

"I'm sorry," he said in a thick, clogged voice. "I don't know why I did that. I mean, I do, I *meant* to, but not now . . . not tonight—"

"Shhh," Shirley said. She cupped more water from the tap and bathed his eyes with it. "Don't talk."

But he wouldn't be stopped. "I meant to go home. To think about it, just like I said." His swelled, horribly bloodshot eyes peered at me, then they were gone as Shirley brought up another palm filled with warm water. "Next thing I knew I was back here again, and all I can remember thinking is 'I've got to do it tonight, I've got to finish it once and for all.' Then . . ."

Except he didn't know what had happened then; the rest was all a blur to him. He didn't come right out and say that, and didn't need to. I didn't even have to see it in his bloodshot bewildered eyes. I had seen *him,* sitting behind the Roadmaster's steering wheel with the gas can in his lap, looking pale and stoned and lost.

"It took hold of you," I said. "It's always had some kind of pull, it's just never had anyone to use it on the way it could on you. When it called you, though, the rest of us heard, too. In our own ways. In any case, it's not your fault, Ned. If there's fault, it's mine."

He straightened up from the sink, groped, took hold of my forearms. His face was dripping and his hair was plastered to his forehead. In truth he looked rather funny. Like a slapstick baptism.

Steff, who'd been watching the shed from the back door of the barracks, came over to us. "It's dying down again. Already."

I nodded. "It missed its chance. Maybe its last chance."

"To do mischief," Ned said. "That's what it wanted. I heard it in my head. Or, I don't know, maybe I just made that part up."

"If you did," I said, "then I did, too. But there might have been more to tonight than just mischief."

Before I could say any more, Huddie came out of the bathroom with a first-aid kit. He set it down on the counter, opened it, and took out a jar of salve. "Put this all around your eyes, Ned. If some gets in them, don't worry. You won't hardly notice."

We stood there, watching him put the salve around his eyes in circles that gleamed under the kitchen fluorescents. When he was done, Shirley asked him if it was any better. He nodded.

"Then come outside again," I said. "There's one other thing I need to tell you. I would have earlier, but the truth is I never thought of it except in passing until I actually saw you sitting in that goddam car. The shock must have kicked it loose."

Shirley looked at me with her brow furrowed. She'd never been a mother but it was a mother's sternness I saw on her face right then. "Not tonight," she said. "Can't you see this boy has had enough? One of you needs to take him home and make up some sort of story for his mother—she always believed Curtis's, I expect she'll believe one of yours if you can manage to stay together on the details—and then get him into bed."

"I'm sorry, but I don't think this can wait," I said.

She looked hard into my face and must have seen that I at least *thought* I was telling the truth and so we all went back out to the smokers' bench, and as we watched the dying fireworks from the shed—the second show of the night, although there wasn't much to this one, at least not now—I told Ned one more story of the old days. I saw this one as you might see a scene from a play, two characters on a mostly bare stage, two characters beneath a single bright stagelight, two men sitting

Then: *Curtis*

Two men sitting on the smokers' bench by the light of a summer sun and one will soon be dead—when it comes to our human lives there's a noose at the end of every chain and Curtis Wilcox has nearly reached his. Lunch will be his last meal and neither of them know it. This condemned man watches the other man light a cigarette and wishes he could have one himself but he's quit the habit. The cost of them is bad, Michelle was always ragging on him about that, but mostly it's wanting to see his children grow up. He wants to see their graduations, he wants to see the color of their children's hair. He has retirement plans as well, he and Michelle have talked them over a lot, the Winnebago that will take them out west where they may finally settle, but he will be retiring sooner than that, and alone. As for smoking, he never had to give up the pleasure at all but a man can't know that. Meanwhile the summer sun is pleasant. Later on the day will be hot, a hot day to die on, but now it's pleasant, and the thing across the way is quiet. It is quiet now for longer and longer stretches. The lightquakes, when they come, are milder. It is winding down, that's what the condemned State Trooper thinks. But Curtis can still sometimes feel its heartbeat and its quiet call and knows it will bear watching. This is his job; he has repudiated any chance of promotion in order to do it. It was his partner the Buick 8 got but in a way, he realizes, it got all of Curtis Wilcox it ever had to. He never locked himself in its trunk, as Huddie Royer once almost did in 1988, and it never ate him alive as it probably ate Brian Lippy, but it got him just the same. It's always close to his thoughts. He hears its whisper the way a fisherman sleeping in his house hears the whisper of the sea even in his sleep. And a whisper is a voice, and a thing with a voice can—

He turns to Sandy Dearborn and asks "Does it think? Does it watch, think, wait for its chances?"

Dearborn—the old hands still call him the new Sarge behind his back—doesn't need to ask what his friend is talking about. When it comes to the thing in Shed B they are of one mind, all of them, and sometimes Curtis thinks it calls even to those who have transferred out of D or quit the PSP altogether for some other, safer job; he thinks sometimes that it has marked them all like the Amish in their black clothes and black buggies are marked, or the way the priest dirties your forehead on Ash Wednesday, or like roadgang convicts linked together and digging a ditch of endless length.

"I'm almost sure not," the new Sarge says.

"Still, it saved its biggest horror show for a time when this place was almost completely deserted," says the man who quit cigarettes so he could watch his children grow up and bear him grandchildren. "As if it knew. As if it could think. And watch. And wait."

The new Sarge laughs—a sound of amusement which contains just the thinnest rind of contempt. "You're gaga on the subject, Curt. Next you'll be telling me it sent out a ray or something to make that Norco tanker crash into the schoolbus that day."

Trooper Wilcox has set his coffee aside on the bench so he can take off his big hat—his Stetson. He begins turning it over and over in his hands, an old habit of his. Kitty-corner from where they sit, Dicky-Duck Eliot pulls up to the gas-pump and begins filling D-12, something they will not be able to do much longer. He spots them on the bench and waves. They give him a little of the old right-back-atcha, but the man with the hat—the gray Trooper's Stetson that will finish its tour of duty in the weeds with the soda cans and fast-food wrappers—keeps his gaze mostly on the new Sarge. His eyes are asking if they can rule that out, if they can rule anything out.

The Sarge, irritated by this, says: "Why don't we just finish it off, then? Finish it off and have done? Tow it into the back field, pour gasoline into her until it runs out the windows, then just light'er up?"

Curtis looks at him with an evenness that can't quite hide his shock. "That might be the most dangerous thing we could do with it," he says. "It might even be what it wants us to do. What it was sent to provoke. How many kids have lost fingers because they found something in the weeds they didn't know was a blastingcap and pounded it with a rock?"

"This isn't the same."

"How do you know it's not? How do you know?"

And the new Sarge, who will later think, It should have been me whose hat wound up lying blood-bolted on the side of the road, can say nothing. It seems *almost profane to disagree with him, and besides, who knows? He could be right. Kids do blow off their fingers with blastingcaps or kill their little brothers with guns they found in their parents' bureau drawers or burn down the house with some old sparklight they found out in the garage. Because they don't know what they're playing with.*

"Suppose," says the man twirling his Stetson between his hands, "that the 8 is a kind of valve. Like the one in a scuba diver's regulator. Sometimes it breathes in and sometimes it breathes out, giving or receiving according to the will of the user. But what it does is always limited by the valve."

"Yes, but—"

"Or think of it another way. Suppose it breathes like a man lying on the bottom of a swamp and using a hollow reed to sip air with so he won't be seen."

"All right, but—"

"Either way, everything comes in or goes out in small breaths, they must be small breaths, because the channel through which they pass is small. Maybe the thing using the valve or the reed has put itself into a kind of suspended state, like sleep or hypnosis, so it can survive on so little breath. And then suppose some misguided fool comes along and throws enough dynamite into the swamp to drain it and make the reed unnecessary. Or, if you're thinking in terms of a valve, blows it clean off. Would you want to risk that? Risk giving it all the goddam air it needs?"

"No," the new Sarge says in a small voice.

Curtis says: "Once Buck Flanders and Andy Colucci made up their minds to do that very thing."

"The hell you say!"

"The hell I don't," Curtis returns evenly. "Andy said if a couple of State Troopers couldn't get away with a little vehicular arson, they ought to turn in their badges. They even had a plan. They were going to blame it on the paint and the thinner out there in the hutch. Spontaneous combustion, poof, all gone. And besides, Buck said, who'd send for the Fire Marshal in the first place? It's just an old shed with some old beater of a Buick inside it, for Christ's sake."

The new Sarge can say nothing. He's too amazed.

"I think it may have been talking to them," Curt says.

"Talking." He's trying to get the sense of this. "Talking to them."

"Yes." Curt puts his hat—what they always call the big hat—on his head and hooks the strap back of the head the way you wear it in warm weather and adjusts *the brim purely by feel. Then, to his old friend he says: "Can you say it's never talked to you, Sandy?"*

The new Sarge opens his mouth to say of course it hasn't, but the other man's eyes are on him, and they are grave. In the end the SC says nothing.

"You can't. Because it does. To you, to me, to all of us. It talked loudest to Huddie on the day that monster came through, but we hear it even when it whispers. Don't we? And it talks all the time. Even in its sleep. So it's important not to listen."

Curt stands up.

"Just to watch. That's our job and I know it now. If it has to breathe through that valve long enough, or that reed, or that whatever-it-is, sooner or later it'll choke. Stifle. Give out. And maybe it won't really mind. Maybe it'll more or less die in its sleep. If no one riles it up, that is. Which mostly means doing no more than staying out of snatching distance. But it also means leaving it alone."

He starts away, his life running out from under his feet like sand and neither of them knowing, then stops and takes one more look at his old friend. They weren't quite rookies together but they grew into the job together and now it fits both of them as well as it ever will. Once, when drunk, the old Sarge called law enforcement a case of good men doing bad chores.

"Sandy."

Sandy gives him a whatnow look.

"My boy is playing Legion ball this year, did I tell you?"

"Only about twenty times."

"The coach has a little boy, must be about three. And one day last week when I went overtown to pick Ned up, I saw him down on one knee, playing toss with that little boy in left field. And I fell in love with my kid all over again, Sandy. As strong as when I first held him in my arms, wrapped in a blanket. Isn't that funny?"

Sandy doesn't think it's funny. He thinks it's maybe all the truth the world needs about men.

"The coach had given them their uniforms and Ned had his on and he was down on one knee, tossing underhand to the little boy, and I swear he was the whitest, purest thing any summer sky ever looked down on." And then he says

Now: *Sandy*

In the shed there was a sallow flash, so pale it was almost lilac. It was followed by darkness . . . then another flash . . . then more darkness . . . darkness this time unbroken.

"Is it done?" Huddie asked, then answered his own question: "Yeah, I think it is."

Ned ignored this. "What?" he asked me. "What did he say then?"

"What any man says when things are all right at home," I told him. "He said he was a lucky man."

Steff had gone away to mind her microphone and computer screen, but the others were still here. Ned took no notice of any of them. His puffy, red-lidded eyes never left me. "Did he say anything else?"

"Said you hit two homers against the Rocksburg Railroad the week before, and that you gave him a wave after the second one, while you were coming around third. He liked that, laughed telling me about it. He said you saw the ball better on your worst day than he ever had on his best. He also said you needed to start charging ground balls if you were serious about playing third base."

The boy looked down and began to struggle. We looked away, all of us, to let him do it in reasonable privacy. At last he said: "He told me not to be a quitter, but that's what he did with that car. That fucking 8. He quit on it."

I said, "He made a choice. There's a difference."

He sat considering this, then nodded. "All right."

Arky said: "Dis time I'm *really* going home." But before he went he did something I'll never forget: leaned over and put a kiss on Ned's swollen cheek. I was shocked by the tenderness of it. "G'night, lad."

"Goodnight, Arky."

We watched him drive away in his rattletrap pickup and then Huddie said, "I'll drive Ned home in his Chevy. Who wants to follow along and bring me back here to get my car?"

"I will," Eddie said. "Only I'm waiting outside when you take him in. If Michelle Wilcox goes nuclear, I want to be outside the fallout zone."

"It'll be okay," Ned told him. "I'll say I saw the can on the shelf and picked it up to see what it was and Maced my stupid self."

I liked it. It had the virtue of simplicity. It was exactly the sort of story the boy's father would have told.

Ned sighed. "Tomorrow bright and early I'll be sitting in the optometrist's chair over in Statler Village, that's the downside."

"Won't hurt you," Shirley said. She also kissed him, planting hers on the corner of his mouth. "Goodnight, boys. This time everyone goes and no one comes back."

"Amen to that," Huddie said, and we watched her walk away. She was forty-five or so, but there was still plenty to look at when she put her backfield in motion. Even by moonlight. (*Especially* by moonlight.)

Off she went, driving past us, a quick flick of right-back-atcha and then nothing but the taillights.

Darkness from Shed B. No taillights there. No fireworks, either. It was over for the night and someday it would be over for good. But not yet. I could still feel the sleepy beat of it far down in my mind, a tidal whisper that could be words if you wanted them to be.

What I'd seen.

What I'd seen when I had the boy hugged in my arms, him blinded by the spray.

"You want to ride along, Sandy?" Huddie asked.

"Nah, guess not. I'll sit here awhile longer, then get on home. If there are problems with Michelle, you have her call me. Here or at the house, makes no difference."

"There won't be any problem with Mom," Ned said.

"What about you?" I asked. "Are there going to be any more problems with you?"

He hesitated, then said: "I don't know."

In some ways I thought it was the best answer he could have given. You had to give him points for honesty.

They walked away, Huddie and Ned heading toward the Bel Air. Eddie split apart from them, going toward his own car and pausing long enough at mine to take the Kojak light off the roof and toss it inside.

Ned stopped at the rear bumper of his car and turned back to me. "Sandy."

"What is it?"

"Didn't he have any idea at all about where it came from? What it was? Who the man in the black coat was? Didn't *any* of you?"

"No. We blue-sky'd it from time to time, but no one ever had an idea that felt like the real deal, or even close. Jackie O'Hara probably nailed it when he said the Buick was like a jigsaw piece that won't fit into the puzzle anywhere. You worry it and worry it, you turn it this way and that, try it everywhere, and one day you turn it over and see the back is red and the backs of all the pieces in your puzzle are green. Do you follow that?"

"No," he said.

"Well, think about it," I said, "because you're going to have to live with it."

"How am I supposed to *do* that?" There was no anger in his voice. The anger had been burned away. Now all he wanted was instructions. Good.

"You don't know where *you* came from or where you're going, do you?" I asked him. "But you live with it just the same. Don't rail against it too much. Don't spend more than an hour a day shaking your fists at the sky and cursing God."

"But—"

"There are Buicks everywhere," I said.

Steff came out after they were gone and offered me a cup of coffee. I told her thanks, but I'd pass. I asked her if she had a cigarette. She gave me a prim look—almost shocked—and reminded me she didn't smoke. As though that was her toll-booth, one with the sign reading ALL BUICK ROADMASTERS MUST DETOUR BEYOND THIS POINT. Man, if we lived in that world. If only.

"Are you going home?" she asked.

"Shortly."

339

She went inside. I sat by myself on the smokers' bench. There were cigarettes in my car, at least half a pack in the glovebox, but getting up seemed like too much work, at least for the moment. When I did get up, I reckoned it would be best just to stay in motion. I could have a smoke on the way home, and a TV dinner when I got in—The Country Way would be closed by now, and I doubted that Cynthia Garris would be very happy to see my face in the place again soon, anyway. I'd given her a pretty good scare earlier, her fright nothing to mine when the penny finally dropped and I realized what Ned was almost certainly planning to do. And my fear then was only a shadow of the terror I'd felt as I looked into that rising purple glare with the boy hanging blind in my arms and that steady beat-beat-beat in my ears, a sound like approaching footfalls. I had been looking both down, as if into a well, and on an uptilted plane . . . as if my vision had been split by some prismatic device. It had been like looking through a periscope lined with lightning. What I saw was very vivid—I'll never forget it—and fabulously strange. Yellow grass, brownish at the tips, covered a rocky slope that rose before me and then broke off at the edge of a drop. Green-backed beetles bustled in the grass, and off to one side there grew a clump of those waxy lilies. I hadn't been able to see the bottom of the drop, but I could see the sky. It was a terrible engorged purple, packed with clouds and ripe with lightnings. A prehistoric sky. In it, circling in ragged flocks, were flying things. Birds, maybe. Or bats like the one Curt had tried to dissect. They were too far away for me to be sure. And all this happened very quickly, remember. I think there was an ocean at the foot of that drop but don't know why I think it—perhaps only because of the fish that came bursting out of the Buick's trunk that time. Or the smell of salt. Around the Roadmaster there was always that vague, teary smell of salt.

Lying in the yellow grass close to where the bottom of my window (if that's what it was) ended was a silvery ornament on a fine chain: Brian Lippy's swastika. Years of being out in the weather had tarnished it. A little farther off was a cowboy boot, the fancy-stitched kind with the stacked heel. Much of the leather had been overgrown with a black-gray moss that looked like spiderwebs. The boot had been torn down one side, creating a ragged mouth through which I could see a yellow gleam of bone. No flesh: twenty years in the caustic air of that place would have decayed it, though I doubt the absence of flesh was due to mere decay alone. What I think is that Eddie J's old school pal was eaten. Probably while still alive. And screaming, if he could catch enough breath to do so.

And two things more, near the top of my momentary window. The first was a hat, also furry with patches of that black-gray moss; it had grown all around the brim and also in the crease of the crown. It wasn't exactly what we wear now, that hat, the uniform has changed some since the 1970s, but it was a PSP Stetson, all right. The big hat. It hadn't blown away because someone or something had driven a splintery wooden stake down through it to hold it in place. As if Ennis Rafferty's killer had been afraid of the alien intruder even after the intruder's death, and had staked the most striking item of his clothing to make sure he wouldn't rise and walk the night like a hungry vampire.

Near the hat, rusty and almost hidden by scrub grass, was his sidearm. Not the Beretta auto we carry now but the Ruger. The kind George Morgan had used. Had Ennis also used his to commit suicide? Or had he seen something coming, and died firing his weapon at it? Had it even been fired at all?

There was no way to tell, and before I could look more closely, Arky had screamed at Steff to help him and I'd been yanked backward with Ned hanging in my arms like a big doll. I saw no more, but one question at least was answered. They'd gone there, all right, Ennis Rafferty and Brian Lippy both.

Wherever *there* was.

I got up from the bench and walked over to the shed a final time. And there it was, midnight blue and not quite right, casting a shadow just as if it were sane. *Oil's fine,* the man in the black coat had told Bradley Roach, and then he was gone, leaving behind this weird steel callingcard.

At some point, during the last listless lightstorm, the trunk had shut itself again. About a dozen dead bugs lay scattered on the floor. We'd clean them up tomorrow. No sense saving them, or photograph- ing them, or any of that; we no longer bothered. A couple of guys would burn them in the incinerator out back. I would delegate this job. Delegating jobs is also part of what sitting in the big chair is about, and you get to like it. Hand this one the shit and that one the sweets. Can they complain? No. Can they put it on their TS list and hand it to the chaplain? Yes. For all the good it does.

"We'll outwait you," I said to the thing in the shed. "We can do that."

It only sat there on its whitewalls, and far down in my head the pulse whispered: Maybe.

. . . *and maybe not.*

Later

Obituaries are modest, aren't they? Yeah. Shirt always tucked in, skirt kept below the knee. *Died unexpectedly.* Could be anything from a heart attack while sitting on the jakes to being stabbed by a burglar in the bedroom. Cops mostly know the truth, though. You don't always *want* to know, especially when it's one of your own, but you do. Because most of the time we're the guys who show up first, with our reds lit and the walkie-talkies on our belts crackling out what sounds like so much gibble-gabble to the John Q's. For most folks who *die unexpectedly,* we're the first faces their staring open eyes can't see.

When Tony Schoondist told us he was going to retire I remember thinking, *Good, that's good, he's getting a little long in the tooth. Not to mention a little slow on the uptake.* Now, in the year 2006, I'm getting ready to pull the pin myself and probably some of my younger guys are thinking the same thing: long in the tooth and slow on the draw. But mostly, you know, I feel the same as I ever did, full of piss and vinegar, ready to work a double shift just about any day of the week. Most days when I note the gray hair which now predominates the black or how much more forehead there is below the place where the hair starts, I think it's a mistake, a clerical error which will eventually be rectified when brought to the attention of the proper authorities. It is impossible, I think, that a man who still feels so profoundly twenty-five can look so happast fifty. Then there'll be a stretch of bad days and I'll know it's no error, just time marching on, that shuffling, rueful tread. But was there ever a moment as bad as seeing Ned behind the wheel of the Buick Roadmaster 8?

Yes. There was one.

Shirley was on duty when the call came in: a crackup out on SR 32, near the Humboldt Road intersection. Where the old Jenny station used to be, in other words. Shirley's face was pale as ashes when she came and stood in the open door of my office.

"What is it?" I asked. "What the hell's wrong with you?"

"Sandy . . . the man who called it in said the vehicle was an old Chevrolet, red and white. He says the driver's dead." She swallowed. "In pieces. That's what he said."

That part I didn't care about, although I would later, when I had to look at it. At him. "The Chevrolet—have you got the model?"

"I didn't ask. Sandy, I couldn't." Her eyes were full of tears. "I didn't dare. But how many old red-and-white Chevrolets do you think there are in Statler County?"

I went out to the scene with Phil Candleton, praying the crashed Chevy would turn out to be a Malibu or a Biscayne, anything but a Bel Air, vanity plate MY 57. But that's what it was.

"Fuck," Phil said in a low and dismayed voice.

He'd piled it into the side of the cement bridge which spans Redfern Stream less than five minutes' walk from where the Buick 8 first appeared and where Curtis was killed. The Bel Air had seatbelts, but he hadn't been wearing one. Nor were there any skidmarks.

"Christ almighty," Phil said. "This ain't right."

Not right and not an accident. Although in the obituary, where shirts are kept neatly tucked in and skirts are kept discreetly below the knee, it would only say he *died unexpectedly,* which was true. Lord yes.

Lookie-loos had started showing up by then, slowing to stare at what lay facedown on the bridge's narrow walkway. I think one asshole actually took a picture. I wanted to run after him and stuff his shitty little disposable camera down his throat.

"Get some detour signs up," I told Phil. "You and Carl. Send the traffic around by County Road. I'll cover him up. Jesus, what a mess! *Jesus!* Who's gonna tell his mother?"

Phil wouldn't look at me. We both knew who was going to tell his mother. Later that day I bit the bullet and did the worst job that comes with the big chair. Afterward I went down to The Country Way with Shirley, Huddie, Phil, and George Stankowski. I don't know about them, but I myself didn't pass go or collect two hundred dollars; old Sandy went directly to shitfaced.

I only have two clear memories of that night. The first is of trying to explain to Shirley how weird The Country Way's jukeboxes were, how all the songs were the very ones you never thought of anymore until you saw their names again here. She didn't get it.

My other memory is of going into the bathroom to throw up. After, while I was splashing cold water on my face, I looked at myself in one of the wavery steel mirrors. And I knew for sure that the getting-to-be-old face I saw looking back at me was no mistake. The mistake was believing that the twenty-five-year-old guy who seemed to live in my brain was real.

I remembered Huddie shouting *Sandy, grab my hand!* and then the two of us, Ned and I, had spilled out onto the pavement, safe with the rest of them. Thinking of that, I began to cry.

Died unexpectedly, that shit is all right for the County *American,* but cops know the truth. We clean up the messes and we always know the truth.

Everyone not on duty went to the funeral, of course. He'd been one of us. When it was over, George Stankowski gave his mother and his two sisters a ride home and I drove back to the barracks with Shirley. I asked her if she was going to the reception—what you call a wake, I guess, if you're Irish—and she shook her head. "I hate those things."

So we had a final cigarette out on the smokers' bench, idly watching the young Trooper who was looking in at the Buick. He stood in that same legs-apart, goddam-the-Democrats, didya-hear-the-one-about-the-traveling-salesman pose that we all assumed when we looked into Shed B. The century had changed, but everything else was more or less the same.

"It's so unfair," Shirley said. "A young man like that—"

"What are you talking about?" I asked her. "Eddie J was in his late forties, for God's sake . . . maybe even fifty. I think his sisters are both in their sixties. His mother's almost *eighty!*"

"You know what I mean. He was too young to do that."

345

"So was George Morgan," I said.

"Was it . . . ?" She nodded toward Shed B.

"I don't think so. Just his life. He made an honest effort to get sober, busted his ass. This was right after he bought Curt's old Bel Air from Ned. Eddie always liked that car, you know, and Ned couldn't have it at Pitt anyway, not as a freshman. It would've just been sitting there in his driveway—"

"—and Ned needed the money."

"Going off to college from a single-parent home? Every penny. So when Eddie asked him, he said okay, sure. Eddie paid thirty-five hundred dollars—"

"Thirty-two," Shirley said with the assurance of one who really knows.

"Thirty-two, thirty-five, whatever. The point is, I think Eddie saw getting it as a new leaf he was supposed to turn over. He quit going to The Tap; I think he started going to AA meetings instead. That was the good part. For Eddie, the good part lasted about two years."

Across the parking lot, the Trooper who'd been looking into Shed B turned, spotted us, and began walking in our direction. I felt the skin on my arms prickle. In the gray uniform the boy—only he wasn't a boy any longer, not really—looked strikingly like his dead father. Nothing strange about that, I suppose; it's simple genetics, a correspondence that runs in the blood. What made it eerie was the big hat. He had it in his hands and was turning it over and over.

"Eddie fell off the wagon right around the time that one there decided he wasn't cut out for college," I said.

Ned Wilcox left Pitt and came home to Statler. For a year he'd done Arky's job, Arky by then having retired and moved back to Michigan, where everyone no doubt sounded just like him (a scary thought). When he turned twenty-one, Ned made the application and took the tests. Now, at twenty-two, here he was. Hello, rookie.

Halfway across the parking lot, Curt's boy paused to look back at the shed, still twirling his Stetson in his hands.

"He looks good, doesn't he?" Shirley murmured.

I put on my old Sarge face—a little aloof, a little disdainful. "Relatively squared away. Shirley, do you have any idea how much bright red dickens his Ma raised when she finally found out what he had in mind?"

Shirley laughed and put out her cigarette. "She raised more when she found out he was planning to sell his Dad's Bel Air to Eddie Jacubois—at least that's what Ned told me. I mean, c'mon, Sandy, she had to know it was coming. *Had* to. She was married to one, for God's sake. And she probably knew this was where he belonged. Eddie, though, where did *he* belong? Why couldn't he just stop drinking? Once and for all?"

"That's a question for the ages," I said. "They say it's a disease, like cancer or diabetes. Maybe they're right."

Eddie had begun showing up for duty with liquor on his breath, and no one covered for him very long; the situation was too serious. When he refused counselling, and a leave of absence to spend four weeks in the spin-dry facility the PSP favors for their stricken officers, he was given his choice: quit quietly or get fired noisily. Eddie had quit, with about half the retirement package he would have received if he'd managed to hang onto his job for another three years—at the end, the benefits really stack up. And I could understand the outcome no more than Shirley—why *hadn't* he just quit? With that kind of incentive, why hadn't he just said *I'll be thirsty for three years and then I'll pull the pin and take a bath in it?* I didn't know.

The Tap really *did* become Eddie J's home away from home. Along with the old Bel Air, that was. He'd kept it waxed on the outside and spotlessly clean on the inside right up to the day when he'd driven it into a bridge abutment near Redfern Stream at approximately eighty miles an hour. He had plenty of reasons to do it by then—he was not a happy man—but I had to wonder if maybe there weren't a few reasons just a little closer to home. Specifically I had to wonder if he hadn't heard that pulse near the end, that tidal whisper that's like a voice in the middle of your head.

Do it, Eddie, go on, why not? There's not much else, is there? The rest is pretty well used up. Just step down a little brisker on the old go-pedal and then twist the wheel to the right. Do it. Go on. Make a little mischief for your buddies to clean up.

I thought about the night we'd sat out on this same bench, the young man I currently had my eye on four years younger than he was now and listening raptly as Eddie told the tale of stopping Brian Lippy's bigfoot truck. The kid listening as Eddie told about trying to get Lippy's girl to do something about her situation before her boyfriend fucked her up beyond all recognition or maybe killed her. The joke turned out to be on Eddie, of course. So far as I knew, the bloodyface girl is the only one of that roadside quartet still alive. Yeah, she's around. I don't road-patrol much anymore, but her name and picture come across my desk from time to time, each picture showing a woman closer to the beerbreath brokennose fuck-ya-for-a-pack-of-smokes hag she will, barring a miracle, become. She's had lots of DUIs, quite a few D-and-Ds, a trip to the hospital one night with a broken arm and hip after she fell downstairs. I imagine someone like Brian Lippy probably helped her down those stairs, don't you? Because they *do* pick the same kind over and over. She has two or maybe it's three kids in foster care. So yeah, she's around, but is she living? If you say she is, then I have to tell you that maybe George Morgan and Eddie J had the right idea.

"I'm going to make like a bee and buzz," Shirley said, getting up. "Can't take any more hilarity in one day. You doin okay with it?"

"Yeah," I said.

"Hey, he came back that night, didn't he? There's that."

She didn't have to be any more specific. I nodded, smiling.

"Eddie was a good guy," Shirley said. "Maybe he couldn't leave the booze alone, but he had the kindest heart."

Nope, I thought, watching her walk across to Ned, watching them talk a little. *I think* you're *the one with the kindest heart, Shirl.*

She gave Ned a little peck on the cheek, putting one hand on his shoulder and going up on her toes to do it, then headed toward her car. Ned came over to where I was sitting. "You okay?" he asked.

"Yeah, good."

"And the funeral . . . ?"

"Hey, shit, it was a funeral. I've been to better and I've been to worse. I'm glad the coffin was closed."

"Sandy, can I show you something? Over there?" He nodded his head at Shed B.

"Sure." I got up. "Is the temperature going down?" If so, it was news. It had been two years since the temp in there had dropped more than five degrees below the outside temperature. Sixteen months since the last lightshow, and that one had consisted of no more than eight or nine pallid flickers.

"No," he said.

"Trunk open?"

"Shut tight as a drum."

"What, then?"

"I'd rather show you."

I glanced at him sharply, for the first time getting out of my own head enough to register how excited he was. Then, with decidedly mixed feelings—curiosity and apprehension were the dominant chords, I guess—I walked across the parking lot with my old friend's son. He took up his sidewalk super's pose at one window and I took up mine at the next.

At first I saw nothing unusual; the Buick sat on the concrete as it had for a quarter of a century, give or take. There were no flashing lights, no exotic exhibits. The thermometer's red needle stood at an unremarkable seventy-three degrees.

"So?" I asked.

Ned laughed, delighted. "You're looking spang at it and don't see it! Perfect! I didn't see it myself, at first. I knew something had changed, but I couldn't tell what."

"What are you talking about?"

He shook his head, still smiling. "Nossir, Sergeant, nossir. I think not. You're the boss; you're also one of just three cops who were there then and are still here now. It's right in front of you, so go to it."

I looked in again, first squinting and then raising my hands to the sides of my face to block the glare, that old gesture. It helped, but what was I seeing? Something, yes, he was right about that, but just what? What had changed?

I remembered that night at The Country Way, flipping the pages of the dead jukebox back and forth, trying to isolate the most important question, which was the one Ned had decided not to ask. It had almost come, then had slipped shyly away again. When that happened, it was no good to chase. I'd thought that then and still did now.

So instead of continuing to give the 8 my cop stare, I unfocused my eyes and let my mind drift away. What it drifted to were song-titles, of course, titles of the ones they never seem to play, even on the oldies stations, once their brief season of popularity has gone. "Society's Child" and "Pictures of Matchstick Men" and "Quick Joey Small" and—

—and bingo, there it was. Like he'd said, it was right in front of me. For a moment I couldn't breathe.

There was a crack in the windshield.

A thin silver lightning-bolt jigjagging top to bottom on the driver's side.

Ned clapped me on the shoulder. "There you go, Sherlock, I knew you'd get there. After all, it's only right there in front of you."

I turned to him, started to talk, then turned back to make sure I'd seen what I thought I'd seen. I had. The crack looked like a frozen stroke of quicksilver.

"When did it happen?" I asked him. "Do you know?"

"I take a fresh Polaroid of it every forty-eight hours or so," he said. "I'll check to make sure, but I'll bet you a dead cat and a string to swing it with that the last picture I took doesn't show a crack. So this happened between Wednesday evening and Friday afternoon at . . ." He checked his watch, then gave me a big smile. "At four-fifteen."

"Might even have happened during Eddie's funeral," I said.

"Possible, yeah."

We looked in again for a little while, neither of us talking. Then Ned said, "I read the poem you mentioned. 'The Wonderful One-Hoss Shay.'"

"Did you?"

"Uh-huh. It's pretty good. Pretty funny."

I stepped back from the window and looked at him.

"It'll happen fast now, like in the poem," he said. "Next thing a tire'll blow . . . or the muffler will fall off . . . or a piece of the chrome. You know how you can stand beside a frozen lake in March or early April and listen to the ice creak?"

I nodded.

"This is going to be like that." His eyes were alight, and a curious idea came to me: I was seeing Ned Wilcox really, genuinely happy for the first time since his father died.

"You think?"

"Yes. Only instead of ice creaking, the sound will be snapping bolts and cracking glass. Cops will line up at these windows like they did in the old days . . . only it'll be to watch things bend and break and come loose and fall off. Until, finally, the whole thing goes. They'll wonder if there isn't going to be one more flash of light at the very finish, like the final Chinese-flower at the end of the fireworks display on the Fourth of July."

"Will there be, do you think?"

"I think the fireworks are over. I think we're going to hear one last big steel clank and then you can take the pieces to the crusher."

"Are you sure?"

"Nah," he said, and smiled. "You *can't* be sure. I learned that from you and Shirley and Phil and Arky and Huddie." He paused. "And Eddie J. But I'll watch. And sooner or later . . ." He raised one hand, looked at it, then closed it into a fist and turned back to his window. "Sooner or later."

I turned back to my own window, cupping my hands to the sides of my face to cut the glare. I peered in at the thing that looked like a Buick Roadmaster 8. The kid was absolutely right.

Sooner or later.

Bangor, Maine
Boston, Massachusetts
Naples, Florida
Lovell, Maine
Osprey, Florida
April 3, 1999—March 20, 2002

Author's Note

I've had ideas fall into my lap from time to time—I suppose this is true of any writer—but *From a Buick 8* was almost comically the reverse: a case of me falling into the lap of an idea. That's worth a note, I think.

My wife and I spent the winter of 1999 on Longboat Key in Florida, where I tinkered at the final draft of a short novel (*The Girl Who Loved Tom Gordon*) and wrote little else of note. Nor did I have plans to write anything in the spring of that year.

In late March, Tabby flew back to Maine from Florida. I drove. I hate to fly, love to drive, and besides, I had a truckload of furnishings, books, guitars, computer components, clothes, and paper. My second or third day on the road found me in western Pennsylvania. I needed gas and got off the turnpike at a rural exit. Near the ramp I found a Conoco station. There was an actual attendant who actually pumped the gas. He even threw in a few words of tolerably pleasant conversation at no extra charge.

I left him doing his thing and went to the restroom to do mine. When I finished, I walked around to the back of the station. Here I found a rather steep slope littered with auto parts and a brawling stream at the foot. There was still a fair amount of snow on the ground, in dirty strips and runners. I walked a little way down the slope to get a better look at the water, and my feet went out from beneath me. I slid about ten feet before grabbing a rusty something-or-other and bringing myself to a stop. Had I missed it, I might well have gone into the water. And then? All bets are off, as they say.

I paid the attendant (so far as I know, he had no idea of my misadventure) and got back on the highway. I mused about my slip as I drove, wondering about what would have happened if I'd gone into the stream (which, with all that spring runoff, was at least temporarily a small river).

353

How long would my truckload of Florida furnishings and our bright Florida clothes have stood at the pumps before the gas-jockey got nervous? Whom would he have called? How long before they'd have found me if I had drowned?

This little incident happened around ten in the morning. By afternoon I was in New York. And by then I had the story you've just read pretty much set in my mind. I have said in my book about the craft of writing that first drafts are only about story; if there is meaning, it should come later, and arise naturally from the tale itself. This story became—I suppose—a meditation on the essentially indecipherable quality of life's events, and how impossible it is to find a coherent meaning in them. The first draft was written in two months. By then I realized I had made myself a whole host of problems by writing of two things I knew nothing about: western Pennsylvania and the Pennsylvania State Police. Before I could address either of these concerns, I suffered my own road-accident and my life changed radically. I came out of the summer of '99 lucky to have any life at all, in fact. It was over a year before I even thought of this story again, let alone worked on it.

The coincidence of having written a book filled with grisly vehicular mishaps shortly before suffering my own has not been lost on me, but I've tried not to make too much of it. Certainly I don't think there was anything premonitory about the similarities between what happens to Curtis Wilcox in *Buick 8* and what happened to me in real life (for one thing, I lived). I can testify at first hand, however, that I got most of it right from imagination: as with Curtis, the coins were stripped from my pockets and the watch from my wrist. The cap I was wearing was later found in the woods, at least twenty yards from the point of impact. But I changed nothing in the course of my story to reflect what happened to me; most of what I wanted was there in the completed first draft. The imagination is a powerful tool.

It never crossed my mind to re-set *From a Buick 8* in Maine, although Maine is the place I know (and love) the best. I stopped at a gas station in Pennsylvania, went on my ass in Pennsylvania, got the idea in Pennsylvania. I thought the resulting tale should stay in Pennsylvania, in spite of the aggravations that presented. Not that there weren't rewards, as well; for one thing, I got to set my fictional town of Statler just down the road apiece from Rocksburg, the town which serves as the locale for K. C. Constantine's brilliant series of novels about small-town police chief Mario Balzic. If you've never read any of these stories, you ought to do yourself a favor. The continuing story of Chief Balzic and his family is like *The Sopranos* turned inside-out and told from a law enforcement point of view. Also, western Pennsylvania is the home of the Amish, whose way of life I wanted to explore a little more fully.

This book could never have been finished without the help of Trooper Lucien Southard of the Pennsylvania State Police. Lou read the manuscript, managed not to laugh too hard at its many howlers, and wrote me eight pages of notes and corrections that could be printed in any writer's handbook without a blush (for one thing, Trooper Southard has been taught to print in large, easy-to-read block letters). He took me to several PSP barracks, introduced me to three PCOs who were kind enough to show me what they do and how they do it (to begin with they ran the license plate of my Dodge pickup—it came back clean, I'm relieved to say, with no wants or warrants), and demonstrated all sorts of State Police equipment. The most informative and patient of these was PCO Theresa M. Maker—thank you, Theresa, for your kindness.

More important, Lou and some of his mates took me to lunch at a restaurant in Amish country, where we consumed huge sandwiches and drank pitchers of iced tea. They regaled me with an hour of stories of Trooper life. Some of these were funny, some of them were horrible, and some managed to be both at the same time. Not all of them made it into *Buick 8,* but a number of them did, in suitably fictionalized form. They treated me as a friend, and no one moved too fast, which was good. At that time, I was still hopping along on one crutch.

Thanks, Lou—and thanks to all the Troopers who work out of the Butler barracks—for helping me keep my Pennsylvania book in Pennsylvania. Much more important, thanks for helping me understand exactly what it is that State Troopers do, and the price they pay to do it well.

Susan Moldow and Nan Graham, the Dynamic Duo at Scribner, would not let me close this note without pointing out that certain—

ahem!—liberties have been taken with the Buick on the book jacket. GM-ophiles will likely notice that *Eight*'s cover-girl is several years older than the Buick in the story. I was asked if this little cheat bothered me, and I said absolutely not. What bothers me, especially when it's late and I can't sleep, is that sneermouth grille. Looks almost ready to gobble someone up, doesn't it? Maybe me. Or maybe you, my dear Constant Reader.

Maybe you.

Stephen King
May 29, 2002